Tomorrow The Barrow We'll Cross

Joe Murphy was born in 1979 in Enniscorthy, County Wexford where he lived for nineteen years before dying. Then he got better.

He was educated in Enniscorthy VEC, from where he went on to study English in University College Dublin. After undertaking a Masters in Early Modern Drama, he went on to qualify as a secondary school teacher. He has had poetry published in an anthology of Enniscorthy writers, but *Tomorrow The Barrow We'll Cross* is his first novel. His job is teaching.

You wouldn't believe the stories.

First published in 2011 by
Liberties Press
Guinness Enterprise Centre | Taylor's Lane | Dublin 8
Tel: +353 (1) 415 1224
www.libertiespress.com | info@libertiespress.com

Trade enquiries to Gill & Macmillan Distribution
Hume Avenue | Park West | Dublin 12
T: +353 (1) 500 9534 | F: +353 (1) 500 9595 | E: sales@gillmacmillan.ie

Distributed in the UK by
Turnaround Publisher Services
Unit 3 | Olympia Trading Estate | Coburg Road | London N22 6TZ
T: +44 (0) 20 8829 3000 | E: orders@turnaround-uk.com

Distributed in the United States by
Dufour Editions | PO Box 7 | Chester Springs | Pennsylvania 19425

ISBN: 978-1-907593-26-0
2 4 6 8 10 9 7 5 3 1
A CIP record for this title is available from the British Library.

Cover design by Graham Thew
Internal design by Liberties Press
Printed by CPI Group (UK) Ltd, Croydon, CR0 4YY

The publishers gratefully acknowledge
financial assistance from the Arts Council.

1798

Tomorrow The Barrow We'll Cross

Joe Murphy

When twilight falls on north County Wexford it falls in purples and golds. The sun behind the Blackstairs spills the gore of its setting up and over the dark backs of the mountains so that the western sky is a swamp of vermilion, a haemorrhage of red. Yet, above this, the light is less harsh, less angry. Above Mount Leinster the sky pales to a lustrous gold that washes and arcs upwards and eastwards until, seemingly without transition, the doming heavens darken to violet, darken to royal blue, darken so that the first stars dapple and strew the horizon. The day is an emptied church, its columns fire-fluted, its ceiling a sweep of colour.

There is a quiet upon everything. Birdsong and the barking of dogs on lone farms ripple the tranquillity. But they do not rend it. There is a calm, a stillness, deeper than the mere absence of noise. The inkspill of shadow creeps out from the foothills of the Blackstairs and little by little isolated lights begin to appear amidst the woods and river valleys. The day burns itself to ashes, and clusters and swirls of streetlights and sodium arcs flicker and blink into a buzzing existence. Around these earthbound stars, sootsoft whirls of moths gather in silent and dusty agitation.

The ditches, the fields, the discarded tarmac ribbons of the roads, all are limned in the purple and gold of the dying day. All is quiet, all is calm.

In the distance the lights of Kiltealy, Enniscorthy, Ferns, Oulart, New Ross, Wexford, Duncannon, Rosslare, Gorey, the lights of a hundred other villages and towns flicker in the swelling dark. And upon this dusky ocean the moon crests the eastern edge of the world and throws its bloodless sheen over sea and over land.

This is *now*. It is late summer and all is quiet, all is calm.

But it was not always.

When twilight fell on north County Wexford in late summer of the year 1798, it fell in purples and golds. The sun sank in a welter of crimson behind the Blackstairs and upon the patchwork countryside rolling out from their feet. In the distance the lights of Kiltealy, Enniscorthy, Ferns, Oulart, New Ross, Wexford, Duncannon, Rosslare, Gorey, the lights of a hundred other villages and towns flickered in the swelling dark. But smaller then, smaller and a smoky yellow, where the naked flames of lamps and candles wavered and danced in the vagaries of a summer breeze.

Only the sunset was unchanged, the sunset and the bonelight of the rising moon, pallid and grinning and cold.

Katie Furlong sat on a rough stool at the small table occupying most of her kitchen. She trailed her fingers over the table's unvarnished surface, feeling her calluses rasp across the knots and gouges. She trailed her fingers across the wood until they found the deep marks chiselled into one corner. The pad of her index finger followed the grooves of its own volition, tracing the letters *N.F.* Katie did not know her alphabet but she knew these grooves were her husband's mark. Her husband, who had made most of the furniture in this two-roomed cabin. Her husband, who had limed the walls and cut the straw to cover the hard, clay and who had left her and not come back. Her husband, Ned Furlong, gone now for two months.

Until the first briny drop spattered upon the skin of her left forearm Katie had not realised that she was crying.

Without a candle, Katie Furlong sat at her vanished husband's table and cried softly as the twilight gathered at her bolted door and the shadows darkened amidst the rafters. For how long she sat there and wept Katie did not know; but

3

when she was roused, it was by the clatter and hard drumming of horses' hooves.

For the briefest of moments she felt a sea-surge of warmth in her breast. She was on her feet and smoothing down the bodice of her linen dress before she realised what she was doing and the first twitch of a smile began to uplift the corners of her mouth, downturned and morose for so long. Then a terrible instinct quelled the hot tide within her and a frigid core of ice abruptly formed about her heart. The yearning for her husband that had brought her so suddenly to her feet was now a thing of lead, lumpen and cold.

Ned Furlong had had no horse.

Katie's breathing quickened and she found herself straining for any clue as to the identity of the horsemen beyond her little cabin's walls. Her fists balled into white lumps, she listened for the inevitable and she felt her anger and fear rise in equal measure within. She stood like something carven whilst her insides churned and her brain grew frantic. So chaotic were her thoughts that when the hooves finally stilled and the first voices came, she almost missed them.

They were Irish voices, speaking English in local accents but there was something strange about them. Something alien. Something clipped and razor-edged. Something wrong.

Silently, Katie slipped around the table and sidled up to the single window set into the whitewashed wall. The window's wooden shutters were closed and barred but Katie pressed her sorrow-raw eye to the loose join between the shutters and prayed she would not see what she already knew to be there. In the dark, the moonlight painted a band of brightness down her face where it was pressed to the gap in the shutters and in this glowing band Katie's eye widened with an awful terror. She almost stumbled away from the window then but instead, in the shaft of moonlight, her visage hardened. Her eyes that only moments before had brimmed like wellheads were now narrowed and emotionless.

The spectacle that played out just beyond her home's walls petrified her and leached all emotion from her body.

In the moonlight, on the packed earth of her small farm's yard, ten yeoman cavalry stood or sat their saddles. Even now, the sound of their coarse guffawing permeated the stone of the walls like a contagion. The silver light on their Tarleton helmets, the breeze riffling the bearskin coverings, the spilled ink of their coats, all were etched in Katie's mind. Indelible as a scar.

She stood, quiet and unmoving as a leaden fist crashed once, twice, three times, upon the heavy planking of the cabin door. She stood quiet and unmoving, as a voice, a voice in her own Wexford drawl, filled the caverns and empty places of her mind with a dread desolation.

'Open in the name of the King and Lord Mountnorris.'

Katie stood, a study in emptiness, as the voice roared again, 'Open or we'll burn it down around your ears.'

Another voice, less bellicose but in an accent that Katie did not recognise, rose in commendation of the first, 'That's the spirit trooper, we ain't here to mollycoddle.'

The cabin's door shivered like a drumhead on its hinges, rattling and creaking as the fist came again and again and again.

Katie Furlong, in the dark of her little kitchen, felt with each hammering blow a gradual withdrawing of her faculties. Terror, fear, rational thought, had all fled at the yeomen's voices. Only a bleak sort of anger remained. In the dark of her kitchen with the thick smell of the soldiers' horses beginning to intrude upon her senses, Katie Furlong moved numb step after numb step, towards the cabin door. Delicately, her white hand withdrew the simple deadbolt and with a cool sureness that lent her face a startling serenity, she opened wide the door.

Before her stood a young man dressed in the uniform of the Camolin Cavalry. He seemed to Katie to be barely out of his teens and yet his countenance was twisted and puckered about a snarl. His gloved hand was raised to fall once again on the door's planking and as the portal was swept aside the yeoman froze with his fist stalled in its downward trajectory.

Katie's own fist, rising in a tight arc, caught him completely by surprise.

The yeoman fell away, curses exploding from his lips as the flintlocks of nine carbines were drawn back. To Katie they sounded like the breaking of bones.

The spluttering yeoman Katie had struck was now bristling and indignant. His mouth was shrunken into something bitter and outraged and his eyes gleamed like spurs in the moonlight. 'You bitch!' he began before the other voice halted his words and stymied whatever action he was about to take.

Katie stood with the moon washing her of all colour, stood with her white skin and white dress, stood with her lips trembling, stood pale against the empty dark of her door. Through her mind, a comet against icy black, a thought burned hideously. In the silence of her own skull, Katie screamed, I'm going to die.

The yeo she had struck was panting with fury and his gauntlets creaked as his fists clenched and unclenched. And the other voice came again.

'Summers, if you do not step aside from the lady I shall have you standing in irons before a military court.'

The yeoman hesitated and then stood to one side, drawing his midnight blue sleeve across his swollen lips as he did so. Behind him, Katie perceived an officer dismounting from his big bay. The man, with calculated nonchalance, sauntered across the hard earth of her yard. As he drew nearer the voice in Katie's mind howled to a banshee pitch. Under the moon the braiding of the officer's jacket glowed like quicksilver and at his hip his sabre swung with each slow step. Horse sweat, the reek of men and the mouldy waft of wine and stale cologne made Katie suddenly want to retch. As the officer stopped in front of her she could taste the bile scalding the well of her throat.

The officer seemed a young man, no more than mid-twenties, and under his crested helmet his smooth cheeks looked freshly shaved. They were marble into which the coal pits of his eyes were set. Then his wide mouth, a mouth made for smiling, Katie found herself thinking, opened and he addressed her sharply.

'Good woman, my name is Lieutenant Shingleton of the Camolin Cavalry. I have come for your husband. Where is he?'

Katie felt her jaw slacken. Her faculties became lax and her stomach heaved in violent spasm beneath her linen dress. The lieutenant's words had caught her off guard and blown her heart wide open. She felt physically buffeted. Her knees unhinging, every joint of her frame dislocating, she somehow brought her arms up to fold them beneath her breasts and struggled to dull the vibrancy of her emotions. She took in the young lieutenant's handsome face and cold eyes and strangled the cockerel crow of exultation that hammered her insides for relief.

Ned was still alive.

The young Lieutenant Shingleton watched with the shrewd vision of one unnaturally aged. The rebellion had hardened him and honed his wits, had quickened his anger and had bred in him the rapacious demons of hatred and contempt. Beneath his gentleman's refinement, beneath his good looks, something had soured.

A small pink triangle of tongue licked out and along Shingleton's lower lip.

'Have a care woman. For the toss of a pin I'd shoot you where you stand. Do not lie to me, I warn you.'

Katie met his considering gaze with the hot defiance that came so readily to her. 'Ned went off to Carnew to visit his cousin. He's sick,' she said.

Katie did not know she had been struck until she saw the blood emptying out of her nose and mouth and onto the back of her hands. With each hacking breath she took, the gush of warm wet coming from her face became a sticky spray. Each inhalation caught gore in her throat and she sprayed her own vitality over her forearms and over the thirsty earth of her yard.

Shingleton stood over Katie's wretched form and allowed her a moment or two to regain her senses. He stood over her and watched her nose and lips spill blood onto the ground at his feet.

'In the moonlight,' she thought he whispered, 'all blood looks black.'

He watched as Katie struggled to her knees, her clawed hands laced over her ruined face, tears and blood a torrent beneath them. Looking up at him, her blood soaking into the front of her dress, making it cling to her breasts, Shingleton could see the sheen of terror in her eyes. Relishing this, he grinned down at her.

'Not to sully your character madam, but you are a lying rebel whore!' He ended his words in a shout, a roar so savage it should have come from a beast. The yeos' horses whinnied, their hooves pawing at the yard and over them another voice came pleading and insistent.

'For God's sake, Lieutenant let me talk to her, I know this woman. Don't do her any more violence I beg you.'

Shingleton's boot heels ground into the earth as he turned to face his troop. Almost to a man they stared with rapt attention towards the bloodied figure of Katie. Their features were set in expressions of eager anticipation or set-jawed stoicism. Two even stood with eyes downcast and shoulders slumped. One figure however was moving quickly forward. His carbine sheathed in his saddle holster he jogged forward, his left hand gripping his sabre's hilt to stop it tangling in his stride.

Shingleton eyed the man with an air of curiosity and then abruptly moved aside. His lips curling around a sneer he drawled, 'If, Burke, you feel you can prevail upon her to provide the information then so be it'.

He massaged the knuckles of his right hand, 'I find violence towards women rather distasteful.'

Burke was already kneeling beside Katie. He had taken his helmet off and had produced a cotton handkerchief from the cuff of one leather gauntlet.

Katie jerked away from him. Her entire world still reverberated to the concussion of Shingleton's fist. Yet one certainty gripped her mind and bound it close and whole. If the yeos were looking for Ned, then he was still alive.

Through this one crystal thought, through the pain and confusion of the rest of her, a voice came soft and penetrating. 'It's me Katie. Thady Burke. It's me. You know me.'

Like frost under sun, Katie's vision seemed to clear and before her, in the dark of her dooryard with the moon turning the earth into a puddle of silver, crouched a man she had known all her life. Gently he held his handkerchief to her bleeding mouth and nose.

Katie stared at him and words came slurred and soft as marl from between her split lips. 'Thady, why are you still with them? Why are you doing this? You're no Orangeman.'

Thady Burke's expression crumpled as though the bones had been removed from his face. 'Shhh, whisht now Katie. I'm no Orangeman but I'm no rebel either. I'm in the yeomanry to protect what little land and property I have, from God knows what.'

Swallowing blood and almost gagging on it Katie asked, 'You fought against your own people?'

Thady shook his head and smiled ruefully, aware that his lieutenant was standing behind him, 'Cavalry corps find it difficult to engage in such rough country.' He paused then and looked her directly in her tear-swamped eyes, 'We know Ned was a United Irishman. We know he went off with Miles Byrne and the Monaseed boys. No harm will be done to you Katie if you but tell us where you think he is or if you have anyone else at all sheltering in your cabin.'

Katie, kneeling at her own door with Thady's gentle hand stemming the flow of blood from her face, felt the fulcrum of events within her. Her life had reached its perfect point of equilibrium. Her next words would either save her or kill her. She did not know where Ned was and she had never sheltered a soul inside her meagre house. If the yeos accepted this she would see the morning. If not she would lie here until the neighbours came to put out her burning home and bury what was left of her body.

At night, from high hills and the slopes of mountains, all over the country-side you could see the lofty blaze of another torched haggard and if the wind was in the wrong direction, and if you were unfortunate enough, you could hear the screams. This was the price of rebellion against the Crown. This was General Lake's idea of peace.

Thinking this, Katie Furlong stared through Thady Burke, stared through him into an abyss of nothingness and said, 'I don't know where Ned is and I've never sheltered anyone in my cabin but I do know that if Ned is alive he's fighting you crowd of bastards and I only wish I had a hundred fine boys hiding in my kitchen to cut every one of you down'.

Thady Burke's mouth was a hanging black hole in his face and as he took his handkerchief away, soaked and crusted with Katie's blood, he moaned, 'Oh, Katie, Katie, Katie.'

Lieutenant Shingleton's hand on his shoulder brought Thady to his feet.

'You should remove any weight of responsibility from your shoulders Burke.

Every opportunity was afforded this croppy bitch to abide by the law. The consequences of her actions are her own to suffer.'

Katie, still kneeling, her face a broken and pulsing mess, watched as in the frigid light of the arcing moon, the lieutenant turned to his men. In her clogged nostrils and throat, the taste of her own blood made her feel faint and in her ears Shingleton's next words roared like a tidal wave.

'Burn this hovel. If anything comes out, shoot it. What you do with the woman is up to you but I believe precedents have been set as to the example you should make of her.'

And under Shingleton's words Thady Burke's voice sighed like a cornfield in a summer breeze, 'Oh, Jesus. Katie, I'm sorry. I'm so sorry.'

Katie stared, stricken, at Thady Burke, his big shoulders and wide face, his eyes round as plates and his sandy hair plastered to his head from the heat and weight of his helmet. She stared at him as in the half-dark behind him a dozen furious stars suddenly erupted into hissing, crackling life. In the flat-booming instant of their birth she saw painted in their light a congeries of gargoyle's faces. Every face splashed with the red of fire, straggling beards and matted hair like tangles of gorse in the savage flare. Then the noise, the cannibal glare, all was gone and six yeomen were falling dead to the packed earth of the yard.

There were no spastic throes from the men who died, no graceful salmon-arcs to lend elegance to their ends. They simply dropped, like broken puppets, dropped as if their strings had been cut.

Katie's scream was lost in the guttural roar that came from out of the enveloping dark and with that roar came a group of thirty wretched wraiths. All wore ragged clothing, shirts and neckcloths soiled, their woollen coats and breeches rent and battered. Some came on without stockings, some with-out brogues but all came on with that single brutal roar of bloodlust and desperation. In the moonlight, the blades of swords and pikes winked like will-o'-the-wisps.

In the yard, one of the remaining yeos attempted to clamber on to his pan-icked horse but was borne under by the steel-edged tide. One other presented his carbine and loosed a single shot into the mass of attackers bearing down on him. None seemed to fall and the first pike-head drove him backwards while the second transfixed him where he lay. His screams mounted and mounted on wings of broken glass as the pikemen stabbed and kicked and stabbed again. Death at the end of a plunging blade; horrible and cruel and slow.

Without firelocks, both Shingleton and Thady Burke watched thirty men thunder toward them across the cold earth of Katie's dooryard and, without a word to each other, both turned to flee. Thady had almost reached the corner of the cabin when a ball from a pilfered carbine hammered into his left side. Gore erupting from his mouth, ribs broken, Burke collapsed, gasping, to the ground.

It is said that Lieutenant Shingleton evaded his pursuers for a mile and a half until the group of five men ran him to ground in a bog near Craanford. His naked body was found the following day, battered and pierced through with pike wounds.

Katie Furlong, however, was still shuddering from the treatment she had received at the lieutenant's hands when a pikeman knelt and lifted her to her feet. His thin face was filthily bearded and the bones of his skull protruded so much that he appeared to be wearing a death's head on his scrawny shoulders. He examined her battered face and shook his head, not in anger but in a kind of sad resignation, 'Jaysus, they don't rein back, do they?'

Katie felt the hardness of his hands on her trembling shoulders and let herself be supported by their firmness. Casting her gaze about, she watched as most of her tattered band of rescuers stripped and rifled the dead yeomen of anything even remotely valuable.

'Are you United Irishmen?' she said.

He smiled then and in that moment could be glimpsed the man he might have become had the summer of 1798 not erupted in flame and death and horror. He gestured around him, 'This dishevelled rabble is all that is left of a company of the United Irish Army. Us and others like us. The pride of our race.' His blue eyes swept the yard as the others of his band squabbled and argued over coin or jewellery, their weapons dropped, their bony hands grasping.

'Look at us madam. Look at us and tell us how proud you are of us.'

Katie, somewhat taken aback by his bitterness, moved his hands from off her shoulders. 'My husband,' she said at last. 'Can you tell me anything of Ned Furlong?'

The rebel took a step back as though to reappraise the woman in front of him. 'You're Ned Furlong's wife? The last I heard of Ned he was heading north with Anthony Perry and Fitzgerald, I think. But this was shortly after Lake came to Wexford Town. God knows where he is now.'

Katie thought he was about to say more when a shout came from a rebel leaning over Thady Burke. 'Here lads, this one hasn't gone off to his eternal reward yet. What should we do with him?'

Amidst cries of 'Stick him!' and 'Kill the Orangeman!' the man who had been speaking to Katie moved quickly to inspect Thady's prone form. The bullet had pierced his side and even in the darkness the amount of blood streaming from the wound had soaked his jacket, dyeing it from dark blue to a sopping black. Thady's lips were grotesquely smeared with red and his breathing was shallow and gurgled frothily.

The man who had been talking to Katie picked up a fallen sabre and, placing a boot on the yeoman's neck, was about to run him through when Thady's voice exploded forth in a spray of crimson, 'Don't kill me, Tom!'

The man, Tom, gasped and bent to look more closely at the fallen yeo. 'Thady Burke! For the love of all that's holy, Thady, what are you doing here? Knowing your family, I can understand you remaining with the yeos, but butchering women? Rapine and murder? This isn't you.'

'Twelve weeks, Tom,' wheezed Thady. 'Twelve weeks since I saw you riding with Knox Grogan's yeomanry corps. Is three months all it takes to turn two soldiers into butchers?'

Tom bent to comb his fingers through Thady Burke's sweat-lank hair. 'Three months? Is that all it is?'

'A lifetime, Tom.' And then Thady Burke said no more.

A young man whom Katie had noticed off to one side, wearing a military jacket and green sash, moved to stand by Tom's shoulder, 'You knew him, Tom? Was he in the Castletown Corps as well?'

'No, Miles. He was always in the Camolin Cavalry but we're the one age. I knew him as one young lad knows another.'

With that he stirred himself and raised his gaunt frame to its full height. Turning to Katie, he gestured toward the young man beside him, bearded and ragged but strangely unbowed with his short-tailed coat and grubby green sash. 'I'm unsure as to whether you've made acquaintance with this man before, but your husband fought under him. Allow me to introduce him – Captain Miles Byrne of the Monaseed Corps.'

Looking from one bearded rebel to the next, Katie felt a peculiar kind of dizziness curdle the substance of her thoughts. The events of the last half hour on this late summer's night had so agitated and horrified her that she was shaken and rattled right down to her very soul. Yet, in spite of this she addressed the captain calmly, 'Captain Byrne I would be very much grateful if, in a moment, you could tell me about my poor husband but first, if you will excuse me.'

With that she strode over to the corpse of Thady Burke and, forming all the horror and fear she had experienced into a hissing ball inside of her, she spat a mouthful of phlegm and blood and bile into its sightless face. She then linked arms with Miles Byrne and began to sob softly into her cupped right hand.

The eighteen year old captain gazed in helpless terror at the weeping woman on his arm and, clearing his throat, said, 'Tom, assemble the corps. We leave as soon as we are able.'

Nodding, Tom acknowledged, 'Yes, Miles.' But his thoughts were elsewhere, his eyes resting on the body of Thady Burke.

Twelve weeks? Had it been only three months?

Twenty minutes later with the moon nearing its apex and the company of pikemen assembled in two ranks, Tom Banville turned his back on Katie Furlong's farmyard, turned his back on the body of Thady Burke and turned his back on the shattered remnants of the only home he had ever known. At the head of a small corps of pike- and musketmen, Tom Banville marched out of County Wexford and only the tears that spilled from his eyes gave testimony to what he had truly left behind.

PART ONE

THE BOYS OF WEXFORD

CHAPTER I

Oath of Allegiance

The 25th of April, nearly three months before Tom Banville turned his back on his county, dawned bright and blue and glorious. This day, on the cusp of two seasons, was a herald of the golden warmth that would permeate May and flood through to June. Around Coolgreany, between the sea and the mountains, the sunshine was washing a torrent of green across the fields and ditches. Trees were dressed in their first shimmer of emerald and bibulous runnels of birdsong trickled through branch and briar. Under the canvas sky and upon the artist's palette of field and pasture, nothing suggested that things here were wrong, that things within this frame were grotesquely askew, misshapen.

The morning's cascade of sunshine brimmed the Banville stable yard with warmth. Laurence Banville was a Catholic middleman, well-to-do, liberal and respected and, as such, the large two-storey farmhouse he and his family occupied had attached to it, not just a stable yard, but a kennel as well. Even as the sun climbed to mid-morning the Banville pack of harriers could be heard yowling and snuffling. In the stables, however, there was little life. Only five horses remained. Three large hunters and two heavy-headed workhorses. Another five stables were unoccupied save for the mournful creak of hanging tack and the sick-bed buzzing of flies.

This morning the mounting sun caught Laurence's two sons and a companion standing in the stable yard. Tom wore a black woollen frock coat over a high-collared white linen shirt, a pair of buff buckskin breeches, linen stockings and a pair of heavy black brogues. In his hands he held a black tricorn beaver.

Resting his broad shoulders against the wall of his father's house, he regarded his two companions with a wry smile.

'If you would like to reconsider your entering into our wager, Proctor, I won't allow it to affect your standing in my affections.'

Richard Proctor, a heavy-featured young man dressed in the red coat of Thomas Knox Grogan's Castletown Cavalry, was pursing his lips and frowning, his brows like an approaching storm front. His Tarleton helmet was placed on a barrel beside him and he unconsciously riffled one callused set of fingers through its bearskin crest. At his side a light cavalry sabre hung motionless in the morning heat.

Still frowning, the yeoman turned to Tom, 'A gentleman never reneges, Tom.'

He then lifted his head as four of the summer's first flight of swallows bolted over the yard, black lightning strikes against blue.

'However I feel we should hurry. We muster in Gorey at three.'

At this, the third occupant of the yard, standing with his back to the others, snorted out a great explosion of derision and muttered something under his breath. Without another word he busied himself with a task hidden from the others by the bulk of his torso.

Dan Banville was five years older than his brother and, apart from the fact that he wore no coat, was dressed exactly as his younger sibling. However, his carriage was slightly heavier than Tom's, his shoulders wider, his face rounder and the blue-grey of his eyes under dark brows somehow deeper and less sparkling. Under his short hair his high forehead was already a match for his father's.

Tom shook his head in exasperation, 'Dan, just because you wouldn't take the oath does not give you license to offend me or to offer offence to our friends.'

Dan turned around then and in his hands he carried two pistols. Both were primed and both set at half cock. 'That coat ould Richard over there is wearing is an offence to all Irishmen and that bloody oath you're going to take this afternoon is an offence to our family.'

Overhead the swallows screamed and darted, hurling themselves through the honeyed air, oblivious and frantic.

'Now, Richard,' he continued. 'A shilling for the two, or nothing. Are they the terms?'

Proctor, still frowning, nodded, 'They're the terms. But I cannot fathom how you intend to accomplish this, Dan. At the first report they'll be off like scalded cats.'

Dan grinned, winked at Proctor then turned to his brother, 'Just don't drink this all in the one place.'

Smiling, Tom blessed himself and set his lean features in a pose of beatific innocence.

Still grinning, Dan rolled up his sleeves, brought both pistols to full cock and raised his eyes and arms skywards. He had only ever done this twice before but even as he lifted his gaze he felt the old coolness, the familiar sureness infuse every fibre. He knew, everyone knew, that he was the best sharpshooter in three baronies, possibly the county. With one of the long shore guns of Shelmalier he could hit a bullseye at four hundred yards. As he lifted his arms he felt his senses condense into that familiar sphere of ice which nothing and no one could hope to penetrate.

Overhead, the swallows darted and yawed, pitched and swooped in erratic exultation. Watching them, Richard Proctor knew that, no matter how good Dan was, he could never be *that* good. And, watching him, Tom was already counting his money.

In Dan's hands both pistols moved, almost of their own volition and his eyes roved back and forth until, with a gradual application of pressure, he squeezed the two pistol butts. There was no abrupt and violent jerking of Dan's hands, just a seeming caress of the triggers and the black barrels of the pistols erupted almost simultaneously.

Through air made suddenly acrid and choked with powder smoke two small black bundles plummeted to the earth, their joyous hurtling stilled, their tiny bodies broken by the searing hammering of lead.

Into the silent vacancy left by the pistols' reports, into the powder-clouded air, Tom Banville's voice said, 'That'll be a shilling there, Proctor.'

Richard Proctor was just delving into a pocket when the Banvilles' back door was flung open with such shuddering violence that the three young men were startled and spun round. As though the house had swallowed its tongue, there was a void in the wall which was immediately filled by the figure of old Laurence Banville. His balding head with its hatchet nose was a spitting ball of fury and his left fist was clenched into a knobbled mass of white knuckles and vein-scrawled skin. His frame was thin and wasting now, in his sixty-eighth year, but his voice still carried a bellowing authority, 'What in God's name are you two boys doing out here? If I find gunplay carrying on in my yard, I shall horsewhip the both of you!'

Before Dan could say anything, his father's gaze had alighted upon the smoking pistols in his hands. The old man's face flushed puce and Dan was certain that he and his brother were about to be on the receiving end of a verbal cannonade when Laurence Banville noticed the red coat of Richard Proctor, standing dumbfounded with one hand buried in his breeches pocket.

All colour leached from the old man's face as though the very blood had drained from his extremities. His features became still and the fury that had flamed behind his eyes was dissipated and quenched. As Dan and Tom watched their father, he became almost a wax effigy of the man they knew. The unnatural pallor of his skin, the dull pebbles of his eyes, all bespoke of some profound change that the sight of the young yeoman had provoked in him.

Dan and Tom looked on as their father raised one curiously tremulous finger and jabbed it like a pike towards Proctor, saying, 'Richard, I know you and I knew your father, and I hope to God he's not looking down on you now. He was a good Protestant but he was no bigot. That jacket makes you an instrument of the tyrant.'

Proctor winced as though struck and splayed his hands, palms outwards, almost in a gesture of supplication, 'Come now, Mr Banville, Thomas Knox Grogan is a moderate man. He has always concentrated his utmost endeavours to further the well-being of his Catholic tenants.'

He pointed to Dan, who was surreptitiously attempting to push the brace of pistols into the waistband of his breeches, and protested, 'Even Dan there was in the Castletown Corps.'

His finger still pointing accusingly at Proctor, Laurence Banville almost spat the next words, 'And he left. He and the majority of the good Catholic boys. All apart from my noble youngest son. And do you know why?' He paused, 'Because of that thrice accursed oath! It is an open wound on the face of egalitarianism and its sole function is to turn the yeomanry into an Orange-man's plaything.'

Proctor blinked in shocked silence and Dan moved forward, his mouth opening to interject something into the ragged quiet. Then Tom said softly, carefully, 'I'm taking the Test Oath, Da.'

Laurence Banville looked at his youngest son, an expression of contempt and disgust curdling his features and, without another word, entered his house and slammed the door behind him.

Dan stabbed a glance at Richard Proctor, who was kicking at the hardened earth of the yard in awkward discomfiture, and then stalked over to his brother.

'Tom, if you consent to take the oath Da will disown you if you're lucky and most likely shoot you otherwise.'

Tom did not even look his brother in the face. His expression a mocking, haughty, half-smile that set Dan's blood to boiling, he said, 'Da doesn't like any-one with a bit of money. For God's sake he calls Hunter Gowan an "upstart". If you and Mother give him his head he will ruin this family. We will end up scratching in the muck like half the rest of our good Catholic fellows.'

Ignoring Proctor's polite embarrassed cough, Dan glared at his brother and felt the first real saw-edge of anger enter into his voice, 'So you would rather take an oath that renounces your religion? Why do you think forty of us resigned on the spot when we were asked to take it?'

Tom, with the iced superiority of the deliberately insulting, finally looked at his brother and said, 'Because you are fools. The oath renounces the United Irishmen, not Rome. Besides, if you and father are so eager to find slight in empty phrases then I am not.'

With that he stormed into the house, shouting, 'I'm putting on my uniform Proctor. We shall be off presently.'

Richard Proctor, who had been studiously examining the toecaps of his riding boots, now looked up at the sound of Tom's voice and, turning to Dan, he mumbled, 'I'm sorry, Dan.'

Dan's temper still made a blazing fist inside his chest and he fixed the yeoman with a look of molten lead, 'Don't apologise to me Richard. Just ensure that you preserve that lovely uniform from the dust of the road. You must look your finest beside the North Cork Regiment and Hunter Gowan. Who can suppose but perhaps even George Ogle himself might be there to hold some innocent down while you pitch cap them.'

Proctor reeled as though drunk and his jaw slackened in genuine anguish. However the words that came next from his lips were toneless and shorn of any demonstration of emotion, 'I am aggrieved to hear you speak so, Dan, you and your father both. I shall not besmirch your doorstep again. If you do not mind I shall await your brother at the front of the house where my horse is tethered. Good day to you.'

He had spun on his heel and was marching around the corner of the farmhouse before Dan could utter another word.

A few moments later, while Dan was cleaning his pistols, Tom came striding out the back door, buckling on his sword belt as he did so, his carbine tucked under one arm. His red coat glowed in the morning sun and the black helmet on his head cast highlights of deep blue back towards the sky. His eyes looked up from under the bearskin crest and, glancing about, he asked, 'What have you done with Proctor?'

Dan shrugged, big shoulders bunching under his shirt, 'He rambled off around the front.'

Tom grunted and with raking strides crossed the yard and disappeared into one of the stables. Some while later he reappeared leading the big grey mare on which he sometimes accompanied their father behind the hounds. The horse's tack was carefully polished and the long holster for Tom's cavalry carbine gleamed with a greasy lustre.

Mounting the animal, Tom glanced down at his elder brother, 'Tell Ma and Da I won't be home for dinner this evening.'

Looking up at him from where he stood in the yard, an empty and oily pistol in one hand, Dan was suddenly struck by some inexplicable notion. Reaching out his other hand, he grasped the grey's bridle before Tom could wheel her and, taking in his brother's face, his bright eyes and the obsidian stubbornness about his mouth, he stated simply, 'Grogan's lucky to have you.'

Then, like a flame breaking from dead ash, a smile swept across Tom's face and he said, 'Indeed, I should be flattered at that had Thomas Knox Grogan and his ilk any standing whatsoever in my affections.'

Laughing, Tom nudged his mount into a walk and called out, clear under the blue sky so that his voice must carry over the farmstead's roof, 'Proctor, you rascal, you still owe us a shilling!'

Grinning in spite of himself, Dan watched his little brother go, listening to the heavy clop of hooves grow ever more distant, listening to their father's hounds bawl and keen at the horse's passing. Then Dan returned to his cleaning as a thin layer of dust settled like a dry frost on the shattered remnants of two dead summer swallows and the first of the flies began to land.

The road from Coolgreany to Gorey ran roughly due south through the village of Inch and then swung southwest into Gorey. Bordered by ditches on both sides, the road was little more than a wide band of hard-packed clay, a deep brown scar slashing through the countryside. Along this road Tom Banville and Richard Proctor trotted their mounts. Proctor's black gelding was not as deep in the chest and maybe a hand smaller than Tom's big mare but, nevertheless, their animals afforded both yeomen a clear view over the ditches and into the neighbouring fields.

They passed by pasture and smallholding, bawn and cabin, all bright and somehow cheerful beneath the porcelain sky. Most cabins in County Wexford were large in comparison to the hovels found in other parts of the country. The majority contained two or three partitioned rooms within their stout, white-washed walls and every one was in good repair. Windows, some even glazed, were opened to the warming air and from the thatched, low-eaved roofs, the narrow turrets of brick or stone chimneys exhaled hazy membranes of smoke into the sky. Around the cabins, the rich, deep soil of Wexford was corrugated and furrowed with potato drills, whilst a little further away the straining stalks of oats and barley needled towards the sun. Sties for pigs and cattle and even a small barn frequently adjoined these little cottages and each plot of fifty or so acres was farmed by five or six different families. Gorse, briar and copses of trees encroached here and there, creating natural boundaries and barbed impenetrable barriers. Prosperity and industry seemed to radiate from every tilled garden, every fat pig and calf.

As they rode, Tom and Proctor waved or nodded to people they knew. Men in the fields, their short coats hanging on branches and their shirts clinging and damp through the efforts of clearing briar or hoeing earth, grunted in the heat. Women standing at doorways in gay straw hats battled with children who pulled at the dun cotton of their unstiffened, sleeveless bodices, like waistcoats, worn over their blue muslin dresses. Occasionally, some cottier's daughter would smile coyly at them and be cuffed by her mother or father. And all along as they travelled the songs of birds mingled with the rough sounds of agriculture.

It was then, just as Tom was half convinced that he had found paradise under an April sky that a crawling unease began to spread its delicate tendrils beneath his skin.

A burned cabin was the first incongruity.

Then an old farmer, standing at a gate, his gnarled form leaning on his scythe, spat upon the road as they passed by. There, a young mother, seeing their uniforms, shielded her six-year-old daughter's eyes and dragged the child behind her skirts. Here, two young men without hoe or fork, took to their heels at their approach and vanished into the ditches. And now a boy, no more than ten, stood in the growing barley and smiled a slow, lazy smile. A smile that seemed to say, *I know something you do not.*

As Tom rode, his feeling of unease swelled into something black and awful. Behind the verdant façade in front of him, something dark stirred. The people, his people, saw his uniform and were afraid. Here, in his own land, Tom Banville suddenly felt like a stranger.

He had not realised that he was swivelling in his saddle, warily scanning the small paddocks to either side, until Richard Proctor's voice brought him back to himself.

'There are rats in these fields, Tom.'

Tom shrugged noncommittally, 'The people seem afraid, Richard. Have

Hunter Gowan and Hawtrey White over at Peppard's Castle exceeded themselves so badly?'

Proctor nodded, a curt jerk of his chin, 'You know yourself. Ever since those sixteen parishes around here were proclaimed last November, men like those two have been given the whip hand.'

'Can Mountnorris not do something to limit the worst of it?'

Proctor snorted, 'He tries, but a proportion of loyalists are frightened out of their wits by the spectre of the French. The very mention of a United Irishman makes them either wet themselves or spurs them to violence.'

Tom undid the top button of his tunic and rubbed a hand briskly across the back of his neck, trying to dislodge the hard knot of anxiety that had suddenly tangled itself there.

'By God, Proctor,' he began at last, 'I know not one man who has sworn himself to the United Irish cause. Not one. But if I know not one, then the predations of Gowan and White and that idiot Ogle down by Enniscorthy will have the green flag hoisted in Wexford by the end of the year. With or without the French.'

Richard Proctor looked at his comrade and, reaching across the gap between their horses, he placed one gloved hand on Tom's shoulder. 'That's why we need the likes of you, Tom. Stout Papists but loyal. If the yeomanry became what your brother and father think they've become, if all Catholics are driven to the United Irish banner for protection, then this county will go up in flames.'

Tom chuckled and fastened the button of his high collar once more, 'You do know Wolfe Tone is a Protestant, Proctor.'

Proctor's heavy brows scuttled together like fat caterpillars, 'He's a traitor though. When you cut away all the dead wood and obfuscation, religion has little substance in this matter. 'Loyalty', that should be our byword. The Pope or the King can be used as a stick to beat people but if there's a revolt like in France, a priest will go to the guillotine as quickly as you or I.'

'And what pray tell should a people do when the 'stick', as you so put it, is wielded by a bully like Hunter Gowan and his mob?'

Puffing out his cheeks Proctor let slip a sigh of resignation, 'That, my friend, is the rotten heart of things.'

They rode on in silence after that, jogging south towards Gorey. Tom tried to keep his mind from wandering, tried to focus on mundane things and not consider the implications of what he was about to do at the muster in the market town. Tom was neither blind nor numb to the brutality of the county's corps of yeomanry. He knew that a uniform and sabre were, to some men, a license to rape and pillage. He also knew that John Beauman of the Coolgreany Cavalry had avowed to put his corps 'upon a true Protestant and Orange system.'

The countryside between Inch and Gorey was, on the surface, as peaceful seeming as the rest of the county. Yet, even here, amidst green fields and nodded 'Good days', dark coils of smoke would occasionally snake over the horizon, testament to a smouldering atrocity.

The market town of Gorey was built on the slope and crest of a gradually steepening hill. It consisted of one long main street with a number of smaller streets leading off it at right angles. It had no defensive wall or ditch and was in fact one of the few modern, planned towns in the county. The streets of Gorey were all of dark clay, trampled and packed to such an extent as to be almost impermeable. At the top of the main street, where the road crested the brow of the hill, was a market diamond. In the centre of this diamond grew a venerable old beech tree, its bark grey and wrinkled, like cords of cooled lava. The main body of the town was made up of two- and three-storey townhouses, stores and market premises all with slate roofs and high gaping windows. However, all the inroads to this main street were lined with small grubby cabins, some standing singly and others crammed in fetid intimacy against their neighbours, their thatch drooping and ragged.

It was past a row of these dilapidated labourers' cottages that the two yeos entered Gorey's main thoroughfare at two o'clock. Immediately upon entering the town both Tom and Proctor became aware of a number of other yeomen in the uniform of their Castletown corps standing or lounging in the street. One figure, a tall, thickset man with the neck and shoulders of a bull terrier waved to them in greeting and strode over to them.

Both Tom and Proctor saluted smartly from their saddles. 'Lieutenant Esmonde,' they chorused.

Their lieutenant saluted in return and regarded the two younger men with frank scrutiny. 'Proctor, fix your chin strap before the muster.'

He then ran a hand through his hair to slick back its chestnut waves and nodding to himself addressed the two men on horseback once more, 'We are to be all present in squadron files at the diamond before the stroke of three. I would advise you gentlemen to keep an ear out for Pat Healy's bugle. Lord Mountnorris has come up from Camolin Park to inspect us, as a consequence of which Mr Knox Grogan decided to muster here and save his lordship a journey.

'Now boys,' he growled, 'with both those esteemed gentlemen present I shall not be amused to find you too deeply in your cups. Look sharp lads. Do you hear me Banville?'

Tom looked down at his lieutenant, his face a mask of pious sobriety, 'Lieutenant, you may place your complete trust in us as individuals and indeed in the corps as a whole. To offer slight to Mr Knox Grogan or Lord Mountnorris would be to invite ridicule upon ourselves.'

Lieutenant Esmonde studied both young yeomen and simply intoned, 'You have been cautioned. Heed it.'

He then saluted and without waiting for their response he marched off to where a group of six yeomen were gathered outside the Peacock Inn.

Tom slumped forward in his saddle, relaxing the straight-backed posture he had adopted in the presence of his lieutenant. 'Well the old goat is certainly exerting himself today. We'll find it hard to sink a drop anywhere in this town with him galloping about like that.'

Proctor was frowning to himself and then one of his eyebrows rose in a speculative arch, 'Unless we head up to that place off the diamond itself. You know, ourselves and Thady Burke had a nice sup there a couple of weeks back. The Old Beech it's called or something very similar.'

Tom, stretching slightly so that he was leaning out of his saddle, slapped Proctor between the shoulder blades and exclaimed, 'Richard, beneath that bovine aspect, you are undoubtedly nursing a functioning mind. Come then, let's do as much damage as we can before young Healy and his damned trumpet summon us to do our duty.'

Gorey's main street was an odd sight as Tom and Proctor jogged their mounts up its gradual slope. Hundreds of locals strolled or hurried or stood in muttering groups, clenched about some grumbled secret. Occasionally a hot glare would be lanced towards the yeomen from some scuttling urchin or pipe-sucking labourer. The rich in their frock coats and waistcoats, their sun-bonneted ladies sashaying at their sides, the poor with their patched jackets and stocking-less breeches, their bare calves grimed and soiled, all milled and moved, jostled and bumped in the heady Brownian motion of a prosperous town. Yet here and there amidst the civilian scurrying, the uniforms of the Castletown yeomanry gathered in scabrous clusters of red. To Tom this was to be expected but what surprised him, took him so completely unawares that it forced him to rein his mare to a halt, and unhinged the firm set of his lower jaw, was the presence of other uniforms amidst the mundane to and froing of Gorey's citizenry.

Clotted on street corners or strolling along the boardwalk that ran on either side of the roadway, the red coats and black bicorns of an infantry regiment blazed out from the blues and greys of their surroundings. Beneath white cross-belts, clasped at their intersection by a brass buckle, the soldiers' wide lapels were turned back to reveal their yellow facing colour.

Tom found himself shaking his head, 'The North Cork Militia. Jesus, they're everywhere.'

Proctor nodded, 'I believe the regiment numbers about six hundred. They've been arriving in detachments to be billeted around the county.'

Tom's face was expressionless but his eyes, blue-grey as a calm sea, were now abruptly threatening as thunderheads. 'And I believe,' he stated, 'that they marched into Wexford openly wearing Orange insignia and that one of their principle acts was to set up an Officer's Lodge in Wexford Town.

'Damn Ogle's black heart for inviting them into this county. It is like inviting a wolf to your door.'

Proctor was also regarding the infantrymen with a look of vague distrust, 'I stand shoulder to shoulder with you Tom. If the county is put under martial law, those blackguards will be to the forefront of any mischief that occurs.'

Then he turned to his companion, 'I have it on good authority that the pitchcap was never seen in Wexford before the introduction of the tenantry to our good Cork friends.'

'I've heard that also. God in heaven, with the North Corks at people's throats and Catholics leaving the yeomanry in floods, any United Irishman in the district must be awaiting the call to arms sure in the knowledge that every peasant in Wexford will rally to them.'

Proctor set his horse in motion once more, saying as he did so, 'Day by day Tom, things get a little worse. And every new element added to the mix simply brings it all to the boil more quickly. I fear for us, Tom.'

Tom watched Proctor as his horse moved off through the scattered clumps of townsfolk, watched and let the yeoman's words settle into his brain like a corpse to the bottom of a pond. Then, without any conscious thought, without any effort of will, Tom's right hand came up and he blessed himself. In the name of the Father, the Son and the Holy Spirit. It was at that moment, that vulnerable instant when he unthinkingly beseeched the Almighty for protection, that Tom Banville realised he too was afraid.

Almost an hour later, the shrill brassy tone of Pat Healy's cavalry bugle climbed above the hive buzzing of Gorey's streets and alleyways. Climbed and climbed until its piercing note reached a high sustained pitch only to fall again into the chatter and laughter of shopkeeper and storehand.

Squatting on low stools in the smoky murk of The Old Beech, Tom and Proctor looked up from their pewter mugs of whiskey. Proctor's shilling had stretched without difficulty over the distance of half a dozen drinks and both young men had consumed more than was prudent in such a short space of time. While neither was drunk both found themselves struggling to articulate certain words and their eyes were laced with a tracery of red.

Raising a finger to his lips Proctor whispered, 'Do you think they would miss us from the ranks?'

Tom grinned, 'As much as it pains me to say so, I would assume that two such gallant figures of soldiery as ourselves would be immediately noted as absent and almost as immediately drummed out of the corps.'

Tilting his mug and tossing its harsh contents down his throat, Proctor said with a grimace, 'That might not be such an ignominious fate.'

Both yeomen rose to their feet and strode through suspended ribbons of pungent pipe smoke on their way to the door. As they passed a table of motley-looking cottiers, Tom thought that, soft as falling eiderdown, the word *slieveen* was whispered by one of the men. Tom did not slow his stride but his flinty stare was returned by each one of the grimy gathering, unabashed and brazen.

Once the two young men had stepped beyond the inn's doorway and into the afternoon glare of the street, Tom turned to Proctor who circumvented his indignant outburst, saying, 'I heard it too, Tom. But it's best not to get involved in any kind of a brawl in the current climate. The entire population would turn on us. Besides, we can't have bloody noses for his Lordship's inspection.'

Tom regarded his friend with eyes bloodshot from drink and squinting in the sudden light of day, 'I suppose that is true enough but, regardless of this uniform, as a man I cannot countenance such insolence.'

Both yeomen moved toward the splintered hitching rail to which their two horses had been securely tied. Proctor, attempting to appease his friend, gave Tom a light punch on the shoulder. 'If you allow your temper to bubble so, you will find yourself in a bout of fisticuffs with some low ruffian. The insult wasn't public and wasn't directed toward you personally.'

'I suppose,' Tom grunted and then, smiling at Proctor, he commented, 'I hope that my eyes don't resemble the marbles that are staring out of your face or Lieutenant Esmonde will be apoplectic.'

Laughing, the men swung up into their saddles and wheeled their horses about. In front of them, the lane they were now trotting along joined with the main thoroughfare just as it came to the crest of its slope. Turning to the right, the two yeomen followed the street until it levelled off and opened out into Gorey's market diamond.

Before them, much of the yeomanry corps was already assembled. Each red-coated trooper sitting his horse and conversing with his comrades. Occasionally a horse would shy or prance upon the hard clay, sending up little cumulous exhalations of dust. The smell of horseflesh and the reek of men under a hot sun attracted swarms of flies which alighted upon horse and rider and settled on the mounds of dung spattered about that wide meeting place. The huge beech tree rose from the centre of this diamond. Its branches were mostly bare so early in the season but its lower arms were now slung with creepers of bunting. Red, white and blue triangles sewn on to a white length of rope festooned the tree's dark boughs and at its base a rough stage made a rickety platform large enough for three or four people to stand abreast. Even now, as the cavalry gathered before it, two workmen in sag-brimmed hats were hammering the last few nails into the stage's unpainted timbers. The sound of their labour pounded out over the crowd of horsemen, regular as a drumbeat.

As order asserted itself beneath the raised horsewhip and cajoling tongue of Lieutenant Esmonde, the fifty or so cavalrymen in the diamond formed up into five squads of ten, each squad in two ranks of five yeomen. It was then, as he and Proctor moved to join their respective ranks that Tom perceived, gathered on the edge of the diamond, the red-coated forms of several of the North Cork Regiment. Each soldier was armed with a musket and a bayonet hung from a pipeclayed sling at his hip. Even from a distance of fifty yards, Tom could see the sour derision on their faces as they surveyed the horse boys and, as he watched, one placed his Brown Bess between his legs and mimicked a child on a cockhorse, flapping his bicorn above his head like something deranged.

Maybe thirty yards to the left of this group, Tom was astonished to see the mounted figure of John Hunter Gowan sitting astride a massive bay charger. Wearing a scarlet frock coat with fashionably turned down lapels and cuffs over a white, ruffled shirt, white breeches and black riding boots, Tom considered that the old loyalist had firmly nailed his colours to the mast. Upon Hunter Gowan's head, a black bicorn, worn with the points fore and aft, only served to amplify the desired impression of a British military officer. He was casting his condescending gaze over the yeomen and a fatherly smile played at the corners of his wide mouth.

Not for the first time that day, Tom considered the implications of what he intended to do. Around him he could count only seven other Catholics and in that number he included Sir Thomas Esmonde, the First Lieutenant. At the turn of the year there had been forty-seven. All had resigned, some claimed they had been forced to resign, at the prospect of the Test Oath. He himself had been away in Dublin on the occasion of the first swearing, he had not been there to persuade his brother and the others to retract their resignations. He was sure that his pragmatism would have swayed at least some of them.

Yet here he was, as the April sun spread warmth from his black helmet to his already damp scalp and then down the back of his neck. Here he was, with flies buzzing around his ears and his horse nervous under him. Here he was, with a shadow-host of doubts clamouring within his brain.

A crowd of townsfolk had begun gathering at the mouth of the diamond, muttering and laughing, the women bending their heads together and the men taking out pocket watches or glancing at the sun. Then, at the head of the troop, sitting his horse alone and isolated, Lieutenant Esmonde raised his sword in his right hand and in a voice that resonated from building to building over the bearskin crests of the yeomen, he announced, 'Captain Thomas Knox Grogan and His Excellency, the Right Honourable Lord Mountnorris.'

There was a muffled cheer from the crowd which was quickly hushed but Tom was unnerved that a number of hisses and lowing boos went up along with the acclamations. Undeterred, Lieutenant Esmonde continued, 'Three cheers for the captain and His Lordship! Hip-hip!'

And from the ranks of yeomen, 'Huzzah!'

'Hip-hip!'

'Huzzah!'

'Hip-hip!'

And on the last 'Huzzah!' two men emerged from one of the market houses facing out onto the diamond. One man was middle-aged, portly and wore the Tarleton helmet and braided uniform of a yeomanry officer while the second, older and much slimmer, wore the elegant attire and pinched expression of a member of the aristocracy.

The two peasant labourers had completed their work on the platform beneath the beech tree and were even now hurrying off to one side, tugging the drooping brims of their hats as they went. Knox Grogan and Mountnorris, for this was whom the two most recently arrived gentlemen evidently were, mounted the rough-hewn steps of the platform and stood facing the yeomanry while the planks beneath their feet groaned treacherously.

As Tom watched, Lord Mountnorris came to the front of the stage and raised one lined hand for silence. The entire gathering, even the attendant townsfolk and their urchins, fell quiet. Mountnorris's features were pallid in the daylight and wattles of grey skin clung heavily to his eye sockets as he began to speak. And as his words echoed in the spring air, it was apparent to all those gathered there that the biggest landowner in all of Wexford was exhausted and under grievous strain.

In a voice cracked and arid he began, 'Yeomanry of the Castletown Corps, loyal subjects of the King and true friends. You have been called to muster here today to pledge your loyalty to your King and Country and to renounce once and for all any and all activities or organisations of a subversive bent. There are those of our enemies who would seek to pull our great civilisation down about our ears. There are those who would hope to ape the barbarity of the Americans and the excesses of the French. This we cannot, under God, allow.

'For some of you this is your second swearing of this oath and I would implore you not to consider it an insult to your proven character that you must perforce revisit ground over which you have already passed. For that I apologise but I will say that this second round of the oath is a most dreadful necessity.

'Sixteen parishes in this county have been proclaimed by certain magistrates to be in a state of open rebellion. Sixteen, when one is too many! But, my friends, if we prove our loyalty and foreswear all other paths we may continue relatively unmolested during these trying times.'

At this, the aging aristocrat raised his hands and voice and cried out, 'How many gathered here would wish martial law declared on this county? How many?'

From around Tom a scattered few yeomen cried out in the negative but from behind him, from the ranks of the curious townsfolk, a great roar went up, 'No!' and mingled in amongst it were cries of, 'Send the North Corks home!' and, 'Stop the burnings!'

Now, however, from some unknown compulsion, Tom sought out the form of Hunter Gowan amongst the press of people. There he still sat, resplendent upon his great horse, a handkerchief, like an eruption of froth, extravagantly pressed over his mouth. From one laced corner leaked a wrinkle of lip and from the wild gleam of his eyes Tom knew that the man was laughing.

Mountnorris gestured for silence before continuing, 'I am relieved to hear your voices raised so. To impose the rule of the military on such an industrious and peaceable population would be an abomination.'

He addressed the ranks of yeomen sweating in their uniforms, their horses snorting and quivering impatiently, 'Yeomanry, your captain will now conduct you in your oath.'

With that he stepped aside and Captain Knox Grogan, flushed and limping slightly with gout, moved to take his place. In one dimpled hand he held up a heavy, leather-bound bible, the red silk page marker lolling from it like a serpent's tongue. His voice was stronger than Mountnorris's and it boomed out over the crowd, 'Castletown Corps, in God's presence, raise your right hand.'

Along with every other man in his corps Tom Banville lifted his gauntleted right hand. 'Damn you to hell, Da,' he muttered. 'And you too, Dan. I'll do this for us and for our family. I'll not have us ruined in the eyes of the powerful. Men of consequence have only one creed and it comes in a purse.'

From the corner of his vision, Tom perceived Richard Proctor dart him a lightning glance and then look away, smiling.

Then the world seemed to explode into a mass of startled shouts and whinnying horses.

The crowd, choking the point where the diamond became Gorey's main street, scattered like quail. Women screamed and violently hauled bare-footed children, wailing, to safety and from out of this rent in the throng, sitting astride his roan gelding, Laurence Banville thundered like the coming apoca-lypse.

Yeomen fled to either side of his hunter's path, some fighting to control their terrified horses, some drawing their swords, but none, not one, moved to inter-cept the furious old man. For furious he was. Even as his father flew across the hard clay of the diamond Tom could see, could feel, the anger radiating from him. His eyes were twin bullet holes of black rage and his liverstrip lips were pulled back from teeth bared in a yellow snarl. His horse's flanks were covered in the foam of its exertions and in his hand he carried a heavy, straight-bladed sword.

Tom sawed at his mount's reins, striving to steady her as the other cavalry mounts bucked and danced like the waves of a parting sea. His father, amidst all the screams, the shouts, the frantic orders and countermands, his father, with a face like the devil himself, was upon him before Tom could even call on him to stop.

Laurence Banville brought his horse to a rearing halt before his astonished son. The gelding pawed the air for a moment and then stood blowing and huff-ing wetly, its mad rush at last ended. Around the father and son the yeomen simply sat their saddles in stunned silence. Even Mountnorris, Knox Grogan, and Lieutenant Esmonde seemed completely dumbstruck. From the ringing crowd of townsfolk, however, first one child and then another began to bawl their fright up into the uncaring sky.

'Da—' began Tom, but before he could continue or even formulate a proper sentence, his father had cut him off.

'Thomas, I will not let you do this. I have not had a second's repose since you informed me of your decision and I thank St. Patrick that I've arrived here in time. So help me, Thomas, I will cut you down myself before I allow you to give yourself over, body and soul, to this shower of murdering lickspittles.'

At these words some of the yeomen closest to the two men made to heft their weapons. They stilled, however, when Tom's sword flashed from out its scabbard, the whispered slither of its drawing a sibilant promise of death. His horse prancing beneath him, Tom roared, fixing one yeo after another with a glare of inferno belligerence, 'The first man to raise arms against my father will die on this blade.'

In the midst of this, as Tom's horse pirouetted and he held his own comrades at bay, Hunter Gowan's voice raised itself in mockery, 'You see? Gentlemen, this is why Papists and the lower sort should not be allowed to wear the King's uniform.'

Like a whip-crack Laurence Banville dragged his exhausted mount around and faced Hunter Gowan, the sword in his old hands levelled and pointing at the loyalist middleman.

'Lower sort?' he raged, 'I'll 'lower sort' you, Gowan, you upstart cur. There is better blood in my dogs than in you, me old shillicock.'

At this, most of the watching crowd and yeomanry gasped in shocked disbelief. However, Tom noted with a certain glee, quite a few of both yeos and civilians let out a great gust of laughter. Hunter Gowan's face became livid, almost the colour of raw meat, but before he could retort, Lieutenant Esmonde had grasped the bridles of both Tom and his father's horse and was glaring at both men. The Lieutenant was on foot now and so was forced to look up at the two mounted figures above him. As a consequence the sunlight falling across his face made his brown eyes glitter and flash. He was blisteringly angry.

'How dare you gentlemen! The sheer gall of it! First you disgrace yourselves by interrupting the Test Oath and remonstrating in front of the Captain and His Lordship and then you most outrageously insult a most loyal and zealous guardian of the community. For shame gentlemen! For shame!'

Laurence Banville, sword still in hand, stared down at the lieutenant, 'I have come here for my son. I'll not bandy words—'

However, his flow of invective was truncated by Lieutenant Esmonde's volcanic indignation, 'I have not finished, sir! As for your son you are welcome to him. He reeks of whiskey and I cannot and will not stand idly by while a man draws steel on his fellow soldiers. Your son has brought shame on his corps and should consider himself lucky not to be summarily court-martialled.

'As for you,' he continued, addressing Tom, 'I suggest you return home with your father and await the Captain's summons. I am afraid your actions do not sit well with him. I am sorry to say I cannot see this going softly for you. You and your father are a disgrace. A disgrace!'

He turned from them, releasing their horses' bridles with an angry snap of the wrist, 'Now be gone!'

Laurence sat blinking for a moment before gathering his wits, 'I will not sit here on my own horse in my own land and be insulted by that popinjay.'

Tom turned to his father, his sword resting across his thighs, and snapped, 'You will do anything he says because otherwise he will clap us both in irons. You've had your little victory, Da. You've prevented me going against our family's vaunted principles. I'll be fortunate if they don't put me on trial over this.'

He then transferred his gaze from his father to the yeomen, to the townsfolk, to the North Corks and to Hunter Gowan. Every face all at once seemed to belong to a sneering goblin. Pointed fingers and jeering guffaws were all directed toward the two Banvilles. Even Proctor was trying to stifle his laughter.

Seething now, a young man's wounded pride heating his words, he snapped, 'You've had your little victory, Da and all you had to do to accomplish it was make a laughing stock of us both. When the tenants mock at mother on the way to mass, when people refuse to do business with you, you will find their cause in this one clownish act. You are a buffoon.'

His father regarded him carefully, his rheumy eyes devoid of anger. Now they brimmed only with the hurt inflicted by Tom's words. He sighed once, long and slow, emptying his brittle chest in a morose sough of emotion. Then, quietly, he said, 'I would rather see all the leases burned and you dead than ever see you swear yourself over to them.'

For a moment of stunned silence, Tom sat his horse and then, urging it into a trot, brushed past his father and made his way through the ranks of his comrades, who kept their eyes downcast, past the North Corks and the grinning Hunter Gowan. Ears pricked forward, the mare bore him through the lines of sniggering townsfolk and down into the near-deserted streets of Gorey Town.

He needed a drink.

He found an inn on the eastern edge of the town that had everything he could have wanted – good stout, spirits and above all several rooms to rent. Tom had no intention of going home that night. His anger, his battered pride, would not allow it.

As soon as he had stabled his horse, he purchased a room and deposited sword, guns, jacket and Tarleton within, and locked the door. He had carefully stowed the key in his breeches pocket and then had taken up a comfortable, convenient – and permanent – position at the bar.

The common room where Tom found himself was long and low-built. Exposed rafters supported the ceiling above and upon the wooden floor clean straw was spread to soak up spillage and the dragged-in detritus of the patrons. The inn itself sat on the old coach road that ran south along the coast towards Wexford Town and it appeared to the bitter young cavalryman to capture a fair degree of passing trade. The inn's heavy door was opened to the afternoon sun and through this bright and airy rectangle a steady chain of customers rattled in and out. Amongst them Tom sat and breathed in the thick pall of pipe and turf smoke, drinking measure after measure and watching the splendour of the day gradually dim into the velvet of evening.

He had been sitting with his elbows resting on the bar counter and his hands curled protectively around his tumbler of stout for some time before the innkeeper approached, wiping his hands on his apron. With his face composed and carefully blank he commented, 'For one so young to labour under such dejection as you do, sir, sets me thinking that maybe you have a story to tell.'

Tom regarded him with the heavy-jowled frankness of a drunkard, 'I've no more story to me than any other soul who comes through your door.'

The man nodded to himself before addressing Tom once more, 'You see, that's where my difficulty lies. Most souls who do come through my door have a good few stories in them. They usually entertain us with wild fantasies of house burnings and torture, of laughing yeos shooting livestock and soldiers living on free quarters. Yet you sit here and claim no tale of your own?'

Tom took a thoughtful sip from his tumbler, his senses too leaden to mutter anything but, 'That I do.'

The innkeeper, a big man with a heavy paunch like a mortar shell behind his apron, smiled in sympathetic understanding. 'I see. Forgive me but the ostler who stabled your horse, and a fine animal too by all accounts, did happen to mention the cut of your travelling clothes, so to speak.'

Tom, the thick hide of his introspection finally pricked by the barb in the man's words, licked his lips and carefully pronounced, 'My travelling is done for this night at least.'

The big, aproned man before him nodded a single time, a barely perceptible ducking of the chin into the thick roll of flesh swelling out from beneath his jaw, and then he was gone. Occasionally, as he passed to scoop a pint for some other patron from the great keg beneath the counter, he would wordlessly add more to Tom's drink until the young man was comfortably enfolded in a fog of inebriation.

All this time, as he sat there sliding further and further into an alcoholic numbness, he had steadfastly refused to consider his father's actions, had refused to dwell on the anger he felt not just towards him but Dan as well. They were both so blind. Nevertheless, the further he pushed it from his mind, the more it preyed upon him, until at last his jaws throbbed from holding them clenched and his skull ached with tension. Only the deep earthy flavour of the stout gave him any release and with every bitter mouthful he felt his rage and embarrassment, little by little, lose their grip upon him. So he sat, slumped over his beer, until a tiny fragment of conversation snapped his head up and pulled his frame upright as though a ramrod had been slipped into his spine.

Two men had eased open the inn's door, closed for some time now as the early summer nights still retained a graveyard chill, and were removing their trusties, each man beating the dust from his greatcoat's cape-collars and sleeves. Both newcomers wore short jackets with round-buttoned cuffs and the tied neckerchiefs of tenant farmers or well-off labourers. It was from these men that Tom heard the words that so snagged his interest.

One of the men doffed his broad-brimmed hat and, placing it on a peg hammered into the wall, declared, 'Bejaysus, sure every blacksmith in the county's a United man. If Caulfield wants to excommunicate them all he'll have some job on his hands.'

The second man was about to respond to his companion when the inn-keeper abruptly barrelled through the aromatic murk of smoke and caught both men roughly by the front of their jackets. Tom could not guess what sentiments were exchanged between the three, but the innkeeper repeatedly flung apprehensive glances in his direction and, once, he thought he heard the word, 'Yeo', pitched soft and low and hissing.

At length, and without either buying a drink or sitting down, the two new-comers collected their belongings and departed, leaving the proprietor to fasten the door behind them. Wringing his hands in his apron once more, he approached Tom and leaned heavily on the counter beside him. His weight was enough to make the bar's stained planks sag and he listed into Tom so closely that the young man could smell the sour odour of his body through his linen shirt.

The man was missing several teeth and, as he whispered, Tom felt himself hypnotised by the tidal surge and withdraw of saliva through the gaps left behind. He regarded Tom with a gaze like a blade, 'It is almost nine of the clock, young sir, and seeing as you've paid for your bread and board, I can vouchsafe that, should you retire on the instant, you will sleep safe and sound until the morning. That is, unless some of your fellow travellers decide to come a-calling in the middle of the night with steel in their hands and fire in their bellies. Is such a thing likely?'

Tom studied the fleshy face. The man's eyes were clear and earnest and somehow fervent in the tarnished illumination of the room's oil lamps.

Tom found himself shaking his head, 'No fear of that.'

'Well good evening then, young sir. It is not a night to be roaming too far abroad. These are becoming dangerous times and when you find a safe bed, it's best to lie in it.' He made to leave but then paused and, placing a hand on Tom's shoulder, he whispered, 'I hope whatever weight is on you is lifted soon, young Banville.'

He strode off down the room haranguing groups of cottiers and frock-coated travellers alike. He moved like a colour sergeant and swore like a trooper and as Tom watched him conducting his rounds the question came unbidden, 'How did he know my name?'

Confused and still more than a little drunk, Tom heaved himself clear of the counter and lurched through the common room like a ship running against a storm. Blank eyes and cold stares fastened on to him as he passed and he had a vague impression of the innkeeper, now impassive and aloof as a carven idol, standing, arms folded, in one dark corner.

A wooden staircase descended into the common room along one back wall and Tom gripped its age-smoothed banister, afraid to let go. Step by creaking step he mounted the stairs, his left hand ball-knuckled about the banister, his right extended out and down in front of him to ward off the floor should it attempt all at once to arise and clatter into his face. His breath came in short, heaving puffs as he shambled towards his room, unlocked the door and entered.

In front of him, a single straw mattress with a heavy woollen blanket lay, porcelain, under the gibbous moon, rising clean and cold beyond the room's only window. Upon the bare floorboards his equipment still made an untidy pile in one corner and the entire chamber smelt of fresh hay and the lingering saccharine of the last occupant's, or their companion's, perfume.

Tom locked the bedroom door behind him and stripped down to his under-clothes. He was about to collapse into the soft sanctuary of the bed when the events of the afternoon and evening trickled a cold stream of trepidation down his back.

In spite of the publican's reassuring words, Tom felt the drink-gummed cogs of his mind spasm into motion. Checking that his door was locked fast, he shuffled over to where his equipment lay and drew his sword, which gleamed in the moon glow of his little room. Then, yawning with the exhaustion of the heavily drunk, he scrambled into the bed and felt the first dark, lapping waves of sleep wash over him. He lay there with the rising moon casting his room in black and silver and setting the steel of his blade to glimmer in his grip. He lay there, tired and alone, on his left side, keeping his sword-arm free.

CHAPTER 2

The Rising of the Moon

The same moon which set a pale watch over the unconscious form of Tom Banville rose above the uneven slopes of Kilthomas Hill. With ghostly lambency, it grinned cold and white upon the fields below. In this borderland between the counties of Wexford and Wicklow a hectic, thorny stitching of gorse ditches crosshatched the land, black in the moonlight. Between these ragged black seams cornfields and paddocks were a quicksilver quilt under the sky. Shadows seemed fluid and unctuous in the frosty light and along the laneways and cattle tracks nothing living broke the cold stillness of the crowding night.

In a copse of cedar trees, midway up the western slope of the hill, however, something moved in the blackness – two forms under the trees.

Amongst the cedar boles and feathery bracken, Dan Banville turned to the person at his shoulder and whispered, 'Look behind you. Isn't it striking?'

His companion turned to gaze out onto the countryside beyond the trees.

Dan smiled as the woman gasped in surprise and whispered, 'Oh, Daniel. It is beautiful.'

She turned to him and he slipped his hands inside the warm travelling cloak she wore over her high-waisted and narrow-shouldered dress. Without hesitation he bent his lips to hers and felt them moisten and respond as the scent of her mahogany hair filled his senses with yearning.

Elizabeth Blakely felt his arms tighten about her, felt her own need arise within her, but, with iron self-possession, she caught hold of his wrists and forced his hands to his sides. Exclaiming, 'Mr Banville, is this why you insist on meeting in such moonlit and deserted haunts!' she adjusted the fall of her dress. Yet her mock anger was only that and Elizabeth knew, even in the dark, that her

37

green eyes smouldered and her lips carried with their words the hint of an unspoken promise.

Dan laughed and held her hands in his, 'Indeed, Ms Blakely, I bring you here to seduce you utterly and to hell with any owl or mouse that seeks to inform your father.'

Smiling up at him Elizabeth stepped inside the circle of his arms and allowed him to hold her to his chest. Still smiling she breathed, 'That would be an intrepid spy indeed that would travel the six miles to Carnew just to tattle on two such as us.'

Dan grunted. 'I would put nothing past your father. His disapproval of me grows daily.'

Elizabeth gazed into his down-turned face but beneath the canopy of gaunt cedars the shadows blurred his features into a ghostly smudge of white. Only his eyes were precise and distinguishable, their colour deepened to soot black but their character remaining, piercing and profound. To Elizabeth, from the moment they had first met that day of the fair in Arklow town, those eyes had always seemed as entrancing and depthless as the void between the stars.

She clenched her fists at the small of his back and gave him a reassuring squeeze. 'You know my father's liberal leanings. He is merely protective of his daughters. And since you left the yeomanry, he is understandably concerned as to which direction in particular you and your family will lean. Come,' she continued, 'I have a basket prepared.'

Dan had ridden some hours in the gathering dusk to arrive at this rendezvous and was ravenous with hunger. Yet, another hunger gnawed at him like some curious contagion working upon his innards. Elizabeth Blakely was in his blood like laudanum. His wits were dulled in her presence; but he ached for her and in her absence a hot gap opened in his guts that could only be filled by her voice, her touch, her kiss.

He had made his way southwest from his father's house, mostly moving across country but trotting along the roads when they afforded him the most direct passage. To some observers and indeed in the opinion of some chroniclers, the landscape of Wexford was a fertile one mismanaged by bad farming and marred by huge tracts of rough ground, overrun by furze and heather and thorn. To Dan Banville, however, his county was one of splendour beneath that high April sky. The ditches to either side were frantic with life and the emerging gorse flowers, coaxed forth by the turning season, were iridescent saffron against deepest green. He had ridden with a smile on his face for the most part, his thoughts already lingering beneath the cedars on Kilthomas Hill but, occasionally, his smile would falter at the sight of a burned-out cottage, or the galloping mass of a yeomanry squadron would force him onto the verge of some dusty, rutted lane.

On these occasions, or the single time he thought he heard, barely on the cusp of perception, the crackle of muskets in the distance, he felt something inside him grow cold. On these occasions he would grit his teeth and unconsciously his lips would move as if offering up a prayer or framing some awful curse. Then he would move on and strive to fill his mind once more with thoughts of Elizabeth Blakely and a yielding cushion of sprouting fern.

Dan and Elizabeth emerged into the moonlight from out of the cedars at a spot close to where Elizabeth's horse was tethered, cropping the coarse grass between its hooves. A grey woollen blanket had been spread under the frenzied scrawl of a blackthorn's branches and upon it a wicker basket sat, tied with string.

'Elizabeth,' said Dan, 'there was no need.'

Even as the words spilled from his lips however, his stomach made a liar of him by rumbling like the wheels of a laden wagon over cobbles.

Giggling, Elizabeth patted the young man's stomach, 'It seems all the hard work your father has you engaged in has done wonders for your appetite.'

Abashed, Dan seated himself upon the blanket and Elizabeth, still giggling, took her place beside him. Her delicate fingers worked at the knots binding the picnic basket and, as if by magic, she extracted half a loaf of bread, some cheese and a wide segment of apple tart. She also produced a stoppered jug filled with milk as her father, a wealthy brewer, was firm in his disapproval of his daughters partaking of alcohol.

The young couple sat beneath the stars, Elizabeth with both her own cloak and a broad swatch of Dan's greatcoat wrapped about her to ward off the deepening chill, talking and laughing like young couples the world over. Between bites of bread and cheese Dan's voice unconsciously raised itself in exuberance, its baritone carrying down the steep slope below them, before Elizabeth hushed him in good-natured exasperation. They sat untroubled by anything outside the compass of their entwined arms until at last Elizabeth cast a quizzical look at Dan and asked, 'Whatever happened to your curls? You look as shorn as a sheep.'

Dan, who had leaned back to take a swig of milk, darted her a glance from the corner of his eye and, lowering the jug, smiled at her. 'If your temples became as high and wide as mine, my dear, you too would find short hair more becoming than a thin straggling of thatch.'

Elizabeth ran her fingers through his short fringe and said, 'I do find it most becoming, but should Hunter Gowan or Hawtrey White mistake you for a croppy I would be forced to visit you in gaol where the food is not so palatable and the company, or so I am told, is not so agreeable.'

Dan felt the soft flesh of her wrist and palm briefly caress the stubbled curve of his jaw and allowed himself a moment of blissful contentment before he spoke. And when he did speak, there was a timbre to his voice that his brother would have recognised as an echo of their father's arrogance and contempt.

'Elizabeth,' he breathed softly as her hand brushed his face, 'If you are afraid of Hunter Gowan or Hawtrey White, then I would urge you not to be. They are as insects. Nothing but upstart planters and the dregs of Cromwell's butchers.'

At this, Elizabeth drew away from him. Her shoulders slipped from under the heavy folds of his trusty and she sat rigid and distant. In the moonlight, her hands clasping the cloak close about her were like pale spiders and her eyes flickered with the brittle light of the hanging constellations. In an attitude of frozen detachment, she queried, 'Do you consider all Protestants "upstarts" and "butchers" Mr Banville, or just those, like my father, who are descended from planter stock?'

'Elizabeth—'

'Don't,' she interrupted. 'Unless the next words that come from your lips are an apology, you should save your breath and allow me to return to Carnew.'

Dan felt a hot cloud of anger envelop his brain but bit back the words that threatened to slip from his mouth. Instead he levelly intoned, 'You know, Elizabeth, that I meant no insult to you or your family, but if I have wounded you in any way then I truly regret it.'

'Of course you do,' she snapped. 'You regret it with every ounce of the fervour with which I sometimes regret being born Protestant. You have no conception of what it's like, Dan. My father is liberal and is hated for it by the magistrates of Carnew. And is Protestant and is hated for that by the peasantry. Only his money provides him with the respect that should be his natural right. If there is a United Irish uprising tomorrow how will men like him be treated? We are afraid.'

Dan watched as the anguish in her words made a grim bow of her mouth and the tiny rivulet of a single tear sparkled upon her cheek. Shaking his head, he moved towards her and when she did not pull away he placed one big arm about her shoulders and drew her to him.

'Elizabeth, I do not know how men such as your father might fare should there be a Rising in the morning. I do not know how any of us should. But you should not fear because of your religion. In spite of what the yeomanry say, in spite of what vomits from the Orange Lodges, I do not believe the United movement to be sectarian. Wolfe Tone and many other prominent United leaders are all committed, landed Protestants. Almost to a man they deplore ignorant bigotry. They would likely welcome your father into their ranks as a fellow liberal!'

He continued quietly, 'I do not believe that there will be a Rising in Wexford unless the North Corks and yeomanry are given their head. Mountnorris and the likes of the Colcloughs down in Tintern are doing the work of a hundred in taking the heat from any brief sparks that alight in their districts.'

Elizabeth sniffed and cast an appraising eye over Dan's features. His gaze was distant and while his arm was reassuringly draped around her it seemed to her that the young man's thoughts had drifted out to roam over his troubled county and that something odd, almost wistful, had entered into his voice.

'You almost seem disappointed,' she said.

'Disappointed? No, not disappointed. Yet I believe that a people should not be compelled to labour under the twin weights of a fat aristocracy and a conniving church. Do you realise that Bishop Caulfield and almost every other Catholic priest has condemned and damned the very name of the United Irishmen? It sickens me, Elizabeth. It sickens me that such knaves think themselves fit to even tread upon the soil of this land.

'The people of Ireland, Elizabeth, be they Catholic, Protestant or dissenter, the people should be free. Free to shape her destiny, free to set her on her rightful path amongst the nations of the earth.'

Elizabeth's finger, stiff and firm, placed against his lips, stemmed the flow of words. To Dan's surprise she was gazing at him with an expression of fear and awe.

Her lips worked silently. Then she ran her tongue along them and whispered, 'What you say is nigh on treason. You read too much of worldly things. Too much of this American polemic.'

Then she smiled and brushed her hand over his roughly chopped curls, 'Or do I love a Frenchman?'

Her remark slipped past Dan before his mind could fully grasp the implications of her words. Then, like a slow dawn, his eyes grew wide and he said, 'You love me?'

Elizabeth laughed and declared, 'I do, Daniel Banville. I love you be you

41

French, American or Chinaman. I love you dearly.'

Smiling, his face aglow with a warmth at odds with his natural pallor, Dan kissed her gently on the lips, 'And I love you, Elizabeth Blakely. Though you be but an upstart planter.'

Elizabeth's mouth sprang open in disbelief and she slapped him playfully on the shoulder, her eyes gazing into his and her smile mirroring his own.

Behind them the moon continued to rise, frosting everything with an eldritch gleam; each shoot of grass a drawn blade and every thorn a pike head.

The Slieveboys loured above Carnew in a threatening swell like the dark mass of a gathering storm. Upon their lower slopes the lights of isolated farms glimmered with a pumpkin glow and the gentle breeze hissed and shivered through gorse and hedgerow. The town itself was mostly darkened at this late hour but here and there a flicker from a lamp or candle strove to hold back the night. On the streets nothing moved save for a lone black mongrel who limped pitifully down the length of the town's main thoroughfare.

Dan and Elizabeth approached Carnew along the narrow winding roads that netted this hilly part of the country.

Since they had commenced their affair some eight months previously, Dan had demonstrated himself to be gentlemanly and attentive. And since Elizabeth's father had grown suspicious and disapproving of him, Dan had avowed to always escort her home from whatever secret trysts they had arranged. Even if, like tonight, that meant that he would not see his bed until well after four in the morning. But to a young man borne on the heady surge of first love, fatigue is alien, the preserve of the old, like the spectre of death.

As they rode they spoke to each other softly, even their lowered tones loud in the silence. It seemed as if the entire country was sleeping, not even the harsh scream of a fox jarred the tranquillity and, on that moonbright whip of roadway, to them it seemed as though the entire universe was theirs alone.

They rode unhurriedly, neither anxious to arrive at the Blakely homestead on the outskirts of Carnew. This part of the county was sparsely populated and only infrequently did they notice the white bulk of a thatched cabin or see on a distant hill a yellow eye of winking lamplight. Eventually, however, Dan and Elizabeth began to find themselves passing through the more densely populated tracts and townlands bordering Carnew itself. As the number of cottages increased, Dan's heart sagged in equal proportion. The solitude, the absence of prying eyes, the quiet dark of the Wexford countryside, these were his and Elizabeth's confidantes, their unspeaking companions in all they had done since the springtime.

On the outskirts of Carnew the road they travelled split in two, one branch heading into the town, the other swinging north. It was along this northern branch that Elizabeth's father had set up his household and it was at this fork in the road that Dan reined his horse to a weary stop.

Both young lovers sat their saddles in silence for a moment before Dan spat, 'I hate this Elizabeth. This slinking about like thieves in the night. Every time we are forced to part like this it drives a spike into my heart.'

Elizabeth's expression was veiled by the darkness but her voice was strained. 'Oh Daniel, father will relent. The country will come to its senses and when things return to how they should be, father will be sure to welcome you with all the affection he once did.'

Looking at her in the moonlight, her face a petal against the black of the ditches, Dan stated, 'I will marry you, Elizabeth and to hell with family and church and all.'

Reaching out to him with one gloved hand, Elizabeth smiled. 'I know my darling. And I shall marry you.'

When the ditch rustled and a white figure spilled into the roadway, both Dan and Elizabeth almost tumbled from their saddles with fright. Their tender moment so rudely and unexpectedly shattered, Elizabeth stifled a scream and fought to control her startled mount while Dan hauled at his own horse's reins and one hand flew reflexively to the hanging flap of his saddlebags.

The figure before them sprawled on the packed earth of the road. It was wearing a rumpled, white muslin dress embroidered with buds and leaves and upon its head was a shapeless white bonnet. The figure looked up from where it lay and raising itself to its knees cried, 'Oh, glory be to God! It's you, Ms Blakely. I knew I heard your voice.'

Elizabeth and Dan were looking down upon the wizened face of an old woman. Her eyes were wide and staring and every wrinkle of her flaccid skin was swilled with shadow. Her hands, shivering as though with an ague, feverishly made the sign of the cross.

'Chrissie!' gasped Elizabeth. 'Whatever's the matter? Why are you here?'

Dan regarded the withered old woman before him. Taking in the dirt marring the hem of her dress, the tattered rent in one sleeve and the woman's hysterical and terrified aspect, he concluded that any tale she might relate would be one of woe.

Elizabeth dismounted and knelt in the dirt beside the old woman, clasping her quaking hands in her own. She addressed Dan briefly, 'This is Chrissie. She is a maidservant to our family.'

Then she asked the maid, 'Chrissie, what has happened?'

The touch of panic in Elizabeth's voice brought Dan's brows beetling down over his grey eyes and he found himself dreading the servant's next words.

She began in a voice as frail as her old body, 'Oh, Ms Blakely, I've been looking for you for an hour. We could not discover you in the house. The women were let go free but you weren't with us and we were so frightened.'

She began to sob and her words became thick, 'Thank Jesus that you're safe. Your mother and your sister are with Mrs Barber and she sent me and Mary to look for you. I hid in the ditch at your approach, I thought you were more yeos come to murder me.'

"More yeos'?' said Dan.

The woman nodded, 'Oh, young sir, the Carnew Cavalry under Captain Wainwright came to poor Mr Blakely's house and wanted to arrest John Mahon for being a rebel.'

Elizabeth's sharp intake of breath cut across her, 'The scullery lad? Why, he's just a boy.'

'I know,' continued Chrissie. 'That's what your father said and he wouldn't hand him over. That's when Captain Wainwright told all the womenfolk to leave. Oh, Ms Blakely, I've never been so frightened. My poor heart almost burst and nowhere could we find you.'

Elizabeth grabbed hold of her shoulders then, rather more roughly than she intended. She could feel the old woman tremble in her grip and felt her bones, like bundles of kindling, under her dress. 'You said mother is with Mrs Barber. What of my father? Chrissie, you must tell me of my father.'

The maidservant was shaking her head now, her toothless mouth contorted in anguish, 'Ah, my darling young mistress, I don't know anything about what those devils have done to him. The last I seen of him he was standing at his door with a fowling piece in his arms daring the whole fifty of them to get past him.'

Dan's gaze swept the darkness in the direction of Elizabeth's home and he said gravely, 'I see no glow above the ditches, Elizabeth, so the yeos have not set fire to your home and we have heard no sound of shooting.'

Fixing him with a blazing stare, Elizabeth hissed, 'We must go to my house. I must see my father. I must see for myself that he is unhurt.'

Dan, who had ridden with the Castletown Cavalry and who had seen the damage a sabre cut could do without the flash and smoke and, above all, the noise of a firelock, frowned down at her. He was about to suggest that she reconsider when the old woman wailed and flung her arms about her young mistress.

'Ms Blakely, you cannot! The yeos will get you. Come with me to your mother and sisters. Oh, Jesus, Mary and Joseph! Jesus, Mary and Joseph!'

Elizabeth merely rose to her feet, dragging the sobbing scarecrow of a maid up with her. 'Until I see my father alive in his own house I will go nowhere but onwards. Go to my mother. Tell her she shall find me at my own home, one way or the other. Give her and my sister my affections, Chrissie.'

Then in a stern voice like the crack of splintering wood, she ordered, 'Go!'

Chrissie threw a disbelieving look at her mistress then she raised a high keen into the air and cried out, 'The world's gone mad! We shall be burying you tomorrow, Ms Blakely. Oh, God in heaven, my heart, my heart!'

She tottered over to where Dan still sat his horse and pawed at his breeches, 'God preserve you, young sir. Don't allow her to do this. Take her up on this great strong horse and carry her to her mother. I beg you.'

Dan opened his mouth to try and mollify the old woman, when Elizabeth snapped at him in that same stern tone, 'Do not attempt to hinder me, Daniel Banville. I am going to my father.'

She stalked over to Chrissie, who shrank back from her as though expecting a blow, 'You have been told, Chrissie. Go to my mother and tell her what my intentions are. Now be off! My mother is likely anxious for news.'

Still wailing, the wrinkled maid gazed in abject horror at Elizabeth and then staggered off down the road to Carnew, screeching as she went, 'They'll all be killed and then what am I to do?'

Elizabeth climbed back into her saddle and sat with an air of stubborn arrogance that somehow reminded Dan of his brother. She flashed him a quick glance and said, 'I mean what I say, Daniel. Do not hinder me.'

Dan nodded once, silently, and they both moved their horses forward at a trot. Elizabeth said flatly, 'You do not have to accompany me but if he is dead, I shall require you to help me move him.'

Dan was sunk in contemplation, chewing the inside of his lower lip as he had done since he was a child and, again, he nodded once, this time adding, 'If he is dead and the yeos gone I shall help you. If he lives and the yeos remain, then I cannot enter your father's yard at your side.'

Elizabeth's expression crumpled into a frown and her voice was breathless with disappointment, 'Why do you say such things? Would you leave me to face them alone because my father disapproves of you?'

Dan sighed. Ever since the old maidservant had appeared like a ghost

45

from the roadside ditch, he had been struggling with his conscience. He loved this woman. Loved her more than anything in his life. It was the expression of betrayal branding her features that swayed him. That look of hurt and abandonment.

'Your father's disapproval of me matters not one whit, Elizabeth. I would not purchase his approval for the cost of a button.'

Elizabeth looked like she had been slapped and began to splutter some half-formed retort but Dan's next words silenced her. There was something in him now that she had never seen before, something commanding, something harsh, something brutal behind his eyes.

'Elizabeth!' he barked. 'Let me finish. I have in my saddlebags a brace of pistols. From whom I gained them, and to what purpose I carry them, are my own affairs. But I promise you this, before a hair of your father's head is touched by those bastards, at least two of them will be dead.'

Stunned, Elizabeth gazed in amazement at the man before her, his close-cropped hair and sideburns, his trusty with its cape-collar emphasising the broadness of his shoulders and his hands, always so gentle, now sworn to do murder on her behalf. She saw him metamorphose before her vision, stepping out of himself, so that he was no longer the son of a wealthy Catholic middle-man and instead became something darker, something harder.

Dan continued, 'I shall leave the road before the avenue that leads to your home. I will tether my horse far enough away to ensure that the yeos don't hear and then secrete myself somewhere close by.'

Elizabeth's expression was avid now, an alien excitement fluttering at her breast, 'And what shall I do?'

'You shall enter the yard at the front of your house and if your father still lives and if he still contends with the good Captain Wainwright you shall attempt to coerce the yeos into leaving. They might not be so eager to bully and intimidate in the presence of a well-known and respected Protestant lady. Do not be afraid. I will be watching and what one man can do unseen from the shadows may rival what fifty can do standing in the light.'

Elizabeth's gaze was frank and appraising and her tone was level as she said, 'I do not believe you are telling me the truth whole and entire. Yet I assume that if you are not then you must have good reason for it. I trust you Daniel Banville but I will demand a full reckoning in time.'

'Good,' he replied curtly.

Some minutes later, the moon revealed the entrance to the Blakely house's avenue. All along its length, stately beeches loomed against the night sky and at its head, nestled in a knuckled fist of trees, sat the imposing home of Andrew Blakely and his family. Dan thought that, from out of the pitch mass of leafless branches and soaring trunks, came the soft orange flicker of torchlight.

He turned to face Elizabeth, 'I must leave you now for a brief while but do not fear. I'll be no more than a stone's throw away.'

Not waiting for an answer, he kicked his horse's sides and sent it pounding toward a low and thinly growing segment of ditch. With a great heave of muscle, the big foxhunter smashed over and through the foliage. Dan felt a brief whipping of branches against his legs and heard the splintering crash of his mount's passage through the hedge and then he was staring into the wide expanse of open pasture that Andrew Blakely had cleared around his home.

Heeling his mount into a canter, Dan set off up the field and was roughly halfway to the Blakely home when Elizabeth turned onto the avenue. In the dark Dan could barely see her form as it passed like a shadow beneath the skeletal arch of the beech trees' boughs.

As his horse moved softly, silently, across the gentle slopes of the grassy pasture, Dan, for the tenth time since its inception, dissected the Spartan details of his rough-hewn scheme.

He had extended his lead on Elizabeth. He was urging his mount on, pushing it up the slope whilst she was bravely keeping both her emotions and her own animal in check. She did not want to spur, clattering and snorting, into a mass of armed men. One surprised finger on a loosely sprung trigger might spell disaster. So she continued her stately progress along her father's avenue, her jaw clenched and every fibre in her body straining with the effort of self-control.

In a minute Dan had reached the dense hedge that cordoned the house and had tied his horse's reins to a young ash tree sprouting from an explosion of gorse. He was some three hundred yards away and from this point he could clearly discern the wavering sparks of the yeo's torches guttering through the trees. Carried on the breeze the jarring sound of upraised voices stabbed his guts with urgency.

Calmly, but with dextrous speed, Dan pulled his twin pistols from his saddlebags, then loaded and primed them. The acrid smell of the powder was merely a faint presage of the sulphurous stink that arose when the flints struck steel but even at this Dan wrinkled his nose. In spite of his deadly eye and matchless accuracy, Dan had never been fully at ease with guns and their lethal potential in his hands.

He tucked the pistols into his waistband and set off towards the house, his movements precise and deft, a hound on a scent. As he moved, he heard the voices drifting through the dark grow in volume and a raucous laugh tore the quiet around him. At this laugh Dan felt a slight relaxation of the trepidation that had been expanding in his chest like some poisonous bubble. The laugh carried with it none of the rust-edged derision that might suggest some brutality being done in the gusting light of the torches. Instead it was almost comradely, as though a jest had been made, one which raised a communal roar of laughter.

As Dan reached the band of ancient beech trees which mantled the Blakely house and its outbuildings, he doubled over into a crouching run. So far he had been cautious, wary that the yeomanry might have set pickets in place to guard their actions. It was with grim satisfaction that he discovered no watch had been placed against unwanted intrusion. To Dan, it appeared that the yeomen were so confident in their position, and in their assumption that their very presence would cow the population, that they had abandoned whatever military instincts they might have once possessed.

Dan slipped through the stand of beech, flitting from tree to tree, his rustling steps masked by the creaking of branch and bole and the gentle soughing of the breeze. As the torchlight grew brighter, he paused for a moment, his big frame huddled into an expanse of fern and nettle. Soundlessly, he drew both his pistols and, using a fold of his trusty to muffle the snap of their mechanisms, he cocked both weapons.

Around him the foliage hissed and rippled and exhaled its rough pungency to catch at his throat and fill the cavities of his skull with an impression of damp vitality. The surrounding undergrowth foamed and lapped up to the base of a stable flanking the Blakely dooryard and then flowed away to either side. The stable itself was a cold black hulk in front of him, its angled slate roof a testament to the wealth of Andrew Blakely. From around the corners of the building the voices of the yeomen rolled and tumbled, their good spirits apparent and their lack of caution total.

Like a pike through river weed, Dan slid through the ferns and nettles and placed his back against the cold and jagged stonework of the stable wall. Here he was in almost total darkness, yet he sidled to his right with all the poise and surety of a man taking an afternoon stroll. His breathing was coming quicker now and he was aware of the rapid drumming of his heart beneath his ribs. Unconsciously his fingers tightened their grip on the walnut stocks of his pistols and with a deep breath he slunk around the corner of the stable and, striving to remain in shadow as much as possible, he hunkered down and surveyed the scene being played out in the dooryard.

The avenue leading to the house entered to Dan's right, opening out into an almost circular expanse of flat, caked earth. Around the perimeter of this open space, stone-built sheds and stables squatted, grey and silent. The glowering two-storey mansion stood directly opposite where the avenue entered the yard, its myriad windows staring sightlessly onto the space below. At this moment the yard was awash with torchlight that illuminated a troop of perhaps twenty yeomen. The old maid, thought Dan, had exaggerated. Ten of these fellows held flaming brands aloft or had jammed them drunkenly into the hard earth. The majority of the yeos had dismounted and although the fire's light made demon masks of their features, to Dan's surprise, it appeared as though they were enjoying themselves.

The yeos had doffed their helmets and some had slung their swords on the pommels of their saddles. In their hands, to a man, they held a glass or mug or cup brimming with what Dan assumed could only be whiskey or brandy. Wending between the dark blue of the uniforms, a middle-aged serving man hastened hither and thither with a large earthenware jug. The look of terror wrenching his features out of shape was unmistakable as a brand. Frowning, Dan sought out Andrew Blakely amongst the uniforms and found him almost immediately.

Elizabeth's father stood framed in the open doorway of his own home. He wore stockings and breeches and a grey satin waistcoat over a white shirt. He wore no coat however, and in his arms he cradled the dark wood and metal length of a fowling piece. His iron-grey hair was slicked back into a ponytail at the nape of his neck, and his features, although smiling, betrayed some unpleasant subtlety of emotion.

Before him, a heavy-bellied glass of rich brown liquid in his fist, stood a man dressed in a yeomanry captain's uniform. Both men seemed to be engaged in a strident but good-natured argument. Dan moved forward slightly, straining to hear what was being said, hoping to find an explanation.

Over the jollity of his men Captain Wainwright was saying, 'Come Andrew. This isn't a question of your loyalty. If you would just hand over the young whelp we could all be on our way.'

Blakely shook his head, his smile fixed in place as though it were painted on, 'And I tell you again, Mr Wainwright, I cannot allow you to harass my staff without tendering good reason. If you could lay definite charges against young Mahon then I would be the first to have him trussed up and delivered to the magistrates. But on the basis of unfounded suspicion I cannot in good conscience offer up a fourteen year old boy to suffer the tender ministrations of the military.'

Wainwright sighed and took a long draught from his glass, 'You are too soft on these Papists, Andrew. I am sure the boy is of use to your household but Fitzwilliam and the other estate owners do not want the French disease taking root in Carnew. You have been both kind and generous to myself and my men – but for the last time Andrew, you must grant us access to your house.'

At last Blakely's smile disintegrated like ash in the wind, 'And if I do not, you will draw arms against a fellow parishioner and staunch member of the community? Has it come to this, that Protestant will kill Protestant?'

Wainwright emptied his glass down his throat and raised his voice more in exasperation than anger. 'You were the one who, when asked to surrender Mahon, went and fetched your gun instead of your pet croppy. Do not accuse me of producing arms prematurely.'

The serving man who had been preparing to serve a young yeoman sitting comfortably upon a barrel of oats, started at the captain's raised voice and slopped the trooper with liquor. The yeo cursed and made to cuff the servant but his hand stilled as Elizabeth entered serenely from the avenue, her face a study in aristocratic arrogance.

Even in the gloom and guttering flare of the torchlight, even with her face assuming an unnatural and pantomime aspect, even though anxiety tightened her mouth and made her rigid with tension, even through all this, Dan felt his breath sucked from his lungs by her hurricane beauty.

In his fists, Dan's pistols sat heavy and eager and pregnant with menace.

In the yard, the yeomen had all fallen silent and every pair of eyes was fastened like limpets on Elizabeth's haughty countenance. Then the crude whispers and drink-fuelled mutters began in a low susurration. Dan knew that should one of them attempt to lay hands on her, that man would get a bullet between the eyes before he had moved more than an a foot.

Captain Wainwright spun around to see what could have effected such a change in his men and from Andrew Blakely came a great shout of joy, 'Elizabeth! Thank God you are safe. We looked everywhere for you! Where in heaven's name did you disappear to?'

Elizabeth dismounted and, ignoring the yeomen, moved straight to her father, the slight suggestion of haste in her steps the only indication of her anxiety. As she swept past Captain Wainwright he bowed his head with an obsequious, 'Good evening to you, Ms Blakely.'

Swamped in shadow alongside the stable, Dan watched the captain as he addressed Elizabeth. He watched as Wainwright raised his head a fraction too slowly so that his leering gaze roved across the front of Elizabeth's cloak and jacket. Dan felt a cold sort of joy that Wainwright would be the first to drop.

Elizabeth was standing by her father, who clasped both her hands in his left while his right retained its grip on the flintlock. His tone was scolding as he spoke to her but his face betrayed his happiness, 'You must tell me child. Where were you at such an hour on such a night as this?'

Kissing him on the cheek she answered, 'I have been with friends in town father. I was about to leave, as I had already remained absent from my home for rather too long a duration and the hour was growing late, when word reached me that a mob had descended upon my family.'

She then turned to the yeos and said something which caught Dan by surprise and rooted him to the spot, his plan falling to pieces.

Fists on hips, she began, 'I had not known that the rumour of a mob would prove to be so well-founded. Look at yourselves, in particular you Captain Wainwright – you all should be ashamed. Turning my mother and sisters and poor old maidservants out into the dark. There mustn't be a single Christian bone to be found in your bodies.'

Some of the yeos were looking at each other with expressions of acute embarrassment and one or two even attempted to straighten the hang of their jackets. Dan simply crouched where he was, astonished and smiling.

Elizabeth was in full flood, 'Have you nothing better to be doing than abusing the households of good Protestant families? Are there not seditious persons enough for you in this district that you have to go disturbing loyal and God-fearing people as well?'

Captain Wainwright cleared his throat and interjected, 'My dear Ms Blakely, that is why we are here. Now if your father would merely allow us to apprehend the person in question we would have no cause to disturb you further.'

Elizabeth regarded him with an expression of fiery defiance, 'Oh yes, Chrissie mentioned that. Young John Mahon. A fourteen year old boy who cannot even read. Yes, he sounds like the type of scoundrel that could bring the country to its knees. Do not be ridiculous, Captain.

'If you wish to deprive my family of a trusted servant, then you shall have to arrest me or render me senseless for I shall not allow it any more than my father should.'

In perfect harmony Andrew Blakely protested, 'Elizabeth!' whilst Captain Wainwright exclaimed, 'Ms Blakely, be reasonable!'

Dan, in the shadows, watched all this with his eagle's eyes and for the moment held his instincts at bay. He had never thought Elizabeth so capable of such bravery and incandescence. For incandescent she was, glowing from within like a forge.

Andrew Blakely faced Wainwright with a mixture of wounded pride and blustering anger, 'Look here, Captain. For the yeomanry to persecute a well-connected and respected Protestant family such as ours will not endear you to either the magistrates or the community. My pockets are deep but my patience is not and my daughter's presence here only complicates matters further.'

At this, Elizabeth placed a hand on her father's shoulder and in a tone that still smouldered but with a different heat than before, purred, 'Captain Wainwright, I have always held you deep in my affections. Such disregard for my family and my feelings does not become you.'

Wainwright blinked at her while several of his men sniggered into their palms. He coughed abashedly, 'Well Ms Blakely, I am but one of many gentlemen who holds your feelings in the utmost regard and I would hope never to be less than deep in your affections. But I cannot see any route around this impasse. Mahon must be questioned and induced to reveal any rebellious secrets he holds and that is final.'

Elizabeth's father, regarding the captain with narrow-eyed scrutiny, asked, 'Do you question my loyalty, Captain Wainwright?'

Wainwright shook his head emphatically, 'Nobody questions your loyalty, Andrew. You are one of Carnew's most well-respected, devout and, of course, prosperous citizens. There is no question as to the integrity of your character or allegiance.'

'Well then,' continued Blakely. 'What if I were to question the lad on the condition that should he dissemble or hide from me any pertinent fact then he should be turned out of my house and immediately tried at the next assizes?

'Similarly, should he reveal all he knows and give assurances as to his good conduct then he shall remain my servant and thus save himself from both gallows and transportation.'

Wainwright frowned dubiously, 'You are certain he will reveal all to you?'

'I have saved him this night from inducement at the hands of your men, Captain. I shall impress upon him that he owes me a debt of gratitude. He shall hold nothing back.'

'If you are satisfied at that, Andrew, then I must insist that in your capacity as a landed gentleman you transcribe all he says and deliver it direct to me.'

Before Andrew Blakely could answer, Elizabeth responded, 'It will be my pleasure to deliver it to you personally, Captain, should you so desire.'

Over the open chuckling of the yeomen, Wainwright stuttered, 'I . . . I should like that very much Ms Blakely.'

In the dark, Dan quietly uncocked both pistols and grinned a wolf's grin. He must remind himself of this night when they were married; the devil with his forked tongue would be less devious.

Andrew Blakely offered his hand to Wainwright, who shook it and said, 'I apologise for this evening's unpleasantness, Andrew, but these are difficult times. I am happy that matters have been resolved so amicably.'

'I as well,' said Blakely.

The captain took Elizabeth's right hand and bent over it, brushing her knuckles with his lips, 'I am overjoyed to see you again, also, Ms Blakely. I would hope that the next time we meet might be in more convivial and intimate surrounds.'

Elizabeth raised her unengaged hand and spread it at the base of her throat as though on the verge of swooning and said breathlessly, 'Captain, I find it hard to answer such sentiments with mere words.'

The captain rose again and, with a wistful glance towards Elizabeth, ordered his men mounted. The yeos grumbled and drained the last of their drinks before tossing the vessels to the earth to be salvaged by the suddenly relieved serving man. Torches were doused in troughs or stamped into darkness and, almost without transition, the yard went from a haze of guttering orange to a hollow space of pitch and silver.

'Good night to you both,' called the captain as he wheeled his troop with parade ground pomp and galloped off into the night.

Pressed against the cold stone of the stable, Dan heard Andrew Blakely growl, 'And good riddance to you and the rest of your ruffians. And may the gates of hell open and swallow you all.'

CHAPTER 3

The Need for Law

The morning of the 1st of May broke over a land seemingly untouched by anything but the most benevolent human hands. To a stranger, viewing that landscape on that first day of summer, nothing could have hinted that it was a landscape bathed in the cold chill of terror.

Tom Banville heaved himself onto one elbow from where he lay in bed and focused his bleared vision upon his brother. He had no idea how long Dan had been trying to wake him but the ghostly sensation of someone holding his shoulder and shaking, penetrated the residual fog of sleep. He could distinctly feel the imprint of Dan's fingers and thumb embedded in the flesh of his right shoulder. Around him the morning light cascaded through the flimsy curtains. Dust motes rose with his movements to dance crazily in the drenching brightness – but from beneath his blankets came the sour odours of sweat and unwashed bed linen.

Tom tried to say something to Dan, who was sitting on the edge of the bed shaking his head disdainfully, but his tongue felt as though it were made of felt and he had to swallow drily before he could force words to come.

'What time is it?' he asked.

Still sitting there in his shirt sleeves, still shaking his head, mouth set in a lopsided smile, Dan answered, 'High time you asked God in his heaven to deliver unto you some small measure of sense, little brother.'

Groggily, Tom shifted himself into a sitting position and rubbed both hands against his bloodshot eyes, 'What was I doing last night?'

'Well,' said Dan matter-of-factly, 'first you were playing horseshoes with young Isaac Hamilton on the green in Coolgreany. Then you went to play cards and then you came home. Somewhere along this jolly little circuit you also

54

found time to consume roughly a bottle of brandy and a quart of Mr Hamilton's best sherry.'

Tom's thoughts were all of the consistency of porridge and in his mouth a putrid taste lingered. 'Oh God,' he moaned, 'I hope I wasn't . . . sick – do I owe Isaac any money for his father's liquor?'

Dan nodded in infuriating cheerfulness, 'You were and you do. I believe you insisted on leaving an illegible I.O.U.'

Tom collapsed back onto the feathery cushion of his pillow and, staring at the ceiling, commented, 'Da is going to be furious isn't he?'

Dan's silence brought Tom's head around so that he could see his brother sitting now in frowning contemplation. At last Dan said, 'I would prefer it if father was furious, Tom, but when mother and I put you to bed, he merely watched us with a kind of despondent resignation. I fear you have broken his heart, Tom. I do not believe that anything you might do could touch him in his present state of disappointment.'

Lying in his bed, his head feeling like a lump of sweating tar, Tom sighed, 'I am awaiting a court martial on that old fool's account. If it were not for the proclamation of the county I am certain I would be drummed out already.'

Dan whipped around to fix Tom with a hard glare, 'Well then you should thank the stars that, in spite of Mountnorris' efforts, those bastard magistrates have declared martial law. One would hate to see you deprived of your vocation, Tom.'

Dan's voice was as sharp as his gaze and Tom involuntarily jerked away from his brother, fearful of him in a way that he had not been since they were boys. Dan surged to his feet and without another word strode across the room and yanked open the door.

Tom tried to get out of bed, pleading, 'No Dan, don't go. I didn't—'

But he was already gone, the door smashing closed behind him.

'Bad luck to it anyway,' Tom muttered, and flung the heavy blankets away from him. For some minutes he sat in his underclothes on the edge of his mattress and inhaled great whistling lungfuls of air, breathing deeply to subdue a sudden bubbling convulsion of nausea. Unsteadily, he straightened up and lurched over to his wardrobe. Still cursing his family, cursing himself and cursing Isaac Hamilton, Tom struggled into his clothes and prepared himself to face the day.

Closing his bedroom door behind him, Tom walked down the dim length of the outside corridor, his brogues noiseless upon the thick line of red carpet running down the middle. He passed the staircase leading down into the front hall and instead took the back stairs, which descended steeply into the kitchen. As he entered, the smells of breakfast hit him like a sledge and, without even acknowledging Mrs Prendergast, the family's only maid who was busying herself preparing a large pot of stirabout for breakfast, Tom fled into the stable-yard. There he stood for a moment, his stomach heaving before he made his way over to the pump and soused his head, neck and face in a deluge of freezing water.

Gasping, he looked up at the noise of someone's approach; at his shoulder stood Mrs Prendergast with a large glazed mug in her hands.

'Here you go, *mo stoir*,' she said affectionately. 'If you can get some hot tea into you, you'll be grand and set-up for some breakfast.'

Tom smiled his gratitude, 'Thank you, Mrs Prendergast. We would be lost without you.'

He took the mug from her work-worn hands and sat on the lip of the pump's stone basin. Mrs Predergast patted him on the shoulder and bustled back inside. Tom sat with his back to the cold, damp iron pump and sucked warm tea past his parched lips. At the first few sweet mouthfuls Tom felt his guts twist and buck but after one or two steadying breaths his nausea subsided. Not quite managing to finish the tea, he dumped the remainder out onto the dusty surface of the stableyard.

He remained, for a moment, stock-still. His breathing was heavy in the bright May morning and he reflected on how his family might act once they clapped eyes on his newly-roused form. Normally he would expect his mother to ignore the fact that anything at all was amiss, and quietly smother any misgivings or reproach she may harbour. His father would rail and bellow in fist-shaking fury while Dan, always the dutiful eldest son, would simply sit and, if anything, pass a razor-honed comment or two, all the while regarding his brother with scornful mockery.

On this morning, though, all his thoughts led him down blind alleys. If what Dan said was true, if their father expected so little of him that the old man no longer cared about his misdeeds, then Tom knew he would be lost. Had he really wounded his father so badly?

Either way, Tom resolved to face his family.

He rose and entered the kitchen, leaving his mug with Mrs Prendergast, who bestowed on him another one of her bantam smiles. He made his way down a short hallway and through the open door of his family's dining room. The room was high-ceilinged, with a wide bay window looking to the east, through which the morning sun now blazed cheerily. The decoration was modest, well-fashioned but lacking in ostentation. Varnished wood glowed with its own particular life and on the long dark table in the centre of the room, the white and blue of breakfast crockery gleamed in the sunlight. At the table, gathered at the end nearest the window, sat his mother, his father and Dan.

The smell of stirabout, of meat and oatmeal gruel, prompted a last pyrrhic swell of Tom's diminishing nausea.

His mother raised her head, her spoon frozen on its way to her mouth, and said, 'Good morning, Tom. I hope you are feeling well. You had such a case of vomiting last night. A fever brought on by the hot weather, like as not.'

Dan jabbed his own spoon across the table at her, 'Mother, he had a case of the falling down drunk. The only reason he isn't dead is because he so disgustingly expelled most of the vile stuff from his body.'

'Daniel!' snapped his mother. 'What a terrible thing to say. Your brother, I'm sure, is as abstemious as you and your father.'

Tom looked at his father, expecting the old man to make some comment or at least to respond in some form or order. Laurence Banville, however, gave no sign, made no act of acknowledgement, to hint that he knew Tom had even entered the room. He simply remained, his silvered head stooped over his plate, his jaw working quickly and mechanically like a bull's.

Betraying an uncharacteristic air of fluster, Mrs Banville gestured to the empty chair beside her, 'Sit down, Tom. You'll be having something to eat of course.'

Tom moved around the table and seated himself next to his mother. His limbs felt stiff and unaccountably tired as he eased himself down onto the high-backed chair and set about buttering a slice of brown bread, which he plucked from a pewter platter in the centre of the table.

Dan watched him as he smeared the butter evenly over the bread, bit into it and chewed laboriously, as though every drop of moisture had evaporated from his throat. And as Tom tongued what felt like wood shavings and ashes around the arid chamber of his mouth, he saw Dan grin at him across the table.

Tom felt like hitting him.

His father's voice startled him when it came, unexpected and rasping.

Without raising his head, without meeting his son's gaze, the old man growled around a spoonful of meal and gravy, 'Pat Doyle was taken off and pitchcapped there yesterday.'

A heavy silence enveloped the table. All three men had stopped eating. Only Mary Banville continued as though she had heard nothing. The clink and scrape of her spoon against her plate was brittle and grating in the abrupt quiet.

'Who did it?' Dan asked.

Still not looking up, cutlery poised in his fists, Laurence Banville replied, 'The North Corks. The bastards. God's curse on every mother's son of them.'

Then his gaze finally lifted and the opaque blue of his eyes sought out those of his youngest son, 'It's said the brave boys of the yeomanry then set his house afire. Let your mind imagine that.'

The great billow of silence rolled back once more and only the relentless rattle and scrape of Mary Banville's plate and spoon broke through the folds of tension.

Tom sat voiceless as his conscience was held transfixed by the conflicting winds of crossed purposes, unsure of what to say or even how to say it. He had known Pat Doyle nearly all his life. The man was a fine hurler and had often been invited to play on old Caesar Colclough's teams down at Duffry Hall. To hear that he was taken by the North Corks knifed something cold deep into his chest. And yet, for as long as he had known Pat Doyle, he had known a man prone to brawling, to making incendiary speeches, to aggravating strife between tenant and landlord.

It was his father's challenging stare that finally tipped the balance.

Returning his expression, Tom said, 'Da, Pat Doyle's a troublemaker and malcontent. A rabble-rouser. Always has been.'

Laurence Banville's eyebrows rose in twin arches of bristling outrage, and across the table Dan's mouth was an empty O of astonishment.

With flushed cheeks and tears in her eyes, Tom's mother turned sharply towards him. In a voice unnaturally calm for all her obvious distress she said, 'Pray tell, Tom, what is your opinion of Murt Cody, over in Monaseed?'

Both Tom and Dan's features clouded identically. For a moment they were almost twins rather that younger and elder brother.

It was Dan who first coaxed his feelings into words. 'Ma,' he began, 'what happened to Murt?'

To their surprise it was Laurence who answered in a voice that bubbled with venom.

'Those stout fellows of the Gorey cavalry emptied their carbines into him in front of his wife and children.'

Tom felt something curdle inside of him and when Dan slammed his fist into the table, his face a furnace of rage, Tom didn't even flinch. He sat waxen and unmoving as Dan thundered, 'Four days of martial law now Tom. Four days of house burnings and judicial torture. White and Gowan rampant. Are you to become an apologist for tyranny?'

Tom was on his feet before he knew what he was doing. His chair tumbled backward and clattered to the floor and his right fist stabbed a shaking finger at his brother.

'That's right, Dan,' he roared. 'You sit here at our fine table in our fine house and you bluster in outrage at the fate of peasants and tenants. If their treatment is so terrible, then grant them sanctuary in the comfort of your own bed. Let them sup from your ample plate. Tyranny? Is that what you call it, Dan? If it were not for that 'tyranny' which you so bridle against, we would not be sitting in this house. What you call tyranny others call law.'

Tom was aware of his mother's shocked gasp, aware of his brother's face as it blanched from angry red to white. It was upon his father, however, that his words had wrought their most dramatic effect.

Laurence Banville was half-risen from his chair at the head of the table. His aged eyes bulged in their sockets and the veins of his neck and temples were wormed beneath his skin.

The gentle, intruding cough of Mrs Prendergast petrified the family into tableau.

The old servant was lost for words. She blinked her eyes and her lips worked mutely for a moment until Laurence Banville erupted like a cannon, 'What the hell is it you want?'

Mrs Prendergast squealed in shock and grasped the jamb of the doorway in which she stood for support. In thirty years of service Laurence Banville had never before raised his voice to her. Involuntarily her right hand came up to bless herself and her voice came warm and wet, 'Please, your honour, Lieutenant Esmonde is out in the yard. He wants a word with the young sir.'

Without looking at Tom, Laurence answered, 'A word? Tell the blackguard he may have a whole library of words. My son has naught else to say here.'

Tom's anger was still too fevered to allow him to be hurt by his father's dismissal. Dan's gaze weighed heavily upon him but, ignoring it, he turned to his mother and said, 'Good day to you, Ma.' He spun on his heel and marched out of the room. Mrs Prendergast fled before him, a leaf before a storm.

Behind him, Dan's eyes followed his departure, their solemn grey tinged with anguish rather than anger. He sat, robbed of voice and thought by his brother's words; sat and watched as his father began to silently eat his breakfast once more, his wrath palpable; sat as his mother's eyes began to seep forth their tears and in her chest the first sobs began to clot her breathing.

Lieutenant Esmonde was waiting for Tom outside the front door. He was dressed in his coloureds rather than his uniform and his finely cut frock coat was only a little stained from the dust of his travels. As Tom came down the hallway the lieutenant touched the front peak of his gentleman's tricorn.

'Good morning to you, sir,' said the lieutenant as Tom came to a halt on the threshold.

'And the same to you, Lieutenant,' replied Tom.

To Tom, the officer appeared far more pallid than when they had last spoken. Although only thirty, Lieutenant Esmonde seemed to have caved into himself. Wan folds of flesh creased around his eyes and his lips were chapped and peeling. Even his cheeks were sunken. It was as though the man were slumping into an awful premature decay.

Looking at the cadaver before him, Tom was certain that Sir Thomas Esmonde had come to bring news of his court martial. In that instant a hot gust of anger flamed within him. He imagined that his father and brother were laughing like jackals.

Sick to his stomach from something far more bitter than the after-effects of drink, Tom asked, 'What brings you here Lieutenant? Surely you bring with you news of my disciplinary charges. What has Captain Knox Grogan resolved?'

Esmonde sighed in response and raised his arms to form some half-conceived gesture but then dropped them. They hung at his sides, like weighted chains.

In a voice every bit as tired as he looked, he began, 'This does not sit well with me, Banville. In fact,' he added, 'I am quite put out. Quite put out. But the fact remains that circumstance necessitates the reinstating of your name on the roll of the Castletown Corps of Yeoman Cavalry.'

Surprised by this unexpected turn of events, Tom spluttered, 'My name reinstated? Returned to the roll? What events would compel your honours to disregard my father's admittedly heinous actions?'

At these words some bright fleck of their old steel entered the lieutenant's eyes, 'Do not saddle your father with the entirety of blame. It was you who drew your sword on your fellow soldiers. It is not something I shall easily forget.

'Be that as it may,' Esmonde continued, 'there have been a number of absences during the past week. The imposition of martial law delivered unto us a great many onerous responsibilities. Some of less stalwart disposition would rather abandon the country to insurrection than enforce the will of our rightful government.'

Tom eyed the lieutenant with the shrewd appraisal of a horse trader. 'Defections or desertions, Lieutenant?'

Esmonde's lips cracked as he smiled coldly, 'You're a bright one, Banville. In that, at least, you take after your father.' He paused before continuing, 'Some have gone into hiding and so are presumed to be in league with whatever rebel agents there are in this district. Others have resigned their posts, being too delicate for the rough matter of restoring order. Those that are left are both zealous and brave.'

Tom frowned, 'Yet you wish to unreservedly admit an unapologetic Papist back into your ranks?'

His eyes still glinting, Esmonde said, 'Not unreservedly, Banville. There are some who hold your family high in their suspicions. However, and this is the marrow of things, there are more who hold your family high in their esteem. Through your intervention you might be able to avoid some of the more unpleasant aspects of the duty that we have lately been forced to perform.'

Tom's mouth twisted wryly, 'You wish me to persuade people, by dint of my name and my religion, to give up their arms?'

The lieutenant nodded, 'Indeed that is the bare bones of it. Young Lieutenant Bookey and the Camolin Cavalry are gathering pikes and handing out protections by the dozen. He is having considerably less trouble than many other corps. His is an example worthy of emulation. Thomas Knox Grogan is a reasonable man and is fervent in his desire to maintain both the law and his reputation as an able magistrate.'

Tom nodded, almost to himself, as though resolving some inner argument, 'Then, Oath or not, you will grant me re-admittance to the corps and my family and its interests will remain protected by my demonstrated loyalty?'

'Oath or not,' said Esmonde.

In his mind, Tom could imagine his family's dissatisfaction. He could hear his father's excoriating comments – or, worse still, feel the blistering cold of his silence. He could hear Dan's intellectual apoplexy and see his mother regarding him with her heavy, sad eyes, her gaze plumbing his depths, sounding the dark hollow of his soul.

'What would you have me do?' he asked.

Esmonde, moment by moment, seemed to be recovering some of his former vigour, yet in his eyes and in the slight curl of his lips he betrayed his abiding disdain for the young man before him. Unconsciously he rubbed his hands together in a manner Tom found unctuous and distasteful and said, 'There's to be a bit of a to-do tonight and the corps has need of your arm, your name and your presence.'

Tom looked at him quizzically, 'A 'to-do'?'

Esmonde observed him warily and each word that came from his mouth was now weighed and measured, his eyes gauging their effect, 'We have been requested to augment a detachment of North Corks. They are an infantry regiment and as such have no cavalry. Their Colonel Foote is in some anxiety as to the state of the countryside.'

Tom laughed sourly. 'The state of the countryside has not been helped by that particular regiment's activities. Don't you think, Lieutenant?'

If half of what he had heard about the red-coated infantry was true, then every member of their ranks openly wore Orange insignia while their officers wore the sash even beyond the doors of their Lodge. The coming of the North Corks had roughly coincided with the establishment of three other civilian Orange Lodges in the north of the county. The coming of the North Corks had brought the pitchcap and terror. Now, every day, Tom found himself more and more in agreement with Richard Proctor. His home, his people, were drifting into disparate camps, the one repellent to the very idea of the other. Tom found himself contemplating the grim vista of two traditions that would rather hurl themselves into oblivion than remain shackled to each other in claustrophobic rancour.

His county was falling apart.

Tom asked, 'Augment them while they undertake what action, Lieutenant?'

'A raid down near Kilanerin. It seems some stubborn souls are refusing to surrender arms. I believe they do not trust the government's protections. No more than a pike in the thatch I'd wager but with the countryside in such a state of agitation every magistrate in the county is urging caution.'

Tom sighed and raked his fingers through his still-wet hair, tangled from his night's revelry.

He answered, 'I shall come, Lieutenant. But I warn you, I'll not be party to the excesses of those Cork bastards.'

Esmonde nodded once, sharply. 'I shall re-roll you on the instant, Banville, with all the attendant rights and privileges of a loyal servant of the King. We marshal in Castletown at seven.'

Neither saluting nor offering a word of farewell, Lieutenant Esmonde mounted the slab-sided white hunter that stood placidly in the dooryard and trotted off.

Standing in the empty doorway, Tom Banville lifted his face to heaven and closed his eyes. The warmth of the sun draped itself in kindly folds over his features, his cheeks, his damp forehead. And in the darkness behind his eyelids, in that blank solitude of doubt and silence, Tom Banville prayed he was doing the right thing. Before him, in the yard of the place he sought to protect, a blackbird trilled in bright alarm. Behind him, from the house of his father, came only a smothering silence.

CHAPTER 4

The Rule of Law

Above Mount Leinster the plummeting sun was cradled in the russet gush of its own dying. Dusk emerged like a grey mist from under stones and the tangle of tree roots and ditches.

Castletown's main street was neither as large nor as urbanised as Gorey's. It consisted mainly of two rows of opposing cabins, all whitewashed and thatched, most with two dark windows staring across the road. Towards the northern edge of the village the street bellied out into a small marketplace before narrowing and crumbling away into a countryside of gorse and long grass. This slightly wider marketplace was flanked along one side by the only slated building in the whole village, a large forge whose heat and light spilled out onto the hard earth of the street. At its door a heavy man in a leather apron looked out, arms folded and face bitter.

In front of this building, a detachment of thirty North Cork Militia stood in two ranks of fifteen. Their red coats glowed in the failing light and the white of their pipeclayed crossbelts was dyed a burning rose from the glow of the forge. At their sides long muskets were held upright and their faces bore expressions ranging from boredom and impatience to casual good humour. Above the black bicorns worn on their heads, floating over the roofs of the cabins and rasping like autumn leaves in the breeze, the muttered argument of officers could be heard.

Some yards behind the two ranks of infantry, Lieutenant Esmonde sat his saddle and listened while Lieutenant Musgrave of the North Corks vented his ire.

'Twelve horse? You bring a grand total of twelve horse? This is an outrage, Sir Thomas.'

At the head of a group of twelve yeoman cavalry, Esmonde observed Musgrave's purple features, his jowls rippling beneath his sideburns, his forehead lined with fury beneath the peak of the cocked hat worn fore-and-aft upon his head. He stated calmly, 'I bring twelve horse Lieutenant, because twelve horse is all I have. One cannot simply conjure men and animals from the stuff of imagination.'

The infantry officer, sitting his own horse, spat on the ground and with difficulty kept his voice from rising above a snarling undertone, 'The pertinent matter is why you cannot bring more than twelve. Where have all your men gone?'

Esmonde allowed the lilting yaw of the Corkman to fall into silence and said, 'I was confident up until this moment that the corps had retained its unity in the face of the present strife. But since the proclamation of the county there have been a number of Catholic resignations. Captain Knox Grogan is much put out by this turn of events.'

'And so he should be,' railed Musgrave. 'You bloody yeos are as artful and deceiving as the lowest croppy and as inconstant as any blasted Papist.'

Esmonde's face was again tired, his skin slack but at these words his jaw clenched and he hissed, 'I would have you know that Doyle over there, Banville beside him and I, Lieutenant, are all Papists. Do you question our loyalty? Do you dare question mine?'

Musgrave was visibly taken aback by this and his next words were devoid of aggression.

'I apologise, Sir Thomas, but Captain Knox Grogan must then recruit from his Protestant tenants to replenish the ranks. To have a shortage of mounted troops would be disastrous in such a climate of insurrection.'

'There will be no insurrection, Lieutenant,' countered Esmonde. 'None whatsoever, so long as arms are collected and troublemakers interred. And if thirty soldiers and twelve cavalry cannot affect a search of the peasantry in absolute safety then I myself shall resign. We are the King's troops, Lieutenant, and this is Ireland, not France.'

Behind Esmonde his small corps of cavalry slumped over their saddle horns and strained to listen to the argument of the officers.

'That Cork officer, for a gentleman he is queerly difficult to understand,' whispered Richard Proctor.

Tom nodded, 'It's the accent. I hear a lot of the North Corks are even speaking Gaelic.'

Proctor stared at him in disbelief. 'Don't talk nonsense, Tom. Nobody but the people of the blackest bog speak Gaelic anymore.'

Tom shook his head. 'They still speak it across in Bantry, Richard, and around the Blackstairs. Not everyone is as English as you.'

Laurence Doyle shushed him into silence and flung him a look with blades in it. 'Thank you, Tom. I was trying to eavesdrop and now I've missed what they were saying. That Cork Lieutenant said something about Papists. If he offers any one of us insult I believe we would be quite within our rights to call the blackguard out.'

'I'll second you,' came a voice from Doyle's left.

Tom and Proctor exchanged glances and Tom pinched the bridge of his nose between his gloved fingers. 'God give me strength,' he breathed into his cupped palm.

Proctor touched Tom on the shoulder and gestured towards the blacksmith who stood at the open door to his forge. He was a bald man and his head and bare arms were streaked with the grime of his trade. Facing the two ranks of soldiers, he wore an expression of naked and derisive defiance.

Tom regarded the man and a trill of unease sounded at the back of his mind; here was a man confronted by a strong detachment from an infamous regiment and he faced them as if they were boys. His demeanour was an unspoken challenge, an assertion of his own authority – he was lord of his surroundings.

Tom knew it was only a matter of time before one of the bored soldiery took his haughty attitude as an insult.

'I think he's looking for trouble,' muttered Proctor.

Tom nodded in agreement. 'And I think those Cork boys are the ones to give it to him.'

It was then that Tom remembered the brief tatter of conversation he had heard at the inn in Gorey.

Sure, every blacksmith in the county's a United man.

Perhaps fortunately for the blacksmith, Esmonde and Musgrave decided to get their troops moving. The officers wheeled away from each other and went to the heads of their respective columns.

Esmonde turned in his saddle and called over his shoulder, 'We'll go ahead of the North Corks and provide a vedette for their march. I would ask one or two of you good fellows to also advance as best you can through the fields on either side of the road and so guard our flanks.'

As Esmonde addressed his men, Musgrave's instructions to his own echoed and struck unpleasant harmonies in the quiet gathering evening.

'We shall march in good order and I shall not countenance any man falling out of the ranks for private gain or plunder! Now, by the left!'

And with that the militia detachment followed their mounted lieutenant out of the little hamlet of Castletown. The infantry marched in two disciplined lines, the left-right of their tread metronomic in the dusk.

'Come on then lads,' urged Esmonde, and he spurred his horse forward. Immediately the boot-fall of the soldiers was buried under the rolling thunder of thirteen heavy fox-hunters. The cavalry surged past the marching infantry in a torrent of flesh and muscle and jangling tack.

Behind them, unnoticed by all, the blacksmith cursed the name of Loyalist and Orangeman and spat a viscous mouthful of phlegm into the dust.

Sir Thomas Esmonde led the Castletown Corps of Yeoman Cavalry roughly west and north out of Castletown village. Behind them, Lieutenant Musgrave had given his North Corks the order to march at ease, and they now walked behind their lieutenant, their muskets dangling from shoulder straps or trailing in one hand. The yeomen, however, were a furlong or so in front and were peering into the gloaming with anxious concentration.

Marking this, Tom turned to Proctor and asked, 'Why is it that the boys are all so nervous?'

Proctor was following the progress of one of the corps making his way through the cornfields to their left. His answer was slow in coming but when it came it made Tom's heart sink a little.

'No rebel would ever stand against a uniformed soldier in open battle, but recently the Shelmaliers and some of the Enniscorthy lads have been shot at by men hiding in the fields.'

Tom studied Proctor as his eyes flicked to and fro over the countryside, glittering like a hunted animal's.

'Rebels? Proctor, do you not think people would shoot at anyone who came to ransack their homes? I do not think the colour of the jacket one wears is much of an influence. A man will shoot a croppy come to steal as quick as a yeo come to search.'

Keeping his eyes on the fields, Proctor answered, 'Any man who bears arms against agents of the crown is a rebel, Tom. Keep a sharp eye out.'

Tom gazed at his friend's intense profile and sighed long and deeply. He had heard the stories – the indiscriminate retaliation for a blind shot taken at a mounted patrol – but until now he had not believed them. Now, looking at the tension, the fear like a cowl darkening Proctor's features, he realised that these men were no longer seeking to keep the peace. In spite of Esmonde's arguments to the contrary, they were already at war.

The cavalry trotted along, each man preoccupied with his own scrutiny of the veiling twilight. Every man, that is, except Tom Banville.

Tom sat his saddle as his horse's rolling gait bore him further into a private limbo. He was numb inside. Still possessed of all physical sensation, he could feel the chinstrap of his helmet dig into the line of his jaw, he could hear the thud of hooves and to each side the rustle of leaves, but within him emotions had been doused. His mind was heavy and slow.

Esmonde led them sharply west, and after a mile or two they halted at Inch to allow the infantry to catch up. A handful of the yeomen dismounted and stretched their legs but Tom remained where he was, sitting his saddle and staring off into the dark.

Richard Proctor strolled over to him, unbuckled his helmet and turned his round face up to his sombre friend. 'You're beginning to worry me, Tom. Have I offended you in some way?'

Tom smiled down at Proctor, but the warmth in his expression was belied by the lead in his voice. 'No Proctor, you've not offended me. My mind is given over to some rather melancholy thoughts at present.'

Proctor nodded. 'These are melancholy times. Have no fear though, we shall all see the other side of them, God willing.'

'God willing,' Tom repeated mechanically.

Proctor cast Tom a final, concerned look, patted his horse's neck and strode over to where two yeomen were smoking their pipes. The young yeoman listened as his companions conversed in barely audible whispers, their words guarded, their eyes ever-roving. Strangers in a strange land.

Tom could not prevent himself wondering whether Proctor now saw croppies and Papist plotters in every ditch and behind every tree. He could not prevent himself wondering whether he had shot any livestock or burned any houses.

It was dark by the time the North Corks arrived. The lights of the tiny village of Inch began to gild the windows of its cabins and cottages. Yet not a soul stirred abroad as the soldiers and cavalry passed briskly through, making for the empty countryside beyond. Dogs barked and howled from hidden kennels and to Tom it seemed as though the night was teeming with ghosts of his own creation.

As they marched through the village one of the North Corks fell out of the column and crept up to a loosely-fastened cabin door, around which a narrow shaft of light fell out into the street. Holding his musket in one hand, he pushed his bicorn back on his head and leaned his weight against the rough gap between door and jamb. The door creaked but held and a woman's voice rose from within, 'Get away ya rascal or I'll set the dog on ya!'

This shout brought the column to a ragged halt, some men even reaching for their powder belts in expectation of an ambush.

The soldier stood frozen in an expression of shocked idiocy, like a child caught raiding the kitchen cupboard, suddenly the focus of forty-three pairs of eyes.

'You there!' roared Musgrave. 'What do you think you are doing?'

The militiaman came to ramrod attention and struggled for words. Finally he said, 'I thought I saw something suspicious, Mr Musgrave, and I was just taking a look for myself.'

Musgrave trotted down the line while the man spoke and reined in his horse before the frightened soldier.

'Who gave you permission to fall out of column?' he asked.

'Nobody, Mr Musgrave,' said the soldier.

Regarding the man with contempt, Musgrave lifted his riding crop and held it before the red-coated figure below him. 'I should have you flogged. Do you realise that?'

'Yes, Mr Musgrave.'

'But I shall not. This time. However, if you or any of your fellows should attempt to disobey an order in the future, then that man shall receive fifty lashes. Do I make myself clear?'

'Yes, Mr Musgrave,' answered the soldier, visibly relieved.

As the man rejoined the ranks, Musgrave tapped him lightly on the back of the head with his riding crop, which had the effect of resettling his hat. The lieutenant trotted back to the head of his men, calling out as he did, 'I am a fair and compassionate man. I wish for no blood but that of Popish plotters to stain my hands.'

'Stay where you are, Doyle,' growled Tom without looking around.

Behind him, Laurence Doyle released his grip on the handle of his sword.

The countryside north of Kilanerin was dappled by the same small farms and cabins that characterised the rest of County Wexford. And like the rest of the county the thick gorse and briar of ditch and hedge made a checkerboard of the fields and woods and made a mockery of cavalry, both heavy and light.

Tom spurred his horse forward until he was beside Lieutenant Esmonde.

'Mr Esmonde, is there a particular homestead we shall be calling on?'

Esmonde observed him from under the peak of his helmet. 'There are several,' he answered. 'George Gormley's is the most important, however. He has been labelled United Irish by one whom the North Corks induced to inform. Do you know him?'

'George Gormley,' muttered Tom. 'No, I've never heard of him.'

Esmonde fixed him with a shark grin that glowed like bone in the blackness. 'As well for you that you haven't.'

About midway between the villages of Inch and Kilanerin the little column of troops began to come across closely scattered clumps of cottages and farms, almost a townland in itself. It was here that Esmonde and Musgrave halted their men and held a brief whispered conference, their gestures urgent, their heads bent close together.

Around them, eight cottages clustered at the base of a low hill, all their windows dark, their walls cold and lifeless. It was not this, however, that so perturbed the officers and set the men to scanning the fields with even more than their usual fervour.

What so set the troops', and even Tom's, nerves on edge was that as they moved in a long line through the dark, a blaze had suddenly erupted from a gnarled promontory of stone off to their southwest.

A bonfire of heather and bracken had leapt, roaring into the night, whipping orange tongues and burning sparks upwards in whirling conflagration. Briefly, for the merest splinter of a second, two figures were silhouetted in featureless ebony against the flames, and then were gone.

With their disappearance, however, came a heavy sensation of paranoia amongst the yeomen and militia.

The fire was a warning. The peasantry knew they were there.

And now they halted in the black of a darkened townland and waited while their officers debated in hushed, animated tones.

'It's the big one.'

Proctor's voice came so suddenly that Tom jumped with fright.

'What did you say?' he asked.

'George Gormley's house,' he said quietly. 'It's that big one over there. See how it has the three rooms with the glazed windows and the bit of a cowshed? I recognise it from when I was a boy.'

Tom frowned at his friend. 'How do you recognise it?'

Proctor leaned on his saddle horn, 'Old Gormley used to help on father's land when I was young. He was a fine tinker as well. He could mend anything at all that you put in front of him. Sometimes father would drive over here in the cart to have something patched or a ploughshare beaten into shape and I often accompanied him for the jaunt.'

Proctor's hand came up and the stubble of his jaw made a rough rasping against the leather of his gauntlet. 'Different times,' he concluded.

Musgrave and Esmonde ended their brief discussion and turned around to face their men. In the light of the moon, Esmonde's face beneath his helmet was pallid.

'North Corks,' began Musgrave. 'We find ourselves in a nest of United Irish. Every cabin in this place may be presumed to harbour enemies of the Crown.

'The source of this filth can be found in that hovel, yonder.' At this he pointed towards George Gormley's well-ordered cottage and continued, 'We shall cut off the head of the serpent and so the body will perish.'

He paused for a moment then drew his sword. 'North Corks, fix bayonets and surround that house!'

The infantry scrambled to fix sixteen inches of triangular steel to the muzzle of each musket so that when fully assembled, the entire weapon was as tall as they were. Each bayonet gleamed like a wet fang as the North Corks fanned out around the darkened homestead in a razor-fringed circle.

The yeomen were strung along and across the road in loose skirmish order. As they watched their comrades take up their positions, Esmonde addressed them.

'Castletown Corps, we are to wait in reserve and provide relief should Lieutenant Musgrave meet with violent opposition. We will also prevent any suspect personages from escaping.

'I would remind you that the magistrates and Dublin Castle have a pressing need for informants and intelligence and as such I must insist that you lay hands on before you lay steel on.'

There was a general murmur of assent from the horsemen.

Most of the infantry had by now formed a rough arc around the front of the Gormley cottage and another group were creeping around the side of the cowshed so as to cordon off the rear of the building. One luckless soldier failed to spot a weather-rotted old fence post propped against the cowshed wall and with a curse and flailing rattle he clattered over it. One of his companions hauled him to his feet by his crossbelts and planted his bicorn back onto his embarrassed head.

Even at the awkward, foul-mouthed tumble of the soldier not a stir came from the house. Only a dog barked in the distance, lonely and mindless.

The night was too empty, too lifeless. Tom found himself becoming gradually aware of the growing trepidation. At any moment he expected the flat boom and phoenix tail of musket-fire. His horse whickered to itself, a soft noise that shattered the stillness like a stone shattering a mirror. Every breath he took surged in his ears and every clank and shuffle of infantry or yeo scuttled into the night on a thousand pin-prick legs.

At last Lieutenant Musgrave seemed satisfied with his troops' deployment. He rose up in his stirrups and held his straight-blade sword high above his head.

'Hello the bawn!' he called, the switchbacks of his Munster accent echoing from field to yard and ditch to wall. 'By order of His Majesty's Government in Ireland, I call on you to admit the King's troops to effect a search of your property.'

No answer came from the silent cabin. No movement to signal anything but ghosts within.

Musgrave settled back down upon his mount, which bobbed its chestnut head and snorted in protest. For a moment the officer look unsure what to do next, then he called to a stoop-shouldered soldier to his left, 'Sergeant O'Sullivan, break down the door.'

O'Sullivan saluted smartly and, in the grand tradition of non-commissioned officers, promptly collared two privates and marched with them up to the cottage's heavy wooden door.

'Right lads,' he bellowed. '*A h-aon, a dó, a trí!*'

And on the last syllable the two privates flung themselves against the portal's planking.

The combined weight and violence of the two soldiers hammered the door from both its lock and hinges. A spume of dust coughed out from the joins in the wood as the door fell suddenly into the dark of the cabin's interior, where it smacked onto the straw-covered floor. One soldier had rebounded from the door but his comrade had vanished into the cabin behind it and now pawed his way to his knees, groping for his fallen hat.

The crash resounded in the night and Tom twisted about in his saddle. He was certain he had glimpsed a dull sheen of gunmetal from the roadside ditch. His mind screamed at him that the stand of trees to his left was bristling with pikes. For the first time that evening, Tom realised what Proctor and his fellow yeomen must have been experiencing. The cold horror of knowing that you were hated for the coat you wore, for the laws you kept, the sickening appreciation of your own mortality. This is what spurred them, what drove them to excess.

Tom sat his saddle in nauseated silence and knew, and was disgusted by his certainty that if some peasant did rise from the black of the ditch, he would be the first to cut the man down.

At the cabin, the North Corks were slowly advancing. Their circle of steel contracting around the whitewashed walls. Suddenly, the soldier who had disappeared into the vacant doorway re-emerged, his musket slung over his shoulder, his hands batting dust from his black hat. His abrupt reappearance into an atmosphere of such tension almost had him killed. Several of his messmates cocked their muskets and took aim before they recognised the figure standing in the doorway. At the sound of the flints being drawn and at the sight of so many raised Brown Besses, the soldier froze. Gaping like a landed trout, he finally stammered, 'There's no one here.'

The infantry lowered their weapons and Musgrave brusquely and with a certain petulance ordered a thorough search of the abandoned homestead.

The yeomanry watched blandly as the North Corks set to ransacking the Gormley cottage. Tom turned to Proctor and with revulsion lacing his voice, he said, 'It's lucky Gormley isn't here. God knows what they'd have done to him.'

Proctor's eyes were blank and unfeeling as he replied, 'The rebels caught wind of our approach. Doubtless they're off hiding in the fields somewhere. We shall have to hunt for them as we've done before. Have no fear, Tom. Business is not concluded here yet.'

As his words ended, a sudden bright reflection sprang into life in his eyes and an orange blush animated his brow. Tom turned in his saddle to see the tinder-dry fringe of Gormley's thatch crackle into a tossing inferno. A handful of North Corks stood beneath the eaves, jabbing more blazing torches into the roofing. Musgrave sat and watched his men work, their shadows grotesque and capering in the glare, a demons' ball.

To right and left, strings of four and five infantrymen filed off along ditches and grikes, jabbing their bayonets into the bushes and peering under the hunchbacked stands of gorse. The yeomen watched the search parties, their horses dancing nervously, restlessly. They had been standing still for far too long. Lieutenant Esmonde's voice came levelly, 'Steady, lads. Steady.'

Then, all at once, one party, working their way through a field rising off behind the burning cottage, broke into a lurching run. Their pale breeches and white crossbelts bobbed and weaved in the dark and, for a moment, Tom could not discern what they were chasing. As they crossed an open space, however, their warning cries gaining in volume and desperation, they were cast in the amber seepage of light flooding out from John Gormley's flaming property. As they crossed this open space, their long shadows skittering alongside them, the object of their mad dash was also revealed.

A grimly-dressed young man was fleeing across the field's ridge, some fifteen yards in front of the stumbling soldiers. The harried terror of the fox before the hounds was evident in his frantic stride and flailing arms.

Lieutenant Esmonde stood in his saddle and raised his right arm, signalling the cavalry to advance and, as he did so, Tom felt a coldness twist inside him, his heart convulsing in his chest. Esmonde lowered himself back down into his saddle and slowly returned his hand to the reins of his mount.

On the hill the fleeing form had barrelled directly into a tangle of red-coated men who leaped upon him and bore him to the ground. Above the roar of the fire, Tom could see the heavy musket stocks driving into flesh like hooves into soft plough or an axe into wood.

Tom watched the militiamen lift the dazed figure by the armpits and half-carry, half-drag him towards the fire-lit yard. Tom's thoughts were a swarm of hectic contradiction. To see the battered figure so treated at the hands of the North Corks appalled him; at another, more terrible level, he was relieved that the infantry had caught up to the man before the cavalry were forced into action. The thought of riding that man – any man – down like an animal filled him with an odd dizziness and his forehead became slick with sweat.

'Thank God for that,' he heard himself sigh.

'Indeed,' agreed Proctor. 'The rascal very nearly showed them a clean pair of heels.'

Tom did not respond to this. He could not.

The entire contingent of infantry had now reassembled in the ruddy pulse of the blaze. The entire roof of what had once been John Gormley's home was now a coruscation of unbroken flame. Burning fragments of thatch and flickering clouds of embers twirled into the sky. The higher the flames mounted, the stronger the upward draught it generated and the brighter it glowed. And so it went, gorging itself on the remnants of the family's home and billowing with the heat of its own angry existence.

The man the infantry had made prisoner was held propped between two soldiers, his head lolling drunkenly on a neck made limp by the violence of his arrest.

Above the howl of the fire, Lieutenant Esmonde's voice came hard as steel.

'Let's hear what the wastrel has to say for himself. Castletown Corps, after me.'

He heeled his horse into a slow walk and the rest of the cavalry followed him, two abreast.

With every step that brought Tom closer to the fire-lit yard he strove to steady himself against what could happen next. The idea that this man was most probably a rebel, or at least spying for rebels, battled for pre-eminence with the oily suspicion that perhaps, just perhaps, this man was simply caught running from an authority he hated and feared. Struggling with himself, Tom could now see against the man's skin the murky rivulets and smeared flecks of blood.

One soldier was now standing before the wretched figure, a swollen water-skin in his hands. One of his comrades tilted back the peasant's head while he dashed water into the prisoner's face and down his throat. The man choked and coughed, his eyes blinking and snapping suddenly into focus. As the yeomen lined up behind the infantry, the soldier attending the prisoner, at a sign from Musgrave, stepped away and allowed him to stand on his own buckling legs.

Sitting his horse in the hellish billow of the burning house, Tom watched the man sway and stagger a step or two to the right like a newborn foal before steadying himself and raising his head to meet the stare of Lieutenant Musgrave. Tom could see the terror crawling across the young man's features.

Lieutenant Musgrave leaned forward in his saddle, his cocked hat and hooked nose lending him all the predatory menace of a vulture, and addressed the man with his customary lilting Cork belligerence.

'Are you one John Gormley, sir?'

The peasant before him, dressed in dark coat and breeches, his forehead and chin still leaking red, gazed up at the officer with eyes wide as a calf's and remained silent.

In the gambolling firelight Tom thought the man could be no more than twenty years old.

The impatience and anger in Musgrave's voice was unmistakable as he rasped, 'I will ask you a second time, you insolent savage, and I warn you there will not be a third. Are you John Gormley?'

The young cottier's jaw loosened in fear and he gushed, 'No, your honour, I'm not Gormley. I'm Paddy Cullen. I live over there in that poor little cabin. Please, your honour, don't treat me harshly for hiding. When we heard of your coming all the people of this place ran and hid. We were afeared, your honour, that's all.'

'"Afeared", by God?' bellowed Musgrave. 'Ain't every seditious man jack of ye got the right to be "afeared"?'

At this the peasant raised his hands in pitiful supplication.

'Oh, Jesus, Mary and Joseph. Your honour, there's no one I know who'd wish any harm to anyone. Have mercy your honour.'

'I am a merciful man,' responded Musgrave. 'If you but inform me where John Gormley may be found, no action will be undertaken against you or your property.'

'Gormley?' The note of confusion in the peasant's voice was unmistakably genuine. 'Why sir, John Gormley upped and left there the day before yesterday. No one knows where he went, or why. He just packed his family into the cart and left. He never said where. That's the God's honest truth, your honour.'

Barely hiding his irritation, Musgrave asked, 'Then why, pray tell, did you and the others of these parts flee at the approach of the King's troops?'

'Your honour, we had no way of knowing what you wanted. We've heard stories of rough handling by the redcoats in other places and we thought it would be safer to hide than be caught in our houses. The people are afeared, your honour. I was coming back to see if you were finished with your business when your men came upon me.'

'So you admit to spying?' queried Musgrave. 'Then tell me this. Do you know of any guns, munitions or arms of any kind secreted in this vicinity?'

'On my daughter's life, I do not, your honour,' said the man, with some vehemence.

Musgrave regarded him with an expression cruelly and grotesquely reminiscent of a father scolding a misbehaving child. 'Secreting weapons in contradiction of His Majesty's law is a heinous offence.'

The peasant frowned in confusion and, as he did, Tom's unease deepened moment by moment.

Paddy Cullen stood silently for a time, perplexed, and then slowly pronounced, 'But I know of no weapons, your honour.'

Tom did not like the direction in which Musgrave was steering events. It was like watching a cat boxing a wounded bird, its claws sheathed but aching to tear. Tom turned in his saddle, looking left and right, but every face appeared either amused or indifferent.

Musgrave was shaking his head now. 'Because we have found none in this cabin does not imply or bestow innocence, sir. You and your kind are United Irish, so therefore you know of weapons. This is simple reasoning.'

Cullen was panicking now, his features contorted, his hands wringing themselves. 'We aren't United Irishmen. For the love of Jesus, sir, I know of no United Irishmen in this district.'

Musgrave sat back in his saddle, an air of resolve coming over him as his coat flared red in the glow of the blaze, and said, 'More lies. Every Papist tongue in this county is forked.'

He flapped a back-handed gesture towards the peasant below him and said, 'Sergeant O'Sullivan, do your duty and then torch the rest of these flea-pits. Examples are to be made and the name of the North Corks is to be made a byword for loyalty and zeal. The croppies will be put down.'

The sergeant stepped from the ranks and made to move towards the figure of Paddy Cullen. For his part, the cottager was dumbfounded and immobile, but at the sergeant's approach he turned on his heel as though to run. However, his attempt at flight was strangled as two soldiers seized him by the arms and one red-sleeved forearm snaked across his throat, choking off his cries as he gasped for breath.

At this, something deep in the centre of Tom's chest cracked. Before he knew what he was doing, he was digging his heels into his horse's flanks. The big hunter was about to leap forward, its muscles balling beneath the sleek sheen of its coat, when Lieutenant Esmonde's gloved fist fastened on the length of rein just behind the animal's bridle and held on with all the force he could muster.

The horse's head slewed to one side and it whinnied its distress, and Tom cast his lieutenant a frantic look, his features stricken, his eyes wild.

Esmonde's features, however, were placid and his voice was quiet, 'Stay where you are Banville or I'll shoot you myself.'

Tom glanced from his lieutenant to where three soldiers were dragging Paddy Cullen behind the burning house.

'For God's sake, Sir Thomas!' he protested in anguished impotence.

Sir Thomas Esmonde appraised him frostily.

'God has no hand in this, Banville. The lowest circle of hell is reserved for rebels and mutineers. You know this as well as I.'

The sergeant and the two privates had now vanished out of sight with the struggling, screaming Cullen. His cries and the violence of his death were obscured by the inferno consuming Gormley's cottage. All about, the North Corks had scattered into three- and four-man foraging parties and were busy rampaging from empty house to empty house. They scurried through the night like vermin, their packs and jackets bulging with loot. As Tom watched, the first flames began to curl up from the thatch of the nearest whitewashed cabin.

'This is the rule of law,' stated Esmonde.

'Release my horse,' said Tom. His voice was level but within him a swarm of fury was tearing at his guts, his lungs, the very stuff of his soul. What he had

Joe Murphy

witnessed repulsed him and, worse than this, his involvement, the horror of his own inaction in the face of such cruelty, disgusted him. He was complicit in this, as bad as Musgrave and as callous as the North Corks; he had killed Paddy Cullen as surely as the bayonets that pierced his flesh.

His brows drawn together in wary consideration, Lieutenant Esmonde relaxed his grip on the bridle of Tom's mount and straightened wordlessly in his own saddle.

Tom nodded to his officer and with a gentle tug of the reins he wheeled his horse around.

'Tom . . .' began Proctor, worry straining his voice and cracking even that single syllable.

Tom ignored him and spurred his horse into a steady jog, his back to the collapsing ruin of the burning cottage and the small group of yeomen. In front of him, a black stain in the orange light, his shadow led him on like a malignant presence, a manifestation of his inner darkness. Around him, in the moonlight, yet more cabins erupted in flames and in the gorse the breeze sighed and rippled like the final exhalation of a dying man.

Dan Banville sat at the heavy writing desk in his father's study and bit the nail of one thumb in growing frustration. Before him, flattened out and held by two obsidian paperweights, a sheet of writing paper glowed in the lambency of a stag's head of candles. It glowed and, for all his efforts, remained stubbornly blank.

All his life he had been lauded for his capacity to speak and write with style and fluid ease. All his life the shackling of one sentence to the next had come to him as naturally as breathing. Yet now, as he bent over the arctic rectangle of the blank sheet, he found it impossible to find the right words. He could not condense, could not warp his thoughts into mere scribbles. What he sought to express was feeling – pure feeling; and syllables, whether prosaic or poetic, were suddenly too flimsy to heft such weight.

He cupped his chin in his hands and stared glumly into the shadows of his father's study. Beyond the wavering sphere of light cast by the yellow candles, shadows throbbed and crawled and erratic flashes licked across the curves of chairs and the corners of bureaus. Upon the looming, glass-fronted bookcase immediately opposite him, the stuffed form of a dog fox snarled down, forever at bay.

As he watched the shadows caper and his own silent reflection gaze back at him from the depths of the bookcase's glass, Dan found something come unbidden to his mind. As he sat there, motionless as the stuffed fox, he thought, You'll never understand, Elizabeth. I'm so sorry.

In that instant he knew, even if he had written page after page of searing honesty and emotion, it would still have been for naught; the pouring of his heart just so much wasted ink. Elizabeth would never understand.

Dan flung the empty sheet of paper from him. It leapt from the table as though alive, swooped and yawed into the dark beyond the candlelight, and see-sawed gently to the floorboards.

Dan rasped his hand across the stubble of his jaw and cursed himself for the decisions he had made.

The entire house was sleeping, so the heavy tread of hooves beyond the room's high, curtained window was as unexpected as it was loud.

Dan's lips curled sourly. He had not been looking forward to his younger brother's return.

Since Tom had ridden off that afternoon, the atmosphere of the Banville household had become thick with tension. Laurence Banville had seethed and stormed from empty room to empty room, seeking for some way to exorcise the fury inside him; the slamming of doors around the house providing his family with an exact map of his progress. Mary Banville had returned to bed at six o'clock, claiming a distempered headache. Dan himself had tried not to dwell on his brother's actions but had instead wrestled with trying to express something that refused expression. All the while, Mrs Prendergast bustled and flustered as though, through stubborn activity, she could dispel the bristling atmosphere that seemed to have settled into the very stones of the place.

And now, as Dan sat in the heat and glow of the candles, Tom returned to the home he had thrown into turmoil – Tom with his uniform, Tom with his sword, Tom with someone else's blood caking his hands. With a cold sort of anger infusing him, Dan grasped the candle stand by its pewter base and left his father's study.

He moved through the house within a globe of pale light; the walls to either side and the floor at his feet were cast in honeyed shades but before and behind him the dark closed around him like a fist.

The kitchen was lifeless and strangely eerie without its daytime chaos. The banked fire in the hearth crackled and slumped as it devoured itself. Standing by the elemental block of the table occupying the centre of the kitchen, Dan set the candles down so that their light would be invisible from the yard. Dan watched through the windows as his brother marched out of the maw of an open stable door. Tom had a bundle of straw which he had used to rub down his mount clenched in one fist and, as Dan watched, he flung it to the earth with a violence that was startling. Tom then locked the stable door and stalked across the hoof-scarred clay, his gloved fingers fumbling awkwardly with the clasp of his helmet. Finally, and with evident relief, he unfastened the chinstrap and, to Dan's astonishment, dashed the helmet to the ground and kicked it angrily across the yard to roll against the water pump with a dull clank.

Tom had not noticed his brother waiting for him. He was now struggling with the back door's latch and when he at last opened it he almost collapsed into the dim interior. He stood there for a moment, framed against the open doorway, his left hand still curled around the door handle, and then raised his eyes to meet his brother's.

Tom seemed to transform before Dan's eyes. In the moonlight and the frail radiance of the candles, he had become impossibly pale. His cheeks were stretched across his bones and his eyes had a glazed look of horror in their depths.

Dan lifted and placed the stand of candles upon the worn surface of the worktable and moved towards his brother. Concerned, he asked, 'What happened, Tom? What have you seen? What did you do?'

Tom wordlessly closed the door behind him. The helpless impotence he had felt as the North Corks burned cabins and butchered poor Paddy Cullen still festered in him. Every drop of bile, every ounce of spleen, churned for release. Yet the only person at whom he could vent this fevered frustration was himself. The hot blood of his body roared in his ears like the blaze of burning thatch.

Dan's voice came again, 'What did you do, Tom?'

His anger now replaced by fear for his spectral complexion and hunted eyes, Dan made to grasp Tom by the shoulders. In response, Tom brushed his hands aside and, without saying a word, he picked up the stand of candles from the table, walked mechanically out of the kitchen and further into the house. Perplexed and anxious, Dan followed.

Still without a word and still without even acknowledging his brother's presence, Tom made his way straight to his father's study, with Dan trailing in his wake like a scolded dog. Without hesitation, Tom went to a large cabinet standing in one shadow-shrouded corner and, opening it, extracted a half-empty bottle of whiskey. Then, still as mute and seemingly deaf as lead, he stepped over the paper lying on the floor, pushed past his brother and stepped into the hallway beyond.

He was about to mount the staircase when Dan, exasperated, finally gripped him by the collar of his jacket and spun him round. The candles cast them both in its halo of illumination and the whiskey sloshed and gurgled in its bottle as Tom pivoted with one foot upon the wooden steps. He stared into Dan's face as his brother's voice rumbled, 'I would hear of your actions this night from your own lips, Tom, before I hear them magnified by the wailing of the tenants.

'What did you do?'

Tom remained silent for a moment, his chalky features blank, and exhaled in a bitter expression of self-contempt, 'I did nothing, Dan. Nothing.'

With that he wrenched himself free and lurched up the stairs. Behind him, Dan stood in the dark, confusion and worry marring his brow, and his arms hanging at his sides. On the stairs, moving in a ball of light, Tom felt his stomach heave in disgust and in his head a single thought convulsed, sour and malignant.

The truth was just that. He had done nothing.

Nothing.

CHAPTER 5

Revelations

Eighteen days later and Tom Banville had not surfaced from beneath a wave of alcohol and self-reproach. His father, it seemed, had decided to behave as though his youngest son no longer existed, whilst his mother's headaches grew in frequency and severity as she struggled to hold together the unravelling fabric of her family. Dan Banville, a frown now permanently creasing his brow, had neither sympathy nor understanding for his younger brother.

News of the North Corks' raid had reached the parishes around Kilanerin the morning after it took place. Word of Paddy Cullen's death and the yeomanry's role in it spilled from the tongues of the people; everywhere it entered a new ear it grew in virulence. And this was not the only outrage. Under martial law, Wexford was becoming a butcher's slab, slick and impregnate with blood.

On the morning of the 18th of May, Dan knocked on his brother's bedroom door as he had done each morning for seventeen days. And, just as every other morning, not a sound was made in response. Dan stood for a moment and shook his head. His right hand hovered over the door's latch, almost, but not quite, touching it. Then, with a muttered curse, he turned on his heel and walked briskly away.

His father and mother had left just after dawn, rattling down the road with the horse and buggy, the reins held loosely in his father's veiny hands. They had gone to the funeral of an old acquaintance of Laurence's who had died of a burst heart as the yeos raided his cottage. However, the absence of his parents and Tom's continued self-imposed hermitage suited Dan perfectly on this particular day.

He had not seen Elizabeth for nearly a month. Since before the declaration of martial law, in fact, and even the frequent letters they exchanged were not enough. He had resolved to meet her and in her letters she had fervently expressed the same.

They had arranged to meet that afternoon in Newtownbarry, a tryst that would require Dan to travel almost the entire width of the county but he did not mind one whit. Even with soldiers rampaging and intimidating throughout the countryside, he desperately needed to speak to her. He had found no way in the last four weeks to write anything more than platitudes and meaningless commonplaces. Even now he could not fathom a way in which to express what he needed to tell her.

He could not fathom how to break her heart.

He passed through the empty house and, avoiding the dairy where Mrs Prendergast scrubbed and sang snatches of folk songs, left by a side door opening out onto the kennels. At the sound of the door closing the harriers commenced a low, yipping chorus of barks and whines. Since the military had seized the county in its armoured fist, a Catholic seen riding with hounds was liable to attract a hail of hot lead. So for the last few weeks the dogs had remained locked away. Confined to their kennels, the animals were frantic for the open fields and treated anyone who passed by as a potential liberator. As Dan strode past the low, green-painted kennel doors, the wet noses of the hounds could be seen protruding from the gap between wood and ground, snuffling and snorting in the dust.

Dan entered the stables, saddled the roan foxhunter and walked him out into the morning light. As he rounded the corner of the farmhouse he almost barged into the unexpected and puffing form of Mrs Prendergast, who was bar-relling along in the opposite direction, her arms laden with a basket of washing. The old woman was about to ask where he was going so early in the morning, and whether he intended to be gone long, but the dour look on Dan's face stopped her. He passed her by without saying a word, mounted his horse and trotted off into the patchwork countryside.

Mrs Prendergast watched him go and, under her breath, muttered, 'God keep you from those murdering bastards, young Master Banville.'

It took Dan three hours of hard riding to reach the outskirts of Newtownbarry. On the way he had come across several blackened husks of houses but fortunately managed to avoid any encounters with the arsonists. Even in passing though, the charred and crackling remains were dreadful to behold. Walls and thatch were often collapsed into a single smouldering jumble but, strangely, Dan found the most heart-wrenching were the cabins whose walls and roofs had not been fully consumed. These stood or leaned obscenely, their whitewash stained with dark fans of soot and their chimneys jabbing crookedly at the blue skies above.

These half-obliterated carcasses nudged his mind into thoughts of mortality. With their heat-warped timbers exposed and visible through the crumbling flesh of thatch and mortar, Dan found himself thinking of lambs savaged by dogs, their fleeces rent and their ribcages empty and broken.

At each of these ruined cottages a little crowd of people had gathered. The women comforting children whose tears streaked the ash that masked their faces, while the men used pitchforks and billhooks to sift through the glowing charcoal of their shattered lives.

Dan passed these desperate scenes in silence. As he passed, hard stares followed and callused hands tightened on the handles of half a dozen forks and scythes. To some he was Dan Banville, the former yeo, and their ire burned from their eyes. To others he was simply a rich man up on a big horse. To all he was an unwelcome guest.

Newtownbarry was a busy little town sprouting up on the Carlow border. From its elongated market square, the road to Kildare and Queen's County skirted the Blackstairs and twisted off into the midlands. As Dan entered the town from the road leading in from Clohamon, the first thing he noticed was the blue, white and red bunting hanging from several windows. It seemed as though a few good citizens of Newtownbarry were eager to convey their unwavering loyalty to the Crown.

The next thing he noticed was Elizabeth Blakely, standing by the corner of a slate-roofed market house, her mahogany hair held up under a straw sun-bonnet. She wore a high-waisted white dress embroidered with green leaves and flowering buds. At the sight of her, Dan's resolve almost failed him.

Taking a deep breath, he heeled his mount onward. Through a fog of despair he crossed the hard earth of the street.

Elizabeth, he thought, I am so, so sorry.

When he was halfway across the town's main street, Elizabeth caught sight of him and with a gut-wrenching smile she hurried over to intercept him. Dan dismounted and kissed the hand she demurely offered. To kiss her, even on the hand, in such a public place might be commented upon and word would surely reach her father in Carnew.

She smiled at him as they walked Dan's horse over to the hitching rail running along one side of the market house. He tried to smile back but the sour feeling snaking along his nerves would not allow it, and his expression remained stolid and wan.

'Whatever's the matter?' asked Elizabeth.

Dan finished knotting his horse's reins to the rough timber of the hitching rail and said nothing.

Seeing her like this, so close and so warm, her eyes growing more and more concerned under creasing brows, Dan felt himself rudderless. He cursed necessity and damned the day he had first laid eyes upon her. Frozen, petrified by the gorgon's stare of the inevitable, he returned Elizabeth's stricken gaze with his own.

In a million years she would never understand.

At last, he offered her his arm and muttered, 'Would you walk with me, Elizabeth?'

Perturbed, she answered, 'Of course, my love.'

They turned down the street and went left up the little bohreen leading off to Clonegal. Chestnut trees arched over the road, the breeze rustling the first few broken-wristed bundles of leaves that spread themselves under the May skies. The young couple walked silently, neither seeking to intrude upon the quiet. In the distance the clatter and industry of Newtownbarry gradually faded to a subtle undertone beneath the lullaby of the whispering breeze.

Eventually Elizabeth could take no more and suddenly spun him about, snapping, 'What ails you Daniel? You are as melancholic as a widow.'

'Elizabeth—' he began. His tongue felt like a ball of wool in his mouth and his throat closed in rebellion.

'Daniel,' Elizabeth breathed softly, drawing him to where a low dry stone wall bordered the roadway. He let himself be guided by her, a ghost ship towed by a swan.

'Daniel,' she urged again, 'whatever it is that burdens you so, I sorely wish you would tell me. How am I to help you if you will not let me?'

Leaning his back against the uneven, moss-cushioned stonework of the wall, Dan regarded her with the anguish and hopelessness of a drowning man. Then, shaking his head, he said in a choked voice, 'Elizabeth, I do not think it fit that we continue as we are.'

Elizabeth, who had been grasping his right hand tightly in both of hers, abruptly let go and took a quick step away from him.

'What did you say?'

Dan could not raise his eyes to meet hers, and directed his words to the rumpled grass verge at his feet. 'I could not write to you for I could not find the proper words to put down and now, when I see you, I find my mouth is filled with stones.

'I am so very sorry, Elizabeth.'

Elizabeth stood then, with her fists planted on her hips and eyed her companion from under cocked brows. 'You mean to tell me,' she began in a voice fizzing with scepticism, 'that you have come all this way to cast me aside as though I were a rag used to clean your boots?'

Dan's voice was strained as he beseeched, 'Elizabeth, please don't.'

Elizabeth's head tilted to one side and she drew a long breath to speak. Dan was expecting a tirade, tears even, but instead she said, 'What are you up to, Daniel Banville?'

Elizabeth's foot tapped an impatient tattoo on the road and she probed, 'Well?'

Frustrated and floundering in the mire of his own mind, Dan frowned and sighed, 'Elizabeth, you cannot comprehend.'

Before he had a chance to elaborate further, the young woman in front of him exploded.

'Rubbish! Do not dare to patronise me, Mr Banville. You stand here and you sigh and you blow like a leaky bellows and you have the gall to treat me so shabbily. How dare you!'

Her voice mounting like a thunderhead, she continued, 'If you think I am some limp lily ready to wilt at any extremity then you are mistaken. I have stood by you against my father and against the advice of all my friends. I have met you secretly at great personal risk and now, from some obscure sentiment, you seek to push me away?

'Look at yourself!' she snapped. 'You can barely stand let alone force weasel words and falsehoods from that mouth of yours. You cannot deny me. You cannot deny *us*.

'And so I say again – what are you up to Daniel Banville?'

Dan at last met her gaze and the agony in his face made her recoil. His breath came in quick gusts and his hands gripped the stones of the wall against which he stood.

"Deny you'?' he asked. 'I thought I could but now I find I cannot. You have robbed me of the only course of action that may have afforded you some measure of safety.

'Leave me, Elizabeth. For the love of God, leave me and go back to your father's house.'

She stepped toward him, hands reaching for the wide, trembling mass of his shoulders.

'Why?' she whispered. 'What could make you say such things? Daniel, why are you so frightened?'

As his doleful eyes lifted to meet hers, his attention was pricked by a sound that had existed on the fringes of his awareness for some minutes but which only now had grown sufficiently intrusive to jerk his focus away from Elizabeth. Beneath the rippling of leaves, a bass rumble slowly mounted.

Down the road from Clonegal, white crossbelts vivid against deep blue jackets, a cavalry detachment was galloping their way.

Dan watched them for a moment, his eyes suddenly wary.

'The Ancient Britons,' he growled.

The cavalry pounded closer, their tack jangling and the wet, blowing of their horses loud above the hoofbeats. As they drew nearer, Dan pushed himself away from the wall and curled his left arm about Elizabeth's waist.

Without slowing, the horsemen of The Ancient Britons rattled past the young couple, one or two of the soldiers openly leering down at Elizabeth. Close to her ear, the stubble of Dan's jaw scraped against his collar as his head swivelled to watch the cavalry as they clattered into Newtownbary.

'God help whoever they're after,' said Elizabeth.

Dan nodded and growled, 'If the French should land it would cut the legs from under their high horses.'

'Daniel,' Elizabeth began. 'If you know anything of approaching trouble you should inform the magistrates. Collection of arms is underway everywhere. I am not so blind as you think, my love. Please, please, do not put yourself in harm's way.'

Dan frowned, his arm still wrapped around her hips, and meeting her gaze he said, 'I do not think you blind, Elizabeth. I could never think anything ill of you. Do not worry. I know nothing of approaching trouble any more than I can predict the weather. I no more wish to be in harm's way than the next man.

'Yet you must understand that being with me like this places you in an unenviable position. I am the son of an outspoken Catholic. I would not see you or your family persecuted for your association with me.'

She looked at him stonily, her brows lowering, 'It is my opinion that you have as much to fear in your association with me as I have in my association with you. The peasants all around Carnew have taken to sleeping in the fields to avoid the nocturnal visits of the yeomanry. How would your father and your friends consider your consorting with a moneyed Protestant?'

'Let them go hang.'

The vehemence in his voice, the sincerity, was absent. His tone was colourless. For the first time since she had met him, Elizabeth doubted her young farmer's son. Not his truthfulness, but his motives.

It was this that prompted her to step away from him and ask, 'If trouble comes, Daniel, if trouble comes and you have to choose between me and someone, something, else, what would you do?'

Shaking his head, his voice came strangled and agonised as if wrenched from some tortured part of him, 'I would choose you, Elizabeth.'

This was the truth, whole and unvarnished and the reality of that truth made something curdle inside of him. Above family, above friends, above church, he would stand with the young lady before him.

Elizabeth heard the truth in his words. She heard the truth and perceived the determination of his bearing. In saying those words, her lover had almost torn himself in two.

And for an instant she hated him for it and hated herself for forcing him to say it.

'Elizabeth,' groaned Dan. 'We cannot go on. Not like this.'

'I love you Daniel. I pledged myself to you in the private chambers of my heart a million times over,' she replied.

Dan nodded, a crater, tattered and raw, yawning in his heart. 'And I to you. But private passion would make carrion of us both in the eyes of our people.'

Elizabeth's eyes travelled over him as she murmured, 'We could elope.'

The bitterness in his laugh was poison in her ears. He shook his head, 'Penniless and friendless? We'd make quite the dashing couple.'

Her hands lifted then and she rested them against his chest. The first glimmer of coming tears flashed in her eyes until she blinked them away and asked hoarsely, 'What do you propose? What solution? For I will not allow you to make such overtures as you have made and then dash it all to ruins. Please say that you are up to something Daniel. Please.'

Dan grasped her wrists in his rough hands and moved her gently from him, his actions at odds with his desires. The words that came from his mouth spilled like coal from a chute.

'You and I have sneaked about and stolen kisses like poachers in fog. Now even that has grown too perilous. Things are changing, Elizabeth. For two such as us, this state of affairs might very well prove hurtful and ruinous to our families. Until the military is reined in, until a semblance of order is restored or a new order supplants the old, our love is a seed fallen on barren ground.'

'That is a hard thing to say, Daniel. Hard and cruel.'

Dan looked at her. 'It is the truth. The only way to preserve you from harm is to send you home. You must not have any association with me until after this has run its course and the country is less frenzied.'

'This is your solution?' she asked drily. 'You seek to send me away from you because of the danger we place ourselves in?

'For my part I would willingly brave ten times the dangers posed by the likes of the good Captain Wainwright. I did not expect to hear such womanish sentiments from you, of all people.'

The edge to Dan's voice was unmistakable, 'I am no coward madam and I would call out any man who should dare suggest such a thing. How dare you.'

'How dare I?' she spat. 'I dare because I do not believe you in every part of what you profess.'

Dan's brows beetled further and his mouth worked with the beginnings of protest but she cut him short.

'I do believe you wish to keep me safe and I do believe you consider the surest way to achieve this is to send me from you. What I do not believe is that you care tuppence about what either your or my family think and I believe you care even less for the military. I do not call you a coward for fearing steel or shot. I call you a coward for not trusting me enough to tell me the truth.'

Dan gaped at her, 'Elizabeth,' he began at last. 'I have given you no cause to imagine any such thing of me.'

'"Imagine", Daniel?' she said, incredulous. 'I imagine nothing. And the cause you gave me is the very fact of you being who you are. You are glass to me, Daniel Banville. You always have been. I may not know exactly what you are muddled up in, but I know that you are involved in something. It is agony to me that you cannot see fit to even inform me as to what you seek to protect me from. It is hurtful, unmannerly and unbecoming of you. In fact, when you are man enough to be truthful with me, whole and complete, then you may write to me at my father's house.'

Dan stood with the May sunshine falling through a ceiling of leaves, and felt his own heart shatter in his breast.

'You wanted to keep me safe,' Elizabeth snapped. 'You wanted to send me away. Well you've gotten your wish Mr Banville.'

With that she spun away from him, her dress flaring out and her sun-bonnet abruptly askew. Her arms swinging and her riding boots scuffing the clay as she went, Elizabeth stormed off, down the road towards Newtownbarry.

Leaning like a fallen spar against the low stone wall, Dan watched her go with eyes that stung. Even now, as she stalked away from him with chin held high and face haughty as a ship's figurehead, he knew he would do anything for her. Physically he was stricken. And yet something had lifted from his mind. Some weight had been removed. As much as his heart wept to see Elizabeth leave in such anger, his mind rejoiced at her going. Now, he knew, she would be safe. Whatever occurred to change the fortunes of his battered county, Elizabeth would be safe from the worst of it.

And as he watched her go, a small, venomous voice bawled inside him that she was right all along. He was a coward. *There's no choice now*, it seemed to chuckle.

There was now no Elizabeth to place above all else. Suddenly, he was free – free to do what must be done.

Tom sat on the edge of the stone trough and leaned one elbow on the snout of the water pump. Evening was coming in a mounting golden haze, creeping up from the horizons of the world. Overhead, swallows tumbled and plummeted, mocking the leaden shackles that bound all else to the earth's dusty surface.

Tom squinted up at the screaming, angular little birds as they shot through the summer air. He drew one hand across his clammy brow and then looked down to where one of his father's harriers sat with a splintered length of tree branch in its mouth. The dog's saliva dribbled from the branch's kinks and knotty protrusions and the animal whuffed and whined in gormless excitement.

For the love of God, thought Tom, even throwing a damned stick is making me feel unwell.

For eighteen days he had been drinking. Drinking and avoiding all human company with the same assiduity with which he had avoided solid food. He had become a recluse in his own home, a shadow in the daylight. For eighteen days Laurence Banville had not said a word to him whilst his mother nattered into the hollow space between father and son. She fussed and flustered and laughed in the silence as though her family were not fracturing before her eyes. Over the last couple of days Tom had noted the deepening fissures around her mouth and the plough lines across her forehead, and the disturbing edge to her forced good humour.

Every day her headaches grew worse; every day she retired to her bedroom earlier than the day before.

The foxhound at his feet dropped the stick and pawed forlornly at Tom's stockinged calf. Its claws made a series of dusty brown smudges against the white linen. Tom absentmindedly patted the animal's head and stared off into the middle distance, his blue eyes unfocused and his thoughts dulled by the aching in his head.

His formless contemplations were interrupted as the harrier's sharp head lifted and its ears pricked in anticipation. The animal stirred itself and turned to face the hard-packed curve of earth that swept from the stableyard around to the front of the house. A low, excited yipping emitted from the animal's slack muzzle and, a moment or two later, Tom saw the source of the dog's excitement. The scuffling thud of a tired horse's hooves padded into the stableyard, closely followed by the animal and its rider.

Dan sat astride the roan foxhunter with the bearing of a man exhausted. To Tom he looked like a man who had been on the wrong end of a beating or had run too long a race. In short, Dan looked like Tom felt.

Tom pushed himself up from the stone trough with a shuddering and heart-felt sigh that was pathetic coming from one so young. With the hound gambolling about his legs he moved, lead-footed and stiff, towards his elder brother. Dan had reined in his tired mount and had dismounted, his broad back stooped as he examined the roan's back legs and fetlocks.

'He's a bit lame,' Dan offered at Tom's approach.

'That would crown a perfect day all round,' replied Tom.

Dan looked up from where he was bent, his face sheeted in the shadow flung by his brother's presence. It was a face that, in Tom's mind, had somehow altered – almost imperceptibly, Dan's aspect had changed. His broad features were identical to that which Tom had grown up with. The same tight nest of wavy brown thatched his head and his eyes retained their old sea-grey curiosity, still regarded him and scrutinised the world with an academic's thoughtful consideration. Nonetheless, the Dan Banville that frowned up at him from that puddle of shadow was not the Dan Banville of the years, the day, the hours before. His jaw seemed harder, jutting and clenched, and some odd purpose had tightened his mouth, narrowing his lips into thin, humourless strips. It was a face that Tom, all at once, could not imagine smiling.

'Why do you say that, Tom?' asked Dan, as though he were the same Dan as always; always curious, always caring.

It took a moment for Tom to answer, so perplexed was he by the subtle change he perceived in his brother. When he did answer it was with a snort of self-mockery. 'I've been dying sick all day. I think I may have reached a nadir. I don't think I can cope with it anymore.'

Straightening, his hard face stony and grim in the westering sun, Dan asked, 'Cope with what, Tom? The drink? Or is something deeper troubling you? Eighteen days, Tom, you've been hiding in your own misery. You have to come out eventually.'

Tom patted the gelding's thick neck and smiled at his brother. 'I know, Dan.

I'm thinking of resigning my commission in the yeomanry. I haven't been in any state to attend a muster in eighteen days. They probably think I've deserted or become a United man at this stage of things.'

Dan's eyes shone but any warmth in them failed to communicate itself to the rest of his features, and his cheeks and jaw remained cold and tense. 'Good for you, Tom,' he said. 'Those bastards have cut loose completely throughout the entire neighbourhood. The county's in flames because of them and those North Cork scoundrels.

'Although Richard Proctor and one or two of the others have paid visit to you at various hours. "Enquiring after your health" they said. Da ran them off, of course. They were seemingly quite concerned about you. As have we all been.'

Tom regarded his brother and shook his head slowly, 'I do not deserve such sentiments. But tell me, where have you been all day? And what travails must you have come through? You look as though you've been carrying this horse rather than the other way around.'

Immediately Dan's brows darkened and his head dropped forward as though his body had been robbed of its strength. Yet, the eyes that fixed Tom from under those pitch brows, were aflame with something raw, something fervent.

'I was off doing something that must, through pointed necessity, have been done.'

Tom searched his brother's features whilst his fingers bunched and un-bunched in the roan's coarse mane. At length he cocked his head and said, 'It's that Blakely one, isn't it. Elizabeth. The Protestant girl you've sought to keep secret from all and sundry. Something has transpired between you hasn't it? She's turned down your hand in marriage, hasn't she? Well come on, out with it.'

For the merest sliver of a shattered instant Dan's face registered an expression of genuine anguish before it slipped away and was gone like smoke in a gale. He shook his head once sharply and his voice came low and wavering, 'No, she did not deny me. I have ended our correspondence and that is that.'

Tom nodded sagely and clapped a hand on his brother's shoulder. The reason behind Dan's strange difference was suddenly laid out clear before him. Tom sighed, 'Probably for the best, all told. That there was a liaison with every potential for mischief. Probably for the best.'

Dan shook himself free of Tom's companionable grip and tugged the gelding roughly towards the stables. Looking once over his shoulder he spat, 'You do not know her at all. Nor me as well as you might, Tom. Do not presume to know what is for the best.'

With that he vanished into the ragged dark of the stable.

Beside Tom's legs, the harrier whined and nudged his hand with the wet pad of its nose. 'I know, lad,' muttered Tom in puzzlement. 'I have no idea what's gotten into him either.'

Night found Tom awake and staring at his bedroom ceiling. It was half past midnight. For the first time in eighteen days his head rested upon the cumulous bulge of his pillow without the anaesthetic of alcohol to weight his eyelids. He lay there in the moonlight with his bedclothes kicked and twisted into a frothy wave about him. His bare chest was slick with moisture, yet the heat that drove down upon him seemed to clot the air and fill his throat and lungs with mud. He could not breathe and he could not sleep.

In his mind Paddy Cullen's shrieks, rising in frenzied horror, rose and fell and rose again like waves on beach.

The fact of his involvement in the raid, the fact of his complicity in a cold-blooded murder churned in his mind like a ball of broken glass. His father's disdain, his mother's slow descent into mania, all could be traced back to that awful night. He was on the verge of destroying his family and he had wallowed in drink and self-pity and allowed it to happen.

He was left with no choice. He must remove himself from the yeomanry lists. He grinned bleakly into the blued silver wash of moonlight coming through his open window and thought what a grand irony it all was. He had stayed in the yeomanry to save his family, but instead it had almost ripped it asunder.

Still, he was afraid, terrified at leaving his home without protection. His father's mouth, his pantomime blustering, had gained them as many enemies as friends. Tom could imagine Hawtrey White and Hunter Gowan rejoicing at his resignation. He could imagine the whisper of steel as it slid free, imagine the flames reflected in its mirrored surface, imagine the gleaming of its bitter edge. He could imagine his home an inferno.

The low drumming of approaching hooves seemed to already rumble in the quiet of his solitude.

Tom sat up, his mouth pursed as he listened.

In the black and argent chamber of his room he held his breath and froze, his ears straining and every portion of his flesh tingling in anticipation.

He had heard hooves.

Not the imaginary hooves of approaching bogeymen but the real thud and clop of iron upon clay and cobble. His eyes stared, unseeing, and the chords of his bedclothes lay looped at his feet.

He had heard hooves. He must have. He was sure of it.

Then, just as the need to take a breath began to tug at his chest, he heard a voice. Hoarse and whispering, it crawled up from the front dooryard below his open window and spilled across his watchful silence.

'Hush, girl. Easy now,' it said.

In the moon-drenched sanctuary of his room, Tom blinked in astonishment. It was Dan's voice that had come soft-pitched and hissing through the night.

Tom moved quietly, slipping from under his bedclothes and sidling over to his window. Underfoot, the floorboards still retained some of their daytime warmth and as he moved across them his feet made little sticking sounds, tacky with sweat. His breath came in shallow spasms and his hands were cold and numb.

In the dooryard, illumined by a moon bright enough to conjure shadows and draw darkness from the merest wrinkle in the landscape, Dan Banville was quietly leading three horses around to the stableyard. With him, the cape-collars of their trusties lending them the aspect of predatory birds, three men moved in furtive and wary silence. As Tom watched unseen, the group slipped around the corner of the house and were gone.

Tom leaned for long minutes against his windowsill, Laurence Banville's dooryard a dimpled bowl of silver below him. His hands clenched and unclenched as he gripped the white-painted wood of the window frame and his brows remained furrowed and dark. Thoughts and questions wheeled and reeled in his head, each one branching and fracturing, shattering into a thousand competing ideas and considerations, a chaos of confusion and half-formed imaginings.

What was Dan doing inviting people into their home at so late an hour? Why hadn't the house been roused?

Who were those men?

Why were they so quiet, so wary?

Tom was dressing himself before he was really aware what he was doing. His breath was coming more quickly now, like a hound panting after a scent, as he jerked his shirt over his head. Without shoes or stockings he crossed to his bedroom door and eased it open. The slight whine of its hinges made him wince and splintered the silence that seemed to have enclosed the Banville household. From the kitchens below, where Dan and his midnight guests must surely be gathered, there was not a sound. The quiet, downy and inviolate, blanketed all the world.

Tom hesitated for a moment before stepping across the door's threshold. He was unsure of what he was about to do. On the one hand he was certain that Dan must have some reason to allow people, unannounced and secret, into their family home; on the other, the very fact of their anonymity and their cloak-swaddled silence trilled a note of curiosity in Tom's young heart. For a moment he hesitated, briefly contemplating calling out and waking the household, but then the adventure of the mysterious seized him and he padded out into the hallway. It was as though he was transported back to his childhood, eavesdropping as Laurence Banville entertained, or stealing illicit cakes from Mrs Prendergast's pantry. Whatever the reason behind Dan's incongruous little party, Tom would find out through his own initiative. Younger brother he may be, but he was damned if he was going to be kept ignorant of something as extraordinary as a midnight conclave.

He crept along the tongue of carpet lolling down the centre of the hallway. With every step he took he expected to hear a creak of timber and a commotion from downstairs, but all remained silent. The entire household, except he and Dan's party, was sleeping. At the end of the corridor, instead of taking the wooden back stairs down to the kitchen, he turned right and ghosted down the stone steps of the main staircase.

This staircase descended into the modest front hallway of the house and each step felt cold beneath his careful tread. Tom moved slowly now, acutely aware that the door to the kitchen lay behind and below him to his left. He thought he could hear, just on the cusp of apprehension, the muffled voices of men in conversation. He had taken this route because, should Dan go to fetch anything from his room, he would likely take the back stairs, and Tom could not see a reason why Dan or any of his guests would have any business in the entry hall. Nonetheless, once he had stealthily gained the foot of the stairs he chose each step toward the kitchen door with the careful deliberation of a stalking heron. Each step was noiseless, and the mere silken rustle of his shirt, barely louder than a moth's wings, was the only sound he made.

The kitchen door itself was a massive old construction of oak planks and iron rivets, ill-fitting and out of place with the simple elegance of the rest of the dwelling. It was a remnant of an older building, a vestige of a rougher age imperfectly hung on three heavy hinges. However, it was this alien aspect of the door that prompted Tom to press himself against it. A large gap ran between the age-blackened wood and its rough-hewn jamb. In the Winter,

Mrs Prendergast and, indeed, Mary Banville herself, railed that the breeze coming through it would cut you in half; but now it afforded Tom with a perfect listening post from which to spy on his brother.

In the dark, swaddled in a void of empty silence, Tom Banville listened.

Inside the kitchen, a voice with the nasal yaw of Ulster in it was saying, 'Aye, sure it only defies belief. I've never seen weather like this in May before. Every farmer in the county is delighted. We'll have more straw and grain this winter than we'll know what to do with.'

A voice in a Wexford drawl, sounding little more than a youth's but weighted with an undefined yet marked confidence, retorted, 'If there'll be anyone left to take it all in of course. The way things are going there'll not be a soul left in the country except soldiers and yeos.'

The first voice came again, 'My God, where are my manners? Let me introduce you all. Dan Banville, this is Miles Byrne of Monaseed and my other more venerable companion is Peter Bolger from Tomnahely.'

At this another voice chuckled, 'Don't bury me yet, Anthony. I may not be a young buck like Miles here but I've long days ahead of me yet.'

Tom strained to spy the men through the crack between door and jamb as his brother's voice, almost in a whisper, replied, 'Thank you Mr Perry. Mr Byrne, Mr Bolger, you are both very welcome to my home. However, I would ask you all to please be attentive of the fact that my poor family is presently sound asleep and knows nothing of our meeting.'

Byrne, Tom thought it was, more from the swagger in his voice than the youthful musicality, then spoke. 'Your "poor family" in its entirety, Mr Banville?'

The question seemed to Tom to possess a honed edge and he was surprised by Dan's response. His brother's voice carried a note of barely-reined anger as he growled, 'Yes, Mr Byrne. Everyone. Whole and entire. And I shall inform you gentlemen here and now that, should anyone voice any ill intention towards my brother, then I shall set them on the road and wash my hands of this entire endeavour. He has remained with the yeomanry thus far in order to protect his family and his home. He has never raised a hand against anyone.'

Bolger's voice soothingly interjected, 'Mr Banville, nobody questions the motives of a yeoman and I am not about to start delving into loyalist minds. It is widely known that although your brother did not commit any violence on the part of the Orangemen, he did nothing to stop it either. My question to you is this - can he be trusted?'

Into the black of the hallway, from out of the crack between Tom's world and his, Dan's voice, hollow and blank, stated, 'No. He cannot be trusted in this enterprise.'

Dan's response hit Tom like a kick to the stomach. He had no idea what the purpose of this secret rendezvous was, as yet, but his brother's words had wounded him. He had no idea that he and Dan had slipped so far away from each other.

The northern accent of Perry then sounded low and definite, 'Then we should keep our voices down.'

Intrigued and dismayed now in equal measure, Tom pressed himself further against the aperture as though striving to slip through the very door itself. Ears straining, he listened in growing shock as the four men continued their conversation.

'How many have we got in each barony now?' asked Byrne.

'A multitude,' came Perry's response. 'If the blasted military would stop their confiscation of weaponry the whole country might be ours tomorrow. With or without the French.'

'At the same time,' said Byrne, 'the outrages of those red-coated monsters, perpetrated daily against the innocents of the county, is the greatest tool we have in rallying people to the banner.'

'I agree,' Dan added. 'If only the priests could see their way fit to aid the people and not keep them servile beneath the detestable English yoke. Fr Philip Roche was the only one with any spine worth the name and Caulfield has had him suspended for agitation. They're preaching surrender of arms from the pulpit and denying good United men the sacrament of confession. I swear to you now, gentlemen, a day of reckoning is fast approaching.'

'I have heard that Fr John Murphy of Boolavogue is a man of some high-standing and influence in the diocese and amongst the people. Has he then become the bishop's lackey as well?' asked Bolger.

'John Murphy?' snorted Perry. 'That fat prevaricator? Something of dire consequence will need to occur to force his hand. No, I'm afraid we are on our own, without divine light or guidance in our lives.'

A hushed sough of laughter slithered forth from the four men.

Tom, growing more and more tense as his suspicions found more and more purchase, breathed deeply in the darkened hallway. He was becoming cold and his anxiety was stiffening all the muscles of his shoulders and neck so that the first spasm of a cramp bucked in the small of his back.

'Any word from Dublin, Anthony?' asked Bolger.

A long pause followed this before Perry answered, 'Some. But I am unsure of the exact details, as yet.'

'Come now, Anthony,' whispered Miles Byrne. 'If you know anything of any substance or importance at all you should inform us. We are all here committed United Irishmen.'

There it was.

For Tom, standing cold and silent, his ear pressed to a splintered gap between wood and wall, those were the words that he knew would come. To hear them so blithely spoken by one who sounded so young was, to him, vaguely appalling. The deadly freight of those words seemed too heavy to be carried by so light a tone. Miles Byrne had laughingly proclaimed Tom's elder brother a traitor to the realm. He had proclaimed a death sentence on the Banville house and property.

Perry was saying, 'If I knew anything of consequence I would communicate it instantly and without hesitation. However, until I am informed from Dublin, I am as ignorant of whatever plans the executive have as anyone.'

All this was lost on Tom Banville. A furious knot of anger had clenched itself at the base of his skull and his teeth ground with animal rage. His breathing came quick through his nostrils and he thought the sound of it must surely disturb the quiet conversation taking place beyond the door.

How could he? Tom fumed in the cauldron of his mind. How could his brother betray him? How could he trust him so little?

Amidst Tom's anger, the hurt of a little boy derided and ignored by the brother he idolised swelled up inside him. And with the hurt and anger hot tears welled in his eyes, sparkling in the darkness. Soundlessly, Tom backed away from the door and step by agonising step made his way back down the hall and climbed the cold stone staircase. His shoulders stooped, his head bowed. In the empty spaces of his soul, Tom felt like a stray cur, a kicked mongrel.

CHAPTER 6

Confrontations

The military barracks in Wexford Town squatted like a great grey toad basking in the sunshine. From its walls, narrow, slitted windows squinted out over the town and leered, ever-watchful, across the wide, mud-brown expanse of Wexford Harbour. At one such window a frock-coated gentleman in a powdered wig cast his troubled gaze upon the streets of Wexford and with his right hand tugged distractedly at his lower lip. From his vantage point, the town was a hive of peaceful industry. The traders and workmen of John Street called and cursed and spat as the morning sun rose ever higher. Coopers and tanners, jackets discarded, sweated at their stinking labour whilst blacksmiths and farriers, every line of their features silted with soot, haggled and gossiped, their forges throwing all the heat and noise of a battle into the street.

Women and townsmen bustled to and fro in the narrow thoroughfares around the Bullring. Wealthy merchants in rich fabrics mingled with the dashing uniforms of military men. From the docks came the eternal hue and cry of fishermen and sailors and with it came the elemental reek of the sea, that distinctive blend of salt and rot, always present, infusing every particle of the sprawling county seat. Above the steep slate roofs of the market houses and customs buildings ringing the dockside, the immense span of Wexford Bridge could be seen in the middle distance, describing a flat trajectory out and across the mouth of the River Slaney. And nearer, above the roofs, the masts and spars of a score of ships were black against the sky, bobbing and dancing in the breeze like a forest of trees. Or, thought the frock-coated gentleman, a forest of pikes.

From behind him, a voice intruded upon his contemplations. 'You seem troubled, Henry.'

Henry Perceval, High Sheriff of Wexford, turned his back to Wexford Town and faced into the gloom of the barracks room. Before him, two men were seated at a heavy carved wooden desk. One wore the red jacket and yellow facings of the North Corks, his gold epaulettes and red sash marking him as an officer. The other, leaning back in his chair, his greased and gleaming black riding boots crossed at the ankle and resting on the desk's polished surface, wore the blue and red of a captain in the Shelmalier Yeoman Cavalry.

Perceval cast a wry glance at the cavalryman's boots, which was ignored, before he addressed him, 'I am indeed troubled, Le Hunte. I am quite put out by all of this. Every report furnished to me adds a little more to my trepidation. What is to be done?'

The North Cork officer regarded the sheriff with cool condescension and interjected, 'My dear Mr Perceval, what is to be done is the execution of our duties. I fail to see how these reports are perturbing you in such a fashion. The arms collections are progressing tolerably well and any of the peasantry foolish enough to gainsay the King's troops finds out the error of his ways and so provides good example to his fellows.'

Perceval shook his head, 'It is not the progress of the arms collections that disturbs me, Colonel Foote. It is the sheer amount being collected that preys on my mind. My God man, I had no idea that there were so many pikes and guns in the hands of the peasantry. What if they should elect to use them?'

'Henry, Henry,' began Le Hunte. 'They shall never use them. As the good colonel has pointed out, the collections are going well. Young Bookey of the Camolin Cavalry is doing a particularly fine job. Between Enniscorthy and Arklow I doubt there is a rebel with any more than a pitchfork.'

Henry Perceval stepped away from the window and dragged a chair out from under the desk. Sighing, he eased himself down onto it.

'You look tired, Henry,' said Le Hunte with genuine sympathy.

'Tired?' laughed Perceval. 'I am exhausted. I do not remember the last night I have managed to slumber unbroken til the morning. My wife has retired to our home in the country for she cannot abide the constant impositions on my time. Day and night, gentlemen, day and night I am assaulted by talk of insurrection, by people frightened by rumour, by requests for warrants.'

With this he reached forward and picked up a bundle of handwritten papers that was neatly piled beside the crossed ankles of Captain Le Hunte. Disgusted, Perceval noted that, in spite of the boots' polish, the soles were dappled with dried scraps of mud and horse dung. Small flakes of this stuff had detached and made a filthy little pile, which the regular movement of Le Hunte's heels was grinding into dust.

Thumbing through the papers, scrawled over in spidery black ink, Perceval asked, 'And what am I to make of these?'

'Those, my good Sheriff?' asked Foote. 'Why, those are the signed testimonies of loyal subjects providing information on known United Irishmen. What you should make of them is haste. I would favour dispatching elements of the soldiery and cavalry to arrest the men identified in those papers forthwith.'

'On what grounds?' groaned the High Sheriff in exasperation. 'The vast majority of the names mentioned here come from the same tracts of North Wexford that have just been declared compliant. The people of the neighbourhoods from Enniscorthy all the way to the Wicklow border have been turning over their arms willingly, or so the military says. Why then should we arrest them? The gaol is already stuffed to bursting and the prison sloop anchored in the bay is fast becoming so.'

'Mr Perceval,' began Foote, his tone infuriatingly reasonable. 'I do not understand your demand for "grounds". Martial law has been declared. If you must rationalise our actions take it that the volume of arms being taken is testament to the fact that United Irishmen must be present in those parishes. Since only a United Irishman would have a pike, the fact of its surrender is enough to damn him.

'Of course, I do not suggest that the entire peasantry be put to the sword but the select few whose names are mentioned in those missives should be clapped in irons as traitors and the very basest of scoundrels.'

Le Hunte, his tanned face a mask of concentration, steepled his fingers below his chin and said, 'I agree completely with Lieutenant-Colonel Foote. The leaders of this movement should be rounded up and tried immediately. If those men are not leaders then at least they may be induced to inform as to whom they receive their orders from. We are in the midst of a most awful chapter in our country's history, Henry. We must not let it slide into barbarity.'

Henry Perceval, sighed, a long and heartfelt exhalation. Exhaustion and worry could be read in every line of his face. Rubbing one ashen hand vigorously across his forehead, he closed his eyes and was, for a moment, still.

'Very well,' he said at last. 'Do what you will.'

Tom Banville had slept fitfully. He had watched the moon arc up and over the Banville household, its light streaming more and more steeply through his window until it vanished beyond the eaves of the roof. Standing there, Tom felt oddly displaced. The first ashen presage of dawn was greying the world when he finally clambered back into bed. Sleep stole upon him with a poacher's stealth, for when he opened his eyes the sun was above the horizon. He had not heard Dan's guests depart but he presumed that they must have vanished before sunrise to avoid the militia and yeomen.

The house was still sleeping as he dressed himself and made his way down to the kitchen. The banked fire of the night before still smouldered in the hearth and warded off any creeping chill that dawn might have brought. Nothing suggested anything out of the ordinary had occurred during the night, nothing suggested the treason that had been spoken within those four walls.

Tired and angry, Tom Banville sat at the kitchen table and waited.

He had to wait for half an hour before Mrs Prendergast arrived in a bundle of energy and fluster.

'God almighty, tonight!' she gasped and her hands flew to her bosom. 'You frightened the life out of me, young Master Banville. Why are you sitting there at six o'clock in the morning?'

'I'm waiting for my brother, Mrs Prendergast. Waiting and thinking.'

She eyed him curiously, the wattles under her chin quivering with a life of their own, 'Well, as long as you don't mind waiting and thinking while I do the breakfast.'

'Not at all Mrs Prendergast, work away.'

Still considering him out of the corner of her eye she said, 'You look terribly worn out, young sir. Are you perhaps only in? Would you be wanting a cup of warm tea or anything?'

Twisting on his stool, Tom smiled at her in spite of himself, 'I haven't touched a drop, Mrs Prendergast. I'm quite alright. Thank you.'

She patted him on the shoulder as she bustled by, 'You were always my favourite. Even as a little lad.'

Tom sat as Mrs Prendergast pinwheeled about him, a middle-aged dervish of activity. She set the fire to blazing, filled the great black kettle with water and proceeded to make a cake of brown bread. She was the heartbeat of the house, the very stuff of its day to day life.

The next person to enter the kitchen was Laurence Banville. He strode in like a conquering general, loudly declaring, 'What a lovely morning, Mrs Prendergast.'

Then the liquid, old orbs of his eyes took in his younger son sitting, pale and ghostly, at the broad slab of the kitchen table. His voice faltered momentarily but then his eyes swept past Tom to fix Mrs Prendergast, and only

Mrs Prendergast, with a rheumy blue stare. His voice came again, just as bullish as before, as though for one small moment the vision of his son hadn't stolen it from him.

'Good woman, could you see your way fit to making up a bit of a bundle for me today. Myself and Dan have to do some work in the top field. Nothing extravagant, of course. Bread, cheese, some of that ham from yesterday and a pint of milk and water should see us through.'

'Of course I could, Mr Banville,' came Mrs Prendergast's cheerful reply. 'I'll leave it here for you.'

Laurence turned on his heel then and made to mount the wooden stairs at the back of the kitchen when Tom's voice, coming almost unbidden to his throat, said, 'Da.'

With one vein-scrawled hand curled about the worn banister, Laurence Banville paused for the merest instant and was gone.

Tom gazed at the empty staircase for long minutes whilst Mrs Prendergast determinedly busied herself with the morning's chores. He was still staring at it when his mother, dressed in a long linen dress and holding a straw bonnet in her dimpled little hands, descended from upstairs. She smiled when she saw him and swept immediately towards where he sat, her smile growing wider with each step she took. Bending, she kissed him on the forehead, stepped away from him and tilted her head in frank appraisal.

'You look much better when your eyes are blue and not red, Thomas,' she said.

'Thank you, Ma,' he replied. 'I've given up the drink. For a little while anyway.'

Mary Banville frowned delicately and shook her head so that her hazelnut curls bounced about her shoulders.

'Sure, you hardly drank much anyway, Tom.'

With that she opened the back door and stepped into the sunshine of the stableyard. Warbling an old song in a key slightly too high for her, she strolled around the front of the house and left Tom to his contemplations.

When Dan thudded down the stairs to the kitchen, his shirt was halfway over his head and in his haste he almost tripped on the second last step. He blundered into the middle of the kitchen and hauled his garment down over his shoulders. His hair was uncombed and his grey eyes were set in twin puddles of charcoal. The same dour set to his jaw was still apparent, as though it had become a permanent feature. When he saw Tom, however, he beamed, 'Good morning, little brother.'

He was taken aback by Tom's bitter expression.

Tom surveyed him, every fibre of his body aflame with anger. For Dan to be so cheerful, to be so deceitful and to seem so cavalier only served to further stoke Tom's fury. How could Dan even look at him, let alone speak to him, in such a manner?

Unmindful of Mrs Prendergast, uncaring of the consequences of his words, Tom snapped, 'Don't you "little brother me", you dissembling knave. We have need to talk.'

Mrs Prendergast, busy scrubbing a tin pan, began to loudly hum the chorus of an old gaelic ballad.

Simultaneously, both brothers whipped their eyes in her direction.

'The stables, Dan,' Tom barked.

Baulking, Dan raised his hands in supplication. 'Later, Tom. Da and I have work to do. We must be away shortly.'

'Ever the dutiful son,' sneered Tom. 'Does he know you are intent on bringing ruin down upon us all?'

Dan blinked. Shock lacing his words with urgency, he hissed, 'What have you heard, Tom?'

Glaring at him, his face a study in controlled fury, Tom repeated, 'The stables, Dan.'

This time, silently, Dan acquiesced. His broad frame slumped and he walked slowly toward the kitchen door, opened it and shuffled into the yard like a man on the way to his execution. Wordlessly, furiously, every muscle tense and primed for violence, Tom stalked after him. In the kitchen, still scrubbing the pan, Mrs Prendergast stopped humming her tune and followed their steps anxiously.

The stables stank in the heat. The stench of horse and old leather made a fetid cavern of the low, thatched building. The heat was oppressive, an almost physical weight, and in the light flung from the open half-door dust motes whirled in spangled golden galaxies. Flies lightning-bolted through the air and buzzed with insistence and, in one shadow-webbed corner of the stables, a nest of swallows screamed with fear and alarm.

Dan and Tom stood facing each other between the empty straw-scattered stalls. Dan, taller and more powerful, his deep grey eyes stormy; Tom, slighter and more angular, his blue eyes flashing like flintlocks; both seething with temper.

'What do you think you know, Tom?' Dan asked through gritted teeth.

'I "think" I know nothing. What I do know is that you are a sworn traitor to the Crown. My own brother!' Tom whispered hoarsely, as though the words themselves might summon soldiers to the door.

'How—' began Dan, but his brother cut him off.

'I was listening to you last night,' Tom raged in a frantic whisper. 'You and Miles Byrne and Anthony Perry and Peter Bolger. I was there when Byrne said you were all United Irishmen. I was there when Perry was discussing orders from Dublin. I was there when you, Dan, when *you* wished the priests would side with the people so as to expedite a Rising! Jesus, Dan, what are you thinking? The United Irishmen are prohibited. You are set upon a course that could very well get us all killed!'

'You were spying on me?' came Dan's appalled response.

'My God, Dan. Don't presume to climb the higher moral ground with me. You've kept your conniving secret from me for God knows how long because I "can't be trusted". Don't dare to assume that you can lecture me on morality when you have been plotting and scheming for months. Years, maybe? How long, Dan? How long have you concealed the truth of your rebel actions behind that intellectual veneer?'

Dan sighed. 'Since the spring, Tom,' he said slowly. 'I've been a United Irishman for three months or more.'

Tom reeled then as though physically struck. He leaned against the side of the empty stall and felt his anger drain from him. Despondency instead filled him and fear began to eat away at him, curdling his stomach. His hands, of their own volition, went to his face and he breathed into their cupped palms.

'Dan, Dan, Dan,' he sighed. He tilted his head back and looked up into the spider-haunted dark of the rafters. 'What have you done to us? What if the yeos or soldiers come calling? What then?'

'If they come I should rather go with them than bring further trouble down upon our family.

'You don't understand though, Tom. This is our chance. This is our poor, degraded country's turn to stand up and be counted amongst the nations of the world. We could create a new order. One based on equality and rights for all. Surely even you can see the good we can accomplish?'

'What I see,' snapped Tom, 'is see a chance for fat aristocrats to keep their taxes for themselves. I see Irishmen spouting nonsense from foreign shores. I see a Wexford farmer willing to take arms against the greatest empire in the world. What I see, Dan, is a fool.

'I want no part in this and I will not allow you to drag the family into it either.'

Dan regarded his brother with eyes brimming with pain. At length he nodded and dropped his head like some exhausted draught horse, 'So be it.'

With that he turned and, scattering the dry straw as he went, he hastened out of the stable. Tom stood and watched his brother hurry away from him.

Shortly after Dan and Laurence Banville had departed across the upward sloping fields, Tom strode purposefully into his bedroom. He carried with him his pair of horse pistols, his uniform jacket and his cavalry sabre. Awkwardly tossing these onto his freshly made bed, he marched over to his wardrobe and wrenched it open. On the floor of the wardrobe, beside his cavalry boots and spurs, was an iron-bound box containing several score rounds of pistol ammunition, powder and oil cloths.

Hefting this out, he placed it beside his other equipment, opened it and began the slow, methodical task of cleaning his pistols.

He had no idea what had spurred him into such sudden activity. The sun climbing the sky in its blazing arc seemed to instil in him a vague presentiment of danger. While his mother occupied herself with needlework in the drawing room, he had oiled and polished his sword, cleaned his jacket as best he could, and made sure the horses were properly shod and well-watered. It was as though Dan's confession had bred in him a myriad of little nettling demons, each one anxious to prick his mind into consideration of some other terrible possibility.

Reeling through his thoughts were scenarios in which the North Corks, the Camolin Cavalry or even the Castletown Corps themselves came to take his brother. And in each scenario, Tom found himself acting differently. Each action irreconcilable with the one before. Each imagining spiralling around and around; a whirlpool of supposition that merely served to feed his growing panic.

Could he give up his brother?

Could he even allow Dan to give himself over willingly?

Could he watch Dan hang or be shot in the road like a dog?

And in the back of his mind a tiny, poisonous voice asked the awful question – if he sided with the Crown, how would his family stand then? How might he, himself, escape implication in his brother's crimes?

To silence the Judas screech, to consign it to just one voice amongst the hundreds that bawled within him, he checked his pistols' flints, their trigger actions, he counted his ammunition, he oiled their barrels. And then he did it again.

Check the pistol. Cock the hammer. Squeeze the trigger.

Again and again and again.

Gasping, he sat on the edge of his bed and forced great swallows of air into his lungs.

Dan would be taken, it was only a matter of time, and Tom knew from the bitter experience of Killinerin the fate that awaited him. Still the question remained: what would he do? What *could* he do?

At length, as minutes dragged into hours and the sun's blank inferno soared ever higher, Tom's frantic activity calmed. His anxiety remained but the chaos in his mind had stilled somewhat. He found himself staring at his hands laced before him, propped on his knees as he sat. He traced their cuts and old scars, he traced their lines and calluses. He frowned at the powder burns that seemed to have tattooed a blue-black fan into the webs of each thumb and along the backs of both hands. His time as a yeoman was indelible, it seemed.

As he stared blankly at his hands he found himself constructing plans. No mere conjuring of terrifying possibilities this time; now he was constructing certainties.

A bleak sort of smile hooked the corners of his mouth and into the silence of his room, Tom Banville began to laugh, a sound filled with all the sick desperation of the damned.

The afternoon was filled with the warm smell of baking. The kitchen of the Banville household was a sun-flooded grotto. Broad beams of sunlight made a bright checkerboard of the table where they lanced through the windows' leaded panes. The crackle of the fire and quick splash and slop as Mrs Prendergast bent, toiling, over the sink were the only sounds to be heard. All appeared peaceful, all was heavenly beneath the eternal blue of May.

Then, slowly, Mrs Prendergast lifted her head. A deep crease formed between her greying brows and she stood still, wrist-deep in soapy water. Unmoving, Mrs Prendergast listened to a low sound that, with each passing moment, grew in strength and volume, like a rising storm.

Dan Banville's yelling voice, on the edge of hearing, was growing louder and louder.

Frozen, Mrs Prendergast watched through the kitchen windows as Dan came tearing into the cluttered expanse of the yard. His powerful frame was in full flight, every muscle propelling him with a pounding conviction toward his home. He hurdled the fallen traces of an old cart, stumbled and regained his feet. His mouth was a ragged tear in his face and from it, breathless but frantic, came his roaring voice.

'Ma! Mrs Prendergast! Get into the dairy! The yeos are coming!'

The old servant stood, shaking, words of protection tumbling from her lips like eggs from a basket, 'Jesus, Mary and Joseph.' Her right hand moved numbly and she blessed herself, leaving a small splash of greasy water on her forehead.

Dan crashed through the kitchen door, nearly smashing it from its hinges. He exploded into the kitchen in a panting whirl of limbs and noise and sweat.

He seized Mrs Prendergast by her doughy shoulders and, gazing at her with fierce intensity, bellowed, 'Where in God's name is my mother?'

Terrified, every inch of her skin gone grey and bloodless, the old woman stammered, 'She's in the drawing room. She's doing her needlework.'

Dan dashed out of the kitchen and moments later returned, hauling his flustered mother by the arm. His hand was clenched tight about her bicep and his hard fingers made white-lipped trenches where they dug into her flesh. Mary Banville looked horrified and sceptical all at once.

'What are you doing, Daniel?' she protested. 'Have you gone mad? Why would the yeos come here? Sure, Tom's a yeo. You're hurting my arm, Daniel.'

Whirling her about to face him, Dan spat, 'Shut up, Ma!'

Laurence Banville, wheezing like a bellows, was suddenly leaning on the splintered frame of the kitchen's back door. Framed in the late afternoon sunlight, his arms outstretched to either side holding himself up against both door jambs, he looked crucified upon the brightness of the day. Gasping for air, he nonetheless had the wherewithal to chastise his eldest boy.

'Daniel, that is your mother. You must never speak to her in such manner.'

Dan flung the old man a withering look before turning to the two women and saying, 'Get yourselves into the dairy. It's got stone walls, a slate roof and strong doors. Lock yourselves in. The cavalry are not a mile distant.'

His mother opened her mouth to interrupt him but his raised hand, cut and bleeding from his work in the fields, silenced her.

'We have not the time, Ma. Mrs Prendergast, you have the key to the dairy don't you?'

The old woman looked confused for a moment and said, 'Yes, Mr Banville. It's hanging up on a nail beside the dairy door.'

'Then go. Hurry,' snapped Dan.

With stricken looks the two women scuttled into the yard. As they passed Laurence, he caught his wife about the waist and kissed her full on her age-puckered lips. Dan allowed his vision to fall to the floor, strangely embarrassed by his father's show of affection.

With the women gone, Laurence turned to his son, 'Now boy,' he said. 'Whatever occurs here today you are to have no act or part in it. You or that wastrel brother of yours.'

'Da,' he began.

Laurence's fist made a ball of gristle as it bunched in the fabric of Dan's shirt front. The old man's fissured face came close to his and from the snarling mouth Dan could smell the bread and cheese they'd eaten earlier. His father's eyes held him, fixed.

'Do you think I don't know why the yeos are coming, son? Do you hold me so low in your considerations? An old man baffled by the happenings of the world? You do me a disservice, boy.'

Dan's mouth worked silently before his father was moving again. Laurence Banville dragged his son, with surprising strength, up the wooden staircase and down the bedroom hallway. When they reached Dan's room the old man flung open the door and pushed his feebly struggling son inside.

'Da, you can't do this,' protested Dan. 'This calamity is of my own making.'

Laurence considered his son carefully before saying, 'And you are of my own making. You are my son and, as my son, you will do as you are told. Stay here.'

He slammed the door and to Dan's consternation he heard the grind and click of a key being turned in the lock.

In the hallway, Laurence slipped the key back into his breeches pocket and tried to recover his breath. Dan is heavier than he looks, he reflected. The big ox.

A sudden, sharp creak made him look up from where he stood. Some yards down the hallway, Tom's door had inched open. Tom leaned from his room, his face troubled and wan. As Laurence watched, his youngest son made to step towards him.

'Don't,' Laurence cautioned. 'Don't you dare interfere.'

Tom stopped and blinked as though he had been awoken from a dead faint. 'What is happening, Da?' he asked.

'None of your business,' came his curt reply. 'Now get back into your room or, so help me, I shall give you the thrashing that your conduct of late has so richly deserved.'

Tom frowned for a moment but, with the innate obedience of the scolded child, he stepped back into his room and closed the door on his father's bristling glare.

'Now,' muttered Laurence Banville. 'Where's my gun?'

Dan, locked in the bright confines of his bedroom, crept carefully over to his window and looked out onto the dimpled clay of the front dooryard. There was no sign of the yeos yet, but they were coming.

From where he and his father had been working in the top field the countryside fell away into a shallow valley of gorse ditches and barley fields. The brown scar of a narrow road sliced through this countryside until it began a slow ascent, disappearing some three miles distant over the crest of a small rise. It was a gleam of metal from the brow of this small hill that had first caught Dan's attention as he worked. Leaning on his slash-hook, he had squinted against the daylight and the hammering heat, and, to his dismay, his grey eyes perceived a line of blue-coated Camolin Cavalry wending their way along the road. Shouting a warning to his father, he leaped forward, jumping ditches and flattening corn as he barrelled downhill.

He had brought them. The thought horrified him. Tom was right. He had brought them, brought disaster down upon his family, home and all.

Now, sequestered in his room, locked away like a bould child, he cursed himself for his foolishness. He twitched the curtains to one side so that he could cast his vision over the short avenue of rutted earth leading from the road to the Banville household. Everything was silent. The world seemed to hold its breath. Dan thought for a moment that he could hear his own heart pounding over the hush of anticipation. But this thought lasted only a moment before he realised, with a lurch of nausea, that he was listening to the drumming of horses' hooves.

In a torrent of jangling tack and scintillating steel, in a wave of sweating horseflesh, the yeoman cavalry swept into the dooryard.

Two rooms down from Dan, Tom Banville too watched the approach of the yeomen and on his face a cruel smile grew ever wider.

As the brothers watched, Laurence Banville strolled, with all the nonchalance of a house cat, out of his open front door and into the sunshine of his dooryard. Cradled in his arms was the grim length of a fowling piece, his thumb resting with calculated weight upon the hammer of its flintlock. His face was, however, a study in affable surprise and he greeted the yeomen with good humour.

'Hallo, gentlemen!' he cried. 'I'm just off to shoot a few pests that have been making a nuisance of themselves. Care to join me?'

The cavalryman leading the troop, a sergeant judging by his uniform, pushed back his crested helmet and wiped one gloved hand across a forehead soaked with sweat and caked with dust. He regarded the old man before him with an air of wary curiosity. Leaning forward, he gestured toward the gun in Banville's hands.

'You should really have surrendered that firearm, Mr Banville. It would be wise of you to consider allowing me to take custody of it.'

Laurence Banville returned the man's stare and said, 'I don't know that you Camolin boys have much authority here, Mr Cullen. This is Knox Grogan's land. The Castletown Cavalry, of which my son is a member, patrols this neighbourhood.'

'We have the authority of the law, Mr Banville,' came the response. 'As well you know. And it is the very intimacy with which your family is connected to Grogan's corps that necessitates our presence here.

'Now, let us not prattle like women, Mr Banville. Where is your son, Daniel?'

'I am not my son's keeper, Sergeant Cullen.'

The expression of exasperation on the sergeant's face would have been comical were it not for the sword and pistol by his side. Perspiration dribbled in oily tendrils down his cheeks, matting his sideburns and gathering in a slimy film along the thick band of his helmet's chin strap. Around the horses, flies buzzed and droned.

Shaking his head, Sergeant Cullen implored, 'Why must you be so difficult, Laurence? If you insist on travelling the rocky road when smoother paths are open before you, then on your shoulders be it.'

'James Cullen,' stated Laurence Banville, softly, silk over steel. 'I know you James Cullen. I knew your father before you. I see you sitting your big horse with your cavalry coat and your bearskin hat and by God I swear to you, the first sign of action from one of your friends and I'll put a ball between their eyes.'

Behind Cullen the creak of saddle leather betrayed the unease of his men.

Tight-lipped now, angry, the yeoman sergeant drew himself up in his saddle and Laurence Banville tightened his grip on his long firelock.

Then, at the apex of the moment, with all held in the balance, the old man heard his front door swish further open and apprehended the heavy, gritty tread of a man stepping close behind him. Oh, Daniel, he thought, why couldn't you do what you were told?

'Dan's not here, lads.'

Tom's voice made Laurence spin on his heel.

Standing there before the dark throat of the house, Tom gazed upon the yeomen, a hangman's smile twisting his features. He wore his blood red yeoman's coat, riding boots and spurs. In his hands the great bulk of his horse pistols were heavy and black, deadly in the bright sunshine. Sweat plastered his dark fringe to his head but his eyes were ice cold with the certainty of his own demise.

'Sergeant,' he began frostily. 'Go tell Lieutenant Bookey that when Dan comes back we'll have him answer any questions he cares to ask. Until he does come back, Sergeant, the searching of this homestead will result merely in the untimely death of your good self and at least one of your men.'

The snap of his pistols being cocked was deafening in the abrupt silence.

'The choice, Sergeant, is yours.'

Sergeant Cullen's eyes, red-rimmed with fury, roved from father to son and then back. His gauntlets creaked on his horse's reins and over the anxious muttering of his men he addressed the two civilians before him.

'We shall return, Banville. When you least expect it, we shall be at your throat with fire and steel. And as for you, Tom, you have signed your death warrant. This is treason and I'll have every loyal Catholic in the county clamouring for your head. United Irish scum, the two of you.'

He spat a great globule of phlegm at their feet, wheeled his men and was gone in a swirling cloud of dust and flies.

PART TWO

WITH HEART AND HAND

CHAPTER 7

Outbreak

Tom awoke first, shivering. The hour just before dawn was always the coldest and his trusty had slipped from him during the night. The great-coat lay in a slithered pile, rumpled about the roots of the hoary old gorse bush. Daylight, lifeless and anaemic, crept in a dove-grey tide between branch and briar. Through the straining, green spines of the gorse, Tom could just begin to discern the emerging shapes of ditch and stone, field and fen. A fog, luxurious as velvet, clung to the earth and wound from tree to tree, shackling all of nature in its clammy, damp embrace. On the horizon the nebulous ball of the sun was just nudging the skyline into fire. In the distance, to the southwest, a column of smoke mounted the morning.

'Good morning,' came Dan's sleep-gummed voice.

'Is it?' snapped Tom.

Dan, from under the heavy folds of his own greatcoat, exhaled in bovine simple-mindedness, blinked, rubbed his stubbled jaw and asked thickly, 'What's wrong?'

Tom retrieved his coat and wrapped it around his shoulders. He eyed his brother with bilious intent, 'I've a crick in my neck and I feel as though my toes have fallen off. And do you know who I blame?'

Dan blinked again, stupidly, and yawned 'Who?'

'You!' hissed Tom. 'You and your ridiculous French ideas. We've been hiding out now for what, three or four days? No word as to whether Ma and Da ever got to Aunt Helen's, no word from your damnable United Irish friends and nothing for shelter except gorse and tree branches. Thank St Jude that the weather has kept up.'

Dan was sitting up now, scratching the stubble under his chin with obvious pleasure.

'I hope you are infested with fleas, you great lummox,' Tom huffed.

'Look, Tom,' said Dan placatingly. 'I'm sure we would have heard if Ma and Da had been apprehended. Word would have been spread to try and get us to come out. They'd be used as hostages to our good conduct. But I am worried that Perry hasn't tried to communicate or provide us with a safe house. He himself resides just outside of Inch, I wonder have we any chance of making it?'

Tom shook his head with an air of finality, 'None. That's some journey to be undertaking with the cavalry and militia scouring the country. We wait and we hide and we stay alive.'

Dan nodded slowly. He lifted his gaze and regarded his younger brother with doleful resignation as Tom asked, 'Are you certain that was the house that went up last night?'

Dan puffed out his cheeks and nodded again.

The oily dark of the previous night had been rent by a volley of musketry. Both young men, huddled beneath the bristling belly of an elephantine gorse bush, had leapt with terror. With pistols in hand they had crawled through the curling waves of ferns that surrounded them and gazed south and west to where their home had sat, nestled in its natural bowl of fertile farmland. Even across a distance of more than a mile, the magnitude of the blaze was obvious.

In a hollow of midnight the Banville household and outhouses were ablaze. The flames licked and tongued the dark in blistering flickers and howling streams of sparks spiralled into the starlit dome of the night. In front of the blaze, like black toys placed by a demented child, the tiny figures of men and cavalry cavorted like demons in the orange corona. The inferno lit the most grotesque aspect of their home's destruction in vivid, nightmarish shades. As the brothers watched, a group of soldiers lifted their muskets and fired into the squat, stone building that was their father's kennels. Seconds later the report of the weapons reached the Banville brothers, drowning the howls of the poor animals, trapped and dying.

Cushioned by ferns, their nostrils filled with the damp smells of growth and decay, they had watched as their home was consumed.

Now, looking at his brother's wounded face, Tom said, 'You know we can't go back to it. They'll be waiting.'

'Oh, I know,' agreed Dan. 'Anyway, there's nothing there for us now.'

'There's nothing anywhere. Ma and Da are gone to Arklow, thence probably on to Dublin. If the county calms a little we may be able to join them. As it is we're a death sentence to any who should seek to aid us. I can't believe Mick Sinnott's father is being so good to us.'

Dan grinned, 'He's a United man.'

'Well I wish he'd rise up then,' snorted Tom. 'It might have the effect of causing the yeomanry to look after their own skins and not be poking into barns and ditches for the like of us.'

Dan smiled fondly at his younger brother, 'Thanks, Tom.'

'Don't say a word until we're safe and can sleep under a roof again. This entire disastrous turn of events can be laid in your lap and the laps of those friends of yours that have so conveniently disappeared.'

The morning wore on and both men tried to make themselves as comfortable as possible. The gorse's twisted trunk split and snaked in myriad directions but by balling up their coats for padding it made for a not unpleasant hiding place.

The gorse bush was one of a number crawling like some spiny pestilence across the brow of an uneven outcrop of rock. All around them, the land lay somewhat lower than the stony protrusion and afforded the brothers a fair vantage point from which to look out for approaching troops. Every so often a column of soldiers or troop of horses would jog along the road in the distance but not once did they come within musket shot of their position.

At night though, the savagery of martial law was grimly evident.

As dusk fell and night sluiced the countryside with shrouding shadow, fires began to spring up all around them. As the stars spangled the heavens, so too did an infestation of smoky orange scuttle across distant fields and villages. Gunshots and the dull, crackling rush of collapsing thatch drifted on the breeze. And in the morning, with every breath, a vague taste of charcoal, of ash, infused the air and caught in their throats.

Tom and Dan had sat there, side by side, night after night and watched the country burn.

The afternoon of the 26th of May found both Tom and Dan wide-eyed and standing on the edge of their little kingdom of gorse. Struggling up the hill toward them was young Mick Sinnott, a bag of provisions slung over his right shoulder and an expression of fierce determination branded across his twelve-year-old face. His tongue was clenched firmly between his teeth and his left hand sought purchase for his skinny frame by grabbing handfuls of grass to

117

steady himself as he climbed. This fervent enthusiasm, this frantic single-mindedness, had surprised them both.

They had watched the boy come running through the fields from two miles away to their south. They had watched him trip and stumble, dragging his canvas sack through briars and gorse, tangling himself up in thistles and whitethorn. On the little figure had struggled, never slackening his pace, never going around an obstacle when he could go through it.

Now, looking down at him as he battled the last leg of his mad dash, Dan wondered aloud, 'What on God's green Earth has gotten into him?'

'Knowing our luck, it could only be bad news,' said Tom flatly.

Dan smiled wryly and punched his brother playfully on the shoulder. 'Maybe the French have landed,' he joked.

Tom glanced at him with one eyebrow raised mockingly, 'That would be good news, would it?'

Blowing like a church organ, Mick Sinnott reached the crest of the hill and stood in front of the two brothers. He planted the provisions at their feet and then leaned back and inhaled so deeply it seemed as if he was trying to take in the sky itself. His red face gradually cooled, blanching as he got his wind back and his chest ceased its violent gasping.

Dan and Tom allowed the young lad to regain his composure before Dan asked, 'What has you tearing across half the country, Mick? Do you bring news from your Da?'

Mick looked from one to the other before saying, 'I do. But I'm not supposed to tell ye out here. I'm not to be seen with ye and I've a lot to tell.'

'Come on into the gorse, so,' instructed Tom.

Moments later Dan and Tom and Mick Sinnott were uncomfortably crowded into the hollow space below the gorse's tangled spread. Everything was quiet here and only the sibilant soughing of the breeze through the thick green spines gave any indication of an outside world. His back to the gorse's dry and age-warped trunk, Mick took a deep breath and rushed out an avalanche of words.

'Hold your horses, Mick,' ordered Tom. 'Whatever you have to say to us must be very exciting or you wouldn't be in such a confounded hurry to relate it. However, I doubt your Da would appreciate you making a hash of his message, so take your time. Why didn't he just send us a note?'

'He can't write,' interjected Dan. 'Go on, Mick. Take your time.'

'Da said it was important that I learn off what I was to tell you,' began Mick. 'I was up half the night making sure I got it right.

'The first thing he said to tell you was that the magistrates are worse than anyone ever thought. No good Catholic will ever try and find protection under the law again.'

'What has happened?' urged Tom.

Dan knifed him a look and turned back to Mick. 'Go on, Mick,' he said. 'One thing at a time.'

'I'm trying,' complained Mick. 'But if he keeps interrupting me I won't be able to remember.'

'Sorry—' said Tom.

'Now, Da said there's been some awful stuff done in Wicklow. Worse than here. There's been people shot in cold blood in Dunlavin and twenty-eight people were massacred in the ball alley in Carnew, without trial. They were accused of being United Irishmen.'

Mick continued over Tom's low, despairing moan.

'The midlands are risen. Kildare and Meath are all aflame. There was a battle at Carlow as well but the soldiers won, they're killing anyone with so much as a pitchfork. There's hundreds dead all over the country!'

Dan and Tom stared at each other in mingled horror and excitement. Tom shook his head, 'This is a disaster, Dan. A peasant army cannot hope to win against regular troops. They will be butchered. If this Rising spreads to Wexford there won't be enough soil to bury the corpses. If Carlow was a rout what hope have we of carrying the day?'

'We're more organised than Carlow, Tom,' said Dan. His face had hardened, resolve gleamed in his eyes as though he were eager to hear of the spread of rebellion, eager for the call to arms.

'What of here, Mick?' he insisted. 'What does your Da say of Wexford? Surely we must rise or be slaughtered in our beds or shot out of hand like the poor people of Dunlavin and Carnew? Come, Mick, tell all.'

Mick Sinnott was nodding to himself as if to make sure he had left nothing out so far. Satisfied, he went on.

'Da says we can't rise.'

'What?' exploded, Dan

'Thank God,' breathed Tom, concurrently.

'Da says Mr Perry – he said you'd know Mr Perry – he said Mr Perry was arrested a couple of days ago and they're holding him in the market house in Gorey.

'He says without him no one around here knows what to do. Everyone's gone into hiding to preserve themselves from the yeos.'

Dan slumped into himself where he sat. His bones seemed to melt like lard in a fire. It was as though the man who was, only a minute before, so eager for the command to rise, had become wax, unfixed and plastic in the midday heat. His face had become slack and the eyes which had so blazed with anticipation were now dull cobbles set into flaccid cheeks.

'Well, that's it,' said Tom. 'What do you propose we do, and to what end, now that your dream of glorious revolution has been scuppered?'

Dan regarded him with open hostility, snarling, 'You don't have to sound so glad about it.'

Turning to Mick, he patted the boy on the head and said ruefully, 'You did well, Mick. Thank your father for us. Tell him we shall remain here tonight but we shall not need him to furnish us with anything more than he has already. This will be our last night spent in this spot.'

Mick nodded and rose to depart, his narrow frame brushing through the thick undergrowth like an animal born to the wild. Dan and Tom sat for a moment in studied silence.

'What do you propose?' repeated Tom at last.

His eyes still vacant and a wan hopelessness in his voice, Dan replied, 'I do not know, Tom. I fear our only chance is to get away to Dublin. I am worried about Elizabeth, however. If the trouble at Carnew is as bad as Mick hinted at then I feel I should go to her.'

Tom frowned at the bare earth for a moment before addressing his brother.

'I do not think your lady friend is in any danger in Carnew. If Mick is neither exaggerating nor omitting some vital detail then it would seem as though the place has been cowed. I do not think a Protestant lady has very much to fear in that particular part of the country. The worst event that could occur to her would be a known United Irishman paying her a visit. Your concern could have her shot.'

Dan took a long breath and exhaled sharply through his nose, 'You're right. It would not be worth the risk. What do you think we should do?'

Tom laughed bitterly, 'Well, we can't live beneath a gorse bush forever. If we move we run the gauntlet of our enemies' patrols. If we stay here we run the risk of being found. If we could find a way to Dublin we would be safe from Hunter Gowan, Hawtrey White and the lot of them. The question is, how do we close the distance between here and there.'

'We could board ship at Arklow, maybe?'

'Maybe. I think we must get away from here, whatever the case. Wexford is a death trap for United Irishmen. Unless your Rising spreads south from

120

Kildare I cannot imagine the countryside in open rebellion. There will be no wholesale massacre of innocent people until that happens and I think we should thank God for that.'

Dan was forlorn. Wearily, he said, 'And yet the daily outrages continue. A man shot here. A family pitchcapped. A house burned. There has been a reign of terror imposed, Tom.'

'Yes, there has,' replied Tom. 'But there aren't hundreds of corpses rotting in the streets of Gorey and Enniscorthy like there are in Carlow. Be sensible, Dan. Would you have our friends and neighbours die like cattle whilst shaking scythes at cannon?'

'Is it not better that they die on their feet like free men than on their knees like slaves?' said Dan.

'Nonsense,' Tom articulated the word with a tangible relish. 'It is better that they live on their knees and crawl towards some future that lies within their compass than lie dead in a ditch. You asked for my opinion and now you have it. Arklow it is.'

Dan nodded again, like a broken-down carthorse with a load too heavy to bear. 'Arklow it is.'

The market house on Gorey's main street was a barbed cage filled with screams. On the weathered boardwalk outside, two soldiers of the North Cork Militia stood guard, their white crossbelts and brass buckles gleaming in the early afternoon sunshine. Beside them their Brown Besses were held loosely, their bayonet points wavering slightly as the men, every so often, winced at the noises from within. Occasionally, one would exchange a pained glance with the other as the shrieks reached a crescendo before subsiding into a bubbling swamp of sobs. No one but the two soldiers occupied that part of the boardwalk and for the past three days the citizens had been crossing the road to avoid passing it. Nevertheless, a small crowd had gathered from time to time across the way, the men shaking their heads, the women blessing themselves and praying, all listening as the screams rose and fell, rose and fell.

The upper floor of the market house had been converted into a makeshift gaol and it was from the open windows of this floor that the terrible noises emitted. Within, the wide room was open and covered the entire expanse of the building, stretching away beneath heavy rafters for ten or fifteen yards on either side of a wide door leading to a sweeping stairwell. The room was originally used for meetings and business banquets, but since the coming of the North

Corks it had been put to a more grisly use. Around the walls, thick bolts fastened lengths of chain, terminating in iron cuffs, to the brickwork. Fifteen prisoners were clamped by their ankles in this manner, chained and hobbled, sweating and stinking in the summer heat.

Each prisoner however, had moved to face the wall. Each pressed their filthy foreheads to the soothing cool of the plaster and stuffed ragged strips of shirt linen into their ears.

And, for the last three days, each had lofted prayer after prayer towards heaven. Begging the Almighty to make them stop.

Throughout the room, the stench of burning pitch, of burning hair, of burning flesh, was enough to make a person gag. Blue membranes of smoke twined, plaiting themselves through the still air. The chained men tried not to breathe the stuff in. They knew where it came from. They knew that with every breath of the sickening fumes they were taking in the stuff of another human being. Each shadowy tentacle of smoke was a ghostly echo of a man's substance, an ashen manifestation of what had been stripped from him and burned away.

In the centre of the wide room, bound to a chair, Anthony Perry sagged forward. On his head a stiff paper cone, like a dunce's cap, sat at a jaunty angle. From beneath the rim of this cone, thick black ropes of tar bubbled and oozed and, wherever it touched bare skin, lifted it from the bone, blistering and beginning to ooze in its turn. Pus and pitch seeped in vile runnels down Perry's cheeks. Dried blood rouged his lips and plastered the front of his shirt. One eye was swollen shut while the other was masked with a steaming patch of tar. His hands rested limply on the arms of the chair, the pads of his fingers swollen and ruddy, like over-ripe summer fruit.

Mercifully, he was unmoving.

Two men stood over him. Both were bare-chested and drenched in the sweat of their exertions. Shafts of sunlight lanced through the room's large, rectangular windows lighting the scene in abominable detail. Flies hummed and alighted, feasting on spilled blood and brackish sweat. The two men were like pagan gods in the sunlight, bloody-handed and rapt, their chests heaving and their eyes roving over Perry's shattered form, bound and oblivious before them. At their feet sat two tin buckets, one smoking, one still.

At last one of the men moved forward and cautiously toed Perry's shin as though attempting to wake him. Shrugging, he turned to his companion, 'I'd wager you've killed him, Wheatley.'

'Nobody's ever died of a pitch-capping,' said the other man with a show of confidence not quite matched by the anxious cut of his features.

'If you have,' retorted his partner, 'I'll swear that I advised you to relent. Foote will have us both flogged if we've managed to squash his canary before it ever sang a note.'

'Here, mind out of the way,' ordered Wheatley. Stooping, he reached into one of the buckets and drew forth a sopping wet rag. Wringing it out a little, he crouched over his prisoner and allowed a trickle of water to splash the wounded face and sooth the tattered lips.

Perry's one good eye fluttered like a frightened butterfly and he commenced a low, grinding moan.

'See, Rogan, I told you he wasn't dead,' crowed Wheatley. 'We'll give him a minute.'

Anthony Perry slowly regained his senses. With each passing moment his agony grew more and more intense so that, as his faculties returned, so did his capacity to appreciate the horror of his situation. Every shred of his body screamed in pain, every nerve burned with the torture inflicted upon him. His head and scalp seemed to be scorched from the inside out. His one eye focused on the men before him and, to his shame, he began to weep.

He wept not for the hurt that had been visited on him but at the prospect of more hurt to come. He wept because he was not dead.

His torturers leered at him. Rogan turned and retrieved a sheet of paper and a pencil from where they lay on the bare floorboards. He then knelt down to look Perry in the face.

The United man whimpered, the tears stinging the cuts and abrasions that marred his cheeks and jaw. Great ropes of saliva festooned his lips and his throat formed an unintelligible noise, clear only in its terror.

'Now, now, Mr Perry,' soothed Rogan. 'This would have been over without any unpleasantness had you decided to be compliant. All you have to do is tell us the names of the leaders of the United Irishmen in this county. That's all. We'll catch them anyway, with or without you. All you accomplish with your wilful efforts to confound us is further hardship for your poor self. The names, Mr Perry and all this nasty business can be put behind us.'

Perry, feeling as if he was in the depths of a hell beyond description, merely whimpered and felt the loose blubber of his lips spill drool down his chin.

'Is that a "no", Mr Perry?' asked Wheatley, tugging playfully at the pitchcap now welded into his prisoner's flesh.

In despair, in horror, in a chaos of racking pain and self-disgust, Anthony Perry found himself able to speak. He ran a thick tongue along his split lips and, slumped like something dead, he began to mumble names.

'Edward Fitzgerald, Bagenal Harvey, Esmond Kyan . . .'

Hurriedly, Rogan began to scribble down every marly syllable that Perry managed to enunciate. Smiling beatifically, Wheatley reached down and patted the tortured rebel on the shoulder.

'That's a good lad,' he said.

At half past one on that Saturday afternoon a young dispatch rider of the North Cork Militia sprinted, hell-for-leather, across Gorey's main thoroughfare. In his wake the two soldiers guarding the doorway to the market house were forced to grab their bicorns to prevent them flying off and into the street. In his hand an envelope flapped and fluttered, its red wax seal livid as a wound.

Upon reaching his grey mare, tied to a hitching rail amidst a small herd of fine officers' animals, he stuffed the envelope into his jacket and deftly undid the slipknot holding his mount in place. Whispering to the animal, cajoling her, keeping her calm, he hoped that his own alarm did not communicate itself to her. Swinging himself up into the saddle, he kicked her once, so that she reared and whinnied, and was off.

The young rider bent low over the animal's neck. He had never experienced such urgency before, such a crucial demand for speed. He had to reach Wexford Town by sunset or all was lost. The mare leaped forward, hooves thumping the hard earth, sounding like distant cannon or coming thunder.

The Blakely residence sat within its nest of beeches for all the world like a nugget of gold cupped inside the gnarled and hoary palm of a miner. It was a ball of amber in the night, a world of warmth in a cosmos of swelling dark.

Elizabeth Blakely paced the newly waxed and gleaming floorboards of her father's library and muttered to herself.

The library was a narrow, high-ceilinged room located to the rear of the house. Its walls were clad with polished wooden shelving devoid of books. The shelves armoured the walls, lifeless and cold, the expanse of wood pierced in two places by the high, arching framework of twin bay windows. Not yet fitted with curtains, the windows yawned vacantly out onto the stableyard. However, the light spilling from the chandelier and the deepening gloaming outside blotted the panes with black oil. No vista could be viewed through the wavering pitch of the glass. Only the contents of the room were flung back upon themselves in warped and anaemic counterfeit.

From window to window the ghost of Elizabeth stalked; a pallid reflection of her nettle humour.

'You shall have the floor worn to kindling before father has a chance to stock this place with books, sister.'

The voice halted Elizabeth and she rolled her eyes to the moulded ceiling before turning.

Beside the vast mass of a cold granite fireplace a girl, some years younger than Elizabeth but with the same characteristic churn and fall of mahogany hair, sat in a high-backed armchair. In her hands a needle and thread were held motionless and on her lap a red gentleman's frock coat lay like a rumpled drift of rose petals.

Elizabeth's mouth tightened and she snapped with more venom than she intended, 'Sarah, if you cannot sew quietly then remove yourself. I'm not above boxing your ears.'

Elizabeth's younger sister widened her eyes comically and formed her lips into a perfect ring of mock-horror.

'Ooooh,' she mewled. 'Beth's in a bad mood. Oh, heavens spare me from her wrath.'

She then collapsed back into the chair, boneless with giggling, her needle-work forgotten.

Elizabeth stood in the light of the chandelier overhead and glared at her younger sister.

'And heavens spare me from your foolishness,' she said.

Sarah leaned forward and the mockery leached from her voice. Her shoulders stooped and her face, a narrower, flintier replica of her sister's, softened in sympathy and understanding.

'Do not be so vexed, Beth,' she said gently. 'Young Mr Banville has sense enough not to involve himself in these goings on. Those peasants gathered on Kilthomas Hill are a mob without any firm purpose. Captain Wainwright says so himself. They're all terribly frightened of the militia and will all be in their beds by morning.

'Father says there will never be a croppy rebellion,' Sarah continued. 'A crowd of farmers on a hill is not the end of the world. Mr Banville knows this and be assured that he cannot be involved. He is quite intelligent for one of the lower sort. I am certain that father has a kind of sneaking regard for him.'

Elizabeth looked at her sister with eyes that flared with anger. She was not angry with Sarah, she was angry with the man she hoped was sitting in his own parlour, safe and secure, many miles away across the gaping dark.

'Young Mr Banville is a great stupid pig of a man,' Elizabeth growled. She folded her arms beneath her breasts and commenced to pace briskly once more. Beneath her feet the virgin polish glimmered as her white dress, wreathed in green buds, floated over it.

Sarah sighed, 'Oh, so you have said. More than once on one of your many tiresome turns about this room. I believe he is also a "brainless clod" and a "jumped-up ploughboy". Have I left anything out? Perhaps I could invent some insults of my own. It would be more diverting, I should say, than watching you stamp about. Daniel Banville loves you. He would do nothing to bring you harm.'

Elizabeth paused then, her steps shuffling to a halt and her narrow shoulders lifting as she sucked a shuddering breath between clenched teeth. Her sister's words had stung something deep within her. But she was not angry.

She was afraid.

In some awful hidden pit of her soul, a place that she could not look into for fear of what she might see, a terrible thought was growing.

Out in the dark upon Kilthomas Hill a mass of local peasants had gathered all through the afternoon and evening. Through hedges and ditches a horde of labourers and farmhands had swarmed up the hill's slopes until its crown of cedar trees was teeming with an unwashed and dirty-footed multitude.

It had been the sole topic of conversation in the district all day and Andrew Blakely had had several visitors who advised him to ready his firearms and bar his doors. Captain Wainwright, from the back of his dancing mount, had related with disgusting gusto how the forces of the Crown had smashed a rebel band at Carlow and strewed the streets with dead croppies.

And all the while, the crowd on Kilthomas Hill grew ever-larger, spreading like wildfire.

Amidst this turmoil, Elizabeth Blakely knew with a certainty as sharp and biting as frost, Daniel Banville would be found or worse.

'Don't worry,' Sarah was saying, her hands going to work once again on the buttons of their father's old coat. 'When the soldiers arrive, they shall all be dispersed like deer.'

With her back to her sister, Elizabeth's mind was filled with images of Dan, alone and proud, as Captain Wainwright bore down upon him, sword held high and bloody in the rising sun. She was certain, certain, he was there on Kilthomas Hill, with his cropped hair and his French ideas. There, in the middle of farmhands and cottiers, 'Liberty, Equality, Fraternity' droning from his lips like a prayer.

This was why he had sought to send her from him. This was why he had tried so hard to push her away.

Oh, Daniel, she thought. You *are* a fool.

Sarah, frowning as she concentrated on a particularly difficult stitch, hardly noticed when her older sister swept out of the room. All around her the silent, empty shelves frowned down, like ossuaries waiting to be filled.

Elizabeth's bedroom was the finest in the house, even more finely appointed than Mr and Mrs Blakely's own. Andrew Blakely had spared no expense in making his eldest daughter comfortable in a home that expanded yearly. A brass bedstead supported a soft white mattress covered in a snowy dune of pristine blankets. An elegant window overlooking the front dooryard was set into one thrush-egg blue papered wall. Embossed onto the wallpaper, cunningly crafted burgundy ferns unfurled their leaves. A bureau stood to the right of the room's panelled rosewood door, a selection of hair brushes scattered across it. At one end of the bureau, as though carelessly flung, a straw bonnet crowned with dried flowers hung over the edge. At the other, an oil lantern lit the room with an unwavering brilliance.

At opposite ends of the room a large walnut closet and a tall full-length mirror stood. It was into this that Elizabeth Blakely now stared and it threw back her own self, slightly distorted and stained here and there with tarnish and tiny black flecks of discolouration.

She stood silently, grimly. There was a stoop to her carriage and a depth to her eyes that Dan would have frowned to see. A depth that spoke of anguish, of thoughts so poisonous they would swallow the world. Elizabeth seemed borne under by a staggering weight.

Mechanically, her hand rose and her long fingers pushed a curling strand of hair out of her face. Then, her eyes narrowing, she paused and allowed her fingers to dwell a moment on a tiny dimple of gossamer skin just at the corner of her right eye. Delicately, as though stroking something newborn and shivering, she caressed the minute curved scar with the soft pad of her index finger.

She remembered the day she had received this. Though time and age had shrunk the physical wound so that nobody, not even Dan, remarked on its presence, it remained. And in Elizabeth's mind the circumstances that led to a small sheen of blank skin being tattooed indelibly upon her forehead remained fresh and vivid.

As she touched the arc of her scar, that day in the stables came back to her in all its physical reality. The high smells of horseflesh mingled with the earthy stink of their dung. The rustle of hay and the constant hum of flies. This was her space. Twelve years old and queen of a world of bits and bridles, horseshoes and oats.

She did not blame the young ostler. Not even now. She had been too free with her time. Too keen to follow him on fishing trips and on adventures, clambering about the ruins of castles and fairy rings. Too close. Too intimate.

Perhaps he was within his rights to kiss her.

When she pulled away, shocked, her lips still feeling the questing musculature of his, her head collided with a hanging stirrup. The cold metal opened a well of red just where the fine hair of her eyebrow faded into the alabaster of her skin.

She punched him. Her bony fist lashing out, catching him across that mouth which only a moment before had sought her own.

His hands leapt to his face, and the hurt, the betrayal, in his eyes prompted something to twist in the pit of her guts. He backed away from her, from the rich man's daughter, mumbling apologies and ploughing a furrow through the straw of the stable floor. And for an instant, as blood trickled across her skin like a wet strand of thread, as she watched him go, she felt something like regret. Yet, another sensation crowed within her too; one of power and burning defiance.

Her father had thrashed the lad and expelled him from his service. Not for kissing her. She had not told her father everything for fear of what he would do to her one-time friend. But for allowing her to cut her head. The shame she had felt as the boy shambled away into the veiling haze and out of her life had lived within her like a worm ever since.

But whenever she noticed her tiny blemish, whenever she unwittingly brushed against it or caught sight of it winking back from the depths of her looking-glass, that old blaze of confidence heated her insides.

And as she stood, gazing at her reflection in her bedroom mirror, she realised she hated this feeling of being afraid for Daniel Banville. She was not some essence of jelly, spineless and lax.

In that raw moment, Elizabeth resented Dan a little. Resented him for making her afraid. She had never been afraid of anything until she had fallen in love with Daniel Banville.

She turned from her mirror and sat down heavily on her bed. Frowning once more, she gazed around her. The furniture, the fashionable wallpaper, the delicately carved wood, all spoke to her of pampering, of indulgence. The elegance of her home was a thin membrane filming over the sour fistula of her sister's casual arrogance and the bloodlust of her father's friends.

She was not like them. She did not belong here.

The dead weight of that thought sat like an anvil in her brain.

And yet she did not belong with the tattered rabble on Kilthomas Hill either.

She occupied a pathetic interstice. She had fallen into the gap between two cultures that seemed on the brink of mutual obliteration. Everything about her was in flux, her world liquefying and sliding away like grease down a drain.

She breathed deeply and the scents of white lead powder and rouge – her greasepaint, as her father called it – clotted her senses. And something else, too. Something more delicate. Something with the fragrance of roses.

Upon the floor, next to her bureau, a small, squat, thick glass bottle lay on its side. Its cork stopper had loosened and a liquid, clear as rain, made a puddle in which the bottle lay.

Elizabeth smiled against her will.

'How much did that cost you, Daniel?' she wondered aloud.

And simultaneously a voice far back in her mind asked how much their love might cost them both.

Her only certainty was her love for Daniel Banville. He needed her as surely as she needed him; and the girl she used to be, the girl with the horseshoe scar, knew what she should do. Sitting here whilst events trampled her under was not even a consideration. Dan was involved in whatever chaos was engulfing the country. Of this she was sure. And, for all his fine words, she could not see him stand alone. He was hers as surely as that pale curve of skin at the edge of her right eyebrow.

She soon regretted taking such a heavy pack.

Beyond the spill of light from the windows of her father's house, the twilight was brighter than she had expected. An hour earlier she had packed her small, stiff leather travelling case with as many clothes as she could stuff in, crammed her sun bonnet onto her head and, with all the stealth of her tomboy youth, she had sneaked from her home and made her way into the shrouding gloom.

She had left no note for her family. They would never understand. Her love and her passion for her young croppy had eclipsed them all.

When she found him, she thought as she struggled along a narrow rutted lane, she would kick his shins.

Kilthomas Hill rose like a great black wave above her. On its upper slopes, hundreds of camp fires burned like winking devils' eyes in the dark. It was toward these fires that Elizabeth trudged. The sheep-walk on which she found herself traversed the hill as it climbed, and her feet, even in the stout black brogues she wore, slipped and slalomed on wet clumps of sheep manure. From up the slope the chatter of the peasants and the soaring, leaping, whirl of a dozen fiddles and tin whistles skirled through the dusk.

Elizabeth toiled ever upwards, her breath rasping now, her mind straying to the last time she had made her way to the crest of this great slump of heather, gorse and bracken. She tried not to think of Daniel's arms around her, tried not to succumb to those thoughts until he was again in front of her, alive and strong and vital.

The peasant camp on the hill was, even to Elizabeth's untrained eyes, an unwashed tangle of bodies and blankets, leering men and bawling children. She stood on the edge of the main cluster of fires and gazed in frank horror at the scene before her. Women and children crowded around makeshift hearths, their black iron pots and kettles suspended above the flames from green boughs fashioned into cranes. Smoke curled from unwashed cluster to unwashed cluster, wafting through all like the music of the fiddles. The reek of spilled whiskey, the stench of bodies, and the sound of laughter created one uniform mass from the scores of disparate families and groups. Wives, shawls of blue or grey pulled about their shoulders or over their heads, fed squealing children or chastised the men who passed around great glugging jars of poteen or stout. And all was lit in the infernal glare of the leaping fires. To Elizabeth it was like a scene from the Bible; Gomorrah made manifest.

And here and there, to her disgust, the black lengths of pike after pike were lashed together like the framework of some pagan monument.

Her mind recoiled at the thought of Daniel being amongst these people. He was no more a part of this bawdy revelry than she was herself. With a deep breath she squared her shoulders, hefted her case and approached the nearest camp fire.

A tight circle of women sat in the glare of the blaze and a heavy cauldron bubbled and belched on the flames.

Elizabeth cleared her throat. 'Excuse me,' she ventured.

The women, ignorant of her presence, gabbled amongst themselves, one throwing a handful of greenery into the foaming pot.

'Excuse me,' Elizabeth said again, louder this time, so that the circle of women could not fail to hear her. 'I'm searching for Daniel Banville.'

As one they looked up at her, a pale girl, alone on the edge of their firelight.

'Jesus, Mary and Joseph!' the nearest woman exclaimed. 'What has a young one like you out rambling the fields at this time of night? Sure, the yeos are scouring the countryside. Are you out of your mind?'

'No, madam,' Elizabeth replied. 'I am unfortunately in the whole of my mind. I have come to find an acquaintance of mine. A young man from the Castletown district. A Mr Daniel Banville.'

The woman cast a cold eye over Elizabeth's soiled dress with its green embroidery of buds and leaves, her bonnet with its dried flowers. The woman's companions stopped their chatter and gazed on Elizabeth too.

Elizabeth was suddenly acutely aware of the finery of her dress, her lack of a shawl, the pinched vowels of her accent.

The woman was silent and her jaws drew inward as she thought. She then whispered hoarsely, 'I don't know what kind of friend the likes of you would have here with the likes of us. I don't know your Mr Banville. But I'll tell you this, daughter, I'd be careful wandering around looking for people. There's a lot of young fellas here with nothing to be doing of a night.'

Elizabeth's throat tightened at these words and she could feel the muffled drum of her heart throb against her ribs. Nevertheless, she faced the woman with all the courage she could muster and stated calmly, 'Be that as it may, I must find him. He . . . ' she paused for the smallest fraction of a moment, ' . . . means the world to me.'

One of the other women, younger, with a face dark and beautiful beneath a layer of grime, now grinned at her and chided her companion, 'Ah, don't be frightening the poor girl, Mags. She's only trying to find her man. And lucky he is to have such a one as her.'

She then turned a pair of dazzling blue eyes on Elizabeth and continued, 'I don't know your young man either but someone around here might. Ask the women at the cooking fires. Men are dumb beasts at the best of times and when they've been drinking, sure, they don't know their arse from their elbow.'

In spite of herself Elizabeth felt a grin hook at the corners of her mouth and she laughed in relief as much as in amusement at the woman's coarse words.

'Thank you,' she said with genuine gratitude. 'When I find him I'll make sure you are rewarded.'

The first woman snorted and, in an oddly flat tone, said, 'Keep your rewards, daughter. The likes of you will find it hard enough in the days to come without giving away the little you have.'

Feeling a chill twist about her spine, Elizabeth moved away from the group of women, picking her way between slumbering labourers, the detritus of cooking and the odd group of armed men. Everywhere she went, hard eyes followed her movements and voices were lowered in guttural whisper. Still, her determination carried her on and, at every cooking fire, she stopped to ask the women if anyone had seen her Daniel. And at every cooking fire the answer came back in tones of pity, in tones of distrust, in tones of contempt.

Daniel Banville was not there.

From camp fire to camp fire, from one huddled family to the next, Elizabeth slipped like an apparition. As the hours passed she was become a banshee, carrying with her a growing air of loss. And yet the more she searched the greater was her need to find Daniel, the more she yearned to hold him, to tell him that whatever he faced, that whatever future he thought to carve out, it was hers too.

From camp fire to camp fire she flitted until, exhausted and alone, she sank down beside one of the great cedars that ringed the head of Kilthomas Hill. She sank down and stared into the deepening dark as the camp fires, one by one, flickered and died and the fiddles stilled and left a forlorn absence in their wake. In the ashen dusk, to the south and east of her vantage point, a blaze suddenly blossomed like a falling ember. She stared blankly at the distant inferno, her thoughts numbed by fatigue, her mind still fixed on the course she had charted for herself. She had no doubt that Daniel would arrive here eventually. She was sure that it was with such a mass of peasants, of *rebels*, that Daniel saw himself. His glorious revolution had occurred at last; a thousand men, women and children sitting on a hill wondering what to do next. She stared into the faraway dark as yet another blaze sprang up and then, like some dim rip-tide, sleep bore her under.

Staring into the gloaming, Tom Banville squinted and muttered, 'They don't look like soldiers.' Then, turning to Dan, he asked, 'What time do you make it?'

Dan shrugged and looked to the horizon where the sun had set some hours before but which was still all aglow.

'I'd say it's about ten o'clock,' he replied. 'Maybe half-ten.'

The Banvilles gazed off into the growing darkness once more. All about the countryside fires were blooming, hot orange in the dusk. Yet these were somehow different to the blazes the brothers had witnessed with depressing regularity up until now. They were more scattered for one thing and, to Tom's eyes, they did not appear small enough to be individual cabins burning themselves into blackened oblivion. Most of the fires were huge, towering above the countryside around them. Amongst the fields and hedgerows small flocks of tiny dark figures could be seen flitting to and fro. Gathering, splitting, reforming, growing, these bands of men flowed along ditches and cattle tracks. In the distance, something that troubled Tom as much as it stirred a formless hope within Dan, the heather on Carrigrew Hill was erupting in flame.

'No,' repeated Tom. 'Definitely not soldiers.'

'I do believe,' Dan ventured, 'that the Rising has started.'

'How?' wondered Tom, his tone incredulous. 'How, with Perry and God knows who else in gaol? How did this start? How do we stop it?'

Dan was openly grinning now, his mouth a crescent moon as the darkness grew ever deeper. 'It only takes one man to make a stand, Tom. If it is the right sort of man others will stand with him.' He laughed then. 'You know yourself that this county is full of the best and most active gentlemen in the world. Should one parish face down the tyrant then surely all right-thinking people should follow.

'This is glorious, Tom! Can you not feel the bigots and rascals shaking in their boots? Can you not feel the very stones of Dublin Castle tremble?'

Tom eyed his brother in bafflement, 'I cannot see how you entertain any hope of this succeeding, Dan. The first charge by cavalry or bayonet and a good many of those 'best and most active gentlemen' will be lying stretched in their own blood.'

Abruptly Tom's eyes widened and he pointed to the sweep of fields arcing about the foot of their little outcrop. 'Someone's coming—' he said. 'They're not soldiers. Some of them are carrying pikes.'

Below them, in the gloom, a group of ten or twelve men was making its way through the fields, using the heavy ditches as a screen between them and the road. All seemed to wear the drab clothing of peasant farmers and some carried the long lengths of pikes awkwardly in their grip or slanted over their shoulder. Dan and Tom watched them come with both curiosity and trepidation.

As the little group neared the base of the outcrop, Tom, off-hand and casual, asked, 'I presume you have your pistols to hand?'

Dan nodded, 'Don't ask silly questions, little brother.'

The group of men were now scaling the uneven and rocky slope directly beneath the two brothers. The ones with pikes were desperately trying to avoid poking their fellows or tangling the ten-foot pole-arm in their own legs. Their trials would have been comical were it not for the constellation of arson that winked all about from the surrounding countryside.

Eventually the group arrived, puffing, before the two Banvilles, their leader, a middle-aged man with the leathern features and massive arms of a farmer, immediately offering a hand to Dan. 'My heart is glad to see you well Mr Banville. I am overjoyed that you are still here and that we got to you before you upped and left.'

Dan laughed and shook the man's hand. 'By God, William Sinnott! I had not thought to see you again. In truth, since bands of men began roving the countryside we were confused as to what was happening. What *is* happening? Your message said that Perry was arrested and the others were in hiding. You dashed the prospect of any Rising in this part of the country.'

Sinnott's eyes had left Dan and now regarded Tom with a sort of cool dislike, as though the two men were strange dogs come suddenly muzzle to muzzle. Instead of answering, Sinnott growled, 'This must be your yeo of a brother?'

The men behind him, a fist of rancour and shadowed ill-will, grumbled and gestured toward the younger Banville, their voices low, their intentions whispered.

Perceiving this, Dan drew himself up to his full height and glared at the men. 'Indeed, this is my brother,' he snapped. 'This is my brother who stood with my father when the soldiers came for me. This is my brother who has turned his back on tyranny and is shoulder to shoulder with the people in their endeavours. If you do not like the fact that he is here then he and I shall leave and never return and you shall have chased away two men whose fighting arms will be needed before long.'

Sinnott, still eyeing Tom with some hostility, grunted in grudging acceptance. He then turned and pointed out into the countryside below. Night had fallen completely now, shrouding the scattered swarms of men as they scuttled from district to district, emphasising the brilliance of the roaring fires.

'I never thought this would happen,' Sinnott was saying. 'Perry is gone, so too is Miles Byrne. A lot of the other captains are fled. This,' he jabbed one hoary, callused finger into the night, 'this is not of their doing. Word started to come up from around Enniscorthy and Scarawalsh a few hours ago. The captains down there had gotten their men out. Those bastards in Dunlavin and Carnew had forced the leaders to schedule this very night as the time when we exact revenge for years of bloody mistreatment.'

'Why did it take word from down south?' asked Tom. 'Why, you were adamant only this morning that a Rising in Wexford was impossible.'

Sinnott cast him a sour look and replied, 'With Perry's arrest nobody in these parts knew what was happening. The parishes around here were paralysed and fearful. We thought Perry had been induced to inform and that the yeos and Orangemen would be upon us all like a pack of wolves at any moment.

134

God help the man but he must have held out, for the boys of Bantry and Ballaghkeen were in the field before sunset and now we're with them too.'

Sinnott's face had twisted into a zealous mask, the moonlight lending him the aspect of some fiercely animated ghoul. Dan however was shaking his head and his eyes were sad. Slowly he asked, 'How long has Perry been in custody?'

Sinnott shrugged, 'Three days, maybe four. But are you not listening? He held out. He held out so that the rest of his comrades could do their work.'

Dan and Tom exchanged an uneasy glance. They knew the depths a torturer could plumb, they had seen the excesses to which a man might go when removed from all legal fetters and morality.

'The poor man,' whispered Tom. 'Three days at least.'

'I hope he died quickly,' Dan added, blessing himself.

Sinnott was staring quizzically at the two young men before him, his forehead creased and furrowed.

'Everyone is doing as discussed, Mr Banville, sir,' he offered at last.

Now Dan looked confused, 'What is it that you are saying, William?'

'We're taking our weapons back,' he said. 'You were there, Mr Banville, when this was organised. We're raiding the collection centres. All the big houses where our guns and our pikes are kept, we're ransacking them and piking any Orangeman or yeo we find.'

Tom gazed out over the flame-spangled landscape. Magistrates' houses, rectors' glebes, captains' mansions, landlords' estates, anywhere that surrendered arms were being stored, was now aflame and crumbling.

'You've opened a hornets' nest, gentlemen,' Tom intoned wearily. 'Those moneyed gentlemen, whose property you've so proudly made bonfires of, will not rest until every rebellious head in Wexford is decorating a spike.'

'What do you suggest we do?' asked Dan. 'Farmers cannot fight soldiers without weapons.'

'Farmers cannot fight soldiers at all, Dan,' retorted Tom. 'This burning and looting of wealthy Protestants has all the trappings of religious bigotry. Reclaiming arms is laudable and eminently sensible if you expect to fight but torching the houses? Piking people on their lawns? This will look to Dublin like bloody, parochial vengeance – not revolution.'

'Haven't we a right to vengeance?' asked Sinnott, bridling at Tom's words.

'Of course you do,' sighed Tom. 'But there are ways of going about it. You could burn every tyrant's house between here and Carlow and it would provide no compensation and very little consolation to the relatives of their victims. If you want vengeance, true vengeance, you must become more than just a rabble.'

Sinnott was nodding now, regarding the young former yeo with a new respect. 'Will you two come with us? We could do with a couple of trained fighting men. We're heading down south to Ballaghkeen to see what's transpired during the night. If they have been as successful as us there won't be a soldier left in Wexford by tomorrow evening, they'll have all run away in terror.'

Dan laughed, 'I doubt that, William. I doubt that very much. The soldiery are all holed up in the garrison towns for the night, watching and waiting, hoping the people will become fatigued or disinterested, hoping that they will become gorged on violence and destruction and that they won't have the stomach for any more. They'll move in the morning, William. When they do we'd best be ready.'

Sinnott and his group conferred briefly and then each in turn shook Dan's hand.

Dan turned to his brother, his eyebrows raised questioningly.

'I shall come too,' Tom said through gritted teeth. He smiled wryly at his brother, 'All roads in this direction lead to hell but we shall walk them together.'

Dan grinned and threw his big arms around Tom's shoulders, wrapping him up with fierce affection. However, Tom noted with dry perspicacity, no welcoming hands were offered him by the sour-faced peasants, no acceptance was there yet for a man who so recently wore the red coat.

It took only minutes for Tom and Dan to gather their meagre supplies and equipment. It took minutes more for the two young men to instruct the surprised group of farmers in how to march with pike on shoulder and to move as a cohesive body without tripping each other up. Then, with the air of children playing at soldiers, the little corps of peasant farmers marched down the hill and into the dark of the enveloping countryside. The two brothers strode behind them, Dan's face alive and vital, Tom frowning and troubled whilst all about them, on hills and high points, more and more bonfires were sent whooping up into the night sky.

CHAPTER 8

The Coming Soldiers

Whit Sunday, the 27th of May, and another perfect morning had broken across the rolling Wexford countryside. The barony of Ballaghkeen edged onto the sea and there was indeed a tang of salt in the air and, here and there, the clay of the roads was streaked with pale brush strokes of sand. On one narrow roadway, hemmed about by the thick green and yellow of gorse ditches, Tom and Dan Banville stood amongst the twelve farmers from their own Gorey barony and watched as William Sinnott propped himself up on an old, salt-bleached wooden gate.

On the opposite side of the gate, standing up to his shins in the straining emerald blades of growing barley, an ancient farmer leaned on a heavy blackthorn walking stick, almost as tall as himself, and scratched his beard thoughtfully. At his feet a black and white farm dog sat and gazed up at him adoringly, its tongue lolling over its teeth like a wet ribbon.

'John Donovan and Lieutenant Bookey, that's what I heard anyhow,' the old man was saying.

'Jesus Christ, both of them?' asked Sinnott incredulously.

'That's the God's truth,' replied the farmer, shifting his weight from one foot to the other. 'Donovan was shot by his first cousin, Tom Donovan, and Bookey was piked in the neck.'

William Sinnott exhaled, long and wondering, and said, 'Lieutenant Bookey of the Camolin Cavalry killed at The Harrow just last night?'

'That's the long and short of it,' said the old man.

Dan and Tom exchanged curious looks before Dan called out, 'What happened then? What of those that did the killing?'

'Eh?' came the reply.

Sinnott leaned forward and raised his voice somewhat, 'He asked what happened to those who killed the yeomen? Where did they go?'

The farmer's wizened hand went back to scratching his beard and he croaked, 'Well, the yeos all flew back to Ferns and Fr Murphy and his men went about the place collecting guns and pikes. I think old Reverend Burrows up in Kyle Glebe was killed in the middle of it all. Piked to death.'

The old man shook his head morosely, 'He didn't deserve that. He was a good man. He was no tyrant.'

Dan pushed forward now and, as the curious group of peasant soldiers looked on, he too leaned over the gate and said loudly, 'Fr Murphy? Fr John Murphy of Boolavogue?'

'The very one. He gathered together everyone he could and sent young Jerry Donovan dashing about on a horse roaring, "Get up and fight! Or you will be burned or butchered in your beds! The country is in a blaze around you!"' The old man laughed then, a wheezing, brittle sort of sound, 'Jerry Donovan, with his lame leg, rising the country, what has happened to the world at all, at all?'

'Where are they now?' pressed Dan.

The farmer sucked in his cheeks with a smack and tapped his lips with one crooked finger, 'The last I heard tell was from Edward Hanley there about an hour ago. He said there was a huge crowd of people gathered outside Jeremiah Kavanagh's hostelry. That's on the crossroads there at Ballinamonabeg.'

'I know Kavanagh's,' offered Sinnott.

The old man laughed again, rocking himself back and forth on the fulcrum of his stick, 'Young Hanley said he was getting as far away from there as he could before every soldier in the county comes down on the place.'

'Thank you, sir,' said Dan as he pushed himself away from the gate and hurried over to where Tom was frowning at him in puzzlement.

'What has happened to make you so flushed?' asked Tom.

'Nothing,' replied Dan. 'Only Anthony Perry's "fat prevaricator" has single-handedly risen all the parishes around this neighbourhood.'

'Fr Murphy of Boolavogue?' asked Tom, incredulous. 'He's not even a United Irishman, is he? He was one of those priests you made monotonous habit of railing against.'

'Indeed,' laughed Dan. 'He was one of the most outspoken in urging the surrender of arms. It turns out he spent most of last night committing violence to get them back.'

He threw his hands in the air, 'The world has turned upside down.'

Tom thought for a moment before surmising, 'So this sheep of a priest has now become a dyed in the wool croppy? I'd suggest that self-preservation after the murder of the two yeomen was a sharper spur to his actions than the prospect of a republican idyll.'

William Sinnott was now at Dan's elbow, 'It is good that they've all gone to Jeremiah Kavanagh's. It is only a mile or so from here. Kavanagh fought with General Washington against the English and is as fine and committed a United Irishman as lives on these shores. He might bring some order to what is occurring. What do you make of the priest's involvement, Mr Banville?'

Dan squinted into the lofting sun as though to receive divine guidance from its glare. 'I don't know, William. Anyone drawn to a banner of defiance at the current time in our country's sad history must surely be a United Irishman, if not in name then at least in spirit. I would hazard that once the first hot rush of excitement passes and the captains and colonels meet to formulate a plan of action, then the priest will fall away in importance. He must be commended for his exertions thus far, however.'

The short march to the crossroads at Ballinamonabeg was a pleasant one. The heat of the sun lifting to its midday brilliance was tempered by a cooling breeze that came waltzing in off the sea. The men of the little group from the north of the county chatted and joked among themselves as they strolled. They sauntered with their shirts open and the butt of their pikes trailing in the dust behind them, kicking stones and pebbles as they walked.

Tom, however, and Dan too to a lesser extent, remained slaves to their days in the military. Their ears strained for the slightest hint of approaching horses and their eyes scanned the skyline above the hedgerows, searching for the tell-tale curtain of dust that would signal the approach of a body of men.

They could hear the noise of the crossroads long before their little bohreen opened out into it.

Four rutted roads came together at Ballinamonabeg and at this junction a few small cabins had sprung up. It was here that the returning Continental Army man, Jeremiah Kavanagh, had chosen to build his public house. Across from where Dan and Tom stepped out into the open space of the crossroads a large, single-storey thatched building sat gleaming in the sunshine, its white-washed walls reflecting the sun and its yellow covering of straw glowing gold in the afternoon light. Its thick stub of stone chimney jutted out of the thatch and wisps of turf smoke snaked lazily skyward, kinking and twisting in the breeze.

From the open door of the pub a great tumult of people spilled out onto the road and lapped up against its walls and the ditches all about. Some appeared to be sleeping whilst some were animated and arguing. Quite a few, Dan noted, were bandaged and bloodied from their nocturnal activities. Quite a few more held a drink in their hands. All told, Dan was sure that there were well over a thousand men present and in the sloping fields behind Jeremiah Kavanagh's pub he could discern a motley horde of women and children, hundreds and hundreds of them.

All about, bristling with potential, their cruel heads glistening in the sunlight, pikes leaned against whitewashed walls or were stacked in neat piles like wood gathered for building.

Tom tugged his brother's sleeve and nodded curtly to a particular point in the crowd. There, holding their horses' reins and conversing amongst themselves, were six brightly uniformed members of the Shelmalier Yeoman Cavalry.

'It seems you're not the only yeo to have a change of heart,' Dan said.

William Sinnott had moved off with his men and was mixing with the crowds, going from group to group and shaking hands with those he knew and making acquaintance with those he did not. Tom, meanwhile, took one look at the packed entrance to Kavanagh's pub and snorted, 'No chance of getting a drink in there.'

Dan smiled at him, 'I thought you were off the drink?'

Tom shrugged, 'I was. However, present circumstances would drive a nun to drink.'

'Let us find out what the tale is behind this raggle-taggle army,' suggested Dan, and he made his way over to the Shelmaliers. Tom shrugged and followed his brother, wending his way through the hubbub of the makeshift camp, stepping over prone figures, asleep or wounded and striding between stands of pikes pushed together like the frames of Indian tepees.

The former yeomen looked up at the brothers' approach, regarding them warily.

'Good day to you, sirs,' greeted Dan. 'I am Daniel Banville and this is my brother Thomas, both formerly of the Castletown Yeoman Cavalry. I hope we are well met?'

The yeomen all offered their gauntleted hands to be shaken before one of them, a man just reaching his middle years, one hand tangled in the reins of a giant bay foxhunter, said, 'Well met indeed. My name is Morgan Byrne and I find it comforting to know that at least a handful of men here have some military training. If Sergeant Roche had a month to drill these peasants we might make something out of them. They are enthusiastic enough but lack discipline.'

One of his companions laughed softly, 'Shouldn't you refer to the good sergeant as "Colonel Roche" from now on, Byrne?'

Tom, curious, asked, 'Edward Roche of the Shelmaliers? Sergeant Edward Roche? He's a United Irishman?'

All six cavalry men now laughed openly.

'He is indeed, as are we all,' one answered. 'A good proportion of the barony seems to be United Irishmen if the numbers of Shelmalier men here are anything to judge by. Most are fugitives from the militia and yeomanry and most have no arms, not even reaping hooks or hay forks. Some though,' he said with a wink, 'have long-barrelled shore guns and finer shots you will never see.'

'Where is Roche now?' asked Dan. 'Who is leading the people?'

The first yeoman gestured towards the pub, 'Kavanagh, George Sparks, Roche and a few others, including that remarkable priest, are in there having a council of war. They've been in there for over an hour. We'll all be sent home, mark my words. That will be the upshot. We have no cavalry, few firearms and no artillery. There is no sign of Edward Fitzgerald of Newpark, who should be here by now and already some of the poor farming folk have sloped off home, having had enough of fighting after only one night.'

Dan studied the soldier carefully, 'We are in such bad shape as all that?' he asked.

The yeoman nodded, 'Unless some driving purpose unites all upon one course then I'm afraid it is back to their smoking homes for these people and a boat to France for the likes of us.'

No sooner had the words left his lips than a young man, hardly out of his teens, raced into the camp from down the northern arm of the crossroads. His bare feet pounded on the sun-baked clay and his breath was ragged in his chest. His eyes were gaping discs of terror and his lips were as pale as fish bellies.

'They're coming!' he roared. 'There's horses coming!'

Immediately, pandemonium gripped the crossroads. In the adjoining fields, women and children sent up a wailing cry that frightened the birds from the trees, whilst the fighting men, resting in the sun, leaped to their feet, seizing pikes and pitchforks with an eagerness bred of terror. They then milled, however, unsure of what to do, each man looking to the other for instructions, each one suddenly stymied, their imagined course of action hamstrung by indecision. A few individuals began to separate themselves from the main body of the camp, step by step, moving south, away from the approach of the cavalry.

Into this panic and confusion stepped Edward Roche. Dashing and commanding in his uniform of yeoman sergeant he immediately began issuing orders, sword drawn in hand. A large man, broad of shoulder with a heavily jowled face beneath sweeping sideburns, he dominated all those around him.

Like a force of nature he held the gradually disintegrating mass of peasantry together. His orders were obeyed without question; men unused to fighting, unsure of their footing in such an unknown situation, were grateful to be given direction and leapt into action.

Then, beside Roche appeared another figure. Dressed in the simple earthy tones of a comfortable farmer, big-boned and balding but possessed of an indefinable aura of conviction, he too began cajoling and harassing, deriding those few who had the temerity to slink away. Upon hearing his voice, a great many of those who had blanched at the news of the soldiers' approach now gained heart. They surged forward and gathered around the two heavy figures that now seemed to hold the unwavering command of the entire mass of fighting men.

'You see that man beside Colonel Roche,' began the middle-aged yeo, 'the one with the balding head, giving orders like an officer himself? That's the good Fr John Murphy. The people love him, I'll grant him that.'

Then, with a gesture to his companions, he said, 'Let us go and provide Roche with a bit of help.'

Tom and Dan both shrugged and followed the Shelmalier men over to where Murphy and Roche were issuing directions. Roche, the military man, had seized the situation immediately whilst Murphy seemed to be the orator, extolling for his flock the virtues of bravery and honesty.

'You there,' barked Roche, noticing Tom and Dan amidst the uniforms of his cavalry men. 'Do you know how to use those pistols you carry?'

'Of course,' shouted Dan in reply. Then, half-drawing his cavalry blade and ignoring Tom's despairing look, he continued, 'And this isn't just for show either.'

'That's the spirit!' laughed Roche.

Then, becoming suddenly grim, he ordered, 'You men, with me. Fr Murphy here will defend the crossroads and the east side of the road with the men from the Harrow. Shelmaliers, anyone with a full pike or firearm is to make for that steep field yonder.' He pointed with his sword.

On the northwest side of the crossroads, bordering the road down which the terrified sentry had dashed, a sloping field rose grassy and peaceful to the horizon. Hedged by strong ditches of gorse and briar, it was here that Roche would set his ambush.

Roche himself led the way, barging through thorn and nettle, heedless of his fine uniform. After him, a corps of maybe five hundred men streamed into the little paddock and took up silent position along the hedgerow bordering the road. Most carried pikes, but slightly above them, higher up the slope, Roche had positioned those few rebels with muskets and fowling pieces.

In the middle of the line of pikemen, pistols and swords in hand, Dan and Tom Banville waited, gasping in the warmth of the afternoon.

Gradually, an electric silence descended on the rebel ranks. Tension fizzed and crackled as men crouched, their hands balled in white knots about their weapons. Amongst cow parsley and fern, amongst spinning swarms of midges, hidden and noiseless in the long grass, Roche's men waited and watched.

Above the quiet of the pikemen and musketmen the lamentation of the camp followers twisted into the afternoon. Men's names were wailed, their wives pleading with them to come to their families and children screamed for their fathers; but not one man moved from his position overlooking the north road. Not one man turned his eyes from where, perhaps half a mile away, a beige cockerel tail of dust was crawling up into the sky above the fields and hedgerows.

The man beside Dan, grimy and bedraggled with a scabrous bandage bound around his left hand, began to pray. His voice was quick and whispered, the words almost running into one, '*Ourfatherwhoartinheavenhallowed-bethyname . . .*'

The jangle of tack and the sound of hooves on clay suddenly filled the world. Yet under it, like a bodhrán beneath the high treble of a jigging fiddle, Roche's voice rumbled, 'Steady lads. Steady.'

Through the meshing branches of the hedgerow, through the thorns and glorious yellow flowers, the rebel force caught first sight of the cavalry's vanguard. They came on at a steady walk, three abreast with the rest, maybe two hundred if Dan was any judge, filling the road behind. They were a disparate group, motley in their uniform. Dan could recognise elements from Gorey, Ballaghkeen, Camolin, Coolgreany and others. Red coats mingled with blue and black but all were armed with pistols and swords and all wore an air of determination.

Dan frowned then. One of the leading figures, in the middle dressed in red coat and Tarleton helmet, seemed familiar to him. There was a certain set to the shoulders, an arrogance about his bearing that proclaimed his identity louder than any herald. Before Dan could make a sound, beside him Tom spat in disgust into the ditch, 'Hawtrey bloody White.'

As though this were a signal, as though the invoking of his name somehow alerted the loyalist officer, just outside of musket shot, White raised his right hand and called a halt to his column. Down the ranks the order was passed and the two hundred horse came to a huffing stop, animals snorting and their tails whipping at nuisance flies and biting insects.

White then reached into his saddlebag and drew forth a telescope, the long brass cylinder flashing back gaudy highlights as the sun struck its surface. Extending it, he raised it to his eye and scanned the road and ditches ahead.

Shoes and boot leather creaked as pikemen adjusted their positions and even their breath seemed impossibly loud, a tidal roar in the stillness.

'Don't anyone move,' hissed Dan.

White was now in conference with the two other officers beside him. One man was gesticulating wildly, the bearskin crest of his helmet riffling in the breeze. The other leaned on his saddle horn and nodded solemnly, every now and then flinging a suspicious glance toward the rebel hedgerows. They debated like this for long minutes while the sun beat down, coaxing sweat from pores, gluing shirts to shoulder blades and the buzzing of flies grew more insistent. Then, abruptly, a decision appeared to have been made, for at a signal from White the entire corps of cavalry wheeled about and trotted back the way they had come.

White alone lingered for a moment, his eyes flaying the ditches and fields, wary and hate-filled, before he too urged his mount into motion and disappeared into the dust-swaddled distance.

The rebel lines watched the yeomen retreat with mingled feelings of relief and disbelief. A lone voice cried out, 'That's right ye murdering crowd of bastards, off with ye!' A gust of laughter rushed through the ranks at this and then a cheer arose, low at first but gathering in volume as each man took it up and magnified it until the very countryside itself seemed to be bellowing in triumph.

Only Dan, Tom and Edward Roche remained unaffected. They stood together in glum disappointment and watched as the dust of the cavalry's retreat faded into the blue of the afternoon sky.

'That was an opportunity missed,' stated Dan flatly.

Roche nodded, 'It was that. We would have wiped them from the face of the earth had they kept coming, of that I am certain. Horses, swords, pistols, carbines, ammunition, a treasure trove is making its way from us even as these farmers celebrate.'

'It will give them hope,' said Dan. 'By God, it gives me hope to see a black-guard like White beat such a hasty retreat.'

Tom was standing quietly, swishing his sword's blade through the long grass at his feet and staring at the point in the road where the cavalry had halted, a whisker from ambush and annihilation. 'Two hundred cavalry,' he mused. 'Two hundred cavalry, well-mounted and armed, led by one of the most zealous monsters in all the land, turn and run from a field full of peasants? I am dumbfounded.'

He turned to Roche and Dan, a wry smile twisting his lips, 'I may have been wrong,' he laughed. 'This might just be easier than I thought.'

Elizabeth watched the rider with a mixture of curiosity and bemusement. She had been awake since before the seam of daybreak crept along the horizon and spent the morning wandering amidst the camp's groggy multitudes. The fires had all been rekindled in short order and now a haze of wood smoke mingled with the disappearing dawn fog. She had awoken with a thirst roughening her mouth and a hunger gnawing at her stomach but without food or water and without a friend to beg charity from, she resigned herself to an uncomfortable morning, the growing smells of cooking mocking her empty stomach.

The camp had come alive, like a corpse re-animating, stiffly at first but gaining momentum moment by moment. Pots were rinsed and scrubbed and slung above the wan flames of new kindling. Men tramped about with armfuls of firewood or stood on the gorse-stitched flank of the hill and gazed south whilst their children lolloped and gambolled around their legs. It was to the south too that Elizabeth found her attentions first drawn. Out there across the silver swamp of retreating fog, from the black gnarls of copses and along the lengths of leafy avenues, tendrils of charcoal rose against the sky. Elizabeth could easily guess their origin and the jovial agitation these distant testaments to arson provoked in the rebels on Kilthomas Hill frightened her a little.

Of Dan Banville there was no sign and her concern for him grew with every passing minute.

Then, suddenly, a figure appeared at the base of the hill. Wending its way up the slope, its appearance dragged people from their cooking fires like the pole draws a compass point. As the rider moved closer Elizabeth could see that it was a burly man, clad in the fine-fitting but rough clothes of a well-off farmer, a broad-brimmed hat crushed down onto his meaty head.

At his approach the crowd of peasants began to wail. He passed through them like a galleon through the glass waters of a fish pond. His horse, a placid, heavy-chested, dove grey animal, pricked its ears forward and high-stepped as callused hands reached for its rider and a hundred voices cried out, 'Fr Michael! Fr Michael!'

Fr Michael for his part merely smiled a wet smile of pontifical benevolence and rose his hand as though bestowing a blessing on the ragged multitude that now surrounded him.

Elizabeth snorted in derision and shook her head. Here was a mob of people intent on substituting one untouchable elite for another.

From all that Daniel had said, from all that he had inadvertently revealed, it had become obvious to Elizabeth that he was a United Irishman, if not by name then certainly by inclination. This rabble of tenant farmers greeting a mounted priest as though he were Alexander himself was not the vision that Daniel had presented to her. An Ireland free from the power of all churches, a debased people throwing off the shackles of Crown and Cross, a people free from the compulsion to bow and scrape; that was what he had hoped for. The scene being played out before her now seemed like an affront to that ideal.

She curled her lip as her stomach grumbled in protest at being left empty for so long. Smiling wryly, she looked down and patted her midriff, muttering, 'If you are going to complain so, then I think we shall have to lower ourselves to beg a morsel to eat.'

She laughed then, thinking, What would father and mother think? Sarah would have a convulsion!

Still laughing, she raised her eyes and then all mirth died within her. Every cell of her body, every atom of her being suddenly turned to frost. Her mouth worked mutely as a maelstrom of thoughts and emotions pulverised her from within. She blinked deliberately. Once. Twice. She willed her vision to clear, wished that her eyes had somehow betrayed her.

At the base of the hill's western slope, out of the green and gold of the quilted countryside, a creeping red line had bled into being like a laceration. Red coats and black bicorns coloured the paddocks below as they marched. And just on the edge of hearing, the burred rattle of a drum could be heard and above the soldiers' heads their colours were unfurled. Slightly to the right of the infantry, a mass of cavalry were snaking around the flank of the hill, snaking along the road that Elizabeth and Dan had travelled on so many occasions.

The yeos had come at last.

Her heart beating in her ears, Elizabeth breathed deeply and fought to prevent herself from screaming in panic. Daniel, she thought, where are you?

Now, above the chatter of the crowd as it swilled about Fr Michael, a warning cry went howling up into the air. Immediately, every pair of rebel eyes turned towards the west and a brute keening arose from the throats of the women. At this sound a gaggle of children, and not a few of the men, began to edge slowly towards the line of cedars at the summit of the hill. Elizabeth too, to her shame, felt herself take a mindless step backward before she steadied herself and planted her feet. She would not move from here. She had made her choice.

Fr Michael, however, was not so easily thrown off his stride. To Elizabeth's surprise the stocky priest was now standing in his stirrups, haranguing those around him.

'You run!' he cried. 'Why? Is this not why we are here? Is this not why we have left our homes and gathered all together as free people under God?'

At his words every one of the wavering peasants halted as though rooted to the very bedrock. Men raised their heads and looked to him whilst their wives and children paused, pulling at their husbands, their fathers, urging them to come away, to hide amid the fern and timber.

Fr Michael was gesturing now, his arm describing a wide arc, taking in the countryside that lay supine and smoking below him. 'Look!' he roared in his bull's voice. 'See how our comrades have dealt with the tyrants this very night. They must surely bring us to battle else be driven into the sea. We are gathered here to stand. We are gathered here to fight! Why run? Why hide? Fight for freedom or be shot like dogs! Fight for Ireland!'

The hundreds of men gathered in the gold spill of morning gave vent at these words to a roar of defiance that only increased the wailing of their families. The gathering was all at once a frenzy of activity. Where once farm hands and labourers stood stultified by indecision and fear, now they rushed to unlimber pikes and shepherd their loved ones to safety in the woods and bracken. Unnoticed by all, fearful but unbowed like a hind ringed by baying hounds, Elizabeth Blakely leaned against the bole of a cedar tree and prayed silently.

She prayed for herself and for Daniel. She prayed that they might see each other once more, just once before the world was consumed by chaos and ruin.

Fr Michael, atop his horse and grandly instructing the men around him, was by now attempting to form two lines of pikemen, hundreds strong, strung out along the contours of the hill.

Below him, even as his men steadied, the soldiers had formed an unbroken chain of scarlet and steel. As one they lifted their muskets and at a distance of a few hundred yards a coughing eruption of blue powder smoke rippled out along their line. A moment later the fizzing chatter of the gunshots skittered across the slopes.

Elizabeth jumped at the sound, certain she saw more than one of the rebels drop his pike or makeshift polearm. Although no one had fallen at this first volley, Fr Michael's little army seemed to be on the verge of flying to the four winds like a bevy of startled snipe.

'Hold!' the barrel-thick priest roared. 'Hold, in the name of God!'

The soldiers were advancing now, the sound of their drum a brittle accompaniment to the terror they instilled with every step. Elizabeth watched as the yeos steadied themselves and, at a word from an officer sitting his mount at the extreme right of their line, they loosed another volley into the mass of rebels. A stinking wall of powder smoke was flung up between the two opposing lines, everything within its folds becoming nebulous and ghostly.

Again, not a single United man fell, but at the report of the muskets three of their number turned tail and fled, terrified, into the cedar wood. Elizabeth's eyes followed them and in her ears the lamentation of the women mounted ever more desperately. They crouched in the musty fern and snagging briar; crouched and clutched crosses and rosary beads. She stood as still as the trees themselves and heard prayer after garbled prayer make a droning procession through the undergrowth.

And then, suddenly, over the brow of the hill away to the rebel right, the muscled ranks of the Carnew Yeoman Cavalry appeared. Against the pastel blue of the morning sky their coats were a deep, deep red. The red of spilled blood crusting in the heat, Elizabeth thought absently. The red of the slaughter house and chopping block. The red of emptied life.

And there, in the middle of their line, his helmet discarded and his sword a sliver of ice in the sunlight, sat Captain Wainwright. At the sight of him, Elizabeth felt a sensation like a blade, as slim as a feather and as cold as glass, slip into her abdomen.

The cavalry commenced a slow walk toward the rebel pikemen whom Fr Michael was valiantly attempting to wheel in order to face the oncoming wall of horse and steel. Then the thunder of their hooves began to build as the walk turned into a trot. In each saddle a red-coated yeoman rose and fell with disciplined and awful precision, each sabre held at a uniform angle, each face grim beneath identical Tarleton helmets. The cavalry came on, relentless and remorseless as a wave, their thunder building and building under the clear summer sky.

Caught between the infantry and the charge of the cavalry, Fr Michael's pikemen began to fragment. Their only hope lay in unity and yet their instincts compelled them to scatter, to race before the horses like hares before the hounds. From behind Elizabeth, panicked screams crawled up into the air and the woods exploded into rustling life as women and children fled out into the open, wailing and crying the names of their men as the yeoman infantry blazed another volley of whipping lead into the streaming mass of peasantry.

This time, bodies did fall.

Men, women and children bowled over and broken, smashed into oblivion by shot and ball.

Before Elizabeth's eyes the ragged campsite became a place of massacre. The cavalry hit home in an avalanche of violence and all was carnage. She watched, stunned and terrified, as a shining cavalry blade, one amongst a hundred, hammered down onto an unprotected head, flexing as it sheared through scalp and skull. Elizabeth, for so long an alien splinter floating beneath the hide of the body of rebels, was now abruptly part of it. Every terrified scream, every gore-splattered inch of skin, every staring and bloodshot eye, was now a part of her, and she of it.

Someone, somewhere, screamed a scream of septic despair. A scream that was taken up and amplified by a thousand other throats. A chorus of screams to which Elizabeth added her own. And, like some dumb animal, with the rest of the herd she turned to run.

Earlier that morning, Lieutenant-Colonel Foote of the North Cork Militia had bent over his desk and fumed. A map, held down by lead paperweights, crackled as his finger chased mobs of enemies across the faded ink on its surface. As his eyes traversed the map's yellowed expanses his face began to adopt its jaundiced hue. Here and there his finger stabbed, darting into the wide tracts of empty land between the small black squares and church towers that represented towns and villages. Each time his finger came to rest, the name of some obscure place or parish he had never even heard of branded itself into his mind. Tincurry. Ballyroebuck. Ballindaggin.

His complexion grew even more sickly as his eyes read the name of the most fateful little hamlet. The Harrow.

'Is this entire county a nest of damned vipers?' he roared, spittle flying from his lips and flecking the parchment over which he leaned. 'What in blazes have our forces been doing over the last weeks? What in blazes are they doing now? Every whoreson rebel seems suddenly bloated with conviction while the rest of us cower in garrison towns! What of the arrests? The collection of arms? How in the name of almighty God is this possible?'

Regarding him in uncomfortable silence, Henry Perceval and Captain Le Hunte shuffled their feet uneasily.

'Bagenal Harvey and Edward Fitzgerald are in custody, Colonel,' began Perceval. 'That has removed two of their leaders from the field. White up in Gorey has made another number of arrests. The rebels are headless, Colonel. They cannot sustain such furious intrepidity without men to lead them.'

Foote turned to glare at the High Sherriff and barked, 'Really, Mr Perceval? What leads you to make that assessment?'

Perceval swallowed drily, as though his tongue was a cotton rag, and said, 'The refugees that have come in from the surrounding parishes are all of the opinion that the rebels are merely peasants bent on loot and destruction.'

He lifted his right hand, in which he held a bundle of creased papers.

'These reports from the garrisons all convey the same low opinion of the peasant mobs. They are full of passion but in the cold light of day they will not hold together. The militia and yeomanry will rout them in short order.'

Foote, his fury not in the least abated, spun and pointed out through the room's high rectangular window. In the distance, the long flat span of Wexford Bridge was teeming with carts and horses, crawling with families scuttling along on foot. A stream of humanity was hurrying south into Wexford Town from East Shelmalier and the countryside beyond. 'Tell that to them!' seethed Foote. 'Tell that to all the loyal folk who are fleeing in terror at this moment. Tell them we were too late. Late by a matter of hours!'

He stormed over to the table and once more jabbed his finger onto a point in the map with such violence that he tore it free from its weights.

'Tell that to Lieutenant Bookey!'

The sparsely furnished chamber echoed his anger and, in the face of it, Captain Le Hunte was discomfited. 'My dear, sir,' he began, 'we are all much put out by last night's events and we all held Lieutenant Bookey very close in our affections. But Henry is right. We shall take these upstarts down a peg or two over the course of today. Mark my words.'

'Oh, I do mark them,' retorted Foote. 'I mark them well. How do you propose to chastise them so easily, Captain? What's this I hear about your corps of cavalry? How many have you left?'

Le Hunte blinked, embarrassed, and stuttered, 'I do not see how that . . . '

'Answer me!' Foote demanded.

'Sixteen,' replied the captain flatly.

'Sixteen,' repeated Foote, his voice shaking. 'With sixteen horse you want to gallop off into a hostile country? No, my good Captain, that won't do.'

He addressed both men then, his voice at last levelling and the fury that had bleached his complexion now ebbing slightly. 'Mr Perceval, you shall continue to apprehend as many of these vile rebels as you can. Do not limit yourself to the names Perry supplied us with. Tell your men to use their own initiative, I want any chance of conspiracy stamped out.

'Le Hunte, have the remnants of your men mount and be ready to depart immediately. I shall muster as many of my North Corks as I can readily gather. If we are to provide these rebels with a lesson it will be a harsh one. There shall be no half measures, Le Hunte, no lukewarm response to treason. We cannot stand as loyal subjects are most barbarously murdered and property is ruined. We shall meet these peasants with overwhelming force and we shall crush them underfoot. Is that clear, gentlemen?'

Le Hunte and Perceval nodded fervently. 'Yes Colonel,' they chorused.

An hour later and a long line of red-coated soldiers pushed their way northward through the crowds on Wexford Bridge. The civilians bustled to move out of their way, dragging children and handcarts to one side as the North Corks filed past in a tramping thunder of boots and rattling weaponry. Out in front, his yellow jacket contrasting starkly with the crimson column at his back, a teenaged drummer boy beat a lively rhythm. Just behind him, Colonel Foote rode side by side with Major Lombard, his young second in command.

'Glorious day for it, ain't it?' offered Lombard.

Foote merely nodded, his thoughts dark, his considerations already focused on the countryside to his north and whatever rag-bag of revolutionaries it may contain.

Already across the bridge, the desultory remains of the Shelmalier Cavalry tried to look their best as they sat their foxhunters. Amongst them was the magistrate Edward Turner, who had come into the town the previous night bearing hysterical tidings of house burnings and savagery. He had been pressed into service as a guide for Le Hunte's cavalry as they ranged out in front, a screen and vedette for the infantry.

One hundred and twenty soldiers and officers marched out of Wexford Town that day, along with sixteen hardened yeomen, every one of them filled with the expectation of open battle and victory against a peasant rabble.

The day grew steadily warmer as the sun pitched itself further into the azure dome of the heavens. Between the sheltering hedgerows the breeze had died to an occasional waft of sweltering air, only serving to emphasise the clamminess of skin, the sticky damp of shirt and red coat. The column of infantry marched at ease, their muskets held limply in sweaty hands and their boots scuffing up little cumulous puffs of dust with every laboured footfall. Birds, brown and black, flashed from cover at the soldiers' approach and vanished in fluttering alarm over briar-snarled ditches and fences. All talk had stilled, the Corkmen marched in silence along the empty roadway.

At length, a Shelmalier yeoman accompanied by the magistrate Edward Turner came cantering down the road toward where Foote and Lombard rode ahead of their men. Saluting sharply, the yeo reported, 'Sir, Captain Le Hunte wishes to inform you that rebel persons have been seen at the crossroads of Ballinamonabeg running in great consternation from our approach.'

'How many?' asked Foote.

'Only a handful, sir. They seemed surprised to see us and fled northward. But the Captain said to stress that all around we found signs of a large encampment. We didn't give pursuit, sir, as the Captain presumed a rebel trap or ambuscade.'

'The Captain did well,' said the Colonel. As he rode, he turned to Lombard and asked, 'What lies to the north of Ballinamonabeg? What might tempt rebel forces to fly in that direction?'

Lombard considered for a moment, then reached up beneath his cocked hat to adjust the set of his wig before saying, 'Island Demesne might make a good field in which to make camp but from a military perspective the Hill of Oulart is the only remotely defensible position I can think of.'

Foote nodded and then spoke to Turner, 'Might a rebel band seek to make a stand at Oulart, do you think?'

Turner frowned slightly, 'It is indeed the only real point of high ground in the vicinity, Colonel. If they do possess the gall to stand against the King's forces they might very well choose that position.'

'Very well, Mr Turner,' replied Foote. 'You shall stay close with the column and guide us to this place, Oulart.' Then he addressed the yeoman, 'Private, you shall return to Captain Le Hunte and advise him to fall back on the infantry. I do not wish the cavalry to be surprised in the field. You are in such small numbers that a few well-aimed stones could destroy you. We shall drive on towards this hill and see what we can do about these miscreants.'

The yeoman saluted and galloped away, his horse's hooves scarring the earth as he drove the animal on.

Behind him, Foote regarded Major Lombard and raised a clenched right fist. Then he spoke in his lilting Cork singsong, 'When we find these dogs, Lombard, I want every last one of them hunted down and shot. Do you understand? Not one is to be left alive after today.'

'Understood, sir,' responded Lombard. 'Not one.'

Tom Banville stood on the southern slope of Oulart Hill and watched the cloud of dust and smoke rise up from the direction of Ballinamonabeg. As the cooling breeze kissed his cheeks, he sighed and then laughed bitterly, 'I have no doubt that signifies the end of our easy successes.'

'They're burning Kavanagh's,' Dan replied leadenly.

Oulart Hill was a whale's back of grass and heather heaving up like some verdant leviathan from the countryside between the sea and the River Slaney. Its uneven slopes were cross-hatched with ditches and narrow lanes, and cow paths traversed its flanks like scars. Upon the great bald crown of this unlikely salient, four thousand people thronged together, huddling in a mass of bodies. Of these four thousand, no more than a thousand men had armament of any kind. Fear bubbled and spewed forth as children wailed and women keened, begging their men to take their families home. Like a contagion, terror spread so that every face turned south and watched in pale horror as the dust of the King's troops grew ever closer.

In the little village of Oulart, nestled at the foot of the hill, a lone dog began to howl.

'We must do something,' demanded Tom. 'To wait here in such irresolute fashion is to invite calamity.'

Dan shook his head, 'With White and two hundred cavalry God knows where to the north of us, our scope for action is limited.'

Then, as they stared into the distance anticipating the appearance of red-coated soldiery at any moment, a great voice rose behind them, haranguing and chiding.

'Up, up!' the voice commanded. 'You haven't fought all night to be cowed like this! Up, I say, and face the foe that has burned and butchered your people for so long! Up!'

Tom and Dan turned and gazed up the slope to the brow of the hill where Fr Murphy was storming up and down the line of peasants like a drill sergeant.

'Have you no shame?' he was saying. 'Did you men not send Hawtrey White running like a slapped child not three hours ago? Did you not stand up to the tyrant and prevail? Now, after all that, your spines turn to water? I am not afraid. Though I should have my head cut from my shoulders, I shall die secure in the knowledge that I am a man and, like a man, I faced my end without fear.

'Those of you who wish to may go and sit with the women and children and, maybe, the soldiers will spare you when it is your time; but those of you who wish to fight with me, stand up. Stand up and be counted! For here on this ground we fight or die!'

To the brothers' surprise and awe, all along the brow of the hill men rose to their feet, pale hands gripping the shafts of pikes and farm implements, shaking them at the brown veil of dust drawing closer every moment. Men stepped forth and shook Fr Murphy's hand, men kissed their wives and children and then herded them, gently but inexorably, over the brow of the hill and out of harm's way. At last Fr Murphy was surrounded by a thousand men, all pale, all badly-armed but all willing.

Then a cry went up from one of them. Down in the valley the first of the redcoats appeared on the road and the hard crack and patter of the regimental drummer intruded upon the rebels' hearing.

A hollow murmuring began amongst the rebel ranks, only stilled when Edward Roche spoke out above the drumbeat rattling up from below. 'Calm, men, calm. Watch them. Watch what they do. They are not so numerous as us. This is our land. They are the intruders here.'

A little more than a mile away the column of infantry halted. The rebels could clearly perceive the officers leaning together, conferring and gesturing towards their position. Edward Roche laughed as his own Shelmalier Cavalry spread out along a low ridge bordering the road.

Gazing intently down at the North Corks, Tom asked, 'What do you think, Dan?'

'There's over a hundred of them, anyway,' said Dan. 'No artillery though and no cavalry worth the name, in spite of that little group sitting prettily over to one side. That number of horse shouldn't frighten anyone. You know, Tom, if these boys don't break at the first volley of musketry, if they stand and fight, I think we could carry the day.'

'It'll be a damn close-run thing,' answered Tom.

Meanwhile, Fr Murphy had taken the best of his pikemen and ordered them behind a thick hedgerow running across the hill just below its summit. Edward Roche and another man, Dan thought his name was George Sparks, had taken a number of gunmen and placed them behind another ditch to the pikemen's right, this one slanting slightly downhill as it negotiated its way across the rocky contours. With pistols and swords Tom and Dan jogged over to join Roche where he crouched behind a gnarled blackthorn tree.

Fr Murphy was speaking again, striding with sulphurous purpose across the slope between the rebel lines. 'They will wait to see us dispersed by the foot troops,' he thundered, 'so that they can fall on us and cut us to pieces. Remain firm together! We will surely defeat the infantry and then we will have nothing to fear from the cavalry.'

Tom looked at Dan, grinned and gestured toward the energetic priest. 'Did you ever think of pressing him into the United Irish ranks?' he asked.

Dan laughed, nodding in agreement, 'He's some man, of that there's no denying.'

Down in the valley the column of troops and the small detachment of yeomen were moving again, marching down the road towards the village of Oulart itself. As they drew nearer, the rebels on the hill could discern the faces beneath the infantry bicorns lifting to sweep the hilltop with appraising eyes. Once the soldiers had gained the village they again halted and their officers huddled together in discussion. Then, as the rebels looked on, a man in civilian clothes detached himself from the conference and gathered the Shelmalier Cavalry to him. Then, with the yeomen in attendance, he rode first to one thatched building and then to another.

'That's Edward Turner,' said Roche. 'I wonder what he's doing.'

Within moments Turner's purpose revealed itself for, from the eaves of the buildings, white cords of smoke began to curl like cats' tails, drifting off on the breeze. At this sight, an outraged muttering slithered through the rebel ranks. The grumbling stilled, however, as George Sparks, a swarthy man with bright eyes and the rolling accent of Blackwater in his voice, rose to his feet from the middle of the line of gunsmen.

'Stay where you are!' he ordered. 'They want us to come down off our height and play with them down below. They can all go hang if they think we're going to be shot for a few burned sheds!'

A wash of confidence flowed through the rebel bands at his words. The men remained fixed where they were, hatred for the soldiers boiling off them in waves. Hands tightened on gun and pole-arm and a deathly quiet blanketed them. The crown of Oulart Hill became still and silent.

The officers in the valley, seeing that their clumsily baited trap had failed to drag the rebels from their lofty position, now marched their men directly along the road to where it rounded the base of the hill. There they halted while the sixteen yeoman cavalry continued to jog along the road in a wide arc, making for the western slope of the hill. The infantry formed a long red line in the glorious sunshine, their brass buckles and white straps glowing in the light. The North Corks looked resplendent as they fixed their bayonets and prepared to rout the ragged, unwashed horde above them.

At this sight one or two pikemen let drop their weapons and made to run back up the slope to where the women sheltered amongst the hedgerows beyond the hill's brow. Dan and Tom flinched as Morgan Byrne's giant fox-hunter cleared the gorse above them in a surge of muscle and sinew.

'Hold!' Byrne roared. 'Hold, damn you!'

The men froze, stricken and shamed as every pair of eyes turned on them. There they stood on open ground with their backs to the North Corks, with their backs to their fellow countymen who crouched in terror amidst the razor spines of the gorse. Men who crouched and stayed, prepared to fight even whilst their minds teetered on the brink of panic.

Byrne now rode back and forth, driving his mount through the furze so that he could fix each man with a flaring glare. Blood ran down his knees and stained the sides of his great horse in red. He bellowed at them in the tones of a ploughman at market, in the language of fair and field.

'Shame on you!' he cried. 'Are you afraid of redcoats? They're only men like you and not half as good!' He pounded one fist against his chest, yelling, 'They're like me and you inside! If you met them in a fair, man to man, would red coats frighten you? Not at all!'

Gazing up at the former yeo as he harangued and lent spirit, Dan found himself murmuring, 'I believe we are going to win this.'

At his shoulder, Tom nodded, 'You know, I believe we might.'

Major Lombard snorted, 'They think they're going to win this.' He sat his saddle beside Colonel Foote and gazed up the slope at the rebel lines. Before the two officers, the North Corks had drawn up in readiness for battle, elbow to elbow and muskets held upright but loose in their right hands. Each man had affixed his bayonet and a spiked fringe of steel now jabbed skyward from their lines. Lombard was eager for the fray, inexperienced but confident, straining like a dog on the leash.

'Well they might entertain such hopes,' interjected Foote, seeking to curb his subordinate's burgeoning enthusiasm. 'They hold the high ground, have advantage in numbers and know the land better than we.'

Lombard reached up distractedly to adjust the powdered wig beneath his cocked hat, an affectation that intensely annoyed his commanding officer, and sneered, 'They are peasants, Colonel.'

'They are a lot of peasants, Major,' came the retort. 'They are a lot of peasants *with pikes*. I do not wish to come to blows with them until I am sure of crushing them completely.'

'Colonel,' protested Lombard, 'no ragamuffin band of local brigands has ever stood in defiance of a uniformed military. They will turn tail at the first volley of our muskets.'

Foote nodded slowly, 'That is true, Major.' Then, resolved, he addressed Lombard again, 'Would you care to lead the assault? It will be your first action I believe?'

'Thank you, Colonel,' gushed Lombard. 'I am eternally grateful.'

Foote merely gestured curtly towards the two companies of North Corks, 'The command is yours, Major.'

With that, Foote wheeled his mount to the rear and he and Edward Turner watched as Lombard took his place at the far right of the red-coated line. At various points along it, the companies' other officers walked or rode. Foote scanned them all, listing the good ones in his mind, Captain De Courcy, Lieutenants Williams, Ware and Barry and, in the middle, hefting the regimental standard, young Ensign Keogh. Steady boys, Foote thought to himself, steady and careful and the job is done.

The Banville brothers watched the militia as they slowly began to advance up the slope below them. Each soldier marched with discipline, his officers barking orders and the sergeants straightening the line with smart blows from their half-pikes. On they marched, and Tom felt the first tickle of a vinegar tingle deep in his chest, the first stir of mounting excitement at the prospect of violence. His breath came quicker and quicker and he rubbed his hands on the tails of his coat to rid them of a sudden, slippery film of sweat.

Dan meanwhile felt everything fall away from him. The same old sensation of aloneness enveloped him. He was at the centre of a frigid sphere in which any impulse could be achieved, any target hit. He had already chosen the soldiers that he would fell first.

Oblivious, the North Corks came on, until, at a word from the mounted officer on their right, they paused and shouldered their muskets.

Too far, Dan thought, as the soldiers, in perfect unison, loosed a volley toward the hedgerow just below the crest of the hill. Every musket flared and boomed, coughing forth an explosion of smoke and flame. The base of the hill was suddenly wreathed in a blue-black haze of burnt powder and the stink of gunsmoke poisoned the air. To the rebels' delight, not a single musket ball struck home and a chorus of jeers rang out from the behind the ditches. Edward Roche and George Sparks, however, shushed the gunsmen under their command into immediate silence. Into this silence, incredulity fluttering in his voice, Tom whispered, 'They don't know we're here. They haven't seen us.'

Dan nodded dumbly as the North Corks reloaded and again advanced. They were close enough now so that the voices of the sergeants and officers were clearly audible, their see-saw Munster accents sounding alien and somehow wrong in the bright afternoon. Every stubbled face was discernible, every line and wrinkle could be picked out as they moved forward, step by disciplined step. Dan and Tom watched and waited, fingers on triggers and thumbs resting on flintlocks.

The North Corks had stopped again and at a strident command they lifted their weapons and paused, motionless. This time, Dan thought, they were close enough to do real damage. Amongst the gorse and briar, rebels clutched their makeshift weapons and groaned in pained expectation. At any moment their scant protection of earth and bough would surely be ripped away by searing lead. Low to the ground and staring at each other with wide, brimming eyes, each man expected his end to come, tearing and hot, from the mouths of those hundred-odd guns.

'Fire!' howled the officer.

Concurrently with the hissing blast of the guns, this time shrieks rang out from the ditch running in front of the soldiers. Dan and Tom could see figures writhing in pain or crawling frantically away through the undergrowth, desperate to find more substantial cover.

As Dan watched, the mounted officer on the right flank of the infantry, a major if his epaulettes and cocked hat were any indication, shouted in encouragement, 'That's the stuff, my brave boys! They're running, can't you see? Another volley and then a charge and we shall have them beaten!'

The North Corks reloaded and continued their advance, right into the teeth of the rebel line. Another volley, thought Dan, and it would be a massacre. It was at this moment, as the North Corks marched forward in triumph, that Edward Roche growled, soft but menacing, 'Ready your weapons lads. Let's give them a hundred times what they've given us.'

Dan and Tom grinned, vulpine and predatory, as they cocked their pistols.

Out on the slope, still ignorant of the rebel gunsmen's presence, the North

Corks had come to a final halt some twenty yards short of the rebel position. Before the major could issue his command, a rebel with a pair of fist-sized rocks clenched in his hands stepped free of the gorse. With an oath, he lashed both stones toward the North Cork line. One stone, a blur as it hammered through the air, smashed into a Corkman's musket, tearing it from his grasp. The entire regiment stood for a moment staring, bemused, at the fallen weapon. Then the major, drawing a deep breath, stood high in his stirrups, his arm raised to give the final, fatal order.

It was then that Edward Roche's gun line belched forth fire and lead into the red-coated ranks.

Caught completely by surprise, his face a welter of consternation, Major Lombard spun his horse around and around, questing for his sudden assailants. His men, terrified, milled in line, turning this way and that, stumbling over suddenly prone comrades, their eyes sweeping the entire hill top, hands suddenly frozen to their muskets' walnut stocks. Blood and gore spattered some of their faces and a few were desperately trying to scrape the stuff off. With their amazed sight they saw their messmates lying dead on the grass.

The gorse in front of the soldiers then erupted in an animal howl of rage. Men dressed in the muddy shades of tenant farmers stormed through the thorns, faces wild and savage, mouths leering like gargoyles. Before the infantry could react, the rebels were upon them, hacking and stabbing, kicking and tearing with tempest fury. Lombard was borne from his horse, his screams brutally cut short as a pitchfork was slid into his neck.

The North Corks held for a moment in the face of this merciless onslaught. Then one, then another, faces grey with shock and fear, dropped their muskets and ran. The entire detachment broke off the fighting and turned, futilely attempting to flee. Surrounded and outnumbered, the soldiers were hacked down and spitted where they lay. Some produced bibles, some gabbled in Gaelic, all in an effort to prevent the slaughter. For the rebels, however, the pitchcap and the noose, the burned homes and defiled daughters were all too deeply branded in their minds. Hatred and fear found vent in the killing fields of Oulart Hill as the North Corks were hunted down wherever they ran, wherever they tried to hide.

On the road at the base of the hill, the Shelmalier Cavalry had ceased their half-hearted out-flanking. They sat their horses, unmoving, astounded by the massacre of their comrades. Dan Banville watched as a Shelmalier rebel, lying flat on his belly in the blood-slicked grass, took careful aim with his strand gun and blew one of Le Hunte's men from the saddle. At this, spurred by nauseating terror, the captain suddenly urged his men to the gallop and they fled along the road, savagely whipping their horses with bunched and flailing reins.

In the sun-gilded distance, already a mile away, a panic-stricken Lieutenant-Colonel Foote and Edward Turner raced ahead of them, lashing their mounts towards Wexford Town. In the gore-drenched fields around Oulart Hill they left over a hundred dead behind them.

CHAPTER 9

Meetings at Ballyorril

The little village of Camolin straggled in the sunshine, straddling the Dublin Road between Ferns and Gorey. Its entirety consisted of a single street of thatched, whitewashed cottages, a few slated smithies and a lone market house. In the early morning light of the 28th of May, the glowing embers of several of these dwellings sent acrid smoke twisting up into the blue. All along the double row of white-walled cottages, black gaps leered and crackled. Camolin was like a ruined smile, the holes in its terraces of cottages appearing like the rotten teeth of a dying hag or the shattered stumps lining a prize-fighter's mouth. All about these ashen cavities, the thatch of the surrounding buildings had charred and darkened but still dripped where their inhabitants had flung buckets of water to dampen the blaze. This morning however, as the sun began to edge above the eastern horizon, Camolin was deserted. Only a handful of old men and women clustered together in shocked silence at the side of the road while packs of mongrels roamed brazenly, sniffing the smoke and snarling at each other.

On the edge of the village, Tom and Dan Banville watched the nascent insurgent army snake southward towards Ferns. Every face seemed set, every tired eye fixed on the back of the man in front. Every pike and musket, Tom noted, was now determinedly carried slanted against shoulder. It was as though the victory at Oulart had bred in the rebels a strange kind of confidence. Though their clothes were rumpled and their faces worn, they were trying to deport themselves as they thought soldiers should. To Tom, it was a grotesque parody, a children's farce.

'They seem to have taken the notion that soldiering is about not falling on one's face,' he muttered.

Dan studied him carefully before replying, 'If they wish to think that they are soldiers, then let them, Tom. If to perform a role is to fulfil that role then why should we complain that our little force thinks itself an army? I would rather march with an army full of heart and belief, than with the rabble that we were within an ace of becoming on the slopes of Oulart Hill.'

Tom nodded in grudging agreement. Then, changing the subject, he gestured toward the marching column, '"Our little force" as you so put it, is not so little anymore, I think.'

That night they had camped on Carrigrew Hill, a few miles to the north of Oulart. The bodies and the stinking gore, the flies and the carrion crows, had hastened the rebels' departure from the scene of battle. With women, children and bloodied fighting men a ragged, formless mass, they moved quickly along the country roads. Relief and jubilation gushed through the veins of almost every member of the multitude. For Edward Roche, Fr Murphy, George Sparks and the other leaders, a slow dawn of self-assurance, of equipoise, began to break across their considerations. They had faced uniformed soldiers in open battle and had triumphed. Lack of weaponry and training had found its counterbalance in bravery and animal ferocity.

The leaders and men all marched wrapped in a new self-confidence and tried to ignore the low sobbing of the widows of the six insurgents who had died. Tom Donovan's wife, her face a crawling flux of anguish, keened mournfully into her shawl. The man who had killed the first soldier during that fateful clash in The Harrow had been one of the first to lose his life, a musket ball bursting his proud heart.

The camp on Carrigrew had been set up in good order and cattle had been brought in from the surrounding fields for milking and slaughtering; these cattle now followed the insurgents as they marched, herded and kept in order by a flotilla of young boys. Camp fires had been lit and Edward Roche, now being addressed laughingly as 'General' by his old yeoman comrades, had set sentries on all the approaches. As night fell, a spangle of flaming cabins could be perceived guttering – a dreadful reminder that the yeomanry was not gone away.

Yet the first sentry that came scrambling into the camp bore with him tidings, not of approaching cavalry, but of tenant farmers and labourers, committed United Irishmen and ignorant cottiers, all streaming through the night toward the rebel fires on Carrigrew. All were driven from their homes and hounded through the dark by the fluttering bat wings of terror, all were seeking sanctuary from the predations of the vengeful yeos.

Now, as Dan and Tom watched, the body of fighting men filing past them numbered perhaps four thousand. In front of the column, Fr Murphy and Edward Roche rode in animated conversation with each other.

Dan allowed his eyes to rove over the lines of peasants as they marched. Farmhands and ploughboys were transformed into killers by the cruel vagaries of chance. They found themselves rebels against the Crown and murderers of the King's troops. Yet, only the previous week they had handed over weapons and promises to the magistrates, sure in their conviction that a Rising could never occur.

Now they marched, affecting as best they could all the mannerisms of a trained army, through a country ravished by spiralling conflict. Cabins were burned, people gutted on their very doorsteps. Everywhere along the route of that morning's march houses were smouldering, Protestant as well as Catholics, as personal vengeance was meted out and petty scores were settled under the banner of freedom and liberty.

Dan focused his attention on the two standards being borne at the head of the column of men. The one on the left was a green flag with a golden harp embroidered upon it, the symbol of the United Irishmen. The second however was, to him at least, vaguely disconcerting.

A handful of men from the parish of Crossabeg had been sent south during the night to investigate what retribution was being wreaked in the countryside around The Harrow and Boolavogue. They had returned relating how all the cabins had been set alight and Fr Murphy's little thatched church had been reduced to embers. They brought with them a long, flowing chasuble owned by the priest, a vestment worn during funeral masses, now charred and torn. It was a length of pitch fabric with a white cross, stark upon the black, that would have stretched from collar to knee.

It was this macabre remnant that the insurgents now carried beside the United banner, hanging from its pole like something dead.

Dan and Tom moved to join the column, mixing with the men of their own Gorey Barony, and unconsciously fell into step, their old yeomanry habits dying hard.

Smiling, Tom turned to Dan. 'Where do you suppose we're headed?' he asked.

Dan shrugged, 'I have not the faintest but the poor old people that remained in Camolin said all the yeomanry and soldiers as well as every Orangeman and Protestant fled during the night. Our victory at Oulart seems to have quite unnerved the King's troops and they all scampered off north to Gorey or south to Ferns. I'd presume we were heading south. The garrison at Ferns is smaller and to take Gorey might be beyond us.'

At this Tom looked at him incredulously and spluttered, 'Of course Gorey is beyond us. Any market town with streets and defensible buildings is beyond us. Cannon and musket shot in close confines will mow these people down like corn. Beating militia, with no artillery or cavalry worth the name, out in the open where they can be charged with pikes is a far cry from storming a town.'

A few faces in the surrounding ranks knifed Tom uneasy looks and an anxious grumbling filtered through the men closest to the two brothers.

'Would you keep your voice down,' hissed Dan. 'The last thing we need is to be robbed of our courage by poisonous words.'

'What?' whispered Tom, hoarsely. 'I do not see how a much-needed dose of pragmatism can be anything except beneficial to these men. If you wish to take barricades and fortifications you must have artillery. A sickle strapped to a pole is no substitute for a nine-pounder, no matter how strong the arm that wields it.'

Dan lapsed into silence. Tom, ignoring the mutterings of the men around him, marched stiffly onward, his own silence a static charge balling about him.

The small hamlet of Ferns, like Camolin, consisted of a single street bracketing the Dublin Road and, as the four-thousand-strong mass of peasants with its train of cattle halted on the long slope leading up into the village, it appeared eerily quiet. Not a soul stirred abroad and only dogs and chickens scratched and lay in the dust. Overhead a flock of rooks cawed and rustled their ebony wings, scything through the brightening air. On the edge of the village, the palace of the Protestant Bishop of Ferns, Euseby Cleaver, sat in ivy-crawled splendour.

Edward Roche stowed away his pocket watch, its golden chain describing a delicate arc against the brown waistcoat he wore instead of his yeoman's jacket, now rolled up and tied behind his saddle. 'Half-nine in the morning and where have they all run to?' he wondered aloud.

'They've made for Enniscorthy,' offered Fr Murphy, the certainty in his voice prompting those nearest to him to nod in agreement before even considering his words.

Roche was thoughtful, his words weighted. 'I tend to agree. I do not think an entire populace, including Isaac Cornock's garrison of infantry and those from Camolin who fled to this place, could have conceivably passed us northward.'

He scratched his chin, stubbled now from two days in the field, and continued,

'You're right Father, the entire place must either have gone south to the safety of Enniscorthy or vanished into thin air. Is our little army so formidable that the whole of the military flies before us so that we must sweep them into the sea?'

Fr Murphy swept one heavy hand across his sweat-slicked pate and grunted, 'We can only hope that Almighty God grants it as such.'

Roche beckoned the column forward, and with good spirits bubbling amongst the men and camp followers at the sight of Ferns empty before them, they marched happily up the hill.

'I find this incredible,' said Dan as he marched in the midst of laughing men, their children now running alongside and dodging playfully between the ranks. 'The country is empty before us. Not one yeo or soldier has sought to stand and give battle since the North Corks. They must be overwhelmed with fear.'

'I don't doubt it,' agreed Tom. 'But I would be more concerned at their absence. To meet them company by company and dismantle them piecemeal would be more to our advantage than to meet them mustered and ranked on a battlefield of their choosing.'

The village of Ferns opened out before them as they crested the hill and, at the sound of their approach, dogs and farmyard fowl scattered, barking and squawking in the sunshine. In front of the army a lone figure stood in the dust of the roadway, a white handkerchief fluttering in his hand. The mass of rebels had lost its military regulation by now, the absence of enemies loosening men's resolve and prompting the women and children to mingle amongst the fighters. As one, the crowd surged forward around the leaders and the lone figure, pikes and guns rattling and tangling and the two banners grounded in the dirt.

Roche and Fr Murphy looked down from their horses at the slight, pale middle-aged man before them. He did not wear the fashionable wigs of the gentry. Instead, his greying hair was tied back in a short ponytail and his shirt was pristine white beneath his black waistcoat. He lowered his handkerchief and, taking in the desperate throng before him, their blades and guns and pugnacious faces, he swallowed drily.

'Have no fear,' Fr Murphy assured him. 'Not one man will lay hand upon you under a flag of truce.'

Looking relieved the man stammered, 'My name is Charles Haughton and I have no quarrel with you or your men. I am a Quaker with no ties to the military or the magistrates. I have remained here in spite of the protestations of my friends and family. I have remained here when all others have fled at your

165

approach to appeal to you to spare the people's property. The folk of this village have never done harm to any United Irishman and do not deserve the terrible acts being visited upon other places.'

'Terrible acts?' railed Fr Murphy. 'The "terrible acts" of which you speak were perpetrated first by the bloodthirsty yeomanry. These people are defending themselves from the Orange monsters that ran away so cowardly at our coming.'

Then a raised voice interjected, 'Father, I know this man.'

A group of young peasants, armed only with stout cudgels, pushed through the bristling mob. They stood before Fr Murphy and Edward Roche and one of them pointed to Haughton, standing nervously under the watchful scrutiny of every pair of eyes. 'I know this man,' the young rebel repeated. 'The very model of a fine human being. I would not have any person here harm one hair upon his head. Mr Haughton is a most amiable, liberal and honest man who would never conscience the tyrannies that have been undertaken by the soldiers.

'Sure, only a few weeks ago he refused to sell the yeomen a length of rope on the grounds that they were to use it to hang a United man. Mr Haughton is not our enemy, sirs, and none belonging to him neither.'

Roche regarded the Quaker in contemplative appraisal before saying, 'Mr Haughton, do not be afraid, for the safety of your property and the property of your neighbours has been guaranteed by this man's assessment of your character.'

Haughton was visibly relieved and, breathing deeply, said, 'If yourself and some of your comrades would like to come into my home I would be glad to offer you some meagre sustenance. I have not much but what I have is yours.'

Roche thanked him and dismounted, followed by Fr Murphy. Then the two men, accompanied by George Sparks and five or six other men unknown to Dan and Tom, went with Haughton to the door of his well-kept and slate-roofed townhouse. Before entering, Fr Murphy raised his voice above the hive buzzing of the throng.

'Let no man,' he ordered, 'harm the property of this good man or any of his neighbours. I would ask that you brave people take some rest and what nourishment you can – for great things lie ahead. Great things!'

With that he vanished through Haughton's open door.

Dan and Tom exchanged glances as the rebel column collapsed into myriad smaller groups, all sitting themselves by the roadside or sprawling on the hot clay of the road itself. Dan yawned and lowered himself heavily to sit on a patch of desiccated grass that grew by the verge of the thoroughfare. Tom sat beside him, his cavalry sabre resting across his knees.

'What do you make of this?' Dan asked.

'I do not think we can stay here for very long,' answered Tom. 'There is no wall to defend and the countryside is too open. We are vulnerable to attack at any moment and nobody has seen fit to post sentries. It is as though we have already won the war. This playing at soldiers must stop, Dan, and soon, before the people here are faced with more determined enemies.'

The brothers sat for a long minute, feeling the aching of their legs ease with the passing of every sun-brimmed moment. Dan's mind strayed to thoughts of Elizabeth, her hair, her touch, her scent. He hoped she was safe. He hoped he had put her beyond harm. He missed her. He raised his hand to shade his eyes and wipe away the tears that threatened to spill from them. Then, a commotion stirred off to their left and both young men lifted their heads curiously. From the direction of the Protestant Bishop's palace, the sound of breaking glass carried brittle and sudden across the morning air. A ragged cheer went up and more shattering of glass was heard.

Tom and Dan exchanged looks, Tom frowning at Dan's reddened eyes. Ignoring his brother's quizzical look, Dan asked, 'Should we not intervene, in some way? They're ransacking the Bishop's house. I'm well aware of his prose-lytising against the United Irish cause but a man of the cloth is a man of the cloth all the same.'

'Don't be ridiculous, Dan,' growled Tom. 'If you think anyone would thank you for defending the property of a known bigot then you are sore mistaken. Give them their head. If the leaders wish to put a stop to it, they can come away from the fine breakfast they are undoubtedly enjoying.'

Dan nodded glumly, 'But this isn't what the United Irishmen are about. It was never envisaged that senseless reprisals should take place like this.' He looked around despairingly. 'My heart quails at the emptiness of this place. Honest and true persons are seeking to flee from us as though we were a band of brigands. Charles Haughton was terrified that he would be spitted where he stood. What do the people think we are?'

Tom gauged his brother carefully before replying, 'They think that, for the most part, we are an ill-disciplined throng of zealots bent on looting and the extermination of Protestants and, for the most part, they would be wrong.'

He jabbed his thumb in the direction of the mocking roars and goading shouts drifting to them from Cleaver's palace, 'Unfortunately, Dan, there are persons amongst these peasants who would gladly sacrifice your noble enter-prise for a chance to punish those who have caused them even imagined offence. Not everyone here is a United Irishman, brother, and not everyone is possessed of your fine sensibilities and lofty ideals.'

Dan stared at the hard ground at his feet before finally admitting, 'I am afraid for Elizabeth, Tom. What if such people decide to punish her family for some fantasy of their own making? What if a bloody mob is all that we can expect?'

Tom smiled reassuringly at his stricken brother, 'Have no fear, Dan. Elizabeth is far from here and Carnew, and a den of Orange malfeasance is probably the safest place she could find herself.'

Dan was about to reply when an explosive cough, deep and vibrating, echoed down the packed street. The two brother's leaped to their feet in time to witness the thatch of a cottage some hundred yards away burst into flames in the morning light. Smoke billowed skyward as another flaming lantern was flung onto the pyre, splashing hot tongues of lamp oil as it smashed.

'What in God's name are they at?' cried Dan.

'Revenge,' stated Tom simply.

From Haughton's house the leaders spilled into the street, weapons drawn and faces demonic with anger. The Quaker's door rattled on its hinges as first one and then another barrelled forth into the suddenly smoke-filled street.

'What is going on?' yelled Roche, spying Dan and Tom standing rapt in the roadway.

Tom merely pointed wordlessly down the street to where rebel hands were wrenching open the locked doors and windows of known loyalists and yeomen. Drunk with a feeling of impunity, rebels were busy strewing belongings and crockery out across the street. As delft smashed like eggshells a joyous shout went up from those gathered outside. Yet the exhortations to violence were not universal. Vast tracts of the horde remained silent and merely regarded the rioters with a wary disdain. Nobody interfered, though, nobody called a halt to the vandalism.

Then Fr Murphy was amongst them, opprobrium lashing from his tongue just as violence lashed from his fists. He shoved and pushed and kicked the individuals in each of the destructive little mobs until he had herded them into the middle of the street. Then in his great voice he excoriated them as they stood amidst the jetsam of the homes they had destroyed.

'How dare you?' he railed. 'How dare you take it upon yourselves to commit so gross and cowardly an act in the face of the hospitality we have been shown thus far?

'How many,' he continued, 'how many of you who have made such disgraces of yourselves this morning were at Oulart Hill? How many of you fought and bled when the soldiers came?'

Neither voice nor hand was raised in answer to him.

'Not one of ye!' bellowed the priest. 'And yet you think it fit to loot and despoil, to break and burn? I see some of you now looking down at your shoe buckles with shame, and well you might. By God Himself, if you think that all that lies in front of you between here and Ireland's liberty is robbery and pillage, then you are mistaken. Let any man who puts plunder and greed, who puts the grossest sins above our cause, quit the ranks now, for such a man is not wanted.'

The gathered crowd watched him with bovine stupidity. One of them, anonymous behind a wall of his fellows, began saying, 'But Father, they're all Orangemen around here . . . '

Fr Murphy cut him short with words as sharp as cavalry sabres, 'If they were demons from the very pit of hell, I would not care tuppence. No good Wexfordman shall stoop to such petty acts as destroying a man's property without trial or recourse to law.'

He flung his gaze about then, taking in as many of the assembled throng as he could, 'Get every man back to his company. We march on Enniscorthy this very instant. We will see how brave you are then, me buckos, when there's real fighting to be done.'

Tom was shaking his head. 'This is insanity of the most dangerous kind,' he whispered for the umpteenth time.

The long column of insurgents had marched all morning and had reached Scarawalsh Bridge just before one o'clock in the afternoon. The bridge lay three or four miles outside of Enniscorthy and it flung its dove-grey stone across the rushing Slaney in a tight series of narrow arches, so that the span itself was slightly humpbacked, unlike the flat length of the bridge at Wexford Town. From atop its stone parapet a person might lean over and view the churning water as it swept past the great wet feet of the arches. River weed flexed and tossed in the boiling water of the Slaney like emerald banners in a gale.

Just after Scarawalsh Bridge, instead of making directly for the garrison town itself, the rebel army had swung right and followed its two contrasting banners into the maze of narrow roads and thick ditches lying to the northwest of Enniscorthy. Very soon Dan and Tom, unfamiliar with this part of the county, found themselves befuddled by the warren of laneways around Monart and Marshalstown.

The afternoon was blazing and Dan's shirt clung to him with a wet, tenacious grasp. Many of the men around him had plucked leaves from the hedgerows and were holding them in their mouths to protect their lower lips from sunburn. In the sweltering heat, the column had become drawn out and straggling, men stopping to take a drink from whatever bottles and containers they carried. Women hurried to mop their husbands' brows and children dragged the heavy pikes of men who were on the verge of exhaustion.

Dan knew that this detour into the wild country west of Enniscorthy was Edward Roche's idea. He had observed 'the general' and the leaders in a huddled group just as they crossed at Scarawalsh and he had seen Roche point, insistently, to the west rather than the south.

The reason for his obstinacy was a mystery to Dan but, after the visceral and harrowing scenes on Oulart Hill, he trusted the heavy-set United Irishman implicitly.

'Insanity,' grumbled Tom once more.

'You have made your feelings clear on more than one occasion, Tom,' panted Dan as they walked.

'I cannot express them long or loudly enough,' retorted Tom. 'How in blazes do Roche and the good padre expect us to advance on a well-defended town? There'll be a few more North Corks there along with Cornock's infantry from Ferns, the Enniscorthy Yeoman Cavalry under that preening jay Solomon Richards and the Enniscorthy Infantry under Pounden. Able officers, brother, able officers who have surely gotten wind by now of our approach. Every redcoat will have a musket, Dan, and all will know how to use them.'

Dan puffed out his cheeks and expelled a long sigh into the air, 'We have the advantage in numbers and in spirit, Tom. Our cause will carry the day.'

Tom threw his arms skyward in a final expression of exasperation, 'The world's gone mad and you along with it.'

At length the rebel column struggled to the top of Ballyorril Hill, only four miles northwest of Enniscorthy. There they halted and the commanders gathered in conclave. There were no half-measures taken here as there had been at Ferns. Roche and Murphy immediately set up a series of pickets in the surrounding fields and roadways and a young lad, no more than ten, was sent scooting up a tall beech tree where he perched, keeping watch like a sailor in a crow's nest.

The fighting men and their families spread out in the fields that lay all about, verdant and glowing, sheeting the hill's blunt crown in deepest green. Sounds of conversation and laughter began to chatter forth from the sprawling camp but there was a fissured quality to the mirth-making. Strain and worry strangled all talk within minutes of its birth and laughter was made cracked and incongruous by the permeating tension. Everywhere that men and women tried to force themselves into merriment, their efforts collapsed under the weight of foreboding.

Enniscorthy sat in the distance like a weight on the landscape, Vinegar Hill louring over all.

The leadership circle had sat themselves down in a paddock just beside the road and Roche was using stones plucked from the ground as a person might use chess pieces. Each stone still maintained a scabrous crust of earth and he carefully cleaned each one before placing it on the grey woollen blanket he had laid out before him. Sparks, Fr Murphy and the others were listening to him in rapt attention as he moved the stones in quick straight lines and whispered urgently, jabbing his index finger first here and then there.

Dan and Tom leaned on the gate leading into this field and watched the leaders converse.

'Playing at soldiers,' muttered Tom derisively.

Dan flung his brother a withering look but any words that he might have thought to say were robbed from him by the animated rustling of the beech tree's upper branches. The feathered leaves and hoary twigs parted as the young look-out's hands pushed them urgently aside. The boy's round face was framed in glossy bottle-green as his mouth opened wide and he called out, 'Good sirs, there's people coming! Not soldiers either but people like us. They're coming up from the bridge.'

Immediately the camp became a maelstrom of activity, shouts rang out of 'Blackwater men, to me!' and 'Shelmaliers to your colours!', and everything was a whirlwind of action and reaction.

Within a few minutes the rebel army was drawn up along the roads and in the fields. Roche, Fr Murphy and the other commanders were sitting their horses and gazing northward, down the hill. Up the slope a sentry came jogging, his entire face a sun-bright grin.

Gasping, he halted before Fr Murphy and gave an awkward salute. Fr Murphy smiled at the man as a ripple of embarrassed laughter crept out of the ranks. Undaunted, the man faced his superiors and reported, 'There's another column of United men on the way here, your honours. They are much fewer in number than what we are. Not all of them look fighting fit either, it's likely they've had an oul' set-to with the redcoats. There's a good few women and children with them as well.'

Fr Murphy turned to Roche and raised a quizzical eyebrow. Roche merely nodded in satisfaction.

'This was arranged,' muttered Dan to Tom. 'Roche and the other United leaders had this hill marked as a rallying point.'

'So it seems,' agreed Tom. 'Although I'd like to know where they come from, surely there can't be so many eager to rally to the United banner?'

Both brothers watched the road as, in the distance but growing gradually louder, an undercurrent of noise began to make itself heard, the drone of voices in conversation and the sudden, spiking explosion of shouts, came flowing between the ditches. Concurrently with this growing tumult a plume of dust rose above the hedgerows and crawled slowly closer across the sky.

The first of the newcomers then appeared in the roadway. He was a large man, sitting with an air of supreme confidence astride a light grey mare. He wore the dark blues and browns of a merchant but his face bulged with all the ruddy good-health of a lord. Beneath the folds of his chin his broad chest was thrown forward and his eyes, set deep into damp hollows, twinkled with abrasive good spirits.

The same could not be said of the tattered group this fine figure led. The ragged column huddled behind their mounted leader like a pack of starving curs. They were all badly armed, with scythes and pitchforks instead of pikes and muskets and a good many of them had red-splashed bandages binding their skulls or shoulders. Men, women and children shambled forward together, supporting each other as the sun spilled down upon them.

Tom pointed to the bloodied bandages wrapped about the heads of the foremost of the new arrivals. 'Those appear most likely to be wounds made by cavalry,' he stated. 'Sabre strokes down onto head and shoulders make marks like that. I would be of the dismal opinion that these people have been through a vision of hell.'

Only half-listening to him, Dan was regarding the proud mounted figure with intense curiosity. 'I know that man,' he was murmuring, as if to himself.

Then, suddenly, he clicked his fingers, 'That man on horseback is Fr Michael Murphy of Ballycanew. He was pilloried and suspended by Bishop Caulfield for his association with the United Irishmen.'

'Another priest?' asked Tom good-humouredly. 'I am starting to think that your United Irishmen is a Popish plot after all.'

'I am glad to see such a committed United Irishman here, with us,' said Dan.

'I am glad of a thousand more men,' replied Tom. 'If we had some cannon or trained horse, I should be even more glad.'

The two rebel bands were mingling, now. Men and women were helping to tend the wounded whilst some of Fr Michael's flock had collapsed onto the ground, limp with relief and exhaustion.

Dan and Tom were casting around for some way to lend a hand when a voice, shrill and on the verge of hysteria, called out, 'Daniel? Daniel Banville?'

Dan swivelled towards the voice and it was as though all the angles of his face, all the muscles that gave him form and poise were turned to butter. Tom watched as his brother crumbled into himself, turning on his heel and almost dissolving at the same time.

From out of the filthy horde of women and children, a slight, young lady in soiled white linen was coming towards them. A battered straw sun-bonnet sat awry on her mahogany curls, its brim tattered and its dried flowers reduced to shreds.

Tom jolted as Dan breathed one word with the reverence of a prayer, 'Elizabeth.'

Tom pinched the bridge of his nose between the grubby pads of his thumb and index fingers and watched as Dan and Elizabeth flung frantic arms about each other, holding tight, bunching fingers ploughing into fabric of shirt and dress. He watched as their heads lifted and then met, mouths questing, lips yearning for the other's touch.

Tom shook his head despairingly as Dan and Elizabeth kissed long and lingering as, all about them, the flotsam of war huddled in bloodied clumps of humanity.

In the midst of chaos, Dan whispered, 'I love you, Elizabeth.'

The couple were pulling apart now and Dan was appraising Elizabeth with eyes verging on tears. His gaze took in her filthy dress and ruined hat, her disordered curls and her face, pale and worn with fear, her eyes banded by swollen rings of red flesh. She had been weeping. To Dan's mind, she had been weeping a lot.

Dan lightly gripped her shoulders and asked her softly, 'What brought you here, Elizabeth? Why aren't you in Carnew?'

Elizabeth lifted one elegant hand and wiped away fresh tears as they leaked from between her lashes. With the other she punched Dan in the chest with all the force she could muster.

He looked at her, shocked, as she addressed him angrily, '*You* have brought me here, you big oaf. You and your half-truths and recalcitrance.'

She was openly crying now, her tears slicing channels in the grime and dust that powdered her cheeks, 'When the Rising broke out I knew you would be involved. I knew that was why you were being so cruel with me. I went to Kilthomas Hill where a great many peasants and that priest who leads them were encamped. I have never seen so motley a crew, Daniel, and I was so frightened but I thought you would be there. I thought you would try and come to me.'

She wiped the back of her hand across her nose and batted away Dan's offered handkerchief before continuing, 'As I looked for you among the fires and cooking pots a great cry went up that the yeomen were coming. And they did come, Daniel, the Carnew Yeomanry under Captain Wainwright. They put the rebels to flight with musketry and then ran them down with their horses. I was caught up with them and was forced to flee with the rest of the camp followers.

'I have never seen such butchery, Daniel. Scores of people were hacked down. Women and children were trampled under horses' hooves.'

She pressed her face against his chest and her muffled voice came again, 'I was terrified, Daniel. The poor people. The poor people.'

Tom coughed politely and as she looked up at him asked, 'Why didn't you make your way back to Carnew?'

Dan frowned at his brother before saying, 'This rude fellow, Elizabeth, is my little brother Tom. I am sure he is pleased to make your acquaintance.'

Elizabeth stepped away from Dan and, sniffing back the last of her tears, she smoothed the bodice of her dress before offering Tom her hand. 'How do you do?' she said, 'I am Elizabeth Blakely.'

Tom, vaguely embarrassed by his lack of manners, took her hand and shook it once, mumbling, 'Tom Banville, pleased to make your acquaintance.'

Dan, his eyes still flicking reproachful looks toward Tom, then said, 'Tom is right though, Elizabeth. Why didn't you get away back to you father's?'

Elizabeth looked genuinely stricken at this. Her hands splayed wide and her eyes flung to the heavens, she fumed, 'I could not! How could I slink off home when I knew you would be out there somewhere, maybe lying in a ditch with no one to aid you? The yeomanry had the countryside all ablaze and were shooting anyone they found in the fields.' She paused then, her eyes dropping to the ground, 'For the women they found, shooting would have been a better fate. So I came south hoping that I might find you or at least somebody sympathetic to me or who was acquainted with my father, but the country is emptied. Houses and cabins are all in flames and loyal Protestants have seemingly vanished from the face of the earth.

'Oh Daniel,' she concluded, 'I thought you had been killed.'

The lovers stared into each other's eyes for a moment before Tom's voice intruded upon them. 'He might very well have been killed had we ended up on Kilthomas and not Oulart Hill,' he snapped.

'The United Irishmen have been lucky in the field once so far,' Tom continued. 'The other engagement was obviously a disaster. I feel we should reconsider our whole involvement in this, Dan. We should take Elizabeth and make for Waterford port and thence to France or even England where we are not known and where we might forge a life for ourselves.'

'What are you talking about?' asked Dan, incredulous. 'You heard Elizabeth. The country is open before us. We have seen no soldiers or yeos all day. A single defeat is nothing to warrant us abandoning the cause.'

Tom moved close to the couple so that he was standing almost in the compass of their encircling arms. In such close proximity to them that he could smell the sour scents of sweat and grime over the last lingering sweetness of Elizabeth's perfume, Tom whispered savagely, 'Your cause is not my cause, brother. I am here because of you and because I chose my family above loyalty to the Crown. The dream of old Ireland free can remain just that as long as you and I keep our lives, since our land and property is now defiled. I accept that we are rebels, Dan, but I would like to die an old rebel in my bed at the age of eighty, surrounded by grandchildren, than be shot in a ditch surrounded by fantasies and pipe-dreams.

'I am not the only man here whose vision of what we do differs from yours, Dan,' he continued. 'You saw what happened in Ferns. You saw the burned homes of ordinary Protestants. Not landlords, not yeomen but ordinary Protestant labourers. Homeless and wretched because of mindless hate. You are a noble man, Dan and as God is my witness I wish I were as righteous as you, but I am not and neither are a good many of those gathered about.'

As Dan blinked at him in wordless angst, Tom addressed Elizabeth, 'Have you revealed to anyone that you are a Protestant, Ms Blakely?'

Taken aback, her hand rising protectively to her throat, Elizabeth shook her head, her red-brown curls bouncing about her shoulders, 'No I have not. I deemed it a rather indelicate subject to broach.'

Tom nodded grimly, 'Then, madam, you have more sense than this big eejit here beside us. Your lack of judgement in matters of the heart is not mirrored by a similar blindness when it comes to matters of the head.'

Dan regarded his brother with an air of grave acceptance. Unconsciously, he clasped Elizabeth more tightly to himself and said in a low voice, barely audible even to Tom, 'I could not countenance anyone bringing harm to Elizabeth. I should spill the blood of every man in this army before I should allow that to happen.'

Tom smiled at his brother, his hand coming up to rest fondly on Dan's shoulder.

'The awful thing about that prospect is that I would be forced to stand with you. And so instead of this foolishness ending your life alone it would have the effect of dragging me down to hell with you. So, I propose that Ms Blakely refrains from mentioning the very word "religion" until we are safe.'

Elizabeth looked at him with wide, sad eyes and nodded emphatically, 'I shall remain merely a good Christian until this bloody mess is decided once and for all.'

Tom was about to add something more when the brazen wail of a bugle winged its way into the summer sky. Harsh and screaming it brayed forth and died away before lifting again in banshee reprise. Close on the heels of the last fading brassy notes a group of men marched into the camp, a sentry scurrying ahead of them, every now and then tossing his beaver hat aloft and catching it in celebration.

The group of men were all well-armed and marched in good order, their step rhythmical as clockwork and their pikes slanted steeply against their shoulders. At their head rode a young man of mature bearing, his gentleman's frock coat open in the heat and two walnut-handled pistols holstered at his belt, a long sword swung low at his left thigh and every line of his youthful carriage communicated an air of unshakable self-assurance. A green sash, reminiscent of the red one worn by infantry officers, was knotted at his hip.

'Mr Byrne!' called Dan as soon as this splendid figure rode within earshot.

Miles Byrne looked up, blinked in recognition and then swung down from his mount. He strode up to Dan's little group with a wide grin lending his features a boyish aspect despite his military bearing and the weapons festooning his body.

'Daniel Banville,' he greeted, 'I am delighted to see you here. With Perry's arrest and the organisation in the north of the county thrown into such turmoil, I was afraid that you had fled to Dublin.'

'No such luck,' answered Dan, smiling. 'Besides, it would have been a tragedy to miss such a ball as this.'

Still grinning, Byrne turned with his precocious confidence and introduced himself first to Elizabeth and then to Tom.

'Elizabeth Blakely. How do you do?' said Elizabeth demurely.

At the mention of her last name, Byrne's brow wrinkled slightly, as though it should mean something to him.

However, as Tom introduced himself, Byrne's visage curdled into an open scowl and he shook the younger Banville's hand only once, as if it were the breeding ground for some vile, contagious disease. Standing in pregnant silence, the two young men faced each other before Byrne said softly, 'Tom Banville of the Castletown yeos, I presume.'

'Formerly of the Castletown Corps of Yeoman Cavalry, yes, I am he,' Tom replied.

'What brings you onto the side of the people?' the young rebel captain asked.

'I am on the side of my brother, Mr Byrne. It is because of him that I find myself numbered among the ranks of the United Irishmen. Because of him I pulled trigger against the North Corks on Oulart Hill.'

Byrne nodded warily before saying slowly, 'I regret not being on Oulart Hill to see those Cork butchers dispersed with such gallantry. I also regret that you had not joined with us before that date, for men of you and your brother's esteem might have swung the tide on Kilthomas Hill and saved a host of poor wretches from the flashing steel of the Carnew Cavalry.'

Tom eyed Byrne thoughtfully, contemplating whether the olive branch that the Monaseed youth had offered him was worth accepting. At length he smiled grimly. 'More like I would have been arrested, and myself and Dan here would be swinging from that Cork blackguard Tom the Devil's walking gallows before the dust of our struggles had settled,' he said.

'The good Sergeant Tom is still spreading terror around Gorey, last I heard,' said Byrne. 'I believe he is orchestrating the torture of United prisoners.' His voice dropped then and a guttural fury bubbled up from his chest, 'A good many of my fondest fellows have run afoul of the North Cork's inducements. I have not seen them since.'

Dan then asked, 'Were you at Kilthomas yourself, Mr Byrne?'

Byrne shook his head, 'Please, call me Miles, Mr Banville. To answer your question, no, I was not. I was gathering men to me around Monaseed at the time that the redcoats marched out from Carnew. Fr Michael Murphy was in charge on the hill, I believe. He is one of the finest and most active gentlemen in the country but is inclined to bluster and, for all his energy, I doubt he has ever given any real thought to leading armed men in the field.'

Dan was nodding in agreement, 'At Oulart, we had Edward Roche and Morgan Byrne, both military men, as well as that priest from Boolavogue, Fr John Murphy. He has shown himself to be a most capable leader and the people hold him high in their affections.'

'I had heard that,' said Byrne. 'Perry's "fat prevaricator" has come down on the right side after all. Good for him.'

He then turned and gestured to where his men were mingling with the other corps of rebels on the broad sward of the hill top and said, 'I will talk to you later, Mr Banville. I must go and see to my men.' With that he turned on his heel and led his horse off through the throng, accepting acclaim and scattered cheers as he walked.

'Dashing, isn't he?' commented Elizabeth.

Dan threw her a look as Tom erupted in laughter.

The rebel army struck camp at around two o'clock in the afternoon and marched, corps by corps, down onto the road slashing through the countryside from Enniscorthy to Bunclody. They marched silently now, each man cocooned within the muffling threads of his own contemplations, each one considering the terrible prospect of the battle to come. The ranks had been further strengthened by a contingent of United men who had come down from Kiltealy, led by another priest, the boisterous – and suspended – Fr Mogue Kearns. The Kiltealy men were all born and reared under the stone-stubbled slopes of Mount Leinster and all were hardy and fiercely determined, their leather faces dour in the sunlight. The rebel column now numbered perhaps five thousand fighting men and, coupled with the cattle train and the long huddled multitude of camp followers, it stretched a mile long from steel-edged tip to shawled and anxious tail.

At its head rode Roche, Sparks, Frs John and Michael and Mogue Kearns. Ranging out in front with his Monaseed men, Miles Byrne could be seen flitting from field to field, crossing and re-crossing the hard earth of the road, providing a vedette for the main mass of pikemen.

In front too, carried high against the blue sky, the two banners, one green and one black, fluttered in a rising breeze.

As Dan marched he knew that behind him, somewhere amidst the horde of women and children, his beautiful Elizabeth would be walking too, her sun-bonnet awry and her eyes fixed, resolute, on the road ahead.

CHAPTER 10

Enniscorthy's in Flames

Captain William Snowe of the North Cork Militia stood in the dust and noise of Enniscorthy's market square and watched his men throw barricades across the five narrow streets that connected it to the main sprawl of the town. Red coats and bicorns discarded, the soldiers laboured with the frantic tenacity of men who knew that their lives depended on their labours. Sergeants and officers bellowed and cursed, ham fists shaking as men, slick-skinned with perspiration, let slip barrels or the traces of carts, delaying the fortification by vital moments.

Enniscorthy Town straddled the River Slaney in a picturesque series of terraces. Thatched cabins and slated roofs climbed the slopes of the river valley, crawling up and away from the river and the six arches of its stone bridge, each roof over-topping the next, stepped ever higher up the defile. The main bulk of the town sat snugly in the steep gorge that the Slaney ploughed for itself beneath the frowning edifice of Vinegar Hill, which sat like a slumbering titan just to the east of the town's most outlying suburb.

Houses of this suburb, like the ones extending north beyond Irish Street, were doleful little tumbledown affairs, often windowless and their thatch mildewed and sagging. In the middle of the town, just off the market square, the iron-grey towers of Enniscorthy Castle bludgeoned the heavens with the gap-toothed thrust of its towers. To the northwest, the town mounted the ever-steepening gradient until the ground, with surprising suddenness, levelled off. It was here that the remains of an ancient barbican, the Duffry Gate, slumped in shattered disorder, a morbid reminder of bygone days.

It was through the Duffry Gate that the sentry, now sitting his winded mount before Captain Snowe, had galloped moments before.

Snowe returned his gaze to the mounted yeoman before him.

'Could you please repeat that, Private?' he asked.

The yeoman, breathless himself, huffed, 'Sir, there's a large force of rebels bearing down on the Duffry Gate from the north. They have all the appearance of attacking the town, sir.'

'Where are Captains Pounden and Cornock?' asked Snowe.

'Captain Pounden has drawn up the Enniscorthy Infantry in front of the Duffry Gate, sir, with the Scarawalsh Infantry in reserve. They mean to make a fight of it, sir.'

Snowe nodded in satisfaction, 'That is good to hear. With Richards's hundred horse we should have two hundred regular troops at the gate to chastise these croppies and expose them as the rabble they are.'

The North Cork captain cast his vision around the square. Here, brick market houses gazed down onto the hard-packed clay, their windows reflecting the sunlight and stabbing brilliant slivers of gold to sear the eyeballs.

'Lieutenant Cusack!' called Snowe, and a red-coated North Cork officer turned from where he was directing soldiers to man the barricades.

The lieutenant saluted. 'Sir?'

Snowe pointed to the windows overlooking the square. 'Have as many sharpshooters as you can find placed at the windows of the market houses. If you cannot spare the men then press as many loyal civilians as you can quickly find. Battle is upon us, so be quick about it.'

The officer saluted and dashed off, rounding up men as he went.

Snowe once more addressed the sentry, 'Have the officers at the Duffry Gate know that they must drive back these rebels with as sanguinary an effort as possible. The niceties of war are not to be applied to traitors and renegades. Have them know that myself and seventy of my North Corks will hold the bridge as a reserve or in case of retreat to Wexford. Have them know that this last contingency is one too awful to contemplate and that retreat in the face of farmers and mischief-makers is something that shall not be tolerated.'

The sentry saluted, sawed his horse about in a whickering wheel of horse flesh and was gone, pounding up the main street toward the Duffry Gate. Captain Snowe watched him go before making his way downhill to the bridge, barking orders as he went.

Captain John Pounden listened as the sentry related Captain Snowe's orders, then grunted and turned to his brother, Joshua, a lieutenant in his elder sibling's corps.

'What do you make of this?' he asked.

Joshua Pounden's eyes were shaded by the sharp beak of his cocked hat but even in the gloom John could see the anxiety scuttling within them. 'I would surmise,' he said at last, 'that Captain Snowe has enough faith in the yeoman infantry and cavalry that he does not see the necessity to reinforce us here. We have upwards of two hundred men and horse, John. We should disperse this rebel band like seeds in the wind.'

Captain Pounden watched as his vedettes came running down the road, the mounted cavalry pickets thundering ahead and merging with the rest of the horses, waiting just behind the infantry. His own foot troops came after in small bands, a sergeant saluting as he passed and saying, 'They are very numerous, sir.'

In the distance to the north, a brown haze began to rise into the afternoon air, shimmering as though a mirage or a vision from some terrible dream. The two Poundens and their assembled troops watched it grow darker and more menacing as it approached. A cold feeling of dread began to weigh heavily on the infantry men. For many of them, house burnings and the apprehension of suspected United Irishmen had been the limit of their experience of battle. The tale of what had occurred the previous day at Oulart Hill had trickled into town over the course of the night like the vile seepage of an infected wound. With each ear the story had grown so that the rebels had become monsters in the minds of the soldiers. Staunch loyalists all, they watched the dust cloud approach with a sense of coming apocalypse.

Perceiving his men's distress, Captain Pounden walked down the ranks, saying, 'Steady boys, steady. God is with us and with his guidance we shall exterminate the rabble to the very last man. Be steady is all. Steady.'

Lieutenant Joshua Pounden, his brow a swamp of moisture, raised one gloved hand to his face and dragged his fingers down his cheeks and along his jaw. He stood, deaf to his brother's words, merely watching as the dust cloud drew ever closer and felt his stomach heave and the cold hand of fear claw at his rib cage. In the distance, but growing louder, he thought he could hear the subterranean thunder of marching feet – thousands of them.

In sight of the Duffry Gate, Fr John and Edward Roche called a halt to the rebel column's march. In front of them, arrayed before the decrepit remains of the gate itself, the ranks of the Enniscorthy Yeoman Infantry stood in a bristling line of steel and scarlet. Behind them, over the bicorns of the infantry, the gentlemen of the yeoman cavalry could be seen sitting their foxhunters, serene as judges at a fair. The heavy ditches on either side of the road seemed to trammel all vision so that every insurgent gaze was directed in ever-narrowing perspective toward the redcoat line.

The rebel leaders conferred for a moment before Fr John ordered that the first corps of gunsmen, amongst them those who had been on Oulart Hill the day before and who were coming to think of themselves as veterans, to form up on the road ahead. With a great rattling of pikestaffs, and with prayers droning up from the ranks in a soft, bass murmur, the detachment of two hundred musketeers moved forward between their comrades, weapons held ready in both hands and eyes glinting in febrile anticipation. Amidst them, Tom and Dan, with pilfered North Cork muskets in their hands, breathed heavily and looked straight ahead to where the red line of the soldiers laid waiting.

To either side of this frightening block of weaponry, Edward Roche had instructed two corps of pikemen to assemble and guard the flanks against cavalry charges. These men held themselves low to the ground, those bloodied from the action at Kilthomas eager for revenge.

Then, as Pounden and his officers looked on, the rebel army began apparently to fall asunder. One group of close to a thousand split off from the main bulk and disappeared through the steeply sloping fields, making, it seemed, for the river or the hovels of Irish Street. A second contingent, more numerous than the first, swept away to Pounden's left. The main body of rebels, cattle train in tow, however, remained firmly on the road facing the Duffry Gate, its bulk a roiling mass of gunmetal and the lacerating heads of pike and hayfork, sword and slash hook.

'They're trying to outflank us,' Captain Pounden said, bewilderment lacing his voice.

'Nonsense,' dismissed Joshua Pounden. 'You give them too much credit. They are either off to find something to loot or are quitting the field.'

Dan and Tom looked on as the soldiers ignored the movements of the two smaller rebel divisions. 'That's a piece of luck,' muttered Tom.

Dan turned to watch Thomas Sinnott, a sixty year old cousin of William's, lead his detachment through the blossoming fields and ditches leading down to the Slaney, and said, 'They'll need more than that.'

To their front, the Banville brothers suddenly became aware of movement in the red-coated ranks. A grumbled agitation filtered through the rebel lines like a breeze through drifting leaves. The yeoman infantry had moved forward into the open, wheel-scarred expanse of ground that lay in a rumpled triangle before the Duffry Gate. Generations of traffic, merchants from Dublin, farmers from Kiltealy and Marshalstown, all had converged at this point over the years so that, before the town, the hedgerows crumbled to dust and three roads funnelled into one. It was upon this tract of trampled earth that the yeomen had formed, perhaps a hundred yards in front of the old gate.

'Hold!' barked Roche as, behind him, the rebel troops began to move forward in response, eager to close the distance.

Dan grinned bloodlessly where he stood, tense, amidst the gunsmen. The prospect of the coming conflict was a cold barb inside of him. He watched the men around him strain with barely held enthusiasm, only anchored to their spot by Roche's harsh tone. His chest ballooned with pride that this moment had come, that his fellow countrymen had risen against the barbarous usurper and now stood keenly awaiting the word to advance. When the French come, he thought, we will sweep all before us, the green flag shall float from shore to shore.

Tom, meanwhile, watched the same men and experienced the same eagerness for the fray as his brother. Yet his thoughts were different. He glanced at the ragged figures around him as they rocked on their heels, every fibre of their beings screaming for permission to charge forward, to remove themselves from under the grim threat of massed musketry. He glanced at them and thought that they were right and sensible. To close the distance and bring the pikes to bear was much better than sitting in the open where musket and cavalry might tear them to shreds. If he were an untrained farm labourer, he would desire to be out of the way of musket balls with as much fervency as the men about him were demonstrating now.

'Hold,' Roche repeated. 'They wish us to advance without heed to the cavalry that they hold in reserve. If we move and become exposed, if we do not hold our discipline, the horses will ride us down. We hold and we wait. They will not intimidate us with their red coats and fools' hats.'

For long minutes the two sides faced each other across three hundred yards of earth and wavering heat. In the air, butterflies whirled and waltzed like torn lace in the breeze.

It was the soldiers who faltered first.

Solomon Richards, his red cavalry coat blazing in the afternoon sunshine, its gold braiding a scintillating splash across its front, moved his men beyond the lines of Pounden's infantry and drew them up in a broad front across the road. To a man, each cavalry trooper held his sabre in a gauntleted fist and each horse snorted and danced in the dust. Richards twisted the ends of his perfectly waxed moustache so that they curled like the blue-black wings of an insect, then raised his sword high above his head.

'Ready?' asked Dan

'As I am ever likely to be,' replied Tom.

The cavalry commenced a slow trot directly toward the rebel centre. The yeomen were unhurried, confident that the very sight of their horses and uniforms would be enough to make the insurgent rabble turn and flee in panic. When it was obvious that the herd of peasants was intent on standing its ground, at a word from Richards, the cavalry began to canter and then to gallop. Across the final hundred yards the cavalry thundered, the ground vibrating beneath the heavy hooves of a hundred snorting foxhunters. In their saddles the yeomen leaned forward, sabres outstretched, polished steel already questing for the soft flesh of neck or shoulder, the satisfying scrape of blade on bone.

For their part, the rebels stood, fear as much as duty keeping them in their ranks. If they ran now they would be hunted down and butchered like all those at Kilthomas, like the North Corks at Oulart, like so many innocent victims who had been chewed up and spat out by the conflict so far. They held their ground not through duty or loyalty but through chilling necessity.

Roche had dismounted and, accompanied by Fr John and Miles Byrne, had positioned himself to one side of the gunsmen. As the soldiers' horses ploughed ever closer, the burly former yeo called out, his voice belling above the terrifying hammering of the hooves, 'Hold, men of Wexford! Stand together!'

Then, as the horses came within half a musket shot, he roared, 'Now boys! Let them have it!'

From the rebel ranks a disordered, loose volley chattered into the air, spitting forth a hundred individual splashes of flame and smoke. The insurgents had never before fired in a single concentrated mass; they had never before been asked to let off a volley in the manner of a real army. For them there was no disciplined single discharge, no one explosion of lead and smoke along the whole of their line. Instead each man picked a target and fired in his own time. The impression was one of ragged amateurism. Without the single intimidating boom of a trained regiment firing as one, the rebel volley seemed almost pathetic, as each musket yapped in isolated defiance and the cavalry bore down in a tidal rush of muscle and steel.

Yet, in spite of the tattered nature of their firing, some musket balls found their mark. Men were flung from their saddles and horses reared screaming in agony, pitching their riders to the ground. In spite of their discipline, in spite of their uniforms and fine horses, yeomen were lying dead in the dirt. And still the insurgent gunsmen kept up their rattling spray of ball and fire. More yeomen slumped in their saddles or clung, desperately wounded, onto their mounts' necks.

After what seemed an age, the cavalry charge broke up, lost all momentum and, to the disbelief of rebel and soldier alike, stopped cold in its tracks. Solomon Richards, his face a gore-streaked mask where a ball had dug a furrow along one cheekbone, wheeled his men about and led them hurriedly back to the lines of infantry standing dumbfounded by the Duffry Gate. Here they regrouped and set themselves for another charge, striving terribly to ignore the jeers and whoops of the rebel column as its members celebrated their little victory, striving terribly to ignore the eight dead yeomen who lay sprawled and unmoving like clots of blood on the roadway.

Dan and Tom, in the midst of the mass of cheering rebels, breathed deeply and clapped each other on the back. The muskets in their hand were exhaling blue powder smoke from their bores, sending a thick stream into the brighter blue of the sky. All about them, their comrades' faces were made indistinct by the reeking pall that had vomited from the column's weapons. The stench of powder was thick in every breath and their ears still rang to the lethal percussion of their firing.

Edward Roche's voice came through the fog of smoke with all the clarity of a hunting horn.

'Look to the hedgerows!' He shouted. 'They are not beaten yet. Let us all push on and drive them into the town!'

At this, the rebel pikemen and musketeers leapt over or barged through the ditches to either side of the road, using them as a natural screen to prevent the cavalry charging again. As they drew closer to the infantry and the abruptly stymied cavalry, a Shelmalier man who had already managed to reload his long-barrelled strand gun took aim and blew one of Pounden's foot troops into oblivion.

At the Duffry Gate, Captain Pounden was arguing with Richards, 'What do you intend to do then? Sit here whilst they creep ever closer? You spend all year chasing foxes through heavier cover than that!'

The cavalry man was sitting his horse, stiff-backed and holding a handkerchief to his lacerated cheek. 'We cannot charge men armed with pikes and guns when they are massed behind a wall of briar, Captain Pounden. It would be tantamount to suicide,' retorted Richards.

Pounden was about to respond when the Shelmalier man's bullet took one of his sergeants square between the eyes, punching into his brains with the sound of a spade biting into wet soil. The Enniscorthy Infantry stood in line, resolute and unflinching, but Pounden noticed that a few of his men were calico pale and that their eyes could not be drawn away from the sergeant's corpse where it twitched grotesquely.

Pounden turned his back disdainfully on the battered cavalry corps and instead addressed his foot officers, 'Gentlemen, have the men form two ranks and prepare to defend the passage into the town.' Then he spoke to Richards once more, saying, 'You can at least tell Cornock to come up with the Scarawalsh and cover our right.'

Richards saluted sullenly and sent one of his men galloping down the hill into the town.

Dan and Tom meanwhile had advanced with a large group of gunsmen to within musket shot of the infantry. Dan's blood felt like ice in his veins as he raised his weapon and sighted along the barrel. This was the moment he had been waiting for all his life. As a boy, sitting at the fire listening to the old people tell stories of Cromwell's massacres and the influx of his lackeys to take the land, he had fancied himself at the head of a victorious army of green. Now, here he was, kneeling in a ditch choked with nettles, feeling their needles sting him through shirt and stockings, a stolen musket braced against his shoulder. It was not quite how he had imagined it, but at its most fundamental, its most visceral, this moment felt *right* to him.

Tom crouched just behind his brother, his face intense and his eyes ablaze. He watched the line of infantry move forward and form two ranks facing the steadily approaching rebels. He would not die in this ditch, he vowed, face-down in nettles and tangled in briars. What was more, he would not allow Dan to die here either.

The steady lines of infantry now commenced a musketry duel, with the rebels hiding in the hedgerows and lying in the ditches across the dry swathe of open ground before the Duffry Gate. Within minutes, men were falling on both sides and Isaac Cornock's detachment filed up the hill from the town and anchored Pounden's right, their withering musketry adding to the hail of blistering lead.

Tom and Dan found themselves under a concerted barrage of musket balls. Men in front and behind them gasped and fell or screamed in agony as bones broke and flesh was punctured. Dan, to his consternation, actually felt a bullet fizz past his nose like some hideous droning wasp. Tom gripped him by the shoulder, yelling above the sound of gunfire, 'We have to pull back from here. We can't advance across that killing ground when their position is so advantageous.'

Dan nodded, his face wan and drained, 'We may tell Fr Murphy or Roche. While the other detachments make their way around to the flanks we are being shot full of holes trying to get in the front door.'

Running in a low crouch, both brothers darted along the ditch and scrambled up into the road beside where Roche, Fr John and Byrne were huddled in conversation. About them was gathered a group of around ten or twelve pikemen, most of them Oulart men.

'Miles!' called Dan, unmindful of protocol or good manners. 'We must break through those lines quickly or else go around them. The soldiers are winning this duel.'

The leaders all regarded the two Banvilles with momentary surprise before Fr Murphy smiled roguishly. 'Have no fear, my son,' he said. 'The Lord provides for all things.'

With that he set off hurriedly into the mass of camp followers, closely followed by the group of pikemen.

'If he expects to find a park of artillery in the middle of all those women and children, he will be sorely disappointed,' grumbled Tom.

When Fr Murphy returned though, it was at the head of a much stranger sight than a row of cannon.

Tom stared on, astounded, whilst Dan felt a broad grin stretch his lips.

The women and children had parted as Fr Murphy strode through them and at his back, coaxed on by the small band of pikemen, thirty or forty of the youngest and wildest cattle lowed and bellowed in aggravation. When the priest drew level with the two Banvilles, he stepped to one side and let the pikemen goad their bovine charges forward along the road directly toward the lines of yeomanry. Bounded on both sides by thick hedgerows, the animals trotted in a great river of muscle and sinew as pikes prodded and slapped at them, urging them on.

Dan and Tom were regarding Fr Murphy with open and unabashed awe.

'How did you ever dream of such a thing?' Tom asked.

'I am a student of history, my son,' replied the priest. 'It constantly surprises me the uses to which it can be put.' He tapped his doming forehead with one index finger, 'No knowledge is ever wasted, lads.'

Along the road toward the Duffry Gate, the rebel gunsmen who had remained in the open had moved aside in bafflement at the approach of the herd of cattle. The drovers behind now jabbed at the poor beasts with genuine force, the steel of the pikes darting into rumps and haunches and trickles of blood matting the hair of the slowest animals. The cows and bullocks were now roaring in genuine anger and their forward momentum was gaining the force of a stampede.

In front of them, the terrified yeomanry were directing all their fire at the looming wave of heavy, horned heads that bobbed and weaved in their frenzy to escape the sharp tormenting of their herders. The shot merely served to rankle the beasts further and only increased their panic and fear. On the cattle came, now running at full tilt, their massive weight an avalanche smashing into the infantry lines.

Captain John Pounden rose from where he knelt, distraught and cradling the mortally wounded body of his younger brother Joshua, shot through the chest by a rebel musket ball. He stood and faced the onslaught of the stampede as though he meant to absorb all of its violence into himself. Over the wide backs of the cattle he could see a mass of pikemen pressing forward, ready to sweep his men from the face of the earth. Pounden felt his mouth go dry as the first of the lowing animals barrelled into his carefully arranged defensive line. The yeoman infantry scattered to let the beast through but immediately another slab of meat and fury hammered home, this time flinging a soldier aside with a toss of its massive head. Like a river of boulders the herd of cattle swept through the redcoats and in its wake came the steel-edged flood of the pikemen. Behind his men the yeoman cavalry had dispersed, floundering in terror. Pounden stood for a moment as his men were seized by the same dread alarm, scattered and helpless as the rebels closed on them, screaming garbled battle cries, eyes wide with bloodlust.

Drawing his pistol, Captain John Pounden of the Enniscorthy Yeoman Infantry stood and prepared to sell his life dearly.

From a few hundred yards away Dan and Tom Banville watched the cattle stampede crash into the yeoman line. They watched the infantry hold for a moment in the face of the pikemen's charge and then they watched the red-coated line collapse and break, the soldiers sprinting and tumbling down the hill as the wave of steel broke over them. As if the taking of the Duffry Gate had been some premeditated signal, the sound of fresh gunfire came crackling through the air and a cheer like a mounting gale carried over the thatched roofs on the western side of the town.

Dan nodded in satisfaction, 'The flanking parties have hit home.'

Tom, however, was uneasy. 'They are meeting with resistance by the sounds of it. I don't doubt that there are reserves of men and supplies down in the town. I only hope that they don't have cannon.'

Captain William Snowe of the North Corks sat his horse behind the bulwark of his men and surveyed the market square with an appalled air of wounded self-regard. If only he had cannon. He could not fathom how the rebels had driven in the defenders at the Duffry Gate and had, simultaneously, so easily outflanked the town. The stray cattle thundering through Enniscorthy's narrow streets might explain how the infantry were overrun but nothing yet presented itself to explain the sheer gall and effrontery being offered by the insurgents. They were fighting as though possessed and, although hopelessly out-gunned and dying in droves, they would not concede defeat.

When news of the collapse of the defences at the Duffry Gate reached Snowe on the bridge he immediately marched the North Corks up into the market square to provide both a reserve for the men posted there and a counter to the rebels that he expected to see flooding down the main street. What he was not prepared for was that the western approaches to the town had also been overrun. Vicious and desperate assaults were being launched by the rebels against the barricades on his left as the smell of burning and a thin haze of smoke began to drift up into the square from the junction with Irish Street.

In front of him a vast band of insurgents had indeed stormed through the Duffry Gate and were now the target of sustained and deadly fire from the sharpshooters positioned at various market house windows. Rebels fell and writhed in the gutter but still their comrades came on. Doors were smashed open and carts were upended and used as cover by the peasant musketeers as they attempted to return fire. As Snowe watched, a high, third-storey window set into the brick facade of a tall town house, coughed forth in a glittering spray of splintered glass. He looked on horrified as a red-coated soldier followed, his arms wind-milling and his despairing scream silenced as he crunched into the street below.

Snowe's lip curled as, from the vacant and jagged-edged hole that was the window, a pike shaft extended, a length of green fabric tied to it in the manner of a flag or banner.

All about him, pandemonium reigned. The incessant flare and boom of musketry was deafening and, mingled with the screams of the dying and the wails of civilians, it lent the entire scene a hellish quality. The stink of black powder and the stench of punctured innards was a grotesque blanket through which the acrid tang of burning thatch was laced. From the direction of

Irish Street the sound of firing coincided with the darkening of the smoke that now billowed in great rolling sheets across the square. The cavorting orange of towering flames licked above the roofs to his right. From the alley leading down to Irish Street a handful of yeomen stumbled, coughing, scattering like leaves in the wind.

Snowe regarded the scene for a moment with the cool detachment of a career military man. He saw the wooden barricade to his left erupt in a cloud of splinters as a rebel volley hammered into it. He saw nine of his own North Corks, positioned to bolster its defences, fall as the yeomanry began to retreat back into the square. He saw the Duffry United men spill like a wave towards him, each house being cleared of snipers by the gore-streaked efforts of the pike-men. To his right, Irish Street was an inferno, nothing could approach along it but neither would it afford an escape route.

Cursing under his breath, Snowe at last addressed the men formed up about him, 'Fall back to the bridge. Enniscorthy is lost but we must hold the crossing and the road to Wexford Town.'

Tom and Dan leaned panting against the doorframe of a slate-roofed town house. It had been this way for the past two hours, moving from building to building while musket balls thudded like lethal hail around them. Dan had no idea how many United Irishmen had died so far but he shuddered to consider the severity of the losses. William Sinnott, he was sure, had perished as he entered through the Duffry Gate, cut down by sniper fire. The building housing the hidden assassin had been broken into and the man had been killed on the spot by Sinnott's furious companions. The same had been the case as the rebel column advanced deeper into the town. Scattered groups of soldiers had stood and formed brief skirmish lines before being driven back as sharpshooters felled men to the left and right. And still the sun mounted the heavens, glorious and innocent, drenching both rebel and loyalist in sweltering heat.

The two brothers crouched with swords and pistols in hand as the massive bulk of a Kiltealy United man smashed into the door between them. The portal bounced on its hinges and flung open with a sound like tearing stitches. Immediately, Dan and Tom were through it and racing up the stairs within, ignoring the family that were huddled in the hallway, the father of the house holding a bible before him like a shield. The stairs creaked as they powered from step to step and as they gained the second floor they slowed and treaded more softly.

The stairs gave on to a short stretch of wooden landing leading to a red-lacquered doorway. Even on their side of the door the smell of gunpowder permeated the air. Glancing at each other, careful not to make the slightest sound so close to their quarry, Dan and Tom sidled up to the doorway.

Tom slipped his pistol back into its holster and, gentle as falling snow, he placed one hand on the door's brass handle.

The splintering crash of the musket ball as it punched through the wood not six inches from his head made Tom yelp and fling himself in abject shock against the wall behind him.

Dan moved then with grim and deadly purpose. He raised his foot and smashed it into the door's panelling just beside the handle. The door whipped away from him with such force that it rebounded and almost flattened Dan as he stormed into the room.

It was a child's nursery, the wallpaper soothing, and a painted white cot placed against one wall. In the other wall was set a window overlooking Enniscorthy's market square and beside it a yeoman was feverishly attempting to reload his musket. Against the window the man stood in silhouette and Dan could not discern what expression he wore but at the sight of Dan the yeo stilled. He became a carven effigy, ramrod held motionless in one hand whilst the other hand was petrified even as he clawed for his ammunition pouch. Smoke wreathed the room with the incense of the battlefield.

The yeo opened his mouth to say something, to offer defiance, to plead for his life.

Dan's pistol blew his teeth out the back of his head.

Tom approached from behind Dan, his step unsteady and his breath shaking as it sluiced between his gritted teeth. Both brothers looked down on the dead yeoman and, at last, Tom ventured, 'He could have killed me. Quick as a wink. Six inches to his left and my brains would surely have been blown out.'

Dan nudged the dead sharpshooter with the toe of one riding boot before saying, 'Our friend here would not have affected much of a change in your circumstance in that case.'

Tom was silent for a moment, the fact of his scrape with death dulling his wits, before Dan's words registered somewhere deep in his brain. He grinned at his elder brother, 'I fail to see how my near death is a matter for levity, dear brother.'

Dan clapped him on the shoulder, sighing, 'If you don't laugh, you cry.'

The two brothers made their way cautiously back down the stairs. The family who had clustered in the hallway were gone. Outside, the fierce fighting in the market square had been replaced by an unnerving quiet. The barricades had been stormed at last by the advancing rebels and the defenders had fled away into the choking veil of smoke that was slowly enveloping Enniscorthy. The entire northern approach to the town was burning furiously.

From out of the shrouding smoke, Miles Byrne strode imperiously, directing men with all the authority of a general.

'Make for Vinegar Hill!' he ordered. 'We are to get out of this smoke. The soldiers and the cowardly yeomen have fled! The town is ours!'

Dan and Tom exchanged startled glances as around them the corps of pike-men and musketeers sent up a howling cheer of jubilation. Through the swirling black blizzard of ash and cinders, Byrne spied Tom and Dan.

'Mr Banville!' he cried. 'You must see this. It is something I had never thought I'd witness even in my fondest imagining.' He beckoned to Dan with an urgency that prompted both Banvilles to break free of their celebrating comrades and approach the young captain with twin expressions of curiosity.

'What is it, Miles?' asked Dan as he drew closer to the Monaseed man, whose eyes were watering now and his breath caught in his throat with every inhalation. Around them, vague shadows in the burgeoning gloom, men were streaming out of the flaming carcass of the town and wending their way toward the dark mass of Vinegar Hill. Strewn across the square, unmoving smudges in the charcoal haze, the bodies of soldiers and rebels lay side by side in the cold intimacy of death.

'Hurry,' instructed Byrne and with that he turned and jogged off in the direction of the castle. Wordlessly, Dan and Tom followed in his wake. Enniscorthy Castle was perched on a rocky spur, dourly overlooking the Slaney. On the far bank of the river, the road to Wexford Town wound beneath the Turret Rocks, a looming limestone cliff crowned with a copse of cedar trees and streaked by centuries of oozing rainwater. The other Wexford Road, this one following the nearer bank of the river, looped about the castle's foot and lanced off into the countryside around St John's Wood and Edermine. It was at this vantage point, hard by the grim towers of the castle, that Byrne and the two Banvilles halted.

Silently and with deliberate haughtiness, Miles Byrne raised his right arm and pointed into the defile below. Floating puffs of smoke wafted across their vision as Dan and Tom stared in wonderment at the scene below them.

Along both sides of the river, long chains of carriages and handcarts made a rag-and-bone shop of the roadways. Families and the contents of houses were all piled high on flatbed wagons. Screaming children clung desperately to their mothers, who in turn clung like limpets onto their husbands. Lone figures on horseback threaded their way through the hurrying throng, lashing with their riding crops should an urchin or stray animal impede their path. All were vanishing southward toward Wexford Town with as much haste as they could muster. Thousands of loyalist refugees clogged the hinterland around Enniscorthy as they sought to flee the brutal vengeance of the rural poor.

Yet, as Dan's eyes took in the crowds gushing in exodus from the burning town, he could not help but notice the lack of red coats amongst those travelling the roads southward. 'What of the garrison?' he asked Byrne. 'Why do I see no sign of the North Corks or yeomanry amongst the populace?'

Byrne laughed contemptuously, his gaze still travelling out over the frantic refugees, imperious as Caesar. At length he explained, 'We had the yeos and militia beaten in the town and Captain Snowe had positioned himself quite advantageously on the bridge, hoping to secure the crossing point and keep the way to Wexford Town out of the people's hands.'

He smiled then and pointed to the left, where, beyond the ponderous bulk of the castle, the River Slaney flowed down from Scarawalsh. 'Thomas Sinnott and his boys crossed the Slaney upstream from the town,' he continued, 'and they gained the far bank. They had fought as far as Lett's distillery before Snowe realised he was in danger of being surrounded and annihilated. When he did, he decided to beat a hasty retreat to Wexford Town. He left before most of those poor wretches down there knew that the battle was over.'

He laughed again, a harsh sound to come from one so young, like the soulless clanging of a smithy, and said, 'I have never seen such an inglorious departure. His men turned their coats inside out and flung away their weapons. His officers tore off their epaulettes for fear of retribution. Every man jack of them should be ashamed of himself.'

Dan was smiling too now, basking in the glow of a hard-fought victory. Tom, however, was squinting through scalding eyes towards the gnarled, humped back of Vinegar Hill, where companies of insurgents could already be seen reforming after the bloody mayhem of the urban fighting. On the crest of the hill the broken stump of a ruined windmill was ragged and dark against the blue sky. Onto the highest point of this old relic a rebel hand had fixed a huge green bough which danced in the breeze, its leaves ruffling and trembling.

'Roche and the others want to us to make for that?' Tom asked.

'The town is in a state of utter devastation,' answered Byrne. 'The smoke alone is choking. The hill will also provide us with a good vantage point to watch for the approach of any body of men sent against us and, furthermore, I think Roche and Murphy are correct to get our men away from any temptation to exact senseless revenge on the poor people left in their homes.'

Tom was nodding in grudging agreement but still felt the need to say, 'If we were not so fatigued, and if the men were not so bent on looting and personal grievances, we should have mounted a pursuit of those Cork blackguards and swept them into the Slaney.'

Byrne regarded Tom with something akin to respect and responded, 'I urged the leaders to consider that very course of action but the men are utterly exhausted from the long march and the bitter struggle, they cannot do much more than recuperate and refresh themselves.'

Tom scrubbed one hand across his stubbled jaw and sighed earnestly, 'I could do with some refreshment, myself.'

An hour later and on the western slope of Vinegar Hill Tom, Dan and Elizabeth sat about a little cooking fire and watched the town of Enniscorthy burn. Some of the park of cattle had been slaughtered and meat was being handed out as quickly as possible to the rebel army now blanketing the hill's slopes and seething across its crest. Tom had managed to borrow a tin pot from the well-provisioned Monaseed men under Miles Byrne and, in no time at all, had a lump of beef stewing over the fire. So now they sat in the middle of a victorious army, listening as songs were sung about them and watching the smoke drift and curl down in the valley.

Here and there throughout the town, moving with the brazen confidence of bestial yahoos, gangs of opportunists roamed, jars of whiskey and jugs of porter slopping from their fists. Dan refused to think of them as United Irishmen for the mobs seemed bent on only one thing. Through the shifting smoke these packs of men and women scoured the town, searching for any remaining loyalists. When they came across these individuals they hauled them, struggling, into the street and piked or bludgeoned them in front of their families, oblivious to the pleas for mercy, inured to the crying of children. Even the dead were not safe from their outrages, for as the little group on the hill looked on, the bodies of familiar local yeomen were hacked at and mutilated, skulls caved in and pockets rifled. The mobs were drunk and vicious and the sight of their savagery made Dan sick to his stomach.

'How are Roche and Murphy allowing this?' wondered Dan aloud.

Tom snorted, 'Because if they do anything about it, they will be forced to take responsibility for it. It is much better if they keep their heads down and pretend that those miscreants are simply evil-natured carrion crows taking advantage of a victory rather than elements of our own glorious little army.'

'It is most horrible,' breathed Elizabeth and she curled her arm tightly around Dan's bicep.

Instinctively, he drew her close to him and kissed her tenderly on the small horseshoe shimmer of her scar. 'It has nothing to do with the aims of the United Irishmen,' he whispered in reassurance.

Tom shook his head mournfully, stirred the beef with the point of a knife, and sighed. 'You are dealing with people, not ideas, Dan. Your United Irish creed may have set this course of action but it is people, with their petty jealousies and ignorant cruelty, who will carry it forward.'

'You're from Carnew, ain't ya?' the question came in a woman's voice, saw-edged and nasal, drawing each vowel out in the distinctive Wexford drawl.

Tom, Dan and Elizabeth whipped their heads about to see a large woman standing over them. Her face was a crimson, cumulous pillow of blubber and her arms, like bags of sausage meat, were folded across her bulging stomach. Her gimlet eyes stared at Elizabeth with glassy hostility.

'You are from Carnew, I seen ya there,' she insisted.

'My good woman,' replied Dan, 'We are from the Castletown district. My name is Daniel Banville, this is my brother Thomas and this is my wife, Elizabeth.'

At this, Elizabeth's eyes widened slightly and her breathing quickened and, yet, she somehow retained her composure as the woman glared at her with even greater intensity. The fluttering happiness that trilled within her breast at Dan's words caught her completely by surprise.

'Are you originally from Carnew, then?' the woman pressed. 'Have ya anyone belonging to ya up there because I'm sure I seen you at a fair all dressed up like a lady, with a yeo on your arm for company.'

Elizabeth shook her head and contrived to look as innocent as physically possible, 'No, I'm not from Carnew. I have cousins up there but I myself am rarely in the town.'

The vast woman was about to say more when Tom waspishly interrupted, 'Bloody hell woman,' he snapped. 'You're as bad the damned yeos yourself with all your questions.'

The woman bridled at his words, great ripples of indignation spreading out from the oceans of her cheeks and jowls, 'Good day to youse,' she said curtly and then barrelled off.

'Thank you,' Elizabeth said softly, reaching out to touch Tom's arm.

'And you thought I was being overly cautious,' he muttered.

Dan was watching the bulk of the woman as she stomped from campfire to campfire on the way down the hill. At every camp she bent to say a few words, her doming shoulders quivering with anger. Now and again she would dart a poisoned glance back up the hill to where the Banvilles and Elizabeth sat huddled together.

'That one is going to be trouble,' Dan growled at length.

'Accidents happen in battle,' Tom offered hopefully.

Elizabeth merely stared into the flames of the cooking fire, saying nothing but feeling a chill wave of trepidation coax every inch of her skin into one dimpled tract of gooseflesh. Dan looked at her curiously, protectively.

'I'm just cold,' she said.

CHAPTER 11

Considerations

As the 28th of May wore on into evening the sun began to sink into the welter of char-black smoke that bellied and roiled above the ruined skeleton of Enniscorthy Town. Above Enniscorthy the sun had become a bullet hole, haemorrhaging its light across emptied homes and gutted cottages, casting the hundreds of unclaimed bodies in a corrupt effulgence that only served to emphasise the horror of what had occurred. In the charnel house of the market square, a lone sow nosed at a dead North Cork militiaman, lapping at his congealing blood.

All through the afternoon rebel bands had flocked to the camp on Vinegar Hill. The pyre that Enniscorthy had become was a beacon that could be seen for miles around. The towering column of smoke rose like the wrath of God over the pastures of central Wexford and at its sight many men who had thought the rumours of a Rising and victory at Oulart to be merely the fanciful ramblings of gossip-mongers and troublemakers, now made their way to the slopes of Vinegar Hill. Captains of the United Irishmen in outlying parishes, who had been waiting for the word to rise, now assembled their corps and marched in groups of twenty and thirty to join the growing muster.

Around the county the military was flummoxed, beaten twice in two days by a rag-bag army of peasants and labourers. Yeomanry units hunkered down in areas they knew to be safe whilst elsewhere whole detachments of cavalry and infantry were in retreat to Wexford Town or Arklow. For a while, at least, the insurgent army above the blackened town commanded the entire central swathe of the county. It was untouchable, impervious and unassailable upon its rocky redoubt.

197

Dan, Elizabeth and Tom lay beneath two furze bushes that had grown together, entwining their thorny limbs like lovers. They had draped a woollen blanket over the entrance to their little den and now all three sat quite comfortably on a warm floor of dry, brown earth.

Through a gap in the branches, Dan watched the arrival of yet another rebel contingent. The men had come in from the wooded country to the west of Enniscorthy, out toward Killoughram and Caim and they marched with all the bearing of strutting peacocks, a hand-sewn banner, green with a yellow harp surrounded by wreath of shamrock, floated at their head. Each man was armed with a pike and a few had fowling pieces strapped across their backs, their white linen shirts were open in the heat and perspiration made cloud-grey fans beneath their arms and between their shoulder blades. Behind them, their hands bound, a gaggle of five or six prisoners stumbled in their wake. The prisoners, all men, panted as they struggled up the slope, blood oozing from split lips and broken noses, and bruises, like streaks of ash, stained their faces. A length of rope was noosed about each prisoner's neck and was held in the free hand of a marching rebel.

'They have brought more,' Dan said, troubled.

Tom was squinting over his brother's shoulder, using a gorse spike to prise a shred of beef from between his teeth and trying to gauge the numbers of men coming up the hill. 'That's another hundred, at least,' he decided. 'If there's not six thousand fighting men on this hill, I would be surprised.'

Dan nodded but his expression remained clouded, 'The ranks are swelling right enough but someone may do something about the raft of prisoners that are being brought in. Each company that rallies to us brings with them persons that they claim to be Orangemen. There's mischief at foot here. As low in my affections as I hold the magistrates and landlords I will admit that not all of them or their tithe collectors are bigots and monsters. It smacks of zealotry.'

'The yeomanry and magistrates have brought this down on themselves,' Tom interjected. 'If you had seen the manner in which the instruments of law and order went about their bloody business you would see from what well of bitterness those country men draw.'

Dan withdrew from his thorn-fringed window and eased himself down beside Elizabeth, wrapping her in his arms, before saying, 'Any man accused of harming the people should be tried then and reason should be provided for their detention. To do otherwise is simple brigandage.'

Still with his back to Dan, Tom said, 'Well, however you want to put it, that makes about thirty fine figures of the establishment now locked Beale's Barn down toward the town.'

'That many?' asked Elizabeth.

Tom turned and nodded. 'That many. I went down there after our dinner and they have them packed into the place and guarded by pikemen. A more miserable bunch of captives you could never hope to see. To a man they are blubbering and squealing like newborn pups.'

'I am sure I would as well should I be in their position,' said Elizabeth.

Dan smiled and kissed her on the forehead, 'That is precisely why you are to remain as my wife for the foreseeable future.'

Elizabeth smiled up at him and kissed him tenderly on the lips.

Tom rolled his eyes and went back to studying the slope below, his gaze taking in the long chains of men snaking in from the surrounding farmland. In his mind he was calculating numbers and capabilities, counting flintlocks, sturdy pikes and arms fit to wield both. His considerations turned to the lack of cavalry, the absence of artillery and the fact that when the counter-attack came six thousand could never be enough.

Night was falling and the three companions were cushioned in the swaddling arms of sleep when a huge guttural roar woke them. The two Banvilles were scrabbling for their weapons before the tenor of the noise fully penetrated the fog of exhaustion. It was a mass of cheering, a hurricane of joy and delight as thousands of voices were raised and sent clamouring into the deepening dark.

Tom and Dan moved to crawl out into the open with an offended Elizabeth left behind; told to 'Stay here' by Dan in a tone that brooked no argument.

They picked their way through the camp, a mass of blankets and makeshift tents, camp fires now cooling to embers and the air permeated with the smells of firewood and eaten meals. Ahead of them, halfway up the slope, a great crowd had gathered. As they watched, more men and their families hurried towards it, swelling its numbers moment by moment. It was from this throng of people that the surge of euphoria had originated. Even now the multitudes of people were hurrahing and flocks of hats and sun-bonnets were being flung up into the night sky.

As the brothers approached, it was clear that the greater mass of the crowd was converged about the ragged stump of the ruined windmill. Dan and Tom pushed their way forward as best they could and craned their necks to better see what was occurring.

As Dan tried to get a better view, a rough, thick-skinned hand was extended before his face. They had halted beside a lichen-speckled boulder on which some peasants had positioned themselves to gain a better view of the mysterious spectacle. It was one of these men that now extended a hand to Dan.

'I recognise you two from Oulart and the fighting down below in Enniscorthy,' the man said. 'Jump up here and have a look at this. I don't know whether I should be cheering or praying.'

Dan looked at Tom, who shrugged and gestured to his brother to lead the way.

The Banvilles scrambled up beside the man, a slim, raw-boned fellow about thirty years of age, and wriggled in amongst his comrades. Before them, over the heads of the crowd, could be seen one of the most pathetic things either young man had ever witnessed.

In front of the shattered windmill, a band of rebels, pikes in hand, faced the cowering form of a corpulent, middle-aged man. The man was dressed in a shirt and breeches but was without jacket, stockings or shoes. His feet were bleeding from where he had been marched through briar and field and his balding head was a slimy ball of sweat. The expression on his face was one of absolute horror, his features a grey tombstone in a forgotten graveyard. In the dusk he wrung his hands together, bound as they were at the wrist, and bleated in sobbing desperation, 'Not that, good sir, my wife gave me that before she passed. Please.'

Standing over him, two narrow-faced rebels were admiring a gold watch which spun and swung on its chain, suspended from one of their knuckled fists.

'Now what,' one rebel was saying in a tone that crawled with menace, 'would you be wanting with a clock like this when you've no time left yourself?'

Then a voice came heavy and authoritative above the murmuring of the crowd, 'Luke Byrne? Captain Thomas Dixon?'

The rebel spun on his heel, the gold watch disappearing as if by magic into the pocket of his breeches. The other rebel, Luke Byrne, hurried to one side, mingling with the other pikemen. Facing Dixon and his men, Edward Roche and Fr John Murphy had pushed through the crowd and now regarded the tableau before them with expressions of suspicion and anger.

'What do you think you are doing?' asked Murphy at last.

Dixon spat into the grass at his feet and then answered with bitterness infusing every syllable of his words. 'This man is a tithe collector. He went about the county like a king, frightening the old and helpless, lining the pockets of the Orangemen and the tyrants. I don't see how any true United Irishman could stand to have Protestant shites the likes of him at large in the countryside and up to mischief.'

He jabbed his pike toward the quailing prisoner, who whimpered and jumped back a yard at the gesture.

'I'd say the oul' bastard bleeds orange as well.'

At this, the majority of the gathered insurgents guffawed in a rough outburst of laughter. Dan and Tom, however, exchanged uneasy looks and Dan saw a number of others in the crowd frown in discomfiture and shuffle their feet.

Fr Murphy regarded Dixon coolly before saying, 'You haven't answered me. What do you intend to do?'

'Do?' asked Dixon. 'Why, Father, we intend to put him down like the dog he his.'

As these words slithered from Dixon's lips the old tithe collector collapsed onto his knees whilst a braying acclamation issued from Dixon's followers in the gathered ranks. Luke Byrne cheered and shook his pike like a man possessed. Dixon smiled like a lurking river pike and Fr Murphy raised one hand, fist clenched and finger extended in trembling fury.

Edward Roche's hand on his shoulder, heavy and cautioning, made the priest pause for a moment as the former yeomanry sergeant looked pointedly at the avid faces leering from the crowd.

'One cannot,' Roche began, 'simply execute a man on a whim.'

'Really?' asked Dixon. 'Says who?'

Exasperated now, Roche snapped, 'Says all goodness and human decency! To have a man put to death without trial is to make the United Irishmen no better than the yeos. You are a captain of the United Irishmen for God's sake. Do you wish to blacken our name, Mr Dixon? Do you wish to turn a fellowship of all men, equal and free, into a cesspool of bigotry, to turn a war of liberation into a religious vendetta?'

Dixon stared at the burly general before him, eyes hot as fever, as conflicting murmurs rippled through the watching multitude.

'Very well,' Dixon conceded at last, 'we shall have him and others like him tried and sentenced. We can't let their crimes go unpunished.'

He hawked again and spat a viscous clot of clinging green onto the ground between where he and the two rebel leaders faced each other. 'We'll keep the Orangeman in the windmill overnight,' he said. 'We don't want him conferring with his fellows down in the barn.'

Roche frowned at this but taking into account the swarm of people pressing in all about he nodded slowly, giving some ground. 'If harm should come to this man before his trial, then I shall hold you personally accountable Mr Dixon,' he said at last. 'You yourself shall be tried by court martial and be shot at dawn. We are an army and we shall have discipline. Do you have me, Mr Dixon?'

Dixon grinned then, his lips drawing back from his teeth in a snarl. Dan thought he saw the man's tongue lick across those teeth once, purple and glistening in the burgeoning dark.

'Have you me, Mr Dixon?' Roche repeated, his voice insistent, almost desperate in the face of the man's hateful insolence.

'Oh, I have you General,' sneered Dixon. 'I have you well.'

Standing on the boulder, looking across the shaggy heads of the revolutionary multitude, both Dan and Tom felt the tight coils of something evil tighten inside them.

'I think perhaps,' breathed the rebel beside them, 'that I should be praying.'

The evening light found Lieutenant-Colonel Foote of the North Cork Militia sitting in a well appointed room on the second floor of a market house overlooking the Corn Market and Bullring of Wexford Town. With him, sitting in various chairs about the room were Edward Turner, Captain Le Hunte, Captain Snowe, and an old man, dressed in the slightly worsted and moth-eaten regimental coat of a line colonel. The old officer sat, a little uncomfortably, in the spongy nest of a velvet-upholstered armchair and sipped the glass of brandy in his hand. Long white moustaches drooped on either side of his mouth but his blue eyes were still bright and thoughtful in the lamplight.

'What do you propose we do, Colonel Watson?' asked Edward Turner, still pale from his shock at Oulart the day before.

The old man pursed his lips for a moment and then, in a voice so full of vigour that it belied his geriatric appearance, he said, 'You can first either call me Jonas or Mr Watson. I am retired from the service these past ten years.'

'And we thank you for lending us your expertise, Mr Watson,' said Le Hunte. 'We are sorry that present circumstance has pressed you back into that red coat.'

'I thought to live here peacefully,' answered Watson, swirling his brandy in its glass. 'I thought to leave all this nonsense behind me in America. And what do I find? My new home goes up in the same flames of revolution I saw over there.'

He chuckled then, 'Maybe it has something to do with me.'

Turner and Le Hunte laughed politely at this, but Foote was silent. The events at Oulart had disturbed him more than he had shown. Uniformed troops should not be beaten in the field so easily and so completely. He had known to be cautious, known to give the rabble the respect that their numbers and position had warranted and yet he had allowed poor Lombard to lead the attack. His men had advanced into the steel maw of a trap and had been wiped out. Wiped out by peasants and farmers.

The bodies of the men who had died had been retrieved earlier in the day and the lamentation of their wives and children still echoed and chased in the corridors of Foote's mind. The bodies, bloated and teeming with flies, their blood a sepia crust in the heat, had sparked a frenzy amongst the loyalist population. The women howled in grief, hands reaching in plaintive yearning for a last touch of pike-pierced flesh. Over a hundred widows keened in the afternoon sun and Foote had stood and offered them nothing but platitudes.

Then at four o'clock, like the first portend of a coming holocaust, a dark finger of smoke curled above the horizon to the north. Men and women, soldiers and yeomen all hurried down to the docks and to the high points of the town. There, with expressions of fear and wonder blanching their features, they stared out in the direction of Enniscorthy. Within minutes of the smoke being seen the first of the fugitives from the burning town arrived across Wexford Bridge, followed closely by others coming in from Ferrycarrig. Consternation and terror was the dreadful freight they carried with them and it spread through Wexford like a plague. People had boarded ships and set sail for Wales, others had fled the town, riding in carts toward the fort at Duncannon; but in John Street, among the tanners and blacksmiths, an awful calm had descended, a calm that felt like anticipation.

Snowe, who had also remained silent, his face wan and his jacket still reeking of smoke and stained with the dust of his rapid retreat, now spoke.

'These rebels,' he began, 'are no mean gang of bandits. They have substantial numbers and fight with determination, bravery and, though I hesitate to say it, no little organisation. There are brains at work here, gentlemen, and the sooner we realise that, the better off we shall all be.'

'How many casualties did you inflict?' asked Le Hunte. 'Did you manage to thin out their numbers any?'

'It is impossible to say,' answered Snowe. 'The smoke obscured much. I would estimate well over a hundred, for our muskets wreaked a terrible toll on them as they advanced up to our barricades. Had we a field gun or two I am sure we would have thrown them back.'

Foote's voice came then, level and with all the weight of a coffin lid, 'How many did you lose?'

'Dead?' asked Snowe, procrastinating.

'Dead,' answered Foote.

'Over a hundred.'

'Ye Gods,' breathed Turner.

Snowe looked mortified and he awkwardly studied the glass of brandy that he held carefully in both curled palms.

In the sudden silence of the lamp-lit room, its heavy curtains and thick wall-paper muffling the sounds from the street outside, Foote exhaled sharply. His fist clenched and released as though in spasm as he said, 'Over two hundred of my North Corks lie stretched and rotting in two days of battle with these rebels. Countless hundreds of loyal citizens are witless with panic. Kildare and Meath are still in uproar. This "nonsense", as you so put it Mr Watson, could very well go the way of your campaign in the Americas unless we put a stop to it soon.'

Watson stroked the white curve of his moustache. 'I have fought irregulars, Colonel Foote, and you are correct in that the King's armies were forced to capitulate at Yorktown. But you cannot infer from the events in the colonies that this rebellion will succeed here in Ireland. The Americans were ably led by General Washington, were well armed and were assisted by the French army and fleet.'

He sipped his drink before continuing, 'The most telling detail of all, though, was the sheer vastness of the Atlantic Ocean. The American rebels had limitless numbers at their doorstep whereas our reinforcements were weeks away. This is not America, my good colonel. The rebels are badly armed, the entire might of the British Empire is no more than a day away and there are no French off the coast.'

'Yet,' said Le Hunte flatly, half-heartedly swirling his brandy.

Both Watson and Foote lanced him vicious looks.

Edward Turner coughed pointedly and asked, 'So what is to be done, here and now? How do we end this nightmare?'

Watson shifted in his chair, his joints creaking, and said, 'The very fact of our defeat at Yorktown is what will win the war for us in Ireland. General Lake, who, as you know, commands all of His Majesty's forces on this island, was also at Yorktown. He will not allow his reputation to be irrevocably tarnished by another loss to revolutionaries. He will crush every rebel underfoot as you would a worm.

'He will need time to muster his forces, however, and to deal with the insurgency around Dublin. It is this time that the rebels could very well use to their advantage.'

He cast another withering glance toward Le Hunte, who was studiously avoiding his gaze, and continued, 'And as Mr Le Hunte has intimated, the French, should they sail, are only a day or two away as well.'

'Do you suggest we take the fight to them?' asked Turner.

At this Snowe looked up from where he was staring in abstraction at the floorboards. His face was suddenly anxious, a hunted expression scuttling across his features. 'We have not the numbers to meet them in the field,' he said a little too urgently.

Watson nodded and then addressed Foote, 'How many men do we have in Wexford Town? Is this place defensible?'

Foote pursed his lips thoughtfully and then answered, 'Including militia, yeomanry and civilian supplementaries, I have about a thousand men at arms.'

'So you have a good-sized force at your disposal,' said Watson. 'What we are lacking is artillery and cavalry in any numbers. Without them, Captain Snowe is correct in his assessment that we cannot meet them in open battle.'

'So we wait?'

'We keep the men at their posts all night and we fortify the town as best we can,' explained Watson. 'And yes, we wait for aid from Dublin.'

'I have also sent word to Colonel Maxwell at Duncannon,' said Foote. 'He and his Donegals should be arriving tonight or early in the morning.'

'That is good,' commended Watson. 'But for him to arrive and be welcomed by a town still in government hands, we must see to it that the defenses are properly constructed and ably manned.'

'John Street shall be barricaded,' said Foote. 'The old town walls will have men placed upon them and what cannon we have will be brought to bear on the approaches from Enniscorthy. Captain Boyd and the Wexford Yeoman Cavalry will patrol the hinterland.'

Watson frowned then, and the wrinkles about his eyes and mouth grew deeper and more pronounced. His face became craggy and hard and he asked, 'Is there likely to be any uprising from within the town? Are there any individuals who should be placed in irons for the common good?'

Turner, some colour returning to his face as the alcohol heated his innards, answered, 'Perceval's clapped Bagenal Harvey, Edward Fitzgerald and John Henry Colclough in gaol on the strength of Anthony Perry's information. As to the general populace of the town I have not perceived the least indication that they would side with the rebels. I would rather be of the opinion that the atmosphere is one of terror that they may succeed. I do not feel the croppies will gain much support from the good people of Wexford Town.'

'That is good to hear,' said Watson, downing the last dregs of his brandy. 'Captain Snowe has related how these revolutionaries were hard-pressed to take stone buildings, stoutly defended, of which we have a plethora here in Wexford. I would wager that a force, even of six thousand, would dash itself to pieces assaulting this place unless they were equipped with artillery.'

'You're confident then?' asked Le Hunte.

'This is not America, gentlemen,' chuckled Watson. 'I can assure you of that.'

Colonel Foote was silent as the men around him laughed in relieved bonhomie, reassured by Jonas Watson's commanding presence. Foote however, was not so easily placated. Nor was his belief in the unconquerable might of the military so unshakable. He had seen over a hundred of his men butchered, massacred before his disbelieving eyes. And now, the very next day, another hundred trained soldiers had been put to the sword and a garrison town had been taken from under the very noses of its defenders. A nauseating sense of foreboding was swilling within him, sour and clinging. In spite of Watson's words, Lieutenant Colonel Foote was afraid.

Beyond the amber-lighted walls of the market house, beyond the smell of cigar smoke and good brandy, Wexford Town was crouched and tense. All through its streets and alleys, redcoats jostled and marched, flowing like blood through arteries. And in barracks and lodgings, cold under the rising moon, the bleak sobs of a hundred and twenty widows and their children spilled wetly into the night.

CHAPTER 12

Hard Councils

Dawn of the 29th broke in pearly translucence over the sprawling camp on the slopes of Vinegar Hill. A summer fog had billowed up from the river during the night and added to the retching smoke of smouldering Enniscorthy. The sun, invisible in the haze, nonetheless ignited the air with a cold fire, setting the mist aglow, filled with a white, seemingly sourceless light. All about Enniscorthy and its environs bands of men were flitting through the dawn like ghosts as more and more detachments of United Irishmen moved toward the hill and its green bough standard.

On the crest of the hill under the ruined windmill, a small group of men, amongst them Miles Byrne and Tom Banville, stood in the damp and watched as Captain Thomas Dixon meted out justice. A mahogany bureau had been brought up from the town and had been placed in front of the windmill's ragged doorway, two of its four legs propped up with lumps of rock to keep it steady on the uneven ground. Behind this desk, Dixon sat with the air of a conquering lord, his lank hair slicked back and his fingers drumming an impatient tattoo. To either side of him, six of his own corps stood with pikes in their hands; in front the old tithe collector shivered in the dank air.

Tom had left Dan and Elizabeth still sleeping in their makeshift shelter, the couple wrapped in each other's arms, oblivious to everything except each other. He left them and made his way through the opalescent dawn, his boots dragging wetness from the grass with every step so that they were soon drenched and glistening as though freshly polished.

He had left because he had known that Dixon would stage his little outrage at dawn. The majority of exhausted men would be sleeping whilst the coming day would lend a grotesque semblance of military regulation to what Tom presumed would be a grotesque parody.

For grotesque it was, with Dixon rabid behind his incongruous desk, playing the part of a military judge and his men sneering horribly as though party to some private joke.

Tom had not expected to see Byrne here but the young captain greeted him with a grim, wordless nod, his features those of a man who had swallowed his own vomit. He regarded Dixon with a cold contempt but, like Tom, thought it wise not to interfere. To divide the myriad rebel factions in any way might undermine the whole teetering edifice of their efforts and bring everything crashing down in an orgy of recrimination and confusion. So the two men merely watched as Dixon, supercilious and preening, addressed the old man who stood quaking in the shadowless effulgence of the dawn.

'So what you're saying is, you're not an Orangeman,' stated Dixon.

'Yes, sir, your honour,' replied the old man, tugging his stringy, grey forelock obsequiously.

'Yet you admit to collecting money and rent for that auld bastard George Ogle?' asked Dixon. 'You admit to working for a man who has dedicated every moment of his waking life to destroying the very idea of the United Irishmen?'

'I cannot deny that,' said the man querulously.

Dixon slammed his hand onto the desktop with such force that the whole thing sprang from off its stone perches and listed like a ship in a storm. He surged to his feet and tossed his head back and he gazed at the old man with the haughty disdain of a lawyer who has speared his opponent on a cold point of logic.

'Then,' he pronounced carefully, 'you admit to working yourself for the overthrow of our proud and victorious organisation?'

The man gaped at this, his mind working furiously and his hands wringing in supplication. 'Why, no sir,' he stammered, suddenly terrified. 'I just did what I was told. I collected rents. That is all. I've never harmed anyone in my life.'

Dixon spat a long stream of saliva at the man's feet, stemming his flow of words.

'The fact that blood-sucking leaches like you are alive at all is an insult to likes of me and mine,' he growled. 'You've stolen the rewards of our blood and sweat for the last time. Your kind is finished.'

'Oh, no, sir. Please,' began the tithe collector. His knees buckled and he collapsed forward onto the damp, shallow soil that crowned Vinegar Hill. His hands were like pale, blind spiders as they clawed across the ground and his face, wrinkled and haggard, was awash with tears. 'Have mercy, sir,' he begged.

And as he lay there, prostrate in the dirt, a single shaft of sunlight burned through the mantle of mist and lit the top of Vinegar Hill like a beacon.

'Kill him,' ordered Dixon, the weight of hatred loading his voice.

Simultaneously, both Tom and Byrne turned away from the scene and walked down the hill. Disgust curdled both their stomachs as the defenceless old tithe collector's screams tore through the air before stilling with gut-wrenching suddenness. The entire trial, if it could be called so, had taken no more than ten minutes.

Tom was shaken and turned to the eighteen-year-old beside him, 'That was as despicable an action as I've ever seen. That was as bad as anything that the North Corks have perpetrated against the peasantry.'

Byrne was nodding distractedly as sleep-muddled heads began appearing from under blankets and hedgerows all about them. 'We must be wary of this,' the young captain cautioned. 'We cannot allow the Rising to become a sectarian circus. If word becomes general that we are executing innocent Protestants under any pretext, then sympathy throughout the rest of the country, especially Belfast, will wane.'

Walking alongside him, Tom asked, 'Do you think the rest of the country is at arms?'

'I don't see why not,' replied Byrne. 'If our people, paralysed by arrests and half prostrate through torture, could rise up and rout the King's forces then I don't see how the brave fellows of Kildare and Meath could have failed.'

'Carlow,' said Tom bluntly. 'And Kilthomas. Both were disasters and both bode badly for the state of the rest of the country.'

'You think we are alone?' asked Byrne.

'I do not know,' said Tom. 'But if Dixon and Luke Byrne are given free hand then any hope of a general Rising, with Catholics and Protestants shoulder to shoulder under the banner of liberty, will be lost.'

He pointed to the two standards stabbed into the earth just to the left of the windmill, with its green branch silhouetted in the haze. The two standards hung limp now, not a breath of air stirred either the green and gold or black and white.

'I would rather we followed the green than the black, Miles,' stated Tom. 'A religious war would tear the country apart.'

'This is not a religious war,' retorted Byrne savagely. 'And Dixon's kind does not represent the vision of our leaders. Wolfe Tone is a Protestant, Bagenal Harvey is too. If Dixon and his followers want to sully our name with matters of base concern then I am certain that the leaders will take action against them.'

'Really?' asked Tom. 'Go tell that to the poor wretch they've made worms' meat of a moment ago.'

Byrne regarded him thoughtfully, then turned and walked away as all about him people roused themselves from slumber and hurried up the slope, curious as to what had transpired under the broken, black tooth of the ruined windmill.

Tom, Dan and Elizabeth sat at the opening of their little shelter and looked out over the Slaney valley. The sun had finally burnt off the cataract of fog and now blazed down upon the earth like an angry eye. Below them, the town of Enniscorthy was a slump of charred timbers and soot-smeared walls, the stone buildings that withstood the fires of the day before clustered mainly about the hollow space of the market square.

The flood of men had continued all morning, pikes and muskets and eager hands pouring in from the surrounding countryside. A particularly fine group of men had come marching in from Killann carrying a green banner with the United harp glittering upon it in gilt thread. At the head of this band was the biggest man either of the Banvilles had ever seen, a blond young man, almost seven feet in height and riding a massive draught horse with the cool command of a born leader.

'Who is that?' Elizabeth had asked in wonder.

'Mount Leinster's own darling and pride. John Kelly of Killann,' Dan answered.

So it had continued. The companies of men bringing with them wives and loved ones and, on not a few occasions, several unfortunate prisoners. As the day grew brighter, it was Elizabeth who first noticed the commotion down where the arch of the bridge flung itself out and over the Slaney's lethargic current. Where the bridge joined with the far bank, a group of rebels coming down from the hill had knotted, huddled as though sharing some hidden secret. Beside them, stretching along the road north toward Ferns and Gorey, was a corps of perhaps two hundred pikemen. It was around the head of this corps that the rebel group had fisted. As Elizabeth pointed, the soft murmur of distant cheering drifted up from the scene at the bridge and the watchers on the hill could see the crowd flinging their hats and beavers aloft in jubilation into the morning air. They looked tiny and black, like flecks of soot, as they fluttered back to earth. Then, with a surge like a gushing spring, the crowd hefted a figure onto their shoulders and began to carry him like a victorious prize-fighter towards the camp.

Even from some distance the bandages whorled about the figure's head were clearly discernible, glowing white and bloody against the earthy drabness of their background.

'Now who could that be?' wondered Tom.

'Whoever he his, he has suffered the tender ministrations of the authorities,' replied Dan.

As the man was borne out of sight below the bulge of Vinegar Hill's lower slopes, the contrast between his reception and the fate of some of the other new arrivals appalled Elizabeth. The cruelty that this war had vomited into being was a spreading slick in her mind. At every turn, just when horror piled on horror to such an extent that it seemed unbearable, yet more depravity followed. It was no wonder she cleaved to Dan and he cleaved to her with such ferocious affection. They were each other's happiness, each other's life-blood. From a deep and festering well of fear and disgust she asked, 'Will they murder many more, do you think?'

The abruptness of the question startled her two companions. Dan and Tom turned to her from where they had begun to debate who the returning hero might be and fixed her with very different expressions. Tom's was resigned and sad whilst Dan was frowning in indignation.

'I do not think these "trials" will be allowed to continue,' said Dan. 'They make a mockery of what we stand for.'

'They make a mockery of what you, yourself, stand for,' corrected Tom. 'Dixon has the whip hand and if Roche wants to stop him, he'll have a deal to do. No one will risk splitting the movement at this stage in the proceedings.'

'So they will continue, in spite of humanity and goodness and decency? In spite of the vaunted *Liberte, Equalite, Fraternite*?' Elizabeth asked bitterly.

'I believe so,' said Tom

'They cannot,' said Dan, simultaneously.

Up the slope, from the direction of Beale's Barn, a handful of bleating prisoners were herded, one by one, to be ensconced within the flinty walls of the shattered windmill. The brothers and Elizabeth tracked the progress of each one with hearts heavy as cannonballs in their chests.

The resurgence of the exultant whooping that they had heard wafting up from the bridge some twenty minutes before brought them out of their introspection. Off to their right, where the fields sloped gently down to the road leading in from Oulart, the excited chatter of men and women buzzed across the hillside.

Shrugging, they rose to their feet and made their way off across the jagged contours, curious to see what had spurred the camp into such good spirits. They stepped carefully between cooking fires tended by women who craned their necks to catch what all the fuss was about, and they had to stop on more than one occasion when gaggles of children cavorted past them, throwing a rag-ball or playing hurling with bits of branches. Wood smoke and the scents of cooking wreathed everything, mingling horribly with the acrid stink crawling up from the valley below.

Eventually, the little group had traversed the hillside and were now standing on the outskirts of a mass of people as they sent a great huzzah roaring into the heavens. In the midst of this crowd, a figure dressed in dark frock coat and breeches was being bounced into the air by dozens of strong arms. The man was grinning in what Dan thought to be earnest and pained good spirits, like an adult humouring a child. One hand was clamped to the bandages that wrapped his head like an obscene turban.

As Dan watched, a slow dawn of recognition broke across his thoughts.

'No,' he whispered incredulously. 'It cannot be.'

'Who is it?' asked Elizabeth as she grasped his arm and stood on tiptoes in an effort to see above the heads of the crowd.

Tom cocked his eyebrow and regarded his brother wryly, 'You know that man?'

Dan nodded fervently, straining his own neck to see now that the throng had lowered the man into their swarming middle. 'I do believe that's Anthony Perry or else my eyes completely deceive me.

'I thought that he was arrested,' he said in a tone suddenly and curiously flat.

'He was obviously in custody at some stage,' began Tom wonderingly. 'How has he ended up here?'

'Why did they let him go when the other leaders, Edward Fitzgerald, Harvey, Colclough, are all presumably still in custody?' asked Dan.

Both brothers exchanged troubled glances.

'What did they do to him under all those bandages?' asked Elizabeth softly.

Tom scrubbed one hand across his stubbled features and said with some bluntness, 'Pitchcap, amongst other things.'

'Is there nothing but barbarity at loose in the world these days? Atrocity piles on atrocity and "an eye for an eye" seems to be the watchword of every man and woman,' Elizabeth said despairingly.

Dan bent to her and kissed her on the forehead, 'There are things much more noble than the outrages we have lately witnessed, my darling. There is beauty and there is laughter and there is love even still.'

'The weather has held up fine as well,' grinned Tom.

The crowd was dispersing now and Perry was being gently shepherded to where the other leaders had pitched a large tent. A green flag hung lifeless from a pole hammered into the ground in front of it.

Tom was about to say something when a narrow woman with a face possessing the hard angularity of a greyhound's, spat as she stalked past Elizabeth.

'Excuse me!' piped Elizabeth, incredulous.

The woman continued walking, silent and purposeful but another woman, heavier than the first and following in her spiky path, hissed, 'It's because of youse filthy Protestants that our men end up like that.' She stabbed a dirt-silted finger back toward Perry and then stormed down the slope.

Elizabeth stood, shocked, her face slack and her jaw unhinging. She felt Dan's big arm enfolding her protectively and his voice came soothing and deep, his baritone filling the empty world.

'Don't mind her, Elizabeth,' he said. 'They don't know who you are and have no reason to harm you in any way.'

Tom watched the women go with smouldering eyes, the blue of his irises seeming to become cobalt as a dark fury rose within him.

'That fat sow from yesterday was sure she recognised Elizabeth,' he growled. 'I'd bet everything we once owned that she has been pouring poison into every ear that would listen.'

The three companions stood as the crowd that had welcomed Perry scattered and drifted back to their own campfires. Like cattle plodding through the fields to be milked, they followed the sheep paths and beaten trackways between gorse and briar in slow, deliberate lines. Fighting men, now well-rested and well-fed, their eyes taking in the gutted corpse of Enniscorthy, which only yesterday had stood before them, garrisoned and defiant, moved steadily down the hill's flanks. Minds turned now toward prospects of further action, to fights further afield, for as every child knew, the devil makes work for idle hands.

Sitting on the threshold of their little bivouac, Dan watched Tom come sauntering across the slope. It had been three hours since Perry's arrival and Tom had decided to go and reconnoitre the state of the rebel army.

He sat down heavily beside his brother and said with an air of genuine disbelief, 'Ten thousand. There are at least ten thousand armed men on this hill.'

Dan's eyes widened and he flung his gaze out over Enniscorthy and into the blue haze of the copse-studded countryside beyond. The county must be emptied, every man who could hold a pike or hayfork must be rallying to them. His heart fluttered in his chest in involuntary excitement. The vast sweep of field and forest before him was crawling with moving bands of men and not one wore the crimson coat of the King, not one soldier or yeo marred the scene with even a fleck of red. Browns and greys and, above all, greens were the colours that filled his vision. Every scrap of pasture, every dusty length of roadway was unburdened by the crushing weight of an alien authority. For the first time in his life Dan looked out on a country free and unbowed.

So filled was he by the momentous nature of this vision that Tom's next words almost passed him by.

'The camp is restless, though,' Tom was saying. 'The men are anxious to be off. They are filled with a high confidence that must be merited considering the successes of the past day or two.

'What troubles me is that the late arrivals seem to be striving to make up for their tardiness through unwarranted zeal. They are demanding revenge against phantom Orangemen and scouring the country for any poor soul hiding in the fields who could not keep up with the general exodus out of Enniscorthy.

'To make matters worse some of our veterans from Oulart and Enniscorthy think that we have the country won already or that our leaders cannot make up their minds what to do next. There's been people leaving already, heading back to their homes, the fools, thinking the job is done. Roche must do something soon or we risk losing a number of good, experienced men from the ranks.'

He looked at Dan in exasperation, 'Are you even listening?'

Dan nodded distractedly, 'So what are you saying, Tom?'

Tom shook his head, 'I'm saying, you day-dreaming idiot, that things are not as rosy as they appear. If we do not regain momentum, and soon, our army is in danger of coming apart at the seams. Dixon's followers will find more innocents to sacrifice and a counter-attack from Wexford or New Ross will disperse us like quail.'

At this Dan nodded gravely, his attention finally coming back to considerations of the practical, the here and now of the sun-honeyed slopes of Vinegar Hill. 'Roche will move,' he said confidently. 'He knows what is at stake.'

'Your belief in Roche is admirable, Dan,' said Tom. 'But neither himself nor the priest has done anything to halt the execution of loyalist prisoners. Another one was hacked to death not an hour ago. Rumour has it that they are going to shoot the next one. The pike as an instrument of justice is too sanguinary even for Dixon's bloody lot.'

Dan's face drained of colour at this and a light seemed to be extinguished in his eyes.

'Ho, the camp!'

The sudden voice, filled with enthusiasm and bubbling good humour, caught the two brother's attention and, as one, they turned their heads to see who had hailed them.

Stepping between lean-tos and tents made from blankets and tree branches, Miles Byrne waved in greeting. The young captain was dressed in an emerald coat with yellow cuffs and collar and a broad-brimmed hat sat jauntily on his head. Its green cockade fluttered as he approached. Altogether he cut quite a dash against the dull tones of his surroundings and a wide smile cut a gleaming segment in his face.

He stood before them and, one hand resting on the hilt of his sword, said slightly breathlessly, 'I've been looking for you for an age. Roche has sent word for captains and officers to assemble at his tent. Something is afoot. I would guess that our next course of action is to be revealed to us, and not a moment too soon.'

Dan looked confused and answered, 'But nobody here is an officer, Miles.'

'Ah,' chuckled Byrne. 'That's where you're wrong. Since poor William Sinnott fell so gloriously in battle, Anthony Perry, on Roche's advice, has elected you as Captain of the Castletown men. Provisionally, of course.'

Tom blinked and began to laugh but Dan's expression soured and he said, 'Tell Mr Perry that I do not deserve such elevation and neither do I desire it. I will fight amongst the men as best as I am able but I cannot lead them.'

Byrne was smiling wolfishly, 'You can tell him yourself, Captain. You must accompany me to the council of war forthwith or we shall be accused of dawdling.'

Grumbling and doing his best to ignore his brother's derisive sniggering, Dan muttered, 'Look after Elizabeth, Tom. She's still sleeping.'

Tom saluted roguishly, 'Aye, aye, Captain.'

Scowling back over his shoulder at Tom, Dan followed Byrne as he made off hurriedly through the maze of cooking fires and blankets. Things could hardly get any worse, he thought.

The tent that Roche shared with Fr John, Fr Michael and George Sparks was a vast, buff-coloured rectangle of canvas, having all the appearance of a military mess-tent. Its peaked roof was stained in a wide sweep, where the fires from which it had been rescued down in Enniscorthy had tongued the material in dark streaks, and its guy ropes had mostly been replaced by pilfered hawsers from the sand cots below on the Slaney. Around the open flaps of the tent a large group of rebel officers in a motley variety of uniforms had gathered. The common and uniting factor amongst the men was the vivid presence of the colour green. On arms, around waists and in the bands of hats, emerald scarves and sashes, cockades of deepest bottle-green to brilliant lime all glowed in the sunlight. And in the midst of it all, Edward Roche, in a jacket the colour of summer foliage, held court.

'Gentlemen,' he was declaring, 'This will be a bit of a squeeze but we shall endeavour to fit us all into the tent for a council of war. We are a brotherhood of affection and as such we shall make this decision together or not at all.'

With that, the mass of men crowded forward through the tent's open flaps. Men doffed their caps and mopped sweating brows as they entered the cool shade of the interior.

Byrne was regarding the men as they filed through the opening with a frown that reminded Dan, startlingly, of Tom.

'I'm not sure that I agree with this,' the young captain muttered darkly. 'Leadership by committee in a time of war is a preposterous notion. Roche and Fr Murphy should make a decision and have done with it.'

Inside the tent, Roche had placed a round table, obviously plundered from some well-appointed townhouse down in the valley. Its heavy frame was carved and polished and its lines curved in elegant sweeps, lending grace to what might otherwise be a clumsy vastness of dead wood. The overall effect, however, was spoiled somewhat by the absence of one of its legs, its place taken by a pile of books, their gilt titles winking out from the leather-bound spines.

About the table sat a group of prominent United Irishmen, not all of them colonels but all of them highly esteemed amongst the men. Amidst them sat Fr John Murphy, looking slightly bewildered by the faces around him, many of whom he had never met before. A graze marred his forehead where a musket ball had zipped past and a violet swelling was bloating beneath one eye. For their part, the newly arrived men regarded the priest in mingled awe and distrust. For some, the memory of him demanding the surrender of arms from the pulpit was still very fresh in their minds. For others the tales of him leading the men at the Harrow and his bravery at Oulart and Enniscorthy were marvels worthy of respect and emulation. Anthony Perry, too, sat amongst the leaders, his eyes downcast and his bandages beginning to discolour from the grotesque weeping of his wounds. To the back of the tent Dan could see the tall form of the blond captain from Killann towering over all those around him, his face a lantern of good cheer and self-assurance. Dan judged that, all told, there were perhaps thirty people packed into a space that could comfortably accommodate twenty. A drone of conversation permeated the air and the heat and reek of unwashed bodies was immense.

'Gentlemen,' began Roche and all others fell silent. 'We are gathered here to decide what steps our gallant army is to take next in the great enterprise we have embarked upon.'

A general murmuring began with voice overlapping voice and opinion drowning out opinion, so that a tidal wave of noise began to mount within the hot cavern of the tent.

Miles Byrne shook his head and leaned close to Dan. 'I knew that this would happen,' he sighed. 'Too many cooks.'

Roche was now banging his fist on the table, at the violence of which Anthony Perry flinched. Gradually a buzzing silence fell upon the gathering and Roche admonished, 'If you cannot comport yourselves like officers then go back to the cooking fires.'

The silence deepened as men looked abashedly about them.

'Now,' said Roche. 'Our next course of action has been complicated by the utter triumph of our successes thus far. There are differences of opinion as to what to do next and without Edward Fitzgerald or Bagenal Harvey to give us leadership we must decide what to do ourselves.'

He paused for a moment in thought. The curled index finger of his right hand pressed to his lips as his mind sought words in which to voice his considerations.

At last he continued, 'We have three broad courses of action open to us. We can take the fight beyond our county and hope to rise Munster and the midlands by taking New Ross and Newtownbarry. Secondly, we might advance on Wexford Town and drive the remnants of our enemies like rats into the sea. Thirdly, we might consolidate our position and await word from Dublin, for the army and yeomanry are in full flight all about us and Mr Perry has informed us that Gorey has been abandoned. We have taken our county, gentlemen, and the King's forces cannot hope to relieve Dublin from where they are beleaguered in the south.'

'That is our current position.'

'What would you have us do?' asked an anonymous voice from amongst the gathered throng.

'I would favour taking Wexford Town and liberating our comrades who are held in gaol there.'

A rising surge of gabbled noise began to swell again from the gathered officers.

Fr Murphy rose to his feet, his broad face and fierce eyes glowing with anger. 'Silence!' he roared. 'You are not children. Speak in turn or not at all.'

'What is your opinion, Father?' asked Miles Byrne.

Startled by the question but revealing no embarrassment at being the centre of so much attention, Fr Murphy stated confidently, 'I would favour taking the fight outside of our borders. I would advocate the taking of New Ross and Newtownbarry, with our enemies corralled and terrified in Wexford Town and all the armies of the land in flight from us, we should have the whole country risen within days.'

Edward Roche was nodding thoughtfully and said, 'That is also the opinion of these two gentlemen. Mr John Hay, Mr William Barker, if you would step forward.'

From behind his chair, two men moved forward hesitantly. They seemed wary and their faces were lined with worry and streaked with the soot of the town below.

'Mr Barker fought with the French army and Mr Hay was a captain in the Irish Brigade. They both advise the taking of New Ross.'

John Hay nodded, cleared his throat and regarded the men gathered about with cautious scrutiny. 'I am an Enniscorthy man,' he pronounced slowly. 'I was not with you at Oulart and I was not fighting with you when you took the town so whatever weight my words might carry, they will not be looked upon with any great affection on your part. However, I will say that I am a military man and that I know military matters. My advice to all here is that you ignore the town of Wexford and that you give up your missing leaders for dead. The town itself is of no strategic importance and its garrison is outnumbered and in no position to offer you battle. You have no stores, no depot for the supply of arms, no way of making ammunition, which is in very short supply after the battle down in the town. The heads of your military and political leadership are locked away behind bars. The only hope is to keep the Crown forces on the back foot. To become embroiled in a war of attrition is to invite calamity, for your men cannot stand against line regiments. Any soldiery knowing their duty will cut them to pieces.'

The man beside Hay, slightly older with a dusting of ash in his hair and sideburns, nodded in agreement. 'I too am from Enniscorthy,' he said. I am a latecomer to your ranks, as are most of the men here and on the slopes outside, but heed me well. The most unfortunate thing that could be done at this moment is to become mired within our own borders. Without the French, Wexford will be our graveyard. We must strike out hard and fast through New Ross.'

'What, and leave the yeos behind us to burn our homes and crops?' came an outraged voice.

This was followed immediately by another shout from across the room, 'Will you ever be quiet, Kavanagh? Your home was burnt the minute you marched off with pike in hand. These men know what they're talking about. Listen to them and shut your gob.'

'I won't stand here and take talk the like of that from you!' the first voice bellowed and with that the entire tent seemed to erupt in cries and shouts. Men quarrelled and flung accusations and the semblance of order collapsed into a bedlam of rancour and conflicting arguments.

Dan and Miles Byrne cast about them in despair as men were shouted down and Roche and Fr Murphy tried to reassert some authority on proceedings. Behind the two leaders, John Hay and William Barker looked at the assembly in glum resignation. At the table, Anthony Perry cradled his wounded head in his hands and said nothing, staring at the lacquered wood between his elbows as though the answers to life's mysteries might be found in the depthless dark of the grain.

As that day's pearly dawn broke over Wexford Town it found Lieutenant Colonel Foote standing, wrapped about in a military greatcoat, in the middle of the Bullring. Before him Captain James Boyd and the Wexford Yeoman Cavalry had formed up to welcome Colonel Maxwell and the Donegal Militia into the ranks of the town's defenders. The Donegals had marched all night from the fort at Duncannon and each man was exhausted, muskets slipping from their shoulders and boots dragging through the mist-thickened dust. Every eye was set into a nest of purple rings and was laced with a tracery of red.

Colonel Foote could empathise with them.

Along with Jonas Watson he had remained awake for most of the night, only snatching an hour of anxious sleep just before dawn. The thousand men of his command had remained at their posts for the entire night as well. Each man had nervously stared out into the black dark of the countryside as the fog rose up like the ghost of a dying man. Each soldier was filled with the bleak expectation that at any moment the flare of torches in the night and the noise of marching feet would presage the arrival of his doom.

Instead, just as dawn was breaking cold and colourless in the fog, the Donegals had come marching and a ragged, threadbare cheer sounded from the walls and barricades of Wexford Town.

Sitting his horse just to one side of Foote, Colonel Maxwell regarded his men with a critical eye. His moustache was impeccably waxed and his sideburns, swept down from below his cocked hat, neatly trimmed and groomed, but the same weariness that lay heavy on Foote also weighed on the Donegal officer, blanching his face and dulling the blade of his gaze.

'They look tired, don't you think?' said Maxwell.

'One cannot blame them, sir,' replied Foote. 'They have made good time and a night march is trying under the best conditions.'

Maxwell was now the superior officer in the town and Foote was careful in how he addressed him. 'There was no sign of the rebels, Colonel Maxwell?' he asked.

Maxwell yawned in spite of his best efforts and said, 'I do apologise, Colonel Foote. I find myself quite wearied, it must be said. To answer your question, I must reply in the negative. There was no sign of any insurgency around Taghmon or in the neighbourhood of Ross. Perhaps this is a local matter that the garrison at Gorey has dealt with.'

Foote snorted, 'Colonel, we have not heard from Hawtrey White in Gorey since his men induced a confession from one of the rebel leaders. That was two days ago. I fear the lines of communication between ourselves and the north of the county have been severed.'

'We can send no word to Dublin?' asked Maxwell.

'No sir,' replied Foote. 'Not by road at any rate.'

'That complicates matters,' sighed Maxwell, as the last of his men filed past and he slumped forward onto his saddlebow.

'Have my men placed at free quarters in the town,' he instructed then. 'They need some rest. In two hours we can start relieving your men who have been on guard all night. It is difficult to admit but should the rebels advance on us now we are in no position to offer any kind of determined defence.'

'Pray God they don't, sir,' said Foote earnestly.

Two hours later and the first detachments of the Donegal Militia were manning the barricades at John Street and taking up position on the old tumbledown walls surrounding the town. Their Cork comrades slapped them on the backs and offered them hearty well-wishes as they sloped off to the welcome haven of barrack and bedroom. Still aching and weary from their night's march, the Donegals blinked stinging eyes as the sun cast aside the shrouding cloak of fog. This close to the sea, a perpetual breeze fanned the cockades of their bicorns and set the forest of spars and crow's nests to dancing above the harbour roofs.

The first of Wexford's civilian inhabitants began to stir and make their way through streets thick with soldiers and yeomanry and all at once it was as though the life had been sucked from the place. The bustle of a busy port town was frighteningly absent and people walked hurriedly, gaze focused on the rutted earth or dimpled cobbles beneath their feet. Only in John Street was there an old familiarity. The steady ring of blacksmiths' hammers chimed like warning bells.

Colonel Maxwell stood shoulder to shoulder with Colonel Foote and stared out the second-storey window of the market house overlooking the Corn Market and Bullring. Behind them an elaborately carved table was strewn with maps and scrawled reports, the paper making dry, rustling drifts where they had been pushed to one side, piling each upon the other.

'What do you council, Colonel Maxwell?' asked Foote.

Without looking at his subordinate, Maxwell stated wearily, 'I council caution and patience. Have the men stand at arms, I don't care if they are falling down with tiredness, and continue the mounted patrols out into the countryside. General Fawcett should be arriving from Duncannon shortly. He assured me that he would be following close on my heels.'

Foote was nodding slowly and glanced surreptitiously at the officer beside him before saying, 'You are certain that he is bringing artillery?'

Maxwell sighed and pinched the bridge of his nose, exhaustion threatening to flare into anger. Foote had asked the same question three times in the past hour.

'Just because the rebels bloodied your Cork nose on two separate occasions,' he barked, 'does not give you leave to witter on like a woman. For the last time, General Fawcett is bringing artillery. Regular artillery, not militia or yeomanry; but His Majesty's Royal Artillery. Do not ask me again Colonel.'

Foote swallowed, his mouth and throat dry, and replied, 'Yes, sir. Of course, sir.'

'We must do something about these refugees,' Maxwell said abstractedly. 'They are doing nothing but spreading panic.'

For the past two days Wexford Bridge had been an almost solid mass of terrified people. Worse was that, once they had reached the town, their fears only seemed to multiply as the confident and imperious military that they so fondly imagined readying to sally forth and vanquish the rebel mob was proven to be a fantasy. The soldiers and yeomanry patrolled the town and guarded its walls but they seemed horribly paralysed, incapable or unwilling to mount an offensive. Several concerned citizens, including rectors and magistrates, had been turned away from Foote's offices with their tails between their legs for having the temerity to suggest that the garrison might meet the insurgents head-on.

The loyalist panic had rippled through the town's population until the trickle of people leaving Wexford by boat or road turned into a flood. As quickly as people entered the town, they left by the terrified cart load. And now, to Maxwell's chagrin, the boats had stopped sailing. Only minutes before, a runner had come pounding up from the docks bearing the message that most of the ships had put out into the harbour and were refusing to accept passengers. Huge crowds had gathered on the quayside, their faces gaunt with dread and alarm, their pleas for safe passage winging across the waves like wounded birds only to be lost in the ominous silence emanating from the ships riding at anchor.

This was certainly what Foote thought, for as the morning had progressed and Maxwell perused crackling maps and officers' reports, Foote had paced back and forth in demented monotony until Maxwell had brought him to the window to gaze out over the town.

Now, with the knowledge of the ship captains' vacillation, siding neither with the rebels nor offering loyal citizens an escape route, biding their time with canny patience, Foote and Maxwell found themselves tangled in the same chains of disquiet. Of the two officers, Foote was obviously the more anxious and he sucked a long breath in a whistle through his front teeth. 'I wish General Fawcett would come,' he said.

Without his mind formulating a response, Maxwell heard his own voice reply, 'I do as well.'

The morning wore on with the expectation of the inevitable rebel onslaught growing like a tumour in the minds of the military. Private soldiers, heads drooping with lack of sleep, were rudely jostled back into wakefulness by comrades whose own eyes were bulging and liquid with fatigue. Men watched the horizon to the north in ever-growing despair, convinced that at any moment the tell-tale plume of dust would arise signalling the rebel advance. The stories of the loyalist refugees, replete with images of savage pikemen dashing out the brains of screaming babies and tearing at soldiers' throats with cannibal ferocity, had filtered through the garrison so that that remaining North Corks and the two hundred Donegal Militia were in a state of utmost anxiety.

And still there was no sign of Fawcett.

By one o'clock the atmosphere in Wexford Town had reached an excruciating pitch. Loyalist panic had been souring all morning and had now turned to a thick and desperate anger.

At the first knock, Maxwell looked up from where he was sitting at the desk, sorting through details of troop numbers and dispositions. Foote, who had been staring out the window, his eyes unfocused and his thoughts elsewhere, jumped as though he had been pinched.

The knocking came again, more urgent this time.

'Come,' ordered Maxwell curtly.

Opposite Maxwell, a large pair of ornate panelled doors swung open and Captain James Boyd of the Wexford Yeoman Cavalry strode purposefully into the room, Tarleton helmet carried under one arm and cavalry sabre swinging at his hip. He stopped in front of Maxwell and saluted sharply.

'At ease,' drawled Maxwell. 'What brings you here, Captain?'

'I come with grave messages from the townspeople, Colonel,' replied Boyd, his eyes staring straight ahead through the tall rectangle of empty window over Maxwell's right shoulder.

Maxwell groaned and rubbed his weary eyes with fingers rough from years of hard living. Instead of replying, he closed his eyes and leaned back in his chair.

Instead of Maxwell, it was Foote who asked, 'What do they want?'

Boyd looked uncomfortable at this and his mouth wrinkled wryly. Every line of his face expressed reluctance at what he was being forced to communicate. He paused, made to speak and paused again as though the words had become lodged in his throat.

'Out with it, man!' Maxwell snapped.

Boyd bridled at this but finally blurted out, 'Many prominent citizens feel we should negotiate with the rebels. Edward Hay and Matthew Keogh, both loyal citizens and beloved and esteemed by all for their fairness and liberal natures, have been inundated with requests to mediate with the rebels. The townsfolk wish to negotiate a truce before the town is lost and their lives and property forfeit.'

'Edward Hay,' said Foote, 'would hardly be considered a model citizen. I have no doubt he has United sympathies.'

'If we had a reason to arrest him, sir, he would even now be lodged in gaol with the other reprobates and malcontents,' Boyd replied.

Steepling his fingers, Maxwell asked, 'The townspeople are so lily-livered that they would negotiate with traitors to the Crown?'

'They are desperate, Colonel Maxwell,' stated Boyd.

Maxwell pursed his lips before musing, 'And desperate times demand desperate measures, isn't that so Captain Boyd?'

Boyd looked momentarily confused, a dark fissure appearing between his black brows, before he uttered a noncommittal, 'Sir.'

'Never mind,' said Maxwell, suddenly smiling. 'What you can do is reassure the townspeople, through whatever spokesperson they are ignorant enough to listen to, that all is in hand. Then get me Edward Turner, Mr Watson and Mr Perceval the High Sherriff.'

'Sir,' acknowledged Boyd, managing to express in that single syllable a whole universe of confusion.

'Do not presume to understand, Mr Boyd,' snapped Maxwell. 'Do as you are told.'

Boyd saluted and hurried from the room, buckling on his helmet as he did so. An odd sense of urgency seemed to grip him at Maxwell's words and he raced down the stairs and out of the building as though his life depended on it. The sunshine flung his shadow out beneath him as he ran, squat and frantic in the high afternoon light. Behind him, in the market house room, he left a confused Lieutenant-Colonel Foote and an unaccountably good-humoured Colonel Maxwell.

'Sir, do you mind if I ask what you have planned?' asked Foote.

'I intend to upset that rabble in Enniscorthy for as long as I possibly can, giving Fawcett and his cannon time to get here, whilst at the same time keeping the damned population here from rioting in panic and costing us the town through hysteria.'

Intrigued now, Foote made his way to one of the deep armchairs and eased himself down into it, the peaks and switchbacks of his Cork accent now soft as he almost whispered, 'I am puzzled, sir, as to how you hope to accomplish both.'

A smile crept slowly across Maxwell's face like something crawling from under a stone. 'If the townsfolk wish to negotiate then we shall let them,' he said slowly. 'But we shall also send word with all possible speed to Fawcett informing him of the seriousness of the situation and advising that we link our forces and come at the rebels from two sides.'

He made a sign with his right hand, index and fourth finger extended and jutting aggressively, 'We shall spear them on the horns of a bull.'

Foote was regarding the senior officer with an expression of appreciation.

'Then you do not mean to abide by the negotiations with the rebels?' he asked.

Maxwell scoffed, 'Rebels in arms against a sovereign power are to be treated with neither the respect nor the delicacy that one might reserve for a regular army. The rules of war do not apply here.'

'And who shall we send as emissary?' Foote pressed, eager now and leaning forward in his chair. 'It is a task fraught with peril for at the very sight of a known yeoman or magistrate they will like as not tear them limb from limb.'

'Keogh or Hay, perhaps?' he suggested.

Maxwell's hand went to his mouth and he smoothed the dark wings of his moustache. 'I would suggest Harvey and Fitzgerald,' he said at last.

Foote stared at him with eyes blinking wildly and blustered, 'But, sir, both those men are under arrest for plotting against the Crown. Harvey has been implicated as the supreme figure behind the United movement in the county whilst Edward Fitzgerald was named as chief amongst the others. Why would you send these men back to the very people who must desire their release?'

Maxwell leaned forward now too and hissed, 'Because, my dear Colonel Foote, if we break Harvey and Fitzgerald then we break the back of the United Irishmen. Ourselves and General Fawcett can then sweep them back into the bogs where they belong.'

'Pardon the impertinence, sir, but you are a shrewd man,' said Foote.

'I am a soldier, Colonel,' came Maxwell's reply. 'Nothing more.'

An hour later Maxwell, Foote, Perceval, Turner and Jonas Watson all crowded into the guard room of Wexford Gaol. The gaol itself was a squat, thick-walled building possessed of the same ponderous, elemental quality of boulders and cliff faces. It occupied a site backing onto Meadow's and Cardiff's quays but its grim facade loured over the narrow, cobbled defile of Barrack Street. All about the building, the reek of the docks was a miasma and from its handful of narrow, barred windows, red-brown stains washed with disgusting implication down the stonework of the exterior walls.

Within, the gaol was very much of utilitarian design, lacking all decoration or any sign of warmth or comfort. The cells occupied most of the structure, their heavy wooden doors age-blackened and iron-bound, chipped in a myriad of places by the ebb and flow of human misery.

The guard room was a small, claustrophobic cube of undressed stone. Whitewash made the walls glare back the light of two lanterns that provided the only real illumination in the place, the only source of daylight being a small, empty aperture set high up in the eastern wall through which a gouge of blue sky showed, like the promise of something unattainable.

A splintered, unvarnished table sat in the middle of the guard room, which usually provided a grimy beach on which the detritus of the guards' meals fetched up and were left to rot. At this piece of furniture, Maxwell, Foote and Perceval sat on creaking chairs. Behind them, Edward Turner and Jonas Watson leaned against the dusty white of the walls.

On the opposite side of the table sat two men. One was well into his middle years, quite heavy-set with the rotund physique of a well-moneyed aristocrat. A powdered wig, now mouse-grey from his time in the gaol, was incongruously perched on his head. He wore a simple white shirt, buff breeches and black shoes. His stockings, which had been silk and very finely made, had been confiscated by one of the guards almost as soon as he had entered the place. His soft calves were streaked with dirt and his loose jowls quivered as his eyes flew from face to face before him.

The other man was slimmer than the first and younger, though a slackness about the jaw line and gut betrayed the fact that he too enjoyed a life that, until now, had not been ravaged by hardship. He wore no wig and his brown hair curled thick and full away from his temples and was held at the nape of his neck by a small black bow. His eyes twinkled with intellectual vitality and there was a certain pugnacity to the set of his shoulders and the line of his jaw that might have been deemed foolish considering his present circumstances.

This second man now spoke, his attention fixed on Henry Perceval, the High Sherriff.

'My dear Henry,' he said. 'How pleasant to see you. Such fine company you're keeping. May I be so bold as to enquire when you intend to let us out?'

Henry Perceval sighed in exasperation, 'Mr Fitzgerald, while I commend you for your bravery it would go better with you were you not so flippant.'

Fitzgerald raised an eyebrow and retorted, 'Flippant? You think me flippant? I would like you then to provide me with any reason why myself, Mr Harvey here beside me, and Mr Colclough are being detained here without trial or opportunity to defend ourselves. I am a trained magistrate, Mr Perceval, and you are acting unlawfully.'

Perceval shook his head but, before he could answer, Colonel Maxwell spoke slowly and levelly, 'Martial law holds sway here, Mr Fitzgerald, and I would be more worried about your very soul than the niceties of courtroom etiquette.'

'And you are?' asked Fitzgerald, his mask of bold impudence still in place, only undermined by the slight pallor that crept suddenly into his cheeks.

'My name is Colonel Maxwell,' came the reply. 'And I am a person not to be trifled with. I have news of your rebellion – your "Rising", I believe you croppies call it.'

'I will not listen to lies,' began Fitzgerald, but Harvey's hand gripped his forearm with surprising fervour.

'Hear him, at least,' the plump aristocrat advised.

Fitzgerald glanced at him in open confusion but relented, motioning for Maxwell to continue.

The vaguest hint of a smile hooked at the corners of the officer's mouth and then was gone as he said, 'Your little Rising has taken place without you. Of that I am sure you are glad.'

Fitzgerald and Harvey exchanged amazed looks and Fitzgerald leaned forward, forearms resting on the grease-smeared table. 'I have no idea what you are talking about, Colonel. But let us assume for a moment that I am in league with these dastardly United Irishmen. How might the outbreak of rebellion give you cause to visit us here in gaol?'

'Because I am going to tell you something that might change your opinion of matters and rob your eyes of their sparkle, Mr Fitzgerald.'

Both Fitzgerald and Harvey regarded Maxwell cautiously. 'Go on,' instructed Fitzgerald.

'Dublin did not rebel,' stated Maxwell. 'The little fighting that there was in other counties was petering out by yesterday. Your county and the foolish people that reside within it are fighting, unsupported, against the entire military apparatus.'

He grinned then, blatantly and cruelly, and in a voice carrying all the weight of a falling axe, he said, 'You are on your own.'

Fitzgerald was dumbstruck but Harvey shifted his weight uncomfortably and dabbed his sleeve against the folds of flesh that swelled about his open collar. 'Let us imagine for a moment that what you say is the truth,' the portly aristocrat said quietly. 'Let us furthermore imagine that I or any of my acquaintances may be in any position to influence the rebels. What would you have done?'

Fitzgerald was spurred into outrage at this. 'This is all lies, Beauchamp!' he exclaimed. 'It is a plot engineered so that we might incriminate ourselves and save them the trouble of a trial.'

He addressed the military men in front of him, 'If you wish to hang us, then have done with it. We are not objects for your entertainment.'

'Mr Fitzgerald,' replied Watson, his odd accent soothing and placating. 'We do not wish to visit violence upon any person. It is violence and bloodshed that we are so strenuously attempting to avoid. A rebel band has attacked and burned Enniscorthy and now seems bent on threatening this very town. There is a garrison of over a thousand men here, gentlemen, there is cannon and cavalry and a wall we can defend. Peasants and farmers cannot hope to take this place without soaking the entire neighbourhood with their blood. You cannot hope to win this war.'

Fitzgerald drummed his fingers on the table.

'You wish us to become emissaries,' he said at last. 'You wish us to tell the rebel forces to disband.'

'We wish to offer terms,' said Maxwell delicately. 'If the rebels surrender their arms and return home, we shall overlook the more grotesque actions of their rank and file. Only the leaders shall be held to account.'

'What about our position?' asked Harvey, his eyes darting from one hard face to the next. 'What can we hope to gain from such an action?'

Perceval, with a pained expression on his face, reluctantly replied, 'You shall save yourself from the gallows. If you bring this whole sorry mess to a satisfactory and speedy conclusion you may escape even the need to make reparations.'

Fitzgerald looked stricken and his eyes cast this way and that, as though questing for some bolt-hole or escape route. At length and with the palpable ache of a man conflicted in his own mind, he pressed, 'As officers and gentlemen, upon your honour, you swear to me that what you say is true.'

Maxwell nodded in a melodramatic parody of sympathetic understanding, 'I swear to you that you have no hope in the coming fight. Your cause is already lost.'

'I will not go,' Harvey's voice came thick and wet as porridge. 'I will not go. They do not know me and will shoot me on sight for betraying them. I will not go. Send Colclough in my stead. Tell them that I remain a hostage here to their good conduct. Colclough and Edward, here, will go. Won't you, Edward?'

Fitzgerald seemed to have withered where he sat and wore an expression of heartbreak. He glanced at the men before him, gaze lingering lastly on Harvey's heavy features, his eager eyes and sweating brow. 'It seems as though I have no choice,' he mumbled at last. 'I will take John Henry with me and I will go to Enniscorthy.'

'Good man,' breathed Maxwell whilst, concurrently, the other officers around him smiled and clapped each other on the back.

To Edward Fitzgerald though, the most dreadful and shameful thing of all was the slow, relieved smile spreading across Bagenal Harvey's face. It was like something leaking from an abattoir.

CHAPTER 13

Events at Three Rocks

On Vinegar Hill, the council of war that had made a cauldron of bad temper and ill-will under the canopy of Roche's tent, continued with all the vehemence of a faction fight. The graceless bawling that had threatened to destroy the entire enterprise had died down and Roche and Fr Murphy had placed at least temporary rein on the emotions of their captains. The round table still remained surrounded by the chief commanders whilst about them the captains and chiefs of the parishes and townlands made another, more sullen ring. The air was crackling with tension and barely-restrained ire as arguments and proposals were hurled across the tent. For nearly two hours now the conclave had been in session and still was no closer to consensus. Men came forward to show the bubbled scars of pitchcappings and claimed that the entire army should march in haste to deliver retribution on the heads of those who perpetrated it. Others claimed they should avenge the dead of Carnew and Dunlavin by straightaway adding those dens of Orange iniquity to the list of towns set to accompany ravaged Enniscorthy. On and on it went, as men with no concept of military strategy were given free hand to throw whatever half-baked conceits or personal grudges they harboured into the general melting pot.

'This is ridiculous,' stated Dan bluntly.

'A waste of time,' added Miles Byrne.

It was at this moment, when Dan felt that no direction would ever be found and that the vast army camped outside would surely fragment and drift away, that a growing uproar penetrated the walls of the tent. The din intensified as one of the men guarding the tent's entrance pushed the canvas flap aside and called, 'General Roche, you should see this.'

'Adjourned, for the moment, gentlemen,' stated Roche flatly, sweat glistening on his upper lip and matting his sideburns to his cheeks.'

At his words the captains, grumbling and muttering amongst themselves, filed out.

Dan and Miles blinked in the sudden effulgence and raised their hands to shield their eyes. They scanned the lower slopes to ascertain what might be prompting such a happy swell of noise. For happy it was, with no sense of panic or alarm about it. Just a multitude of voices raised in good cheer.

Then, over the shoulder of hill to the south, the first small, ragged figure of a crowd of people came walking lightly, his young face aglow and calling out, 'Edward Fitzgerald! It's Edward Fitzgerald! He's escaped and come back to us!'

Behind the boy, surrounded by a flux of admiring forms, rode two men. One was older, with ascetic features and a weak chin, dressed in a once-lavish jacket that had seen better days. The other was splendidly mounted and dressed, wearing a gentleman's tricorn and a frock coat that seemed brand-new, stained only here and there with the dust of his journey. He waved to people as he jogged his mount forward, smiling and gracious as a lord.

At a little distance from the gathered leaders the crowd fell away, laughing and joking and crying, 'Three cheers for Lord Edward and Mr Colclough!' as though they were returning friends or long-lost relatives.

Alone, the two horsemen covered the last twenty yards of stony ground and, without their flotilla of admirers, their faces assumed a much graver aspect. As Dan watched, Edward Fitzgerald, seemingly without thinking, reached down to where excited hands had twined a green ribbon into his horse's mane. Unconsciously he loosed the piece of fabric and it floated elegantly to the ground to be trampled by his mount's heavy stride.

Dan frowned, troubled.

Fitzgerald and Colclough dismounted in front of the assembled captains and immediately Edward Roche rushed to shake their hands. 'By God, I am happy to see you! What of Harvey?' he gushed.

Fitzgerald was silent, his eyes roving from one captain to the next, seemingly transfixed by the sheer number of men that had flooded to the United banner.

Colclough however, coughed politely and said, 'Bagenal is unfortunately still detained at Wexford Gaol.'

'Come,' instructed Roche. 'Sit with us and tell us how you executed your escape. I must say, you look in tolerable good health for a prisoner of the military.'

Colclough and Fitzgerald exchanged awkward looks but followed Roche as he led them into the tent. The other captains trailed after, the ones who knew

Fitzgerald happily informing the others that now, with 'Lord Edward' to lead them, they would storm Dublin Castle itself.

'There's something not quite right here,' Dan muttered to Miles Byrne.

Byrne's young face was twisted around a fretful scowl. 'I agree,' he said. 'I don't like the condemned expression on Fitzgerald's face. He is one of the most active and able gentlemen that I am acquainted with but to see him so cowed makes a mockery of everything I know him to be.'

Dan lifted the tent flap, the canvas warm and rough, like a callus, to the touch, and allowed Byrne to go ahead of him. Inside, the tent was filled with a downy quiet that seemed to smother all noise at its conception. The colonels and General Roche were sitting at the round table with the captains spread out around the walls. Every eye was latched onto Edward Fitzgerald where he sat with Colclough, a little apart from the other leaders. Every eye except Anthony Perry's, who instead directed his gaze into the blank lustre of the table top as though lost in his own thoughts.

Fitzgerald coughed, paused, swallowed drily and then rubbed the heel of his palms across his closed eyes.

Roche was frowning now and he urged, 'Come on, Edward. Out with it.'

Fitzgerald sighed and with a grimace said, 'The numbers on this hill surpass my wildest dreams of what a United Army might look like in the field and your triumphs at the Harrow, Oulart and Enniscorthy are on the tongue of every person that we have encountered from here to Wexford. I had not hoped that we would be so successful and so soon.'

'Why then, with a victorious army before you, do you seem so melancholy?' asked Fr Murphy suspiciously.

Fitzgerald cast his gaze aloft in despair and moaned, 'Because we are alone. Because the rest of the country is subdued.'

An outburst of anger and dismay flared through the gathered leaders before Roche silenced all by surging to his feet.

'How can you say that?' he demanded. 'How could you possibly know?'

'Colonel Maxwell who now commands Wexford Town with over a thousand men swore to me it was so.'

'Lies!' spat Fr Murphy, rising to stand with Roche. 'Damned lies, spawned to dilute our spirit and cool the fire of our purpose.'

Roche was leaning on the table, glaring at the men before him with a terrible discernment. 'They sent you here, didn't they?' he asked, jabbing a thick finger first at Colcloough and then at Fitzgerald. 'This Maxwell sent you here to ask for our surrender. And you consented to be his pigeon. For shame, gentlemen!'

Colclough lowered his eyes, unable to meet Roche's glare, but Fitzgerald's face remained stoic and determined.

'They sent us here with terms, Edward,' explained Fitzgerald. 'If you disband and go home now the rank and file along with their families and property will be spared. Otherwise, most terrible war will be unleashed upon every man woman and child in the county.'

At these words a rolling thunder of fury and indignation rumbled through every one of the gathered captains. It was Miles Byrne's young voice, however, that cut through the rumbling anger and belled forth strong and clear, ringing with his irrepressible self-assurance.

'Gentlemen,' he began, 'the sheer gall of you to express such sentiments astounds me and beggars belief. Are you aware of the absurdity of telling a victorious army to disperse and go to their homes, and there wait until they might be shot in detail?

'What these "terms", and I would hesitate to put such a name on what amounts to mere doggerel, serve to indicate is how panic-struck the garrison of Wexford Town really is.'

A general murmur of agreement rippled about the tent at Byrne's words.

'If we were to descend on Wexford swiftly, like the wrath of God Himself, we must surely take the town and all its supplies,' stated Fr Murphy hammering the table with his fist.

Another captain, unknown to Dan and wearing an ivory cravat, most likely stolen from some gentleman's wardrobe and badly knotted about his own grimy throat, roared in approval, 'I'm for that! We should drive them across the water to Wales!'

A great cheer went up from the gathering at this and, as Dan watched, cohesion and accord began to gel men together who had, only minutes before, been about to fling the entire United Irish enterprise into oblivion rather than have their individual vendettas thwarted. Hands were shaken that before had been balled into fists and men were suddenly galvanised and eager, anxious to be on the road to Wexford Town.

Amongst them, however, John Hay and William Barker frowned and said nothing. Their advice and their good sense had been washed away on a flood tide of enthusiasm and anger. The terms offered by Maxwell had pricked the leadership's pride and given direction to all the pent-up frustration and energy that had moments before been without any obvious outlet.

Edward Fitzgerald and John Henry Colclough watched in awe and despair as the men they had sought to protect from an all-out war were now set inflexibly upon that very path. The guilt that Fitzgerald felt in the pit of his stomach was like something alive and squirming.

Outside Roche's tent, Colclough was unceremoniously dumped into his saddle. All about and on the slopes sweeping down to where Enniscorthy smouldered, spitting and coughing like a dying man, corps of insurgents were raising banners and cries went soaring into the air: 'Bargy men to your colours!' and 'Shelmalier men, to me!' Over and over the calls rang out, multiplying and re-echoing until Vinegar Hill was a swarming mass of men coming together by company and forming about the emerald banners of their own parish and barony.

Colclough looked about him in mingled pride and fear and then turned to Edward Roche who stood at his horse's head. 'Are you sure you wish me to communicate those exact words?'

Roche nodded deliberately, just once, his chin ducking into the flesh of his jowls and said, 'Those exact words. Tell Maxwell that as long as he holds Harvey, then we keep Fitzgerald and that no terms on his part will be listened to other than the complete surrender of the town.'

Colclough nodded, took one last look as the vast camp mobilising about him and replied, 'As you wish, General.'

Then he was gone, spurring his horse southward toward Wexford, dust and flies left hanging in his wake.

Dan watched the man thunder away and considered how simple, once a purpose had been decided upon, it had been to marshal the men and delegate duties. Within minutes, committees had been established to oversee the supply and welfare of the men. A semblance of order was to be restored to the desolate hell that Enniscorthy had become and Vinegar Hill was to be the main depot and rallying point for all United forces. William Barker was elected to oversee the repair and defence of the town that he loved and had grown up in. Officers from each parish, with a small cohort of pikemen each, were immediately tasked with providing supplies and provisions for the fighting men. The swollen bulk of Vinegar Hill was to become the main reservoir of food, with the women and children remaining to bake bread and cook the meat. The garrison at Enniscorthy under Barker was to be replenished and relieved at regular intervals by men newly arrived at the camp. Vinegar Hill was to become a symbol of abstract defiance, a place not just of upheaval but of organisation and self-reliance as well. A new order was being born; bloodied and bawling in the sunlight.

Dan was pleased that Roche and Murphy had been at pains to order

Thomas Dixon and his men to join the long column facing south. The two leaders had separated Dixon and his fellow zealot, Luke Byrne, by virtue of the fact that they belonged to separate corps. Byrne was left behind on the hill, stewing in chagrin, whilst Dixon stood grumbling at the head of his men, craning his neck back towards the windmill and the prisoners within.

Elizabeth, however, was to prove an entirely more difficult problem. She stood outside their little den of blanket and gorse, arms akimbo and eyes flashing.

'Don't be such a fool, Daniel Banville,' was her response to his request that she remain at Enniscorthy.

'Elizabeth,' he said, infuriated, 'why must you be so stubborn?'

Her eyes widened at this and her lips tightened with anger. 'And why must you be such a fuddy-duddy?'

Tom, who was busying himself with buckling on sword and pistols, sniggered derisively.

Dan ignored him and pleaded with Elizabeth, 'This might very well prove to be a most bloody encounter. There are over a thousand troops at Wexford and here, at least, Mr Barker shall have crews of men rebuilding the town. You shall be safe here amongst the women.'

'No, I shan't,' she replied. 'Half the women here will not even look at me let alone afford me any assistance or kind words. I am coming with you Daniel and I am not for turning on this.'

Dan knew it was pointless to argue further.

Tom then stood and pointed, his expression curdled into a snarl. 'That horrible termagant is coming too, it seems.'

Down the slope towards the fighting men, the bloated form of the questioning woman from the other day stumped through the gorse and long grass. Her lumpen arms were enfolded about a bundle of clothes and a cooking pot swung by a length of twine from one meaty shoulder. Her gaze swept the hillside in half-lidded disdain as though to offer challenge to the world, as though she were at eternal war with life itself.

As she passed the assembling column of rebels, which now stretched from Enniscorthy to more than a mile beyond its southern boundary, she paused and, bending all of her great bulk forward, she kissed Thomas Dixon on the cheek.

'Well, glory be to God,' exclaimed an astounded Dan. 'Will you look at that.'

'Shite will always attract flies,' commented Tom, for which he received a chiding slap on the arm from Elizabeth.

With everything arranged as best they could, the little group moved down into the valley amidst a horde of others, men leaping over hummocks, pikes in hand, hurrying to their companies. As they reached the foot of the hill, Elizabeth made to turn right, intending to join the still numerous flock of women and children who had decided to remain with the column rather than stay in the relative safety of Enniscorthy and its environs. As she took her first step away from him, Dan seized her by the shoulder, turned her and kissed her passionately. Tom directed his gaze downward and scuffed at the dirt with the toe of his boot.

'If Dixon can get a kiss before marching off in the hot sun,' Dan said rather breathlessly, 'then I don't see why I shouldn't.'

Elizabeth stared up at him with a stunned expression, her eyes somewhat dazed, her mouth slack. She swallowed once and replied, 'Mr Banville, how indecorous of you.'

With that, she adjusted her battered sun-bonnet and made her way off to the rear.

Laughing, Dan and Tom strode quickly to take their place at the head of the Castletown men. A green standard, stitched with harps and shamrocks and emblazoned with the word 'Liberty', hung from a banner pole above their front rank. The banner man was a young farmer who recognised them immediately. 'Captain Banville,' he greeted with a nod. 'Young Mr Banville. I hope you are well.'

Tom stared at the man in frank surprise and said, 'Jim Kehoe! And I thought you were a peaceable young fellow with no interest in anything except barley and potatoes, and you a United Irishman?'

Kehoe nodded, 'That I am. Me and Captain Banville took the oath at the same time, didn't we Captain Banville?'

'That we did, Jim,' said Dan. 'Now stop calling me "Captain".'

Tom was shaking his head, flummoxed. 'Am I the only one in the whole parish who wasn't a United man?' he asked.

Dan patted his brother on the back, a wide smile breaking across his broad features, 'You know, I think you may very well have been.'

The minutes dragged on as stragglers were rounded up and added to the ever-growing multitude of pike- and gunsmen. The column was now a formidable thing of vast numbers and honed steel. At its core were six thousand men who had stormed a principal town and wrested it from a well-armed garrison. At its core was a fearless determination.

And yet Tom was troubled.

In spite of the rebel army's successes thus far, in spite of its burgeoning numbers, there was a blank where there should have been something vital. The lack of cannon, cavalry and ready supplies of ammunition were unfortunate, and to Tom, insurmountable – but something else was dragging a saw blade across his nerves. The prevarication shown by the leadership over the best course of action, the arguments and the parochialism as related by Dan did not bode well for the future. John Hay and William Barker had been forgotten in the rush to exterminate an already beaten army, huddling and afraid in Wexford Town.

New Ross, he thought. We should be marching on New Ross.

At length a bugle sounded from the vanguard of the rebel army and corps after corps of men began the march to Wexford Town. Above the column, pikes and pole-arms made a rattling forest of needling black, swaying and weaving in rhythm to the men's gait. Each pike head glistened where oil and whetstones had done their work, polishing the blade and hook and sharpening their lethal edge. Thousand upon thousand, rank on rank, the United Irish Army snaked along the road, men binding neckerchiefs about their noses and mouths against the dust of their passing.

Out ahead, Miles Byrne and his Monaseed contingent had taken up the familiar role of vedette for the mass of fighting men behind. They ranged along the road and criss-crossed the fields to either side but no word of ambuscade or counter-attack came back from them.

To the army's right, the River Slaney ploughed lazily along, languid in the afternoon heat. On its wrinkled surface, a family of swans sailed proudly, their pristine white elegance balanced upon the pale smear of their own reflections. Abandoned gabbards and sand cots were left beached against its banks, a reminder of peaceful times, seemingly gone forever.

Enniscorthy soon became only a smoking memory behind a turn in the road and still they marched, feet grinding the earth in a long, harsh continuous growl. No one marched in step and it was all the men could do to keep each individual corps from splintering and merging with the one behind. Every so often, Roche or either of the Fr Murphys would come riding along the flanks, exhorting the men and chivvying along those inclined to dawdle.

Twilight was beginning to purple the horizon as the rebel army tramped across Ferrycarrig Bridge, two miles west of Wexford Town. Along the march no sign of soldiers, cavalry or civilians had been seen. It was as though the whole world had been gutted. At Ferrycarrig, the head of the column veered not east towards Wexford Town but rather southwest, towards the hulking, dusky, heather-bruised mass of Forth Mountain. They passed beneath the old Norman watchtower, venerable and grizzled on its granite tor and then swung right.

Dan was confused. 'Why are we making for another campsite?' he wondered aloud.

'I cannot fathom,' answered Tom. 'I do not see why we should not sweep into the town under cover of darkness and carry the place by storm. This, to me, smacks of another needless waste of time. The men are fresh, they have rested and eaten well all day.'

'Perhaps Fitzgerald has given them cause to delay?' ventured Dan.

'Perhaps Fitzgerald should be flogged and sent back to the garrison that he professes such intimacy with,' replied Tom acidly.

Dan scowled at him but said nothing.

In the gathering folds of darkness Roche and Fr Murphy led them up the bordering slope and through the surrounding bracken and briar. Above them, like blots of ink against the red gouts spreading across the sky, the outcropping of the Three Rocks loomed ominously. Underneath these fists of rock and dry moss the rebel army spread out on the swathe of heather and made what shelter they could from blankets and swatches of canvas. The road below was lost behind the uneven swelling of the mountain's slope and above them there was only the vast, gemmed cloak of the night.

Tom, Dan and Elizabeth sat out in the open, cushioned on a feathery mattress of heather, and watched the men and women around them construct tents and lean-tos, using the hafts of pikes for scaffolding. No fires were lit; orders had been passed down that light of any kind was to be immediately extinguished. Nevertheless, here and there, men who had never bowed to authority in all their days surreptitiously sucked on glowing pipes.

Tom was about to say something, to caution Dan about the danger posed by fire amidst the tinder-dry undergrowth, but Dan raised a hand, cutting him off.

'Let them,' the elder Banville whispered. 'They have seen and sacrificed enough to allow them the simple pleasure of a bowl of tobacco of an evening.'

Tom grunted but still felt the need to add, 'If they set fire to the hillside around us or give warning to any eagle-eyed yeo, then all their sacrifice will be for naught.'

Elizabeth yawned and held Dan closely to her and on her face a contented smile played at the bow of her mouth. 'You worry too much,' she said.

The following morning broke across Wexford Town like a gentle wave. A mackerel sky of dappled, sea-blown cloud gaped overhead and seemed to widen and deepen as the light gradually grew.

The Colonels Maxwell and Foote stood tiredly on the quays and looked out across Wexford Harbour where a freshening breeze tossed the waves into saw-edged flux. Gulls, angular and screaming, scudded across the combers, delighting in the toss and tumble of the wind. The flat, wooden thrust of Wexford Bridge lanced out across the water to terminate on the East Shelmalier shoreline opposite; a long, tarred, skeletal arm clawing off into the distance. About the toll house sitting on this northern end of the bridge, a large group of people had gathered. Unlike the loyalist refugees of the past few days, these people made no effort to cross the water or make for the town. Instead, they milled about on the wave-sluiced shore and busied themselves ransacking the abandoned toll booth. Foote fancied that he could hear glass breaking, delicate and almost musical.

Behind the two weary officers was a small detachment of equally weary North Corks. Foote regarded them with eyes that felt filmed with sand and then turned to Maxwell.

'Should we order those vagabonds on the bridge to disperse?'

Maxwell exhaled heavily and rubbed his chin with a gloved hand. The rasping sound the leather made against the stubble of his sprouting beard startled him and he looked down at his palm in surprise. Slowly, he removed the glove, smoothed his moustaches and replied deliberately, 'No.'

Replacing the glove and flexing his fingers within he explained, 'With those thousands of ruffians encamped at the Three Rocks, those people yonder are most likely a ruse to split our forces. They cannot cross the bridge without being cut to pieces by our musket shot and they cannot do any mischief to us from so great a distance.'

'They can cut us off from any retreat northward,' said Foote cautiously, his eyes flickering to his superior and away again like midges across water.

'If we do abandon the town,' answered Maxwell, 'it will be to make for the fort of Duncannon to the south.'

He paused and looked to the west, though the crowding buildings of the busy port blocked any view of the countryside beyond. He squinted at the sky then and took a gold watch from out of his waistcoat pocket. In the dawn the inscription, *With all my love, A.M.*, was swilled with sepia, the letters curling darkly against the bright metal.

'Fawcett should be here,' he growled angrily. 'What is keeping him?'

Foote considered for a moment before saying, 'When that messenger, Sutton, arrived in from Fawcett just an hour ago he related that he had grave difficulty avoiding the mass of banditti on the slopes of Forth Mountain. He was but one man alone. Fawcett's column must surely number in the hundreds and must find it impossible to negotiate the countryside around the rebels without drawing them down upon him.'

Maxwell watched the crowd on the far bank of the harbour mill and swirl in agitated bursts of movement. He stood for a moment in silence before musing, 'If we were to fix the rebels in place, then that would surely allow Fawcett to get through.'

Foote frowned at his commanding officer, his face anxious, 'Sir, that would necessitate leading a large body of men out through John Street and into open country. The rebel camp at the Three Rocks is said to number over ten thousand. If they were to fall all at once upon the men I am sure that we must come out the worst of it. Captain Snowe was, last night, most vociferous in his opposition to any engagement with them without at least parity of numbers or cavalry in support.'

Maxwell sniffed derisively, 'I feel Captain Snowe has been most abominably unmanned by his defeat at Enniscorthy. We have Boyd's cavalry along with Captain Cox's two hundred horse from Taghmon. We should be able to out-flank the rebel position and keep them perched amongst the heather and stones.'

'And if Fawcett still cannot get through, or if the rebels fall on us like a wolf on the fold, what then?' wondered Foote.

Maxwell smiled grimly, 'That will not happen. If the rebels were possessed of the intrepidity they pretend to, they would have come close on the heels of Colclough and forced us to give battle immediately. Instead, they dally. I think that three hundred troops and two hundred cavalry should be enough to cool any rebellious fervour. With Fawcett at their back I am sure that they must be positively bamboozled.'

Foote nodded contemplatively before stating, 'I believe you should have Mr Watson ride with the men. His experience in fighting the colonists might be of great value in our current predicament.'

'Capital idea,' agreed Maxwell, his mood visibly lifting and the fatigue that dulled his eyes seemingly fleeing with the dawn. 'I do believe that our position might not be as dire as first we thought.'

Foote eyed him dubiously. 'Sir,' he said.

The same dawn that found Maxwell and Foote standing on the Wexford quays illuminated the Three Rocks in shades of dove-grey. Through the bracken and ferns, leaping over briar and knuckled stone, a figure came running through the cold morning light. He scrambled up the western slope of the hill and knifed between snoring bundles of blankets and ragged tents whose canvas coverings were beginning to snap and rumple in a mounting breeze. The man's breath was coming in gasps now and he hauled himself toward the summit by balling his fists amongst the dew-slick undergrowth and pumping the burning muscles of his legs. At the crest of Forth Mountain, Roche's tent hulked against the brightening sky with the two banners rippling out from their poles, the green and the black, the harp and the chasuble.

The pikeman sitting at guard outside the tent's entrance rose at the man's approach and staring hard into the grainy dawning he called in greeting, 'Thomas Cloney! What's a Bantry boy like you doing running around so early. Sure, aren't youse late for everything?'

Then the man took in Cloney's breathless face, his bracken-soaked clothes and asked bleakly, 'What's wrong?'

'I may speak with General Roche,' Cloney panted, his hands on his knees. 'There's soldiers coming from the west. They're bringing cannon.'

Minutes later and Edward Roche was hurriedly tucking his shirt into his buff-coloured breeches and asking, 'What would you have us do, Father?'

Fr John Murphy was also frantically striving to dress himself in the grey twilight of the tent's interior. He pulled on his heavy brogues and replied, 'I am not a military man, Mr Roche, and know nothing of artillery but I do know that if we allow them to come close enough to unleash shot and shell then it will go badly for a lot of the men out there.'

Sitting up from where he lay swaddled in blankets, Edward Fitzgerald raised his hands and commented, 'I have not been amongst you for long enough to voice any opinion on the strengths of the fighting men nor do I feel it appropriate that I should offer any military advice in my current circumstances.'

Roche flung him a caustic look before addressing Cloney. 'How many are there?'

'A hundred, maybe more,' replied Cloney. 'It doesn't seem to be a full regiment and the soldiers are led by a lieutenant. They look like a support column.'

'So where is the main body of the regiment?' asked Roche, loading his pistols.

Cloney shrugged, 'There's no sign of them. Our lookouts report this column with the artillery moving against us but the country out as far as Taghmon is free of the soldiery.'

'Perhaps they hope to trap us somehow?' asked Fr Murphy.

Cloney shook his head, 'I think the artillery column has just ranged too far ahead of its regiment. John Kelly of Killann wants us to trap them on the road as they cross over from the west and wipe them out. I would favour that too. The men of Bantry have missed Oulart and Enniscorthy, let us taste victory here.'

Fitzgerald was now standing and pulling on his breeches, his face branded with a doleful expression, the outward manifestation of the conflict raging in his heart. He sighed and asked, 'You are sure this could not be an ambuscade?'

Cloney nodded fervently, 'There's not a redcoat around to bring them succour. They're ignorant and unmindful as a new-born lamb. Kelly has a thousand of the boys assembled already. All he's waiting for is the word from yourselves.'

Murphy and Roche exchanged a long glance whilst Fitzgerald stared at the heather-carpeted floor.

'Have it done,' Roche said flatly.

Captain Adams of the Meath Militia rode in some confusion at the head of his marching column. Forth Mountain rose about him in a great swollen bulge of fern and furze. To his left the slope fell away into the lightening gloom, scattered with a patchwork of rough fields that God alone knew what crops or animals could be sustained by. To his right, the hillside rose in a chaos of whipping briar and clutching bracken, dismal and painted in shades of grey and brown by the breaking day. The road his column moved along ran west to east along the flank of the mountain, dusty and overgrown, its neglect and disrepair evident in its ruts and washed-out potholes. A more desolate place he could not imagine.

He frowned beneath the peak of his cocked hat and cast his eyes back over his column and into the silvered countryside below. His Meath infantry, all sixty-six of them, stomped along stoically with only one or two yawning from the tiredness of marching through the night. Behind the red coats of his own soldiers came the dark blue of the twenty or so men and officers of His Majesty's Royal Irish Artillery, the silver braiding of their blue coats glowing like spider webs in the morning light. Amongst them, on heavy carriages drawn by four deep-chested horses, sat the toad-like bulk of two howitzers with all their supplies of ammunition and powder.

And yet there was no sign of General Fawcett.

Adams was beginning to think that he had been duped.

The night before he and his detachment had paused for rest at Taghmon, where General Fawcett had supposedly already placed his men at free quarters, a necessity that the peasantry despised and resented. When Adams and his column had arrived however, they were informed by a group of apparently concerned villagers that Fawcett had pushed on immediately, such was the gravity of the situation in which the garrison at Wexford found itself. Taking them at their word, Adams had ordered his men to march on into the darkness, without sleep and without reconnoitring the land ahead of them.

He had allowed himself to be made a fool of, he reflected bitterly.

A sudden grumbling bubbled through the ranks of his men and the column came to a ragged halt, the soldiers muttering amongst themselves and one or two pointing down the slope to where the bracken and briar bristled about splintered outcrops of rock. Beside Adams, Lieutenant Wade shrugged in his saddle and called out, his voice echoing and gross in the silence, as though it were a violation of the dawn.

'You men,' he cried, 'who gave you the order to halt? Have you something to say for yourself, O'Hare?'

A sergeant, who was peering down-slope with a hawkish expression, started at the mention of his name and saluted sharply.

'Sir, one of the men here thinks he saw something moving below on the slope.'

Adams's frown deepened and he twisted in his saddle to scan the hillside with eyes suddenly wary, all thoughts of Fawcett abruptly supplanted by more immediate circumstances. It was at this moment, just as the leather of his saddle creaked and he adjusted his weight to cast his gaze over the rough expanse of ditch and brush below him, that a white rag, tied to the shaft of a pike, was raised aloft from the blanketing undergrowth some hundred yards down from their position.

The men of the Meath Militia immediately spurred into action. Flintlocks were drawn back with a sound like the crackling of autumn leaves as men aimed their muskets toward the tattered white flag that had vanished as suddenly as it had appeared.

A silence fell over the column. Into that silence, for the briefest moment, Captain Adams breathed in panting anticipation until a cold fist abruptly seized his heart and squeezed as if to burst it.

'Turn!' he yelled in sudden realisation. 'Turn, for the love of God! Face up the slope!'

He was a fraction of a second too late, for as the words sprang from his lips, so too did a spitting roar of musketry spring from the gorse and fern and thick undergrowth behind the soldiers. Smoke suddenly coughed across the roadway and filled the space between the ditches with a roiling blue-black fog.

Adams had no idea how many of his men had fallen to that first volley but he knew that his column was in bedlam. Within the fog of gunsmoke men had no idea from where the rebel guns had opened fire and some stood staring blankly at their fallen comrades whilst others fired blindly in the wrong direction.

'Up the slope!' Adams shouted, spurring his mount down the length of the column. 'They're above us!'

At that moment the entire hillside above the troops seemed to explode into lethal animation. Men spilled out of the bracken as though the very land was spewing them forth. The foremost of all was a blond giant who leapt with one bound over the low ditch bordering the road and hammered into the column with all the force of a charging bull. Adams watched, horrified, as the man's pike punched straight through the nearest soldier so that its brutal steel point exited between his shoulder blades in a sickening spume of crimson. Adams's men were being butchered.

Wheeling his horse, he yelled above the terrified screams of his men and the guttural whoops of their murderers, 'Spike the guns! Don't let them take the artillery!'

His eyes sought out the park of cannon and its blue-coated defenders and his face slackened in despair. The rebels had already seized them. Several of the artillery men were being held, pinned and struggling, to the ground whilst a group of peasants danced around the cannons, slapping them and rejoicing as though the each weapon were some fond pet or faithful hound.

Adams wheeled his mount once more, sawing savagely at the reins, his despair and panic rising to a hectic pitch. He could not reconcile what he was witnessing with what he knew of the world. His uniformed soldiery were being massacred, their cries obscenely desperate in the smoke and fumes.

Through the pall he saw the horde of the rebels standing over the bodies of his men whilst others chased off through the bracken, scything down those Meathmen who had tried to run, spitting them where they begged on their knees for mercy. Frantic and dismayed, Captain Adams spun his horse and thundered off to the west, lashing the animal with every atom of his strength. Behind him a huge roar of triumph and exultation swelled and climbed, soaring into the sky, huge and joyful, like the sun rising above the brow of Forth Mountain.

Dan beamed in satisfaction, 'That was some victory.'

Tom was shaking his head in bafflement but nonetheless a smile made a broad curve of his lips. 'I am amazed by our continuing success and good fortune. Our little army now has artillery. Who would ever have believed such a thing possible?'

The two brothers and Elizabeth were watching as the twin howitzers were wheeled forward through the ranks. The men of Bantry, who had won so valuable a prize and had been led so ably by John Kelly, were being feted throughout the camp as heroes and warriors on a par with the Fianna and Red Branch Knights. Songs and laughter rolled across the slopes of Forth Mountain as scouts came in from the countryside to the west reporting that Captain Adams and a few terrified survivors of the ambush at Three Rocks had continued their flight until they had run headlong into General Fawcett. At the news that the column had been annihilated and the cannon captured, Fawcett had immediately turned about and headed back to Duncannon. The general, it seemed, had decided to abandon the garrison at Wexford to its fate.

The rebels had now arranged themselves so that the bulk of the army was positioned on the eastern slope of Forth Mountain, overlooking the approaches to and from Wexford Town. A slight rise in the ground obscured the John Street gate which should have been clearly visible only two miles distant. John Hay had immediately taken charge of the newly acquired artillery and, using all the experience he had gained in service with the French, he now directed the placement of the guns so that their great maws overlooked this slight rise. Any sortie from the town or any force seeking to enter from Ferrycarrig must run the gauntlet of Hay's well-directed shot and shell. The gunnery privates who had been taken prisoner were now pressed into operating the howitzers and keeping them supplied with ammunition. The men, beaten and bloodied, had no choice but to comply.

Debates now began amongst the rank and file as to what to do next. Most favoured advancing straightaway to Wexford Town whilst others, with Thomas Dixon and his wife most vocal among them, favoured scouring the surrounding countryside for known loyalists and yeomen. The very sight of Dixon and his wife was enough to send tremors crawling across Elizabeth's skin and as the morning wore on she found herself drawing closer and closer to Dan as though to draw strength from his confidence and good humour. Dan was flushed with the success of the dawn victory and the capturing of the artillery but even for him the silence and aura of indecision emanating from the higher circles of leadership were becoming disturbing. As nine o'clock approached, Tom was spitting in frustration, 'Why are we not *doing* something?'

Miles Byrne approached them, his raking stride carrying him easily up the slope away from the forward lines and the howitzers, now well dug-in behind a ditch. He swept his hat from his head and wiped a hand across his brow saying, 'Good morning, Dan, Tom. Ms Elizabeth.'

'Good morning, Miles,' replied Dan. 'Any word on what the plan is now that we find ourselves in such an advantageous position? What are the prospects of an attack on the town?'

Byrne's young face soured at this and he sighed, 'The leaders are debating what to do next. Every victory that we achieve in the field seems to stymie them rather than drive them on. Instead of greeting this morning's work as the boon it is, they are intent on creating phantom problems for us to overcome.'

Tom kicked at the heather at his feet, growling, 'A ridiculous waste of time. What could they be thinking?'

Just then a shout went up from the outer lines closest to Wexford Town. Over the rise in the distance, a large column of marching infantry and jogging cavalry were advancing. With colours flying and drum beating they came on with the cavalry swinging out to their left to prevent the rebels from flanking them on that side.

At the sight of the soldiers a sudden commotion seized the rebel ranks and men dashed hither and thither, snatching up pikes and muskets whilst women and children began to wail once again at the prospect of more death and violence.

Dan bent and kissed Elizabeth on the forehead. 'Get beyond the brow of the hill,' he instructed.

She smiled up at him, weary and resigned, and trailed her fingers along his jaw line. 'Be careful, my love,' she said.

He nodded and grinned coldly as she walked away before calling out in a belling voice, 'Castletown Corps, to your colours!'

Alongside him, Miles Byrne was crying, 'Monaseed men, to me!'

All about, the slopes of Forth Mountain had become a ringing anarchy of noise as orders were shouted and corps after corps assembled beneath their standards. The din was furious and in the middle of it all Edward Roche appeared beside Dan, Tom and Miles, his fleshy face intense and his eyes rapidly taking in the vista below.

'Have your men move forward with me,' he instructed Dan. To Byrne he ordered, 'Have the Monaseed boys along with the Ballaghkeen contingents move around to our right. Should you get the chance I want you to fall on their cavalry with every ounce of your fury and strength, do you understand?'

'I do, General,' and then Byrne was off across the slope, calling men to him as he went.

'Come along Mr Banville,' said Roche. 'Let us see what Mr Hay can do with our new toys.'

Colonel Maxwell surveyed the rebel position, now barely a mile in front of him. He had led the sizeable column of infantry and horse directly out of the John Street gate and had advanced purposefully and with good spirits into the countryside beyond. On his left Jonas Watson rode a stocky roan mare, on the old officer's grizzled head a wide-brimmed hat cast his face entirely in shadow. Occasionally and with an automatic quality that suggested the absence of any real thought, Watson's gauntleted hand would rise and he would smooth the long white moustache that drooped like willows on either side of his mouth. It comforted Maxwell to have Watson with him, for the old campaigner was glad to lend him the benefit of his experience in fighting irregulars across the Atlantic. It was reassuring that Watson considered the massive rabble blackening the slopes of Forth Mountain far less formidable than the rebels he had encountered in America. At his back marched Maxwell's entire contingent of Donegal Militia. The North Corks, shaken and badly mauled, he had considered unsuitable for any further fighting.

As Maxwell rode along he nodded in satisfaction as the Taghmon Yeoman Cavalry swept out to his left, trotting in squadrons and sitting their saddles in as perfect a representation of martial discipline as one could imagine. The entire picture that the garrison wished to paint in the eyes of the watching rebels was one of military pomp and excellence. Maxwell could imagine the bitter waves of fear and intimidation that would surely flood through the insurgent ranks at the sight of their advance. At the column's head, directly behind Maxwell and Watson, so that the snap and ripple was loud above their mounts' hooves, the Union Flag and the yellow regimental colours of the Donegals were carried, biting and whipping in the gusting sea breeze. Maxwell turned in his saddle to admire the sight of his men stretched out on the road leading back to Wexford Town and his features filled with a fierce pride.

'Your men look well enough,' commented Watson without taking his eyes off the massed ranks of rebels on the hill before them. 'They march in good order.'

'Aye,' agreed Maxwell. 'I have never seen them so eager for the fray.'

'I would hope,' replied Watson, 'that the necessity for a pitched battle might be avoided until we can link up with General Fawcett. These rebels of yours have substantial numbers.'

He pointed then, his hand lifting and index finger pointing inside the well-worn leather of his riding gloves. His liquid eyes were bright in the shade cast by his hat's brim, as he said, 'They have some men of ability with them too, it seems. See how they move to counter our cavalry.'

On the slope ahead of him, Maxwell could perceive a vast block of men moving through the fern and bracken, making towards the southeast face of the mountain, threatening the very cavalry that sought to pen them back. As he watched the rebels move, Maxwell was all at once reminded of starlings, flocks of tiny bodies, numberless in multitude, all moving as though controlled by a single intellect.

'Let them,' he grunted. 'Should they decide to separate further, Cox's cavalry may actually have the chance to get amongst them.'

At about seven hundred yards from the first of the rebel lines, Watson and Maxwell slowed the column's advance, preparing to wait for the first sign that Fawcett had reached his side of the great hulking hill before them.

Watson leaned forward in his saddle and his eyes, narrowed and sharp as pins, scanned the ditches ahead of him with all the wariness and circumspection that years in America had bred in him. He regarded the cavalry strung out to their left and he eyed the tightly packed lines of pikemen strung along the slopes of Forth Mountain and crouched behind its ditches and hedgerows. He spat distastefully into the dust at his horse's side and commented wistfully, 'If only we had a field gun or two.'

Concurrently, from out of the ditches sheltering the vanguard of the insurgent lines, a dragon's belch of smoke and flame vomited out into the morning. Maxwell and Watson had time to frown before the roar of the discharge rolled over them and the ground just to the right of the column leapt upwards in a brown jet of pulverised soil.

The officers' horses whickered and snorted, bucking like ships in a storm, whilst the ranks of the Donegal Milita took staggering steps backwards, shock and fear curdling the features of each and every man. Maxwell, struggling to control his panicked mount, yelled in fury, 'Hold my brave boys! Hold or we shame ourselves beyond redemption!'

Watson, who had managed to settle his mare rather more swiftly, was staring in smiling admiration toward the rebel position. 'By God,' he said softly. 'They have artillery and persons who know how to use it.'

'Could they be Fawcett's?' asked Maxwell, the creaking note of hysteria which he heard in his own voice appalling him.

Before Watson could answer, a second report bellowed out from the rebel ranks and the ground directly to the left of the column's front rank coughed skyward and spattered those soldiers closest to it with a dry rain of stones and soil. The Donegal men shuffled again, their colours dipping and wavering as the ensigns began to quail, their shoulders seeming to cave into their chests as though striving to make themselves as small a target as possible.

'Hold, damn you!' shouted Maxwell.

'Let me take some men,' said Watson, calmly. 'I'll take them forward and we shall see whether those guns are ours and how many these rebels might have.'

'That is dangerous, Mr Watson,' replied Maxwell.

Watson laughed with all the warmth of a funeral dirge. 'Their gunners have rather bigger and better targets than a mere scouting party, Colonel. I shall be safe enough.'

Maxwell nodded, 'Be quick about it, Mr Watson. The men cannot sit here all day and those shots are getting closer.'

Watson saluted, a little too sharply for Maxwell's taste, and wheeling his horse he selected five privates from the front ranks to accompany him. He then jogged off to the right, pushing through the scant gorse that made up the hedgerow at this particular point along the road, and quickly made his way forward through the fields. He crouched low in his saddle and ushered the redcoats with him to dash along the ditches like foxes at hunt, his face urgent, his gestures quick and honed as knives.

Maxwell was quietly impressed by the old campaigner's bravery and decisiveness and, in spite of his own trepidation at remaining exposed upon the road, he watched as Watson and his men gradually closed the distance to the rebel lines.

He could not know that in a hedgerow close to the base of Forth Mountain's eastern slope, one of Edward Roche's Shelmaliers was taking careful aim along the severe length of his long-barrelled strand gun. He could not know that the Shelmalier, who had grown up sniping at barnacle geese as they came whirring high in over the sloblands and marshes of the Slaney's mouth, was tracking Jonas Watson's every bob and motion.

In the distance, Jonas Watson was blown from his saddle, his body tumbling, limp and grotesque, through the bordering hedgerow to lie bleeding and lifeless in the dust of the road.

Maxwell blinked in horror as time itself seemed to stop. The sun became a static ball of fire in the sky and all the world contracted until it consisted solely of the pathetic, rumpled hummock of Watson's shattered carcass.

The rebel cannon flamed again and this time Maxwell felt words bubble up from a venomous wellspring of fear and loathing, bubble up and spew from his lips.

'Back to the town!' he heard himself cry. 'Back to the town or our lives are forfeit!'

The front ranks of the Donegals immediately began a slow wheel. This manoeuvre would, however, have resulted in dragging the rear ranks forward into range of the rebel's smoking cannon. Instead, first one and then another and then a whole flood of red-coated soldiery simply turned on their heels and took flight. Maxwell watched as his column, which had marched forth so proudly only an hour before, now disintegrated and commenced an inelegant scramble for the safety of Wexford Town. Kicking his horse's flanks, Colonel Maxwell joined them and within moments had overtaken even the speediest of his retreating men.

The Taghmon Cavalry, outnumbered, outmanoeuvred and now facing accurate cannon fire, all spun their mounts and joined the general rout. Behind them, dust and rebel cheers chased them home.

Upon the slopes of Forth Mountain Dan and Tom watched the sortie from Wexford Town turn tail and flee. Both men were smiling like proud fathers and before them, sweat trickling from their brows and coursing along the fringes of their sideburns, Edward Roche and John Hay were shaking hands.

Then, from behind them came a shout and Miles Byrne came leaping in boyish effusiveness through the bracken, holding his sword aloft so that it did not tangle in his stride.

'General Roche, sir!' he called. 'We must make after them! We should have every chance of catching them before they reach Wexford. Pursued vigorously, we would surely enter the town with them pell-mell, without the least hindrance.'

Byrne came to a ragged stop before Roche, breathless and eager.

Roche regarded him for a moment before turning with a curious expression of longing toward where the last of Maxwell's column was disappearing in the distance.

'I should speak to Fr Murphy and the others before undertaking such drastic action.'

'No you should not, Mr Roche,' argued Byrne. 'We have no time.'

Roche bridled at this and glaring at the young man before him, a stern echo of the yeomanry sergeant he once was entered his voice. 'Do not contradict me, boy,' he said. 'Or you shall feel the back of my hand before you feel any other procedure of discipline.

'We have time in abundance. The garrison is trapped within Wexford. They cannot hope to face us again and they cannot be relieved. They must sue for terms.'

Byrne looked about in dismay and Dan could perceive the same feeling of chagrin welling up inside John Hay as the old French officer shook his head forlornly and directed his gaze into the heather clumped about his ankles.

In the distance the pale dust cloud of Maxwell's escape gradually faded against the blue of the sky like the gold of dawn fading in the brightness of its own birth. In the roadway, his jacket already crawling with flies, Jonas Watson lay staring at the doming heavens, his eyes wide and sightless. In the centre of his forehead a black hole was punched. He looked vaguely surprised in death and his wound gaped blankly from out of the smooth white of his forehead like the pitiless eye of hell itself, spilling congealing tears of red toward the gull-grey wings of his temples.

CHAPTER 14

Old Wexford is Won

On receiving Colonel Maxwell's summons, Lieutenant-Colonel Foote raced with unseemly precipitation towards Wexford Gaol. News of the morning's disaster had reached the town with the first of Maxwell's terrified Donegals and from the first mouth to speak of it to the last ear which took it in, the tale had grown horribly in the telling. Every loyalist citizen in the town was in a frenzy of utmost terror. Some had flung themselves into the sea in an attempt to swim out to the ships riding so mockingly at anchor out in the bay. To make matters worse for the garrison, the mob of countryfolk which had amassed at the northern end of Wexford Bridge had set the planking alight and cut off all hope of breaking out to Dublin. Even now, as Foote barrelled through frantic crowds of civilians and stunned, wan, knots of redcoats, the trickle of smoke from the bridge's burning began to curl up into the cloud-clotted blue.

To his consternation, the soldiery of the Wexford garrison seemed to be in as much alarm as the civilian population. Once or twice he had passed men whom he knew to be members of the yeomanry without their uniforms, endeavouring to avoid his eye as he hurried past.

When he entered the gaol he found Maxwell along with Henry Perceval and Wexford's mayor, Ebenezer Jacob, gathered around the disgusting slab of the guardroom table. Maxwell looked as though he had been through hell, such was the jaundiced colour of his complexion. Every inch of his flesh seemed to be coated with sweat and the lines of his face seemed to have been ploughed deeper than before. He sat and stared at his hands lying heavy and motionless upon the table.

Henry Perceval was in a state of supreme agitation and was banging one clenched fist into an open palm whilst glaring at Jacob. 'You simply must, Mr Jacob. There is no alternative.'

'I will not,' stated Jacob baldly, his narrow, ascetic head wagging from side to side like a ship's rudder.

The cadaver that Colonel Maxwell had become then interrupted, speaking to Foote, 'Welcome Mr Foote. I am glad to see you so promptly, please have a seat.'

'There is not time, sir,' said Foote. Then he swallowed and his expression betrayed the reluctance he felt at expressing his next words.

'Captain Snowe,' he said, 'and a good portion of my North Corks have abandoned the town. They've fled, sir, gone south out the Rosslare gate.'

At this Perceval sent up a wail like that of a kicked dog and Ebenezer Jacob began to bless himself and mutter the Lord's Prayer. Curiously, Maxwell seemed to receive this news with an air of placid acceptance and, to Foote's surprise, an incongruous smile began to melt the waxen set of his mouth.

Perceval was railing now, 'This makes your obduracy even more ridiculous. You are a liberal and a well-known one at that. You should take Bagenal Harvey and go negotiate with those savages before they burn the town down around our ears. If the military cannot protect us then we must trust to diplomacy and our native wits.'

'Then you talk to them,' snapped Jacob. 'Liberal I may be but I am Captain of the Wexford Yeoman Infantry and am well-known for that too. They'll pike me where I stand.'

'Harvey,' intoned Maxwell, and for the first time since he arrived Foote saw his commanding officer's hand move to smooth the corners of his now ragged moustaches. 'We shall have Harvey sent to them, alone if needs be, but Harvey must go. He is high in the United ranks and will be listened to. If you wish to save your lives and property then he is the one who must go.'

Perceval rose to his feet and roared then in guttural fervour, 'Guards! Take us to Bagenal Harvey!'

A small door in the wall across from Foote swung grindingly open and a ragged, unshaved soldier in the colours of the Wexford Infantry leaned through the aperture.

'Sir?' he asked.

'We wish to see that blackguard Harvey,' instructed Perceval.

'This way, sirs,' replied the yeoman.

They followed the guard to Harvey's cell door. The group of officers stood to one side breathing in the moss-dank air as the guard sorted through a bunch of heavy iron keys that jangled from a rusted ring at his belt.

'Hurry up, man,' snarled Perceval.

At last the soldier selected the correct key, turned it easily in the door's massive lock and swung the portal open. Harvey's cell was quite large and a barred window set high into the wall allowed a cascade of summer sunlight to flood through and splash a tiger-striped lozenge of brightness upon the flagstone floor. Along with the sunshine, the sounds of the quays came clear and vital through the open gap of the window. Straw pallets were shoved against two of the walls and a stained wooden bucket sat in the shadows beneath the window. The place stank. A large fireplace, now cold and strewn with crumbling ashes and the wizened black scrawls of kindling, was set into the left-hand wall.

Of Beauchamp Bagenal Harvey, there was no sign.

The officers crowded into the cell with eyes wide as plates, their mouths gaping in disbelief. The guard stood behind them and scratched his head, a look of dumb, animal confusion clouding his features.

'He was here earlier,' began the man before Henry Perceval pirouetted and seized him by his grubby, yellow lapels.

'If Harvey has escaped,' the High Sherriff hissed, 'your head will be on a spike before the day is out.'

Maxwell's voice then came, emollient and soothing, 'Calm yourself Mr Perceval. Mr Harvey is still enjoying our hospitality. Isn't that so Mr Harvey?'

Silence greeted his words.

'Come now,' he said. 'Childishness does not become a leader of men. I can see your foot, Mr Harvey.'

Then, from the wall above the fireplace a disembodied voice, indistinct but discernible, grumbled hollowly, 'I want nothing to do with you.'

Incredulously, the guard and other officers moved toward the fireplace while Maxwell, tone still languid as a summer pool, instructed, 'Come down from the chimney Mr Harvey or we shall be forced to pull you down.'

'I shall not,' came Harvey's ghostly voice, accompanied by the sound of scrambling within the wall as of someone trying to gain better purchase on a slippery slope.

'Oh, for goodness' sake, get him down from there,' ordered Maxwell at last.

Four pairs of hands reached up into the flue and, in spite of Harvey's kicks and curses, eventually grasped him by the ankles and yanked him roughly down from his soot-caked cubby-hole. Harvey sat in the filthy crucible of the lifeless hearth and blinked at his assailants in outrage. His face and hands and every fibre of his clothes were streaked with black, and pique made a quivering mass of his jowls.

'How dare you gentlemen,' he began before Maxwell, his temper boiling through his affected tranquillity, finally barked at him in frustration.

'Shut up, Mr Harvey! I cannot hope to fathom what games you think are being played but I'll have you know that people are dying beyond the walls of this town. Good Protestants like yourself are being butchered by your rebel compatriots. The town is on the verge of surrender, Mr Harvey. We wish for you to offer them terms.'

Harvey blinked again, his eyes red-rimmed from the effects of the soot, and said wonderingly, 'The United Irishmen have taken the town?'

'Not yet,' replied Maxwell. 'But to avoid bloodshed and needless destruction we wish to offer terms.'

'I will not go,' stated Harvey. 'Send Ebenezer, there.'

Henry Perceval threw his eyes to heaven as Maxwell regarded the man sitting in the ash before him and sighed, 'You are chief amongst the United Irishmen in all of Wexford and yet you will take no role in matters beyond crawling into a chimney?'

Harvey contrived to look offended and explained as though speaking to a child, 'You see, my dear Colonel, I am from the south of the county whereas most of these rebels, from what I can gather, are from the rural north. They would have no cause to trust me or even believe that I am who I claim to be.'

He paused then and commented shrewdly, 'I see Edward Fitzgerald hasn't returned.'

Foote perceived the first red blush of a murderous fury mount above Maxwell's collar and the senior officer's hand began to stray of its own accord toward the pistol tucked into his waistband. Evidently Harvey apprehended this fact as well for he immediately raised his hands and gushed, 'But I do know of two people who would be inclined to go speak with these rebels. Loftus and Thomas Richards are very well known liberal Protestants and are beloved and held in high esteem by everyone. If I were to write them a letter and instruct them to take it to the rebels outside the town then I am sure that would suffice.'

'Anything at this stage,' breathed Perceval in despair. 'If those vagabonds enter the town without bond of good conduct then every loyalist household must surely be ransacked and set aflame.'

Maxwell was nodding now, 'Very good. I shall leave you Mr Perceval and you Mr Jacob to provide Mr Harvey with the necessary writing materials. Colonel Foote and I shall busy ourselves preparing the defences should the insurgents decide to attack whilst negotiations are in progress. Such perfidious rascals are capable of any act, however outrageous.'

'Indeed,' agreed Perceval. 'Thank you for your efforts, Colonel.'

The two officers then turned and left the cell, striding through the gaol and stepping out into the buzzing commotion of Barrack Street. Foote regarded his commander quizzically and asked, 'Do you truly believe those rabid dogs out there on Forth Mountain will abide by any terms that we may offer? I have seen what they are capable of and yet you wish to negotiate a treaty with them, putting our lives, arms and ammunition all at risk?'

Maxwell, his complexion still pale but gradually losing the waxy sheen that had so shocked Foote, smiled at his subordinate. 'I do not mean to do anything of the sort, Mr Foote,' he said acidly. 'I mean to have every member of this town's garrison evacuated before the rebels even know we have gone. Captain Snowe's methods may lack finesse but his idea was the correct one under the present circumstances. The town is most abominably lost and I care not the toss of a pin for the terms offered by rebels. Do you think I would trust the word of a traitor to the Crown?'

Foote frowned slightly, 'But the Richards brothers and the townsfolk will be left at the mercy of those savages. One can only imagine their rancour should they find us gone and our terms worthless.'

Maxwell snorted, 'Can you imagine the disgusting vision of those thousands of bandits with all our arms and munitions? It is a thought most repulsive to me that our own guns may be turned on the King's forces. It shall not stand. Better we save ourselves and leave these vacillating, lukewarm liberals to deal with that ungodly host than be the architects of our own downfall.'

He slapped Foote companionably across the shoulder, 'We shall live to fight another day, Mr Foote. Now ready your men to depart. Swiftly and with silent drum and colours furled. We must be as surreptitious as we can for to alert the townspeople is to alert our enemies.'

Foote nodded slowly, the idea of abandoning the town under such conniving circumstances galled him and gnawed at his pride. Yet, at another level he felt a great surge of relief within himself. He would not be butchered and hacked like poor Major Lombard, would suffer no further humiliation at the hands of the brutal mob of peasantry. He would not end this day lying dead in the dust like old Jonas Watson.

In spite of himself, a slow smile spread across his face like a slick of sewage. 'Give the North Corks an hour, sir. As soon as the Richards boys ride into those barbarians' hands we shall be gone out the Rosslare gate.'

'Swiftly, Mr Foote,' stated Maxwell leadenly, 'and silently.'

'As smoke, Colonel,' replied Foote. 'As smoke.'

Dan, Elizabeth and Tom watched as the two riders drew closer. They wore the frock coats and tricorns of gentlemen but even at a distance of three hundred yards it was plain that both carried a brace of horse pistols. They advanced along the road from Wexford under the eyes and guns of every rebel on Forth Mountain and only the fact that one of them held aloft a white flag saved the riders from being blown apart. They were both young men, their faces pale petals in the distance, blued not at all by any trace of beard or stubble. As they came within musket range, their deportment conveyed their fear. They crouched in their saddles, the one holding the flag now fluttering it desperately.

Standing beside the three friends, Edward Roche muttered softly, 'Thomas and Loftus Richards? Now why would they send those two gentlemen as emissaries and not Bagenal Harvey or an officer of the garrison?'

Tom leaned on his cavalry sabre, striking an incongruously jaunty pose standing as he was amidst fern, briar and gorse, and said simply, 'They are afraid of us.'

Roche looked at Tom, one heavy eyebrow cocked in question.

Tom lifted his sword and pointed at the horsemen. 'The commander of that garrison, Maxwell, is no fool. He does not trust us, since we have managed to hand every soldier in the county a hiding, burned one garrison town to the ground and allowed innocent civilians to be executed.'

Roche looked uncomfortable at his words but Tom continued, 'Would you offer yourself into the hands of such men as us, Mr Roche? For surely I would not.'

The Richards brothers had reached the rebel lines and had been immediately swamped by a sea of grasping hands and shaken weapons. Both men were lifted from their horses and disarmed before being escorted up the slope encircled by a troop of braying pikemen who jeered and mocked their every step. The spectral pallor of their faces and the manner in which their eyes darted constantly from one sneering rebel to the next betrayed the naked terror that gibbered within each of their breasts.

Eventually both men were brought before Roche where the eldest, barely into his twenties, spoke, 'We should like to be conveyed to a senior officer in this—' he paused for a moment, 'this army.'

Dan regarded the men with barely concealed contempt and, ignoring

Elizabeth as she squeezed his arm, he answered, 'Why, the gentleman whom you are addressing might be considered the leading light in our struggle for liberty. You might also seek out Fr John Murphy or Mr Edward Fitzgerald. We have no shortage of leaders and officers.'

The snort of a horse heralded the arrival of Fr John on the scene. He had been riding through the camp and had jogged his mount over to investigate the furore. Now he stared down from the back of his great beast and fixed the two brothers with an intense, searching glare.

'What you have to say may be addressed to the entirety of this camp,' he declared. 'For every man, woman and child deserves to hear what those red-coated cowards have to say for themselves.'

Loftus Richards reached into his coat pocket and produced a piece of paper on which a spidery hand had scrawled a few short lines.

'This comes from one of your own,' said Loftus. 'The garrison awaits your terms but Mr Harvey has seen fit to write to you.' He cleared his throat and read in a voice loud but wavering somewhat with fear.

'"I have been treated in prison with all possible humanity and am now at liberty. I have procured the liberty of all the prisoners. If you pretend to Christian charity do not commit massacre or burn the property of the inhabitants and spare your prisoners' lives. B. B. Harvey, Wednesday, 30th May 1798".'

The entire throng that had gathered about fell into a stunned silence as Fr John regarded the two messengers with such a savage aspect that both men stepped back in terror.

'Christian charity?' he railed. 'I do not know this Harvey fellow and I am under no compunction to do as he asks. I do not know what terms they can expect from me, not after the treatment that I have received.'

His voice grew in volume so that the whole hillside resounded to his words, 'They have burned my house and burned my property. I was obliged to take shelter in the ditches.'

He cast his eyes over the thousands of faces all turned to him, aglow with the vehemence of his words, 'They have put me under the necessity of rising the whole country!'

At this the assembled insurgents issued a cheer like a gale through a forest canopy and moved as one clawing entity to tear the Richards brothers apart. Elizabeth screamed and clung to him as Dan roared, 'They are under a flag of truce, for God's sake!'

Conversely Tom was attempting to haul his older brother from out of any proximity to the doomed men, growling, 'Shut up, Dan, you damned fool!'

To Dan and Elizabeth's consternation, the vulpine face of Thomas Dixon could be seen, hot with zealousness, in the middle of the surging multitude. He was snarling and his voice was raised in a frenzied animal howl.

It was then, just as fury seemed set to pitch the crowd headlong into a mayhem of slaughterhouse brutality, that Edward Fitzgerald cried out in dismay. His voice was deep and sonorous, carrying with it harmonics that cut through the snarls of the mob.

'Stop, I say!' he cried. 'What have these two men done to any of you? They come before us carrying the surrender of the town and the words of our most respected and affectionate friend, now set at liberty. And we thank them with murder and violence. That is the way of the tyrant and despot. That is why we are in the field this day. We fight against the barbarity that you seek now to inflict upon these two innocents.

'Liberty. Equality. Fraternity. If you wish to harm these men, why then you should strike down the very man beside you, aye, and me after; for we are all born one and the same with rights and passions that no man should dare thwart without due cause and reason.

'If you wish to put emissaries bearing a white flag to death, then go find a red coat and join the garrison cowering down below, for there is no place for you within the ranks of the United Irishmen.'

The gathered throng of pikemen were suddenly still and men panted in the afternoon sunlight like exhausted lurchers. Thomas Dixon began to say something, but Fr Murphy interrupted him, stating, 'You speak well, Edward. Very well. You are of course correct in that no man should lay a hand on these two when the real foe is down below us in the town. What would you have us do?'

Just then, John Hay suddenly barged through the rebel ranks and saluted automatically. Breathlessly, he gasped, 'General Roche, Fr Murphy, Mr Fitzgerald. I believe we have been made the victims of a *ruse de guerre*.'

Fitzgerald and Fr Murphy looked at the man curiously and Roche motioned for him to continue.

Hay swallowed, getting his breath back, before ploughing on, 'I have seen garrisons throughout Europe commit to this very course of action when necessity drives them and opportunity grants it.

'We must split our forces and a strong detachment must be led around to the south of the town to cut off the garrison's retreat to Duncannon. Otherwise we may win nothing today but bricks and mortar. No guns. No powder. Nothing.'

Fr Murphy gaped openly at Hay's words and shifted uneasily in his saddle before saying, 'You mean to say that, while these men are sent here to negotiate with us, the garrison will fly towards Rosslare and thence across country to the fort?

'Surely that is a death sentence for these two. Why would any man knowingly undertake such actions?'

Before Thomas and Loftus Richards could begin a terror-stricken defence, John Hay replied, 'Oh, these men are unwitting dupes. Pawns in a stratagem. They are of no importance whatsoever. Are you listening to me? We must drive with some portion of our forces toward Rosslare or this victory will be pyrrhic.'

Roche and Fr Murphy exchanged sceptical glances.

'I do not think that splitting our forces is the thing to do, Mr Hay,' replied Roche. 'The detachment you propose to intercept the garrison would be far removed from the main body of the men and we have no cavalry to lend quick support should it find itself in difficulty. No, we shall stand together as we have always done. It has served us well thus far.

'Besides, I feel that the troops who so precipitately flew back to the safety of the town would not be eager to venture out into the countryside again so soon. The idea of them abandoning the loyalist civilians of Wexford, some of whom are the most grotesque monsters ever to tread the earth, and allowing them to face the wrath of the people without terms is absurd. No, we shall not act rashly in this. The garrison is at our mercy, our enemies are suing for terms.'

Hay's face darkened at this and his next words were weighted with menace. 'Our enemies are professional officers, Mr Roche, and I have seen the cold-blooded nature of professional officers on the battlefields of Flanders. I fear that your ignoring me this day will cost us all our heads in the end.'

He turned on his heel then and without offering salute he stalked down the hill to where the cannon were being cleaned and oiled.

Fr Murphy, Roche, Fitzgerald and the assembled crowd all watched him leave and a malign hubbub began to buzz through the ranks. This was stilled when Edward Fitzgerald raised his hand and declared, 'Since Mr Hay's concerns are great I feel that we should immediately present our terms to the garrison. I presume unconditional surrender of the town and all its arms in exchange for the safe passage of the garrison and civilians are what is called for?'

A roar of acclaim went up at these words and as it died Fr Murphy spoke into the void left behind.

'They are to leave Wexford with their colours cased and drums muffled. We shall afford them no respect. Let them know that they are beaten.'

'Very well,' agreed Fitzgerald. 'In that case, I suggest that Thomas Richards and myself shall immediately return to the town and present our terms. Meanwhile his brother shall be held here as a guarantee against foul play.'

Again the gathered rebel rank and file cheered at this. Dan, however, saw Roche and the priest exchange another dubious look. After a contemplative moment that seemed to stretch just a fraction too long, Fr Murphy nodded once and said, 'Then you must make haste. I must admit that Mr Hay's words have spilled cold water down my back.'

Within moments the little diplomatic mission had been assembled. Fitzgerald, looking splendid on Loftus Richards's black charger, was waving his tricorn as he passed through the ranks like the lord that many of the peasantry thought that he was. Thomas Richards sat his own saddle with a look of terror washing his face of colour, as around him vast numbers of fighting men poured across the slopes to bid them farewell. Hats and neckerchiefs were flung in the air and a wild yell battered his ears. He had never before seen so many fierce-looking vagabonds in the one place. To Richards the world seemed upended, its filthy belly exposed to the light.

Once they rode out of sight beyond the low rise obscuring John Street, the leaders began assembling their corps. Standards were hoisted and the cries of the various parishes and baronies winged about the rugged shoulders of Forth Mountain. Bodies of men converged and meshed. Those who had been on the march now for four days formed ranks and files with a precision whose execution seemed alien in men so ragged and unkempt. The newer corps valiantly attempted to emulate the veterans, the Bantry men who had won the howitzers taking their cue from the Scarawalsh men alongside them. Women and children extinguished cooking fires and gathered up bundles of cloth and blankets. Babies wailed.

Very soon the entire thrusting bulk of the mountain, usually a glowing edifice of purple heather and green-golden gorse, was a black mass of bristling weaponry.

Dan watched as Anthony Perry walked down the line of men from the Gorey barony. He had placed a broad-brimmed hat on his head over the white knot of his bandages but in the shadow of its brim, crawling down across his left eye and cheek bone, the pale sheen of a scar glimmered hideously. Yet there was more life about him than there had been the previous

day. He moved with greater animation and the doleful welter of emotions
that had swam constantly across his features was replaced by an expression of
granite resolve. Though, as he drew closer to Dan, it was clear that there was
sadness in his eyes. Men looked to him in good cheer, offering words of support and welcome and Perry returned them readily enough, but those great,
sad eyes refused to meet the faces of his comrades. His gaze scudded past, a
stone across water.

Assembled in their corps, the multitude of the United Irish Army stood
ready, waiting for the return of Edward Fitzgerald and their chance to enter
Wexford Town. Edward Roche, Fr Murphy and a dozen of the main chiefs were
engaged in animated discussion just ahead of the front ranks.

'Probably arguing over the best place to get a pint,' commented Tom.

The rebel army stood for an hour before Roche, with a perplexed frown
marring his forehead, ordered a detachment of the Shelmaliers to advance to
the Windmill Hill, a small knoll halfway between their position and John
Street, to await the senior officers of the garrison and to receive the stores and
arms and ammunition that were theirs through right of conquest.

The Shelmaliers marched off and took up position within cannon shot of
the rebel lines but still no word and no messenger issued forth to greet them.

Still they waited while the sun tumbled from its zenith, falling westward
through the eggshell sky, and men began to grumble and shuffle in the heat.
Pikes were grounded and here and there men actually sat themselves down on
the heather at their feet. The camp followers began to come forward, curious as
to the lack of activity, and the children began to cavort between the files and
tumble across the empty ground separating one corps from the next.

Dan was craning his neck to see if Elizabeth still remained at the rear of the
column when Tom spoke softly.

'Fitzgerald is dead or deserted,' he whispered.

Dan regarded him in shock. 'What makes you say that?' he asked.

Tom's face was a frowning picture of frustration as he muttered, 'We have
been standing on this God-forsaken hill for nearly three hours now. If the garrison had accepted our terms word would have reached us ages ago. Something
is not right here Dan.'

Suddenly a gasp went up from the column to Dan's right and men lifted
arms and pikes to point off to the southeast. There, on the horizon from the
direction of Rosslare, a mottled haze of smoke was drifting up into the sky,
floating across the blue like a bruise. As the men watched, the dark trail of

smoke began to creep westward towards Mayglass and Duncannon. The men began to mutter amongst themselves and abruptly the entire hill was a sibilant hive of buzzing conversation.

All of a sudden Elizabeth was at Dan's side. Her face was filmed with perspiration and from under the band of her sun-bonnet the delicate curls of her hair spilled unheeded and tangled. Her eyes were filled with an intense excitement as she exclaimed, 'Daniel, you must see this! I was up at the Three Rocks and the whole country from Rosslare to Mayglass is in flames!'

Dan looked at her, appalled. His face full of consternation, he asked, 'Are you sure? You are sure it is smoke?'

She nodded fervently and Dan cursed with a passion that startled Elizabeth. Tom merely groaned and pinched the bridge of his nose as though a headache thundered through his cranium.

At that moment John Hay came dashing up the slope from where the guns had been harnessed to the traces of four heavy horses awaiting the order to move.

He approached the group of leaders and began arguing in growling tones pitched just low enough to avoid eavesdropping. Every now and then he would gesticulate with sword-thrust vehemence in the direction of the trail of smoke to their south, his finger stabbing and his face scarlet with fury. Before him Roche, with his hands joined as though in prayer, was trying to explain something, glancing towards Wexford with wide, insistent eyes. What their exact words were neither the two Banvilles nor Elizabeth could determine.

Eventually Hay turned away and, kicking heather and bracken with each incensed stride, he stormed back down the slope.

Roche and the other leaders were muttering and shaking their heads, some morosely, others, Fr Michael Murphy chief amongst them, angrily. Then, loud enough so that he was heard by any pair of ears on the surrounding slope, Roche barked, 'I know!'

He turned to face the men and ordered, 'Get these women and children to the rear. We march on the town.'

No cry of joy greeted his words. No roar of bravado and fellowship filled the day with noise. Only a glum rumble of assent rolled through the ranks and the brittle clacking of pikestaff against pikestaff rattled across the desolate tracts of Forth Mountain as weapons and equipment were shouldered. An odd laugh rang out from one or two individuals but their empty isolation in the general gloom only served to emphasise the bleakness that had suddenly descended. In the midst of victory, on the verge of taking the county seat and all that entailed, every man felt a sullen resentment blacken within them.

Dan, Tom and Elizabeth, every man, woman and child who had seen the mocking plumes of smoke drifting up from the southern horizon, knew that they traced a swathe of arson, a trail of burning left by the fleeing and vengeful garrison of Wexford Town. Dan, Tom and Elizabeth, every man, woman and child, knew that they had been cheated.

It was a victory that felt like a funeral.

CHAPTER 15

Debates and Divisions

Dan, Elizabeth and Tom sat on the steps of the market house and looked out across the Cornmarket and down into the Bullring below. The morning of the 31st of May had broken with a flurry of ragged grey clouds trawled across the sky by a buffeting south-westerly wind. The wind had a bitter edge to it and the three companions huddled together unconsciously, Elizabeth with a heavy blue woollen shawl wound tight about her narrow shoulders. Dan lovingly leaned his head against hers and occasionally filaments of her hair would catch in his stubble and scrawl across the air between them.

Tom, scratching his own stubbled jaw, said distractedly, 'As soon as I get the chance I am going to find a hot bath and I am going to soak in it until I shrivel into a prune.'

Dan laughed, 'We must stink to high heaven.'

Elizabeth shook her head, wrinkling her nose, 'You always smell like this.'

The majority of the rebel army had spent the night before encamped on Windmill Hill just outside the John Street gate, soaking in a confusion of chagrin and disappointment. They had entered the town earlier to a rapturous reception. Green boughs and every scrap of emerald fabric in the place had been fashioned into banners and flags that were held flapping from windows and balconies. Every single inhabitant seemed to be grinning maniacally and cheering as though their lungs would burst, green cockades and sashes decorating every item of clothing they could be pinned to. Out in the bay the ships riding at anchor had run up green and white flags and had fired their cannon in salute as the leaders rode out onto the quays. Everywhere good cheer reigned and food and drink had been brought out on massive platters for the famished fighting men. Wexford Town had become a carnival, a celebration of life, of vitality; and a gurning prostration at the feet of a victorious army.

The various corps of rebels had been immediately detailed to ransack the barracks and any prominent loyalist houses they could find. The men had returned without a single soldier or arms in any great quantity, a lone cask of gunpowder and a few fowling pieces were all that three hours of searching had revealed. The garrison had fled; Maxwell's ruse had worked.

The search parties had, however, uncovered a number of loyalists who were either resident in the town or who had fled there over the previous three days. People who thought they had escaped the butchery of Enniscorthy, suddenly, and to their horror and panic, found themselves abandoned by those they thought might protect them. All over the town loyalist middlemen and landowners were frantically clothing themselves in green, acclaiming the rebel army as though it were the Second Coming.

Thomas Dixon had immediately convened an *ad hoc* court martial in the Bullring. Sitting behind a pilfered table, the dusk falling about him like a miasma, he was intent on pronouncing justice on a number of these unfortunates until Roche and Fr Murphy had excoriated him and had the prisoners removed to the gaol. The cobbled mall of the Bullring, now lined with abandoned traders' carts and empty flour barrels, in times of peace was an elongated marketplace. The people of Wexford would congregate here in noisy knots of commercial frenzy, haggling over barley and corn, beef and butter, its covered arcade a chancel for knavery. Now, as the unfortunate prisoners stumbled and staggered their way to a miserable confinement, the space was filled with raucous jeers. Over a hundred people now packed the cold cells on Barrack Street and their wails and terrified pleading echoed all along a thoroughfare thronged with celebrating peasants.

Beauchamp Bagenal Harvey and a frightened, blubbering Ebenezer Jacob had met the rebel vanguard as it spilled into the Cornmarket just above the Bullring. Jacob had ducked behind the United man as Fr Murphy loomed over them both, proud upon his heavy mount. Harvey had found the time to return to his town house and was now resplendent in a green frock coat, black breeches and ivory waistcoat. On his head a perfectly coiffeured wig perched in a mass of powdered curls, silk stockings sheathed his calves. He greeted the rebels like the aristocrat he was.

'Gentlemen!' he had said with a flourish. 'Old Wexford is won. I have seen to it that all our brave patriot fellows have been set at liberty.'

Fr Murphy looked down at him saying, 'Bagenal Harvey, I presume? I am Fr John Murphy and because I do indeed "pretend to Christian charity" I will not say to you what I have thought of saying over the past hours since receiving that rag of a letter you wrote.'

Harvey blinked, stunned, whilst Jacob cowered even further.

Roche leaned out of his saddle and gripped the priest's arm while explaining, 'We are all very weary, Beauchamp, and the last day or two have been very trying. Not least because of your arrest.'

He gestured around him then, taking in the ragged, battle-worn rural rebels as they danced and gambolled with the smiling citizens of Wexford Town. Somewhere a fiddle struck up a jig and a torrent of laughter spilled through the streets. Roche's voice hardened slightly as he continued, 'I do not know what orgy of violence you or your captors expected Beauchamp, but we are not savages. We are United Irishmen, like your good self. We have not become murdering monsters overnight. We have no cause to ape the yeos and the North Corks.'

He had said this with all the blunt finality of a hammer blow.

Harvey swallowed and stuttered, 'Well, yes, indeed. I never once thought that my good fellows would stoop to slaughter and rapine but the people of the town, even the liberal ones, were haunted by tales told by those from Enniscorthy. Obvious falsehoods, in my opinion, but one cannot help ignorance.'

Fr Murphy grunted, his face still a quarry of unforgiving stone, and lifted his head to fix Ebenezer Jacob with a flinty look.

'Ah,' Harvey said. 'Let me introduce Ebenezer Jacob, Mayor of Wexford Town. He and I have been relentless in our efforts over the past few hours in calming the panic of the populace. Every man jack is now fully behind the United movement, Catholics, Protestants, peasants and merchants, everyone can be glad that the days of the tyrant are numbered.'

Jacob moved slightly to one side of Harvey, nodding gormlessly.

Roche sighed, 'I know Mr Jacob, Beauchamp. I am glad of your efforts in assuaging the fears of the population but we must act quickly to ensure law and order is maintained.'

Harvey and Jacob had nodded fervently in unison, whilst about them the town was erupting in a bubbling fountain of camaraderie and good spirits.

It had taken an hour for the first murder to happen.

John Boyd, the brother of Captain James Boyd, had been recognised as he was jostled along the quays. Set upon and piked, he lay bleeding, begging for help and for water. A crowd had surrounded him, curious but unfeeling, like a cat inspecting a bird mauled to the point of death. They stood silently as he groaned in a pool of his own spreading blood until a heavy-set rebel stepped forward with a hatchet and dashed his brains out.

The second murder had followed close after; George Sparrow piked to death in front of a screaming, horrified crowd of onlookers, his body lying rent and gushing red onto the parched and trampled earth of the Bullring.

And then a calm had descended.

The febrile mirth, the strained hilarity, all gradually slid from their hectic peak into a trough of awful realisation. The murders were the first things to chill the carnival and rime over its fires with a grim reality. The second was the complete absence of arms or supplies. The fighting men who had remained sober enough to gauge the significance of these events soon found their spirits dampened and their exhaustion dragging at their limbs like iron chains. The town had slowly emptied, the rebels moving out to the Windmill Hill in flotillas of tired flesh and hanging heads. Men from the same parish, men who had grown up together and now had fought shoulder to shoulder, supported each other as they swayed off into the black of the night.

Eventually, as dawn was breaking, only Edward Roche remained behind. He stood on the quays and gazed out along the dark length of Wexford Bridge. The burned spars at the northern shore had been replaced by rough-hewn planks hours before the rebels had entered into the town and it was over this patchwork causeway that Edward Fitzgerald had vanished.

Roche allowed Ebenezer Jacob's words to roll about the inside of his skull like dice in a cup.

'Fitzgerald was asked to disperse the crowd on the far side of the bridge. They had burned the toll house and the soldiery had torn up the planks to stop the spread of the fire. When the soldiers left, the rabble, I mean the people, threw timbers across the gaps. Fitzgerald tried to stop them making for the town when they saw how close you were. They ignored him for the most part and just when I thought he was about to wheel his horse and return, he instead drove the big beast on and galloped off to the north.'

'His estate of Newpark is in that part of the country,' Roche said. 'Perhaps he has returned to his family for a night.'

'Do you think he will be back?' asked Jacob. 'His presence is very comforting to the Protestants of the town. The murders of Boyd and Sparrow have put people quite on edge.'

Roche had said nothing at the time, but as dawn broke across the harbour he had pursed his lips and exhaled slowly through his nose, 'I hope so. For our sakes and his own, I truly hope so.'

The morning had advanced with the wind tossing clouds across the sky like tattered bandages. Vast, unravelling skeins of cotton seemed to trail across the heavens. Now, at mid-morning, Elizabeth Blakely shivered and said, 'I fear a change in the weather.'

Tom glanced upward from where he sat beside her on the worn granite step and nodded slowly, his mind elsewhere.

All through the morning the insurgents had filtered back into the town so that its narrow streets were now packed with thousands of men and women who, for the most part, seemed to be drifting aimlessly. They were atoms in a stream of humanity that slid sluggishly between whitewashed banks. The quays were also thronged as children who had never before seen a ship were hoisted up onto their fathers' shoulders and stared with amazed eyes out across the foam-flecked width of Wexford Harbour. Infants and toddlers were wrapped against the cold and pushed their pudgy, pink fists into mouths running with drool, too young yet to comprehend the importance of events or the horrors through which they had lived.

The Bullring chimed like a belfry. Edward Hay, John's brother, had been greeted by the rebel leadership as a comrade in arms as soon as he had met them, a circumstance that would have provoked the righteous ire of Colonel Foote had he witnessed it. He had immediately been asked to turn the Bullring into a massive smithy; he was instantly become the master of armaments. Every blacksmith and farrier in the town had converged on the Bullring with apprentices and tools and good iron and steel and set to hammering out pike heads by the dozen. Swords and muskets were oiled and repaired. Wood turners were busy sanding and lacquering long straight lengths of ash to replace broken pikestaffs. The place was humming with the breathless industry of a hive.

Then, above the ring and clatter of the blacksmiths, above the hustle and bustle of the thronging multitude, a hunting horn sounded shrill and piercing. The crowd stilled for a moment, silent and apprehensive and then a huge cheering mounted in volume from the direction of the quays. Dan, Elizabeth and Tom looked at each other quizzically and then wordlessly joined the flood of people slipping through streets and alleys toward the sea.

The quays were already choked with onlookers by the time the three companions arrived. Everyone, country rebels and frock-coated townsfolk alike, all were waving a green branch or scrap of fabric. Tom and Elizabeth stood on tip-toe to catch a glimpse of what was provoking such a joyous outpouring. Dan, however, by virtue of his height, commanded a good view of events and his eyes widened in astonishment at what he saw.

In from the Rosslare gate marched column after column of fresh pikemen.

They carried themselves proudly although none had the lean, battered look of the men who had taken Enniscorthy and Wexford. Most were well-armed and some carried the long-barrelled guns so emblematic of the coastlines of Shelmalier and Forth.

At their head rode an extraordinary figure on a massive white foxhunter. An old man with the air of royalty, he was dressed from neck to black riding boots in dark green, even the frothy billow at his throat and cuffs were of emerald lace. On his head sat a black broad-brimmed hat with a green cockade set into its golden band. He waved royally to the crowds as he passed, bestowing smiles and nods like favours at a party.

'Who is it?' asked Elizabeth, her lack of height meaning she had to grip Dan's shoulders and bounce on her toes to even catch a glimpse of the unfolding scene. Irritated and sharply aware of the inelegance of her actions, she pressed, 'What's happening?'

'It's Cornelius Grogan of Johnstown Castle,' breathed Dan incredulously. 'I had no idea he was a United man.'

Tom was grumbling under his breath, bobbing up and down and side to side like a prize fighter as he tried to snatch glances between people's heads. 'How many does he bring with him?' he asked.

Dan studied the long lines of rebels for a moment before replying, 'Two thousand, at least. Those red-coated rascals who so lately burned and murdered all along the road to Duncannon have brought the whole south of the county into the field.'

Tom had ceased his manic bobbing and whispered, 'Two thousand? God almighty, every man in Wexford must be up in arms.'

Just then a voice called out over the din, 'Captain Banville?' It was young Jim Kehoe and he was waving at them from the back of the crowd. 'General Roche would like to talk with you in Mr Harvey's lodgings. He's calling a muster of the officers.'

Dan frowned slightly and turned to Elizabeth, saying, 'Does that relative of yours still reside on Chapel Lane at the junction with Back Street?'

Elizabeth nodded cautiously, 'My Great Aunt, yes, although I have never been held very high in her affections. I presume the old goat still lives there. All the demons with all the pitchforks in hell couldn't strike fear into her withered heart.'

Tom laughed at this, 'You have been in the company of soldiers for too long.'

Dan ignored him and continued, 'Go to her now on the pretext of seeing to her comfort. Tell her you were worried for her safety. We must make haste, for Mr Harvey's house lies at the far end of Main Street beyond the junction with George's Street, and with every thoroughfare so crowded it may take us time to reach.'

Tom's laughing expression died on his face like something eviscerated. He regarded Dan with a look of suspicion. '"We"'? "Us"?' he asked. 'I am not an officer and have no intention of becoming one.'

Dan slapped him on the shoulder and said curtly, 'Miles Byrne and a few of the others think otherwise. You are coming.' His voice was stern, as though he were chiding his little brother for a childish wrongdoing. In his tone the years rolled back and they were boys once again.

Elizabeth was now opening her mouth in protest until Dan covered it with his own. He kissed her for a moment before she pushed him away in exasperation. 'Daniel!' she blustered, indignant.

He seized her by the shoulders then and looked deep into the depthless black of her pupils. 'Go to your aunt,' he whispered fiercely. 'And for God's sake stay away from that monster Dixon and his wife.'

With that, he flashed her a grin of boyish enthusiasm and spun away from her, blundering his way through the crowd. Tom shrugged his shoulders apologetically and then he too vanished into the mass of people. Alone, she stared after them, the hub of a whorl of empty space that slowly collapsed inward, gradually drawing tight about her.

A broad wooden boardwalk ran along the quayside and as the two brothers made their way along it, Tom called out loud over the tonguing waves, 'Hold on a second there, me bucko. What has you thinking that I might be willing to take on a position which no one but madmen and martyrs would want?'

Dan looked back over his shoulder and grinned. 'You have the trust of everyone in our corps and you have proven yourself to be as true a United Irishman as Wolfe Tone himself. Even Miles has set you on a pedestal, he considers you one of the most able and eminently sensible gentlemen he knows.'

'I *am* an eminently sensible gentleman,' agreed Tom, shoving his way past two hulking farmhands. 'That is why I must view this as idiocy.'

He hauled Dan by the collar of his jacket so that he spun around and stopped in his tracks. All about them the clamour of Grogan's arrival still resounded but Tom faced his brother without any enthusiasm softening his features.

Uncaring of who might be listening, Tom pointed back the way they had come and continued, 'Do you think that peacock on his white foxhunter is a leader? That is the calibre of our officers. Where was the like of him at Enniscorthy and Oulart?'

Ignoring the startled expressions on those faces near enough to have over-heard, Dan smiled at his brother, 'At what time did you become so blood and thunder a croppy, Tom?'

Tom sighed then and his anger drained from him as he said, 'Since the yeos came for my brother. I am not a croppy, Dan, but I am a pragmatist. Should our raggle-taggle army fail to carry the day, we are all dead men.'

Dan nodded to where Grogan's green-clad torso and the arctic slab of his mount's broad head were visible above the gawking assembly. His voice was low but earnest as he said, 'Well then, Tom, it is to the like of that "peacock" that we must entrust all our hopes. The leaders are not dandies or fops, Tom. They are great men. Bagenal Harvey is one of the truest and most patriotic gentlemen on earth.'

Tom gripped his brother by the shoulders then and shook him as one might shake a sleeping child who is tossing, lost, in the midst of nightmare. His eyes roved across Dan's broad face, his bright sea-grey eyes, and he said, 'Apart from Roche and John Hay not one of your "leaders" has even a feeble grasp of the most simple of military fundamentals. How many can instruct a column of men to form line and to fall from that into square, or to wheel and pivot in the field? None. They are politicians and romantics, Dan. They are not soldiers.'

Tom felt Dan's finger jab him hard, three times, in the breastbone. Once for every syllable: 'But you are.'

Tom blinked as Dan went on, 'That is why you must accept a commission. Miles Byrne, John Kelly, Thomas Cloney; all are mere captains yet it is they who are most intrepid in the field. It is they who the men look to. It is *they* who will carry the day, Tom. Without them, without men like you, we are doomed.'

Tom considered this for a moment. About them the excitement of Grogan's passing had died away and now only the heavy tramp of his marching column sounded above the individual conversations as men and women, bored with the spectacle, began to drift away back to the Bullring or John Street. At length a wry smile tugged at the muscles of Tom's mouth so that Dan was reminded of him as a ten-year-old, his face slathered in jam and brazenly unrepentant as Mrs Prendergast scolded him and threatened him with her mixing spoon.

Tom spoke then, 'You know, you left yourself out of that list of luminaries.'

Dan grinned too and asked, 'So, you'll do it?'

'I will, Dan,' came the answer. 'But only because you are my brother and you have invested yourself, heart and soul, in this madness.'

'Good chap!' exclaimed Dan. 'Now, we may hurry. Roche must have something important to say.'

Bagenal Harvey's townhouse was situated at the north end of Main Street, just beyond the junction with Monk Street. Its facade was as grand and ostentatious as its owner. The brick walls were clad in neatly squared blocks of stone and the windows were wide and towering, reflecting back in pale and rippling counterfeit the ebb and flow of the street before them. The door to the house was a heavy, oaken chessboard of carved panels and the steps leading up to it from the dust of the road were hewn from Forth Mountain quartzite and glinted milkily in the sun. In front of this stately abode a large group of rebel leaders had congregated, puffing on pipes.

At the two brothers' approach Miles Byrne detached himself from the other officers of his Monaseed contingent and crossed the street to meet them. He paused in front of Dan and shook his hand warmly. Then he nodded to Tom asking, 'Well, have we roped him into our tattered little brotherhood?'

Dan grinned, 'He says he will take a commission but is endeavouring to be as curmudgeonly as possible about it.'

Tom rolled his eyes and said, 'A child could not have been more insistent than your pleading.'

Byrne laughed but immediately sobered, his face taking on a curious expression as he replied, 'I am glad you have decided so, Tom. We all of a sudden have more regiments than we have men to lead them. We cannot have the likes of Dixon over there, or Luke Byrne up at Enniscorthy allowing our victories to descend into depravity.'

He jerked his head to one side indicating where Thomas Dixon, his greyhound face warped into a perpetual sneer, was conversing with some of his aides. He leaned against the wall of Harvey's house like a scarecrow in a field, all hard angles and cold button eyes.

'How many men do we have now, anyway?' asked Tom.

Byrne smiled then and a suggestion of his eighteen years flickered once more in his eyes, a youth bloodily and prematurely birthed into adulthood, made sport for an instant across his face.

'The country must be emptied,' he said. 'The entire county from Gorey to The Hook must be in the field for there are at least twenty thousand fighting men camped in and around this town.'

Dan gaped incredulously, 'Twenty thousand?'

'At least,' Byrne beamed.

Tom nodded consideringly, 'And what are we to do with so formidable a force?'

Miles looked over his shoulder to where Harvey's townhouse loomed over the bustling street, 'We are waiting on Grogan to arrive and then we shall see. I just hope that this council is far more decisive than our last.'

The three young men then crossed the street to where the officers from the northern part of the county, with whom they were most familiar, were clumped together in a swirling blue haze of pipe smoke. Within minutes a shout went up from down the street and every head was turned to see Cornelius Grogan striding through the throng toward them. Like the sea before the painted stern of a galleon, bystanders and United men were ploughed to one side by the flamboyant old man who, in spite of his white hair and furrowed visage, bore himself erect and proud as he walked.

Nodding 'good day' to people as he approached, Grogan mounted the steps to Harvey's house before pausing with his hand on the latch. He then turned and with bravado spoke over the heads of the assembly. 'Gentlemen,' he declaimed, 'this is the beginning of the end of tyranny. Liberty! Equality! Fraternity!'

This was greeted by a loud huzzah from the watching officers. Tom was disgusted to hear even Dan add his voice to the clamour, his face radiating optimism and zeal.

Tom merely shook his head and curled his lip as Grogan whirled and disappeared into the silent house.

Long minutes stretched out and men began to fidget and grumble before the door opened again. One of Harvey's servants stood in the empty doorway and gazed out fearfully upon the crowd in the street. He was a young man, born and reared in Wexford Town and he was mightily afraid of this mass of country farmers who had butchered soldiers and carried all before them on a tide of steel and shot. His fear found expression in his voice as it wavered, caught in his throat and failed him again.

'Would you speak if you're going to say something,' spat a voice from the street.

The serving man swallowed and finally croaked, 'Mr Harvey will see you all now in the drawing room.'

Laughing gruffly, the mob of rebel officers tramped up the steps and past the bewildered servant, who had no choice but to step aside as they tracked dirt and the refuse of the street across the threshold. Once they had passed he sighed softly and bent to polish the scuff marks from the floorboards.

Bagenal Harvey had set the scene for this latest council of war between the long expanse of his dining room and the comfortable surrounds of the drawing room. The double doors in between had been flung open and lamps and candles had been lit to provide more light. Both rooms were wallpapered in feathery designs and a hunting scene hung on the wall above the drawing room fireplace, its dark shades and sepia browns contrasting sharply with the pastel green of the walls. The two rooms formed one large space into which the officers of the various corps now piled, many of them casting wide-eyed stares at the unimaginable luxury of the place. One or two ran trembling fingers across delft delicate as sea shells, or blinked at the extravagance of silver candelabra.

Dan looked about as the men filed in and noticed that at the head of the heavy, darkly lacquered dinner table seven or eight chairs had been set and behind them the standard of the United Irishman, gold harp on green, hung leadenly from a pole hastily lashed to a coat stand. As Dan watched, Bagenal Harvey, Edward Roche and, surprisingly, Edward Fitzgerald walked through a side door and sat at the three top chairs. Behind them John Hay, George Sparks, Fr Michael Murphy, Anthony Perry, Cornelius Grogan and one or two others took up the other chairs. Lastly, Fr John Murphy walked into the room and stood confused, staring at his fellow leaders but without a seat at their table.

An agitated muttering began to swell amongst the gathered captains at this sight until Harvey himself arose and fetched a spare chair from another room. Fr Murphy's face had become a shade of bruised purple and his nostrils flared in indignation but he accepted Harvey's mumbled apology with a dignified silence and sat down.

Byrne frowned at this dumbshow and whispered to the brothers, 'That's a disgraceful way to treat so brave a soul, unsworn United man or not.'

The angry murmuring continued amongst the men until Harvey raised a hand and a gradual silence drifted down upon the gathering. He spoke slowly, rising to his feet as he did so, 'We are here convened to formulate a plan of war and to discuss its execution for the betterment of our people and the spreading of liberty across the entire island of Ireland.

'The people's army has so far been triumphant and has caused the flight of the King's forces from our little corner of the country. But this is not enough, I have been told. General Roche has assured me that we must continue apace or we risk losing the initiative.'

He was interrupted at this point by a vigorous, 'Hear, hear,' from Miles Byrne.

Harvey nodded and continued but Dan detected an almost mocking tone in his voice, as though he felt a slight disdain for the words he was forced to utter, 'To this end the leadership of the United Irishmen, and of course the esteemed Fr John Murphy,' he added hastily, and which Fr Murphy ignored completely, 'have therefore designed a stratagem to further our goals.'

A voice then rose from the midst of the congregation and a man stepped forth. He was a peasant farmer and almost a week's growth of beard made a grey-flecked pelt of his face and neck. Dan thought he recognised the man from Oulart Hill and his words immediately confirmed this fact.

'I've been with Fr John here since The Harrow,' he drawled. 'I don't know why he was left standing when the likes of "Lord" Edward Fitzgerald there had a chair. I don't see why we have to listen to any plans that Mr Fitzgerald has had a hand in. Where did he go yesterday? Let him answer that first if he's not too afeared to be honest with us.'

Harvey looked uncomfortable, his flabby face quivering as he raised a placating hand. 'These are trying times for us all, my good fellow,' he began but Edward Fitzgerald rose elegantly to his feet and stemmed his flow of words.

'Don't antagonise them, Edward,' Harvey cautioned before sitting back down.

Fitzgerald cleared his throat and faced the farmer with an air of nobility that seemed to outshine even the sunlight streaming through the high, leaded windows. He then glanced around the assembly saying, 'I went home, gentlemen. I found Wexford abandoned by the military and I went home for the night.'

A horrible noise slithered from the officers' throats and Dan thought he heard the word 'coward' bleed forth into the air.

Fitzgerald merely stood for a moment and then responded, 'Call me "coward" if you will. Call a man "coward" for wishing to spend a last few hours with his wife and family. For make no mistake about it, gentlemen, we have reached the turning point. I do not expect to see my home again unless it is under the banner of Ireland free and the tyrant's yoke removed forever. I have come here from my last night with my family sure in the knowledge that it is liberty or death for us all from now on. The government cannot allow us to humiliate them and the French must come to our aid. We are at war, total and utter and with all the horrors and brute necessities that that sorry circumstance carries with it.

'Therefore I have returned, committed and four-square behind every man here, after one brief respite at my poor home. If any man should think me milk-livered or lukewarm for doing such, then let him speak and I shall remove myself from this entire enterprise.'

A silence greeted his words and with a muttered, 'Thank you,' he sat down.

Into the silence another voice intruded, this time anonymously from the rear of the crowd where it spilled through the open doors into the drawing room. 'I thought the plan was to rid Wexford of soldiers. Surely we have accomplished all that our instructions set out. To go further without word from Dublin is to go beyond our remit.'

Harvey again rose to his feet, a pontifical smile playing at his blubber lips, and replied, 'My dear man, I have only, since my recent release from incarceration and from my Herculean efforts to ensure the liberty of our fellow patriots, been made aware of these militant manoeuvrings. I was committed to a course of political emancipation without any inkling of an armed insurrection. General Roche here informs me that the original aims of the United Irishmen for County Wexford have indeed been accomplished.'

A murmur of agreement and wonder filtered through the assembled officers as Roche added, 'We were to defeat and blockade the Crown forces within our county and so prevent reinforcements reaching Dublin. That we have done with an intrepidity and alacrity which must be considered miraculous. According to our original scheme we should now engage in restoring order and providing food and shelter for the dispossessed and those brutalised by the fighting, Catholic and Protestant both. Mr Harvey here was to be foremost in this process. If other counties have been as successful as we have been then word should be reaching us from the provisional government in Dublin soon.'

The anonymous voice rose again, lifting above the heads of his companions, who shuffled to move out of his way, 'Then why don't we simply wait for word?'

Again a buzz of agreement rattled around the room.

Harvey answered him, still smiling condescendingly. 'My dear fellow, I am of the same opinion as you are. I feel the time for bloodshed is over. Conciliation must begin at some point, must it not? However, our good friends who sit around me are not in so optimistic a frame of mind.'

Roche nodded and growled, 'I do not think we have taken Dublin. We would have had word from the surrounding counties by now.'

It was then that Anthony Perry spoke, his voice low but mounting with every word like a gathering storm. 'I also do not think Dublin has fallen. I believe we must carry the fight to them. We must rise the country or die in the attempt.'

His hands then went to the bandages that turbaned his scalp and, snarling,

277

he ripped them from him. Underneath, his head was hairless apart from at the nape of his neck and at his temples where a few desultory straggles hung limp and sweat-slicked. The bare surface of his scalp was a devil's parody of human flesh. The entire dome of Perry's skull was livid with fresh scars and oozing pustules were pale pouches of corruption bubbling across his head. As the bandages came away with a horrible rasping sound, thin trickles of blood began to seep from the myriad lacerations that wound between his sores.

At the sight of his maimed skull many of the surrounding men averted their gaze and stared blankly at floor or ceiling. Dan however could not tear his appalled eyes from the marks of Perry's torture.

'Look at me!' Perry snapped, his Ulster accent harsh and barking. 'Look at me, damn you!'

Every face reluctantly turned to regard him with mingled pity and horror.

When he was sure of his audience Perry continued, 'You who speak of rest, of conciliation, know nothing of what was done to me. What I endured. What I was forced to do. I will die and take every man here with me before I fall into their hands again. We must move and move quickly.'

Harvey was scowling and began to speak in a mollifying tone, 'My dear Mr Perry, we all sympathise—'

Roche cut him off viciously, 'Mr Harvey, sympathy will not carry the day. We must mount an offensive and strike out of the county before the government can gather its wits and before line regiments start arriving from England. If we can hold them until the French arrive then the country must surely be ours.'

Harvey's scowl deepened and he sat down into his chair with the air of a scolded schoolboy.

'What should we do, General?' asked a voice to the left of Dan.

Roche cleared his throat and explained, 'Our numbers are now very great and we have amassed a large store of firearms. Unfortunately our powder is in short supply and its manufacture is proving difficult. We do however have artillery and men who are trained in its use. We also have untold thousands of pikes and strong arms and stout hearts with which to wield them.'

A small cheer greeted this comment but was immediately hushed into silence by the majority.

'The plan is to divide our force into two. I will command one division while Mr Harvey will assume command of the other. Mr Fitzgerald, Mr Perry and I will march north with ten thousand men and move on Gorey and Newtownbarry, striving to break out into the midlands or across into Wicklow.

Mr Harvey will lead the southern division of thirteen thousand to attack New Ross and move into Kilkenny, thence to Waterford and so rise the Munster counties.'

Tom leaned into Dan and Miles and whispered hoarsely, 'That's what Hay and Barker suggested two days ago.'

'I am aware of that, Mr Banville,' growled Roche, overhearing. 'Since I am reliably informed that you are taking provisional command of the Castletown Corps I shall tell you now that I expect any misgivings you may have on our march north to be directed solely to me.'

Tom frowned in confusion and looked at Dan, who stared fixedly ahead whispering out of the side of his mouth, 'Later.'

The meeting continued for a few minutes more with Matthew Keogh being named provisional governor of Wexford Town with the liberal Ebenezer Jacob as chief medical officer. Provisions were made for law and order, for munitions manufacture, and, finally, it was agreed that a printing press was to be commandeered to be used for the printing of pamphlets.

The council concluded with Fr Murphy leading the men in a short prayer while Harvey and the other Protestant members present blessed themselves and listened silently. Finally Roche ordered, 'Everyone to their regiments. Await runners bearing orders. The Northern Division will march with me this very afternoon. Make ready.'

The mass of rebel officers filed out of the rooms, passing the serving man as he scrubbed the floor by the front door. In the street Miles Byrne turned to Dan and asked, 'What do you make of that?'

Dan nodded, 'I feel that a firm course of action has at last been decided upon. The leaders lead and we follow. It is as it should be.'

Tom spoke, his voice low, his expression dark, 'What did Roche mean by saying I had command of the Castletown Corps?'

Byrne looked uncomfortable, his youthful face twisting and his eyes finding unnatural interest in the flight of a swallow flitting over the slated roofs in this well-to-do part of town. Dan, however, faced his brother with all the frankness he could muster and said, 'You are taking the corps and heading north with Roche. I have been asked to look after a new body of men come in from Mayglass. They have no captain and have no experience, yet they and their like will be sent to accompany Mr Harvey in his taking of New Ross.'

Tom looked at him quizzically, 'So you are to babysit novices?'

'I am to lead men who were unfortunate enough to miss the victories thus far,' Dan retorted.

279

'Preposterous,' snapped Tom. 'You are coming north with me. I only became involved in this lunacy because you were. I will not allow you to get yourself killed for some far-fetched romantic notion.'

'Liberty is hardly a romantic notion,' said Dan somewhat stiffly.

Tom pinched the bridge of his nose in that familiar gesture of exasperation, and said, 'Do not sloganise me, big brother. I have never been the idealist that you are. I do not see why you just do not come north. Roche strikes me as a far better bet than this Mr Harvey.'

He turned to Byrne then and asked, 'What say you, Miles?'

Miles Byrne shook his head, saying, 'I do not wish to become involved, Tom. We are soldiers and so we may follow orders without question.'

'And where do your orders take you, pray tell?' wondered Tom.

Byrne shrugged, relenting, 'The Monaseed Corps are to go north with Roche and Fitzgerald.'

Tom nodded bitterly, his lips twisting as though a hook had lodged in the soft flesh of his cheek, 'So we are to abandon Dan to his fate, is that it? It will not stand. I will not leave my brother behind.'

Dan smiled at Tom. His brother's loyalty was touching, in spite of his stubborn refusal to accept the nobility he himself found in the United Irishmen.

He patted Tom on the shoulder and said, 'John Kelly and the boys from Killann are staying with the Southern Division as far as I know. As is Thomas Cloney. There is work to be done here, Tom. Experience and bravery to match Mr Harvey's political guile. Should we break through at Ross, why the whole of Munster will rise with us.'

'Then I shall stay with you,' argued Tom a little petulantly. 'I only accepted a commission because I thought you and I would be fighting together. I shall walk away from it before I leave you to fend for yourself.'

'For shame, Tom,' hissed Dan. 'You cannot abandon the men like that. You bring dishonour down upon us both. Roche would be furious. He was most happy to have you numbered amongst his officers.'

Tom astutely eyed the two men before him, 'I have the distinct impression that the good General Roche was aware of my "decision" long before I was.'

Byrne sighed then and pitching his voice low so as to avoid any would-be eavesdroppers, he said, 'Tom, you know as well as I do that to sit and reflect on our victories thus far amounts to nothing. To break out into the provinces is what is required. We cannot do that without men of utmost capability. Both you and Dan are needed in different places, Tom. Either you seize this chance or you risk disaster for us all. Mr Harvey's choice as commander-in-chief is a political one. Being a Protestant of the highest respectability and chosen thus by his Catholic countrymen should be sufficient proof that this is not a religious war. Yet it is not Mr Harvey, nor even General Roche who will win the day. That task falls to the fighting men, ably led by gentlemen the like of you.'

Tom stared at the young captain intently before turning to Dan with a cold sort of anger blistering the well of his throat. His words came with all the spitting defiance of a cornered wildcat and in that instant Tom Banville was more his father's son than Dan could ever hope to be.

'I will take the Castletown Corps north,' he hissed. 'I will take them and I will fight the English to the very wharves of Dublin Port if needs be. But both of you mark my words, I do this not for the green-painted fantasies of the United Irishmen, I do this not for Harvey, nor for Roche nor for Fr Murphy, not even for you, Miles. I do this for my family and for my honour.'

He stared at Dan then, his eyes brimming with fury and fierce affection, 'I do this for my brother.'

CHAPTER 16

With Brave Harvey

In Wexford Town, the early afternoon of the 31st of May was a shifting heave of bodies and material. The breeze had been constant all morning, whipping cloaks of spume to swish up off the waves of Wexford Harbour. Now though, as well as the waves and the slither-slap of ships' sails, the breeze pawed at the banners of a hundred different parishes and townlands. The banners were mostly homespun and roughly stitched, the embroidery awkward or mawkish, shamrocks and crosses and lumpen slogans scrawled across their fields. Yet each and every one was green, green, green. The universal impression was of a great primeval host set to advance as though stepping from the pages of history or the wild terrain of myth.

Rough cries mounted the heavens, competing with the splintered calls of the wheeling seagulls, 'Oulart men, to your colours!'

'Ballaghkeen, to your colours!'

'Monaseed, to your colours!'

Wexford Town was a hive of teeming forms as men and women streamed out through John Street, towards Windmill Hill and Ferrycarrig beyond. The Northern Division of the great rebel army was on the march, pike-heads scintillating in the sunlight.

Behind them Wexford, although far from empty, had stilled. Like a vast animal of brick and mortar, slate and thatch, the town seemed to draw in its breath, its arteries less choked, its heart less fevered.

Dan Banville stood upon the high stone wall surrounding St John's Church and looked out over the departing ranks. Below him, amidst a throng of cheering onlookers, Elizabeth did not watch the marching insurgents but instead directed her anxious gaze upward, fearful for Dan ten feet above her and buffeted by the breeze. From her perspective his face was pale, his jaw set in a hard line that betrayed his loss, his pain, at his brother's absence.

'Come down, Daniel,' she called.

Dan glance downward and smiled at her in a manner which he thought might be reassuring but instead imbued his expression with a haunted sort of desperation. She had availed of her aunt's hospitality to wash and change her dress and as her face tilted up to him, her beauty struck him with palpable force.

'In a moment,' he replied. 'I want to see them gone.'

Them, thought Elizabeth ruefully. Her beloved was a terrible liar and she had not been exaggerating when she had described him as glass to her. She saw to his very core, could plumb his depths as easily as if he were a bucket of water. Now he stood high up on a wall that he had clambered with the urgency of a man escaping gaol, clambered so that his knuckles were skinned and dripped blood in a soft pat-pat onto his boots; now he stood and looked out over the heads of ten thousand marching men but seeing just one.

In that moment Elizabeth discerned truly, and perhaps for the first time, the love that Daniel bore his brother. That and the blazing pride that burned within his chest as he gazed to the point in the distance into which Tom had disappeared.

'You can't see him anymore, Daniel,' shouted Elizabeth in a manner she found most unladylike. She craned her neck and held her worsted sun-bonnet onto the crown of her head. 'Come down before you slip and break your leg. They'd likely put you down at this rate.'

At last Dan turned his eyes to her and smiled a smile of genuine warmth. Stirring himself, he bent and lowered gradually down the face of the wall until he stood, breathless, before Elizabeth. He shook his bleeding knuckles distractedly and raised his right hand to his lips to stem the flow of a particularly deep gouge.

Elizabeth reached up and smoothed the lapels of a clean coat across his broad chest, saying, 'We must be at my dear Aunt's in Chapel Lane for tea at four o'clock. She is simply straining at the bit to catch a glimpse of you. She has even granted permission for you to use her bath should you so require! Imagine that. Hot water, Daniel!'

He grinned and kissed her quickly. 'And soap,' he said. 'Most importantly, soap.'

She grinned back at him, tasting the slight metallic tang of his blood on her lips.

They turned left and walked arm in arm down John Street as the last of the rebel detachments moved past. As they strolled, Dan noticed that several of the smithies and tanneries that lined John Street were closed. An unusual quiet swaddled the rough buildings and their empty windows nudged the mind into thoughts of ancient ruins and pagan tombs. Their proprietors had joined the United ranks almost as soon as the army had entered the town. The John Street Corps were now moving past Windmill Hill, eager for Bagenal Harvey or Edward Roche to signal the advance on New Ross and Arklow and the open tracts of Ireland beyond. On John Street no horses whinnied and kicked as they were shoed, no merchants argued with filth-streaked leather-makers. Even the stink of life was fading. It was as though the street had been gutted and now lay vacant and without a pulse upon some great cold slab.

Elizabeth wound her grip tighter about Dan's forearm and looked up at him, smiling in spite of the odd atmosphere. 'Tom will be fine, you know. He is careful and daring in equal measure. I cannot see him doing anything rash that might endanger himself or the men around him.'

Dan nodded silently. It was not Tom's ability to look after himself that bothered him but a gnawing sense of guilt that he had somehow forced his brother into this course of action. It was as though he had preyed on Tom's dedication to him, had used the knowledge of Tom's loyalty to goad him down a path he hadn't chosen.

Yet even this, private and hidden though he thought it was, did not escape Elizabeth's scrutiny.

She narrowed her eyes and said softly, 'It is not your fault, Daniel. He left to ensure this Rising succeeds. It is the only way you have of returning safely to your home.'

Dan snorted, 'Our home is burnt to the ground. We have land but it will take time to make it what it once was.'

'It will take time for us all to make something from this trauma,' Elizabeth replied.

Dan, however, wasn't listening to her. His attention had been abruptly snagged by a group of men and women clustered at the junction with Chapel Lane. All wore the dirty greys and ragged browns of poor townsfolk, their calves stockingless and their dirty feet without shoes, caked in the grime and dust of the streets. They had been engaged in a raucous, scuttling jabber of conversation but at the couple's approach they quietened. A stillness came over them and they directed hard stares towards Dan and Elizabeth. There was a threat in those stares that Dan found chilling, a nasty belligerence married to a brutish swagger.

As the young couple passed, the frigid zone of silence wrapping the group seemed to extend and enfold them so that even the mere thought of speech or gaiety was snuffed out like a guttering candle. Dan felt the hairs at the nape of his neck lift in apprehension and he silently thanked God that Elizabeth was at his left and that his sword arm was free. For her part Elizabeth sensed something of the foreboding in the air as she leaned into him, angling herself away from the shabby clot of people whose eyes fastened onto her like claws.

Dan had shepherded Elizabeth past the last member of the group when the noise of someone hawking up a lungful of phlegm rasped from behind them. Dan spun just in time to see one of the townsfolk, a balding, sunken-cheeked fellow with a nose slanting crookedly across his face, spit a glistening rope of snot and spit onto the road just short of the hem of Elizabeth's dress.

Dan was moving before he realised it. Outrage and fury spurred his muscles into action before his mind had even fully grasped the situation. Only the weight of Elizabeth swinging from his arm like a sort of anchor kept him from drawing his sword in a shining arc of violence and bloodshed.

'No, Daniel!' she cried. 'Let them be. They know not what they do. When things become less fraught I am sure they will regret their actions this day.'

Dan halted and regarded the group of people before him. In spite of their pugnacious attitude they had all taken a step backward at the sight of Dan's anger and one or two of the women – and not a few of the men – seemed poised for flight.

Dan pointed at the man whose spit now dried in the dust and growled, 'I will not ask for an apology from the like of you. But I assure you that what my wife says is true. You will regret your actions this day.'

Elizabeth whispered, her voice soft as snowflakes, 'Don't, Dan. They are too many.'

The man merely laughed in a bitter cough of sound, devoid of any light or joy. 'Would you go 'way out of that. You'll find yourself floating in the harbour like a lot of the others will soon enough.'

Elizabeth's grip upon Dan's arm stilled his urgent impulse to gut the man.

Without another word Dan and Elizabeth walked away from the crowd and turned down Chapel Lane. Behind them the crow cackle of laughter rattled into the street.

'Don't mind them,' breathed Elizabeth at last but her voice was thin with the strain of false courage.

'I don't like this,' Dan muttered. 'For the last few hours, ever since the Northern Division was assembled to leave, something terrible has been occurring to me. The town is changed, the air has darkened. Have you seen the looks directed at some of the citizens by their fellow townsmen? Have you noticed the whispering cabals gathered on every corner?'

Elizabeth looked into his face, her expression clouded with concern, 'I see ne'er-do-wells and rabble-rousers who have naught else to do but spread gossip and engage in bullying those whom they think might be intimidated. Mr Harvey and Mr Fitzgerald are themselves Protestant, Mr Keogh, who has been established as Mayor, also. No man can surely be ignorant enough to act on bigotry in such circumstances.'

'I would not have thought it,' replied Dan. 'But I fear that Tom may be right. Human nature is a gutter-bound thing no matter what ideals one might aspire to.'

Elizabeth shook her head then, her mahogany curls unfurling from beneath her hat. 'Oh Daniel, do not allow the actions of a stupid, oafish gang to colour your thoughts like this. Be happy. You will soon meet my charming aunt.'

Dan laughed sourly. 'From bad to worse. I wish Mr Harvey would decide to act. We should be away. Idle hands will always find evil work to do.'

Twenty minutes later Dan was forced to admit that Elizabeth may have been unfairly harsh on her aged relative. He had not met the woman as yet for she expressed a wish to see him 'as befits a good Catholic gentleman and not some vagabond who spends his life in ditches'. They had been met at the door by her manservant, a dour old man with a stooped back and whose breeches seemed to be forever on the brink of slumping about his ankles. He had allowed Elizabeth to enter and go straight down the hallway but had ushered Dan into the pantry where a tin bath sat steaming and where a razor, mirror and soap had been placed on a shelf. Dan had gushed his thanks and when the old servant had shambled out he undressed and sat soaking up to his middle in the lapping warmth of clean water.

As he scrubbed at himself with the soap he reflected that any woman who could be so hospitable to a guest of different religion and who had arrived at the head of a conquering army could hardly be the dragon that Elizabeth had described. The water around him began to fog with the detritus of days living in fields, of smoke and fighting and death. Clawing for the razor and mirror he commenced to scrape away the bristles that had come to mat his jaw and had lately began to itch with an irritating heat. Soon he sat in what amounted to little more than a brackish puddle, a scum of filth fouling the surface.

Wrinkling his lip he heaved himself out, dried and dressed himself. The new coat, shirt, riding breeches and stockings that he had procured felt fresh against his newly scrubbed skin but the effect was somehow counterpointed by the battered state of his old yeoman's boots and the mottled wash of bruising that seemed to swim below the surface of every patch of skin. A narrow, crimson line beaded with scabs arced below his right eye where a briar had hooked at him. No wig and no tricorn might count against him but overall he felt he looked as well as he could hope to, considering everything.

Breathing deeply he left his weapons in a dark corner and opened the pantry door only to find the old serving man waiting for him.

'I feel much better, now,' Dan remarked. 'A hot bath does wonders.'

The serving man merely cocked his head to one side and wordlessly looked at him with a mix of pity and contempt. He then shuffled down the corridor, leaving Dan to follow in his wake.

Mrs Abigail Brownrigg, née Blakely, was the childless widow of a prosperous grain merchant who had fortunately passed to his eternal reward long before the grain prices collapsed in 1797. Upon his death she had found herself alone in a large townhouse with only her two servants, Pat and Molly, for company. To while away the hours she spent her time composing withering letters to her closest relatives and calling upon them unannounced to belittle their housekeeping or terrify their wives. Elizabeth had not seen her for seven years and yet her last visit to Carnew was still spoken about in the Blakely household in hushed tones, as though it were some awful tragedy. Nobody had ever sought out the old crone of their own volition and none had ever thought to pay her a visit in her cold, echoing house, her clocks ticking away the seconds to the grave.

She had greeted Elizabeth earlier in the day with detached surprise and a dry civility which had left Elizabeth fearing that worse was to come.

Now the two women sat in Mrs Brownrigg's drawing room, both perched primly on the edge of high-backed armchairs, a small wooden table the colour of Elizabeth's curls positioned between them. Upon this table, a dainty china tea set was placed with a plate of bread and apple tart beside it. Each woman held a small cup of tea in her right hand, a saucer in her left, and both sat in complete silence. Between the two tall rectangular windows opening out onto the back garden, a grandfather clock stood with its pendulum measuring out life spans in brief, swishing, slices of time.

The old servant paused at the open door to the drawing room and coughed politely. 'Mr Daniel Banville, ma'am.'

The old woman nodded and Dan entered. His first impression of Elizabeth's aunt was one of poise. She sat in her chair with all the elegance of a sculptured swan. Her back was straight, her neck long and her chin jutted forth with a regal air above the lip of the teacup suspended from delicately pinched fingers. She was old, of that there was no doubt, for wrinkles chasmed the skin of her throat where it climbed out of the modest bodice of her charcoal dress, and her hands were wormed with a blue tracery of veins. Brown spots speckled the pale skin of those hands and her bones tented up through the flesh like white knots. Her eyes, however, were jewel-bright and regarded Dan with the probing scrutiny of a hawk.

'Mr Banville,' she greeted, 'I have heard so much about you that I felt I must see you in person.'

Still standing, Dan offered a bow and replied, 'I am delighted to meet so close a relative of Elizabeth's. She speaks of you with great fondness.'

Mrs Brownrigg sipped her tea demurely before saying, 'Poppycock. Young man, if you seek my approval you would do well to mind your tongue. I am universally loathed among my relatives and well I like it.

'However, blood is the tie that binds and since my niece is in need of succour and seems unaccountably fond of you then I am forced to accept you into my home. What I am not forced to accept is balderdash from any young man, let alone a croppy.'

Dan blinked and Elizabeth gasped, 'Aunty!'

'Come now, child,' replied her aunt, and Dan thought he could detect the merest hint of humour in those bright, birdlike eyes. 'Mr Banville is a grown man and seems quite used to fighting. I am sure he is neither thin-skinned nor devoid of wit enough to necessitate your springing to his defence. What say you, Mr Banville?'

Dan smiled. 'I am a stalwart croppy, Mrs Brownrigg, of that you are correct. However, if you can forgive that one trifling flaw I can assure you that I hold your niece very dear in my affections.'

Mrs Brownrigg motioned for a chair to be brought in and the servant plodded over to retrieve one from beside a bookcase packed with volumes, their spines fissured from decades of constant use. He placed it before Dan with a grunt of effort.

'You may go now, Pat,' instructed Mrs Brownrigg. As the old servant shambled from the room, his brogues scuffing the floorboards, she continued, 'Mr Banville do sit down, your great bulk is intruding upon the elegance of my drawing room.'

Elizabeth smiled at Dan apologetically as he seated himself with the odd feeling that, in spite of her tone and words, he liked this old woman.

'You have not been formally introduced to Elizabeth's parents, I presume?' she continued.

'No, unfortunately,' answered Dan. 'The circumstances at the time prevented such a meeting.'

Mrs Brownrigg grunted and said, 'Circumstance is an ever-changing thing. Please, Mr Banville, help yourself to tea and cakes. Molly makes exceedingly good apple tart.'

Dan thanked her, carefully poured himself a cup of tea and placed a sliver of apple tart onto a small saucer with all the delicacy of a man lighting a fuse.

'He has good manners, at least,' commented the old woman.

Elizabeth remained silent but her eyes constantly flickered to Dan's face, her expression tortured, her shoulders now hunched.

'Oh, do sit up straight, girl, and stop making faces,' snapped Mrs Brownrigg before addressing Dan again.

'As I said, circumstances change and I feel we have reached one such change of circumstance in this town, if not this whole country.'

Dan nodded, 'I feel you are correct.'

She nodded, 'We are Protestant. You are Catholic and a rebel. Only days ago the very thought of having you under my roof would have appalled me.'

'I shall not stand for this!' interrupted Elizabeth, her voice almost shouting. 'I love this man, Aunt Abigail.'

She had sat through this charade for longer than she felt necessary. The lidded mockery in her aunt's voice, the arch superiority of her bearing, all grated on Elizabeth's nerves like a rasp across a knot. She had sat here now in her aunt's sepia-shadowed lair for over an hour as the many clocks measured out every second in brittle chops of noise. And every second she sat, sipping at her aunt's weak tea, she felt the gloom of the place wrap her more closely. She could not sit here and have Daniel baited like some doltish child.

Sensing her protectiveness, hearing the outrage in her voice, Dan responded, his own voice level, his thoughts flat and calm, 'Let your aunt finish, Elizabeth.'

Elizabeth's lips tightened almost imperceptibly and she flung him a shrewd look, the dark of the room making her eyes glimmer in brilliant imitation of her relative's.

Mrs Brownrigg nodded, a brief dipping of her chin and a dry warping of her corrugated skin, 'Of course you love him, my dear. You are young and he is a fine figure of a man. What you and all the rest of my unfortunate relatives have in common is neither foresight nor common sense. Mr Banville here seems to know when to speak and when to listen, perhaps you should learn from him.'

Elizabeth bridled and rattled her cup and saucer onto the table before her.

Seemingly oblivious to her chagrin, her aunt continued, 'The fact of the matter is that the old order seems about to topple and you, Mr Banville, are an officer of the new. I am too frail and too cantankerous to leave this house and my dear niece is too silly to make her way in this new world without protection. What I would like to know, Mr Banville, is what your intentions are in light of our changed circumstances.'

Dan frowned, unsure of what the old woman expected. Honesty was called for, he felt, and so with a deep breath he plunged on, 'Mrs Brownrigg, my intentions are to marry Elizabeth. I love her sorely. I am also duty-bound as a United Irishman to defend and liberate the people of Ireland be they Catholics, Protestants, labourers, servants or old, bitter ladies living out their days like spiders in a web.'

Elizabeth gasped in shock but Mrs Brownrigg laughed with a sound like dry leaves in the wind.

'Oh, he is a rare one, Elizabeth!' she exclaimed. 'A rare one, indeed.'

Just then the old servant, Pat, came shuffling into the room once more, his hands wringing and his brow a swamp of glistening sweat. Dan spun in his seat to look at the man and the sight of his trembling form had the young captain half out of the chair and groping for his absent pistol before he could think.

'I am sorry for interrupting, ma'am, but the croppies,' here he knifed Dan a glittering look, 'have set fire to Mr Boyd's house and have surrounded Mr Harvey's. They want Mr Edward Turner. They're going to lynch him.'

Mrs Brownrigg sipped her tea, her equipoise undisturbed, 'Well, Mr Banville,' she asked. 'What do you intend to do?'

Dan, who was on his feet now and anxious to retrieve his sword and pistol, regarded the old woman with piercing awareness. 'Edward Turner is deserving of justice,' he replied levelly. 'I was there when he fired the cabins at Oulart.'

His eyes moved from the venerable aunt who sat serene and unmoving, gazing at him in cool detachment, to Elizabeth and back again. He cleared his throat and said, 'However, justice must be meted out in the proper way and not by the hands of a mob.'

He turned away from them then, his face set and grim, 'I will see what I can do.'

The black, cumulous tower that rose above Captain James Boyd's former residence was the first sign that anything was amiss in the streets around Selskar Church. The house had been ransacked and set alight and now flung sparks and butterfly wings of ash whirling up into the afternoon sky, the wind breathing life and ferocity into the flames. All along the length of George's Street the stench of the inferno coupled with the blanket of smoke made passage impossible. Choking fumes and particles of cinder clogged the throat and blinded the eyes.

Around the corner, in front of Bagenal Harvey's house, a mob had gathered. Pikes were brandished and burning torches, the flames almost invisible in the sunlight save for the wavering of the tortured air above them, were waved aloft. Men roared and bellowed and the entire assembly seemed to sway and roll as one body, like the sea. The din was raucous and ill-tempered and the stink of unwashed bodies and alcohol mingled with the acrid discharge from Boyd's flaming abode. Every face was that of a demon, twisted and hate-filled, warped with a mindless lust for violence.

The mob arced out from Harvey's front steps leaving an open space, like an amphitheatre, some ten dusty paces wide. Before the quartzite steps, seeming to fill all the available space like some fiendish dervish, Thomas Dixon paced back and forth.

'Justice!' he cried, his arms raised above his head, his hands tensed into talons. 'All we ask for is justice!'

The crowd brayed in approval.

Dan Banville had hurried there as fast as he could, running against a large number of others who sought to distance themselves from the mob at Harvey's door. When he arrived, panting and sweating, he had asked the first person he recognised in the assembly what was happening.

The man, a broad-shouldered veteran of Enniscorthy, had answered without tearing his gaze away from the bundle of angular energy that was Thomas Dixon, 'Bagenal Harvey, our good commander-in-chief, has elected to hold a dinner party for all men of substance in the town.'

That's what Harvey is up to, thought Dan. Why in God's name could he not just assemble the corps and march on Ross? Why did he dawdle so?

'And?' he prompted the man.

Still without looking, the rebel answered, 'There's half the Orangemen of Wexford in there, including that bastard Edward Turner. Captain Dixon wants him turned over to us.'

Dan frowned darkly. 'In order for him to be held accountable for his actions against the people?'

At last the big man turned to him and Dan saw that across his right eye a scorch mark had left his brow and cheek bone a red swathe of scar tissue and had turned the eyeball into a blind, milky white sphere. The man stared at Dan with his one good eye but all the malignancy in his gaze seemed to emanate from the other sightless, pus-filled blank.

He considered Dan's words and then his lips wriggled into a sneer. 'To kill him,' he pronounced slowly.

Dan had moved away from the man then and worked his way into the crowd so that he was only a person or two away from the pacing Dixon.

'Justice!' Dixon cried again and then turned to the closed building behind him. 'Hand us over Edward Turner! Give him to the people or we shall take him by force. A new era is upon us, no more will Ireland shelter the despot.'

Dan fancied one of the curtains framing the house's tall windows twitched like the fluttering of an eyelid.

'Liberty and vengeance!' roared Dixon.

And the mob echoed, 'Liberty and vengeance!' Every throat flung its words against the stone-clad edifice like the ocean flinging waves.

Across the space that had formed about Harvey's doorway Dan could see the burly form of Dixon's wife, her sack-like arms folded and her ham head violet with heat and fervour.

Then Harvey's door opened and Beauchamp Bagenal Harvey stepped forward into the maw of the crowd. He was sweating profusely and his sideburns were damp against his heavy jowls. With a face pale as the belly of a frog, Harvey looked about him. The assembly fell silent and Dixon stepped smartly back into the ranks like an animal seeking safety in its pack.

'Ladies and gentlemen,' the United Irish leader began, his voice trembling and struggling to be heard over the cries of people trying to extinguish the flames of Boyd's former residence in George's Street.

Harvey coughed and began again in a slightly stronger voice, 'Ladies and gentlemen, please, you have no reason to disturb my dinner. I am entertaining citizens who may be of much benefit in rebuilding our stricken county.'

'You're feeding monsters!' yelled an outraged voice and the crowd surged forward a step or two.

'Please!' pleaded Harvey. 'There must be a time for conciliation, the two traditions cannot be enemies forever. Please return home and we shall be off presently towards another great victory over the tyrant.'

This was greeted with a stony silence that extended and deepened as the moments passed. Harvey swivelled anxiously, questing for a friendly face, the heels of his shoes horribly loud on the hard ground as he turned and turned about.

'Mr Harvey,' came Dixon's voice, like something crawling out from under a corpse. 'I do not think that the good people of Wexford can be so easily mollified by trite words.

'With all due respect, you were not with us at Oulart or Enniscorthy. You sent us a letter pleading on behalf of the creatures who persecuted us for so long. And now you stand and seek to thwart the will of the people? How do you expect us to follow you into battle, Mr Harvey? How can we hope to storm the gateways to Ross when you display such concern for the comfort of our oppressors?'

He paused for a heart beat before repeating, 'With all due respect.'

A moist segment of tongue ran out and along Harvey's lower lip and he stood stock-still for a moment, unsure of what to do.

Dan felt the weight of providence bear down upon him. He knew that were this exchange to continue that Bagenal Harvey would be piked and every one of his guests massacred. In the interstice between one second and the next, the seeds of the Rising's failure were sown and about to burst into miserable life. With Harvey's death the United Irishmen would tear themselves apart and Dixon and his ilk would reign supreme on a tidal wave of terror and butchery. Wexford would eat itself like a fox caught in a trap until the government finally put it out of its misery with musket and bayonet.

Dan moved reflexively, barging out into the open and stepping quickly to Harvey's side. It was a measure of the man's fear that, when he perceived Dan meant him no harm, he clung to his sleeve like a child to its father.

A murmur went up from the surrounding insurgents but Dan let it wash over him as he bent close to Harvey and whispered, 'Mr Harvey, unless you hand over Edward Turner to these people then you and everyone in your house must surely be murdered. Think on it.'

Harvey looked at the tall young man before him with eyes brimming with confusion and terror. 'But they will kill him.'

Dan growled, 'He might deserve such a fate. To entertain such an avowed loyalist in your house was ill-judged, sir. His only hope is to stand trial and so present some form of defence.'

Harvey sighed, 'I will send him out.'

Dan turned to the crowd as Harvey disappeared back through his front door.

Every face before him was masked with suspicion and bubbling fury. A dark muttering began to circulate and as Dan faced them he felt the first twinges of the terror that had stupefied Bagenal Harvey.

All moisture seemed to have evaporated from his mouth and his gums and tongue felt as though they were made of leather. He knew he must say something, anything, to stem the flood of rancorous grumbling that surrounded him. Thomas Dixon was staring at him with a poisonous sneer that soured further moment by moment.

'Mr Harvey has gone to fetch Mr Turner,' Dan heard himself say. 'He has agreed to surrender him for trial.'

At this a large number of the gathered rebels let out a huzzah but some remained mired in sullen silence.

Dixon spat, 'What need have we for a trial? The man is a monster.'

Dan nodded calmly, keenly aware of the knife edge he walked. 'I was at Oulart, Mr Dixon, and I am aware of his reputation but only the yeos and soldiers execute people without due process. Would you place us in the same category as our enemies?'

Then, in a voice louder and more commanding he asked, 'Who here would wish to be like the yeos and North Corks?'

There was a general murmur to the negative and a few limp shouts of, 'No one' and 'Not I'.

Dixon scowled but said nothing. His wife, however, lowered her great soft head and whispered something into Dixon's ear. The man's expression changed subtly. The scowl remained but it darkened somehow, becoming more intent, more pointed. His wife lifted her face then and a wide marly smile stretched across her lips.

Dan watched this tableau with a growing, sickening repulsion. All at once, a cold dread for Elizabeth had opened, gaping, beneath his ribs.

When Bagenal Harvey's door opened once more it was to reveal the pasty features of Edward Turner peering out into the street.

At the sight of him, a wild whoop ululated up from the crowd and the head withdrew a little as though Turner had decided to barricade himself into the house rather than face his persecutors. Instantly however, and with a violence that suggested unseen hands had propelled matters, the door widened further and Turner seemed to spill clumsily out onto the steps. Behind him the door slammed shut like a falling guillotine.

Turner regarded the people before him with a face that had taken on the colour of ashes. His wig was askew and his frock coat rumpled, his hands crawling over his paunch like white crabs as he attempted smooth out the wrinkles. A bellicose spew of insults flowed from the watching rebels and Turner's wide eyes drifted from face to vicious face.

Dan growled at the quivering magistrate, 'Say something, Mr Turner, or they will likely pike you where you stand.'

Turner whimpered but managed to stutter, 'I offer myself up to the justice of the people, where neither the house nor the interference of my friends nor the chief commander can offer me protection.'

A feral howl greeted his words and, as one, the mass of rebel bodies swarmed forward. Dan moved quickly to one side as urgent hands quested for Turner's terrified form. His coat was stripped from him and, as though through some magic trick or infernal conjuring, a gash was opened along the raised contour of his cheek. Blood flowed down the man's face and was smeared and grotesquely smudged by hands which punched and slapped, tearing the wig from his head and battering him like a storm.

'To the gaol!' someone cried.

'Pack him in with the others!' another voice answered. 'We'll have his head on a spike by tomorrow!'

Through the mêlée of bodies, prodded and jabbed by the brutal steel of pike-heads, Turner was goaded down the street. His face hung from his skull like empty sacking, every line loose and nerveless, his eyes doleful puddles. The mob of insurgents flowed around him, swirling like dirty water down a drain, hurling spittle and vitriol, cat-calls and curses. Amongst it all, within this maelstrom of barbarity, Edward Turner made a pathetic figure. Abandoned by his friends, surrendered to his enemies, he was doomed.

Dan watched the mob depart with an odd flux of emotions warring within his mind. He knew what Turner was, he had watched him burn cottages, had heard of his pronouncements of flogging and transportation, he had lived hand in glove with the North Corks and had turned a blind eye to their excesses. Dan knew all this, yet he could not help but feel a sort of sympathy for the man, hounded and humiliated as he was, baited like an animal. Dan thought that if Dixon was presiding over his trial then Turner could expect nothing but the same perverse bigotry that he himself had visited upon others. He was a man reaping the whirlwind.

'Feel sorry for him, don't you?' a voice asked from over his left ear sending a soft feathering of foul breath across his cheek

The question was asked in a sticky whine, nasal and grating and Dan knew that Dixon's wife stood behind him; he could sense her oppressive bulk pressed close to him.

'Madam,' he said without turning, 'I would advise you never again to sneak up behind an armed man. It is inadvisable and likely to precipitate a nasty accident.'

Mrs Dixon moved around Dan like a leviathan sluggishly rolling in the deeps and looked at him with brazen disdain leaking from her hooded eyes. 'You'll get yours, too,' she grunted and then turned to follow her husband and the mob he led, moving through the thickening smoke like a figure in some awful dream.

Dan stared at her blurred back as it faded from sight, his mind a ball of ice. Behind him, Harvey's house was silent and cold, its windows staring blindly out onto the street. A curtain, unnoticed by anyone, twitched and then stilled, leaving all motionless, only the roiling smoke and a lone, screaming gull lending any life to the scene.

CHAPTER 17

Ambitions

The afternoon of the 1st of June crumbled slowly into a purple sea of dusk. A mackerel sky was all aflame with the bloodlight of the dipping sun and its high clouds were spun gold across the heavens. The rough prominence of Carrigrew Hill was swamped in the effulgence of the dying day and upon its summit Tom Banville gazed southwest across the countryside, a frown darkening his brow.

That morning, full of laughter and arrogance, the Northern Division of the United Irish Army had split at Scarawalsh Bridge. Fr Mogue Kearns, a redoubtable, bumptious United man, had been given command of two and a half thousand pike- and musketmen, a howitzer and a handful of ship's swivels. Roche, Fr Murphy and Edward Fitzgerald had instructed this force to take and occupy Newtownbarry and from there to scout in force into Carlow and Wicklow and ascertain the state of the rebellion in those two counties. With Kearns went Miles Byrne and his Monaseed Corps, ranging ahead in the now-familiar role of vedette.

Tom had stood at Byrne's stirrup as the young officer had prepared to depart. Scarawalsh Bridge flung itself over the Slaney to their right and the dusty hump of its back was thronged with the dark masses of the rebel army. A forest of pikes made a rippling porcupine of the fields and paddocks all about and green flags flapped sullenly in the fading breeze.

'Mind yourself, Miles,' Tom had cautioned.

Byrne had smiled roguishly and replied, 'The fiends that occupy Newtownbarry are the ones in need of minding. Our fine boys will make them run as far as Maryborough. We'll be into the midlands and have the place risen around us before the end of the week.'

Tom had patted the sinewy neck of Byrne's mount and repeated simply, 'Mind yourself.'

Miles had sobered then, and nodded, 'Thank you, Tom.'

He paused and added, 'Speak to Roche and Fr Murphy about the goings-on at Vinegar Hill. Luke Byrne can't be left there. Thirty-two done to death in two days is inordinate.'

Tom's face had clouded and he had said, 'I will do what I can but I fear the leaders have no stomach for discipline. They will not risk driving a wedge between moderates and fanatics.'

Miles had wheeled his horse, saying, 'I fear you are right but do what you can. I shall see you tomorrow or the next day when the land around Newtownbarry has been swept free of redcoats.'

Tom had waved goodbye to the young captain and watched him trot through the ranks, a wave of cheers and thrown hats marking his progress like the wake of a man-o'-war.

The rebel detachment moved off then, with flags flaring in the few shallow gusts of wind before settling against their flagpoles like dead game hanging from a nail. Men laughed and joked and wives and children blew kisses and waved handkerchiefs, sure that nothing could stand before them. Enniscorthy and Wexford had fallen and so no earthly thing now exceeded their grasp.

Now Tom stood on the crest of Carrigrew Hill with the main mass of the Northern Division encamped all about him, thousands of men standing as he did, staring southwest with horror blanching their countenances. Tom stood and counted the corps as they returned in bloodied dribs and drabs. Exhausted men stumbled along the road and flung themselves over ditches, scrambling through the fields beyond, frantic to gain the safety of the camp. Wounded, supported by their comrades, they lurched step by agonised step out of the gloaming. In scattered groups of twos and threes, in battered clusters of ten or twelve, the remnants of Fr Kearn's detachment struggled through the twilight. In their movements and in the relieved faces of those who had already returned was a ghost of the panic they must have experienced mere hours before, the latent venom of defeat.

The wailing anguish, the keening of the widows and children of those men killed or missing wreathed the hill and filled the dusk with heartbreak.

And still Miles Byrne had not returned.

Tom waited silently, a sour sense of foreboding curdling his insides.

He had not expected this. To his shame he had allowed his optimism to strangle his good sense. Miles Byrne had rode off and with him Tom's thoughts had flown to images of struggle, a hard-fought victory with hundreds of casu-alties, a garrison pitted in desperation against a horde set to destroy it. He had not once considered defeat. He looked out over the fields and hedgerows of central Wexford and considered the fact that this was much worse than a defeat. The insurgent regiments had not come marching home, bloodied but unbowed. They had streamed through the countryside up from Scarawalsh as though the devil himself was at their backs, panicked and ragged and shattered. It had been a disaster.

Something here was not right and he was sure Roche, Fitzgerald and Fr Murphy had grasped it the moment the first survivor fell into the arms of an outlying sentry. The man had been brought into the camp and within minutes his story was snaking from fireside to fireside, twisting and warping as it did so but maintaining the hard core of its essence.

Fr Kearns and his men had taken Newtownbarry with all the bravery and enthusiasm that the United Irish Army had so far demonstrated. Then things had gone wrong and Tom felt compelled to point the finger of blame squarely at the good Fr Kearns. His men had watched the red-coated garrison flee along the road to Carlow and had then set about burning any loyalist house they could find, raiding cellars and pantries for whiskey and porter with every bit as much abandon as they had attacked the King's troops.

Minutes stretched by as Fr Kearns sat his great white charger in the middle of Newtownbarry's main street with a beatific air and the indulgent expression of a benevolent Pope. Men drank and blustered and looted and no one noticed that the garrison had rallied.

Strengthened by a detachment of Queen's County Militia that had come marching down the road to support them, the soldiers had rediscovered their spines and had turned around. They had stationed themselves on the high ground overlooking the smoke and bedlam of Newtownbarry and had moved a heavy nine-pounder into position. Its black bore glared down upon the rebels like the baleful eye of an ancient cyclops.

Not a soul in the town perceived the danger until grape shot and musket balls tore into the celebrating multitude. Again and again the guns sounded as rebel captains roared orders at drink-numbed subordinates and Fr Kearns pirouetted his mount, dumbfounded and bewildered. Men fell like cut weeds, spilling gore onto the packed earth, and an awful panic gripped the survivors as the yeoman cavalry and soldiers charged them.

A fighting retreat had turned into a rout and this in turn had become a massacre. In the countryside around Newtownbarry, scores of dead insurgents blighted the fields in pathetic tangles of mortality.

Tom sighed and thought of Fr Kearns, sequestered now with the leaders in their tent, engaged in heated debate, as the evening wore on and men and women continued their mournful vigil, waiting for friends and loved ones to plod, bleeding, out of the sunset. Tom wondered if Kearns had any idea of the importance of his defeat, the gravity of what it had revealed.

Even if one were to ignore the ill-discipline and downright stupidity of the rebel actions at Newtownbarry one must be forced to confront the fact of the involvement of the Queen's County Militia, the blue facing of their red coats distinctive as a banner. How had they been dispatched? How had the garrisons of the midlands found the men to reinforce Newtownbarry when they should have been busy fighting their own battles?

Tom squinted as the plummeting disc of the sun arrowed forth one last burst of molten gold before it dipped below the horizon and was gone. Concurrently with the dying of the light a cry arose from the outer pickets. Tom stared into the gloom as a sentry came hurrying through the fields, his path eating a black trough through the hazy yellow of the ripening barley. Behind him trailed a ragged group of five men but even at this distance, down the slope and five hundred yards across the ditches, Tom recognised the proud, almost swaggering stride of Miles Byrne. He moved without hindrance although the absence of his horse testified to the hectic nature of the retreat. Two of his companions however were visibly struggling through the clinging corn and Byrne paused for a moment to allow one man to lean on his shoulder.

Tom felt relief flood through him – a sensation he had not experienced since that first survivor, his shoulder lacerated by a cavalry sabre, had come stumbling into the firelight.

At length the men reached the camp and Byrne strode purposefully across the slope, making for the leaders' tent. Tom intercepted him and greeted him with a handshake.

'I thought I told you to mind yourself,' he said, smiling.

Byrne smiled wryly in return, 'That, my friend, was easier said than done.'

Tom regarded the young captain critically. His green jacket and white shirt were as dapper as ever but it was on his face that the events of the day had wrought the most pronounced change. His complexion had the same yellow cast as tallow or lard and weariness had ploughed deep furrows around his eyes and mouth. The muscles of his jaw seemed weaker somehow, more slack than when he had ridden away so gallantly that morning.

Taking all this in, Tom asked, 'How did this happen? We have heard differing reports that all cement into one awful impression.'

Byrne's shoulders appeared to slump but with a visible effort he straightened himself and assumed his familiar manner of vital exuberance. 'The day was won,' he began. 'That is what makes the whole sorry story so galling.

'We had taken the town and I had advised Fr Kearns to send a detachment of men along the road to Carlow and so act as a picket or to catch the soldiers as they retreated.'

Tom frowned. 'What did the old braggart say?'

Byrne laughed bitterly, 'He cut me short. He sat his horse and held up a whip, which was his only weapon. "Tell all those you have any control over," he says, "to fear nothing as long as they see this whip in my hand." He then led us in a prayer.'

Byrne shook his head sadly, 'For want of foresight, a hundred men lie dead in the lanes and gardens of Newtownbarry.'

Tom scowled, 'The story is the men were drunk.'

Byrne's young face became an open mask of surprise. 'For my own part, I must declare that I did not see a single man intoxicated during the time we occupied the town. Besides, the strongest liquors could scarcely have caused drunkenness in the short space of time we were in the place.'

Tom nodded dubiously, one eyebrow lifting of its own volition. Regarding the young captain searchingly, Tom asked, 'What make you of the Queen's County Militia? What of the Rising elsewhere?'

Byrne raised his right hand and scrubbed his palm across tired and smoke-raw eyes. From his lips there issued a dry, cold laugh possessing all the warmth of a draught from a pagan tomb.

'I fear we are alone, Tom.'

The following morning was one of fog and mist in the town of Carnew, huddled at the base of the Wicklow Mountains. Cloud rolled down through the valleys in great voluminous folds and pearled gorse and fern with beads of wet.

Colonel Lambert Walpole looked out onto the town's main street and thought that for the day to be in any way good, the sun would have to burn off the vapours overhead and soon. He stood framed against the rectangle of sourceless white flowing through a ground floor sash-window of Carnew's market house. Like most market-houses in this part of the world, the building was finely built, slate-roofed and its interior contained a number of sizable chambers. Its white-framed windows with their winking checkerboard panes looked out on Carnew's main street, warping the world onto which they gazed. In the pallid dawn, local labourers were unloading casks of butter and sacks of meal from two wagons, their draught horses standing placidly between the traces. Walpole's contingent of men had eaten the town to the bone over the course of the previous day and night.

Walpole was young to hold the rank of colonel. Only in his early twenties, his dark hair was combed back in a dashing hazel wave and his sideburns described two perfect rectangles down either cheek. His uniform was pristine in every line and element and he carried himself with the grace of a courtier, one more at home in the great palaces of London than the confines of a dreary little market town in Ireland.

'Colonel,' came a voice from behind him, 'General Loftus is most desiring of an answer.'

Walpole turned his back on the window and swept the room in which he stood with an imperious gaze. Several of his staff officers lounged in chairs and couches that had been requisitioned and placed around a broad circular table on which stood a glass decanter of sherry. Beneath the vessel, as though held there purposefully by this incongruous paperweight, a variety of maps and reports were spread.

In front of the table and the object of every stare in the room was a dusty and fatigued-looking dispatch rider. He stood to attention with his cavalry helmet tucked stiffly under one arm. His eyes were focused directly ahead but every so often would flicker to the sheet of paper held nonchalantly in Walpole's right hand.

One of Walpole's officers, a Major Jackson, swung his leg down from where it draped across the arm of his chair and commented drily, 'Ain't old Loftus an eager one? He is determined to lead the charge, is he not?'

Walpole laughed hollowly and a cold sneer crawled across his face. Lifting the paper he wagged it as though it were a piece of incriminating evidence before saying, 'The man wishes us to link up with him at Arklow. Ain't that rich, my boys? He quotes from General Fawcett at Duncannon who is of the opinion that "any attempt that was not next to a certainty of succeeding against them should never again be attempted."'

His voice took on a disbelieving tone as he read from the letter in his hands, 'They are no longer to be despised as common armed peasantry. They are organised and have persons of skill and enterprise amongst them.'

Walpole shook his head and snorted in derision, 'What do you make of this, gentlemen? Has Fawcett taken leave of his senses or is Loftus trying to put the wind up us?'

The dispatch rider coughed pointedly and with his eyes still carefully focused over Walpole's left shoulder he said, 'General Loftus has asked me to impress upon you the urgency of his request, sir.'

'Damn General Loftus!' Walpole barked.

The dispatch rider blinked and shifted uncomfortably as a charged silence filled the room. Walpole's lackeys sat a little straighter in their chairs and one or two exchanged knowing looks.

Walpole was pacing now, his boots hammering on the floorboards, punctuating his words with hollow thuds and harsh scrapes as he spun on his heel. His young face was storm-racked and his eyes flashed in the opalescent morning light.

'Loftus over-reaches himself,' he raged. 'I have not ingratiated myself with those fools in Dublin Castle, I have not *demeaned* myself with their company, to be ordered about as though I were a scullery boy.

'I have not seen anything in the midlands to suggest that these Wexford louts will be anything more than a leaderless rabble. We taught those others a lesson at Gibbet Rath and by God I shall teach these rebels a lesson here. I will not allow Loftus to claim the credit. By Jove, I cannot countenance it in the slightest. My blood is boiling at the very thought. The sheer effrontery of the man!'

One of Walpole's lieutenants, a pudgy man with the cherubic face of an infant, raised a hand timidly.

His colonel ceased pacing and snapped, 'Have you something to say, D'Arcy?'

D'Arcy cleared his throat before venturing, 'General Loftus is quite experienced, sir, and these rebels have been quite a nuisance. Perhaps personal ambition should be put aside for the common good.'

Walpole stared at the man as though he had begun raving.

'D'Arcy, you are a fool,' he stated simply. 'If you cannot add something of value to my thoughts then remain silent.'

He tapped the letter to his chin in a manner one might expect to see in an amateur actor who feels his minor part must be exaggerated, 'I do not think that General Loftus is fully aware of our situation. I feel he underestimates our numbers and capabilities.'

With that he addressed the dispatch rider who remained standing silent and dutifully stone-faced, 'Tell General Loftus that I have five hundred fine fellows with me in this dreary little hamlet. Tell him that I am sure this force sufficient to our present need and that, with his permission of course, I wish to push into the county myself. Can you remember all that?'

'I will do my best, sir,' said the rider flatly.

'Tell him I shall await his favourable response,' Walpole concluded. 'You may go.'

The dispatch rider saluted, spun on his heel and hurried from the room, buckling on his helmet as he went.

Walpole regarded his officers for a moment and a look of contempt stole across his features, 'Who would have thought Loftus to be afraid of farmers and bog savages?'

That evening of the 2nd of June found General William Loftus incandescent with rage. The same tired dispatch rider who had that morning stood before Colonel Walpole and listened to his railings was now an unwilling witness to another officer's temper.

General Loftus had procured for his offices a large room in a finely appointed townhouse, south-facing and overlooking the bridge at Arklow. Beyond his windows the Avoca river, speckled with the grey and white of squabbling geese, moved with lazy ease to the sea, sliding under the bridge's arches like brown oil. The town of Arklow climbed up and away on either side of the river's banks, its slopes gentle and rolling, the roofs of the buildings edging only gradually one above the other. The sounds of civilian life drifted through the air, mingling here and there with the harsher drum and rattle of his thousand men. The soldiers and townsfolk mixed freely, no blood was spilled, no bodies lay strewn and broken. This was a town untouched by events to the south, unscarred by a war that seemed set to consign Wexford to an abyss of flame and slaughter.

General Loftus, however, was in no mood to appreciate the tranquillity of the scene.

'The pup!' he roared. 'The unabashed gall of the cur is quite unbelievable. How dare he!'

'He seemed quite adamant, sir,' offered the dispatch rider.

Apart from the messenger, only one other officer occupied the room, a thin lieutenant-colonel with the ascetic bearing of a scholar. No gaggle of acolytes attended Loftus and the charts and reports that covered his heavy desk were arranged neatly. Everything in the room was set precisely, every angle was squared and each chair perfectly equidistant from the other. This was a room of method, of reason, and Walpole's insubordination introduced an uncomfortable twist to its straight lines and hard edges.

Loftus stood in simmering fury and hissed, 'I don't care if he quoted from the Bible. I shall not have a mere colonel dictate my plan of action.'

The narrow-faced lieutenant colonel spoke, his voice soft and thoughtful, 'Walpole does have influence in Dublin, General.'

'Be damned to his influence!' fumed Loftus. 'His friends have no sway here. I will not be played for a fool by a courtier and a dandy.'

He turned then and cast his gaze out the tall window giving onto the Avoca and the town beyond. His eyes took on an unfocused aspect and he swivelled his head to the right as though through sheer force of will he could penetrate the intervening miles between Arklow and Carnew, boring through hill and mountain to spear Walpole with his anger.

'Dare we advance without him, Jones?' he asked at last.

The lieutenant-colonel's melodious voice came again, 'We have a thousand men and horse and are well-supplied with ammunition and artillery. The men are rested after the march from Dublin. It would take a force of considerable size and fortitude to oppose us.'

Below Loftus the Avoca slithered silently along. The long drought had lowered its level but even so the river was still wide and its current strong. Here and there however, stones and detritus, fallen trees and the spoil from middens broke the wrinkled surface. At one point, just before the bridge, hard by the south bank, the skeletal spars of a sunken boat clawed forth from the water like the monstrous ribs of some nightmarish sea monster.

Loftus sighed, 'But do we know the rebels' disposition? Do we know their numbers and their intent?'

Jones reached for a bundle of papers on Loftus's desk and began hurriedly flicking through them.

'I have read them all,' stated the general, his eyes still staring out into nothing.

'The rebels have taken Enniscorthy, of that we are sure. There is no word yet from Wexford Town but it is utterly inconceivable that it should have fallen as well. A rebel advance on Newtownbarry was repulsed early yesterday and thus far they have remained camped on the hill of Carrigrew. They number in the thousands and the bloody nose that L'Estrange gave them yesterday will hardly dent their numbers, although it has seemed to have cooled their ardour.'

Jones frowned at his superior's words and cast an appraising glance at a map lying weighted on Loftus' desk. 'They have not moved on Gorey?' he asked.

Loftus shook his head, 'Not as yet, though if we dally further they could be in possession of that town within hours. Damn Walpole and his infernal lust for glory.'

Behind him Jones shrugged, 'We could advance without him, sure in the knowledge that he must hurry to catch us in order not to miss the show.'

'Advancing into the teeth of the enemy without five hundred men that should be added to our strength is not ideal, Mr Jones.'

Loftus's eyes came abruptly back into focus and he allowed them to take in the vista of Arklow Town under a summer sky. He saw the Dublin road knifing over the great bridge and sweeping around the sharp corner that led to Main Street. He saw the buildings, thatched and whitewashed but with a cluster of slated roofs at the market diamond, stepping gradually higher as they mounted the crest of the hill, obscuring the outlying districts from view. Behind that hill a rebel army waited, a rebel army that had already butchered hundreds of uniformed soldiers. General Fawcett was wary of them, that much at least was clear.

And yet they had waited on their hill now for two days. Waiting for what?

Turning away from the window Loftus was suddenly resolute. 'Mr Jones,' he ordered, 'we will draft letters to Colonel Walpole and Ancram and L'Estrange at Newtownbarry. We have wasted enough time. Action is called for. I want my orders in their hands by tomorrow morning.'

Behind Lieutenant Colonel Jones, his face streaked with dust and his lips cracked and parched, the dispatch rider groaned softly to himself.

Another sunset cast a topaz glow over the gorse-furred hump of Carrigrew Hill. Tom Banville and Miles Byrne sat side by side and looked out across the expanse of countryside to their west. Each man was silent, each held a slab of rough brown bread in one hand while a battered tin jug, filled with milk, was passed between them. The milk, still warm and thick, drawn from a cow's udders only minutes before, glugged and gurgled as it was set down and lifted again, the only sound that disturbed the men's tranquillity. Both Tom and Byrne wore identical expressions of apprehension.

'Why do we wait?' Tom asked at last. 'We sit and the priests say mass and we drill the men and we advance not at all. For two days now. Why?'

Byrne slowly chewed a mouthful of bread before washing it down with a swallow of milk. His eyes squinted into the sunset. 'The leaders are awaiting word from some other quarter, I would imagine. They are afraid that the Rising has failed everywhere except here.'

Tom plucked at a blade of grass distractedly and replied, 'If the midlands has been subdued and Dublin has not been taken, then who do they expect to have word from?'

Byrne sighed and closed his eyes, momentarily allowing the sun to wash over his face, before saying, 'They are debating what we should do.'

'What issues can they possibly be debating?' said Tom. 'Surely only two courses are open to us. Either we retreat to Wexford Town and break out through New Ross or we descend with our entire force on Newtownbarry and press on into the midlands.'

Byrne nodded, 'I think Fr Murphy and some of the lads from Wicklow wish us to take to the mountains.'

Tom flashed him an incredulous look, 'I will not take to the hills like some brigand, Miles. I will not live hand-to-mouth, surrounded and on the run. I will not leave Dan with no hope of seeing him again.'

Miles was silent for a while as the sun fell ever-further westward and shadows unfurled themselves, questing out from the boles of trees and tangles of gorse. At length he said, 'Dan should be across the Barrow by now. Word should arrive from Waterford or Kilkenny soon.'

Suddenly uncomfortable, the thought of his brother surrounded by smoke and fire filling him with a terrible dread, Tom asked, 'What word is there of Vinegar Hill? Has Fr Murphy elected to do anything about the murders?'

Byrne shook his head, 'Oh, they were all suitably appalled, none more so than Fitzgerald, who waxed lyrical about the necessity of keeping law and order and yet none suggested that Luke Byrne be court-martialled or that a detachment be sent to procure the safety of prisoners. Meanwhile, at Enniscorthy they are massacring any man with even a hint of Orange sympathies.'

The young captain continued, 'What Mr Harvey and the others should have done was use that press in Wexford for the printing of proclamations, which should have been issued and distributed in their thousands, prohibiting pillage or plunder of any kind, but particularly against taking the life of even the greatest criminal before he was tried.'

Tom snorted disdainfully, 'I feel your ambitions for old Ireland free are foundering, Miles.'

Byrne sighed, 'No, Tom, they are as strong as ever but we must remove ourselves from these doldrums. We must learn that not every setback is a mortal blow and that the initiative must be seized. We esteem our enemies too much.

We have bested them over and over. Even Newtownbarry was won before we let it slip away. While we wait and second-guess their motives and movements, while we wonder what has occurred throughout the rest of our poor, degraded country, our enemies are no doubt actively engineering our downfall. Every minute we sit on this hill is a moment closer to our doom.'

Tom closed his eyes, wondering at the joyless fates that had conspired to land him here on the slopes of Carrigrew Hill. He found himself thinking of Dan and hoping with every fibre of his being that he had fought his way through New Ross and that he was somewhere now on the road to Waterford. He thought of Elizabeth, the Protestant girl whose smile made Dan's face glow. He hoped that whatever world might exist after this war might embrace those two with all the warmth they deserved. If he fought for anything it was for his brother; and his brother fought for an Ireland united without recourse to creed or colour.

As the sun died in a welter of crimson and the stars began to dot the heavens with pin-pricks of winking silver, Tom Banville found himself praying. Silently, under the vault of the night sky, Tom prayed for Dan and for Elizabeth and for Ireland. But most of all he prayed for himself, that he might have the strength to see this through.

CHAPTER 18

Walpole's Horse and Walpole's Foot

Gorey lay prostrate under the evening. Its long main street was a channel of golden warmth and the few members of its civilian populace who had not fled north to Arklow sweated, seeming to melt, in the heat. The 3rd of June had been the hottest day of an already remarkable summer and the country was gasping beneath the glare of the sun. The least movement squeezed perspiration from every pore and welded shirts and stockings to clammy skin. The blue sky, seeming so high and eternally distant for so long, now seemed to drape itself over roofs and chimneys, a sapphire tarpaulin under which the world sweltered.

As the evening spilled syrupy light over the town of Gorey, General William Loftus stood in the reception hall of the market house and looked in disbelief from Lieutenant-Colonel Jones to the now-familiar dispatch rider who was swaying where he stood. Dust caked the rider's uniform and his hair was sweat-soaked into a single oily slick that clung to his head like tar. Fatigue dragged at him like an anchor and it was all he could do to face his general without falling flat on his face.

Loftus transferred his gaze to the scrap of paper in his hand and with an oath balled it up and flung it to the ground.

'He says he shall be with us this evening or tomorrow morning at the earliest! The insolent scoundrel!' Loftus' face was infusing with a deep beetroot red that darkened to bruise purple in the hollows of his cheeks.

Jones nodded placatingly, 'How has the good Colonel Walpole couched such disappointing words?'

Loftus was furious, his usual precision torn to shreds and flapping loose through Walpole's recalcitrance.

'The bounder has the temerity to chastise me for not allowing him to take the county on his own! He writes that if his talents are to be wasted, then we can go without! I shall flog him to within an inch of his life!'

Jones coughed delicately and nodded toward the dispatch rider who was stifling a yawn and striving manfully to ignore the raging of his commanding officer.

'Yes, yes, very good. You are dismissed,' said Loftus absent-mindedly.

The messenger sagged in relief, his face splitting in a grin of gratitude. Saluting with all the elegance that his aching bones could muster the man fled the building, closing the door behind him.

'We should press on without him,' advised Jones slowly, the sing-song of his voice soothing in the blistering atmosphere. 'The Gorey Cavalry have reported that the camp on Carrigrew is big but that they lack warlike stores and seem reluctant to attack.'

'Between the Antrim Militia and local yeomanry, I have a thousand men under my command, Jones,' replied Loftus. 'I am not about to risk their lives by rashly venturing out into hostile country when we should have half as many again. We shall allow Walpole until first light to arrive but if he does not I shall have him shot for dereliction of duty, do you understand me, Jones?'

'Perfectly, sir,' he replied.

Loftus thought for a moment before saying, 'The prisoners held in this market house, have they been induced into providing information about the rebels?'

Jones nodded, 'Exhaustively.'

'And?' Loftus prompted, 'I am in no mood for games, Colonel.'

Jones blinked and continued hurriedly, 'None are talking, though a one-armed fellow named Esmond Kyan is supposedly a high-ranking United Irishman. Anthony Perry named him in his confession.'

'One-armed?' asked Loftus, suddenly curious.

'Yes, sir,' replied Jones. 'Lost it in duel. He's a former Royal Artillery Officer. He could prove useful.'

'As a hostage?' asked Loftus archly.

Jones smiled, 'Needs must, Mr Loftus, sir. Needs must.'

Darkness had cooled the furnace of the day and the sun had torn the whole western horizon into a ragged tatter of red when a shout of alarm barked out from one of Loftus's southern pickets. Colonel Walpole had arrived at last. He rode a dashing grey stallion with a high-stepping gait as though on parade. His cocked hat was crisply tailored and freshly blacked and the red of his coat glowed in the twilight like a coal fallen from a hearth. Behind him his men trailed in two well-armed files with the baggage train bringing up the rear.

As soon as he had entered the limits of the town, passing below the vast spread of the venerable beech rearing regally above the market diamond, a runner appeared, issuing a summons from General Loftus himself.

Walpole reined in his mount while his men filed past and regarded the messenger with aristocratic condescension. 'You should tell the general,' he replied, 'that I must see to my quarters before I see to his requests.'

'Begging your pardon, sir,' answered the runner, his Antrim accent dulled and softened through fear of the mounted officer before him, 'General Loftus wants you immediately. He said that if you refuse to come before him he would consider you in breach of a direct order, sir.'

'Would he now,' said Walpole slowly, rolling the words around in his mouth as though they were some exotic delicacy. He shouted towards a sergeant who was just then marching past, his half-pike shouldered and his face a leather mask of controlled belligerence.

'Sergeant O'Connor, pass the word that the men are to be placed at free quarters in the town. If any of my officers should ask, tell them I am at a very important meeting with General Loftus. Stratagems and such, as it were.'

The sergeant saluted with a grin like a gash in tree bark.

Walpole turned to the runner and gestured with a delicate flick of his wrist, 'After you, Private.'

General Loftus looked up from his desk as Walpole entered the small room that he had commandeered for use as his offices.

The room had once been a sort of library adjoining the main chamber of Gorey's market house and one wall was entirely filled with a series of shelves occupied by volume upon volume of old books. Loftus had taken the time, in his thorough way, to leaf through several. He found old histories and tracts on farming, almanacs and tables of the tides, all coated with a sumptuous powdering of rat-grey dust. He then carefully arranged three chairs around the room's solitary table, each one as perpendicular as possible to the table's edge. He placed a lantern on the left side of this table and by its yellow gush of light he arranged his maps and journal neatly in one corner. He set his pocket watch on top of this stack of paper and, while the minutes ticked by, thumbed through a pamphlet produced by the Ordnance Survey.

Now, balled in the golden sphere of illumination cast by the lantern, Loftus greeted the walking nuisance that was Colonel Lambert Walpole.

'Don't bother saluting, you buffoon. I should have you shot.'

Walpole's face took on the indignant look of a cosseted brat who has suddenly been chastised. His mouth gaped and a little quiver of anger rippled along his jaw.

'That is an insult, sir,' he eventually spluttered.

Loftus stood and in the honeyed light of the lantern dark shadows abruptly swam forth from the hollows of his eyes. 'Your behaviour is an insult,' he replied. 'The very fact of your existence is an affront to the uniform which you wear. You are a dangler at court, sir, but I will not have you dangle here. You will respect orders or you will be court-martialled, is that clear?'

Walpole's chin worked back and forth as he fought the sentiments that threatened to explode from him. The impression he gave off was curiously that of a cow chewing cud.

'You do realise who you are speaking to, General?' Walpole asked.

Loftus's eyes narrowed, but he persisted, 'I know full well, Mr Walpole. I know you purchased your commission and have friends at all the best parties. I know what you do not have is military experience. I know that if you counter-mand my orders again you shall regret it, I assure you. You find yourself a long way from Dublin, Colonel.'

Walpole, his lips twin, bloodless worms squeezed tight together, breathed deeply through his nose. A silence crept upon the room and in its vacuum the young courtier weighed his options carefully.

At last he said, 'I apologise, General Loftus, I was remiss in my duties. It shall not happen again. I am your humble servant from this day until the rebels are crushed.'

And then, Loftus thought, you shall use every nasty little trick you have up your perfumed sleeve to revenge yourself upon me.

'Very well,' the general said aloud. 'Since we are to conduct this action in tandem I shall inform you of the plan of attack.'

He sat and indicated one of the vacant chairs so precisely positioned at the little desk, 'Please, Colonel.'

Walpole eased himself onto the seat, flowing from his former attitude of attention into a languid sprawl, his skeleton seeming to liquefy and the chair creaking as he lounged like a house cat.

'I think you should allow me to have at these brigands, General, whilst your column remains in reserve,' he said with a lazy arrogance. 'From what I have seen of these croppies, they fall to pieces at the sight of a uniform.'

Loftus smiled humourlessly, the lamplight now lighting one side of his face whilst swilling the nooks and hollows of the other with liquid dark, and said, 'These croppies, sir, have taken two garrisoned towns and hold the entire county from here to Duncannon in their sway.'

Walpole was about to respond but then blinked and straightened in his chair, 'Two towns? I thought they were repulsed at Newtownbarry?'

Loftus's grin widened in direct proportion to the leaching of warmth from his expression, 'They have taken Wexford. It was the first thing told to us as we arrived in Gorey.'

Walpole frowned then, his conceit giving way to caution and his conception of the situation slowly turning on its head, and said, 'That cannot be.'

'Oh, it can,' replied Loftus, enjoying Walpole's sudden discomfort. 'These particular croppies are like none you have seen before.'

Walpole had recovered his sang-froid somewhat and, pursing his lips, said, 'Still, we have a force of fifteen hundred horse, foot and artillery. Peasants cannot hope to stand against it.'

Loftus nodded slowly and unfolded a map which he plucked from the stack at his left hand. The paper popped and rustled as it opened with a noise like a fire beginning to catch. In the gold spill of the lantern the lines and shading of the map were jaundiced as Loftus used the tips of his splayed fingers to spin it about so that Walpole could read it more easily.

The young colonel leaned forward avidly and asked, 'What is it that I am looking at here?'

Loftus tapped the map where a dark spatter of geometrical squares was marked with the label *Gorey*. 'We are here,' he said.

His finger then traced two black, inked arrows which swept south from Gorey across the flat abstraction of the Wexford countryside. One made directly south along the Enniscorthy road, the other forked to the east and snaked along the coast road to Wexford. Between these two ebon curves the hill of Carrigrew sat in a whorling nest of sepia contour lines.

Loftus's finger jabbed again, 'That is where the rebels are.'

Walpole nodded as understanding lighted his visage, 'You mean for us to encircle them?'

Loftus appraised his subordinate for a moment before answering, 'I mean for us to drive them before us and to annihilate them if needs be. If they flee south, then I have passed orders to L'Estrange and Ancram at Newtownbarry to move up from Scarawalsh and so intercept them. This "Rising" ends tomorrow.'

Walpole let a smile worm across his features, a limp, simpering thing and said, 'Congratulations, General, it seems you have out-manoeuvred them. What role shall I have in this great victory?'

Loftus sniffed, his thoughts clamouring that the young colonel could not give a fiddler's curse for either the success of their endeavour or the state of the country should they fail.

Keeping his voice level Loftus replied, 'You shall move south along the road to Enniscorthy, through the village of Clogh and from there turn left to approach the rebels' western flank.'

'And I shall have full autonomy?' Walpole pressed. 'What numbers shall I have?'

Loftus sighed and cursed the fates that had landed him with such a grasping upstart for an ally. 'You shall have half the garrison, Mr Walpole. Six hundred. Horse and foot and a park of artillery. I shall have the rest. Fifteen hundred, all told.'

Walpole could not help but grin gleefully, 'Thank you, General. I shall sweep the brigands before me like chaff before a gale.'

Loftus leaned forward then, suddenly grim, his face hard and all the authority of his rank freighted in his voice, 'You would do well to remember the successes of these croppies thus far, Mr Walpole. You are to remain in contact with me at all times. Co-ordination is the key to this enterprise. Do you have me, Mr Walpole?'

Walpole, still smiling at some hidden vista that only he was privy to, nodded absently and replied, 'Of course, sir. I have you, sir.'

An hour before dawn the camp on Carrigrew Hill was silent save for the rasping, hacking breaths of a lone sentry as he struggled across the slope, blind in the dark. Blundering through furze he stumbled into an area of clustered tents and blankets, cooking fires of the night before now glowing piles of embers between. Careful not to wake the multitude sleeping all about, the sentry now strove to pick his way between the sleeping forms, his movements theatrical and his steps exaggerated in their slow precision.

It was only through enormous bad luck that he happened to place a foot on the outstretched hand of a sleeping Tom Banville.

The sentry jumped even more than Tom as the dark swamp of night congealed beneath a gorse bush suddenly transmogrified into an indignant rebel officer.

Tom, still half tangled in his woollen blanket, hissed, 'What in Jesus' name do you think you are doing, man?'

The sentry squinted in the pre-dawn black before whispering hoarsely, 'Mr Banville? Thank God I've found someone. I'm looking for Roche's tent and I can't find anything in this feckin' dark.'

Before Tom could respond a voice groaned up from a pile of blankets nearby like the sound of some spectre crawling out of the pit. 'Shut up, the two of you,' it moaned wearily.

Tom pitched his voice so that it was almost inaudible, 'What has happened? Why do you want Roche at this hour?'

The sentry swallowed before saying, 'A man arrived at one of the outposts only minutes ago bearing word that the redcoats in Gorey are going to advance on us at nine o'clock.'

At least now we shall be spurred into action, Tom thought, our course is plotted for us.

'Are you sure?' he asked the man.

The sentry nodded, his head a lump of pitch against the slowly lightening horizon, 'He says the soldiers are drinking the place dry, one of their officers is placing wagers that we'll all be dead by midday.'

Tom's lips tightened and he felt his brows draw down in anger, 'Oh is he, now?'

He grasped the man's shoulder and pointed off to the left where Roche and Fr Murphy's tent was a pale cloud beneath a copse of cedars. 'That's what you are looking for,' he said. 'Now hurry. I'll find Byrne and the other captains. We'll rouse the men.'

As the man sped off through the gloom, the anonymous dark let forth another groan, more angry than the first, 'For God's sake would you be quiet!'

Tom smiled, his mind, still sleep-drugged but gradually coming to sparking life, was fastened onto the prospect of action. After three days of inactivity the rebels on Carrigrew now had a purpose. The fact of their being hemmed in by a chain of enemies that threatened to strangle their county suddenly was not of any consequence. Survival was now the imperative. And Tom knew that, should the fight be a successful one, then the breaking of that strangling chain was a real possibility. He dared not think it but the advance of the soldiers might have provided the kick that the United leadership so sorely needed.

Thinking this he faced the greying hollow of the fleeing night and crowed, 'United Irishmen arise! The foe is astir and you shall be butchered in your beds! To your pikes and to your banners!'

From the surrounding gloom grunts and gasps of men abruptly woken changed gradually into the hectic sounds of activity. The distinctive clatter of pike-shaft being separated from pike-shaft and ringing rattle of sword belts and baldrics rent the predawn quiet, submerging the first liquid notes of the dawn chorus beneath an avalanche of military bustle.

Then the first cry went up, 'Monaseed Corps, to your banner!'

'Shelmalier men, to me!'

The sun stood high above the horizon and the masses on Carrigrew Hill, who had been so befuddled and stymied for the past three days, their leaders trapped in a maze of the mind, now were determinedly arrayed in companies and battalions, ranks neat and banners lifting, snagged by gentle zephyrs. Pikes were slanted upon shoulders and every face was lifted to where Edward Roche stood upon a gnarled fist of granite, his voice booming out into the morning.

'United Irishmen!' he cried. 'We are here gathered under the banner of liberty, a free people determined to spread that freedom beyond the safety of our own borders. We are Irishmen. Not Wexford men, not Wicklow men, not Protestant, not Catholic, but Irishmen, one and all. This morning a force moves out from Gorey to end our mission and put out our lives. We will not allow this.'

A great roar greeted these words. Pikes were shaken, the mass rippling like a sea in storm.

'We have beaten the soldiers at every turn and the cowardly yeomen we have put to flight,' Roche continued. 'So shall it be this morning.

'Mr Fitzgerald, Fr John and Fr Michael, Mr Perry and Fr Philip Roche are the men to whom you should look to at this time. We have stood with you at Oulart, at Enniscorthy and at Wexford. We will stand with you here. We will destroy the forces moving against us and then the whole country must surely be open to our advance.'

The host blanketing the slopes of Carrigrew Hill cheered again at this. Every face was suddenly ablaze and eyes glittered in anticipation of the coming violence. At the head of his corps, Tom cast his gaze across the myriad ranks that spread out around him. Thousands of tattered forms strained to hear Edward Roche, strained to catch a glimpse of the famed Fr Murphy. He was in an ocean of fervour. The bastardised conception of the Wexford Rising, the commingling of the political with the religious, had spawned something terrible and awesome. All around, the multitude of fighting men were possessed of a blazing zeal that yearned to be set free. They were hounds on a leash, rearing to be loosed.

Tom wondered whether this was what Dan had envisaged when he thought of a United Irish uprising. Had he imagined an army of unwashed peasants shaking pikes at the sky like a heathen horde? Had he imagined the blood and gore, the atrocities? Had he imagined that black chasuble hanging like a smear of charcoal from its cruciform pole?

Thinking of his brother, Tom once more hoped he was safe. That New Ross had fallen and the counties beyond were aflame with rebellion. If they were not, if New Ross held, then they were doomed.

Roche was declaiming again, 'We march, north. We march to take Gorey and to secure the release of the prisoners held there by the bigots and tyrants who oppose us.

'We march now!'

With that he bounded from his rocky platform, his stocky frame slightly heavy in its movements, depriving his actions of the dash and drama which he had sought to instil in them.

Within minutes the vast column of rebel soldiery was on the move. A rising fog of dust crept into the air above Carrigrew Hill as countless feet ploughed the hard earth into powder. Miles Byrne and his Monaseed boys assumed their usual role as vanguard, followed by Roche's own Shelmaliers with the main insurgent body snaking away behind, wending through the lanes and ditches that laced the countryside at the base of Carrigrew.

At the head of his own corps, just behind the Shelmaliers, Tom Banville marched alone and watched the back of Anthony Perry as he rode a few yards in front. As Colonel of the Gorey Barony, he was held in high esteem by the other leaders. As a man who had been tortured by the yeos he was beloved by the rank and file, who saw him as the embodiment of vengeance. For them he was a walking, talking avatar of the degradation the peasantry had suffered at the hands of the North Corks. He was a symbol of the oldest arbitrament the world had ever known – blood for blood.

Yet Tom sensed something else in the man. Perry could not meet the eyes of his men and in the presence of the other leaders his gaze remained fixed on the ground. Every so often he would fling Edward Fitzgerald a stricken look before hastily turning away again. Tom felt that something had passed between these two, some secret thing that weighed upon Perry like a yoke, stooping his shoulders and dragging his gaze into the dust.

Tom felt something else, too. Something grim resided in the rebel colonel, something baleful and sour. To despise an enemy as an enemy, as someone to be overcome for the sake of a military goal, Tom could appreciate. But the wanton hate that radiated from Perry at the very mention of the Gorey Yeomanry or North Corks was frightening. Tom could not imagine what torment he had endured to fill him with such bile. It seemed to extend beyond his physical hurt, mere wounds could not bubble such venom through a person. Humiliation and shame were what fed Perry's hate, of that Tom was certain.

As he marched, Tom thought that twin demons must reside within Anthony Perry, one battening and growing fat on the putrid flesh of the other. Bitter hatred of the Crown flowed in his very veins and yet a contempt, just as bitter, for himself seemed to sour him further. Perry was a maelstrom of anger, a bedlam of despair.

'Captain Banville, sir?' came the voice of Jim Kehoe from over Tom's shoulder.

'Don't you "Captain" me, Jim,' Tom replied. 'That nonsense may have worked on my brother but I can assure you I am a different prospect.'

'Yes, sir,' answered Keogh. 'I was wondering will there be many soldiers coming to meet us. The boys are anxious for the fight.'

Tom turned so that he was marching backward and grinned rakishly at his banner man. 'Jim,' he said. 'There'll be more soldiers than we've seen so far. Roche has said they mean to destroy us. They won't do that with the handful we saw at Enniscorthy.'

Jim Kehoe's young face blanched slightly and his knuckles whitened on the flagstaff held upright before him.

Tom's grin widened and he laughed, 'Don't be worrying, Jim. It'll make a better story to tell the grandchildren.'

Anthony Perry's voice cut through his merriment like a saw through bone, 'A rider approaches.'

A murmur filtered through the ranks as the rider, one of Miles Byrne's Monaseeds, reined in his mount, first to speak with Roche and Fr Murphy and then to converse with Perry before moving on to Fr Roche who had taken command of a detachment of Ballaghkeen men.

Perry turned to Tom and said, 'Have your men climb the ditch to our right and make their way along the inside of the field. Our vedette reports the approach of a column of redcoats. We are to flank them and catch them before they know we are even here. Be quick about it. They're nearly upon us.'

Ahead of the mass of rebels the ground rose steeply to the left and upon this slope Tom could discern the dark forms of rebel musketeers crouching down behind ditch and gorse. All along the road the advance guard of the rebel army was scattering into the surrounding fields, positioning themselves in ditches and hedgerows, moving forward slowly like wild things at hunt, cat-footed and wary.

At a gesture, Tom led his men over the hedge to his right, a blackthorn drawing a shallow curve of red across the back of one hand as he did so. Wincing and muttering he watched as his corps filed through behind him, silent and watchful. Jim Keogh had furled his banner and stowed it in the undergrowth, now waiting for the order to advance, tense and stoic.

Tom wondered at the change that had come over these men in the few short days they had been in the field. Peasants and labourers were now soldiers. Ragged and ill-equipped but determined nevertheless. Confident in their abilities and in the righteousness of their cause. He felt a flutter of pride within his breast and fought to still it with a savage force of will.

He was here for Dan and for his family, he reminded himself. He led these men for his future, not for Ireland or the cross.

He waited until his corps had settled amongst the nettles and briars that thronged the base of the hedgerow, one company amongst fifty that crouched in ever-narrowing perspective until the ditch turned and blocked them from sight. When they were all assembled he nodded curtly and began a crouching run along the narrow defile that lay along the inside of the ditch. Briar and snarls of gorse clawed at them him as he darted along but he was oblivious to them. Behind him, the rustle of a thousand men moving sounded in the hot air like a whispered argument. Yet this was the only noise the men made. No conversations. No laughter. Only the panting of exertion and the snap and rattle of dried twigs and bracken gave notice of their advance.

Ahead, through gaps in the undergrowth, Tom could see the rising ground rearing above the hard scar of the road, its ditches and fields packed with waiting rebel gunsmen. Then, along the road, the first ranks of the soldiers came marching. At their head rode a dapper colonel on a tall grey horse.

Silence enfolded the insurgents as the red-coated mass moved closer. The storm-weight of anticipation settled down like a blanket of warm lead and under its smothering oppression Tom Banville held his breath.

Then, as the soldiers passed beneath the looming shoulder of the rise, the entire countryside seemed to explode into barking spasms of musket smoke. The ditches to the right of the red-coated column spewed forth pikemen by the dozen.

Caught off-guard, the soldiers began a panicked defence. Their colonel wheeled his mount yelling and waving a coutier's small sword as though he were a conductor of an orchestra. About him his troops tried to form line and offer a volley in return. The pikemen that had sprang from the surrounding fields hammered into them and the line fell apart, soldiers firing in ones and twos, terror-stricken and dismayed.

Gunsmoke, dense and choking, clogged the road between the ditches, moving lazily in great viscous swirls. Within its obscuring folds the battle became a hazy chaos of phantasmal forms. The infantry colonel, sawing desperately at his horse's reins, was a towering figure in the fog until a musket ball caught him in the temple with the flat smack of breaking bone, spilling his brains onto the blood-soaked earth below. Like a falling statue the colonel crumbled from his saddle, toppling to lie in a shattered heap amongst the bodies of his men.

Tom moved his little column along the ditch to outflank the soldiers and cut off their line of retreat. On the road brutal fighting was under way around the park of artillery. Anthony Perry was at the heart of it, his face a mask of fury and a hideous scream issuing from a mouth that opened like a tear.

Tom appraised the situation as musket balls crackled through the undergrowth around him. Just a little away from the violence around the cannon, a company of redcoats had steadied themselves to loose a volley into the rebel ranks. Their muskets were levelled and each man sighted along the dark length of his barrel with a steadiness imbued through parade-ground discipline.

Smiling, fatalistic and cold, Tom bellowed, 'Castletown Corps, secure those guns!'

With a roar his men surged forward and flung themselves upon the soldiers who had prepared to fire. A few had the wherewithal to discharge their weapons into the savage mass of men bearing down on them and then turn to flee. Others held their ground and sought to stand against the tempest of pikes by presenting their bayonets and frantically trying to form square.

Tom's men swept over them like a wave scouring a beach, leaving rent bodies and tattered uniforms as flotsam in their wake.

By now the main body of the rebel division had entered the fray and soldiers were scattering through the fields and pastures. Red jackets were torn off and flung into the long grass where they lay like bloodied scabs in the afternoon light. The Gorey Cavalry had turned and fled at the first eruption of violence and now streams of terrified infantry followed them, sprinting away along the Gorey road, weapons and dignity abandoned.

General William Loftus sat his horse on the coast road to Wexford Town and listened to the sounds of battle come heaving across the fields to his west. Behind him the Gorey Infantry and detachments of the Antrim Militia formed a dense column of red between the hedgerows.

'What do you make of that?' he asked

Beside him Lieutenant Colonel Jones frowned slightly, 'It would appear as though Colonel Walpole has engaged the rebels.'

Loftus too was frowning, a harsher expression than his subordinate's, his brows heavy above anxious eyes. 'It appears as though the action is hot, does it not?' he said.

'It does, sir,' acceded Jones in his distinctive sing-song. 'I would expect as much though, for the enemy is numerous and they have proven themselves valiant. They might take time to break.'

'I do not hear the cannon,' Loftus muttered almost to himself, his lips pursing. 'I hear cries and musketry but no cannon. Why not?'

Jones regarded his commander with something approaching concern, 'Perhaps he has no need. Perhaps the engagement is at such close quarters the artillery proves useless.'

Loftus snorted disdainfully, 'If that fool court dangler has allowed his men to engage at close quarters, then he deserves the whipping he shall undoubtedly receive.'

Jones nodded, 'The fighting seems to be dying away.'

Loftus's eyes took on an unfocused aspect and he stared into space as though attempting to see something beyond the mere physical. At length he said, 'We shall take the column across to Walpole. Any rebels we encounter along the way are to be shot out of hand.'

Jones wheeled his mount but before he could pass the orders on, Loftus continued, 'I want the cavalry sent out well ahead. This country is a warren of ditches and laneways. I want long warning of anything that might be an ambuscade.'

Jones saluted, 'Yes, sir,' then jogged his mount down the line, passing on Loftus' directions.

Loftus hoped that Walpole had been as cautious.

Half an hour later General Loftus stood among the ruin of Walpole's column. The bodies of men and horses strewed the area like some ghastly pestilence and blood congealed in sickening spatters upon the dust of the road. Flies buzzed in morbid excitement and crawled across sightless faces, tonguing the open red wet of wounds and gashes.

Loftus shook his head in disbelief as his men picked through the corpses, salvaging what little weapons and ammunition the rebels had left behind. Here and there a wounded man was found groaning in a ditch or field but overall a horrible stillness had descended. Loftus's men searched in silence, their movements grotesque and incongruous in this place of quiet death, this place stinking of gunpowder, blood and punctured innards.

Jones voice came drifting over the field of bodies, 'I have found Mr Walpole, sir.'

Loftus made his way over to his subordinate, gingerly stepping over bloodied corpses as he went, determinedly avoiding looking at their twisted faces. As he drew beside Jones he saw that Colonel Walpole had been struck twice by musket balls, once in the thigh, once in the right temple. His handsome face was pale now, gore matting his hair and pooling horribly in the socket of one staring eye. He had died with a look of supreme horror racking his features.

'The man was a fool,' muttered Loftus. 'But to die like a dog in the highway is a most cruel end. Most cruel, indeed.'

Jones was praying silently but at Loftus's words he roused himself and asked, 'Do we follow them? Our scouts say the rebels have made for Gorey, hard on the heels of what is left of Walpole's column.'

Loftus lifted his gaze to squint at the sun and then checked his pocket watch before answering, 'We cannot allow them to gain possession of another town. If they take Gorey they can advance on Arklow with impunity. After that, Wicklow and then Dublin. We must stop them before they spread this madness further.'

He paused and breathed deeply before continuing, 'Gather the men. Organise a burial detail from amongst the yeomen and then pass the word that we march on Gorey. If we can catch the vagabonds before they have a chance to fortify the place or while they are still celebrating their victory we may be able to turn the tables on them.'

Jones coughed delicately before replying, 'The rebels have taken Mr Walpole's artillery, sir. Esmond Kyan whom we have detained in Gorey is an artillery man, sir.'

Loftus sighed, a long exhalation of doleful exasperation, 'Then we must catch them before they have him set at liberty.'

'Very good, sir,' answered Jones, dashing off to carry out his orders.

In less than quarter of an hour Loftus's column was on the march once more. They left behind them a grumbling squad of yeoman infantry who gazed about them with sour expressions and tapped the baked earth with the blades of trenching spades.

Just short of Gorey Town, Loftus reined in his mount. The road here rose in a gradual climb toward the crest of Gorey hill just to the south of the town. It was down this gently sloping road that a cavalry man came careering, his helmet askew and his face and blue coat veined with dust.

He halted in a tan cloud of scattered earth and saluted briskly. 'We are too late, General,' he panted. 'They have taken the town and are stationed on Gorey Hill. They're waiting for us, sir.'

Loftus nodded slowly before asking, 'In what numbers and how are they disposed?'

The cavalry man gulped drily and ran a thirst-thickened tongue over cracked lips, 'They have about two thousand on the hill itself and more in reserve in the town behind.'

He paused slightly before adding, 'They have cannon, sir.'

Loftus turned to Jones who was sitting his horse impassively by his side. 'Have the cavalry brought in and the men ready themselves,' he said. 'We advance on Gorey with all due caution.'

Jones saluted and turned to ride down the line.

From the Enniscorthy road Gorey Hill was hardly worthy of the name. It formed a low hump of scrub and gorse that the road wound around like a fallen length of buff ribbon before falling away into the market diamond of Gorey Town proper. However, to General Loftus's eyes, it was an impenetrable rampart.

He sat his horse some four hundred yards south of the hill and regarded its squat bulk through a brass telescope. Arrayed along the crest a large body of pikemen made a spiked wall against the sky and out in front, gathered about a brass six-pounder, a smaller group of rebels was a silent ball of distant activity. In their midst, dressed in a bright blue frock coat and with bruises marring his features, a man was pointing and gesticulating vociferously. Loftus noted how he only gestured with one arm. His left was carved from wood and hung loose by his side, burnished and worn to a dull shine through constant use, nerveless and dead.

'I believe that is your Mr Kyan,' said Loftus to Jones.

Jones merely grunted his agreement, his eyes fixed on the happenings on the summit of the hill. At length he commented, 'I believe they mean to discharge that thing.'

Concurrently with his words the cannon on the hillside belched forth a roaring swirl of blue smoke and the trees arching above Loftus and Jones rattled and clattered as though in a hail storm. Behind the two officers their men exchanged uneasy glances as fragments of branches and torn leaves pattered down from the over-arching canopy.

Jones brushed a shattered twig from where it had lodged on his epaulette and said, 'Grape shot. Interesting. Their elevation is rather too high, though.'

Loftus was shaking his head in dismay and he sighed, 'Their next shot will not be. Have the men retreat. We shall fall back across the county to Carnew. We have no artillery and we cannot hope to gain Arklow with them astride the road like this.'

Jones cocked one eyebrow, 'Are you sure, General?'

Loftus regarded him then with an expression that carried all the despair of a drowning man, 'The county is lost, Mr Jones. If we dally here further we shall all join Mr Walpole in death.'

Jones nodded curtly, his face inscrutable, and rose his melodious voice into the afternoon sky. 'The column will about face!' he ordered. 'We make for Carnew!'

General Loftus cast one glance back towards the rebels on Gorey Hill before wheeling his mount and trotting after his men. The army he had led to smash the Rising was in tatters, his noose to strangle the croppies unravelling before his very eyes. And in his ears from the direction of Gorey Town the sound of mocking celebration clamoured like an ache, and the faces of his men, shocked and pale, were like ghosts in the sunlight.

CHAPTER 19

An Evil Stirs

It had been four days since Dan Banville left Elizabeth behind in Wexford Town and he could still feel the feathery ghost of her lips on his. He sat on the steps of Talbot Hall, a large slate-roofed house squatting on the upper slopes of Corbet Hill, and gazed out over the countryside below. The afternoon sunlight spilled down upon the fields and hedgerows around New Ross with all the warmth of a welcoming hearth. The squares of the fields, each separated from the other by the dark sutures of heavy ditches, glowed gold where barley ripened hourly in the season's glare. Meadows of grass rippled in elegant emerald combers as a light breeze soughed across the landscape. It was this detail that struck Dan with a chill realisation. Echoes of his former life, now seeming so distant and blurred through a fog of terrible experience, played upon his mind. All those green rectangles, all those paddocks and fields of grass should have been cut for hay a week ago. Should have and would have been cut were it not for the savagery and violence that had ripped the country open from nave to chops.

Down below, not two miles to the north-west, the town of New Ross straddled the River Barrow in a helter-skelter of jumbled buildings and narrow laneways, its streets scrawling defiles that fell steeply down to the quays and the porter-dark rush of the river. The long drawbridge that linked the counties of Wexford and Kilkenny described a shallow curve of black in the distance, stepping out across the water on the spindly legs of its supports and trusses. The town was clustered predominantly on the Wexford side of the Barrow with only a straggling few cabins desultorily clinging to the bank at the Kilkenny end of the bridge. The old medieval wall of New Ross still stood and flung its lichen-stained arms in a protective embrace around the town. The fortification was pierced in three places by the ragged apertures left by what were once ancient barbicans, to the south the Priory Gate, at the south-east corner the Three Bullet Gate and at the north-west corner the Market Gate. All three gates were now barricaded and dammed against the rebel flood by the chocolate crescents of trenches and earthworks.

As Dan watched, a red, white and blue Union Jack stirred against its flagpole above the barracks in the centre of the town and lifted, tugged by some impulse of the air, before falling flaccid once more.

'What date is it?'

Dan looked up and around at the sound of the voice. Behind him, John Kelly leaned his towering frame against the doorpost of Talbot Hall. His blond hair was in shadow now and looked like a thatching of dirty straw bundled across his skull but his blue eyes held a sapphire intensity that radiated command. He was at home in any environment, the world seeming to shape itself to his expectations, to bend about the sheer weight of his personality.

Dan smiled wryly and replied, 'It's the fourth, John.'

Kelly pushed himself away from the wall and sat down beside Dan. He sat a step lower and leaned forward, yet even so his eyes were level with Dan's own.

He shook his head in exasperation, 'So for three days we have been overlooking that shaggin' place while they build their damned ditches ever higher?'

Dan nodded mutely.

'What of the men?' asked the blond colonel. 'Have they answered Harvey's summons?'

Dan frowned then, the conflict that had been clamouring in his mind for the past two days threatening to spill from his lips. He cleared his throat uncomfortably and said, 'Mr Harvey was rather more insistent with his last messages. The corps are coming back. They should be assembled by tonight.'

Kelly regarded the stony ground between his splayed feet for a moment before commenting, 'You hold Harvey in high esteem, don't you?'

Dan felt suddenly uncomfortable, the folds of his shirt seeming to cling like burrs to his sweating skin. He looked at the side of Kelly's face but the boy from Killann had his eyes fixed on the earth beneath his feet.

At last Dan sighed, 'I believe Mr Harvey is a most passionate United Irishman. He is a Protestant gentleman who struggles for the rights of the down-trodden and degraded. He is the ideal that Wolfe Tone might have imagined. When the French come I am sure he will be well-received into the new parliament.'

Kelly looked up then, his blue eyes narrowing, 'And as a military commander?'

Dan was silent for a moment before answering, 'General Roche or Fr Murphy have more about them in that regard.'

Kelly turned his head and flung his gaze out toward New Ross, saying, 'Harvey is a man of integrity and zeal, yet integrity and zeal may not be enough. He has a very delicate constitution for one chosen to lead in the rough-and-tumble of war.'

Dan's lips tightened, words and thoughts buffeting him and holding him fast in the conflicting winds of crossed purposes. His loyalty to Harvey, to the dream that Harvey represented, had come under a sustained battering over the course of their stay on Corbet Hill. While Dan remained as fixed as ever on the course of rebellion, as committed to the ideals of Liberty, Equality, Fraternity, the human vessels through whom those ideas were to be spread had become increasingly frail to his anxious eyes. While the beacon of Ireland free burned as brightly for him as it had always done, the men to whom this sacred light had been entrusted seemed to pale, to grow wan, the vitality of the cause replaced by something pastel and washed-out.

Kelly was regarding him now with an expression of concern on his features. 'We will carry the day, Dan,' he said. 'It is to the likes of us that the task ahead falls. When Harvey gives us our head we shall fall upon that town like a lightning bolt.'

From out of his gloom Dan answered, 'We may get all the corps back first. I don't know why Mr Harvey and Mr Colclough allowed the regiments to go home. They must assume that the war is over and that the French have already landed.'

Kelly grinned savagely, 'I don't know what their thinking was but it has taken two days to get everyone back. Those Forth and Bargy men haven't fired a shot in anger yet and they want to run off back to their beds.'

Dan nodded in agreement, 'There are two thousand foot and horse down in that town. They've been coming over the bridge since we arrived here. If we had taken the place on the first night we might have the whole province of Munster risen around us by now. We will need every man we can muster when the time comes.'

A warmth had crept into Kelly's face as he listened to Dan speak, as though he discerned the misgivings that plagued his thoughts. Putting a massive paw on Dan's shoulder, he replied, 'We will be victorious, Dan. As we have been in every engagement so far. The Kilkenny lads have been sending messages across

Joe Murphy

that they will be waiting to ambush the garrison as soon as we push them across the bridge.'

He pointed, his long arm lifting like a spar, his fist like a cannon ball. 'All we have to do,' he continued, 'is drive them from the town and across the bridge. The Kilkenny men will be waiting and we shall have them caught between us. I hope they can swim for surely some will be in for a dunking.'

He laughed then, a barking explosion of genuine good humour, and Dan found himself chuckling in spite of himself.

Then from around the hunched and gorse-pelted shoulder of the hill a broad, bullet-headed figure rolled. He was dressed in a collar-less, white linen shirt that clung to him as though painted onto his wide torso and buff breeches that terminated just below the knee. No stockings sheathed the thick hawsers of his calves but a pair of worsted brown shoes bore him across the slope. He moved with a sort swaying gait as though the land itself echoed the pitch and toss of the sea.

'Ho, there, Captain Banville!' he cried, the Hook Peninsula yawing in his voice.

'Mr Rouse!' responded Dan, clambering to his feet, a sudden gust of wind whipping at his coat, setting it to clatter and snap like a sail. 'How are the men?'

Rouse was now standing before Dan and he raised a leather-brown hand in salute to John Kelly. 'Captain Kelly,' he stated as formerly as he could muster, 'I'm Seán Rouse of the Hook. I'm one of Mr Banville here's men, so I am.'

Rising to his feet, Kelly towered over the man like a cliff but he saluted with the deference that had led him to be held in such high esteem by all in the United ranks. 'Mr Rouse,' he acknowledged simply.

Smiling now, Rouse addressed Dan, the countryside spread out behind and below him like some fantastical backdrop to his words, blue and green and gold.

'The men are grand, Mr Banville. I've had them hard at it from first light. They can carry themselves as well any of the Scarawalsh or Bantry lads now, sir.' He paused for a moment, marine-grey eyes slipping mischievously to John Kelly's face. 'Begging your pardon, sir,' he concluded.

'You see,' smiled Kelly, his amusement at Rouse's audacity breaking from his face like sun through clouds. 'Tomorrow the Barrow we'll cross and all will be well.'

'I hope so,' breathed Dan, while in his head a sudden voice mewled like something lost in the dark, *I miss you, Elizabeth.*

The river Barrow flowed through the town of New Ross deep and brown and stinking. The detritus of the place, with its narrow streets and fisheries, its tanneries and its hundreds of hovels, all washed down its steep streets into the sliding waters. Along the riverside the quays of New Ross were crammed with the heavy hulls of sea-going ships, their spars drifting to-and-fro, metronomically in time with the heave and subdue of the Barrow's waves. Along the quays, scores of red-coated soldiers gathered and milled, guffawing and spitting, their officers striking elegant poses whilst they debated how to garrison their men. For garrison was the only word for it. The entire town had become a military camp, its earthen laneways and thoroughfares become veins for an influx of red, steel-spangled blood. Hourly, across the Barrow's single drawbridge, cavalry and infantry poured into the town, displacing the poor and battered populace so that they bolted themselves into their own thatched cabins and prayed that the soldiers would not come knocking. Hourly, the military din increased as horses neighed and champed at the bit and cannon rumbled into the place on wheeled carriages. War, terrible and utter, had come to New Ross.

The four-storey Custom House overlooked the Barrow and its seething quays and, within its spacious interior, Generals Henry Johnson, who now commanded the town, and his immediate subordinate Charles Eustace, consulted with their officers.

The room that they had commandeered was a vast drawing room on the second storey. Flowers and ivy leaves, moulded from plaster, ran along the join between the coral-painted walls and the gaping white expanse of the ceiling. A beech-wood floor, lacquered and polished to a hard glare in the sunlight reflected the high windows that pierced the west-facing wall. Clusters of mismatched tables and chairs stood at various points about this floor, the elaborate carvings of several showing they were native to this grand chamber. The others had been procured and dragged in here, the scrapes and gouges in the floor's varnish testament to the hurried nature of their arrangement. Maps and rustling dunes of paper drifted over everything.

Johnson, a tall, rangy officer in pristine red coat and powdered wig stood in silhouette against one bright window and cupped his chin with his right hand. Behind him four men sat at a table and rifled through a series of documents.

At last, one of them lifted a white sheet exclaimed, 'Ah ha! I have it, sir. Twenty barrels. The building that the yeomanry call the Main Guard has twenty barrels of powder in its stores. That should suffice, surely.'

Johnson nodded slowly. His long face a mask of concentration, his blue eyes unfocused, staring off across the river as though he perceived something ulterior in Kilkenny's undulating hills. At length he replied, 'Send another two just to be sure, Eustace. And set up a piece of artillery at the meeting place of Mary's Street and Michael's Lane. In fact set up two. Should we lose that junction, we lose the Main Guard. If we lose the Main Guard then we shall lose the town.'

Eustace nodded sombrely to himself and added in tones as dark as the waters of the Barrow itself, 'If we lose the town, we lose Munster.'

The figure immediately to his left shifted uncomfortably in his seat. He was a middle-aged officer dressed in the red coat and green facings of the New Ross yeomanry and although once a fine figure of a man, he was now going to seed. Fine wines and dripping roasts had begun to spill his gut over the top of his breeches. He coughed pointedly, 'I say, General. I feel we are being far too cautious with this scheme of yours. These rebels should be met in the open field. The gall of the rascals really does set my teeth on edge. We should have at them, I say.'

Eustace ducked his head whilst the fourth member of the group said nothing but merely stared at the slew of documents on the table before him. His mind elsewhere, his narrow, ascetic face troubled.

Without turning, Johnson addressed the speaker in a voice harsh with contempt, 'Mr Tottenham. You are captain of the New Ross yeomanry and as such I am compelled to afford you all the respect that position demands. However, although your brio is commendable, these rebels have whipped us at every turn in open battle. Now they sit like a plague of locusts of Corbet Hill and they wait and do nothing. It baffles me. We add to our strength by the minute and yet they watch us and do nothing. I fear some wickedness is at work.'

He turned then and gestured to Eustace, 'You are sure they do not seek to circumvent us? They have no parties on our flanks?'

Eustace nodded curtly. He had known Henry Johnson for long enough to know his meticulous nature, his shrewdness and his razor intelligence. He also knew that Johnson regarded these rebels as the greatest threat to the Crown since the Armada. His superior mulled daily over reports of rebel movements and chewed on the gristle that was the prospect of a French landing. Henry Johnson was a worried man.

'Yes, sir,' Eustace replied. 'I am certain.'

'Then I am at a loss,' Johnson sighed. 'Their inaction flies in the face of all military sense.'

Charles Tottenham tugged his waistcoat so that the buttons were placed under slightly less strain and snorted, 'I know these people, General. They are farmers and fishermen and school teachers. They are not soldiers.'

Johnson regarded the man with irritation darkening his brow beneath the grey fringe of his wig. He sat down heavily on a vacant chair and explained as though he were addressing a particularly dense toddler, 'Every army that has been met these "farmers", as you describe them, in the open field has been destroyed, sir. We cannot risk the loss of this town through vanity and the ridiculous impulse to fight these miscreants among the hedges and ditches that they spring from. Should we lose New Ross then the entire south of the country is open to them. Do you understand this, sir?'

Tottenham nodded slowly, his jowls over-lapping the collar of his coat, 'I understand, General, but it is an affront to me to sit here and do nothing.'

At last the fourth member of the group stirred himself and cleared his throat. His red and blue infantry officer's coat was by far the most finely-tailored in the room, out-shining even those of the two generals. Upon his head a wig sat, dusted with white lead. Slowly his hand lifted and he lifted this wig free, tossing it onto the table with a palpable air of relief. With his other hand he smoothed back a frizzled thatch of hair.

'I am fifty-three years old,' he said at last, wearily. 'In all my days I have not seen such calamity as this. How is it that Irishmen have all, without warning, lost the ability and inclination to talk with their fellow Irishmen?'

He turned his slim head to fix Charles Tottenham with a thoughtful stare, 'You say you know these people? And yet you have done nothing to parley with them. Perhaps they can be convinced to return home. Perhaps the wrongs they perceive can be righted in the courts?'

Tottenham frowned at this but it was Johnson who answered, 'Lord Mountjoy,' he began.

Mountjoy's raised hand interrupted him, 'I would prefer if you called me Luke, General. I was christened Luke Gardiner and I would fain die as Luke Gardiner.'

Johnson smiled then, warmly and without contrivance, and continued, 'Lord Mountjoy, Luke, I appreciate your presence here and the Dublin City Militia are without doubt some of the finest men under my command but you are far from home. These croppies do not wish for representation at the bar. They do not care for the niceties of proper conduct. They would seek to supplant our way of life with superstition and barbarism. They would have a guillotine at every crossroads and a Popish priest in every church. These people do not "parley".'

Mountjoy looked at Johnson with an unmistakable sadness sluicing through his eyes, 'So we wait and pile cannon upon cannon. We wait until we have the opportunity to blow our fellow countrymen to atoms? Is that it?'

Johnson nodded as beyond the windows of their elegant room a roar of coarse mirth rose from the soldiers on the quays.

'We wait,' he said.

Abigail Brownrigg sat at her elegant coffee table and sipped strong tea from a white porcelain cup. Late afternoon sunlight flowed in from the garden at the rear of her house, yet there was a constant air of the crypt about her drawing room. The shadows formed more thickly in the space beneath table and chairs, and in the corners of the room murk was webbed more densely than seemed natural. It was a gloom which Mrs Brownrigg had accentuated through the deployment of dark carpets and wallpapers, all the wood lacquered to an ink-like intensity. She enjoyed the dark. It brought deep thoughts.

Now, over the white rim of her teacup, she watched her niece pace the floor.

'My dear,' said Mrs Brownrigg, 'your pacing is most unladylike and is quite likely to wear a hole in my carpet. Do sit down, child.'

Elizabeth flung her aunt a look of exasperation and continued to stalk back and forth, her skirts swishing and her forearms knotted beneath her breasts.

Mrs Brownrigg continued to sip her tea, a study in placid serenity.

Eventually Elizabeth had had enough and she stood before her aunt, bristling like an angry cat. 'Why won't you let me go to him? He must be made aware of this.'

Mrs Brownrigg smiled at her niece with all the pleasantness to be found in the upturned mouth of a hunting pike. Placing her cup carefully upon its saucer she asked, 'What would you have him do? Your young man is a rebel officer and might certainly sway them if he were here. However, he is not and until his return you should sit yourself down and fret less over events you are powerless to influence.'

Elizabeth sniffed, 'If Daniel were to hear of this he would come flying back to me like a bird. He could not countenance it. He would not allow it.'

Mrs Brownrigg regarded her coolly before saying, 'Your young man is no fool, Elizabeth. There will be terrible business at New Ross and he will not abandon it for the petty skulduggery that we have heard reported last night.'

Elizabeth stared, wide-eyed, at the old woman.

'Aunty!' she exclaimed. 'I would hardly call it petty skulduggery. They are killing prisoners!'

Mrs Brownrigg lifted one gnarled hand, the translucent skin taut over white bone and gristle, marbled with the blue of veins. Smiling, she extended one crooked finger, the joints swollen with the onset of rheumatism.

Holding this solitary finger aloft, she stated flatly, 'They have killed one prisoner my dear. The noun is in the singular.'

The previous morning, just as dawn was glimmering in the eastern sky, Captain Thomas Dixon and a group of ten men had forced their way into the town's gaol. There they had seized a loyalist prisoner by the name of Francis Murphy and had dragged him out into the street past the guards who mumbled some half-formed protestations, impotent in the face of Dixon's hate. The mob had harried Murphy down the street and into the Bullring where Dixon promptly accused him of informing on his cousin, his voice ringing in the cold steel of the dawn light. Without ceremony and without recourse to any defence, Murphy was piked to death, his body hauled off to the quays and dumped in the sea. Blood, bright red and frothy where it had come in a gout from Murphy's punctured lungs, had pooled in the drains of the Bullring until one of Dixon's men emptied a bucket of sawdust over it. Indignity piled on indignity.

The news had spread through Wexford Town like a disease.

Matthew Keogh, the town's newly-installed governor, came into the streets to decry the outrage, his voice trembling with indignation.

And yet nothing was done.

No move was made against Dixon. The captain stood across the street from Keogh and listened while his actions were lambasted. He listened as he was declared an enemy of civil accord and a man whose lawlessness was an affront to everything the United Irishmen stood for.

He listened and smiled a slow, creeping smile.

It was the lack of resolve in the face of such evil that so appalled Elizabeth. How Keogh could stand and castigate the actions of a handful of brutes while one of them stood and sneered at him was beyond belief. Action was needed, not platitudes, and while Dixon was at large, while the new authorities were floundering in indecision, an outright massacre drew ever closer.

In the face of such outrages Elizabeth could not understand her aunt's dispassion, her lack of urgency.

Offended now, she addressed Mrs Brownrigg with something like genuine anger in her voice, 'I cannot fathom you, Aunty. How can you be so cold?'

The old woman sighed then, the rigid set of her back relaxing slightly and her shoulders sagging. She regarded her niece with twinkling eyes and asked, 'My dear, does your father know you are here?'

Elizabeth frowned, 'No, he does not. And do not even consider sending me back to him for I should rather brave battle alongside Daniel than be sent back to Carnew now. Daniel tried to keep me safe by abandoning me, I will not have you do the same.'

Mrs Brownrigg allowed her to finish before stating, 'That is all well and good my dear, but safe you shall be kept. I shall not send you to your father through a countryside filled with bandits and God alone knows what. Neither shall I allow you to even suggest such idiotic actions as haring off to New Ross.'

She paused and breathed deeply before continuing, 'I asked if your father knew of your whereabouts because I am sure it would cause him incalculable distress to know that you have placed yourself in such danger. I asked because, although he and I are of a different cut, we are of the same material. You are my niece, girl, and I will have you remain so.'

'But—' began Elizabeth.

'But nothing,' interrupted Mrs Brownrigg. 'No matter how many poor innocents those ruffians put to death, you shall remain quiet and placid in my home. You shall allow all this unpleasantness to pass over us until your young man and his croppy army return to impose a little order on things.

'Until then, you will wait, safe and sound. To take public umbrage at the actions of murderous savages is to invite notice. A thing that in the current climate might be most unwise.'

Elizabeth deflated, the anger that had filled her sails suddenly dispelled. She sat down across from her aunt with a sigh like a ruptured bellows.

'Have a cup of tea, dear,' said Mrs Brownrigg.

That evening Elizabeth sat at the dressing table that stood beside her narrow bed. Before her, a large square mirror was propped against the wall and she stared into its depths without her mind truly apprehending what it saw. In one hand she held her mahogany fall of hair tightly and with the other she dragged an ivory-backed hair brush through the curls. Her bright eyes were now vacant, her thoughts centred on a hill overlooking New Ross.

'I miss you Daniel,' she murmured.

She placed the brush on the dressing table and focused her attention on the face staring at her from out of the fathomless silver of the mirror. She looked clean and healthy and for the first time in a week, she reflected, she felt clean and healthy too.

Never in her wildest imaginings had she ever thought she might see and experience the brutality she had bore witness to since the day she climbed Kilthomas Hill in search of Daniel Banville. Her mind recoiled from the memory but she forced herself to hold it in her mind's eye. The charge of the cavalry thundered through her thoughts and the screams of women and children were clawing talons against the inside of her skull. Her despair at not finding him, the horror that he might have lain amongst the dead scattered in the fields and along the roads around Kilthomas, came back to her as raw as ever. And another feeling crept upon her from out of the well of her memory. The feeling of disgust, of terror as she made her way south toward Ballyorril, surrounded on all sides by a wretched flotilla of human agony. She was not one of them, with her pale dress embroidered with green buds, her sun-bonnet, tattered but still betraying the expense of its craftsmanship. She was not one of them and they knew it. The nicking flicks of flinty eyes, the sullen stares, the resentment boiling off the other women in waves, all this spoke of her alien nature, her freakish difference.

And then she had held Daniel tight to her bosom and all concern fell away. His strength, his deep, deep eyes seemed to lift her from the tangle of bitterness and discord into which she had fallen.

And what was more she knew it to be true for him also.

When he looked at her he changed. His fierce passion for the Rising, the brooding melancholy with which he contemplated outrages perpetrated by both sides, all transformed into something gentler in her presence. When he looked at her he was filled with a different light, something as bright as anger, as intense as fury, yet somehow not as consuming. Something that grew and swelled with the promise of more growth to come, something warm and passionate, something suggestive of future days and long nights shone from him like a lighthouse through fog.

All this communicated itself through every line in his face and body. Every angle of his big carriage belled forth, 'I love you.'

And every atom of her answered, 'I love you, too.'

This she knew and it made her sick with grief that things as profane and grotty as politics and religion had reared between them like a wall. When this was all over, she found herself hoping, when the Rising had swept away the old order of things, then they would be married and be damned to anyone who raised an objection.

This was the most frightening thing of all. She had abruptly found herself invested in Daniel's great enterprise. With a creeping subtlety that had caught her completely unawares she had suddenly discovered that she wished for the revolution to be a success. She wished for all the old chains to be shattered and all the oppressive shackles to be broken.

She wished to be free. Free of the label of Protestant. Free from the yoke of

Catholicism. Free from the ancient feud that had made a killing field of Ireland and for so long kept Daniel and herself apart.

And yet the women's eyes on that long flight from Ballyorril and the harsh words on Vinegar Hill and on the streets of Wexford Town, flung themselves into her thoughts like a vile pestilence. What if human nature was that awful, she found herself contemplating. What if every change possible was wrought in the system of government and still that animal hatred persisted? What would that speak of a humanity determined to consume itself and sink into a morass of vulgarity, senselessness and barbarism?

What if the Rising solved nothing?

She was stirred from her reverie by a swell of noise that permeated the stones of the house. Frowning, she stood and made her way out onto the landing. Turning right she made her way down the hall to where a small window over-looked the street at the front of the house.

Below her, thronging the street, a mass of townsfolk had congregated. Gone were the fighting rebels who had packed the town with rural accents, and now only trouble-makers like Dixon or administrators like Keogh were left to shape the place as they saw fit. The crowd below in the street seemed to consist entirely of the poorer citizens, their ragged shirts and dirty bare feet proclaiming that they hailed from John Street and Oyster Lane. On an upturned crate, the object of every single peasant gaze, Thomas Dixon was giving an impromptu sermon. Standing on the ground beside him, her bulk accentuated by a dark blue shawl girding her shoulders, Dixon's wife beamed like a queen greeting her subjects.

Gingerly, Elizabeth cracked open the window and, stepping well back into the concealing shadows of the house, she allowed Dixon's oratory to waft up to her.

'And I would not hesitate to do it again!' he was braying in his nasal manner as a wave of cheering and wild applause erupted from the mob before him.

Dixon theatrically adjusted the lapels of a suspiciously well-tailored frock coat that he must surely have purloined rather than bought, and continued with the air of someone who had found his proper place.

'I ain't one to stir up trouble mind you. But I think that Matthew Keogh and the others who are suddenly in charge should take a good hard look about themselves. I don't see any poor Catholics such as you and me getting anything out of this Rising so far. Meanwhile the Orange monsters who squashed us underfoot ever since Cromwell are treated like kings in the gaol. They aren't held there for punishment says I. They're there to protect them from the justice of the people!'

At this the crowd roared in acclaim but silenced as Dixon raised his hands and said, 'Now I ain't one to stir up trouble but I think that Mr Keogh is allowing his religion to cloud his judgement. I say there should be money for the poor and hang the lot of those rich scoundrels who have our backs broken while they drink the best wine and eat the best meat.'

As Elizabeth watched and listened the crowd collapsed into a frenzy, howling, 'Hang them!' and 'Dixon for Governor!'

Before Elizabeth's disgusted gaze a wide grin split Dixon's hatchet face and he waved his hands frantically for quiet. Eventually the shouting and outcry died to a few drunken yelps which provoked scattered bubbles of laughter amongst the gathering.

Dixon had adopted a conspiratorial air now and leaned forward over the mass of people, his voice pitched at the level of an exaggerated stage whisper, 'Let you and me go our separate ways for tonight for even at this distance from his house Mr Keogh's lackeys might seek to intrude upon us. But bear in mind what I have said this day and if any you fine people should be in need of me, you know where I am.'

With that he leapt down from the crate and was enfolded in the clay-soft arms of his wife.

As Elizabeth watched, the crowd gave one last cheer and was soon rapidly dispersing, coursing through the lanes and alleys as though escaping from something terrible.

'Now you see why I am so concerned about you.'

Elizabeth jumped at the sound of her aunt's voice.

The old woman had ascended the staircase on cat's paws or else Elizabeth's horrified attention had been so completely captured by Dixon's speech that she had failed to hear her approach. Mrs Brownrigg now stood before her, tall and angular, her body a collection of sinew and bones, and regarded her niece with eyes filled with subtle emotion. A smile creased her lips and her expression somehow lay halfway between mockery and compassion.

'Child,' she said, 'you are safe here.'

Elizabeth was embarrassed at the relief she felt at those words.

CHAPTER 20

The Gateways to Ross

Nightfall on the 4th of June made Talbot Hall on the slopes of Corbet Hill a beacon in the darkness. All about, drawn up in battalions and companies, the men of the Southern Division of the United Irish Army had assembled at last. Yet something had gone abysmally wrong. Where fifteen thousand men had marched out of Wexford four days before, just over ten thousand remained. Where the five thousand others had disappeared to, no one seemed to know. The one fact that remained as the darkness deepened, was that Bagenal Harvey's dithering had proved disastrous.

Behind one glowing window in the looming edifice of Talbot Hall, black silhouettes moved back and forth and voices, dulled and muffled by the stone walls, were raised in anger.

Inside the room, a long dining table standing on lion paw legs was a no man's land between John Kelly of Killann and Beauchamp Bagenal Harvey. The other occupants of the room were sitting in chairs around the table but had removed themselves from the discussion so that Kelly and Harvey seemed to be the only figures of consequence. Harvey was sitting in his chair at the head of the table, his face haughty and his arms crossed above his bulging stomach. John Kelly, a giant of a man with blond hair, was positioned halfway down the table, half-risen to his feet, resting his entire weight on the pillar of his left arm while his right was pointing at Harvey. Oil lamps and a wrought iron chandelier lit the tableau in smoky yellow light.

'Allowing the men to go home was lunacy, Mr Harvey. Thousands have not returned,' Kelly railed.

Bagenal Harvey curled his lip and replied, 'You cannot hold me responsible for simple farmers refusing to fight.'

Kelly rose to his full height, his anger flaring like the candles overhead, 'I hold you responsible for discipline, Mr Harvey. We have sat here for days while you dithered about a plan of attack. We watched as New Ross was reinforced hourly. The English have built trenches and breastworks. Of course the men refused to return! They are not as simple as you think. You have thrown away the initiative entirely. We will have to take New Ross over a mound of bodies because of your hesitancy.'

He quieted as Thomas Cloney, sitting in a chair to his left, placed a cautioning hand on his forearm.

'We were all guilty of complacency,' interjected Cloney softly. 'I honestly thought that the country must be in up in rebellion and that the King's troops would be in open flight all around us. It seems that this is not so. The Kilkenny United Irishmen have sent word across the water that we are definitely alone in our struggle but all it will take is a spark to ignite rebellion in their own county. If we cross the Barrow they will come out into the field with us. No matter the delay, the imperative is still that we take New Ross.'

Here he flung a dagger glance towards Harvey, 'The unfortunate fact of the strong position in which the garrison now finds itself, is, however, worthy of debate.'

Harvey's face settled into a petulant scowl and he muttered, 'What are we to do, then?'

The captains around the table exchanged questioning glances and John Kelly sat down, shaking his head and casting an exasperated glance toward Dan Banville sitting toward the far end of the table. Dan, for his part, shrugged and nodded in understanding. To his mind Bagenal Harvey's authority was unravelling like a beggar's shawl.

At length John Henry Colclough pointedly cleared his throat.

'Perhaps we should ask for the garrison's surrender? Perhaps an emissary of some sort should be sent?' he suggested.

Dan felt a wave of nauseating despair sweep over him at these words and John Kelly sneered, 'We saw what sending messengers did at Wexford. You're awful fond of messengers, Mr Colclough. You and Edward Fitzgerald both.'

Colclough bridled at this and said, his voice harsh with indignation, 'How dare you, sir! Explain yourself Mr Kelly.'

All around the room voices rose, some in agreement with Kelly, others shouting, 'You go too far, John.'

Dan Banville sighed and placed his head in his hands, his eyes closed, the rancour of the room washing over him.

Harvey's voice crested above the din, 'Gentlemen, please. There is no need for this. Remember who our enemies are.'

Gradually a taut silence fell and Harvey continued, 'We shall have no more of this. We are here to spread liberty across our poor country and to overturn tyranny. Whatever antipathy exists between us as individuals must be set aside for the sake of our enterprise.'

A low grumble of assent trundled around the table.

Harvey nodded, the rolls of flesh at his chin bulging, and said, 'We must decide a plan of action. We cannot simply fling ourselves pell-mell against a fortified town.'

He paused for a moment before continuing, 'I was not at any of our great victories so far. I was not at Oulart Hill or Enniscorthy. I was a prisoner when Wexford fell. Some might suggest that I am a diplomat, not a warrior, but I assure you my breast is filled with as much passion for the cause as any man here.'

'No man doubts that,' said Cloney.

Harvey's eyes flicked reflexively to the Bantry man and his face radiated a fleeting gratitude before he went on.

'I will not make any pretence to knowledge of stratagems or tactics. I will not play at soldiers. So I open it up to those here amongst you who have soldiered and fought for Ireland or for liberty beneath a foreign flag. How might we take the town?'

'The gates,' Dan heard himself say. He was surprised at the sound of his own voice.

He found himself the focus of every stare in the room and he felt his face flush. John Kelly grinned at him and nodded for him to continue. Harvey gestured urgently, prompting, 'Go on, Mr Banville.'

Dan coughed and spoke as clearly as he could manage. 'The three gates are vulnerable. We should detail a portion of our force, divided into three, to take them. There are no physical gates to close against us, so those gateways are simply holes in the wall. Once we hold the gates, the advance forces must pause and wait for reinforcements. Once the three divisions are in position we then move into the town simultaneously. I am not familiar with New Ross but the streets look narrow and winding. I fear this may well be a long and bloody fight. We will not take the town as easily as Enniscorthy.'

The men around him were nodding consideringly and an officer Dan did not know asked, 'We only need them to cross the bridge. Even if we can put a bit of a fright into them so that they retreat across the water, the Kilkenny boys will have them on the far side.'

'Will this work?' asked Harvey.

Another man, John Boxwell, to whom the rebel artillery had been entrusted, answered, 'It should work. If our forces can drive them onto the quays, they may take the route across the water to regroup or rally. At that point the town will be ours. It's getting them across the bridge that might prove to be butcher's work. They have cannon in those streets and I've seen the havoc that grapeshot can wreak at close quarters.'

Harvey pursed his lips in thought and said, 'Perhaps Mr Colclough's idea for an emissary might be worthwhile. Bloodshed should be avoided at all costs, particularly if it might spill in such torrents as you men have implied.'

John Kelly's snort of derision made Dan wince. 'If you think that a British general is going to surrender a walled town because we appeal to his better nature, you are sorely mistaken. A more sanguinary class of blackguards is yet to walk the face of the earth,' he growled.

'We must at least make the attempt, Mr Kelly,' replied Harvey.

There was a subtle harmonic in his voice that Dan did not like, a note of despair, of anguish. Dan could appreciate his commander's concern for the lives of his men but the yearning to avoid violence that seemed so desperate in Harvey struck him as being too raw, too overwhelming. It was excessive.

How could anything, let alone a nation, be birthed without blood?

Yet, a murmur of assent buzzed about the table. The image of cannon in the street, of pikemen blasted apart by shot and shell, the prospect of a battle more fierce than any before, seemed to affect the officers deeply. The reality of the coming violence had weighed suddenly down upon the room.

And, all at once, Dan was aware of how many of the gathered officers were newly arrived at Wexford Town. How many had faced redcoats as they lifted their muskets to fire? How many had felt the hot whipping of lead a hair's breadth from their face?

Dan knew now why he had been asked to stay with the Southern Division, and the terrible realisation of the inexperience, the callowness, around this room horrified him. Such vacillation appalled and terrified him in equal measure.

'What terms should we offer?' asked Colclough.

Harvey rubbed one hand along his stubbled jaw before replying, 'Unconditional surrender, of course. We shall allow them to leave the town with colours flying as befits an army undefeated in the field but anything other than a total surrender of the town and all its arms might suggest that we are in some way lukewarm about our prospects of victory.'

'I agree,' said Colclough. 'Very insightful of you Mr Harvey.'

Across from Dan, John Kelly closed his eyes and suppressed the urge to curse.

At four o'clock in the morning, just as dawn crept into the eastern sky, young Matthew Furlong of Templescoby rode down the steep slope of Corbet Hill towards New Ross Town. In his breeches' pocket he carried a letter drafted by Bagenal Harvey requesting the immediate surrender of the town and all its stores. His right hand was bunched about the reins of his mount and in his left he carried a white flag. On the slopes above him, the ranks of the United Irish Army watched him wend his way around outcrops of rock and between clusters of gorse, charting a sinuous course to the first of the bracelet of defences thrown out around the Three Bullet Gate.

At the head of his new corps, trained and drilled over the past four days so that they at least knew how to march in order and fall from line into square, Dan Banville leaned forward and squinted into the lifting night.

Dan could not imagine the thoughts that crawled through Furlong's mind as the young man approached the lines of soldiery arrayed before him. He had answered Harvey's request for a volunteer almost immediately and had seemed happy to play such an important role in what might very well be a bloodless victory. He had smiled before riding away, and there was something awful about the vista that made Dan want to retch.

As the boy drew near the scimitar arc of disturbed soil which the soldiers had flung across the approaches to New Ross, it was clear that a frantic commotion commenced around the yawning maw of the Three Bullet Gate. Scrambling red coats swarmed and over the earthwork's brow the black flecks of bicorns and tricorns floated above the pale dots of watching faces.

Young Furlong was a hundred yards from the town walls, his white flag stirring in the first fumble of a drowsy breeze, when the foremost trench hawked forth a spray of blue smoke. Like something made of clay, Furlong teetered and tumbled from the saddle, boneless and robbed of life. His body struck the ground at the same moment as the crack and rattle of the muskets struck the ears of those on Corbet Hill.

The effect was immediate.

A vast roar emanated from the rebel ranks, like the dull rushing of a tempest somehow with an animal howl. It was a noise of outrage and anger and fear all balled together and flung across the mile of empty ground separating the hill and the town. Pikes began to sway and shudder, and like a slow avalanche the thousands of furious rebels began to slip gradually down the slope, the lust for vengeance blistering through their veins.

Dan spun on his heel and faced his corps, his sword drawn and his face pale. 'Hold!' he bellowed. 'Hold!'

All about frantic officers desperately tried to restrain their outraged men. Gradually, the rebel line steadied.

Dan faced his men, his breath coming hard through clenched teeth, and growled, 'We shall be on them soon enough. Now, though, we hold here until the order is given.'

The men before him were waxen faced, their eyes burning. Horror and anger seethed in every inch of their bodies.

'They shot him, Mr Banville,' Seán Rouse exploded in disbelief. 'He had a white flag and all and that shower of bastards shot him. How are we supposed to stand still and watch that happen, sure?'

Dan smiled grimly, 'They want us to come down. They want us to come on without discipline or order so they can cut us down with fire. When we turn to run then they'll set the cavalry on us. We won't oblige them, gentlemen. We hold and we follow our orders.'

Rouse breathed hard through his nose, like a bull about to charge. But he held his ground, the fury in his face a perfect replica of those thousands around him.

At the door of Talbot Hall a frenetic conversation was taking place between the senior rebel leaders. All were on horseback and all seemed as furious as their men. Harvey sat in the middle and slumped in his saddle like a broken puppet. Eventually the leaders split apart, leaving Harvey to remain sitting his horse, alone before the empty house.

John Kelly rode to the head of his battalion, his huge frame towering in the saddle. His men, along with the companies under Thomas Cloney, were to take the Three Bullet Gate. To him would fall the task of revenging Matthew Furlong.

John Boxwell was given command of the force to attack the Priory Gate, the southernmost entrance to New Ross, and he jogged his mount off to the left flank of the army. Dan watched him go with a sort of regret; Boxwell was an experienced soldier and artillery man and Dan would have liked to have been following him or Kelly into battle. Without an Edward Roche or Fr Murphy, Dan was beginning to feel rudderless in the plunging stream of events.

He looked up as the man detailed to lead his own division brought his mount to heel on the slope to Dan's right. John Henry Colclough sat his saddle with palpable unease. His green coat was buttoned to the neck and belted with a wide yellow sash. In his white-knuckled right hand he held a cavalry sabre as though it were an animal that might at any moment squirm free and bite him.

Then, just as the sun heaved above the horizon, the shrill blast of a hunting horn came high and long and the three advance divisions of rebels moved like a landslide towards New Ross.

Boxwell's division swung immediately to the left whilst Kelly and Cloney marched their men with lethal single-mindedness towards the Three Bullet Gate below them. Colclough walked his horse forward, bearing slightly to the right, leading his companies out in an arc around the town to fall on the Market Gate, a mile and a half distant.

Dan marched at the head of his hundred and twenty men but his eyes were fixed on Colclough. The rebel colonel swayed elegantly in the saddle yet the set of his shoulders was stiff and his head swivelled constantly to the left, flinging apprehensive glances at the town below.

At the base of the hill the countryside was a mesh of ditches and hedgerows, the characteristic *bocage* of County Wexford. Around the base of the town walls however, the ditches had been hacked down and levelled to open up a killing ground, a hundred yards across which the rebels would have to run before being able to use their pikes.

Seeing this, the men with Dan began to mutter apprehensively.

'Steady boys,' he said reassuringly. 'We'll be on them before they can blink. Falter now and we're lost.'

The muttering fell into a tense silence as Colclough led them out into the countryside, making for the narrow tongue of dusty road that licked out from the Market Gate. Behind the column, from the direction of the Three Bullet Gate, the first brittle crackling of muskets could be heard.

Kelly must have hit home, thought Dan. All around him, however, the men of Colclough's division were turning their heads towards the sound of battle, each face pale and branded with fear.

Frowning, he sought to focus their thoughts, to hone the edge of their anger. 'Listen!' he called, 'The Bantry boys are setting-to. Kelly will have young Matthew Furlong avenged before long!'

Dan knew that the Castletown Corps or the Monaseed or any of the Northern Division would have shaken the heavens with a cheer at these words. They would have roared in defiance and joy that the men who had murdered a teenager under a flag of truce were being made pay in blood. He knew that

Roche would have raised a huzzah or Fr Murphy would have roused his own men in response, urging them to emulate the men at the Three Bullet Gate.

Yet from around him no cheer arose, and no call to action came from the lump of tallow that Colclough had become. There was only terror.

'Mr Colclough!' called Dan, feeling the slippage of events within him, feeling their fixity of purpose liquefy and slide away like fat in a fire. 'You must say something – your men look to you, sir!'

Colclough, his eyes starting and his lips so white they seemed rimed with frost, merely sat his mount and said nothing.

And in that moment of inertia, as the sounds of gunfire intensified behind them and the first screams climbed the morning, the rebel column under John Henry Colclough began to disintegrate. Slowly at first and then with a terrible, inexorable momentum, the insurgents dropped their pikes and muskets and began to slip away through the fields.

A voice came from behind Dan, Seán Rouse's choppy sea-birthed vowels. 'What do we do, Mr Banville?' he asked.

Turning, he saw that his own company had remained together while all around them their comrades were flooding away from the assault. Every man regarded Dan with sad-eyed loyalty. Looking at them with a slimy, sickening clot of dismay lodged in his throat, he replied, 'We take New Ross.'

Turning again he made to address Colclough, only to have the older man lean down from his saddle and thrust the handle of his cavalry sabre towards him. Dan stared at Colclough in shock as he said dolefully, 'Take my sword Mr Banville. I am not worthy of it.'

'Mr Colclough—' he began, but Colclough's shaken head silenced him. There was a dread, leaden aspect to the colonel's bearing, a grotesque absence of vitality and spirit. He was a broken man.

'Take my sword,' he sighed. 'I shall have no further use for it.'

Dan lifted his arm and closed numb fingers about the proffered hilt.

'I am sorry Mr Banville,' Colclough said with an abstract and awful simplicity. 'I have to go.'

With that, he wheeled his mount and made after his men, following them into the obscure fields and hedgerows between New Ross and Wexford Town, vanishing in the sunlight.

Dan stood for a moment, stunned, before a harsh eruption of jubilation brought him back to his senses. From the Market Gate, only four hundred yards distant, a series of joyous hurrahs sallied forth. The garrison was celebrating, relieved that a column numbering in the thousands had broken and run without a shot being fired.

Furious now, Dan dashed Colclough's sword to the ground and spun to face his own small corps who stood huddled together, terrified and exposed, a long musket shot from New Ross's eastern wall.

'What were you told?' he snapped. 'Group together like that and you make a bullseye for any man with a cannon. Form line.'

Wordlessly, his men began to spread out into a long ragged line, their movements automatic, their faces a series of pale leather masks.

Dan watched them, his mind boiling but his voice possessed of an arctic calm, and said, 'Now lads. We are not in force enough to take the Market Gate on our own, but we can lend a hand to Kelly and Cloney. We shall join with them as quick as we can. The British commander in New Ross is no fool and as soon as he sees that our right flank has collapsed he'll send out cavalry to sweep round and cut off our forward elements. We have to get back to the main body or we shall all be cut to pieces. Does everyone understand?'

To a man the company nodded, some muttering, 'Yes, Mr Banville.' Rouse, as self-appointed drill sergeant, puffed out his chest with pride.

'Right,' said Dan. 'In good order, we hurry back to the Three Bullet Gate.'

They skirted along ditches and filed through gaps and stiles, following the rumpled terracotta of cattle tracks and sheep walks. He marched at the head of his men with all the confidence he could project but his mind was a quagmire of doubt and misgiving. How could Colclough had left two-thirds of the army behind? How could he abandon a struggle in which men fought and died, slipping away like a common thief?

Under the blue of the morning, Dan was baffled by the circumstance in which he found himself. For the first time since the Rising began he felt his soul crowding with reservations. For him not just the prospect of success but the very nobility and motives of the United leadership were abruptly undermined and tottering.

He and his ashen company of panting pikemen had almost reached the Three Bullet Gate when the noise of the conflict waging in and around its ragged arch grew to a spitting crescendo. The soldiers' musketry snapped forth in volleys that ripped into the rebel ranks as they crossed the open ground. The foremost of John Kelly's column had flung themselves upon the defenders at several points and here the gunfire was replaced by the shrieking of men spitted by pike or bayonet and the hollow clacking of musket stock against pikestaff. Smoke made an acrid dry fog before the gate, swaddling all in its choking folds.

Yet Dan perceived that all was not as it should be here, either.

A narrow lane ran along the base of Corbet Hill and beyond it, retreating up the slope and away from the battle, Dan's disbelieving eyes could see battalions of panicked insurgents. Anger flared within him; anger and moral outrage that these men would leave their companions to be hacked to pieces and picked-off by musket fire.

As all this passed through Dan's mind, a despairing cry went up from the tail of his column.

'Cavalry, Mr Banville! Jesus Christ, we'll all be killed!'

Dan whirled and roared at his men, 'Steady, damn you! If we run we'll be slaughtered.'

They had by now crested a low tongue of scrubland lolling out from Corbet Hill, and from this vantage point Dan watched as a long snake of red-coated cavalry slid from out of the Market Gate. Each horseman wore a crimson coat with white crossbelts gleaming across his chest. On each head sat not the familiar bearskin crest of a Tarleton helmet, but a broad black bicorn with a white and red pom-pom that danced to the strides of the horse. Their collars were a deep blue and in their wide, white gauntlets they carried the brutal, glittering lengths of heavy straight-blade cavalry swords. Their horses bore them on relentlessly.

Dan addressed his men, his heart pulsing, 'Make for the gate. Form square and provide a rearguard for Kelly's battalion. If you do anything else we are damned.'

Hectically, his men barrelled past him, racing for the narrow laneway across which ragged groups of rebels were still streaming away from the battle. The laneway and paddocks below it overlooked Kelly's position and Dan knew that the cavalry men were galloping for this same narrow stretch of road. If they gained it before his men had a chance to cross the ditches and intercept them, Kelly and Cloney would be caught between the hammer of a cavalry charge and the anvil of the soldiers' bayonets.

Breathing deeply, he watched his column thrash their way through the gorse and briar, Rouse cursing the men fleeing in the opposite direction as they went. He turned his head and saw the cavalry moving faster now, noting the corps of pikemen who sought to block their charge. The coats of their heavy mounts glistened in the morning sunlight, the coils of their muscles slewing beneath their skin.

For a brief, splintered moment, Dan thought of Tom – before his body seemed to leap forward of its own accord.

Across the slope and down towards the Three Bullet Gate he flew, vaulting hedges and ditches as briars snagged his coat and nettles whipped at his shins. The thumping of his heart roared in his ears and his breath was a bellows fanning flames through his muscles and searing his lungs.

Above him, he could see his men forming a ragged square, their pikes bristling from the four-sided block. Below him, around the Three Bullet Gate, a sort of stalemate had developed. The soldiers held their ground, their muskets spitting defiantly at the pikemen who charged, repulsed again and again. The ground in front of the gate was stubbled with the rotten crop of bodies and blood and shattered limbs. Here and there clumps of rebel musketeers tried to return fire, attempting to suppress the soldiery long enough to allow the pikemen to come to blows, their volleys ragged and their homemade powder fizzing feebly.

In the midst of one such group of gunsmen, John Kelly towered like a lighthouse in a maelstrom, his blond hair glowing and his face infused with the ruddy gush of his exertions. It was toward this giant of a man that Dan dashed, unmindful of thorns and thistle and hissing shots.

Skirting the back of the pikemen, Dan came within hailing distance of Kelly. Just as he opened his mouth to yell his warning, however, a volley of musketry from the gateway drowned out his words in a flood of smoke and flame. Dan saw the ranks of pikemen waver but hold firm and he raised his cupped hands to his mouth.

Uncaring of the frantic desperation that tore at his voice, he roared, 'Cavalry, John! Cavalry are behind you!'

John Kelly remained turned away from Dan, his proud face directed towards the mass of redcoats that barred his way into the town. A slight farmer with a whiskered, pointed face tugged at Kelly's elbow and pointed to where Dan stood in the middle of a patch of empty ground between two blocks of insurgent pikemen; ground that spat up dusty coughs of earth as musket balls pattered about his feet.

Dan saw Kelly turn, his great head lifting in his direction and saw the frown that darkened his wide brow. Following Kelly's gaze, Dan flung a glance over his right shoulder and what he saw transformed his nerves to threads of ice.

Along the laneway, beneath the retreating rebels, a hundred heavy horse had assembled, their red coats blazing and their horses dancing in expectation of the charge. Below them his own small corps looked like the desultory scrap that it was, huddled together in fear, its pike-heads trembling like a fevered pulse.

Gasping, breathless from his race across the fields, Dan was suddenly torn between his men and the relative safety of the rebel companies surrounding

Kelly. Anguished, he turned from his little block of infantry and flung a beseeching gaze towards John Kelly. If the blond colonel swung his gunsmen around, it might give Dan's corps a chance to fall back without being hacked to pieces.

As his eyes fastened upon Kelly he was shocked to see a slow smile open across his features. John Kelly stood and pointed with his sword, its tip jabbing the air insistently.

Confused, Dan spun on his heel, drawing his own sword and pistol, convinced that Kelly meant to warn him of some danger now bearing down on him.

Instead, what he saw dragged his own lips into a deadly grin.

Beyond the cavalry, on the slopes above the lane, the rebel flight had stalled. Groups of men were rallying and forming ranks and files. All across the hill, the general retreat was halting. As if stemmed by a tourniquet, the haemorrhage of men slowed to a trickle and then ceased altogether. Corbet Hill reared against the morning sky like the rough shoulder of a slumbering Titan, its wrinkled flesh matted with a spiked pelt of pikes.

To Dan the contrast with Colclough's division could not have been more marked. Here were battalions and companies standing and rallying not through loyalty to a cause but through loyalty to their friends. The sight of the cavalry had roused in them the instinctive protectiveness of a pack animal at bay. They would not condemn Kelly and Cloney and the multitude who followed them to a merciless slaughter. They were suddenly resolute, banners waving and pikes steadied.

Mere moments too late, the cavalry spread out along the laneway realised their predicament.

With a guttural roar, the serried horde of pikemen flung themselves down the hill, falling upon the cavalry's unguarded rear like an avalanche. The savage charge consumed all before it, horse and rider were sent tumbling, transfixed by the bitter length of pike and bayonet. Within seconds twenty cavalry men lay dead and the others were flailing at the steel-frothed tide of humanity lapping at their knees, frantic to get away. Eventually those of the horsemen not speared by the initial charge fought their way free and thundered in hectic disorder back towards the Market Gate.

For a long moment Dan was stunned and then a massive, whooping roar went up from the regiments on the hill, a roar that was taken up and magnified by the relieved men before the Three Bullet Gate. Dan swelled with pride as he watched his own little corps fan out into line and march down the hill, leading the victorious mass of insurgents on. It was as though the entire rebel hillside had rediscovered its spine and heart.

For the first time that day, Dan felt that victory was within their grasp.

Around the Three Bullet Gate, the suddenly demoralised defenders had begun a slow retreat in the face of Kelly's renewed advance. The flames from the muzzles of their muskets had set the thatch of the shouldering cabins alight, and now the gateway itself, as well as the street beyond, was filled with smoke and ash and heat.

As Dan's men arrived at his shoulder, the last soldier, his face blackened and eyes watering from spent gunpowder, was edging backwards into the town.

'Did we do well, Mr Banville?' Seán Rouse asked, his face blazing with conviction, his eyes shining as though with tears.

'You have done more than well,' said Dan. The sight of his motley corps so proud and steady when so many others had simply turned tail and fled, filled him to the brim with gratification. Clearing his throat, he said, 'The town is ours now lads. The soldiers are running.'

And so it seemed, for Kelly and Cloney's men were surging through the Three Bullet Gate like a swollen river through a weir and to the left a pall of smoke was rising from within the town walls, behind the Priory Gate. The two remaining insurgent columns had smashed through the first ring of defence and were inside the town. New Ross was surely theirs.

But, as Dan watched, instead of holding the gate until the Southern Division was ready to move on the quays in its entirety, Kelly had pushed his men on. Even now they were invisible behind the belching smoke. Musket fire and cries drifted out through the muffling haze like the screams of a banshee or the ghostly, disembodied thunder of a distant storm.

Dan hesitated only a moment before stabbing his sword at the fog-choked throat of the Three Bullet Gate. 'Onward!' he bellowed. 'For Liberty and Ireland!'

General Henry Johnson stood at the Custom House windows and watched a throng of red-coated infantry gush across the bridge and into the Kilkenny countryside. He swallowed drily and asked, 'We are sure that there are no Kilkenny rebels in the field?'

Behind him, his uniform singed and his face blackened by the soot of burning thatch, Charles Eustace replied, 'We are certain, sir. The loyal subjects of Kilkenny have decided to obey the King's peace. This Wexford rabble are without support.'

'And yet they drive us back,' growled Johnson. He spun away from the window and began to pace the room. His riding boots hammered into the floorboards as he spun, marched and spun again. 'I have never witnessed such blind courage. You have pulled the men back, yes? The cannon are positioned? The cavalry in reserve? You have done all this?'

Automatically Eustace nodded, 'Yes, sir. We have abandoned the southern half of the town and established ourselves around the bridge. The cannon are all deployed and the Clare Militia have recovered their spine and are turning the tables. Our grape shot is felling them by the hundreds, sir.'

Johnson, still pacing, his hands gripped tight at the small of his back, shook his head, 'We cannot lose this town, Eustace. We cannot.'

Smoke drifted in banks across the windows at Johnson's back and feathered flakes of soot spun on the fire-fanned winds like an infernal fall of snow. The room was filled with the sounds of musketry and the dull dragon's roar of cannon.

But most horrible of all to Johnson's ears were the screams. High above the military thunder and penetrating the stones of the building and the walls of his mind, the screams of the dying could be heard. Cheers and huzzahs swelled only to dash themselves to pieces and collapse into a swamp of agonised wails. Johnson knew every boom and chatter of cannon and musket, every roar and rallying cry, signified the deaths of dozens. The streets of New Ross were slimed with the gore of Johnson's own deliberations. He had planned to invite the rebels on to his cannon. It was he who had turned this place into a vision of utmost horror.

In spite of his military discipline, in spite of his years, Henry Johnson was disgusted at what he had done. And yet, he found himself thinking, he had no other choice. To meet the rebels in battle, outnumbered and on alien ground, would be suicidal. And so in doing his duty he had turned himself into a butcher.

Standing awkwardly, Eustace transferred his weight from foot to foot. He cleared his throat, paused, and cleared his throat again.

Johnson, perceiving that his subordinate had some other item of information that he was reluctant to impart, stopped his pacing and regarded him with shrewd calculation. 'Out with it, Eustace,' he urged, his voice kind, his anger reserved for himself alone. 'What else is there?'

Eustace licked his lips, tasting the salt of his sweat and the gritty char of the ash that covered him, and said, 'Lord Mountjoy is dead. He was killed at the Three Bullet Gate.'

Johnson sighed like a breeze across a graveyard, 'The poor man. Where has his talk of parley got him now? Another mark against me, Eustace. And every minute, more are added to the tally.'

Eustace frowned at his commanding officer.

Johnson turned to face the smoke and fire beyond the windows. Across the bridge he could see his troops rallying, red coats like embers in the veiling pall.

'We hold the town,' he said, almost to himself. 'We hold this place or else what is it all for?'

Not on Oulart Hill, nor at Enniscorthy, had Dan felt anything like the exuberance that coursed through him as he entered New Ross. With his men roaring behind him, he plunged into the blinding mass of smoke and flame and was for a moment wrapped in a purgatory of grey. The vague, lumpen shapes of the dead and wounded bulged up out of the ground all around as he moved between the carcasses of burning, crumbling cabins.

Suddenly he was free of the smoke, and stumbled into a scene of the purest hell.

Before him, an open space splayed out into four separate streets which then wound off between rows of tall, slate-roofed townhouses. At the entrance to two of these streets, lines of terrified soldiers had formed crimson dams against the rebel flood. Two ranks deep, they lifted and fired their weapons in disciplined volleys and from the upper windows of bolted houses sharpshooters turned the ground below into a sodden mire of blood.

As he watched, a detachment under Kelly rallied and charged headlong at one of the red-coated companies. A blast of musketry flung more than a dozen of the Bantry men backwards in a bloom of gore before the others crashed home. In the centre, John Kelly was a whirlwind of violence, his sword rising and falling like a butcher's cleaver and with every blow it arced back more slick and more red. In the inferno of the fighting, Kelly's handsome face had taken on the aspect of a man in the throes of madness.

The soldiers stood for mere seconds before being flung back, breaking and running with Kelly's men at their heels. At the same moment Thomas Cloney led a charge against the other troop of soldiers who turned and fled without waiting for the impact of the pikes. With a cry of brutal bloodlust Cloney's detachment barrelled after them, as all around Dan more and more rebels swarmed into New Ross.

Dan stood for a moment before deciding that Kelly, for all his intrepidity, would face the stiffest opposition by making directly for the quays. Gesturing to his men, he ordered, 'We follow Kelly of Killann, if the soldiers have established redoubts he may need our help.'

As these words spilled from his lips, to his right the deep boom of a cannon rolled through the streets, drowning out the lesser crackle of musketry.

At this sound many of the rebels closest to Dan exchanged uneasy looks but he snapped at them, 'You'll hear worse than that today. And the slower we set about harrying these scoundrels into the Barrow the quicker they will be loading their damned cannon.'

The men before him, still looking apprehensive, filed past, ducking as the soldiers occupying overlooking windows commenced a chattering, harassing fire down upon them. Trusting speed and the cover of the smoke to keep them safe, Dan and his men pressed on. Behind him he heard the snapping clatter and tinkle of doors and windows being smashed, and the crack of muskets and the bubbling screams as house after house was cleared of defenders.

Swinging to the left down Michael Street, staying close to the wall as he went, Dan saw the massive figure of John Kelly pressed as far as he could be into a shallow doorway. All about him his men had taken what shelter they could find in the desolate expanse of the street. Bundles of insurgents had crammed themselves like roosting bats into niches and alcoves, wedging themselves behind decorative door pillars or crouching low behind the raised doorsteps of houses.

A man beside Dan suddenly doubled over, his face curdling with pain, a gust of agony soughing from his twisted mouth – and Dan knew why Kelly and the others were so desperately seeking the least bit of refuge. Down the street, a formidable stone-faced building hulked amongst the more elegant townhouses and from its windows a veritable battery of musket barrels weaved to and fro, tracking the smallest movement in the street below.

As Dan watched, one of these muskets puffed a breath of gunsmoke and the wall just at Dan's ear spat forth a spume of russet brick dust.

Ducking low, he muttered an inaudible curse as his heart sought to clamber up his throat. Blinking his stinging eyes, he called to his men, 'Keep against the buildings, if you expose yourself for even a moment they shall have you in their sights!'

Above him the sun was a pale, spectral ball in the smoke and in the surrounding streets the sporadic rattling of musketry was gradually cohering into long drum rolls of shattering noise. Most terrifying of all was the rumbling thunder of cannon. Screams rose and flocked together creating a pall of noise just as dense, and infinitely more horrible, than the smoke and ash. Dan could imagine the damage that grape shot would create in such claustrophobic confines, and he whispered a prayer for the men who faced the big guns.

But for the moment he could do nothing to help the other corps who threw themselves upon the barricades and cannon. He focused his attention on storming the building from whose windows a withering fire was being directed into the street below.

'John!' he called. 'John Kelly!'

Kelly half turned to him, his body flattened against a heavy door, and shook his head almost imperceptibly. 'We are pinned here!' he roared. 'They repulsed our first attack and have made a killing ground here – we must flank them somehow!'

Kelly's mouth moved then as though he were issuing instructions but his words were lost in the chattering fire of another volley of lead from the building ahead.

Gesturing to his men to remain where they were, Dan dashed forward, bent almost double and half-expecting to be hammered from his feet by a musket ball at any moment. Then Kelly's shouting voice brought his head up.

'Get back, Dan!' he yelled. 'Come around with Cloney!'

And in that instant, that tiny fragment of time in which Kelly directed his full attention at Dan, he leaned forward slightly. Dan had neither time to scream a warning nor a chance to avert his eyes.

The musket ball shattered Kelly's thigh like the fall of a sledge.

With a roar of agony and rage, the Bantry man collapsed forward into the street where the earth immediately began to whip up in angry wisps of grit. The men closest to Kelly reached out, scrambling to seize him before the soldiers could complete their work and hauled his massive frame close in to the sheltering wall.

Dan remained rooted to the spot for a moment before the droning hiss of lead and the words 'Move, Mr Banville!' brought him to his senses. Diving forward, he skirted along the right-hand side of the street to where Kelly lay.

Kelly was surrounded by a small group of his men who were busy knotting their jackets about pikestaffs so as to make a makeshift stretcher for him. Dan saw the distress on their faces, the numb disbelief and terrible fear at the loss of Kelly.

Kelly lay clutching at his bloodied thigh, red gushing from between his fingers, drenching his clothes and clotting in the calluses and wrinkles of his hands.

Dan bent over him, trying as best he could to look the wounded man in the face without leaning too far into the street himself. 'John,' he said. 'What should we do?'

Kelly looked up at him with eyes glazing in shock and anguish. He drew in a long shuddering breath before reciting his words in a rush.

'Have Cloney come around from behind. That barracks is separating us from Boxwell. Unless it is taken we cannot gain the docks. Damn Harvey for this. He has done for me.'

He groaned then as a kneeling rebel strove to unhook Kelly's bear paws from about the yawning pit of the wound.

'Go!' Kelly's voice quivered. 'Find Cloney.'

Dan nodded once and placed a gentle hand upon the bleeding man's shoulder. The deplorable inadequacy of the gesture galled him but he could do nothing more.

Turning, he ran back along the wall against which his men were pressed in a long, wary line. Even the irrepressible Rouse was panting and a cold pallor swam below his tan skin. 'What do we do now, Mr Banville?' he asked through gritted teeth.

'Join with the Bantry men,' Dan ordered. 'Do as they do. I shall return with reinforcements as swiftly as I am able.'

The men regarded him grimly as he went, the last in the line, a young lad of no more than fifteen, muttering 'Be careful, Mr Banville' as he passed. Dan smiled his thanks to the boy and flung himself into the coiling smoke.

Cloney's column had gone right when they entered the town and so Dan now darted left. All about him the dead and dying lay piled in rumpled heaps, red coats mingled with the drab coloureds of the peasantry, all alike in the terrible equality of death. From out of the smoke came cheers and huzzahs, screams, and the clashing of steel on steel.

Sprinting now, Dan entered Neville Street and physically recoiled at the carnage he saw. Rebel corpses stacked one upon the other, felled like logs or sheaves of wheat. The ground itself was a rich burgundy of spilled blood and under the acrid tang of powder smoke the coppery stink of death lodged in the back of his throat.

Nevertheless, amidst the rebel corpses, the scarlet coats of soldiers were visible even here. For all their casualties, Dan thought, they were pushing back the garrison.

Blundering through the smoke, almost tripping more than once over a prone rebel or the groaning agonies of a dying soldier, Dan stumbled into the junction of Church Lane and Mary Street. In every direction violence was a hectic universal, vile in its intimacy as muskets barked and men screamed, bayonets and pikes clashed and slid home. Such visceral savagery on so grand a scale had not been witnessed at Oulart or Enniscorthy. Insurgents charged barricades and were blown back by musketry and cannon, tumbling in groups of twenty only to be replaced by others, screaming in fear and frenzy, driving on because they couldn't now turn back. Men died and bled and howled and Dan stood at the gore-splashed crossroads and cast about frantically for the figure of Thomas Cloney.

Ahead of him Church Lane was a slaughterhouse clotted with powder smoke. But as he watched, through the choking mist, he thought he saw Cloney fling himself to the ground, thought he heard his voice bellowing out over the scream of battle.

Dan took two steps forward, his mouth already forming the first syllable of Cloney's name, when a fey whim of summer air caught the curtain of murk and rolled it to one side. Through the empty, curling whorl that opened before him like a tunnel, Dan saw several things. He saw a shredded band of rebels standing, dumbfounded, before the maw of a massive, brass nine-pounder. He saw their comrades fling themselves to one side. He saw Thomas Cloney lying flat against the ground, turn to look at him, horror flaying his features. He saw the gunner behind the cannon touch a fizzing fuse to its touch hole. He saw the desultory feather of burning powder as the charge ignited.

All this he saw in crystal clarity, each piece complete and whole in and of itself. And then Dan Banville saw no more.

PART THREE

THE SLANEY'S RED WAVE

CHAPTER 21

Taking Leave

The rebel camp at Gorey Hill on the 8th of June was a place of carnival. The sun had risen and now hung heavily in the late afternoon sky pouring a bright, permeating heat over the countryside. The town of Gorey was alive with activity as throngs of people laughed and lounged, confident that they were masters of their domain.

Tom Banville, however, was in a venomous mood.

The now familiar failings of the insurgent leadership had resurfaced since the victory at Tubberneering, and he was sick to his teeth with it. In the two days since Edward Roche's departure, the bickering and arguing amongst the men he had left behind had become a festering canker of rancour and ill-feeling.

Roche had ridden off late on the 6th to procure a much-needed supply of gunpowder from Wexford Town and to discover the reasons behind the disturbing silence that had emanated from the south of the county since the 4th. Nothing had been heard from either Matthew Keogh in the town itself or from Bagenal Harvey who, by this time, must surely have been at the walls of Waterford.

He had ridden off leaving two of his closest friends in nominal command of the massive army sprawled in and around Gorey Town. Anthony Perry and Fr Philip Roche were to lead in his absence, a prospect greeted with blustering outrage by Fr Michael Murphy and with grim resignation by Fr John, a man who seemed to be growing steadily more marginalised. It was as if the country curate was a source of vague embarrassment to the United Irishmen around him, like he was an uninvited guest.

Of course, Miles Byrne was indignant at Fr John's treatment. The young captain had become a staunch supporter of the priest from Boolavogue ever since Enniscorthy and was appalled at the supporting role he was being forced to play.

And the toing and froing, the twisting and endless arguments about strategy, had begun all over again.

It was assumed that a march on Arklow was inevitable and so the entire army had set out on the 7th to ensure that General Loftus had indeed abandoned the county and was not lurking somewhere behind them. They had reached Carnew without incident and were told that the good general had retired all the way to Tullow in County Carlow. The entire north of the county was theirs. The men celebrated by burning every loyalist home they could find.

It was at this point that the first cracks began to web darkly through the insurgent command.

Fr John Murphy and Fr Michael Murphy had almost come to blows. The latter demanding an immediate advance on Arklow whilst Fr John and the majority of the men from Wicklow argued that a war of stealth waged from the safety of the Wicklow Mountains would keep both north Wexford and the road to Dublin free of Crown forces. The French, Fr John was adamant, must be given time to land. The rebels must remain in the field long enough to give the French a chance to come to their aid. Risking everything in set-piece battles was foolishness. Fr Michael stopped just short of accusing him of cowardice.

And yet, reflected Tom, something had altered in the bearing of Fr John Murphy. For a man renowned for his peaceable nature, a man determinedly opposed an armed Rising mere days before he himself sparked the conflict that had consumed his county, the violence being done must surely have been terrible to behold. He was a priest, first and foremost; he tended to his flock. The fact of his responsibility, his complicity, in the slaughter of hundreds of innocents squirmed like rats in his brain. Tom thought the man was at breaking point, labouring beneath a yoke of guilt.

The executions had not helped matters.

Just after Carnew, two prisoners were brought before Anthony Perry. He greeted them both like old friends, throwing his arms around them in a fierce embrace. One was Rogan and the other was Wheatley, the men who had boiled Perry's flesh from his scalp, the men who had driven him to the brink of madness.

It took Perry some time to kill Wheatley. Rogan less so; Wheatley's screams echoing in his ears had dulled the edge of Perry's cruelty somewhat. Yet the relish with which he had dispatched them had disturbed all who witnessed it. No matter the scars, no matter Perry's constant suffering, the joy he took in slaughtering them was terrible to watch.

After this, Fr John silent and pale, the United Irish officers had decided that Arklow must be taken and after that Dublin would surely fall. Tom remembered that Fr Michael had smiled at this and had flung a gloating look towards Fr John.

Now, a day later, Tom sat in the shade of the tremendous beech tree that spread over Gorey's market diamond and flicked pebbles into the dust of the thoroughfare. His mind was mired in black contemplation, his thoughts wandering south to where his brother was doing God knew what. The silence from the Southern Division had grown in his imagination, from being a source of vague unease to a full front of malignancy.

He should never have left his brother behind. He should never have allowed himself to be taken in by Dan's words. He was not needed here. He was an appendix of the greater organism, and the Northern Division would unravel with or without him, it was only a matter of time. He flung another pebble with a force that sent it skittering off into the distance.

From behind him the sound of pounding footsteps brought him to his feet. Tom stepped around the furrowed bole of the tree and watched a young boy of no more than twelve come lolloping down the rutted earth of the market diamond. His bare feet kicked up little clouds of dust as he pounded along. The boy's face bore the fierce determination of one to whom a great mission had been entrusted, and his little forehead was creased in concentration. So intent was the boy on the object of his mad dash that he nearly collided with Tom.

The boy looked up at him with wide eyes and panted, 'Do you know where Fr John is, sir?'

Tom frowned in curiosity, 'He was saying mass an hour ago. I would presume he's retired to his rooms. Why are you looking for him?'

The boy considered this for a moment before answering with brazen confidence, 'I'm only to talk to Fr Murphy.'

Tom regarded the boy levelly and asked, 'Do you know me, lad?'

The boy nodded slowly, 'You're Captain Banville, sir.'

Tom grinned, 'That I am. Now, I was thinking of heading down to Fr Murphy myself, so you might as well tell me and save yourself the journey.'

The boy considered this for a moment before relenting. He pointed back the way he had come, toward the mass of bodies on the crest of Gorey Hill, and said, 'There's a messenger come from the south. Mr Perry wants Fr Murphy straight away.'

At the boy's words Tom's heart bucked with excitement and dread. Fighting to keep his voice calm, he said to the lad before him, 'Thank you, son. I shall go and fetch Fr John immediately.'

The boy grinned at him impishly, 'Mr Perry said I'd get a ha'penny for my troubles.'

Tom fished the small copper coin from out of his pocket and distractedly tossed it to the boy, who spun and barrelled away, his ha'penny held high like a trophy.

A messenger from the south, thought Tom as he turned and hurried down into town. Surely he must have news from New Ross. Surely Munster must have risen. Surely Dan must be alive.

Fr John Murphy had taken up residence in a rather finely appointed town-house on Gorey's main street. He had been heard to remark that it was poor recompense for the loss of his own modest home and chapel. Outside the house a man Tom recognised as James Gallagher kept careful guard.

Gallagher saluted as Tom approached, 'Captain.'

Tom returned the salute and asked, 'Is the good padre within?'

Gallagher smiled, 'He is, sir. I believe he is upstairs.'

Tom thanked the man and passed through the door, already open to allow a cooling draught to help lift the stifling heat of the house.

Immediately inside the door, a wooden stairway climbed the right-hand wall. Tom mounted them carefully, the well-worn heels of his riding boots making small clunks on the varnished wood. The stairway opened out at its head to a long corridor lined on one side by the doors of four bedrooms. The nearest door was slightly ajar and a narrow band of light, slim as a finger, glowed out from the room.

Through this gap, narrow though it was, a voice could be heard as though engaged in quiet conversation.

Tom approached slowly, his footsteps silent and delicate. Words came to his ears, soft and fluttering but weighted with an urgency and raw emotion that startled him. In the privacy of his room, Fr Murphy was praying.

'Forgive me, Father. I have wronged you and brought havoc down upon all I held dear in my life. Please, God, grant me the strength to see this out.'

Then, in a manner completely unlike the usual dull drone of a man intoning his prayers, Fr Murphy began to recite the Act of Contrition, investing every word and syllable with a fervour that took Tom's breath away. Standing outside the little bedroom, Tom felt embarrassed. To listen as a man bore his soul in such a fashion was an intimate thing and one which he was sure he should not divulge, even to Fr Murphy himself. Tom was in no doubt that the curate from Boolavogue would not be at all happy having his privacy so shattered.

Tom waited a moment before coughing politely and rapping his knuckles on the panelled bedroom door.

There came the quiet, moth wing sounds of a man composing himself and then Fr Murphy's voice came with all the old bravado that Tom had come to expect, 'Come in. Come in. What's the matter that you must disturb a man at prayer?'

Tom entered the room and began to salute reflexively before the priest snapped at him, 'Enough of that, Banville. Come now, what's the news?'

Tom regarded Fr Murphy for a long moment. The man was pale and unshaven, his eyes nestled in a cushion of dark wrinkles. He stood with one elbow resting jauntily on the mantelpiece of the fireplace, yet his bearing had all the weary slackness of a man who had not slept in an age.

'Father,' said Tom at length, 'a message has come from the south. Mr Perry desires your presence.'

Fr Murphy breathed deeply, puffing out his barrel chest and squaring the loose set of his shoulders. Suddenly bluff and bullish once more, he replied, 'Then lead on, Mr Banville.'

Only the slight roughness that burred his voice betrayed the depth of his exhaustion.

On Gorey Hill a ring of the United leaders had formed about a lone horseman. Tom and Fr Murphy squeezed through the outer ring of captains and were greeted with handshakes from Anthony Perry and a dour-faced Miles Byrne.

'That appears to be everyone,' said Perry in his northern twang. 'On with you, so.'

The horseman, a young man with a long scab slashing across his right jaw, cleared his throat and read in a clear voice from a piece of paper held aloft in his left hand.

At a meeting of the general and several officers of the United Army of the county of Wexford, the following resolutions were agreed upon:

It is ordered that a guard shall be kept in the rear of the different armies, with orders to shoot all persons who shall shy or desert from any engagement; and that these orders shall be taken notice of by all officers commanding in such engagement. All men refusing to obey their superior officers, to be tried by court martial and punished according to their sentence.

It is also ordered that all men who shall attempt to leave their respective quarters when they have been halted by the commander-in-chief, shall suffer death, unless they shall have leave from their officers for so doing.

It is also resolved that any person or persons who shall take it upon them to kill or murder any person or prisoner, burn any house, or commit any plunder, without special written orders from the commander-in-chief, shall suffer death.

By order of: B. B. Harvey, Commander-in-Chief
Francis Breen, Sec. and Adj.
Head Quarters, Carrickbyrne Camp
June 6, 1798

Here the messenger stopped reading and gazed about him as the ring of rebel officers erupted in a cacophony of fury.

'Why in God's name should we protect people who have treated us like vermin?' cried one, and then other voices were added to the chorus.

'They flogged my brother to death!'

'They burned my farm to the ground!'

Anthony Perry reached up and snatched the paper from the astonished messenger's hand and a silence fell over the gathering as he shook it in one fist.

'What does Harvey mean by this?' he asked. 'Does he seek to hamstring us in our efforts?'

Before the horseman could answer, Tom stepped forward, his anxiety spurring him into action, and asked, 'What of New Ross?'

At Tom's words the man seemed to sag in his saddle and a sickening expression washed over his features.

Shaking his head slowly as if he could not believe his own words, the man answered, 'That scrap of paper is Mr Harvey's last command. He has resigned as commander-in-chief.'

At this a huge rippling sigh seemed to pass through the rebel leaders. Tom, however, was silent, every word the man spoke driving into him like a nail, crucifying him where he stood.

'New Ross is still in government hands. The Southern Division was thrown back with great loss. The Kilkenny men abandoned us.'

Into a deepening well of blank silence the man continued, 'There were massacres. The soldiers burnt a house in Mary Street where our wounded were being cared for. They all died. All of them.'

The outrage that this ignited in the men was quickly smothered by the man's next words.

'But that's not the worst of it. Some men fleeing the battle came across a Mr King's farm at Scullabogue. We were holding over a hundred loyalist men, women and children there. These men, they shot thirty people on the lawn and then locked everyone else into the barn.'

Beside him, Tom could hear Fr Murphy mutter, 'Oh, God no.'

The rider glanced about him for a moment, swallowed hard and said, 'They burned it down around their ears. Women and children, sirs, all dead in the ashes.'

Perry lifted one hand to a jaw hanging limp with shock. Licking suddenly-parched lips, he asked, 'What did Harvey do?'

The messenger nodded to the paper now rumpled and torn in Perry's bloodless hand, 'He issued that order and then resigned in dismay. He is most distressed, for I fear his constitution is not at all suited to circumstances such as these.'

Miles Byrne spat onto the ground in disgust, 'No one's constitution is suited to circumstances such as these. Who commands now? What of the Southern Division?'

The messenger nodded, 'General Roche has assumed command and he requests that Fr Philip Roche ride south with me and take specific charge of what's left of the Southern Division. The English are in total command of the countryside around New Ross and all efforts are to be directed towards stopping their advance on Wexford Town.'

A multitude of eyes then swept to Fr Philip Roche, whose tall frame towered over the men around him. Fr Roche's eyebrows rose in surprise but he nodded his head in reluctant acceptance.

Tom had felt a pressure swelling inside him, squeezing his lungs so that it seemed he must burst. As the gaze of the officers was directed on Fr Roche his own had remained locked upon the young rider before him. Stepping forward he seized the horse's bridle and glared fiercely at the startled man above him.

'What of Daniel Banville?' he asked. 'He is a captain. Does he live?'

The young messenger blanched at Tom's savage aspect but eventually stuttered, 'I am not familiar with the name, sir. A great many of the captains lost their lives at New Ross. They were cut down at the heads of their corps. I cannot say if your brother was amongst them or not.'

Tom nodded once, curtly, and his eyes fell to where his hand had clawed about the tack of the man's horse.

'I apologise,' he said.

He turned and moved through the circling officers.

Miles Byrne watched Tom with narrowed eyes before slipping after him. He left the officers, like battered scarecrows, gathered around the pale horseman and hurried in Tom's wake. Once clear of the hill and making his way down into Gorey proper, Byrne caught up with Tom and placed a hand upon his shoulder.

'Where are you going, Tom?' he asked.

Tom shambled to halt like a ship foundering in rough seas and blinked at him as if he were a stranger. Shaking his head like a man rousing from sleep, he found he could not say anything.

'Come sit down,' said Byrne.

He guided Tom to the splintered edge of the boardwalk and forced the stupefied captain to sit.

'Dan is lost, Miles,' his voice fell from his lips like something wounded.

Byrne knelt before him and gripped his shoulders and said, 'Tom, there is no guarantee that Dan is amongst the fallen at New Ross. A man of such valour and activity as your brother would surely have been noted had they managed to bring him low. Take heart, Dan. Edward Roche will instil a new eagerness for battle in our southern comrades. A better man in a time of crisis one could not hope to find.'

A red flash of anger sparked in Tom's eyes and he growled at Byrne, 'I have been duped by Dan and your good self on this matter before and I tell you again, I care not a whit for Roche or your "Liberty" or for your damnable green flag. The only thing I cared for has been robbed from me. Our home is destroyed. My parents are in exile. How am I to tell them that I allowed Dan to die alone in some pigswill street in New Ross? How am I to tell them I cannot even point to a grave over which they may grieve?

'No, Miles, you and Dan were both mistaken. The United Irishmen does not need captains like you and I. It needs leaders, real leaders, men who would not have sent my brother to his death.'

Byrne looked at him with troubled eyes, 'What are you to do?'

Still sitting, a great seething welter of anguish churning inside him, Tom felt the first tears for his lost brother trickle from his eyes. He raised a hand and dashed them away ashamedly. Byrne looked away.

'Do?' sniffed Tom. 'What can I do?'

The Northern Division of the United Irish Army marched through Gorey on the 9th of June with an air of confident joy scarcely dulled from the day before. Perry had ordered the advance on Arklow the previous evening and Bagenal Harvey's last command had ensured that all fighting men had reported promptly to their corps. In spite of New Ross, in spite of the massacres at Mary Street and the disgusting brutality of Scullabogue, in spite of the fact that the country had largely abandoned the Wexford Rising to its own fate – in spite of all this, the army was in high spirits. Were they not victorious? Were they not the masters of the entire north of the county and much of southwest Wicklow as well? Had they not met the English in open battle and sent them flying before their pikes? The setback at New Ross was, to most minds, merely that, a set-back; a thing easily remedied. Edward Roche would work his magic on the administration of Wexford Town and thousands of fine fellows would soon punish the garrison at New Ross for their temerity at seeking to thwart the will of the people. Meanwhile, Arklow would have fallen and the road to Dublin would be wide open.

The men marched as though to a victory celebration rather than a battle for their very existence. Only among the leaders was a terrible grimness apparent, an urgency and will to action that had not communicated itself to their men. The precarious position of the Rising weighed upon them. If they failed to take Arklow then they would be pinned within their own county, trapped like birds in lime.

Perry trotted his mount up and down the line of march, haranguing and lambasting, goading men to move more quickly. The men nodded and smiled and roared in greeting at his approach, then simply ignored him.

They passed out of Gorey and into the quilt of barley and grass that was the countryside beyond, the army stretching for two miles along the dusty road to Arklow. More than once, battalions crowded hard on each other's heels, forcing the entire column to come to a ragged halt while the captains and colonels strove to untangle the mess. Curses and harsh words rattled back and forth in the sweltering air.

The march to Arklow should have taken three hours; the awful realisation began to dawn on some of the leaders that it could take twice that.

At the head of the Castletown Corps, beneath Jim Kehoe's limp green banner, Tom Banville walked in numbness. He marched when the column marched. He stopped when it stopped. Yet nothing touched him.

During one idiotic halt he gazed in abstraction as Fr Murphy railed bitterly at Perry and Esmond Kyan, 'You are going to be defeated, it is too late in the day!'

Tom knew that Fr Murphy's words should have trilled some shudder of unease in him, yet it failed to penetrate, failed to get inside his bones and allow him to contemplate what was to come. For Tom, the march was never-ending now, an eternal moment in which he was trapped, past and future swallowed by loss. Each footstep pounded a word through his head, over and over.

Dan. Is. Dead.

After four hours of marching, the rebel army arrived at Coolgreaney, the last village before Arklow Town. The men were exhausted, and flung themselves down on any patch of open ground they could find. One enterprising group entered an abandoned pub and began raiding its stores for porter and whiskey. All about, men lounged with shirts unbuttoned, their heads tilted back as though all this were a simple Sunday stroll. Pikes were steepled together in skeletal bundles, forgotten as their owners laughed and talked and swilled mouthfuls of pilfered beer.

'Mr Banville?' came Jim Kehoe's insistent voice.

Tom had no idea how long the man had been calling his name but his words carried the firm edge of someone annoyed at being ignored. 'Yes, Jim?' he answered.

'May we fall out, sir?'

Tom shrugged dispassionately. Behind him, grumbling darkly, his corps fanned out and sat themselves down on the grass and earth.

It was then that something finally pierced his bubble of introspection. Halfway down the rutted tract of dirt that formed Coolgreaney's only street, Fr John Murphy and the thirty men who had remained with him since that fateful night at The Harrow, stood and faced Perry and Fr Michael Murphy. The entire scene had an air of confrontation about it that stirred something within Tom. Fr Michael stood with arms crossed while Perry was half-turned and gesturing for Fr John to come with him inside the ransacked public house. Fr John, however, remained rooted to the spot and his men crowded around him, protective and anxious.

Tom walked slowly towards the peculiar gathering, skirting Fr John's men as surreptitiously as he could.

'I will have no part in it,' Fr John was saying. 'I made my feelings clear last night and against my better judgement my men and I have followed where you have led. My conscience though will not allow me to throw their lives away for no good reason.'

'For God's sake man, keep your voice down,' hissed Perry. 'If you insist on arguing in the street then let you at least have some consideration for the morale of those men you abandon.'

Fr John scowled at this, rasping witheringly, 'How dare you! Where were you the night of The Harrow? Tell me that!'

Perry blanched at these words and Fr Michael blessed himself theatrically, snapping, 'God forgive you, Father!'

Fr John continued, 'I abandon no man but I shall not watch while you sacrifice hundreds of lives to bloodlust. We should be making for the mountains, not flinging ourselves on barricades. Arklow will be another New Ross, mark my words.'

Perry's expression filled with a thunder-cloud darkness and he exclaimed, 'You are an insufferable, stubborn man, Father! But if you insist on following this course of action then you are most welcome to join us on the road to Dublin after our victory.'

For his part, Fr John smiled grimly, stating, 'And you are welcome to join me at Castletown, if you survive battering your brains out against the barricades of Arklow.'

With that, he and his men turned and made off through the scattered clumps of lounging rebels, heading south for Castletown. Troubled stares followed them as they went and cries of 'Where do you go, Father?' were ignored by Fr John and his column. Sitting astride his mare like a Roman general, he stared at the road ahead, his features impassive, his carriage proud.

Hesitating for only a moment, Tom Banville ran to where his Castletown Corps were spread out like a pride of lions basking in the heat. For the first time since the news came from the south, his limbs were invested with something like their old energy. The strange fog that had clouded his thoughts was lifted and the tortuous path forward that he had envisaged was now laid out before him with childish simplicity.

He skidded to a halt before his men, who regarded him with a sort of amused curiosity, and blurted, 'Lads, I won't ask you to go to Arklow if you do not want.'

The men before him began to mutter and exchange uneasy glances. At length, Jim Kehoe asked, 'Why wouldn't we want to go?'

Tom felt his temper rise but forced himself to remain calm, 'Because if you lose at Arklow, you will be trapped. New Ross is garrisoned, as is Newtownbarry. Should Arklow hold against us we are surrounded. Arklow is not our fight. I will not order you to go where I will not.'

At this another man, a man whom Dan had told him was named Forde or Foyle or something along those lines, said, 'You are not going, Mr Banville?'

Tom shook his head, 'I am not. This is not my cause. I have lost my brother in one futile battle. I am reluctant to sacrifice either myself or my men in similar fashion. The course on which we are set is doomed.'

'Mr Banville,' the reproach in Jim Kehoe's voice was like an anvil, 'Dan, God be good to him, will be spinning in his grave to hear you say such things. We are United Irishmen, every one of us. We cannot leave off now when success is so close.'

Tom nodded slowly, his heart heavy, 'So you are all resolved to continue with Perry's assault on Arklow?'

Every one of the Casteltown Corps, now all sitting up, their eyes as intent as hunting hounds', nodded mutely.

Tom sighed, 'So be it. Should you carry the day at Arklow then I do not think I shall join you at Dublin. Take Arklow and the country is yours. If you are defeated then you shall find me with Fr Murphy at Castletown or at the camp on Gorey Hill. Today you follow Miles Byrne as though he were Moses himself. He is the best we have left. I wish you well, lads.'

Saying nothing, the men he had led against Walpole at Tubberneering, the men who spilled blood for him and who adored his brother, watched as Tom Banville walked away from them. For his part, Tom felt a vast sadness enfold him. They were Dan's men, he knew that deep down. They followed him because he was Dan's brother. He had never taken the United Oath, he had never invested himself in the illusion of liberty with the same conviction as Dan or Miles. He had never truly belonged. Without Dan he was a stray dog, battered and homeless.

He found himself hoping fervently that the men of Castletown might some-how survive the coming battle, that their bravery might be rewarded with glory rather than grape shot. He hoped Perry and Fr Michael were right. He hoped that by tomorrow morning both he and Fr John would be confirmed as the cowardly fools that some must certainly think them. He hoped all this and yet he knew the desperation of their situation. He knew they were alone in their struggle. And he knew that the Crown would be waiting for them at Arklow.

His dearest wish as he left Coolgreaney behind was that he might have time to find Dan's body before a red-coated soldier tightened the noose about his own neck.

At Castletown the sounds of the battle in Arklow were like the muffled thundering of waves against distant cliffs. For an hour the unabated din echoed across the countryside. For an hour Tom and Fr Murphy stood facing northwards in Castletown's deserted street. Only the clash of steel on steel was inaudible, that and the wet tearing of flesh, the sobbing screams of the dying.

At eight o'clock the brittle, autumn-leaf crackle of musketry died to a graveyard silence. An unbroken hush draped itself across the land. Over field and hedgerow, ditch and gorse, not even the singing of birds fractured the calm.

Then the first of the survivors came. Ragged and wounded, a tattered scarecrow of dirt and gore, he shambled down the road leading in from the north. His face was a devil's mask of black powder burns and his shirt was slit along one red-sodden sleeve where a cavalry sabre had slashed him. He carried no weapon, only the weight of defeat and the horrors of what he had witnessed.

Tom and Fr Murphy approached the man who stumbled towards them in a daze.

Seizing Fr Murphy by the lapels, the ragged refugee babbled, 'They're killing the wounded. Their cannon cut us down like wheat. Fr Michael is killed. My God, Father, what are we to do?'

Fr Murphy exchanged a glance with Tom before calmly asking the man, 'How did Fr Michael die? What happened?'

The man shook his head as though befuddled and answered, 'He was blown from his horse and fell close to a burning cabin.'

His face when grey as he continued, 'The Ancient Britons, they stopped and used his fat to grease their boots.'

Fr John's face became hard, as though chiselled from unyielding rock. 'Go on,' he said.

The man breathed deeply, his senses slowly returning now that he was safely away from Arklow, 'We flung ourselves against their barricades and they were breaking, by God they were breaking. You could see them running across the bridge and up the Dublin Road. Byrne and his Monaseed boys were masters of the right flank but we were being tumbled in twenties by grape shot and muskets. And then we started to retreat and they set their cavalry on us. There was butchery in the fields. Forgive us Father but we had to leave the wounded behind. We left them to be shot like dogs.'

The man was close to tears now but Fr Murphy pressed on, 'Who gave the order to retreat?'

The man shook his head, tears streaking through the black that caked his face, 'I don't know, Father. Everyone and no one.'

Fr Murphy stepped away from the man and turned to Tom, saying, 'This day spells our doom, Mr Banville.'

Tom felt a cold vice grip his heart at these words and he asked, 'What should we do, Father?'

Fr Murphy looked at him levelly, 'We do what we can, Mr Banville.'

Tom let out a long, shuddering breath. He lifted his eyes to a sky slowly filling with the amber wash of the falling sun and thought of the collapse of his world. He thought of the fields around Arklow, strewn with the dead and dying. He thought of the alleys and laneways of New Ross, stinking charnel houses in the heat. He thought of the barbed ring that was suddenly thrown around his county, cutting them off and sealing them in. But most of all he thought of his dead brother, rolled into a pit, unnamed and unremembered. He thought of all this, closed his eyes and strangled the racking sobs that threatened to shudder from him.

CHAPTER 22

Evil Ascendant

Mrs Abigail Brownrigg sat in her drawing room with all the poise and haughtiness of a mother cat. She sat on the edge of her familiar, high-backed armchair and balanced a cup and saucer in her right hand. Every angle of her bearing was stiff and the wrinkles about her mouth were gouged even more deeply than usual. She would not be swayed.

In front of her, Elizabeth Blakely stood, arms akimbo, and said, 'I am going up and you cannot stop me, Auntie.'

Mrs Brownrigg's left eyebrow arched in surprise, 'I should mind my words a little more carefully, child. This is my house and if I desire you locked in the pantry for the afternoon, then so shall it be. The fact of the matter is I do not wish you to intrude in that room and that is the end of this debate.'

Elizabeth would not be put off, however, and she frowned sullenly.

'Don't pout, girl,' snapped her aunt. 'It makes you look like you are concentrating. Deep thoughts are fundamentally unattractive in a lady.'

Elizabeth's eyes narrowed and she retorted, 'You may be my aunt, but the devil himself could not keep me from that room.'

Mrs Brownrigg raised her teacup to her puckered lips and delicately sipped from it. She placed the cup back onto its saucer and smiled.

'Nonsense,' she purred. 'Why must you be so melodramatic? Your presence in that room would be positively indecent.'

Beneath the whip of her aunt's scorn, Elizabeth felt herself redden. An itching tide of heat climbed up from the hollows of her collar bones and seeped in an ever-rising wash of colour beneath her chin. Behind her eyes, her mind burned with incandescent anger.

Elizabeth spat, 'This may be your house, you old crone, but I'll be damned

373

if I allow you to keep me away as though I were some foolish girl or a bould child!' And with that she whirled from the room.

Mrs Brownrigg took another sip from her teacup and said into the empty air, 'It appears as though the girl has some backbone after all.'

Out of hearing and with the gushing thunder of blood in her ears, Elizabeth Blakely mounted the wooden steps leading to the upper floors of her aunt's gloomy townhouse. At the turn of the landing a large grandfather clock, the twin of the one in the drawing room, loomed like a grim sentinel. The slow swing of its pendulum, so graceful and unremitting, seemed to mock her erratic, ragged breaths.

She stormed up the last few steps and turned left down the corridor. At its end a dark, varnished door led to a box room. Elizabeth paused here for a moment and smoothed the front of her dress taking a long, deep breath. Then, quietly, she opened the door and slipped inside.

The room was illuminated by a single small gothic window that looked out onto the gardens at the rear of the house. A stillness lay upon the room, a tranquillity that seemed to cocoon this place away from the hellish parade of the macabre that Wexford, day by day, was becoming.

In one corner a narrow bed was placed and on it lay a man's body. The right side of the man's head was wrapped in a red-smeared bandage and a similar one, though less stained, was wound about his left shoulder. The man lay quite still, and his skin was damp and pale. Only the tremulous fluttering of his closed eyelids gave any hint that life still resided in him. On the floor beside the bed was a basin of pinkish water, droplets beading the naked wood of the floorboards. Beside it a bowl of half-eaten soup slowly congealed in the summer heat.

Elizabeth approached softly and stood looking down on the wounded man and in that instant he opened his eyes.

For the briefest of moments a smile played across the man's lips and his pallor seemed to lift somewhat. Then a sudden realisation appeared to seize him, snapping his grey eyes into a panic and sending spasms through his muscles.

'Elizabeth,' whispered Dan feebly. 'Why are you in New Ross?'

Then, as though the effort of these few words had sapped him of what strength he had, his voice died away and his eyes began to slide shut once more. For long minutes Elizabeth sat on the edge of the bed and gazed at him with helpless angst.

At last, Dan's mouth opened and, though his eyes remained closed, there was a familiar timbre to his voice. For the first time in days there was a lucidity about him, a hint of awareness.

Hoarsely, he asked, 'Where am I? What of New Ross?'

Elizabeth smiled and lifted her hands to wipe away the tears that sluiced down her cheeks. Shakily, she replied, 'You are at my aunt's house in Wexford, my darling. You are safe. Do not concern yourself with New Ross.'

Dan's eyelids pulsed and opened, his gaze seeking her face and finding it floating only feet away from him. Sighing almost in contentment he whispered, 'You are so beautiful.'

Grinning now and still trying to stem the flow of tears, she chided, 'Flattery is a despicable way to induce me into troubling you with news, Mr Banville.'

Dan smiled back at her, moment by moment feeling strength growing in his limbs, 'You know me too well, Elizabeth. How long have I been here? Tell me that at least.'

Elizabeth frowned then and sniffed away the last of her crying before saying, 'This is the 11th of June. You have been here four days. All the while drifting in and out of fever.'

Dan blinked in astonishment and made to sit up before being prevented by Elizabeth's hand placed gently on his chest. Her joy at seeing him move in so determined a fashion was tempered by the knowledge that energy enough to sit up would surely be followed by energy enough to heft sword and pistol. Since they had brought him here, bloodied and feverish on the back of a broken door, he had seemed nothing but a shell, a mewling, boneless thing, squirming in the grip of infection.

Dan swallowed and lifted his right hand to touch first his wounded shoulder, then the side of his head and finally gripped her hand in his. 'Four days? What happened to me? How goes the Rising? Is Munster risen?'

Elizabeth's frown deepened and she shook her head. 'I will have no more of Risings in this house. You were wounded and brought here. That is all you should know. You need to convalesce, not go dashing off again.'

Dan nodded and eased himself down onto his pillows.

Elizabeth smiled then and rose to her feet, saying, 'I shall have Molly prepare you some more soup. You have eaten next to nothing over the last few days.'

Dan's stomach rumbled at the very mention of food and he said, 'That would be nice. Thank your aunt for me. She had no reason to shelter a croppy under her roof.'

To Dan a fleeting darkness seemed to pass across Elizabeth's face before she answered, 'She had very many reasons, my love.'

Dan waited until Elizabeth had left the room, listening as her footsteps receded down the corridor and padded down the stairs. Then, wincing with the pain in his shoulder and with his head filled with silent, throbbing thunder, he swung his legs out of the bed. He was weak, his muscles quivered with every motion, but the dull ache of broken bones was absent from his wounds. His scalp had been lacerated to the skull, of that he was sure, and his damaged shoulder was in agony. He lifted his left arm carefully and found that, apart from the darts of pain that screamed out from the wound, he could move his arm quite freely. Flesh wounds, he thought. And still he could not recall how he had come to receive them.

Like a tottering foal he got to his feet and was startled to find that he was naked. For a moment he wondered who had undressed him and tended to his wounds. Surely not Mrs Brownrigg? Feeling ridiculous and embarrassed, he wrapped a sheet about his waist and made his way, one slow step after another, to the door leading onto the landing. It creaked softly as he opened it but the corridor outside was deserted. A high window at the end of the corridor gave onto the street below.

Grimly, moving like an old man, Dan made for this window and undid the latch. Leaning out over the street, he watched people go by, willing for someone he knew or who was obviously a United Irishman to pass.

After five agonising minutes, a young man approached from the direction of the Cornmarket. He held a pike in his left hand but his right arm was cradled in a dirty grey sling. Dan thought he recognised him from the day spent camped at The Three Rocks, a day that now seemed like months ago.

As the lad drew closer, Dan called, 'Here, chap! Up here!'

Dan was appalled at the dead-leaf rasp that his voice had become and was not surprised that the young pikeman did not hear him as he continued obliviously up the street. Desperately, Dan tried again, 'Up here, boy!'

This time the youthful rebel paused and looked up, frowning. When he saw Dan, a half-naked man, swaddled in bloodied bandages, waving at him from an upstairs window, he took a startled step backward.

'Do you know me, boy?' called Dan from his lofty position.

The lad blinked before replying, 'If it wasn't for the bandages I'd say you were Captain Banville. But, sure, everyone knows you were kilt in New Ross.' He swung his right arm in its sling, 'Sure, I was nearly kilt meself. You're looking well for a dead man, sir.'

Dan nodded bleakly, 'You can tell everyone that I am very much alive. Now, listen. Go find Thomas Cloney or one of the other captains. Tell them to come here and ask for me as a matter of urgency.'

The young insurgent raised his eyebrows and said, 'I could get Captain Dixon for you. He'd be better than one of them Protestant ones, anyway.'

'Not Dixon,' snapped Dan, and in those two words all of his old baritone authority came flooding back. 'Not Dixon. Anyone else but him.'

Shrugging, the young man said, 'Yes, Captain,' and hurried off down the street.

Dan closed the window and shambled back to his room, feeling an unaccountable wave of fatigue wash over him as he did so. Now, he thought, if only I could find some clothes.

Some hours later, Dan was stirred out of a doze by the sound of voices floating up from downstairs. The taste of the soup Elizabeth had brought and spoon-fed to him still remained, savoury and delicious in his mouth.

He sat up as the voices resolved themselves and became clearer. One was Elizabeth, the other seemed to be the silken tenor of Thomas Cloney.

'You will not, sir!' Elizabeth's voice was raised to just below a shout.

Cloney replied in emollient tones, 'My dear Ms Blakely. If Dan wishes to see me, then I must insist that I am allowed to. He is a fellow officer in the United Irish Army and I am duty-bound to see to his needs.'

'Mr Cloney,' snapped Elizabeth, 'Daniel is wounded and convalescing. The very last thing he should experience is agitation and excitement. He should rest without disturbance or news of calamities.'

Cloney replied now with a hint of iron in his words, 'Madam, I am aware of the wounds your Daniel has suffered. It was I who had him taken out of the bloody streets of New Ross and removed to your presence, where I thought his chances of recuperation might be increased. He spoke of you often.'

There was a pause then, broken at last as Elizabeth said more calmly, 'If it was you who rescued him, then I owe you a debt that I shall find impossible to repay. If you wish to see Daniel, then you may, so long as you give me your solemn word that you shall not upset him.'

Louder now, as though already on the stairs, Cloney replied, 'I shall do my best, Ms Blakely.'

Seconds later, Thomas Cloney knocked softly on the wood of Dan's bedroom door and quietly pushed it open. He beamed as he saw Dan sitting up and grinning back at him.

'Dan!' he exclaimed and crossed the room in three quick strides, plonking himself down on the side of Dan's bed as though it were a favourite armchair.

'Thomas,' greeted Dan, 'I am glad to see you. Maybe you can tell me something of substance without resorting to treating me like a child.'

Cloney shook his head good-humouredly, 'Ms Blakley wants only to see you well. You are a lucky man, Mr Banville.'

He glanced at the bandages wrapped around Dan's head and shoulder and added, 'A *very* lucky man.'

Nodding, Dan replied, 'How did I come by these, Thomas? There is a hole in my memory.'

Cloney sighed and pointed to Dan's wounds in turn, saying, 'Grape shot. You had come to tell me of John Kelly's wounds and stepped out in front of a nine-pounder. Fortunately for you the majority of the blast was absorbed by my luckless Bantry men. You had your head split and hole bored in your shoulder but the injuries themselves were not that severe. Fever was your greatest enemy.'

Dan frowned then, 'What of John Kelly?'

Cloney shook his head sadly, 'He lives. He was brought to his sister's house here in town but his leg is badly mangled. The sawbones want to chop it off but of course he's having none of it. He has a bullet lodged in the bone.'

'And what of the battle?' asked Dan. 'Did we take the town?'

Cloney paused for a moment and a heavy silence fell down around them before at last he said, 'We are straying onto ground that I promised Ms Blakely I would not cross.'

Dan was leaning forward now, his shoulder protesting, and he seized Cloney by the lapel of his green jacket. 'I have spilled enough blood for the cause of Ireland to be able to stomach some bad news, Thomas,' he said. 'Now out with it, for your expression and your reluctance have already told me half the truth.'

Cloney flung a surreptitious glance toward the closed bedroom door before continuing in a soft rush of words, his voice pitched low, 'We had the town won and the garrison was in retreat across the Barrow where the Kilkenny men were to surprise them. No ambuscade was set however and they rallied and flooded back into the town. Our men were exhausted and sick with fighting and could not hold them back. We left behind us three thousand dead and wounded.'

He shook his head morosely, 'We had no answer to their cannon. They turned the streets into a butcher's window.'

Dan felt a horrible sensation creep over him. Rasping, he asked, 'What of the army now? What of my men? Who leads them?'

Cloney looked uncomfortable as he leaned forward, supporting his forearms on his thighs, 'Most of it has dispersed. Some back here to Wexford Town. Some have simply gone home. We still have a substantial force in the field on Lacken Hill, enough to threaten the garrison if they decide to come out. Seán

Rouse led your corps out of New Ross. They are in good order. You trained them well, Dan.'

Dan grinned wanly but then frowned as Cloney turned and sighed hollowly before continuing, 'I returned here this very morning from a raid on the village of Borris. We had entertained some hope of capturing arms there, but the soldiery and yeos have invented a new and cowardly stratagem. They will not give us open battle. They fly before our pikes and make strong points from slated houses. Without heavy cannon, we cannot dislodge them.'

Dan's expression was souring by the moment and he asked, 'What of the Northern Division? They have surely taken Arklow. What of my brother?'

At this Cloney looked stricken and Dan whispered, 'Good God Almighty, Thomas. What has happened?'

Cloney, his eyes on the floorboards and his voice cracking, explained, 'Arklow is held by the Crown. The Northern Division was thrown back. Their losses, though, were not as great as ours and they are still in the field in some numbers. But I fear it is only a matter of time before they are forced to retreat to Vinegar Hill.'

'And Tom?' asked Dan leadenly.

'There I have good news,' he said. 'Some of the Enniscorthy lads with me at Borris listed the officers that were now prominent in the north of the county. Your brother's name was amongst them.'

Dan sighed with relief, 'That is indeed good news. What do the English do now?'

'They sit behind their fortifications and gather their strength,' growled Cloney. 'They refuse to come out and fight us and we cannot drive them from their redoubts. Until they are in sufficient strength to destroy us utterly they have simply set a ring of bayonets around the county, biding their time. Unless the French arrive soon we cannot hope to hold out for much longer.'

Dan was nodding solemnly and said, 'Mr Harvey will see that something is done. He has surely learned the lessons of New Ross.'

Cloney coughed in discomfiture and, rising to his feet, he crossed the little room and stood with his back to Dan, one arm braced against the pointed apex of the window frame, his gaze directed out onto the gardens beyond. He was silent for a moment and then spoke rapidly, 'Mr Harvey has resigned as commander-in-chief. General Roche has taken overall command.'

Dan was perplexed, 'Surely this is good news, Thomas? General Roche is a very able commander and some might consider him more able for our current situation.'

Still with his back to Dan, Cloney answered, 'It is the circumstances in which Mr Harvey resigned that are so very hard to relate, Dan. There was . . . unpleasantness . . . in the aftermath of Ross. The soldiers butchered our wounded and, whether in reprisal or out of some native spite, some of our men at Scullabogue burned a barn full of a hundred Protestants to the ground. Men, women and children. Mr Harvey seemed broken by it.'

Dan's face grew deathly pale. Struggling for composure he stammered, 'But how? Surely there must be some mistake, some exaggeration by our enemies?'

Cloney's head shook once and he said, 'I saw it myself. I saw the men shot to death on the grass. I saw the black remains of the barn. I saw the charred corpses still standing upright, they were so tightly packed in.

'Worse is that it is all Mr Keogh and Mr Roche can do to stop the same thing happening here. Dixon is rabble-rousing like a prophet from a mount and people are openly going about speaking of how all will be fine now that a Catholic is in charge. The boys up in Enniscorthy have been slaughtering loyalists like cattle ever since the town was taken and Dixon's followers want the same thing here. They heard what the soldiers did at Ross and they think Scullabogue is something worth emulating. There is a growing panic, Dan.'

Dan's mind contorted like something tangled in a snare. It horrified him that while he lay, supine and useless, his county had turned on its head. In a few brief days the Rising had become a foetid mess of atrocity and barbarity. Victory had been theirs for the taking and now it seemed to be slipping, day by day, from their blood-slickened grasp. Here in the warm chamber of this room, comforted by Elizabeth's ministrations, it was appalling to think that beyond these plastered walls Wexford was becoming a witch's cauldron. His world had become suddenly filled with gore and despair, as pathetic as the bowl of red-tinted water that cleaned his wounds.

Frowning, Dan replied, 'If you find me some clothes, my sword and my pistol, I shall lend my good arm wherever it is needed.'

Turning on his heel, Cloney came forward and placed his hand on Dan's good shoulder. He smiled warmly at the injured captain and said, 'I will not lie to you, Dan. To have you back, either in the field or to keep peace within the town, is something that I dearly wish for. But you are of no use to anyone for a day or so more. Listen to Ms Blakely.'

Cloney continued, 'I must be away now, for I fear that I have put too much of a strain upon you too soon. You look as white as those sheets you lie on. I am off to Lacken Hill. When you feel properly able, and only when you feel properly able, you will find me there.'

'See you soon, Thomas,' said Dan wearily, suddenly aware of a blanket of tiredness settling around him. 'Thank you for the news. Have heart. We are not defeated yet.'

Thomas Cloney watched Dan Banville slip into slumber as he finished speaking. Smiling wryly, he left the room and closed the door gently behind him.

The next two days passed for Dan in a blur of sleep and soup and dressing changes. Elizabeth had assumed the role of nurse and through her gentle touch and careful hand he felt vitality returning minute by minute. His strength grew exponentially and on the evening of the second day, as Elizabeth unwound the white gauze from around his head, he said, 'I believe we should go for a stroll tomorrow. I feel quite better.'

Elizabeth regarded him critically and then leaned to the left to inspect the wound that had gouged a furrow along the side of his head. It was healing nicely, scabbed over already, his hair, growing again after so long, falling so that it was hardly visible.

She pursed her lips and frowned, replying, 'Your head does not need a bandage any longer, my love, but I fear your shoulder is still too open to go traipsing about the town.'

Dan lifted his left arm and flapped it like a wounded bird. 'Look,' he said. 'It is fine. I will not pretend it gives me no pain but the shot went straight through the flesh. The best thing for me is to get some exercise.'

'We shall see,' was all she said.

To his surprise, early the next morning Elizabeth arrived in his room with a bundle of clothes folded over one arm. She dumped them unceremoniously onto his bed and stated, 'If you wish to go for a walk, you will need to make yourself decent.'

Dan's broad face broke out in a grin and he said with roguish impudence, 'You become more like your goodly aunt every day.'

She arched her eyebrow at him and flounced from the room.

Dan dressed himself as best he could, his shoulder screaming in protest as he slipped his shirt over his head. Eventually he stood and looked down at himself. Shoes, stockings, breeches, shirt and coat, all were exactly as they should be; no mean feat for a man who had been shot by a cannon only six days before.

He walked to the door with a steadiness that surprised even himself and opened it to find Elizabeth waiting for him, her eyes bright and a smile fluttering at the edges of her mouth. Seeing her there, with her hair pinned in a bun at the nape of her neck and her sun-bonnet predictably askew, he felt a surge of warmth in his chest.

'I love you, Elizabeth Blakely,' the words were out of Dan's mouth before he even new they were there.

She blinked at him, surprised by the sudden expression of affection, then linked his arm and kissed him on the cheek, 'And I love you.'

The sun glowed beatifically in the high blue of the sky with only a few sea-tossed clouds to contend with. A cooling breeze, seemingly the one constant in Wexford Town, slipped across the waves of the harbour and slunk along the alleys and laneways leading up from the quays. All about the town, hanging flags and bunting still cast everything in shades of emerald. The green boughs that had been lashed to shop fronts and railings had, however, turned to brittle brown shreds in the heat. Now, as Dan and Elizabeth strolled past, they shed their leaves in rattling drifts, their heads bowed, their once-vital branches become mere kindling.

At every step through the streets of Wexford Town, Dan felt his strength grow and his legs become more confident. Gone was the palsy that he had felt trembling in his muscles only two days before. Apart from the fact that he carried his left arm curled into his side, there was nothing to suggest that he was in anything but perfect health.

They walked down Main Street, its shops and merchants' premises all closed but their places taken instead by carts and wagons, peasants and farmers selling wares. Women queued in chattering lines of muslin and linen, waiting their turn. Even in the midst of war, families needed to be fed. As they walked, Elizabeth noted that the only men they encountered were those too old or too young to carry a pike or gun; too old or too young or too hurt. Here and there, clustered in small hobbling groups, wounded men leaned on crutches or compared blood-crusted bandages that swathed arms and heads. Unconsciously, Elizabeth gripped Dan's arm even tighter. Leaving Main Street behind, they turned right onto the quays, the sea air in their noses.

There on the quays, a mob of people had gathered around a young man who sat, stunned, on the ground, his nose bleeding and an expression of distilled horror paling his face. Another man stood over him, facing the crowd with a scrap of fabric clenched in his right fist. The fabric was orange.

This second man, a short fellow with the blistered face of a blacksmith or tanner, held the orange cloth aloft with a triumphal screech and shook it as though it were a military banner.

'Look at this!' he was yelling, whirling about as he did so. 'This was torn from the inside of this blackguard's coat. Look at it! Orange, orange, orange! What good patriot would suffer himself to wear orange?'

The crowd roared their approval as he swung a kick at the young man at his feet.

'Off to the gaol with him, lads!' the man ordered, and fifty pairs of grasping hands hoisted the unfortunate, bleeding wretch to his feet and began to drag him down the street.

Elizabeth's grip coiling about his right forearm was the only thing preventing Dan from springing forward to the young man's aid.

'God almighty, Elizabeth,' he argued. 'We can't just stand here and allow a man to be carted off to gaol simply because the lining of his jacket happened to be orange. This is madness!'

Elizabeth looked up at him, 'It would be madness to intervene – you can barely move your arm!'

Dan watched the mob disappear around a corner and growled, 'I shall have words with Roche about this.'

As he climbed into bed that night, a heavy weariness stealing over him, he thought that Bagenal Harvey and Matthew Keogh had much to answer for allowing the district to descend into such chaos. He would go to Roche first thing and ask for the immediate arrest of that scoundrel Thomas Dixon; then he would ask for permission to travel north with Elizabeth. All day, a cold worm of trepidation had fattened itself in his brain and now sat swollen and unspeakable, deep in his skull. Scullabogue, the lust for revenge, the petty cruelty of the people, all this meant that Wexford Town was no place for Elizabeth. The longer they remained, the closer they were to something awful.

Edward Roche was away at Vinegar Hill when Dan called on him the next day. The British had flung their cordon ever more tightly around the county and the need to find a defensible position was occupying the mind of the commander-in-chief. The plan to hold the advance of the government forces until the French arrived was consuming Roche and he spent every minute of the day poring over maps and charts and sending messengers out to Fr Roche to the west and Anthony Perry to the north. And still the government columns merely sat and waited, swelling their forces in anticipation of General Lake's order to advance. No matter what the rebel leaders did, the garrisons around the county held their positions, stubbornly refusing to come into the field.

With Roche gone, Bagenal Harvey was next on Dan's list. His rapping on the former aristocrat's door was answered by a footman who informed the exasperated captain that Mr Harvey had retired to his bed for the afternoon. As for Matthew Keogh, he was nowhere to be found.

Dan went home that evening to a genteel dinner with Elizabeth and her aunt, his shoulder burning and a string of curses wheeling through his mind.

The next day, the 14th of June, was not so uneventful.

Dan and Elizabeth walked arm in arm through the Cornmarket. Dan's health was returning at an astounding rate, in direct contrast to his falling spirits. Matthew Keogh, the town's notional governor, seemed to have taken a leave of absence, while Roche had taken up almost permanent residence on Vinegar Hill, striving to simultaneously coordinate the movements of both rebel armies. Into this gap in authority Thomas Dixon and his followers were pouring a stream of bilious invective. Houses of Protestant citizens which had remained untouched throughout the Rising were now being ransacked at the least pretence. Whole streets were now composed of defiled homes, windows broken and their doors hanging from their hinges like torn limbs. Dixon's mob had turned more than a few into public latrines and the stink of human faeces now crawled from out the once-perfumed boudoirs of fashionable ladies, long fled. The town's gaol was packed to bursting.

Worse still were the continuing deaths on Vinegar Hill. The cry of blood for blood could not be silenced.

Dan had resolved to see if John Kelly was in any way close to recovery. To his mind the United movement was wavering, rudderless and alone and surrounded by enemies. In such circumstances, men of John Kelly's character would be needed more than ever.

As they turned down the short ramp of street connecting the Cornmarket with the Bullring, a commotion caught Dan's attention. Outside The Cape of Good Hope, a pub of deserved renown, an altercation suddenly flared between two opposing groups of rebels. Civilian townsfolk drifted anxiously away from the scene, women hurrying in a swish of skirts, hands clamping straw hats to their heads, men striding quickly with fearful backward glances.

A dozen Wexford Town insurgents, identifiable by their see-sawing accents, were facing a hard-bitten band of Enniscorthy men, their own voices accented more sharply than those of their southern comrades. Between both groups a terrified and bleating handful of shackled prisoners were the subject of pointed words and shaken fists.

Inevitably, Thomas Dixon and his wife were standing close by. Dixon's face was creased in a weasel-like sneer and his arm was draped casually around his wife's bulbous waist. As the townsfolk slipped away, a trickle of Dixon's men began to converge on the Bullring like vultures flocking to a carcass.

'Let us go around them,' Elizabeth whispered, tugging at Dan's sleeve.

Dan frowned down at her and replied, 'No, let us wait. This may be revealing.'

One of the Wexford Town rebels was pointing a quivering finger at the leader of the Enniscorthy men, saying, 'You know full well that Matthew Keogh wants these prisoners lodged in the gaol. You aren't taking them back with you now.'

The Enniscorthy man, a twig-thin figure with eyes like bullet holes and a mouth like a wound, snarled back, 'And you know Luke Byrne has tried these men already. They're to be done to death and that's it. Keogh can go be fecked.'

The prisoners, four men all deep into middle age, quailed at the Enniscorthy man's words.

Around Dixon there had now gathered a good-sized group of pikemen, well-armed and looking on with expressions of cruel mockery.

'Let the Orangemen go back to Vinegar Hill,' Dixon interjected loudly. His nasal whine cutting through the air made both sets of rebels look towards him.

His wife's great, yielding face split into a grin, her teeth standing crookedly in her gums.

'Let the Orangemen go to hell,' she cackled and around her Dixon's followers laughed uproariously.

The insurgent contingent loyal to Matthew Keogh looked about them in the sudden realisation that they were outnumbered. The four chained prisoners seemed shocked, their faces draining of colour and their eyes staring like frightened animals.

Dan was moving before Elizabeth could stop him, tearing himself free of her grasp and heedless of her stricken expression.

'Daniel, don't!' she hissed, but he ignored her and marched down the slope to stand between Dixon and the prisoners.

'Good day to you, Captain Dixon,' said Dan, almost pleasantly.

'Not dead, after all, Banville?' replied Dixon.

Dan smiled at him and said, 'Why do you want to send these prisoners back to Vinegar Hill, Mr Dixon? Luke Byrne will have them killed on the spot. Mr

Keogh wants them to be locked away in the gaol and Mr Keogh is still governor of this town, is he not?'

Dixon hawked up a mouthful of phlegm from deep in his narrow chest and spat with relish into the dust, 'Keogh is a puppet. A Protestant puppet. Why should we feed and mollycoddle the enemies of the people?'

Dan's smile grew chill and, as Elizabeth watched, the set of his shoulders stiffened and his weight shifted to the balls of his feet.

'"Enemies of the people"?' scoffed Dan, eyes ablaze. 'I'll "enemies of the people" you, Dixon. Where were you at New Ross? When have you even crossed swords with the enemies of the people? You rant and you rave and you terrify the helpless but you remained safe here in Wexford when the real fighting had to be done. Some Protestants may be bad neighbours, Mr Dixon, but you are a bully.'

Dixon's men bridled at Dan's words, but the few townsfolk who had remained to gawk were now turning and walking away, and from Keogh's loyal guards there came no sign of support for Dan. They stood with eyes downcast, embarrassed by their own inaction but too afraid to become involved. Dan was alone, Elizabeth realised with horror, alone and wounded.

Dixon was livid and he spat, 'You are a fool, Mr Banville and a lackey of Harvey and his kind. They who have led us to the very brink of disaster. If you were at New Ross then you know the soldiers massacred our wounded. No prisoners were taken. Men were shot where they lay. And you want us to let Harvey and Keogh protect the butchers who have bled this sorry country dry for so long? Your kind makes me sick.'

From the crowd gathered around Dixon a murmur of acclamation arose and from behind Dan one of the Enniscorthy men quipped, 'Maybe we should pike this fellow too.'

The prisoners merely whimpered, their lives like a ball of rags being kicked about between two opposing goals. Keogh's men still said nothing.

Dixon's wife then spoke, the words sleeting from between her clenched teeth, 'You're some man, Mr Banville. A Protestant lover and a busybody. You stopped us piking Turner but you won't stop us now.'

Dixon nodded and smiled cheerily, 'Things are changing, Mr Banville. You won't find anyone who lost friends and relations in the streets of New Ross so eager to protect Orangemen anymore. Things are changing. Roche is organising his brave last stand. Harvey has lost his nerve and Keogh is toothless. My time has come. Me and men like me. Those prisoners are going back to Enniscorthy and there they will die.'

Dan ground his teeth, the knowledge of his defeat bitter in his stomach. Wordlessly, he turned from Dixon and approached the four chained prisoners.

'I am sorry,' he said.

One of the men, whey-faced and whose sad eyes were filled with a sort of depthless grief, replied, 'Thank you for trying, young sir.'

Then, with a whoop, the Enniscorthy rebels surrounded the prisoners and marched them down Main Street, roughly jostling and goading them as they went.

Dan watched them go and then knifed the silent cluster of Keogh's guards a look of savage disdain. The men stared at the ground, shame-faced and humiliated by their own inaction. Without a backward glance he ascended the sloping plot of hard-packed earth to where Elizabeth waited for him, her face pensive and her hands balled in the fabric of her dress.

Behind him, outside The Cape of Good Hope, Dixon mused almost whimsically, 'We must do something about the good Mr Banville.'

The following afternoon found Dan Banville staring into a looking glass held in his right hand. His shoulder wound had been cleaned and stitched and now the black threads of the sutures dug tiny furrows in his flesh. All around it the yellowing haze of a bruise floated beneath the skin and the last red haze of infection was cooling to a dusky pink. Even now, ten days after the grape shot had punched through him, a bandage had to be applied daily to soak up the amber fluid that leaked from the knotted centre of the wound.

It still hurt like blazes too, although, he reflected, probably not as badly as poor John Kelly's thigh.

After yesterday's altercation with Dixon he had gone to visit Kelly. Dan's mood was further soured by the sight of the blond colonel from Killann propped upon a nest of pillows in his sister's bedroom. He sat in his bed a pale wraith, so far removed from the commanding presence of old. The change that the wound had wrought within the Bantry man made Dan feel uncomfortable, nudging his mind along dark paths reeking of death. Kelly had left a part of himself in the dust and smoke of New Ross and the continuing bad news from the west and north only served to depress him further. With an unexpected feeling of awkwardness, Dan had made his excuses and left. They had lived a dream, had come tantalisingly close to realising it, only to have it reduced to splinters before their eyes.

Dixon and the disheartening sight of Kelly's splinted leg made Dan consider the very existence of the United Irishmen. What had they accomplished, apart from violence and vengeance? Unless the French came – and what was keeping them? – might the heroism he had witnessed, the spilled blood and the campaign of terror that had prompted it, be consigned to mere footnotes in history?

Wexford *must* hold, he thought.

A light knock on the bedroom door snapped him out of his bleak reverie and he quickly pressed a wad of gauze to his shoulder and pulled his shirt over his head, calling, 'Come in,' as he did so.

The door opened and Pat the manservant stood on the threshold bent and wizened. He regarded Dan from under his brows with the same gruff dislike that he had conveyed ever since first clapping eyes on the young rebel captain.

'Ms Blakely wants to know if you're ready for your afternoon exercise,' he intoned flatly.

'She treats me like a race horse,' replied Dan in an effort to coax even the suggestion of a smile from the man.

'I'll tell her you'll be down in a minute,'

Dan finished dressing and then, without thinking, he reached under the bed and dragged out his sword. The leather of its belt and scabbard was worn and battered and the blade was nicked in half a dozen places, but its weight was reassuring.

Wincing at a twinge from his shoulder, he belted on the sabre, its presence at his thigh like a familiar and loyal hound.

Elizabeth frowned as he came down the stairs. Her eyes fastened onto the sword and she asked, 'Why are you wearing that?'

'He wears it because he is sensible.'

Mrs Brownrigg stood in the open doorway leading to her drawing room and cast a withering gaze down the length of the hallway. Her arms folded and her features hard, she continued, 'Any man who antagonises the likes of Thomas Dixon must arm himself.'

Dan came to the foot of the stairs and nodded towards Elizabeth's aunt, 'Mrs Brownrigg.'

'Mr Banville,' she replied. 'I trust you have not forgotten your undertaking to keep my niece safe?'

'Of course not, Mrs Brownrigg.'

'These are dangerous times, children. I would have you both be very careful.'

Dan smiled and replied, 'I will look after her, Mrs Brownrigg.'

Elizabeth's arm snaking around his waist surprised Dan, but her words broadened his smile and set his eyes sparkling.

'We will look after each other,' she said.

When they left, Mrs Abigail Brownrigg stood for a moment in the hallway of her cavernous house and listened to the ticking of clocks in the gloom. She blessed herself and walked slowly into her drawing room, closing the door behind her.

The afternoon sun was pitching from its zenith as Dan and Elizabeth strolled along the quayside. To their right the tall ships at anchor creaked and heaved against their hawsers, the sea sucking toothlessly at their barnacle-studded hulls. The boardwalk along the quay was crowded with people, wounded rebels and townsfolk all mingling freely in the afternoon warmth. Yet there was a palpable tension in the air, the laughter a little too forced, the smiles a little too like grimaces.

'We shall go to France,' Dan was saying. 'If we cannot hold this port in readiness for a French landing, if the French do not come, then we shall go to Paris. I have never seen Paris.'

Elizabeth smiled up at him, 'My love, you can barely speak English, let alone French.'

Dan laughed and squeezed her to him, saying, 'I wish the English would come out from behind their walls and end this stalemate. The people grow more and more frustrated and every day more and more slip away home. This inertia is a killing thing. General Lake is smothering us, defeating us through claustrophobia and fear, rather than through force of arms.'

Elizabeth said, 'I fear we may all need lessons in French.'

In the middle distance, wending through the crowd, a man who Dan vaguely recognised was making his way towards them. He wore a tricorn on his head but every so often, from under its peak, he shot a furtive glance to where the couple were walking. It was the wariness of these glances, the birdlike abruptness of them, that had caught Dan's eye.

Elizabeth, however, was oblivious.

'If the Rising does not succeed,' she was saying, 'we will need to get safe passage to Dublin and thence to France. My father has many relatives in Dublin, some of whom are quite well-to-do, once there it should not be difficult to book passage.'

Dan nodded distractedly, his attention taken up entirely by the oddly familiar figure that was now quite close. The man was pushing through the crowd with a little more urgency than was normal, as if he were in a hurry to make some vital appointment.

Where, Dan thought, had he seen him before?

The man was almost upon them, when the sudden realisation burned through Dan's mind like a bullet. He was one of Dixon's men.

Dan tried to untangle his sword arm from Elizabeth's grasp as the man rushed closer, his last few steps taken at a half-run, something glimmering bitterly in the grip of his right fist.

It was at that moment, on the raw edge of that jagged lip of time, that Elizabeth Blakely stepped in front of Dan. Her face was smiling, warmer than any sun, and her mouth was just beginning to open, readying to chide him for not paying attention. She stepped between him and Dixon's man and Dan's face whitened in horror and his right arm convulsed, questing for his sword's hilt.

The man in the tricorn's right hand drove forward. His glittering eyes were fixed on Dan's face, not even aware of Elizabeth as she slid in front of his plunging blade.

Elizabeth gasped in surprise and pain. Her bright eyes opened wide and she stared at Dan as his big arms enfolded her, supporting her, as the strength seemed to leak from her body all at once.

For a moment all three figures stood in shocked silence. Dan, his face an open wound, embracing Elizabeth as she sagged, her eyes beginning to roll and a trickle of red leaking from the corner of her mouth, the assassin with his blade still lodged in her back, a look of surprise masking his features.

All three stood in mute horror and then the last of Elizabeth's strength drained from her.

Dan lowered her to the ground as a ring of bystanders formed about the horrible tableau. He leaned over her as tears sprang into his eyes and a battery of cannon seemed to erupt in his chest.

'Elizabeth!' he sobbed. 'Elizabeth! Don't leave me. Don't leave me.'

She lay with her eyes half-closed, her sun-bonnet awry on her nest of mahogany curls. A few strands of her hair had come loose and spiralled out around the pale curve of her neck and a spreading pool of deepest crimson began to spread out from around her shoulders.

Dan bent and kissed her lips. A warmth still resided within them but that was the only residue of life that remained. It was like pressing his lips to warm clay.

When he arose his mouth was smeared with her blood.

The assassin still stood before him, the centre now of an anxious circle of townsfolk. He was a young lad, no more than a teenager, and beneath his too-big tricorn his skin still bore the scars and pits of ravaging acne. He faced Dan in trembling terror, the bloodied filleting knife still held in his right hand.

'Jesus Christ,' he mumbled. 'I didn't mean to stick her. She stepped in the way. Jesus Christ.'

The first cut of Dan's sword caught him across the right bicep.

The lad screamed and dropped his knife, turning to flee. Dan hamstrung him with a vicious snap of his forearm and the boy fell to the boardwalk. Away back in some dark corner of his mind, locked there by grief and fury, his conscience screamed that this was wrong. This lad was no more the author of this work than Elizabeth herself. And yet his muscles worked of their own brute volition, his shoulder screaming in agony. Not a word escaped his lips as he flailed at the scrawny figure beneath him, only the grunts of his exertions gave testament to his emotions. The wet chop and slap of Dan's blade as it rose and fell sent gouts of gore spraying into the crowd of onlookers.

One by one, slowly at first and then with gathering momentum, the crowd turned and began to stream away, the women sobbing and children bundled into the blinkering folds of skirt and shawl.

And still Dan hacked in blind rage, his arm growing tired and the wooden planks at his feet becoming slick with blood.

'Captain Daniel Banville, I arrest you for the murder of William Delaney, a fellow United Irishman. I further charge you with consorting with the enemy and seeking to thwart the will of the people.'

The nasal whine of Thomas Dixon made Dan pause. Dixon's voice cut through his anger, refocusing it and giving it new form.

'You!' he spat. 'You did this! It is you who should be lying under my sword, not this wretch.'

Dixon stood amidst a gang of a dozen pikemen, his face snarling with grim glee. He watched Dan with the wariness of a man confronting a wounded but predatory beast and said, 'You're coming to gaol, Mr Banville. And delighted I am for you, too.'

At these words Dan surged forward, unmindful of the pain in his shoulder that told him his stitches had burst open, uncaring that the men before him were armed to the teeth and waiting for his charge. Only Elizabeth, lying pale and beautiful, robbed of life by treachery and hate, meant anything to him now. He had lost her and with her he had lost everything.

Dixon took a frightened step back at the abandon of his charge, at the wild hate that crawled across Dan's face.

For Dan the world had collapsed into an all-encompassing need to tear Thomas Dixon limb from limb. He did not see the pikestaff of one of Dixon's men until it had smashed bluntly into his jaw. He was on his knees when the next blow landed, cracking across the back of his skull and sending him sprawling, dazed and in helpless anguish, across the quayside.

The last thing he saw before his senses left him was Elizabeth, her face tranquil, her skin porcelain. He had loved her with everything good he had in him. And everything good had not been enough.

CHAPTER 23

Liberty or Death

General Gerard Lake sat behind a desk in his field tent and ate his break-fast from a pewter plate. The day before, the 18th of June, had been the first truly overcast day in a month and a half and now the rain was coming down in sheets. On the canvas roof of the tent the rain drummed in a relentless roll and flowed from the eaves in wind-flung waterfalls. Before him a dripping infantry captain stood to attention.

Lake was fifty-five years of age, a tall man and grey-haired beneath his pow-dered wig. His lantern jaw worked like a horse's as he chewed a mouthful of porridge, and his dark, hazel eyes were narrow as he ruminated. At length his pinched mouth opened and his voice, in its clipped Harrow accent, came from around a ball of cud, 'You are sure of this, Captain Dalhousie?'

The shivering captain nodded, 'Yes, sir, quite sure. The rebels have begun a general retreat towards Enniscorthy.'

General Lake was an uncomplicated man, but he had seen enough of insur-gent armies in America to make him doubly cautious. He gestured with his fork to his subordinate, saying, 'You're sure they ain't feinting?'

'Very sure, sir.'

'Splendid!' exclaimed Lake. 'The fools have saved us the trouble of a fight in the open countryside.'

Despite the weather, General Lake felt his spirits lift immeasurably. The Rising in the midlands and north had been put down and the French were not on the sea. The little county of Wexford was surrounded, its immense rebel peasant armies matched in numbers and overwhelmed in firepower by the Crown forces now ringing them.

For the first time in a month he was confident that he would not lose

Ireland as the colonies in America had been lost.

But the spectre of the French remained. If – and he prayed it would not be so – the Wexford rebels could hold a beach head against him and if the French were to land even a token force of two thousand men, then all would be placed in the balance. He had spent the last ten days since New Ross and Arklow patiently building an army of twenty thousand. And now at Arklow, Newtownbarry, New Ross and here, just below the slopes of Kilcavan Hill, his forces were ready to advance.

A smile made a crescent of bone beneath the fleshy hook of his nose and he asked Captain Dalhousie, 'The other general officers have responded to our orders, yes?'

Dalhousie nodded, his eyes fixed on a patch of vacant air about a foot above his superior's left ear, and replied, 'Yes, sir. General Johnson is marching north from New Ross so as to take Enniscorthy from the west, and Brigadier General Moore with the Light Division has moved out of New Ross and is making towards Wexford Town. General Needham has committed to move south from Arklow and Generals Loftus and Dundas together with Sir James Duff have all confirmed receipt of your orders. They should be converging on Scarawalsh Bridge within a day.'

Lake's smile grew wider and he said, 'I am very pleased at the manner in which this is being brought to a close, Captain Dalhousie. General Johnson at New Ross and Needham at Arklow deserve to be well-rewarded for their actions in stopping the rebels breaking out. God help us if they had marched on Dublin. It would have spelt our doom.'

He leaned back in his chair then and raised his left hand to scratch his long jaw thoughtfully. 'Let this be known, Captain,' he said. 'The taking of prisoners is not to be encouraged. Any man found under arms is to be shot. These people are rebels against the King. We afforded the colonial irregulars far too much respect. It will not happen here. I want every man jack of them scoured from the face of the world. Is that clear?'

Captain Dalhousie saluted, 'Very clear, sir.'

Then he turned and left General Lake to his breakfast, slopping out into the downpour, splashing through the puddles as he hurried to spread the general's word.

The same bellying sky over the tents of General Lake and his staff hissed down upon Tom Banville as he and the battered remains of the Northern Division of the United Irish Army floundered south towards Camolin. The rain came down in a cold, iron-grey curtain. The roar of the rain as it thundered into the ground was interrupted occasionally by the squelching splatter of men slipping in the muck and the phlegmy suck and slurp of mud dragging at men's feet. All along the rebel line, men walked stoop-shouldered like poor beasts. Already the depressions and ruts in the road, the hollows of the surrounding fields, were filled with dark lakes that mounted moment by moment, growing and consuming as their creeping edges met.

Tom Banville reflected gloomily on the circumstances that had brought him to this rain-soaked point on the Gorey to Camolin road.

After the defeat at Arklow, both he and Fr John were accepted back into the ranks without any rancour or ill-feeling. The men were too exhausted to harbour grudges and were only too glad to have experienced officers among them again. Fr Murphy had once more argued the merits of marching into the Wicklow Mountains, for they mustered still around seven or eight thousand strong. However, he was ignored again and a frustrating stalemate had ensued with the garrison at Arklow refusing to be drawn into battle and the United Irish Army becoming more and more exasperated.

The fact that they were surrounded and alone had filtered through the ranks like a poison. Desertions had accelerated and the lust for vengeance to be taken on loyalist prisoners grew with every passing hour.

Word arrived of government armies at Carnew and Newtownbarry almost at the same time as orders from Edward Roche called them south to Vinegar Hill. They were to provide a bulwark against the Crown's advance and keep Wexford Harbour free for a French landing for as long as possible.

Again Fr Murphy railed against this prospect. Another set-piece battle could only succeed with huge numbers of guns and supplies, in which they were sorely deficient. Yet this time, overruled by both Edward Fitzgerald and Anthony Perry, Fr Murphy consented to lead his men into battle once more. With government armies ringing the county, there was nowhere left to go.

When Tom had informed his Castletown Corps of the intention to make a last stand on Vinegar Hill, a wounded Jim Kehoe, his left arm in a sling, asked, 'And you will stand with us, Mr Banville?'

Tom had laughed bitterly at this and replied, 'If you had broken out of the county, lads, I would have wished you well and turned south to be with my dead brother. Now with the county infested with redcoats once more we are all chained to each other out of fearful necessity. I am afraid, lads, that we will either be shot together or shot separately. It would be my pleasure to die with you in battle rather than at the hands of some patrolling yeoman in a country lane somewhere.'

'We could defeat them at Vinegar Hill,' replied Kehoe.

Looking at him, Tom's expression softened. He took in Kehoe's young face, the desperate hope that kindled in his eyes, the yearning in him for something to hold on to.

'We could,' said Tom. 'We've beaten them before.'

Jim Kehoe had smiled at this and the other Castletown men had slapped each other on the back with renewed confidence. And, watching them, Tom felt his heart slip even further into despair.

Now they slogged south from Gorey, abandoning the whole north of the county to a razor-edged tide of red. Around them, refugees stumbled through the mire; Catholics and peasants this time rather than the frightened lines of loyalists that had so recently thronged the roadways of Wexford.

Tom marched in silence, his head bowed and water dripping from hair that was slicked and clinging to his scalp like river weeds. Behind him, he knew Miles Byrne was harassing the enemy outriders, his Monaseed Corps providing a resolute rearguard for the mass of pikemen and civilians that clogged the swampy roads around Camolin. As he marched, each slewing step bringing him closer to Vinegar Hill, he found himself wishing that Dan was with him.

Soaked and cold and exhausted, Tom Banville missed his big brother.

Dan spent four days on board the makeshift prison ship docked at Custom House Quay before Thomas Cloney found him. Four days of misery had passed with him crammed into a locked cabin with a dozen other men. All were loyalists, known informers or yeomen, and Dan was disgusted that he was interred with them. The cabin was a gloomy cavern of damp and dirt, the gaolers content to allow their prisoners to fester in the dank swamp of their own filth. The place reeked of vomit and faeces and puddled urine. He had neither eaten nor spoken one word to his cellmates since he had first been flung in there, bloodied and unconscious. He spent the hours curled up on a stinking pallet, facing the wall and thinking of Elizabeth.

On the third day, the 18th of June, the day on which she must have been buried in the graveyard of St Iberius' Church, Dan had wept uncontrollably. It was as though a void had opened beneath his ribs that threatened to consume him utterly. The other men in the cell had moved well away from him. Grief, depthless and irremediable, had dragged him under. He wondered briefly if it were possible to be driven mad by sorrow before realising that he did not care.

Mrs Brownrigg, prudent as always, had not sought to contact him or pass him any message. Any association with one so hated by Thomas Dixon could only bring more disaster down upon her unfortunate family. Dan could not fault her for it.

When Thomas Cloney found him, he found a ragged scarecrow.

A key rattled in the cabin's lock and Cloney barged past the astonished guard, barking at him as he went, 'I'll remember you if any harm has come to Captain Banville.'

Ignoring the loyalists, who cowered in a huddled mass, Cloney strode straight across to where Dan lay on his pallet, his forehead pressed into a corner.

'Jesus, Mary and Joseph,' breathed the rain-drenched Cloney. 'What have they done to you?'

Dan soughed forth a great shuddering breath and said, 'She must have been buried yesterday, Thomas. Put into the hard ground where I can never see her again.'

Cloney knelt beside him and sought to turn him over but was rebuffed as Dan shrugged his shoulder away from him.

'I heard what happened,' said Cloney, his throat gagging. 'I will have you out of here by tomorrow, as soon as I can get hold of Edward Roche. You have killed a fellow United Irishman, Dan, no matter what the provocation there's no getting away from that fact. We cannot start turning on our own.'

'They killed her like an animal,' snarled Dan. 'They stuck a knife in her back.'

Cloney nodded and said soothingly, 'I know. That's the fact that may save your life.'

Stirring himself, Dan sat up and regarded Cloney with eyes that were red-raw and staring. A swollen, ink-dark bruise blurred the line of his jaw and Cloney was taken aback by the madness that seemed to crawl within Dan's expression. Here was a man, Cloney thought, who had nothing left to live for.

Dan growled, low and threatening, 'I would give my life, and yours as well, to have that bastard Dixon's head on a spike.'

'You may yet get the chance,' replied Cloney. 'For the moment however, you are safe here. You will have no court martial and myself and Mr Harvey are determined that you should be released as soon as the present crisis is finished.'

Blinking, his intellect roused for the first time in days, Dan asked, 'What is happening?'

Cloney sighed and lanced a grim glare towards the loyalist prisoners crowded like sheep against the far wall. 'There is a large force of soldiers moving out from New Ross. Fr Roche wants however many men we can press to march out and meet them at Goff's Bridge, by Foulkesmills. I wanted you beside me but some thought it might not be sensible to have amongst the ranks one who slaughtered a lad hardly grown out of childhood. You have become a monster in the eyes of some, Dan.'

'I have been made a monster,' came Dan's anguished response.

Cloney grunted in agreement and said, 'Have no fear, Dan. I shall return and have you at liberty as soon as I can. We have met the English before and thrown them back. We shall do so again.'

Dan nodded, his throat dry, 'Thank you, Thomas.'

Cloney pointed to Dan's left shoulder where blood and pus had caked and hardened the folds of his shirt, gluing them to his tattered flesh.

'Look after that,' he said. 'Wash it with salt water. I shall return.'

Dan watched him leave, heard his angry words of admonishment for the guards, muffled and indistinct through the thick wood of the cabin's door. Then there was silence, disturbed only by the rain lashing at the room's single narrow window and the creak and groan of the ship as it rolled on the waves.

Dan slept that night in a hot frenzy of nightmares and half-imagined horrors. In the black behind his eyelids Elizabeth's face floated like a petal on dark waters, her eyes accusing, her lips stained red with blood. A grotesque phantasmagoria lumbered through his sleeping mind, laced with the last despairing wails of William Delaney as Dan's sword fell and rose and fell again and again and again.

He awoke the next morning filmed with a greasy patina of sweat. His cellmates regarded him with troubled eyes. Each man flicked wary glances towards him and then away, their gaze sliding across his features, never lingering for long. Dan presumed he had been talking or screaming in his sleep. He cared not a whit and for a moment wondered if this was the liberty that madmen felt, this blithe disregard for everything.

For the first time in four days he ate, a breakfast of cold stirabout provided for him with rather more civility than he had come to expect from the guard. Cloney's words must have worked.

He waited as the sun climbed higher above the rumpled blanket of the murky sky. The rain held off and the day allowed a gusting breeze to dry the land. He waited, dwelling on what he would do to Thomas Dixon when Cloney released him from this prison ship. He would do a variety of things, using all of his old yeoman's exquisite expertise. And above all he would do them slowly.

He waited until midday had come and gone and the first braying roar from the dockside told him something was wrong. A thousand voices rose in yelping acclamation, the mass of sound laced with hysteria.

Yes, something was very wrong.

Unmindful of the man's feeble protestations, Dan leaped up onto the pallet of another prisoner's and pressed his face to the narrow window that gave onto the choppy surf of Wexford harbour and the long, squat span of the bridge stretching left to right across his vision.

What he saw brought a burning surge of bile into his throat.

To his right, where Wexford Bridge joined Custom House Quay, a massive, jostling mob of people had gathered beneath the metal arch commemorating the bridge's construction. A long table had been placed on the quays alongside the bridge and seven men sat at it, in the manner of judges at a court-martial. Among them, the vulpine face of Thomas Dixon was prominent as he leered and guffawed, his words lost between the distance and the heaving sea. Above their heads a flag waved, snapping in the wind, black as coal and embroidered with a pale cross. Beneath this white cross was the legend, LIBERTY OR DEATH.

Before this grim court-martial a group of ten loyalist prisoners were ringed round with leering pikemen. The prisoners' hands were bound and they had assumed the slump-shouldered attitude of men resigned to their fate.

As Dan watched, Dixon smashed his fist on the table and the gathered throng yelled their approval, every face opening up like bursting stitches and their great shout of zeal thundering across the waves. The prisoners were marched solemnly onto the bridge's planking where they knelt, surrounded by Dixon's pikemen. Then, at a signal from the men presiding over this macabre parody of a court, each prisoner was spitted in turn. Four pikes were driven into their chests and backs and they were lifted, struggling in tortured agony, high above the delighted faces of the mob. Their screams clawed heavenward until at last, mercifully, they expired and the murderers pitched the still-bleeding bodies into the dull waters below.

On the quays a frenzy of bloodlust had gripped the crowd and each onlooker writhed and wailed in an ecstasy of pagan savagery. Before Dan's astonished eyes they became ghouls, cannibal grotesques bent on nothing but slaughter and destruction.

'Mother of God,' Dan breathed as another group of unfortunates was led up the quays from the gaol.

In the absence of the fighting men, in the void left by the battle that Thomas

Cloney and the others were even now waging, Dixon's rabble had seized the opportunity to murder and butcher with impunity. While others braved the musket and cannon of the soldiers, the flashing steel of the cavalry, Dixon was conducting a massacre.

Dan leaped down from the pallet and rushed to the cell door.

Behind him, his fellow prisoners were murmuring anxiously and one was climbing up onto the pallet. Dan heard him retch convulsively.

Dan, meanwhile, was hammering his fist against the heavy door. 'Let us out!' he roared. 'Have you all taken leave of your senses? Can you not see what is happening?'

Not a word was uttered in response. Only an ominous silence communicated itself through the wood, a wordless promise of coming death.

Then, as Dan leaned his forehead against the door in resignation, a voice at last answered, soft but penetrating, as though the man spoke with his mouth pressed against the portal's planking. The voice was unfamiliar to Dan, possessing the hard, aggressive edge of Enniscorthy.

'I see what is happening, Banville,' the voice said. 'And I saw what you did to young William on the quays as well. You hacked him apart all because of some Orange whore. Well, all you pieces of loyalist filth are going to get it in the neck this day. Just you wait and see.'

Frightened now, Dan stumbled away from the door as, behind him, another of his cellmates was made sick by the awful scenes on Wexford Bridge.

The hours passed slowly, and the screaming agony of those dying on the bridge flooded the cabin like a pestilence. Each wail was greeted with a roar from the quays and each death lingered like a gallery of ghosts.

How had it come to this?

When they came for Dan, they came in force.

Dan sat with his head in his hands until he heard the grinding sound of a key in the lock and the door swept open. In the hallway beyond, a mob of men carrying muskets, blunderbusses and pistols made a demonic escort for him and his fellow condemned.

Dan looked up at them and growled mockingly, 'Not taking any chances this time, boys, are ye?'

As they poured into the room Dan surged to his feet to meet them, his arms stretched out to either side like a man crucified, his face branded with a sneer of cold defiance.

'Take me to her!' he yelled, the tendons standing out on his neck in white ridges of gristly fibre. 'Take me to her! I am ready!'

His hands were bound and, at the head of the dozen pale wraiths with whom he had shared a cell, he was paraded down the length of the quays. By the time he reached the seven judges he was drenched in spit and phlegm, the crowd baying and howling like banshees around him.

Dixon and his cohorts lounged in their seats like lords. Every one of them ragged and every one of them reeked of sweat and alcohol. Behind Dixon, his hulking wife leaned forward and whispered something to her preening husband.

Dixon smiled up at her and kissed her passionately on the lips, his narrow face sinking into the cushions of her cheeks.

Dan could hear his cellmate begin to retch once more.

Dixon at last ran his gaze across the doomed men before him. His eyes were unfocused with drink and, like the six other men around him, he had assumed the supercilious bearing that he guessed a judge must convey. He had become a parody of a parody. And in that instant Dan perceived him for what he truly was.

'What are you grinning at, Banville?' Dixon snapped.

'Indeed,' interjected another judge. 'You may respect this court or you'll live to regret it.'

Dan felt his smile grow wider as a wild abandon seize him and he crowed, 'Why must I respect anything fools do? When brave men are even now flinging themselves against English guns to preserve the dream of liberty we have fought for, you set up an assizes to persecute innocent people. Why must I respect men such as you?'

Dixon was on his feet in a flash, 'Do you call me a fool, Banville? Do you dare?'

Dan grinned in a lethal rictus and replied, 'I asked why I must respect fools. Do you think perhaps that you are a fool, Mr Dixon?

'Do you think that for your entire life thus far people have seen you as nothing but a pathetic little man, worthy of no more respect than something you might scrape off your boot? Do you think they follow you now because they are afraid of you? That you are like a rabid dog?

'Tell me, Mr Dixon, when you lie beside your wife and you stare into the midnight dark, does it occur to you that you are nothing but a parasite?'

Dixon was apoplectic now and a ghastly silence descended over the crowd close enough to overhear Dan's remarks. As Dixon fumed, the silence spread in downy ripples until he and Dan faced each other at the centre of a growing, pregnant hush.

Dixon's face had become as red as brick dust and he trembled visibly. In the face of Dan's maniacal grin he roared, 'Kill him! Kill them all!'

A muted murmuring came from the surrounding crowd, their blood cooled by Dan's defiance and the eagerness and relish with which he had excoriated Dixon. The pikemen circled all about exchanged uneasy glances, their faces frowning, their actions unsure. Overhead, the black flag whip-cracked in the squalling air.

Again, Dixon bellowed, 'This man killed one of our own! You have all seen it! The people demand his death in return!'

This time, the pikemen stirred themselves and with slow, almost shameful movements, prodded the men forward, goading them in a pale, shambling line towards the executioners on the bridge. Dan, however, needed no goading.

He gathered all the hatred and bitterness that had bred in him over the last five days, battening on his grief. He gathered it all and spat onto the table in front of Thomas Dixon, his voice belling out over the crowd, 'I accuse you, Dixon, of betraying the aims of the United Irishmen. And you will be held accountable for your actions this day. If not in this life, then surely in the next.'

Then he tossed his head like a wild stallion in full flight and flung his gaze out across the watching multitude. 'I accuse you all!' he cried.

With that he marched, stiff-backed and proud, along the line of the Custom House Quay and strode out onto the bridge, his guards hurrying in a graceless jog to keep up. Dixon's eyes followed him as he went, his moment of triumph robbed of its relish, his standing in the eyes of his followers diminished. The tawdry spectacle, the grotesque circus that had played out on the bridge had been exposed as the orgy of petty hatred it was; one small, cowardly man's attempt to stand centre-stage.

On the bridge Dan knelt as four pikemen surrounded him. He felt the smooth, wet timbers soaking the fabric of his breeches. Water mingled with the afternoon's spilled blood drenched his knees. He felt the breeze, snapping in off the harbour, buffet him as he bowed his head. He could feel Dixon's hatred and he rejoiced in it. His breath was coming quicker now. His shoulder burned. It would be a slow death, he knew, hoisted by his rib cage over the Slaney. He prayed that he would not scream.

One of the executioners walked down the row of condemned men, his pike and his forearms caked with blood, and said, 'You better ask for forgiveness from the Lord, boys. You'll be before him soon.'

I am coming to you Elizabeth, thought Dan. I am coming.

Then a cry arose from the opposite end of the bridge. A shout of horror and outrage and anger.

Dan felt the planks beneath him shake like a drumhead and the sound of hooves came to his ears, hammering ever closer. His would-be executioners had fallen away from him now and were running frantically back towards Wexford Town. A frightened, milling agitation seized the crowd on the quays and handfuls began to hurry away, swarming up the narrow laneways leading into the town. The long table that had been occupied by the seven abominable judges was empty. Of Thomas Dixon there was no sign.

To either side of Dan his fellow condemned began to sob in relief.

Heaving himself to his feet, his hands still bound behind him, Dan turned his head towards the Ferrybank end of the bridge, where the east Shelmalier countryside rolled down to the Slaney's mouth and Wexford Harbour. From out of that countryside, marching hurriedly across the bridge, came a detachment of Shelmalier marksmen, their long-barrelled guns carried easily in practiced hands. And ahead of them, whipping a huge black charger as though his life depended on it, rode Edward Roche, his face incandescent with fury.

He reined his mount to a clattering halt before Dan and, leaning down, exclaimed, 'Jesus, Dan, what has happened to you? What has occurred here?'

Struggling to free himself from his bonds, Dan replied, 'Abomination has occurred here, General. Massacre and murder. Thomas Dixon has engineered a slaughter of the prisoners.'

'And why are you among them?' asked Roche, his face pale.

'That is a story that must wait, General,' said Dan. 'We must apprehend Dixon immediately before he can instigate any more savagery.'

Roche cast a stricken look towards Wexford Town and rumbled, 'I wish we could, but time is of the essence. We must gather as many fighting men as are available and return with them to Vinegar Hill. The English are on the verge of surrounding Enniscorthy and the Northern Division with it.'

Dan shook his head in despair, 'The fighting men left at Fr Roche's orders to hold back the enemy at Foulkesmills. They are in action there as we speak, I would guess. The only people left in the town are that murderous rabble you see sneaking away like kicked curs.'

Roche frowned and said, 'I will have some of my corps see to the safety of any prisoners not yet put to death, but the real substance of things is to the north of here. Perry and Fitzgerald need men within a day.'

He paused then, his broad frame dark against the pearl sweep of the sky and the ragged iron of the river. He paused and surveyed the blood-swamped timbers of the bridge, the sobbing line of prisoners, the dozens of lacerated bodies bobbing like wet sacking in the water. A grim realisation seemed to grow within him and with lead in his voice he said, 'This was bad business done here today, Dan. Any chance we may have had of reaching a settlement with Lake has been torn asunder by Dixon's madness. It is liberty or death for any United leader after this, Dan. Liberty or death.'

CHAPTER 24

United in Blood

Tom Banville awoke with a start. Night had fallen on Vinegar Hill some hours before and now the summer sky was an open maw out of which the black wind sobbed. All across the hillside campfires burned low into flaring embers, their light pulsing with the vagaries of the air as though possessed of a febrile life. Every man able to bear arms within ten miles had congregated throughout the evening of the 20th of June, thronging the slopes and packing the gutted town below. Refugees, fugitives from the predations of Lake's military, had followed suit and again the motley thousands of families and relatives, wives and loved ones, swelled the numbers of the rebel host.

Across the Slaney valley, in a wide scimitar of flickering orange, the fires of General Lake's army arced from south-west to north-east. Thousands upon thousands of fires dotted the fields and pastures around Enniscorthy; the landscape was aflame, the countryside infested.

Tom had been woken by the hollow sound of calling voices drifting up from the sentries stationed at the base of the hill. Shivering, he wrapped his trusty around himself, buttoning it tightly under his chin like a cloak. Yawning, he set off to see what the disturbance might be, threading his way between the slumbering hummocks of exhausted rebels.

With his mind still fuddled from sleep and his tired eyes focusing on the rutted sheep walk in front of him, he almost collided with Miles Byrne stalking up the hill in the opposite direction. Byrne and his men had been fighting a rearguard action all day, skirmishing and withdrawing through the dense hedgerows, frustrating Lake's vanguard as it marched. His return, and that of his men, was the evident source of excitement among the sentries.

Realising it was Tom who had nearly blundered into him, he said bitterly,

405

'I see they have dragged you here as well.'

Shaking the woolly feeling from his mind, Tom fell into step beside Byrne, asking, 'Where else was there to go, Miles?'

Byrne was cold and tired and his voice sounded far older than his eighteen years, 'I don't doubt that we have to make a stand somewhere, but there are no defenses prepared. Scarcely anything has been done to make this hill formidable against the enemy. What in God's name were the Enniscorthy lads doing for the past three weeks, besides slaughtering prisoners? Now our little army must be drawn up en masse and await the arrival of the English with their vast parks of artillery whilst we have but two six-pounders, a howitzer and scarcely a round of ammunition between them.'

Tom smiled and a bleak sort of laugh clattered from his lips, 'I agree. The English are in a hopeless position. They must surely surrender.'

Byrne grinned in the dark, 'I am glad you are here, Tom. I am only sorry your unfortunate brother is not by your side.'

Tom was silent then, the mention of Dan opening even wider a raw wound that still gaped, not yet beginning to knit or heal. Both men walked quietly, wet grass and weeds drenching their boots.

Eventually Tom said, 'You are tired, Miles. My camp fire still has heat in it and you may want some rest before tomorrow's excitement.'

'Thank you,' Byrne replied. 'I was dreading the notion of making a cold camp beneath some dripping gorse.'

General Lake, Commander-in-Chief of His Majesty's forces in Ireland, stood at the open flap of his tent and stared south-east across the two miles dark countryside to where Vinegar Hill stood, a black stain against the night sky. On its slopes and in the town at its granite foot, fires flung glimmers of orange and red which were immediately swallowed by the hungry wind. As Lake watched, a distant camp fire guttered and winked out of existence. He smiled grimly.

Behind him, his field tent was brimming with the saffron light of half a dozen oil lamps and a hubbub of voices spilled out into the rain-scented dark. Around Lake, the voices of his soldiers raised in song carried on the wind, growing and fading like the groans of ghosts, half-heard and bodiless. He drew a long breath, as though to inhale the essence of his men's exuberance, and the smells of mess-tins and cooking pots and the stink of open latrines coated his nose and throat. This was his centre; his place in the world was here, surrounded by the squalor of soldiers and the reek of their lives.

And soldiers they were, he thought as he surveyed the dove-grey tents that disappeared away into the night like irregular rows of teeth. Line regiments and Royal Artillery. But he had had enough of the bloody yeomanry with their arrogance and complacency. Their ineptitude and incompetence. All he required to bring this country to heel were regular regiments and since they began pouring in from England through the ports of Dublin and Kingstown, he knew that he had gained the advantage. Now that these Wexford croppies had failed to break out of their own county they were done for as surely as a man with his neck on the executioner's block.

Yet what a close-run thing it had been! This thought disturbed more than anything else. It had been a matter of days, hours perhaps. Had the Wexford peasants captured New Ross, the entire south of Ireland might be in flames at this very moment. Had they captured Arklow, then the horrible vista of a horde of rebels marching on Dublin, on the capital, presented itself to his appalled imagination.

Lake narrowed his hazel eyes against the gust and considered the forces under his command, spreading in a vast arc across shadowy fields and blackened, weeping ditches. General Henry Dundas who had put down the Rising in Kildare, Johnson's battered battalions who had fought so gallantly at New Ross, Loftus, reinforced and eager for revenge after his men's thrashing at Tubberneering, Needham marching south from Arklow, out there in the gloom somewhere between Enniscorthy and the sea. All veterans of this war; for as much as it galled him to say it, this was a war, with all its attendant baseness and brutality.

Lake had been at Yorktown when it surrendered to the French and Continentals and as he stood on this patch of muddy sloping ground in the heart of County Wexford he found himself borne back to that moment seventeen years previous. Seventeen years and still the shame of that surrender curdled something in the pit of his stomach. Now, on England's very doorstep, he was threatened with the very same circumstances. If he failed to crush the rebellion here, if twenty thousand soldiers, artillery and cavalry were beaten by a rag-bag rabble of farmers and bogmen, then Ireland was lost. If the French were to arrive before the croppies were put down then that grossest of horrors, a French invasion of Britain, opened out before him.

His hand slipped down his jaw and every rasp of bristle communicated itself to him through the pink tips of his fingers. He had grown yielding in those seventeen years, he thought. At Yorktown, his hands had been callused, roughened through a soldier's tough existence, his pride and vanity equally rough-hewn.

For all his Harrow education, he had always possessed a burred and ragged edge to his being. Now, as promotion followed promotion and his purse became fatter and fatter, he had come to lose that bitter edge.

When, he wondered, had his hands become so soft?

Standing in the weeping cold of this damp Irish night he vowed to himself, promised the man he had been at Yorktown, that Vinegar Hill would not be another surrender. He could not allow himself to hand over another colony to traitors and allies of the French. He would drown the land in blood before accepting that fate.

A polite cough from behind him spun him on his heel, his boots gouging shallow grooves in the earth. Captain Dalhousie was leaning through the opening of the field tent. Over his shoulder the interior of the tent was an amber cavern of lamplight and several officers were visible leaning over a map.

'It is time, sir,' Dalhousie said simply.

Lake nodded once, silently, his face like flint.

Tom and Miles Byrne had hardly been asleep for an hour when a series of great booming coughs rumbled across the Slaney valley. They sat up immediately, their hands fumbling for their weapons while all about them men struggled from under damp blankets, lurching to their feet to turn pale faces out into the crowding dark.

Like a wave, a ripple of massive detonations roared in the distance, impossibly loud in the silence of the early morning. Beginning in the dim countryside to the left of where Tom and Miles stood, to the south-west of Enniscorthy, a cannon belched its violence beneath the cloud-clotted sky. Then, in a wide arc following the sickle of camp fires, cannon after cannon exploded in the night.

Men started and women cried out at each report. Dogs barked and yelped around rebel camp fires and howled hauntingly in the streets of the shattered town below.

Tom and Miles listened to the cannon, faces grim with resigned comprehension.

'Their corps are signalling their positions in preparation for the attack,' stated Byrne.

Tom nodded, 'It will come with the day.'

Then, as the two young captains listened, an odd thing occurred that made them exchange startled, incredulous looks.

With numbing, inexorable uniformity, the cannon signals reverberated in a whumping chain from south of Enniscorthy towards the Blackstairs and then back around to the north and east. And here it stopped. No guns sounded from the east or south-east of the rebel position. Only hollow silence came from over the ragged spine of Vinegar Hill, and in that silence there was a cause for hope.

In the swamping dark, as men comforted their wives and children, as dogs howled and bayed, Miles Byrne smiled wolfishly.

'They've left a gap,' he said.

The assault came as dawn broke on the longest day of the year 1798. The serried ranks of the rebel army were waiting for it, while the women and children, the aged and infirm, retreated across the southern slopes. Fr Murphy, Edward Fitzgerald and Anthony Perry held command of the various corps stationed on the hill itself, while down in the valley, William Barker and Fr Mogue Kearns led the defence of the blackened shell that was Enniscorthy Town.

On the slopes of the grim eminence, louring blackly in the dawning, row upon row of pikemen moved in blocks of bristling weaponry. In spite of the numbers facing them, in spite of the guns that ringed them, the insurgents were in boisterous form. For all the days since Arklow, the Northern Division had failed to bait the redcoats and their officers into open battle. Now they had the chance to meet their foes once more in the field and not one believed that they could not best them as they had done so many times before. If the battle of Vinegar Hill was won, the back of the military in Ireland would be broken. The chains that bound for so many generations would burst. And so the pikemen waited with eager anticipation, willing the troops on while rebel musketeers positioned themselves behind ditches and husbanded their meagre stores of ammunition.

Standing side by side on the north-western slope of the hill, Tom Banville and Miles Byrne watched the slow tide of soldiers seep through the fields and ditches. It was as though the countryside were bleeding, staining the ripening barley, the deep green of the meadows, with a creeping wash of red.

Fr Murphy's great voice bellowed in the morning light, 'Steady, lads, this is the moment we fight or die!'

Miles Byrne turned to Tom and asked, 'Where are Roche and his Shelmaliers? We have a forest of pikes but very few guns. Where are his marksmen?'

Tom's gaze remained fixed on the advancing columns darkening the fields below as he replied, 'He went south for reinforcements. I had assumed he had returned. If he doesn't hurry, he will miss our great victory.'

Byrne smiled wryly, his eyes now flashing from one detachment of redcoats to the next. 'If the soldiers came but a little closer,' he mused, 'we could fall on them and cut them apart.'

Unfortunately for Miles Byrne, General Gerard Lake was no mere militia commander. The regular army, the world of line regiments and cold assessments, rang in his blood. He had no intention of allowing the rebel pikemen to crash into his men to gut and hack and slaughter. He had read the reports, he had heard the stories of Oulart and Enniscorthy, The Three Rocks and Tubberneering, the desperate valour of Arklow and New Ross. The rabble on the slope and in the town before him did not lack for heart or intrepidity, and so he would not best them with heart or intrepidity.

He would best them with cannon.

Almost simultaneously from the west of Enniscorthy and the north of Vinegar Hill a shattering bombardment commenced.

Barker and Kearns had their men take cover from the storm of shot and shell around the Duffry Gate, but on Vinegar Hill a terrible new weapon announced itself in a hail of fire and death.

The insurgents were drawn up in tight ranks and as the cannon balls came skidding through the dawn, churning the ground as they skimmed across the ditches and fields, the rebels simply moved aside to let them pass. Occasionally a ball would crash home and a screaming man might lose an arm or leg but at distance the cannon were easily enough avoided. The pikemen moved slowly forward, waiting for their opportunity to strike, while on the lower slopes a musketry duel suddenly sprang to spitting life.

And then Lake's howitzers barked and from out of the sky tumbled black balls the size of human heads. These rained down onto the insurgent ranks like meteors but where they dropped the rebels scattered so that they thudded harmlessly into the damp soil of the hill's slopes. Puzzled, the rebels converged about these strange, black lumps of hissing cast-iron.

Then the first of the explosions happened.

The heavy metal hail that seemed to harmlessly thump earthwards, ponderous and clumsy, now erupted in a shredding blast of gunpowder and shrapnel. The rebels clustered around the first few were blown to pieces before they could even voice a cry. Their corpses were mangled, the wounded scorched and bleeding amid the gorse and briar on the hill. Smoke began to billow across the sodden hillside, and within its murky folds the sudden, rosy flower of detonation after detonation blossomed and withered and the dull crump of the cannonade drowned out all but the wails of the dying.

The other companies saw the danger now and ran hectically to avoid the blasts, flinging themselves flat upon the wet bracken in the hope that the flame and shrapnel might pass over them.

A despairing cry went up, ragged and panicked, 'They spit fire at us!'

Midway down the slope, Tom ducked involuntarily as a corps of fifty pikemen was entirely consumed by a series of lethal blasts. Beside him, Miles Byrne roared over the clamour of the detonations and the screams of the wounded, 'We shall be cut to pieces before we have a chance to engage!'

Tom was afraid the young captain was correct, for under cover of the artillery barrage battalion after battalion of infantry advanced in line through the mantle of scrub and undergrowth that furred the base of Vinegar Hill. Every so often these lines would halt, discharge a tight, disciplined volley and advance once more, all the while encircling the beleaguered rebels more and more tightly.

Realising the danger, Fr Murphy rallied a contingent of pikemen and threw himself and his men against a wall of red. The soldiers had time to fire off a single volley before the rebels were upon them. In disorder they fled away through the fields, leaving Fr Murphy's men exposed in front of a park of artillery. Grape shot and shell poured into them and they were forced to withdraw behind trenches hastily prepared the night before.

In Enniscorthy Town a tumultuous battle raged. Barker and Kearns's defensive line had been smashed by the brutal power of the artillery and now vicious hand-to-hand fighting waged between the charred and smoke-stained walls of the town. General Johnson's cannon were being hauled laboriously down the narrow length of Main Street and a six-pounder was already in position in the Market Square. Barker, assessing the danger with all of his experience in service to the French, immediately ordered a counter attack and suddenly the gun was in rebel hands, its crew lying dead around it. Every street was raked with grape shot and musketry, every lane and alley became a choking defile, swimming with powder smoke.

And yet, little by little, the insurgents under Barker were driven back to the Slaney, running oily and dark under the pall of smoke. Street by street they fought and died, funnelling towards the bridge and the only escape route left, the Wexford Road.

For Tom Banville, standing with his Castletown Corps alongside the Monaseed men, the longer the battle continued the more frustrated he became.

The artillery barrage had pinned the entire insurgent army back into a steadily shrinking arena. The pikemen were next to useless and the musketeers lining the lower slopes had been badly mauled by cannon and muskets.

Then, abruptly, the cannonade ceased and from the massed ranks of redcoat infantry came the sound of fifes and drums. Over the shoulder of the hill, from the north-east, a sea-surge of a roar lifted into the sky. A people's defiance filled the space between heaven and earth with echoing noise.

Tom yelled to Byrne, 'They're pressing from the north and east!'

Byrne grinned savagely and spun to face his Monaseed Corps, who had remained steady and unscathed throughout the artillery barrage. 'Men of Monaseed!' he called. 'Now's the time for pike work!'

With that he led the charge across the slope, unmindful of the whipping lead about his ears. Just behind him, Tom Banville led his Castletown men; even Jim Kehoe with his wounded arm, bellowing like a bullock as he ran.

Over the brow of the hill the main mass of Lake's and General Dundas's columns had concentrated their efforts in a determined assault upon the right flank of the insurgent line. Here Edward Fitzgerald and Anthony Perry had their hundreds of men lined up, ready to meet them. The two colonels were conspicuous as they marched up and down in front of their men, Fitzgerald in his bright green coat and Perry with his bandaged head, both exhorting their men to hold their ground and meet musket fire with heart and hand.

General Lake sat his horse in the midst of chaos and watched as men were torn apart all around him. He had known the rebels did not lack for heart but the desperation of their charges, the bravery of their efforts in the face of cannon and musket shot was a terrible and pathetic thing. On the jagged slopes of Vinegar Hill his artillery had wreaked a bloody harvest and churned earth blended with spilled blood, turning the ground into a bog of viscera.

General Dundas rode his horse beside him while in front, the Light Infantry, with its howitzer in tow like some ghoulish pet, hurried forward along a narrow laneway. Behind him Dundas's brigades marched in deliberate parade-ground files. The noise was excruciating; the wild and savage battle-cries of the rebels almost indistinguishable from the screams of their dying. Bugles and drums rattled and blared and all was a confusion of smoke and clamour.

However, General Gerard Lake was a man of experience. He had seen battle before, although few had come close to this grotesque carnival. His troops were slowly advancing, throwing back desperate rebel assaults, bayoneting the traitors where they found them wounded and mewling in the fields and ditches. The croppies could not hope to stand against such concentrated fire and steel. Yet, here, and there where the peasants hit home, there was such a frenzy to their efforts, such a recklessness to their actions, that they carried all before them. Soldiers and militia were sent sprawling, fleeing or else transfixed by the rough, whetted steel of pike-heads and pitchforks. British screams commingled with Irish, their accents indistinguishable in torment, the gurgling slurp of dying breaths a universal and intimate language.

This was what caused Lake some measure of alarm and set the great, obsidian edifice of his conviction to totter. If the rebels could come to close quarters, if they broke through the ring of red surrounding them, if they should capture a park of artillery, then they had the numbers and audacity to confound his plans. Within himself, Lake felt his world balance on the edge of a cliff fathoms deep.

Beside him, Dundas turned in his saddle and yelled above the bark of musket and howitzer, above the clash of steel and wails of pain, 'There is still no sign of General Needham, sir. The rebels may attempt to effect a retreat south towards Wexford Town!'

Lake lifted his hand to his jaw and trailed his fingers along its stubbled, horse-muzzle length. Needham's continued absence was a bur beneath his skin. Inexplicably, he had failed to be in position at the commencement of the assault and now a gap yawned to the east and south through which a slim thread of hope might lead the rebels to safety. It was a gap that Lake was endeavouring to close before the traitors and Papist preachers who led this mass of peasants could discover it and escape.

Lake realised with a horrid start that he was not just irritated by Needham's mistake, he was frightened by it.

The spectre of Yorktown seemed to suddenly float above Vinegar Hill on such vast skeins of batwing leather that it threatened to eclipse the world.

Lake swallowed thickly, his throat suddenly clogged, and made to answer Dundas.

And then the world turned upside down.

His horse's scream cut through the surrounding din with such a piercing quality that it drove a spike into the ears of all those near it. Lake suddenly found himself lying flat on his back, his eyes staring vacantly at the grey clouds overhead. A lazy tissue of smoke trailed past his dumb gaze, languid and dislocated from the earthly chaos below.

As he lay there on the thin, damp soil of Vinegar Hill, General Gerard Lake could feel the unmistakable warmth of blood saturating his breeches. His thoughts came quickly, a skittering procession across the forefront of his mind, *ohgodmylegstheyvetakenmylegsohgodmylegs*.

As he lay there on the thin, damp soil of Vinegar Hill, General Gerard Lake was paralysed by terror, cold and breathless and primal.

Tom Banville and Miles Byrne brought their corps into position on the left side of the defensive line and were in time to join in the whoop of delight that fluttered across the hillside at the sight of General Lake tumbling from his horse. The cry of delight died as quickly as it had risen, however, for it was only the general's poor horse that had been shot, its barrel belly opened by a cannonball. The man astride its back had been flung to the ground by the violence of the animal's death and he lay there for long moments, stunned, drenched in his mount's steaming gore. Nevertheless, even after the hours of death and destruction that had been visited upon them, a gust of laughter rushed through the rebel lines at the sight of Lake being hauled gracelessly to his feet and scurrying for safety behind the ranks of his infantry.

Fitzgerald then gave the order to charge and a thousand furious pikemen threw themselves down the slope only to be met by a firestorm of bullet and grape shot.

All around Tom, the Castletown Corps stumbled and fell. Men simply folded as they ran, crashing to the ground, boneless and spraying blood. And still the charge continued, even coming to blows with the redcoats at several points, but its momentum was stolen by the overwhelming ferocity of the soldiers' gunfire. Reluctantly, the rebels first halted and then retreated back up the slope, dragging their wounded with them.

It was this that horrified Tom the most, the sheer amount of wounded. Men with limbs blown off, or ragged rents torn in stomach or chest, this face a disgusting swamp of gore, these eyes white and sightless.

How were they to get the wounded away? How could they prevent a massacre? Where were Edward Roche and his Shelmaliers? These thoughts jostled through Tom's mind as he struggled back up the slope, supporting a grievously injured Castletown man on his left arm as he went.

Below, on the bridge arching over the Slaney, a stalemate had developed. Back and forth the battle ebbed, with the soldiers gradually gaining the upper hand. This was the case until Barker rushed forward to prevent a cannon from being positioned against his men and had his arm torn off for his trouble.

Bearing their mutilated commander to the rear, the insurgents dug in and their tenacity, if anything, increased. With frenzied abandon they flung charge after charge back across the corpse-littered expanse of the bridge, howling defiance with every breath. Under the arches of the bridge the churning froth of the river began to run red.

For the moment the east bank held firm.

Unfortunately for the insurgent cause, the same was not true for the men on Vinegar Hill. Fitzgerald, Perry, Fr Murphy and Miles Byrne and Tom with them, were being pushed back across the summit. Gradually they retreated, blood-soaked field by blood-soaked field. Step by step, hauling wounded and dying with them, the rebel army made for the gap they knew existed in the circling mass of soldiers and artillery. Close by Beale's barn and southward through Darby's Gap, the insurgent troops broke and fled. Behind them, gaining rapidly, Lake's troops raked the wounded with musket fire, and his cavalry rode down the women and children, who now scattered through the fields, as though they were hunting foxes.

In the middle of this retreat Tom Banville stooped and hoisted a bloodied Monaseed man to his feet and wondered where in Christ's name Edward Roche had gotten to.

The first booming of the dawn assault on Enniscorthy and Vinegar Hill sounded like thunder to the men camped with Edward Roche at Garrylough. The house itself was reminiscent of the Banvilles' former home, a large two-storey construction of brick and wood, its proportions grand but not ostentatious. In its dooryard and stables, its parlours and kennels, Roche's force of Shelmaliers now made it a military camp. He had nearly a thousand men assembled with him but it had taken the rebel commander far longer than he might have wished to get them all into the field. His men had marched for nearly two days gathering troops from around Shelmalier and South Ballaghkeen and they were exhausted. Most of the new men hailed from the coastal sloblands, sharpshooters, smugglers and poachers, their strand guns well-oiled and well-used.

Roche, lying in his own soft, four-poster bed for the first time in weeks, had stirred in his sleep at the first rumble of the storm to the north-west but had snapped wide awake, blinking and drawing a long shocked breath as Dan Banville barged into his room and snatched the sheets off him.

'That's cannon!' Dan declared. 'They are shelling the camp at Vinegar Hill as we rest here. Get on your feet, General!'

Roche shook his head and immediately began to fumble for his clothes. The night was a hollow of black. Exhaustion weighed upon him and every inch of his body seemed to ache from the exertions of the last few weeks of battle and hardship. Every year of his life now dragged at his limbs, his age finally taking its toll. Wearily, he pulled his shirt over his head and yanked on his breeches. Dan, an elemental thing dark as night itself, helped him by impatiently tossing him his boots and jacket.

In Roche's eyes the young captain had changed immeasurably since they had parted company after the fall of Wexford Town. Something had frayed within him, some cord of sanity was close to breaking. There was an urgency about him, a frantic lust for activity that bordered on the surreal.

The loss of his young lady and the butchery he had borne witness to at Wexford bridge might provide an explanation, as might the news from Foulkesmills that they had garnered earlier that evening. After a closely fought battle only the personal intervention of Brigadier General Sir John Moore had swung the day in favour of the Crown. The Southern Division under Fr Philip Roche was in good order but in retreat towards Wexford Town. There was open talk amongst the leaders in the town of suing for terms from General Moore, who was, by all accounts, a humane and kind Scotsman.

For the Rising to have any last hope of succeeding, the battle looming at Vinegar Hill must be swung in favour of the United Irishmen. For the United men to have any bargaining position at all, they must throw Lake and his armies back into the midlands and back onto the quays of Dublin. To be caught between the forces of Lake and Moore was to be seized in a vice, one that would crush the life out of anything held in its cold jaws.

Dan, for his part, could not have known how accurately Edward Roche had gauged him. Elizabeth was an ever-present in his mind and the yearning for revenge flared and died, only to be reborn like an illness in his breast. The guilt he felt was a thing of constant, twisting agony. He had died that afternoon alongside Elizabeth as surely as if William Delaney's blade had struck true and pierced his heart instead of hers.

There was another element, though, that Roche had overlooked. Tom was at Vinegar Hill. For Dan, all the war and sacrifice, the agony and upheaval since the yeos had come for him, simply could not end with the death of his brother as well. He had lost everything, and he would be damned before he added Tom to that list.

Now, with eyes glittering like pike-heads in the dim light drifting through

Roche's bedroom windows, he growled, 'I'll rouse the men, the sooner we march, the sooner we get there.'

That mad dash through the dark, rain-washed Wexford countryside remained with many of Roche's men forever. The smells of damp clay and straining growth, the weeping drip-drip-drip of branches and leaves, beaded with water from the scudding showers that passed over, fleeting and chilling as apparitions. The moon, setting the edges of ragged clouds to glow as though coated with phosphorus, tumbled out of the rack only to hide itself again, cold and distant and bone-white. The men panted as they marched, Dan among them, their strides hurried and their faces set.

It was an hour from the moment Roche was disturbed in his slumber to when the column of Shelmaliers passed through the village of Ballymurn. The sun was rising by then and the world was cast in shades of steel and opal. Another hour from Ballymurn brought them to Oylegate, just south of Enniscorthy.

Long before that, however, they had come across the first refugees. Women and children, sick and wounded, all were bundled onto handcarts and stolen jaunting cars or piled in disorder onto wagons drawn by donkeys and slat-ribbed horses. All were in a panic, terror-struck and desperate to escape the onslaught of General Lake's army. Just like at Wexford Bridge, the vulnerable were the first to feel the pain.

Roche and Dan spurred the men on, driving through the fugitive flood that slowed them infuriatingly, clutching at them and begging for protection. As though given new impetus by the human jetsam that swirled around them, as though the immediacy of their mission was newly reinforced by the sight of every crying child or wailing widow, the marksmen of Shelmalier and Ballaghkeen pressed on.

Then, as they drew closer to Vinegar Hill, the din of the battle grew loud in their ears and on the horizon a black veil of smoke drifted up, mingling with the tattered grey of the morning. Between Oylegate and Enniscorthy, just before Edermine, the first of the fighting men appeared, hastening away from the charnel house that was the valley under Vinegar Hill.

Dan stopped a bleeding figure, a lean man in his fifties, his face a sweat-slimed contortion of panic. Glancing over his shoulder, panting and frightened, the man told them that the town was lost and that the rebels were fighting a steady rearguard action along the quays to protect the men fleeing from the hill. The English had left a gap, he said, and thousands were streaming through it.

'Save yourself,' he finished. 'The soldiers are shooting anything that moves.'

Dan looked from the terrified man to the smoke that bruised the sky to the

Joe Murphy

north and replied stonily, 'Do not concern yourself about me, sir. I have only one person more to lose in this life and I should sooner take my own than turn my back on him.'

The man blinked at him dumbly, then scurried off down the line of pike- and gunsmen, his actions frantic with terror. Dan watched coldly as he disappeared from view then pressed on, his eagerness seeming to drag Roche and the gasping column along in his wake.

A mile further on and casualties began to strew the road. The wounded, who could run no farther, lay in broken heaps, lining ditches and gullies. Horses lay also, their necks broken and their carts with women and children under them, either dead or dying in the road where the desperate haste of their flight had overturned the carts.

Still they marched until the sound of chattering muskets and ringing steel seemed to drown the world and more and more pike- and musketmen rushed past, their faces black with smoke or scabbed with wounds. Every figure was blood-stained and powder-scoured. The desperation in their movements was a terrifying thing to behold. Above and beyond this ragged flood of humanity, Vinegar Hill was swathed in tattered coils of gunsmoke. As Dan watched, a lazy shred of smoke withdrew from the hill's summit and, tiny in the distance but clear as day, the green bough that had been lashed to the ruined windmill was torn down by red-coated forms.

All is lost, Dan thought. Lost utterly.

In the battered barrel of his chest he could feel what was left of his heart dissolve.

Then, without warning, the rearguard of the United Irish Army appeared on the rise just above the road. To Dan's shock and to Roche and the Shelmalier's delight, the men marched with grim discipline. They did not run. No panic fevered through their actions. Dan recognised Fr Murphy, mounted and haughty, at the head of this resolute little column and then, to a great cheer from the Shelmaliers, the men of the rearguard turned and fired in loose order on the red-coated infantry pursuing them. Ahead, on the road leading to the bridge, another group of insurgents retreated foot by foot, blazing away with their muskets, determined to keep the soldiers at bay.

Edward Roche spurred his horse forward and wheeled it theatrically in front of his men.

'This day,' he bellowed above the gunfire and clash of steel, above the huz- zahs and screams, 'will live long in the annals of our poor country's quest for

418

liberty. And it is not done yet. The men of Shelmalier have still a part to play. Ready your muskets, my boys, for if the English have left this gap by which our brave fellows may escape, then we shall plug it against their pursuit.

'Form ranks!' he cried. 'Cover the rearguard!'

The Shelmaliers immediately spread across the road and into the fields to their right, presenting a long line of crouching pikemen, behind which two rows of gunsmen stood and primed their long fowling pieces.

At this sight, both contingents of retreating rebels quickened their stride and were soon running at full tilt towards the newly-established defensive line. The soldiers sent up a great huzzah at this and began to pursue them pell-mell until they perceived the formidable hedge of pikes and guns that blocked the Wexford Road. Cheers dying in their throats, the soldiers halted.

As Fr Murphy trotted his horse past Edward Roche, he inclined his head slightly in a wordless expression of thanks.

Smiling grimly in the middle of the line of pikemen, Dan Banville did not notice the colours of the Castletown Corps come dashing down the hill to his right. He did not notice his old comrades as they slalomed between the guarding pikes and dashed down the road to safety. He did not notice the young man who stopped, stupefied, in front of the Shelmaliers with a look of the purest joy breaking across his features like dawn upon a golden shore.

'Dan!' Tom yelled, the syllable exploding from his throat like a sob.

The raw emotion in that voice brought Dan's gaze up and he locked his eyes onto the beaming face of his brother.

'Tom!' he cried and then, heedless of the danger, he stepped forth into the no man's land between the two armies and wrapped his arms around Tom's shoulders.

Casting a quick look behind him toward where a red-uniformed line of soldiers was massing, Tom said, 'I thought you were dead!'

Dan replied bleakly, 'So did I.'

Tom frowned then. Something in his brother's eyes, something in his bearing hinted at darkness.

'Is Elizabeth safe?' he asked.

Dan's face paled and his eyes brimmed like wellheads. 'I will tell you later,' he said. 'For now we must cover the retreat to Wexford.'

Swiftly stepping into the ranks, the Banville brothers stood with swords drawn, shoulder to shoulder. Tom's eyes were troubled and he cast a sidelong glance to where Dan stood. He was overjoyed to be reunited with his brother but the horrible grief he saw within Dan disturbed him deeply. Then, as Tom watched, tears sprang from Dan's eyes and coursed in full flood down his cheeks.

'Mr Roche!' cried a rebel voice. 'They are bringing forward cannon. We cannot stay here!'

In front of Tom and Dan the soldiers' lines had opened to admit the heavy carriage of a brass nine-pounder. It was wheeled to a halt and its gunners commenced the swarming, arcane operations that readied it to fire. Ramrods and wadding and a bucket of water were all dumped beside it and a wooden case full of grape shot canisters was hefted forward from the rear.

Anxiety rumbled through the insurgent ranks and, beneath the disquiet, Dan said matter-of-factly, 'They killed her, you know.'

Tom blinked and he whispered in outrage, 'Elizabeth is killed? By whom?'

Dan swallowed drily and stated, 'A man called Thomas Dixon. I would have you kill him if you find him.'

Tom Banville's stomach pitched with nausea. Dan's words seemed to pinwheel about his mind without ever finding real purchase. The fact of Elizabeth's murder sickened him physically and yet it was an unreal thing, like a distant scream on an empty mountainside.

Tom regarded his brother fiercely, his lips suddenly dry, stitched onto his face. He rasped his tongue across them and he said, 'I'll kill him for you, Dan. We'll kill him together.'

But Dan did not answer. Mute tears merely snaked through the grime that marred his face. He was suddenly a creature of moist, white clay, soft and sobbing.

Then, Roche's voice rose in command, 'Shelmaliers, in good order, fall back to Wexford!'

With a rattling of pike and musket, the men under Edward Roche began a grudging retreat from Enniscorthy. In front of them, the lines of redcoats remained where they stood, unwilling to risk a confrontation with so many well-armed men. As they marched, Tom Banville glanced once more at his brother. Dan's eyes projected an unsettling bleakness; it was as though, with his brother safe, he had lost the will to live. Silently, Tom marched and with each step towards Wexford Town, a desolate foreboding grew within him. The battle had been lost, the Rising had been lost, and now he feared his brother was lost too, trapped in the all-consuming quicksand of grief.

CHAPTER 25

What is Left Behind

❧

Wexford Town was an altogether different place this second time the Wexford Army of the United Irishmen entered it. Gone were the green banners and the platters of food, gone were the kisses and the emerald garlands. It was as though the men who had fought at Vinegar Hill and Foulkesmills, the men who had come within a whisker of overthrowing the King's Government in Ireland, carried a plague. They were like lepers and outcasts, and the townsfolk could not be rid of them quickly enough. They were frantic to erase any association between themselves and the banner of the United Irishmen. Even Bishop Caulfield had made an appearance, mewling and bawling from his high windows that they would bring disaster down upon the town if they stayed. In short, Wexford Town awaited Brigadier General Moore with open arms.

A large column of rebels including Fr Murphy and Miles Byrne had filed out of the town and waited on the Windmill Hill or at the old Three Rocks encampment. Some, Anthony Perry, Fitzgerald and Roche among them, had decided to head north along the Coast Road and try to slip past General Lake's dragnet. All the leaders, from captain to colonel, realised that to be taken by the military on this day, so soon after the Battle of Vinegar Hill and the murders on Wexford Bridge, was a death sentence.

Tom Banville stood in the cemetery of the Protestant Church of St Iberius and watched his brother weep over the heaped loam of a fresh grave. Dan was on his knees and the convulsions that racked him spoke of a hurt too raw and too physical to imagine. One hand was clawed into the rich, sandy chocolate of the soil while his other was pressed to his pale and tortured forehead.

At the head of the grave-mound a simple wooden cross stood slightly askew, a brass plaque tacked to it. In hard, engraved lines the inscription read, ELIZABETH BLAKELY, DIED 15TH JUNE 1798. KILLED BY A UNITED IRISHMAN.

There was something pointed in that inscription that cut at Tom, something acid in those words that he did not like.

Beneath the cross, a rain-battered bunch of purple wild flowers lay forlornly, sinking into the soil.

Tom stood for long minutes while Dan hacked his grief out onto the deaf clay of Elizabeth's grave. Then, as his brother's sobs abated, he said slowly, carefully, 'Miles Byrne has gone out to The Three Rocks. He says Fr Murphy wants to lead some of the men out into the midlands. We cannot stay here. We shall all be hanged.'

Dan was silent.

'Dan—' began Tom, but he was cut off by his brother's words.

'I will not leave her,' he croaked, his voice still gummed with grief. 'I cannot.'

'Then we shall both stay here,' replied Tom. 'We shall both stay and be made crow's meat by Lake. I thought you were lost once, Dan. I will not see you lost again.'

Dan exhaled then, a long expulsion of breath as though he sought to purge the sorrow that lay so heavy in his chest. 'Go with Miles, Tom. Help him get the men out of Wexford. You are all that Ma and Da have left. Get away from here. Go to Dublin. Find them. Tell them I love them dearly. Tell them I regret the pain I have brought them.'

Tom let the sea breeze whisper, feather-light, past his cheeks. The breeze brought with it the organic, rotting stench of the docks and the calls and cries of those desperately striving to hook from the water the bodies of the ninety-seven men and women whom Thomas Dixon had piked to death.

'You are sure you wish to stay?' asked Tom, his mind recoiling at his own question. How could he allow his brother to remain behind, to face a rigged court-martial, friendless and alone?

'I am sure,' replied Dan, and in those three words was all the dragging weight of purpose that Tom needed to hear.

Dan meant to die here, by the side of his beloved. He would be shot, stretched on her grave before he allowed himself to be taken from her. When the soldiers came they would find a man already six days dead.

As Tom regarded his brother he knew he could not save him; and all the while those five damned words spat accusingly out from the brass plaque on Elizabeth's temporary cross.

Killed by a United Irishman.

Tom knew that his brother felt every syllable of those five words were for him and him alone.

'I will be at the camp, Dan,' Tom said, hating the pleading, bleating note that had entered his voice. 'I beg of you to reconsider and join me there. Please, do not do this. You're my brother.'

Dan turned his head then and Tom almost staggered back a step at the vision his brother's face presented. Before his eyes, Dan had become empty, his flesh grey and slack, his gaze dead.

Dan's mouth worked slowly, 'You are all I have left, Tom. I kept you safe. I came for you in the end. Tell Ma and Da that, would you? Tell them I came for you.'

Tom's own eyes now overflowed and he stepped towards his brother, hugging him fiercely to his chest, 'I love you, Dan.'

Dan's right arm came up and wrapped around Tom's shoulders but his left hand did not lift from where it was buried in the soil of Elizabeth's grave. 'And I you,' he whispered.

Tom wrenched himself away from his brother and ran from the graveyard, the tears streaming unashamedly from his eyes. He wept for Dan and he wept for Elizabeth. He wept for himself. He wept like a child for his county and for his country. He wept for the future and all that he had left behind.

In the silence of the graveyard, Dan Banville knelt as though made from the very clay banked and piled in a low heap before him. He knelt by his darling Elizabeth and waited for the soldiers to come.

'I am coming soon,' he whispered. 'I am ready.'

Acknowledgements

The past is a strange place. The only way you can find a path into it is by standing on the shoulders of those who have gone before. Therefore, I am indebted to all those scholars and historians who have dedicated far more time than me to exploring the events of 1798. Also, I have to express my gratitude to the staff and personnel of the National Library in Dublin, Enniscorthy Library and Wexford Town Library. To Dan and the staff of Liberties Press, thanks for your faith and hard work. To my friends and family who read the manuscript and who have helped me along not just this path but others too numerous to mention, a massive and heartfelt cheers. To my parents and brother, I owe everything good in my life to you three. And to my darling wife, Áine, your patience deserves more words than I could ever write. This, and everything else, is for you.